W9-BDY-716

Best of Hair Trigger
Second Revised Edition

A Story Workshop Anthology

Columbia College Fiction Writing Department

Chicago, 1992

ISBN 0-932026-31-1

Copyright © 1993 Columbia College Chicago

Story Workshop is a service mark of John Schultz (U.S. Patent and Trademark Office Registration No. 1,343,415) and may not be used without his permission.

Columbia College Fiction Writing Department
600 South Michigan Avenue
Chicago, Illinois 60605

Table of Contents

Freshman Writing and English Usage

Preface and Acknowledgements

The Best of Hair Trigger collects undergraduate and graduate prose in *Hair Triggers 1–14*. *Hair Trigger 3* and *Hair Trigger 8* won first prize as the best college literary magazine in the country, in the Coordinating Council of Literary Magazines 1979 and 1986 national contests. *Hair Trigger 12* received a Silver Crown award from Columbia University's Scholastic Press Association, 1990, and student pieces in several *Hair Triggers* have won a variety of the Scholastic Press Association's Gold Circle Awards.

This anthology is the latest in the bloodline of such widely acclaimed anthologies as *The Story Workshop Reader, Angels in my Oven, It Never Stopped Raining, Don't You Know There's a War On?, f*[1], and *Hair Triggers 1–14*. The selected prose came from Story Workshop® Fiction Writing and Prose Forms, Writing I and II (freshman composition), Novel Writing, English Usage, and other Story Workshop writing classes.

In making the selections, the editor was forced to choose among writings of virtually equal merit, because the size of the book would not allow for the publication of all the eligible pieces. Many of these stories and essays have repeatedly demonstrated their usefulness in the writing classroom, in helping students learn how to write. A wide range of content is available in this collection. The writings are characterized by respect for the reader, for content, form, point of view and language.

A few essays appear here that were written when the authors were enrolled in undergraduate classes and their writings were, for one reason or another, never a part of the *Hair Trigger* selection process. Since they superbly fulfill particular forms, they are included in this anthology.

NOTE: A selection may be included under the heading of one form, yet fulfill other forms in some part of its execution. For instance, in the How-It-Happens sequence, how-to-do-it-betters, model tellings, letters on behalf of the opposite, letters on behalf of one's self, and other forms may appear.

This is the appropriate place to acknowledge department administrative assistant Deborah Roberts for indispensable help in the making of the book. Thanks are due again to the former President of Columbia College, Mirron Alexandroff, for his encouragement of this program, and to President John Duff for his support.

The lively, affecting, sometimes outrageously funny writings in this book have already demonstrated that they are a delight to read and stimulating to use in the teaching of writing.

John Schultz
Editor and Chairperson
Fiction Writing Department

Shawn Shiflett
Editor and Faculty
Fiction Writing Department

How-To

HOW TO MAKE LASAGNA
Phyllis Crowley

To fully appreciate the Italian flair for creating works of intricately interdependent layers, levels, strata and tiers, examine a pile of several kinds of fruit in any Italian grocery or St. Paul's Cathedral or the Mafia or The Church or Dante's *Inferno*. Lasagna is built somewhat along the same principles.

If your kitchen is makeshift, substandard, defective or outmoded, never mind. A dash of outrageousness in its immediate environment mysteriously brings out more of the essence of lasagna than do completely circumspect accoutrements. Let's say you're guilty of owning one of these kitchens, that 25 guests are expected at seven, and you haven't straightened up the house. Well, don't. Relegate that task or forget it. Lasagna will tolerate nothing else but your total conscious state for the four hours it takes to make.

You may use the recipe that follows as a shopping list. But remember, you can't pin down lasagna in a recipe, just as you can't assure that gin, vermouth and olives, however flawless their combination, will always result in a classic martini. There has to be something in the martini besides gin, vermouth and an olive. There has to be gestalt. Lasagna requires a lot of gestalt, but since nobody knows what it is, gestalt doesn't appear below. Do not proceed without it however.

The meatballs:
> Ground chuck, 3 pounds*
> Parsley
> Eggs, 3
> Bread crumbs, about two cups (Use really good bread.)

The seasonings:
> Salt
> Pepper
> Garlic
> Bay leaves, 2
> Oregano
> Basil
> Thyme
> Vinegar, about half a cup
> Table sugar, a tablespoon and some
> Chili Sauce, half a bottle of the good stuff
> Chianti, half a bottle
> Parmesan cheese

Other things you use:
> Butter, about ½ pound
> Purple onions, about 6
> Canned tomatoes, 3 large cans

Water, as you go
Green peppers, about 4
Mushrooms, 2 large packages
Table celery, finely cut—5-6 stalks
2 pounds of ricotta

So here you have the general makings of one of those freewheeling, imprecise, impertinent dishes that tell you what they need as they cook along. Just imagine you're Pavarotti, stepping on stage to do King Gustaf. You know he respects Verdi but is not going to be confined by him.

All Italian dishes begin with garlic, even spumoni. So get two fat, gleaming garlic cloves with outer skins just the tiniest bit brittle. Flick at each with a fingernail and check the noise for tone. A sound thunk tells you a clove is sound inside. Whichever knife isn't as dull on one side as on the other will have to do, as will the hand-sized carving board you probably own, with the large, unsanitary, black crack. As you chip away at the garlic, toss a stick of butter into the frying pan. Don't let the butter get past tepid. Before adding the roughly chopped garlic, swish the butter around once. Throw in another butter stick and turn off the gas. That stick will get absorbed at the other ingredients' leisure. Chop six purple onions you have, it is to be hoped, chosen only after comparison with several dozen other purple onions. No one can really afford six purple onions but you must have them today for they are to their pale cousins what crabmeat is to tuna fish.

You might imagine, because lasagna does not require dainty handling, that your course for the afternoon will be easy. But the dish makes subtler demands. What they are, no one can define precisely. Be alert for them.

Right now, melt yet more butter in a saucepan and add the onions. Then just hack around, swirling the entire purple mixture over low heat. Toss it, after a couple of minutes, into the garlic. Set the combination aside, on the sink, maybe. If the butter congeals, that's perfectly okay. Just don't let it get hot because then it will render.

Order the cat from the room. Her interest in your adventure is not innocent.

Produce three one-pound four-ounce cans of tomatoes and toss contents into the huge dented pot suspected of having Macbeth's coat of arms on it somewhere. Again, low heat. Half a cup of vinegar follows the tomatoes into the pot summarily as does the tomato paste from three eight-ounce cans.

Next, a scant tablespoon of sugar. Oh, keep stirring. Use a wooden ladle. Never, never stir lasagna with a metal implement. Use your wooden ladle even if it couldn't pass any known Board of Health test; use it if, withal, it has authority, character, tone, air, countenance, the complexion of a mercenary in the Sahara, and if it is strong enough to keep your brew from sticking. If this occurs, senora, you had best lose yourself in the night or, worse, profane this peerless dish by attempting to substitute for its sauce some unspeakable red plastic substitute from a jar. At this juncture, you need salt and two crisp, fragrant, shiny, unfragmented bay leaves. Toss in oregano as the bay leaves sink into your sibilant, warm, red mess, and some basil. And throw in half a bottle of chili sauce if you keep a decent brand about the place.

With an eye on all, chop, seeding first, four green peppers and pile them over the onions and garlic that are cooling their heels on the sink. Stir in the peppers but not violently, or you will have spillage since your heap is six inches high by now, or should be.

To the sauce — you kept stirring, didn't you, while chopping and adding the peppers? — add a half cup of water. Ride constant herd on this sauce now.

Since you must hang around in the kitchen for the next two hours anyway, you can make little clean-up dashes in between stirs, but this is tricky. You can also amuse yourself by getting together your mushrooms and celery. Use a lot of mushrooms, a cascade of them. After all, how often do you make lasagna? You don't want to be counted among those lasagna makers who, because of some weird, subservient attitude toward money, skimp.

By the way, have you got everything for the last stages? It isn't a bad idea to turn off everything while you check because you probably haven't. If you do have to return to the store, shut the kitchen door, not that we don't trust the cat.

Now that you're back with the Parmesan and the ricotta, get busy. Jesus, you haven't much time. Get the sauce going.

You're not letting it bubble? A tad more water, quick, and ply that wooden ladle. Get at the bottom of the cauldron. Stir downward toward upward, not the other way. Don't let anything stick down there. A scorched bottom is fatal.

A potentially serious crisis point approaches, the moment you choose to dump the garlic mushroom celery etc. mix into the sauce. If you break down, if panic seizes you, the fact that you won't be the first confronted by this challenge to do so, might make your disgrace easier to bear.

Having chosen, you stir and fold the mix into the sauce. Taste. You'll find you need more salt, much pepper, more oregano. Take out the bay leaves. Add half a bottle of Chianti. Add a little thyme, perhaps. A little dill — fresh is nice. Fool around for a while.

Assuming you have been clever and have done a few preparations this morning, get the things from the icebox. You used four or five pounds of ground chuck, lots of parsley, snipped with a scissors, three eggs, pepper, paprika, bread crumbs, shredded, salt, and all of this resulted in meatballs. They are tiny and round and hard. You used a teaspoon of meat mix for each. You have thousands. Brown them in the pan, batch after batch, and toss each batch into the sauce from the pan. You had better have a *very* high pot.

The noodles you know about. You'll need two packages. When they're cooked, get over to the sink with them as best you can—they have required a large pot and boiling water and are fairly dangerous. Flush the noodles with cold water. Drain very efficiently or you will have runny lasagna.

Get the ricotta. You have the sauce, you have the noodles, you have the cheese. The moment has come when you begin to build, to integrate. Steady. Here again, what proportion of what ingredient is correct in relation to the position, texture and tone of another ingredient, or several, cannot be conveyed. However that may be, you have to know.

Layer two brownie pans with noodles. Trim the noodles to size with scissors. Let us hope they were cooked and drained carefully and therefore did not pull apart, or fuse, or act up otherwise. Carefully pour some of the sauce over the noodles. During the building process it might be a good idea to give the sauce a stir now and then—just because you turned it off doesn't mean it's stopped cooking. Its internal temperature is so hot it's probably cooking itself, to an extent. If all of the meatballs during this stirring and building don't keep their shape, don't worry. They sort of tend to merge anyway but cooking the meat meatball style is infinitely preferable to free form, and you will reap rewards in flavor and texture, for your effort. You begin to suspect this since the aromas in your kitchen are sheer magic and cause an occasional passerby to pause and stare at the window.

To the noodles and the sauce, add ricotta, in dollops here and there. Apply another layer of scissored noodles, then the sauce, then the cheese. Remember layers, levels, strata, tiers. Repeat the process until the ingredients are incorporated. You have now built your dish. Shake the can of Parmesan over the two pans for quite a while.

Forty minutes in the oven will do to interlock all components and charge the air even more fragrantly.

Very soon after the pans are brought forth, the diners will arrive. When the hushed crowd eddies around your magnificent, gently steaming golden-brown autumn-orange, beige ochre and sienna complex, remember the old Italian proverb, "Art is the concealing of art," and to all entreaties reply you will be glad to give them the recipe but they must understand that you have in this dish a secret thing you are not prepared to reveal at the present time.

*Don't think ground meat is the only form of protein that can be used here. Ground meat can be supplanted by seafood, poultry, or almost anything in the vegetable kingdom.

SO YOU WANT TO DRIVE A TRACTOR
Cliff Wilkerson

"So you want to be farmer for the summer, do you Bud? I pay six dollars a day and room and board. If you had experience I'd up it to eight, but I'll have to put in some time undoing some of what you did wrong, no offense, and some time showing you how to do things. You will make mistakes, but that's how you learn. First thing you'll be doing is helping me finish up the plowing, so I'll have to put you on the tractor.

"I want you to know about that tractor, though, Bud, before you start to drive it. It looks tame enough sitting quietly out there by the implement shed, but don't let that fool you. A tractor is a lot like a horse. They're both tamed but underneath their skin and metal hides they're still brute, brute strength, and they have no power of reason. Underestimate them or get careless and they will turn on you, stomp you, plow you under, or kick you into the dust. I've seen men hurt and killed by both horses and tractors.

"You being a city boy and all makes it harder. My boy's been riding a tractor with his old daddy here since before he was out of diapers and by the time he's ten or twelve he will have a sense of the power and the danger. He learns one thing at a time and he has a lot of time to learn. He can take a tractor out without any of these instructions because he'll have learned by watching and listening to me. It'll be a part of him. But you are a stranger to the land and to the ways of the country so you don't know the dangers and pitfalls. But you can learn, if you pay attention and listen to what I say. But you have to learn it all at once, so it won't be easy. Now let's go out there and take a look at what's to be done.

"The first thing about a tractor is its care. A worn bearing will cost you from a half a day to three; running out of gas means a long walk across plowed ground; not enough oil in the motor can put a tractor out of commission for a month. So first thing you do in the morning is rouse out of bed and while the steak is sizzling in the skillet and ma's biscuits are browning in the oven you skat down here and service the tractor.

"You start by greasing her. There are ten grease zerks that I want you to remember; they have to be pumped full twice a day. This here metal contraption that looks like an oversized cake decorator is a grease gun. The grease gun is made of two parts that screw together, the head and the barrel. The head, or pump, is like a fancy lid you might screw on to a mustard jar. It has a twelve-inch long, thin neck coming out of the center of it with a nozzle on the end that moves in just about the same way your own head swivels on your neck. The comparison ends there, except that the hole on the end of the nozzle is its mouth. You stick the nipple of a grease zerk into the mouth in order to pump grease from the gun into the tractor bearings.

"Now on the side of the lid there is the pump handle. It has the look of a man's shoulder and arm cut off at the elbow. When fastened to the barrel the whole contraption may look like a grasshopper that some young lad has pulled one leg and an antenna off of. What you have to do is grab that leg and make it kick the grease into the bearings. That little pump handle will put out forty pounds of pressure which is enough to grease any contrary bearing you can find, even when the zerk is clogged.

"The barrel is a metal cylinder two and a half inches in diameter and eighteen inches long. It has a spring plunger on its bottom end that you use to suck the grease into it. You have to give the plunger a little twist to lock it when you've filled the gun to capacity. But if you forget to unlock it after the head has been replaced you may think you have a stuck grease zerk because you can't pump the grease without the pressure supplied by the spring in the plunger.

"But something that will try your patience even more than spilling a quart of honey on the kitchen floor is if you accidentally trip the lock before the head is in place. Then you will watch a foot and a half long grease snake slither onto the dirt.

"See that little nipple sticking out the side of the wheel? Well, that's a grease zerk. You have to fit the tip of this here grease-gun nozzle over that. Just put it on the nipple and push. That's right. Now pump the handle and force the grease into the wheel bearings. Pump until you see the grease squirting out of the cracks around the bearing. Good. Now move on to the next one. The big wheels take a lot. Now sometimes the nipples won't take the grease because dirt gets clogged in the opening. If that happens, give a quick sharp pump on the handle and that will unstop it.

"Now give the ends of the steering rods a pump or two, the fan needs some, there are a couple up under the engine there, and once a week give a shot to the steering wheel.

"Filling the grease gun is fairly easy but messy. See that five gallon can of grease? You have to screw the head off the gun, stick the open end of the barrel into the grease and then pull the plunger here on the end of the gun all the way out. It sucks up the grease like you would suck a malt up a straw. Take your finger now and run it all around the lip to collect the grease that sticks to it and twist the whole goopy mess onto the end of the gun so you have a little heap on top. Screw the neck and head back on and she's ready for another day's work. Tuck the gun up there in the tool box so you will have it in the field with you this afternoon.

"Just one last thing, be sure and keep that gun in the shade because if you try and pick it up in the middle of the afternoon when the sun's beating down, that piece of greasy metal can get hot enough to blister your hand. Of course the best thing to do is to wear gloves, but most folks don't seem to want to bother with them.

"The next thing we have to consider is the gas and oil. We have to change the oil in this old horse every two weeks. The oil gets dirtier than a hog wallow in no time at all and will wear the engine out before you know it. Cuts a tractor's life in half to use dirty oil. So you have to get that old piece of oil drum over there and stick it under the oil drain. That's right, down there under the tractor. Get down here on the ground and take a look up under. See that plug with the square-nut on it? Unscrew that with a pair of vice grips and watch the black oil fly. You got to get your arm back quick or you'll be black to your elbow. Now when you've let it all drain out you have to put that plug back in and snug it in good and tight. You lose all the oil out of the motor because the plug shook loose and she'll freeze up on you so tight it will take a stick of dynamite to move her. And after the dynamite she ain't much use to anybody. Now, when the plug is in good, you take six quarts of oil out of that oil drum over on the trailer there and pour it in this hole here on the side of the motor. Don't forget to put this cap back on either, or you'll be changing the oil again most likely before the day's out.

"My daddy used to complain about all the hay and oats those old mules and horses of his used to eat over a year's time. It was a lot, but you can bet it wasn't anything to the gas you have to feed this old tractor. Now it's true that it's got a lot more horses under its hood than ever my daddy owned in a lifetime, but even so, when you figure it guzzles 40-60 gallons a day, well that ain't hay.

"Excuse the joke. Come over here by the trailer a minute. See those three barrels? They are all filled with gas, 50 gallons apiece. That one in the middle has the gas pump sticking out of it. That cap up on top of the tractor just in front of the steering wheel is the gas cap. You take the nozzle on the end of the gas pump's hose and stick it in there. But never, and I repeat, never, while the engine is running or you'll have one hell of a fire on your hands some fine day.

"To pump the gas you have to turn the handle you see there on the side of the pump. You turn it like you would the handle for a car window and you fill that 30 gallon tank to the top but don't run it over. You'll get to where you can tell, by the sound of the gas splashing in the tank, how near the top you are. It starts out sounding like when you pour water in an empty bucket, than after a while like water running in the creek and when it's nearing the top it fades to a whisper. When you don't hear it whispering to you any more you know it's time to stop turning that crank.

"Now there's one more thing. When you empty one barrel you have to move the pump to a full one. All's you do is turn the pump counter clockwise and it screws right off the barrel. There is a pipe attached to the pump that extends down to the bottom of the barrel and you have to pull that all the way out. If you've had the foresight to have unscrewed the cap from the full barrel you just lift the whole contraption over into it, screw it down, use the cap to plug the empty barrel and you're ready to pump again.

"But mind you, you must be very careful. That empty barrel, when it's open, is like a stick of dynamite. One spark and I'll be scraping you off the side of the barn over there, and you won't be in one piece either. A full gas barrel would just burn like a torch but one that's the least bit empty will explode in a minute. So don't ever change that gas pump when a piece of machinery is running, don't ever light a match or smoke around the barrels, and when you lift that pump from one barrel to the other, do it gently. You pound or scrape metal against metal and you're going to get a spark. One spark and I'll have to go looking for me a new field hand.

"By the way, try not to let the gas get so low in the tractor that you're pulling gas from off the bottom of the tank. There's always a little water and sediment settles and you get that in the carburetor you'll be thirty minutes trying to get her started again.

"Speaking of water, you best check the radiator every morning. She'll usually be down a little. If you see the water below the overflow just take that bucket with the long neck on it and fill it over there at the horse tank. Don't dip it out of the tank, though. The water gets too many impurities in it. Turn on the windmill and pump fresh water. You have to snap back that wire catch on the radiator lid and lay it aside. But for goodness-sake, don't forget to put it back on. You wouldn't get halfway around the field till she would be blowing like a sperm whale. Which reminds me, don't ever take that lid off when the tractor's hot or you'll end up with your hands and face cooked like boiled cabbage. That would put you out of commission for quite a spell.

"I think that about does it. Are you ready to crank this old buzzard up? Good. But there is one thing you need to know about cranking a tractor. That crank can kick like a mule. So when you go to crank it you have to stand directly in front facing the tractor. It's easier to stand to the side so you can put the weight of your body into it. But I want you to picture what it would be like holding both arms over the back legs of a jackass when somebody juices him with a cattle prod. This old Case tractor here can break both arms and if you're unlucky enough to have your head bent over can knock it clear into the middle of the south eighty over there.

"The other thing about cranking is how you take hold of the handle. If you take hold of it like you were shaking hands you will be minus a thumb if she kicks. Did you ever see a monkey take hold of its bars? Its thumb wraps around on the same side as its fingers. That's the way you have to grab the crank handle. Then, if she backfires, the crank will kick out of your hand and you will be all in one piece.

"All right now, you've got her serviced and cranked up so let's take her out and do a turn around the field. You sit right up there on the fender and hold on tight while I drive. First thing is that you have four forward gears and one backward. If you look close you can see the positions have been marked there by the shift stick. There are three low gears, and road gear. The only time you want to put her in road gear is when you're out on the highway. Driving country roads or in the field is too rough for this gear. So all the driving you will be doing will be in third gear unless we hit a spell of wet weather and then you might have to shift down to second or even first. Be sure and always stop the tractor dead still before you try to shift or you'll strip the gears right out of her.

"O.K. I'm putting her in third gear. See this pedal here on the far right? It's the clutch pedal. You push that in and gradually let it out. Bucks a little don't she? Still a little cold, I guess. Now, while we're riding out to the field I'll tell you a little about the brakes. The pedal of the left brakes the left back wheel and the pedal on the right, the one next to the clutch pedal there, brakes the right back wheel. When you go to turn a corner you have to get some help with the brake but I'll show you that when we get to the field.

"There is one thing I want you to remember above everything else, though, so listen real careful. You're going to be sitting on this tractor one fine afternoon and the sun is going to be baking the back of your head. The heat will be so thick that the flies can't even buzz in it. You'll be going around and around some field watching that front right wheel follow the furrow. The roar of this old motor will start to sound like a mother's lullaby and the lurching and heeling back and forth of this old horse will begin to feel like the gentle rocking of a baby's crib. Your mind is going to be dulled by the sheer monotony of having watched wheat stubble roll under the blade of the plow for eight to ten hours. Your belly is going to be full from a noon meal of fried chicken, corn on the cob, green beans, gravy, hot bread, milk, chocolate cake and a quart of iced tea. All the blood's going to be down digesting that and forgetting your brain. And at times like that is when more people get killed than any other time. They fall asleep and one of two things happen. The first thing is that they fall off the tractor and a plow breaks their back or a disc chops them into little pieces. The second thing is that they come to the end of the field and hit those corners in third gear. Do you know what happens when you hit the corners in third gear? Well, I'll tell you. The front end of the tractor bounces up, the back wheels dig in and they catapult that tractor right on its back on top of you. There is many a good man and boy lying up there in Fleetwood Cemetery today, son, because they caught forty winks on the back of a tractor. I sure want to tell you that shouldn't happen to you. Your mama would never forgive me if I had to tell her that boy of hers pulled a tractor over on himself or plowed himself under. No sir. You get sleepy you crawl off that critter and get a drink or take a leak or, if you have to, lay down in the shade of the tractor and sleep for a spell. But be sure and shut the motor off. If that shift should happen to jiggle into gear you'd be a sorry sight with wheel marks across your middle.

"Well now, here we are. We'll just back up to the plow and hook up. Easy now. There we are. Jump down and put the pin in. Hand me up that rope, too. That's what trips the plow in and out of the ground. You give a good hard jerk and she's in the ground again. This plow is called a Molhboard plow, it's a three bottom plow. Each of its three shares, or bottoms, takes a foot and a half swatch. That means you will be reducing the size of this field by nine feet every time you go around. Takes about 80 rounds to finish off this 80 acre field. I'll tell you one thing, you won't finish up today.

"Now all you have to do till we get to the end of the field is hold the two right tires of the tractor right next to the furrow. We are turning over about 4-½ to five inches of dirt and if we have the plow set right those shares will throw the dirt so we have a smooth field. If you see the dirt starting to ridge you want to stop and set the plow in a notch, or otherwise I will have a field of ditches and I can't farm ditches. If the plow is digging that furrow deeper than five inches I want you to set her out a notch. One other thing, if you bring the plow in when the field is finished you have to pin the hitch over to one side or the plow will start swinging back and forth and snap the hitch. But when you get ready to plow again you have to undo the pin or your plow will ride out of the ground. Won't get much plowing done that way, I can tell you.

"O.K. now, here we are at a corner. Watch me. See how I use the brake to pull the tractor around. When we get about two feet from the end spin this bugger hard to the left and ease her around. There we are. If I had let her travel another three feet, though, we would have ended up out in plowed ground. If I had turned sooner, I'd have a corner so big I'd spend half my summer trying to disc it out. That's what you do, by the way, is disc out those corners when you're through plowing.

"There's a lot more to be learned, son, before the summer's out, but I think that's enough for today. I'll take it a round or two with you and then let you loose. You got any questions?"

THE PRINCESS OF THE PLANT WORLD
Tony Del Valle

"Its fruit is edible at almost every stage of ripeness, and the number of castaways who owe their life to it is legion." The best known tropical plant is the palm.

An American pilot after his rescue from the South Seas declared: "Without the palms on my atoll I should be dead. Every day I picked my breakfast, lunch and dinner from the top of a coconut palm. The green fruit contained a gelatinous flesh, which immediately quenched the thirst. The ripe fruit contained the hard shelled edible coconut, which had the cool milk in it. When I was found after fifteen days, I had eaten thirty-two coconuts and was in the best of health." (*The Art of Survival*, Cord Christian Troebst)

So?

Did you say, "So?" You know what? I was inspired to write this piece by a person like you who would have said "So?" to a piece of information as precious as the one I have just given you.

I heard this person tell a story about a man stranded on an island who, in order to get coconuts, all he had to do was to grab the palm with both hands by its trunk and shake it a few times, then clear the way for the falling coconut. That's the most ridiculous thing I ever heard! Imagine wiggling a trunk three feet thick and solid as a concrete pillar. What if your survival depended on this erroneous knowledge about palms!

So maybe you'll never have to survive. (Don't bet on it. You never know where you'll be a year from now, a month from now, a week from now—if you travel a great deal. And with the possibility of nuclear holocaust hanging upon our heads...Forget it. Like I said, don't bet on it.) Anyways, I insist that you listen to this piece about the palm tree and how to get coconuts. Hopefully all you'll need this knowledge for is fun and personal advancement.

Pick the lowest palm. I should mention at this point that not all palms bear coconuts. But the ones that don't, they have another life sustaining source. But more of that later.

You'll notice that the trunk is made up of these rings stacked one on top of the other from major to minor all the way to the top. The rings at the bottom of the trunk can be up to four inches wide and slightly concave. The higher you go the smaller these rings get. The texture they give the palm provides a perfect grip as you climb.

The reason for picking the lowest palm is quite simply because if you slip and fall there's less chance of you getting fractured bones or (God forbid) of you getting killed.

Palms near the ocean are curved into graceful bodies. They can grow up to one hundred feet—that would be as high as an eight story building. The curve is always towards the water. Perhaps not so much because of the strong winds but—according to the Botanical Gardens of Chicago, Horticultural Society—because of genetic or hereditary traits. These curved palms are the easiest to climb. Inland, the palms are straighter and some of them don't bear coconuts. This one is known as the Royal Palm—a national symbol in Puerto Rico.

Before you begin climbing take off your shoes and socks. Take five deep breaths and begin as high as you can from the ground. You'll notice some moss growing at the very bottom of the trunk. This is very slippery, so avoid it. Another thing to avoid is walking around once you've taken off your shoes. You don't want to lose that moisture on the bottom of your feet because it helps you get a better grip of the palm at the beginning of your climb. Once you are on the palm, hands on the back of it as if on the back of your lover's neck, and your feet at diagonal angles, climb as fast as you can. Go with the original impulse. And when you reach the thin part of the palm, at which point you won't be able to use your feet anymore—the area being too thin and too awkward to plant both feet on it—embrace it. Embrace the palm with your arms and your ankles crossed behind it while taking a deep breath. While holding that breath in, grip. The expansion and tightening of your chest is an important part of your grip. Then reach up higher with your arms. Grip. Deep breath again and pull up your thighs. Grip. Reach up with your arms crossed behind her back.

The reason you have to go with the original momentum and climb as fast as you can is because you want to get as far as possible before your body shifts into low gear—if I may put it that way—and you slow down. I've seen some weight lifters do this in most of their masochistic games. All the ones that tried this technique won. Whether they were pushing five hundred pounds on a wheelbarrow or winding a cable with a thousand pound weight hanging at the end of it using only their hands and wrists, this technique worked.

Now you are at the top. There is a feeling of triumph compared to that of having scaled Mount Everest, or having crossed the highest tight-rope. The wind makes the palm leaves flutter and the palm swings gently. Reach up to the stem of one of its leaves and make sure it's not a dry leaf. All a dry leaf needs is the slightest weight to send it thundering to the ground. They can be quite heavy. Get a good grip on a green leaf and while still embracing the palm let your muscles relax a little.

The black hairy spiders that live on the crown of palm trees are ugly and they feel creepy when they walk on you but don't let them scare you to the point of opting to jump off and break your neck. They live in houses made of white silk, little tents which they stretch over any suitable crack or cranny. Avoid placing your hand directly on any of their houses. If by some chance the spider does bite you, don't panic. You're not going to die or be paralyzed like in the Hollywood movies. Romantic as it may seem, it won't be worse than a bee sting.

There's another insect which you might find inhabiting a palm tree. These you should really have respect for because they can bite you anywhere and in many places at the same time. If one stings you on an eye and you try to swat it away with your hand, death will greet you at the foot of the palm.

The best way to avoid bee hives is to listen. Make a halt before you reach the leaves and listen closely for their buzzing.

Yet another animal that you might find living on a palm tree is the proverbial rat. These are less dangerous than bees because they scare easy. But a bite from a rat can cause many infectious diseases like diphtheria.

Tony Del Valle/13

While the rat itself can be a nutritive meal, one must not eat the head because it is the teeth that are usually dangerously infected.

You can tell if a palm is inhabited by rats if there are a lot of dry clusters between the leaves. But you can see these from the ground and dismiss the palm altogether.

Once you're a little rested, and you've used your animal instincts to explore the palm, get as close to the leaves as you can. You can get both arms into the foliage while you grip the trunk with your legs. Now it's all a matter of pushing the coconuts off to the ground. They are connected to the palm by these rope-like stems. Never attempt to carry any coconut down with you. It's impossible to do. Watch where the coconuts are falling as you push them off, and look around for a point of reference as to where each one landed. *This especially if there's a lot of undergrowth.*

Coming down from the palm is easier than going up. All you do is reverse the procedure. You grip the palm with your arms and you lower your legs. Grip with your legs and lower your arms. I've seen experienced palm climbers let go once they are at what they think is a safe distance from the ground. Boy did they regret it! You see, once you let go, you can't stop sliding down. And the friction of those rings on the palm, on your arms and legs and chest—which you hadn't counted on—just sands them down like sandpaper. Even your chin will get part of it.

It is better to stick to a systematic descent.

Now about getting at the meat of the coconut; the hard fibrous outer husk of the coconut is the fruit's only disadvantage; opening it without a machete or a good knife is quite a problem. But there is the so-called "wedge method"; you ram a stake into the ground and grind the top end to a wedge; grasping the coconut with both hands you can bring it down on the wedge until the green husk is pared off.

Another American pilot who ditched his plane one'night off the coast of the Dutch East Indies swam to an island where he found several ripe coconuts in the sand. "He looked for his knife to open them and was furious to find he must have lost it in the water. So with the aid of a propelling pencil he began to peel the thick husk off the first coconut fiber by fiber. He reached the nut proper after almost four hours of peeling and then it was easy to break it up with a stone." (*The Art of Survival*, Cord Christian Troebst.)

If he would have started with the stone it would only have taken him an hour. If you still think half an hour is too much just to eat a coconut, think of the Mexican "mojados" who work on American berry farms near the border for twelve hours for just one meal at the end of the day.

The oil obtained from coconuts can be used for frying, cooking, and as lamp oil for earthenware lamps (this is still done regularly today in Africa and the South Pacific).

The simplest way of getting this oil is by boiling the coconut meat. This brings the oil to the surface of the water, then all you have to do is scoop it off.

A palm can be used in 999 different ways. The palm that is usually found inland, the Royal Palm, has at its heart a substance known as "palmillo". This is usually found at the very top where the trunk of the palm turns into a soft green segment much like the metal band that encases a section of an ice-pick handle. Inside that segment is where the leaves begin to form. And these leaves in their 'foetus' state are a real delicacy; sweet, soft and a bit dry, also very satisfying. So you see, even the palm that doesn't bear coconuts serves a more basic purpose than just adorning landscapes with awesome nobility and beauty. With palm resin you can polish cars, floors, furniture, and shoes, make carbon paper and phonograph records. Palm oil is used in the making of metal plating, (e.g. in food cans) and of toilet soaps and other cosmetics, lubricants, varnishes, and weatherproof coatings. Palms serve as a basis for the manufacture of syrups, sweets, and aromatic substances.

Indeed the palm is "the princess of the plant world," "a gift of God."

HOW TO MAKE CHIT'LINS (CHITTERLINGS)
Cris Burks Lewis

Down home, when the hogs are shiny with fat, the neighbors gather in my grandma's backyard to watch the slaughtering of her hogs. Each year four or five hogs are changed into porkchops, pork roast, pickled pig feet and ears, neckbones to be boiled and smothered with white potatoes, cracklin for bread, ham and lean bacon sugarcured, sausage seasoned with plenty of sage and kidneys for stew. The women bargain with grandma for the surplus fat while the men wait, impatiently wait, for grandma to announce the chit'lin dinner date.

The main attractions are two ancient black kettles that steam with fresh cooked chit'lins. For two days the stank of the chit'lins assaulted the air with rudeness. Yet no one minded as they knew each morsel would be tender and succulent, full of flavor.

The problems with having a chit'lins dinner in the city are the lack of fresh chit'lins. You can buy chit'lins in 5, 10, and 20 pound pails. However, since they have been chemically treated and frozen some of the original taste is lost. Please note—the best time to purchase chitterlings (frozen or, if you are lucky, fresh) is the winter months. It is during this time that pigs are slaughtered, but also the heat of summer adds to the risk of trichinosis and spoilage.

In order to cook chit'lins you must possess two things: a huge pot and a strong nose. If you are squirmy when it comes to a foul smell I suggest you have porkchops for dinner as chit'lins give off an offense odor, like an outhouse in the summer.

It's also wise to plan the dinner for a Sunday so you will have ample time to cook and clean them. A pail of chit'lins is packed tightly and frozen. They require more time than other meat to defrost. Generally 12 to 16 hours. It's advisable to leave them out overnight.

I feel it's most comfortable to clean them in a spotless kitchen after a nice hot bath. This insures that the meat is clean and also prevents your stomach from turning at the filth.

Pour the defrosted chit'lins into a clean sink. Each chit'lin is one long intestine of the hog. It is wiggly and split down the middle like a busted balloon. The frozen chit'lins are freed of the waste matter except for a few specks here and there. Fresh chit'lins are caked with a huge amount of waste matter and require more time and a steel stomach to clean. Therefore, if this is your first time cleaning chit'lins I advise you use frozen ones.

Run cold water into the sink. COLD, not Hot, as hot makes them slimy and activates the odor before it's necessary.

Annie Banks used hot water the first and only time she attempted to cook chit'lins. The smell was so strong that she became dizzy and vomited on top of the chit'lins. She threw the 20 pounds of chit'lins and waste out, and has not eaten another bit since.

Therefore, I urge you to USE ICE COLD WATER.

You may want to sprinkle a little salt over them. I don't know why! There are several wives' tales for this:

    1. According to grandma, salt kills any filth.

2. Aunt May says salt helps remove the fat.

3. Mama says it's just the thing to do when cooking chit'lins.

But, as I've said, it probably don't make a difference. I've never not done it, so I can't tell you.

Add two cups of vinegar to the water as this helps loosen the fat; also if you let this set for two to three hours it will cut down the odor later. Be sure to keep changing the water and adding the vinegar as it is important that the water stay ice cold.

After they have soaked, hold one chit'lin at the tip. Stretch it open with both hands. Once it's open, you will see globs of white fat dotted with black, brown and green waste matter. Using the fingers of one hand like a claw, firmly grip this and pull it off. You will have to repeat this several times in each spot. The spot is cleaned when the skin is faintly translucent. You will see tiny web design inside the skin. Do this continuously along each intestine. You may wish to cut the chit'lins in half as one intestine is sometimes two feet long. Also, since the intestine is full of dips and curves, you should be particularly attentive to these areas as a small particle may be curled there.

Once the chit'lins are freed of fat and waste matter, rinse them carefully under running water with quick spot checks. Place them in a large pot, approximately 10 to 12 quarts. Cover with water, add two cups of vinegar per 20 pounds, place over a high heat and cover with a lid.

While waiting for the chit'lins to boil, skin and cut four onions in half; place these on top of the boiling chit'lins. According to your own personal taste you may want to add crushed red pepper.

The onions and vinegar will tone down the smell of the chit'lins, but for an added measure you may do the following: unscrew the top of the lip (the handle), place a pared apple on top and drop a grain of salt on the inside of the apple.

Allow 10 to 12 hours cooking time. I prefer a low heat overnight. If the chit'lins is covered with plenty of water they will simmer into a mellow flavor. Add salt to taste.

HOW TO SLOW DANCE WITH A COWBOY
Kim Geller

If there is one thing I am grateful for in my life, it is that I was born a female. Not because I love pink and party dresses, and not because if there was a war I wouldn't have to go, but because being born a female I automatically acquired the opportunity to experience a thrill no male child could (or would want to) feel, the thrill of slow dancing with a cowboy. It is not an experience most girls know about or have had, and this is a shame because they are most certainly missing out. So, although it will not be fair to the males who read this paper, I am going to explain to the girls the absolute right way to slow dance with a cowboy.

First and foremost one must realize that slow dancing with a cowboy is not merely a few minutes of meaningless grappling to a warped ballad—it is an art. If you keep this thought in mind at all times, your quest for the ultimate in titillating thrills will become much more attainable.

The very first thing to take into consideration is where to go to meet your cowboy. This is an important decision because if you choose the wrong bar the consequences could be disastrous. You might have to be willing to do a little traveling. In my opinion, the best place to meet the most rugged REAL cowboys is a little place called The Dirty Boot in Kerreville, Texas. I choose this as the ideal place because any guy who hangs out at The Dirty Boot is not someone you would ever bring home to your mother, which by the way brings me to my next rule: if a cowboy asks you to dance and he looks like someone you'd introduce to your mother, not only refuse the dance but leave the bar immediately—you're definitely at the wrong place.

Rule number two has to do with dress. There is no particular dress code; HOWEVER, it is important to exude the right sort of sleazy-but-sweet attitude. If you are at the right place, it will be dark, so colors are unimportant —but make sure the clothes you wear are snug. Also, I like to wash my hair with Spring Rain shampoo and conditioner because I have found that cowboys love the smell. I don't recommend a lot of make-up, but it is important to be tan because tan skin is warmer to the touch than pale skin. Only one who has slow danced with a cowboy knows how important heat is.

When you first walk into your cowboy hang-out it is important to make eye contact with and smile to the bartender. Once you have the bartender on your side you pretty much have it made in the shade. It is the bartender who most probably will be responsible for getting you noticed by saying things like, "Whew! Get a load at what just walked in!" (Not the sarcastic version of that saying. If you're somewhere where the cowboys are smart enough to get into sarcasm, leave immediately—you're in the wrong area.) Or, "Now there's some flesh I'd like to get into." It is these comments to the regulars he is bringing beers to that will start the ball rolling.

Remember, when you walk in, don't sit at the bar. Take a seat at a table for two between the bar and the little dance floor. The jukebox should be diagonally in front of you and around twenty feet to the right. The first drink you order should be a shot of something strong (I strongly recommend Jack Daniel's) and never on the rocks. Not only will this drink relax you, but it will also establish you as the kind of woman who can drink Jack Daniel's straight and for some reason this will impress the bartender. Whatever you do, no matter how bad it tastes, drink it in three swallows and DON'T MAKE A FACE!

After the shot, order a beer and sip it slowly while soaking up the atmosphere. Do not get drunk. Getting drunk will turn your slow dance with a cowboy into a "taking out the garbage" kind of thing. Also, if you're drunk you might end up getting a lot more than a slow dance and, well . . . that's another book. Anyway, while you're sipping your beer (actually you oughtn't sip but rather nurse) don't be afraid to glance around and see what the scene is. Don't look at anyone or in any direction for an extended period of time as you want to give the impression that you're a little bored. It is important, however, to remember who is where and which cowboy appears the most interesting.

Slowly glance back at him. You needn't stare because he will notice this second look right away and most likely act upon it. Now focus your attention to the floor in front of the jukebox. Keep your eyes there until you notice a pair of beat-up, scuffed, broken-in cowboy boots. Again glance up at your now-chosen cowboy. Make eye contact and give the smallest smile that you can give. He will turn around and put a dime (yes, if the jukebox costs 25 cents a play you're at the wrong place, and leave immediately) in the machine. He will punch in two rectangular buttons and a man with a deep voice, singing a very sad, very slow song, will be heard.

Now, and this is important, focus your eyes on his boots again. Notice how they are slowly striding towards you and revel in the rhythmic dull tapping sound they make. When they are finally directly in front of you, have your gaze move lazily up to your cowboy's face. On your way up notice the faded softness of his jeans and the hardness of his rodeo muscles underneath. Notice how many times the T-shirt looks like it's been washed and pause for a moment on the tanned, well-developed arms. Look at his thick neck and now look at his face straight on. The perfect cowboy face is handsome but weathered. His features will be almost clumsy-looking but not in an offensive way. He should look comfortable—like a worn-in, faded flannel sleeping bag on a chilly December night.

When he asks you if you'd like to dance, his voice will be low and direct. Look him square in the eyes and nod your head "yes." He will now hold out his large, cattle-steering hand, and you take it fearlessly. Follow his slow, cockroach-killing boots to the dance floor and now face him. He will take your left hand and put his other arm around you. If his palms are sweating, excuse yourself to the women's room or telephone because real cowboys do not have sweaty palms. His arm will feel strong around you and he will pull you in close. If you listened to my advice about the shot, now is the time you will be glad you did.

There is no use giving any more instructions now as the cowboy takes over and there is very little else to be done. The only other tips I can think to tell you are: don't breathe hard, don't ask him if he has a girlfriend, and don't ask who's singing. When your face is close to his neck be sure and smell him—in my opinion there is no better smell than the neck of a cowboy. It will smell clean and a little spicy with the faintest bit of sweat (NOT perspiration—sweat). If you detect that teensy, faint smell of sweat, then congratulations! You have caught yourself a real live cowboy!

THE FINE ART OF TEQUILA SHOTS
Jennifer Sheridan

You're fifteen now, almost a man, so it's time for you to learn to do shots of tequila. Your friends will know pretty soon if you aren't doing them. They notice these things.

I will tell you now that you will become intoxicated drinking tequila to an extent you never dreamed in your kiddy rum-and-Coke drinking days, and you will become cocky. You will think you can do them without lime, without salt. If you're like me, you're a showman, you want to impress the ladies, who doesn't? However, you will regret the forfeit or jumbling of any of my instructions when you are puking your guts out in the bushes, but I'll get back to that.

Let me begin by telling you a couple of things to watch for. First of all, there are two main brands of tequila. You have Two Fingers, which comes in the black, frosted glass bottle, very stylish; babes love it. The problem with Two Fingers, however, is that you cannot see how much tequila is in the bottle at any given time during the evening. This is an important fact to be aware of, as it is imperative that all the tequila be consumed in one sitting. Only a bunch of wimps fail to finish their bottle. The drinker who monitors the bottle is able to pace himself and still insist on taking the last shot, thus appearing to be a more serious drinker.

The other top brand is Mescale. This brand does not have the disadvantage of the black glass, but, as you know, there is the worm to consider. Mescale is famous for the dead worm fermenting at the bottom of every bottle. The coolest dude at the tequila shot party always eats the worm at the end of the night. This is you, pal. Your friends will notice if you don't.

Imagine, if you will: a roomful of drunken teenage boys, your closest chums, the men who will one day make or break you on that slow, steep climb to success. Mike and Woody, today snot-nosed bullies, will one day land you your first job. These men have sisters you will seduce, college research papers you will buy. The opinion of these guys is your future. They will turn on you now, an angry, uncontrollable mob, if you try to wave away that worm, saying, "I have a sensitive stomach. Maybe next time, guys." There'll be no next time with these guys; they don't forget the big mistakes, the ones you must avoid tonight. The countdown to your future begins now. Read on.

There are three basic elements in proper tequila shot taking: the lime, the salt, and, of course, the tequila itself. The lime must be cut into quarters. You don't want too sharp a knife because, as your vision begins to blur and your speech to slur beyond your control, you could very well cut your fingers or slice off your hands or those of your friends and be unable to phone for paramedical aid. Not a good way to impress the gang, my friend. But don't use a knife that is too dull, either. No butter knives here, pal, okay? This is serious. Limes are not as easy to cut as you might think. You may want to prepare them at home beforehand.

So, quarter the limes, and by the way, lemons are not a substitute. We are not baking sugar cookies here. The size is important. Focus on bite-size, because that is the name of the game in tequila limes. Halves won't fit in your mouth. You don't want that much lime anyway; it's nasty and it takes the enamel off your teeth. But no skimping, either. Buy enough limes to have one quarter for every shot taken by each participant and then some. This is adulthood. This is alcohol. Dental health is not our main concern.

Now that you have your limes prepared, I have a few words of advice about salt. I myself prefer Morton, especially on those stormy autumn evenings so perfect for a cozy night around the hearth with ten or twelve of your closest rowdy buddies. Please resist the temptation to use your mother's salt substitute. She may be sodium conscious but come on, you are young and strong, in your prime really, and if you're so worried about your health at a time like this, then let's just forget the whole thing now.

I'll pause now to tell you why we use lime and salt when taking shots of tequila. It has been suggested by some researchers that by distracting the taste buds with these dramatic flavors, one is able to keep the stomach bile from rising to the throat, but as far as I know it's just tradition to do it this way.

Sitting in front of you now are the following: quartered limes, box of salt (no shakers allowed, too much spillage), a clean shot glass, and a full bottle of tequila. Are you ready? Shall we begin?

Fill the shot glass to the rim with tequila. Set it aside, but keep it close— within arm's reach. Now, if you bend your thumb back in an exaggerated hitch-hiker position you will see a small indentation just above the wrist.* This space was prepared genetically for tequila shots!

Fill that dimple on your left hand with salt. With your limes and shot at the ready, steadily bring your left hand up to your mouth and, like a cow at a salt-lick, lick that salt off your hand. Really swipe it with your salt-thirsty tongue, and while the salt is melting down your throat, pick up your shot with your right hand, being careful not to spill any; remember that the boys are watching like buzzards waiting for a carcass to drop on the desert sand. Drink it down. Really chug it. For God's sake, don't sip it! You'll never make it to law school if you sip. Pretty girls will never take off their monogrammed blouses, moaning your name. You will never marry or procreate, and your father's name will slide into oblivion, so please, KICK IT BACK!

Now bite into the lime quarter with all your might, really chomp down. You're biting a citrus bullet. Don't eat the peel, you numbnut, it might be poisonous or something. You only want the juice.

There, you've done it, your first shot. Congrats. Repeat procedure, passing the bottle around the room until it is empty. Don't forget to laugh at and totally alienate anyone who makes the slightest mistake. Remember they would do the same to you without hesitation if you had not had the benefit of reading this manual beforehand.

What do you think? No problem, right? Well, you'll learn to love it eventually. Now, cut loose! Work with it, enjoy it. This is your youth. You will look back on this time of your life with tearful joy once you hit thirty and your body is too worn out to have this much fun, believe me.

*Some find the space between the thumb and forefinger more suitable for holding salt. These people may have physical deformities that do not allow for the traditional method described above. For individuals having such problems with dexterity, this second salt location is acceptable, though not necessarily preferable.

Once the bottle is empty and you are totally soused, don't pass out. There is still plenty of party left.

Remember the worm.

There are those who insist that the worm is an hallucinogenic. Be sure to tell everyone that you saw the furniture breathing, that colors spoke to you in ancient languages after you ate the worm, whether or not it is true or you even vaguely remember anything like that two days from now when you are able to stand without assistance.

Which brings me to barfing. You will be lucky if you wake up tomorrow having expelled some of the alcohol from your system, so don't hesitate. Here are a few pointers that will keep you relatively embarrassment and mess free.

Think of your parents, even if you are not in your own home. At the first real signs of nausea—not just that nagging little gag you will undoubtedly feel as the tequila passes your taste buds—make your way calmly but quickly, "in an orderly fashion," to borrow grade-school fire-drill lingo, to the bathroom. Phrases like, "Gotta hit the can, man," and "Be right back, gotta take a leak," mumbled, so as not to invite anything to leap up from your stomach too soon, will excuse you without too much notice. If the bathroom is occupied, make for the bushes. A clump of dark, quiet shrubbery will suit your needs nicely. Stay off the driveway. If all else fails and you feel the need to ralph where you stand, just be sure to stay off the carpet, at all costs. It is also not a great idea to throw up on people, animals or furniture, but rugs somehow get remembered. Picture this:

> "Oh man, remember when that jerk lost it on my mother's new Persian carpet?"
> "Oh man, yeah. What a nerd!"
> "Oh man, you said it. I'll never party with him again."

So watch it.

At the same time, you can and should exaggerate the details of your vomiting experience. Use phrases like: "worshiping the porcelain god," "technicolor yawn," and "tossing salad." These phrases, until now, have been reserved exclusively for use on the finer college campuses around the country. Make the best of them.

In general, think of tequila shot parties as a natural rite of passage, not unlike circumcision and getting slammed in the stomach during third-grade dodgeball. It is something that everyone goes through. Enjoy it! You will surely laugh a lot at any number of jokes concerning farting and the female anatomy. Do elaborate imitations of teachers and television personalities. Remember, be safe, don't drive or operate heavy farm machinery, and above all, don't suggest making margaritas, the wimpiest of all tequila drinks. What do you think this is, a girl's slumber party? I mean, come on.

HOW TO CREATE A SUPER-HERO COMIC BOOK STORY
Jim Batts

I suppose I started being very interested in comic books when I was about 10 years old. Mind you, I'd been drawing since I was old enough to hold a pencil. Of course, I'd read "Casper," "Little Lulu," and other "baby comics" up till then. But I didn't really become fascinated by comics until the "Batman" TV show. Looking back at that show, I find it embarrassing, dumb, and cute, but in my 10-year-old mind it ignited something. I immediately subscribed to "BATMAN COMICS." I was disappointed by the blandness of the art and stories. When they ran out, I shopped around for different comics. I then discovered the heroes of the "MARVEL COMICS GROUP," Spiderman in particular. These stories, with their involving plots, bold artwork, and unusual characters, sent me to my drawing pad. It was then that I knew when I grew up I would create super-hero comic book stories.

What's the first step in doing a super-hero comic book story? First you must have a star of the tale, like Spiderman or Batman. He (or she) must be original and unique enough to grab the reader's attention. In most cases the star carries the story. For my first character I thought up Captain Kermet. Cap is inspired by the Marvel Heroes, Captain Marvel, and the grand-daddy of them all, Superman. As Leroy H. Kermet he's a short, balding, chubby, bespectacled pipsqueak of a guy who is given a power belt by alien visitors. By pressing the belt he is transformed into the tall, handsome, blond long-underwear hero, Captain Kermet. Not very complex, is he? Well, I created him while I was in fifth grade, so that's the audience I was aiming for. Design your character with an audience in mind. Even if he's totally super-heroic, give him a human quality which everyone can identify with. If you've got a good character to start with, you've got success nearly guaranteed.

The step after that is nearly as difficult: getting an idea. If you've an interesting character, ideas shouldn't come too slow. For instance, Captain Kermet is powerless against, let's say, purple baboons. Bizarre, but you get the picture. Fashion an idea from the personality and powers of your hero. You can also get ideas from current events. Say you've just seen "STAR WARS." Now how would the good Captain respond to similar situations and characters? Don't make it enough like SW to be plagiaristic, just give it that same feeling. This way you can have a good topical adventure story and a clever parody. Keep an open mind and don't throw out anything as too wild.

Plotting is very important. A slow-paced story will lose the reader's interest quickly. Try to get the hero in peril as soon as possible. Most comic book stories have this basic formula: villain does nasty thing; hero meets him; hero gets hell knocked out of him; villain escapes; hero finds out villain's weakness; hero and villain fight it out again; villain gets bejabers beat out of him; police capture villain; hero walks into sunset. Actually, plotting depends on how long you wish your story to be. I've described the most basic super-hero tale. Some stories have stretched as long as ten issues. Don't let it get too wordy or complex; just keep the story rolling along.

Now don't make it all action; keep it very tense and dramatic, but break in every once in a while with a little humor. Plot it as: action—break—small action—longer break—big action finale. The framework should be as basic and simple as you can make it.

Now is the time to think out and design your supporting characters. Actually, the story can be a showcase for the villain. Sometimes the basic premise of the bad guy can give you his personality. For example, Cap's arch-enemy, Crabman, would love the sea and be very irritable. You can also get an idea of his appearance: claw gloves, shell-like torso, and a clam-like head. Most villains are either big, dim-witted, brawny, ugly, or warped: thugs or grotesque scientists. The rest of the cast can be dumb henchmen or friends of the good guy. Most of the friends should be good-natured but not very bright. Some can be klutzy for comic relief. A couple could even suspect that the lovable schmuck is also the amazing righter of wrongs. They also can provide some suspense if the bad guy grabs one of them. A few can be policemen or detectives who can also provide comic relief as they try to help the hero. The henchmen can range from the abused little "Ygor" assistant to the smooth killer who loves his work. Design them for quick identification and keep the original drawings in case you wish to use them for other stories.

The next step is called the Marvel method since that staff pioneered it. Because one writer handled several books, he would give each book's artist a rough outline so he could have more time for his books. Since you'll be doing the art also, you needn't be too descriptive. Set a number of pages and describe what action each page will contain. For example, Page 4: Kermet is knocked cold by Crabman; C picks up K and swims to his underwater hideout; K wakes later to find himself being lowered into the hungry jaws of a giant shark. Also, if any pertinent or clever dialogue should pop into your head, inject it into the outline. Put this framework aside and later you can come back and put in all the dialogue and descriptions.

Now we are ready to begin drawing the story. Nearly all comic art is done on illustration or bristol board about 11 inches by 14 inches. You will also find a ruler and a T-square useful. Of course, you should have a pencil and a kneaded or gum eraser. Position your paper on your drawing board or desk. Now comic book pages are divided into panels. Each panel contains a separate sequence of action. For example, in panel one Cap walks to the door; in panel two Cap opens the door. Don't clutter the page with too many panels. Comic pages should have a maximum of six or seven panels. For huge battle scenes sometimes a "splash" panel will do. A "splash" panel is one which encompasses an entire page. In each panel remember to leave a few dead areas for dialogue and descriptions to be put in later. Vary what goes into each panel. Doing a comic book story is like film-making. Use all sorts of camera angles to see the action: close ups, long shots, medium shots, bird's eye views, through the characters' eyes, ant's eye views, etc. Make each highly dramatic. While drawing the story, experiment and find out what works the best for you.

After you've drawn the story, it's time for lettering. For this you'll need a thin pen or rapidograph and a bottle of water-proof India ink. You should have plenty of room for the word balloons (character dialogue) and captions (descriptions and time indications). Use your T-square and draw them out with your pencil. Each letter should not be over a quarter of an inch square. Limit the amount of balloons and captions. The pictures should be able to speak for themselves. Remember to keep it simple. Now go over the penciled lines with your pen and make the words you wish to stress darker. For example: "HEY! Is that YOU?" Don't forget to ink the borders on the pages and the comic-book sound effects (BIFF, POW, ZAP). And yes, try to keep it neat.

In order for your drawings to reproduce clearly in the comic printing process, you'll need to ink your artwork. Add a good sable brush to your list of materials. Keep most of the lines to a medium thickness. Balance your panels with light and dark areas. Don't overwork with your ink or the art will look dark and muddy when printed. Be sure to practice with your pen and brush until you feel comfortable before you begin. Mistakes can be expected, so don't get upset. Inking is a very specialized aspect of comic book stories.

The next step is optional. Up to this point your story should look good enough without coloring, but it's a good idea to try it anyway. Decide what colors your hero's costume will be. For coloring you'll need a watercolor set and brushes. Choose the colors for all your characters. Don't make them too garish and flashy, and remember simplicity. For backgrounds give them a kind of dull flat tone so your character will stand out against them. Try not to color your backgrounds the same as a predominant color of your character or he'll blend in. Don't just throw the colors on; plan them out. The coloring on a story is like icing on a cake. If done well, it'll make a good comic book story even better.

You're now done with the hard work on your comic book story. Find out how to get in contact with publishers or just somebody with printing apparatus to get your story printed. Be sure to show it to your friends for their opinions. Most of the people I've shown mine are amazed that I've tried such a thing. They seem to be impressed by the thought of an original story told in a visual way. Make note of all comments and use them to make your next comic book story even better.

Comic publishers will also critique your story. Don't get discouraged by unfavorable comments. Everything is helpful. Some people I've shown my stuff can hardly believe that someone would waste time doing comic books. That attitude is changing. Comic art is finally being recognized as fine art and given respect in France and Italy. This new way of looking at comics is spreading across the U.S. fairly quickly. At times when I get disappointed by an unsuccessful story, I remember that ten-year-old who was delighted and inspired by those comic book stories, and I decide to go back to my drawing board and try once more.

How-It's-Done

OREO FATALE
Linda Hamburg

Dear Nabisco,

Before I get to the main issue of this letter, which is my complaint with you, suffer me to explain something about myself.

For thirty-three years of my life, I have been a chubby chick. When I was a little girl, I was cute and cuddly, so everyone called it baby fat. In my adolescence, I was described as pleasingly plump, and my parents began their losing battle with me to lose weight.

When I moved from Champaign to embark on my single life in Chicago, I decided to try all kinds of diets to get skinny. All of my attempts were pretty successful and I usually managed to get within 15 pounds of my goal weight. My will power—what little I have—has always been strong for the first two months of any diet I've tried. This is where we get to the problem —Oreo cookies. Why on earth did you have to invent Oreo Cookies? You see, at the end of the second month I always begin to get a craving for Oreo cookies. First, they seem to loom out of nowhere into my vision. I can be working or driving when all of a sudden I'll see this giant Oreo in front of me, a round chocolate wafer with the Nabisco logo stamped on top. As it rotates like a huge sign, I see the ridges on the rim of the cookie, and then appears the creamy white center peeking out from between the first and second cookie. I blink my eyes and the vision disappears for awhile. A couple of days later, I begin to actually smell the familiar fudgy chocolate fragrance that is truly the Oreo smell. Nothing else smells like an Oreo cookie, and nothing I try to do will rid me of the overpowering aroma. When my mouth starts to drool, I know I've had it. All attempts to stay out of the cookie aisle in the grocery store fail. Suddenly there I am, standing in front of the cookie shelves; hundreds of brands and flavors, all stacked neatly, beckon to me, but I am indifferent to them. Riveted to one spot, I stare longingly at that familiar cellophane package with the appetizing cylindrical rows of chocolate sandwiches. I pick up the package tenderly, fighting with my conscience, but it's a losing battle. As I glance from side to side to make certain that my parents aren't spying on me, I drop the package into my shopping cart and proceed to the check-out area.

All the way home I keep telling myself, "Don't do it. You've come so far, don't blow it now." My other voice says, "You've been a good girl. You deserve a treat. Three cookies won't hurt."

Inside the apartment I put away the groceries and go to the refrigerator. I take out the milk and pour it into a tall glass. I don't drink milk at any other time, but it's a cardinal rule that one must never eat Oreos with anything other than a glass of ice-cold milk. Tearing open the package (I must comment here on your packages. They never open right. I always end up ripping the cellophane under the seal on top and down the side. It's such a mess), I remove the first cookies and hold it in the palm of my hand. Sitting down at the table, I stare at it lovingly. I cup my hand; it fits so snugly. My fingers travel over the surface of the chocolate orb, feeling the raised lettering and design. As I turn it over, admiring its perfection, I draw it to my nostrils and inhale luxuriously. "What a lovely aroma," I say softly with my exhalation. Thoughts of added pounds to my newly slender frame creep in, so I shove the first Oreo into my mouth before I can change my mind. I follow this with a gulp of milk. After a short pause (this is a long drawn-out procedure because I'm only allowing myself three cookies) I reach for the cookie in the second row, so that the three rows will remain even. If I took two from the same row it wouldn't look right. I'm a neat eater. It's the only thing I do neatly.

The second cookie is eaten differently from the first. I hold one side of the sandwich with the tips of the fingers of my right hand, and with the fingers of the left, I carefully pry the other side away from the filling. This can be done with alternate hands, but I'm a lefty. Hopefully, the cookie will separate without crumbling, leaving the icing on only one of the inside surfaces. Sometimes the filling separates, too, and tears, leaving some on one cookie and some on the other. This is okay, too. It makes for more variation in Oreo-eating.

I proceed to eat one half, little nibble by little nibble, drawing the whole event out and making every single bite count. Not forgetting, of course, the milk, which should be sipped in between each bite of chocolate cookie. This is the only way to do it. The first chocolate wafer gone, I proceed to lick the creamy vanilla filling. This can be dragged out to an hour of licking, unless, of course, my tongue gets a cramp. When I get a cramped tongue, I begin chipping away at the filling, or I glide through the middle with just my two front teeth. The chipping method can lengthen the process, but the gliding is more fun. It makes me feel like I'm diving into a vat of creamy vanilla filling. I glide through the center of the circle of filling first, then eat the sides that are left. Following a sip of milk, I toss the remaining chocolate wafer into my mouth, fill my mouth with milk and let the wafer melt. Taking the third cookie from the third row, I eat it in a normal fashion in small bites. I pulverize each delicious bite slowly into powder between my teeth, followed, of course, by milk. I usually end up with no more milk and a couple of bites of cookie. So I pour more milk. Polishing off the cookie with a swallow of milk, I find I have more milk left and no more cookie. This is easily corrected by taking a fourth cookie.

With the fourth cookie eaten, I could be finished, but now the rows of cookies in the package aren't even. This is the crux of the problem because the whole damned procedure keeps starting over and over again. Suddenly I realize that half of the the package has been eaten. "How did I manage to do that?" I cry. "Now I've done it again."

It is with a mixture of despair and grief that I take what's left of the Oreos and go out to the garbage can by the alley and throw the remaining ones away. I've tried just hiding them in the house, but I always weaken again. The only other alternative would be to take them over to Ron Smith's house, but then he'll invite me in for coffee, and the two of us might end up eating Oreos together.

The next day the bathroom scale reads 3 to 5 pounds heavier. So I resolve once more to stay on the diet, and most of all, to abstain from Oreos forever. However, I always crumble when it comes to Oreos.

So, you see, don't you, that it's really all your fault, Nabisco? If you had never invented Oreos, I would have been skinny a long, long time ago.

Tomorrow I am starting a brand new diet. No more putting it off and no more falling into the same pattern. No, no, Nabisco, I shall never succumb to your scrumptious cookies again. So, don't bother sending me money-off coupons or even a case of cookies in gratitude for this letter. I won't eat another Oreo until the next time.

SKYDIVE
Bob Mercer

Every weekend you see them standing there with hands over their eyes, shielding them against the sun, while looking up into the sky, watching, waiting, as the plane ten thousand feet above, a black dot against the sky, bores its way through the air. Then all of a sudden, as if a plug had been pulled from a socket, the plane's engines die, and there's a moment of silence as the plane glides through the air, leaving in its wake a small trickle, which quickly grows into a long line of human flesh and blood. Twelve skydivers thrust themselves from the noisy, vibrating fuselage of the airplane, with their arms and legs spread-eagled, marking the beginning of their mile-and-a-half fall through the sky before opening their parachutes two thousand feet above the ground.

You can hear the people standing on the ground talking to themselves, saying out loud or to the person next to them, "Ma-a-an, it sure takes a lotta balls to do that!" Or the guy standing there with his girlfriend, some hot blonde, and boasting, "Shi-it, I got the balls to do that!"

For skydivers, the real skydivers (not some guy who made five jumps in the military ten years ago and not the guy who made a couple of static-line jumps so he can go back to the bar and impress all the chicks—no, I'm not talking about them—I'm talking about the people, men and women, who eat, sleep, and breathe the sport, the ones who divorce their wives or husbands for the sport), you see, for these people, jumping out of airplanes isn't a matter of how big your balls are or how many you got. For them, jumping out of airplanes is a religion, an addiction. It's the alcoholic's alcohol.

By the time a skydiver has made a hundred and fifty jumps or so, all thoughts of the sport as a thrill or stunt, as something that's going to kill him if his parachute doesn't work, are long gone. Even the thrill of just jumping and freefalling from a perfectly good airplane is gone. Fifteen years ago, a skydiver would probably be giving up the sport with about two hundred jumps, not because the sport was considered dangerous, but more because it became boring. There wasn't anything to do once you left the plane, except backloops and barrel rolls; and after a few hundred of them, even they became boring. But today skydivers with a hundred and fifty, two hundred jumps are still students learning the art of "free fall relative work," the art of flying one's body around the sky on an invisible cushion of air that's created by the skydiver's own body as it falls through the sky, allowing him or her to become their own "body pilot" and master of movement in the third dimension.

Today, more than ever, skydivers fly their bodies around the sky. If you've ever stuck your hand out a car window while driving down the expressway, you've probably felt the same type of air cushion that a skydiver's body creates as it falls through the sky. On this cushion of air, the skydivers, by using different body movements, can propel themselves around the sky. By twisting their bodies to the left or right, they can make turns. Other movements, such as sticking their arms out in front of them while pulling their legs in (which puts them in the same position as a person sitting in a chair with arms stretched upward, only tilted forward about forty-five degrees), allow the skydivers to slide backwards. Although skydivers can't fly upward, they can control the speed at which they fall downward by spreading their arms and legs outward. This allows them to grab more air with their bodies, creating more drag as they fall through the sky and thus slowing down their rate of fall. Pulling their arms in close to their sides, their hands about their shoulders and their legs tucked up, reducing the body size, streamlining it, causes the jumpers' rate of fall to increase. Skydivers can adjust their rate of fall from about eighty miles per hour downward with their arms and legs fully outspread, grabbing all the air they can, to over two hundred miles per hour in a straight head-down dive with their arms against their sides and their legs straightened like a ski-jumper standing on his head.

Today skydivers use this control for doing "relative work," the building of formations by two or more skydivers while in freefall. The skydiver flies himself or herself from the airplane to a formation of other jumpers falling through the sky at the same time. They fly their bodies to predesignated positions or "slots," as they call them, making "grips," holding onto the other jumpers' arms and legs.

Skydivers have this saying, "There is no such thing as gravity, the earth sucks." And because of this fact of life, skydiving, unlike most sports, is learned in small pieces of time. "He who hesitates shall inherit the earth." On a typical skydive, the jumpers leave the plane at about 7,500 feet above the ground. They all leave at once and have about thirty seconds of freefall time in which to fly together and build their formations before they must split apart and open their parachutes at 2,000 feet. Because the actual time in freefall is so short, skydivers have to learn their sport in small slivers of time, as compared to most other sports. A skydiver might make ten jumps in one day and, for all his time (the whole day) and energy (repacking his parachute), only gain five minutes of freefall time to add to his logbook. This makes skydiving a never-ending learning process. The most experienced skydiver in the country has only seventy hours of freefall time, not much when you compare it to other sports like tennis or racquetball, where a serious amateur will put that much time (seventy hours) into his sport every month and a pro every two weeks. Just to learn the basics of relative work—flying down to someone and touching him and then falling at the same speed as him while holding on to each other ("pinning the base," as it's called)—takes about a hundred jumps before being mastered and done with consistency.

As a skydiver and pilot, I've seen a lot of skydives. I've watched hundreds of students make their first jump. A static-line attached to the plane opens the parachute as they fall away from the plane, and after a quick tug, they find themselves hanging 2,500 above the ground in a world they've never experienced before. I've seen students make their first freefalls, some picture perfect, falling away from the plane with their arms and legs spread out in a stiff spread-eagle position with a deep arch in their back, while others go flipping and tumbling end-over-end out of control or flat-spin like human pinwheels. I've watched eighty-jump skydivers, no longer considered students because they've made over twenty- five freefalls (twenty-five freefalls is the magic number that cuts the student's umbilical cord and erases the word STUDENT that stands in front of SKYDIVER), fly down to one another and come within six inches of "making contact" (actually touching another person in freefall), only to begin orbiting one another like the blades of a slow moving fan. They land frustrated, but with smiles on their faces.

I've watched thousand-jump-*plus* "skygods," people who look like any other normal human being on the ground but, when in the air, fly their bodies as naturally as any ground-bound person walks, talks, or breathes. They climb out onto a five-inch wide, two-foot long step that's attached to the plane's landing gear just above the right wheel, while holding on to the strut (a metal bar that's attached to the bottom of the plane's wing and runs down at a forty-five degree angle to the plane's fuselage) with one hand while seventy miles an hour of wind and noise rush past, trying to blow them off. They arrange themselves on the step. The first man out faces away from the plane's door with both feet on the front edge of the step and hangs on to the strut with his left hand, while the next two jumpers climb out after him, each taking a grip on the front person's legstrap with his inside hand while hanging on to the strut or the inside of the doorway with the other. The fourth man, the "tail man," as he's called, stoops in the doorway and reaches out to grab the inside legstraps of the two jumpers in front of him.

When everyone's ready, the tail man shakes the legstraps of the two jumpers in front of him, starting a chain reaction from back to front. The two middle jumpers shake the leg straps of the front man, and he in turn starts a quick swaying motion backwards that begins a domino-type effect, rippling backwards to the tail man stooping in the doorway. This motion changes quickly and suddenly from its ripple backwards to a quick, harmonious thrust forward off the step into a sightless sea of nothingness, sending them for a ride on an invisible, horizontal wave of air created by the plane boring its way forward through the sky. This wave tips the whole formation upward, almost flipping it over, before the highest side of it slowly begins to settle downward and flatten out. Falling straight down, the jumpers still hang on to one another, their bellies flat to earth and backs toward the sky. They let go of one another, twist, turn, and fly together again to make another formation, getting smaller and smaller as they brake, twist, and turn for another formation and then another and another, until they've become tiny specks against the massive backdrop of green cornfields below, having built eight to ten formations before splitting apart and opening their chutes for the final descent to the ground.

The good skydives, the "hot" ones, as they're called, don't just happen. Even after you reach the ranks of "SKYGOD," the hot skydives have to be worked for; they start long before anyone sets foot inside the airplane. They start with good "dirt dives" (practicing the planned skydive on the ground). The jumpers walk through the whole dive, twisting and turning, simulating the same movements they'll do when they're in freefall. These dirt dives are as important as the actual skydive. Without them, the jumpers might as well be throwing their money away. The dirt dives are free. They don't cost a cent and can last all day, compared to the actual skydive, which will cost seven dollars and last only a few minutes. It's during the dirt dives that the jumpers perfect what will actually be the skydive, working out any problems that might occur when changing from one formation to the next. It's the time put into the dirt dive that, in the long run, will make the actual skydive more efficient, allowing for better, hotter skydives in the future. The good skydivers, the ones who get the most formations out of each dive, spend anywhere from twenty to thirty minutes of hard, one hundred percent, concentrated effort on their dirt dives. By the time they climb in the plane, they know their job so well that the transitions from one maneuver to the next—who drops what grip when, and who pivots what way and grabs which leg or arm—become so instinctive they could do it in their sleep.

When a "HOT" skydive has been planned and twenty minutes of work have been put into dirt diving before climbing into the plane, the ride up to altitude is silent, except for the noise from the plane's engine and maybe a question or two from one of the jumpers. Otherwise, they just sit there, in deep concentration, going over the dive again and again, moving their arms and hands slightly, simulating each different maneuver, reaching one arm out, closing it, then letting go and twisting slightly one way or the other, mentally simulating the whole dive over and over again all the way up to altitude.

When the plane's altimeter reads 7.5 (7,500 feet), the jumpers in back twist around, pulling their arms in and ducking their heads, as they pull themselves up into a kneeling position. The space in the back is cramped, and everyone begins one last check of their equipment before the word "DOOR" is screamed out. With everything in place, reserve ripcord handles, pilot chutes, goggles (on tight), the man kneeling beside the door swings it open, filling the plane with the rushing noise and clean smell of the air at seven thousand feet, before climbing out onto the step.

Letters

DORM LIFE
Ann Hemenway

After dinner Elaine went back to her room. She never carried keys because she never locked her door. There was nothing in her room to steal. No radio, no stereo, just a dusty typewriter with keys that stuck. She went over to her bed and flopped on it face down. Without looking up, she reached one hand down to the side of the bed and groped around until she felt the pickle jar. Then she unscrewed the lid and dropped it on the floor and reached into the jar and fished around until she trapped the pickle. With her thumb and forefinger she slid the pickle to the side of the jar and pulled it out. Keeping her arm outstretched she flipped over to her back and then in one quick motion popped the pickle into her mouth. She stared at the ceiling and crunched. She thought, while staring upwards, that ceilings ought to be made more interesting. Michelangelo had the right idea. She thought of drawing tiny pictures all over it with a felt tipped pen, obscene pictures of pricks and twats and animals humping and tongues licking at everything. Better yet, sneak the obscene drawings in with harmless little doodles and hold a contest. Whoever could find the most obscene drawing won a bottle of tequila, a pair of edible underwear, and a penis-shaped lighter. Or else she could get her friend, J.P., the abstract expressionist, to paint incomprehensible designs up and down the ceiling. The thought pleased her so much that she contemplated the walls, trying to visualize pictures and designs. She saw swirling cyclone shapes and ants crawling up the walls. Her gaze fell on her desk and she saw a stamped letter lying there—a letter she had written to George and forgotten to mail. She'd written it about two weeks before so it was old. She got off the bed and grabbed it and returned to her original position. The letter was addressed to:

George (The Happy Wanderer) Luden
1550 N. Fitch
Weston, Mass.
PLEASE FORWARD

Dear George:

I'm writing this in the bathroom. I seem to think better when I shit. I just got back from the Skylark Inn. Remember it? Of course you do, you introduced me to it. How avant-garde you are, old George, now everyone goes there and talks to the lady with the cotton candy hair behind the bar. They're still tying the yellow ribbon 'round the old oak tree on the dance floor, except now they've got a new one. Frank Sinatra singing "That's Life."

How are the Gulf Stream Waters and the Redwood Forests? Still there? Or have you piled them on your roof with all the other junk?

I went to a party last night, my first one in ages, as you may well imagine, after being prostrate with grief after your departure. I haven't felt like doing much of anything lately. My friends are at a loss to figure out why their little Ellie, who was once so vibrant, has sunk into such a lethargic state. Alas, poor Elaine, her libido is lousy.

Well, Elaine, did go to a party—a small "get together" among friends. I expected there to be about ten people but there were only about six, including myself. I knew only one of the people there and didn't even know him well.

I'd been there about two minutes when I had a strange feeling that the other people there knew each other intimately. It seemed as though they had been in some catastrophe, like a flood or an avalanche together. They weren't rude to me; on the contrary, they all smiled and nodded at everything I said and looked at me with bright eyes and acted very interested in my profound comments. They acted too interested, as though they wanted to prove to me that they were open and affectionate people. One girl in particular, with mousy pop-eyes and a brown sweater, was the most warm and open. Everything she said was prefaced with my name. "Elaine, what do you think of this?" and "Well, Elaine, I feel that such and such..." And she kept putting her hand on my arm reassuringly. Don't ask me why she felt I had to be reassured. Do I have that kind of face? You always told me I had a cat face—a Tabby cat face, round and contented. Does a face like that need constant reassurance? Does it, George?

The mousy-eyed girl, Missy (Hurry, hurry, step right up and see Missy, the Mouse-eyed Girl) finally told me why everyone was acting like survivors from the Holocaust. They'd all been on an "Intimacy Retreat" together and were having a get together with their mediator in order to "share" their feelings about what had happened to them since this famous "retreat." I wonder if they beat each other off?

The mediator was a bony, red-bearded guy named Norm. Missy Mouse kept flashing her pop-eyes at me saying, "Norm's pretty neat, isn't he, Elaine?"

Norm had brought a big packing box full of papers and folders and said, "Tonight I'd like to share myself with you."

Miss Mouse's eyes really popped on that one. I think she wanted to get in his pants.

George, they treated Norm like a fragile piece of china, tapping their fingers on his arm, crowding around him when he started to "share" himself. Share what? Share what? To me, sharing always meant sharing half of your tuna fish sandwich with Bobby Biaggio in the grade-school cafeteria, or having to share your sand shovel with your sister when you were playing in the sandbox and you not wanting to so you hit her with it.

George, how do you share yourself? Cut off your finger and give it to them, making sure they give it back?

"I want to share these pictures with you," says Norm.

Why not just say, "Hey, feast your eyes on these, kiddo"?

It's dumb, George, dumb.

Anyway, Norm "shared himself" for the rest of the night. We saw pictures of his parents, of sunlight on water, class pictures of him as a little kid, pictures of his brothers, pictures of a retreat he went on where he painted a naked woman's body to get in touch with it. That was kind of interesting, except he kept talking about it as a "sharing experience." We saw pictures of people I don't know and never will. It got so I just stared at the pictures and then when he took them away to put out some other ones I'd keep staring at the empty place.

Well, old Norm really shared, George, whether we wanted him to or not.

I really had a rip-snorting time at that party. Why weren't you there so we could have walked out together? Why weren't you there so we could have muttered nasty, cynical comments to each other while staring at photograph after photograph. And sipping wine. And eating cheese. And crunching cauliflower buds with onion dip. I'm pissed at you, I really am.

Beware of wine and cheese parties. Especially when Joni Mitchell and Bob Dylan wail in the background. Personally, I got worried when I didn't see a single beer can.

By the way, your postcard was lovely. Furry grey kittens with blue eyes and bubbles floating around really make me go soft all over. I would have liked your postcard, too, if I could have read it. Is "Gleenf" a word? Were you writing in code? I did see the word "Flathead." Did you find Flathead, Wyoming?

My ass has probably got a bright red ring from sitting on this toilet for so long. Write soon, a 3-D postcard this time, please. I collect them.

Yours in Smut,
Elaine

P.S. Find out if people fuck in Flathead, okay? I've been wondering for days. Also, if you can find any pictures of erect penises, let me know. I don't think it's fair. We have this glistening twat that you cut out from that Hustler poster. But no erect penises. And believe me, there's not a sadder or more depressing sight than a drooping prick. So get me a hard one—- preferably one with a little cum on the end.

P.P.S. Duke the dog started humping Olive the mutt in the cafeteria and got put on probation. The next day he shat in the library, so now Reid, his owner, has to send him home.

Elaine decided to mail the letter, even though it was old. She pried the stamp off and put the letter in a new envelope, licked it, and went to the mailbox outside her dorm. She opened the door to the mailbox and slid the letter in.

"Who's the letter to?" said a male voice behind her.

It was Reid Henderson, the guy whose dog got expelled.

"To a friend," said Elaine looking him straight in the eye, ready to spit in it.

"To George?" he said, leering.

"Yeah, I told him I missed the way he cums on my face." she sneered.

He stopped leering. "Elaine, look, just because George and I hate each other's guts doesn't mean that you and I can't at least be civil to each other. Look, George has split, never to return again, so he's not around needing you to defend him. So why don't we just bury the hatchet and be friends?"

Elaine gazed at him. He had a body that didn't quit. "I'll consider it under one condition," she said.

"What's that condition?"

"That you never use another cliche like bury the hatchet around me again." Then she stared at him for a full minute looking him up and down and up and down.

"Do you draw?" she asked him.

"Yeah, I'm an art major, you fool."

"Can you draw obscene pictures?"

"I used to draw obscene pictures all over the bathroom wall in high school. Really gross ones."

Elaine turned and started heading into the dorm, she motioned for him to follow.

"What are we doing?" he said.

"You are going to draw obscene pictures all over my ceiling." And she shoved him in the door to her room.

WARD HEELER, 51ST WARD DEMOCRATIC ORGANIZATION
Andrew Hyzy

Dear Sir,

There comes a time in everyone's life when they realize that they haven't lived up to their own expectations. One will wake up some morning and realize that life is but an empty shell, a skeleton of what it could be. There are many reasons for this: dissatisfaction with one's work, love life, social standing, financial position, whatever. The reason really doesn't matter. What matters is that there is a feeling in the pit of one's stomach that loudly proclaims Failure. I implore you, please continue reading and let me explain my position.

I want to be a garbage man.

First of all, and most importantly, I am a true-blue, loyal Democrat. You will recall, sir, that I was a senior in high school and not yet eligible to vote when I first volunteered to work for the Democrats. At that time I did not have a city job and could have quite easily told you to ring your own doorbells, put up your own posters, do your own campaigning. But I didn't; quite faithfully I stuffed envelopes with campaign literature and sealed them until my tongue resembled a spoon dripping with congealed gravy. I rang doorbells for days on end, relentlessly urging people to support you at the polls. I went into houses that resembled Hiroshima after the bomb; I was attacked by mangy vicious dogs; I was insulted by vindictive Repulicans who would boldly slam their front doors in my face, making me feel humiliated and ashamed. I brazenly wore your campaign buttons as I stood in the hot sun, passing out literature on street corners, the victim of verbal abuse from all angles. I didn't even stop when I was mistaken for an immigration agent and shot at by a group of illegal Mexican aliens who quickly scurried under beds and behind curtains when they saw me at the door of their hacienda. Time and time again I listened patiently as people crabbed about dead trees, potholes, broken curbs, rats, busing, the Arab-Israeli conflict, snow removal, mortgage rates, and garbage cans. In the dead of night I went through the neighborhood, ripping down your opponent's campaign posters and replacing them with yours. I even hung them where it said "POST NO BILLS UNDER PENALTY OF LAW" on the walls. In short, sir, I busted my behind to help you get elected. On election day I stayed at the polls from 6:00 A.M. until 6:00 P.M., being careful to stay 100 feet from the entrance so there would be no trouble and your name wouldn't be blackened. I patiently helped old people crippled with arthritis out of their house, into my car, out of my car, into the polling place, and back again. I said nothing when they complained about the cleanliness of my car and then proceeded to ash their cigarettes on my car floor. When the election was over, and the results were in, there was nobody happier than me when you won. This was several years ago, sir, and I have been doing it ever since. Every time there has been an election I have frantically worked like a peasant for the Regular Democratic Organization. I have bought tickets to your annual golf outing, four of them each year at $30.00 each, and I don't even golf. I, sir, am a Democrat's Democrat. I stood in line for four hours in below-zero weather to view the body of the late

Richard J. Daley. Don't I deserve to be a garbage man?

Sir, I was born to be a garbage man. I am eminently qualified for this position. As a child, my favorite pastime was going through alleys, excitedly poking through muddy coffee grounds, saturated Tampax and moldy blue vegetables, seeking some sort of treasure. My parents' and grandparents' homes still bear evidence of these worthy scavenger hunts. On my grandmother's coffee table rests a large green pottery ashtray in the shape of a leaf that I distinctly remember taking from a garbage can at 88th and Kenwood in my youth. I am not afraid of dirt, sir, especially when it's useful dirt. I live for garbage, sir, and to be quite frank with you, I can no longer tolerate the job I have now. For four years I have been working steady midnights at Police Headquarters. My social life is suffering, the pay I receive is barely enough to live on, and worst of all, I have a desk job in an office with five women and four men. I have done good work where I'm at, exceptionally good work, and I don't steal paper clips, ashtrays, rubber bands, and toilet paper like some of my co-workers, yet have been passed over every time a promotion has come through. I'm trying to finish school and can take only one course per semester. I don't want to leave the city, sir, but I'm afraid that if I don't get something better in the employ of the city, I will have to look elsewhere, possibly in private industry.

In closing, I would like to thank you for reading this, and express my appreciation for anything that you can do to help. As one of your better campaign workers, I feel that I can be rest assured that I will be hearing from you soon.

Yours very truly,
Andrew F. Hyzy

MR. JONES
Elizabeth Sommers

Dear Mr. Jones:

We are an Ad Hoc committee consisting of your pillow cases, bed sheets and mattress. From the onset we must admit that we asked, even begged, for Blue Blanket to join our cause. It hurts our plea, certainly, to admit that he mocked our repeated requests with gales of laughter. While this cannot be remedied, please remember this: Blue Blanket is on top. We are on the bottom.

It is a pleasure to remind you, Sir, of our long, pristine, and uneventful life with you. Your insomnia never bothered us. Every few weeks you tossed us into the washer and dryer, allowing us to luxuriate in what we now must be forced to admit was a fantasy of cleanliness and spiritual purity. The few hours you did sleep were not troublesome to us. You merely slept, mouth firmly closed; the several dreamy comments you indulged in quite interested us. Though you were no stranger to nocturnal emissions, Mr. Jones, or even conscious pre-nocturnal emissions, Mr. Jones (as it were), you did indulge us in this habit. You were clean, neat and careful. Our dignity was never wounded.

While on occasion you were joined in your insomnia by this or that young vixen (and we are not women-haters, Mr. Jones, although our preferences are different from your own), by and large the temporary nature of these liasons rendered indulgence simple. Now, however—and this is delicate, even sticky—we must draw the line. Your unprecedented zeal shows no sign of abating. Nor does her's, whom for our modest purposes we shall appellate X.

Mr. Jones, we beg you. X and you talk incessantly through the night. She squirms and exclaims. You answer back in baby talk. She reciprocates in kind. The two of you sleep together in obscene, convoluted positions. Then, and we know of no euphemistic way to put it, you osculate in your sleep. Spittle occurs. You ignore our revulsion.

Then you wake, en masse as it were. The nightly horrors are small annoyances contrasted to these morning excesses. Need we harp on the situation? Screeching giggles, high-pitched indications of pleasure, and then, Sir, wetness. Lots of it. Everywhere. Often. Nor does it seem to concern you. Indeed, you crow about, enormously pleased with yourself, dreamy, enraptured.

Can this be what you want, Sir? Must we write to your Mother, or to the President of your Corporation? Blackmail is not our purpose, Mr. Jones. Our former amiable relationship prohibits such outrage. But, Sir. At least tend to our hygienic imperatives. Better yet, go to a fourth rate motel for the duration of this insanity. We will wait it through, Sir, and you are in our prayers.

In the interest of total honesty, which seems to be a current obsession of yours, Blue Blanket insists that we mention how he is enjoying every moment of your hysteria. But we repeat: Blue Blanket is on top. WE ARE ON THE BOTTOM.

Sincerely yours,

Monsieurs Mattress, Pillow Cases
and Sheets

MOUTH
Elizabeth Sommers

Dear PJ,

If my mother taught me one thing, it's that I shouldn't ever let my teeth go. She said it once a week for six years on the way to the orthodontist. "You'll be alive for a long time," she said, "and you'll need your teeth. Straight, white cavity-free teeth are my gift to you, and see that you take care of them." Of course I listen to Mother for my own reasons. I don't think I'm ever going to trade in my life for a Lake Shore Drive penthouse—this has been getting more and more clear—but still I've got this refrain echoing through my mind. Yes, mother, even though I ignored your advice about Third World men, drugs, and about social work being a nice career for girls, I always take care of my teeth.

In fact I'm vain about my teeth. They're nice teeth, good color, straight as arrows to boot. If I were a horse I'd be all set. "Now that you've got such nice teeth you should smile more," she said when they yanked my braces off. Well, she can't have everything. I prefer, as you know, a sober, intelligent visage, full of mystery, but I always know if I want to smile, oh can I ever. It's a comfort.

So last month I trudged out to Deerfield to Dr. Roberts when I got my six month check-up card in the mail. At that time I had ten dollars to my name, no job and no prospects, but I went anyway. Breeding always shows, doesn't it? Dr. Roberts has really jazzed up his office since my last visit. He's got Impressionistic prints framed in gold gilt all over and a new sign that says "We cater to cowards," that looks like someone made it with a Christmas wood-burning set. I didn't even have to wait. I went right in, climbed right into his black leather executioner's chair, and the dental hygienist bustled up and said, "Rinse." Why won't she ever slip and say, "Spit," PJ? I liked the old dental hygienist better. She was named Rosa and she got senile and went off to California at sixty years of age. This new one is polite but distant, with a very professional attitude, and you never met a worse bore.

So I rinsed. She put those cardboard X-rays in my mouth and took her pictures as evidence. I wasn't afraid. Dentalphobia is engrained in me. I brush four times a day and never eat candy. Remember that camping trip we took when I forgot my toothbrush and I wanted to drive three hundred miles home but you let me use yours and I wore out the bristles? I was really moved when you said you didn't let just anyone use your toothbrush. It made me nervous when you cocked your head a moment and thought about it. What were you considering—my god, I couldn't figure it out. Thank you, though. Thank you from the bottom of my heart.

Anyway, I was cross-legged in the chair feeling cocky as anything, waiting while she developed my pictures. I made a note in my mind that I'd been there for half an hour already and Dr. Roberts hadn't said so much as how do you do. He's getting too big for his britches, I thought, what with all these new Monets and Manets. Then he rushed in nice as you please, with a bigger pot belly than ever and the same old halitosis. "How's your mother and father and little Maggie and Allen Stein and Pattie Jameson and

Myrtle Wolfson?" he asked. Dr. Roberts knows everyone. In Deerfield all roads lead to Dr. Roberts.

"They're all more or less fine," I said. "They all need checkups," he said. Then the dental hygienist walked in again. I didn't have a single cavity! A clean bill! We were all excited because I haven't had any for six years. "It's my fluoride treatments," Dr. Roberts said. "It's my health food," I said. "It's because she already has a filled cavity in every tooth and there's no room for anymore," the dental hygienist said. Isn't she the Miss Priss?

I tell you I was proud. She cleaned and picked at my teeth for a while. Dr. Roberts vanished again, discreetly. She sank my jaws into the fluoride goo as I watched a movie on proper brushing techniques that lasted exactly the amount of time the fluoride stays in your mouth. Can you beat that? She had that little hose in my mouth sucking up rinse, which wasn't pleasant, but hell, it beats the drill.

Dr. Roberts stuck his nose in to say good-bye. "Remember to tell them they all need check-ups," he said. "Dr. Roberts," I said, "if I don't have my wisdom teeth yet I'm never going to get them, am I?" PJ, I had to know. They're dropping like flies all around me. He hesitated one moment and then he said, "Well, we'll just take a head X-ray."

They fit my head in a big metal machine, clicked four pictures and I was sprung. I made my way over to Jewett Park and met Allen Stein for a softball game. I told him he needed a check-up and he looked at me with new respect. Allen always did think I was omniscient and that clinched it. He's so easy.

The next day I was still asleep when the phone range at 12:00. Imagine my shock and horror when I heard Dr. Roberts on the other side, his matter-of-fact voice saying, "You've got three impacted wisdom teeth. What are you going to do about it?"

I was still groggy and I couldn't believe my ears. Please, not me. Please, there's been a mistake. I was on the verge of tears, but I managed to croak out the obvious question: "Dr. Roberts, what do you mean, what am I going to do about it? You're the dentist."

"I don't do teeth that bad," he told me. "I'll have to refer you to an oral surgeon. Dr. Matthews practices in Northbook. 945-6299."

PJ, I am a proud woman. You know I have control of myself. But that morning I screamed and moaned and thrashed in bed for an hour. Then, because I was brought up by mother, because I have dentalphobia, because I knew I had no out, I got on the phone to Dr. Matthew's office.

I hope I'm not boring you. I kid you not, this is the biggest thing to happen to me since I discovered the Grateful Dead. I know other people's kids and other people's teeth are a big joke, but my teeth are different. PJ—PJ, tell me you're interested in my teeth.

It turned out that each tooth was going to cost me one hundred dollars. One hundred dollars can buy a lot of marijuana. God, I was hysterical. If I wanted to go in the hospital that would be fine too, the nurse said. Well, I don't have dental insurance. In fact I don't have any insurance. I hate those guys, they breed like maggots on people's tragedies. I wasn't about to go in any hospital. We talked over the details and finally I asked how much it hurt. I think she heard my voice shaking. She probably knew I'd been crying all morning, and she was laughing when she said, "Young lady, this is not a pleasant experience, but we've never lost a patient."

HAHAHA. I'm sick of everyone's stupid jokes. I didn't get out of bed that day, PJ. I lay twitching and thrashing all day long. Then towards evening I called mother and I was crying on the phone, PJ. If you weren't such a good friend I'd never admit it. I'm a grown woman and I called, blubbering all over the place. And you know what? She laughed at me when I asked if Daddy would pay for it. "My little socialist wants her nasty capitalist daddy to pay for oral surgery, eh?" she said. I could hear Daddy laughing in the background. Oh God, PJ, the humiliation I suffer. She said she'd talk to him about it, later.

"Mom," I said, "does it hurt as much as having a baby?"

I was serious, too—I've never been so scared in my life. But it got her mad. "How could you even compare the two," she asked. "It's not right. It's disgusting." Then, PJ, she laughed at me again and she never even answered the question.

The oral surgeon had an original Hoffer on the wall, PJ. Do you have any idea how much that costs? I got to know that office very well—soft, modulated classical music, plush shag carpeting, comfy leather couches. Sara begrudgingly volunteered to take me out there, but she wouldn't hold my hand and I dug my nails into his leather couch. I hope he has to have it reupholstered. I lifted three New Yorkers from his office too, so I figure the total bill was only $297. It's the little things, PJ. We've got to get them on the little things.

I know life is full of suffering. I know people survive war, famines, droughts, and plagues. I admit I'm a grown-up suburban brat, hopelessly spoiled, but PJ, I'd never been so scared in my life. They made a mistake when they led me into the office. The last patient was still in the chair. She wasn't conscious yet—they give you sodium pentothal, the truth serum, of all things. Her mouth was still trickling blood and her jaw was already swollen. She was heaving big gulping sobs. The nurses took her by the arms and she staggered on cement legs into the recovery room, taking big lurching steps like a drunk. My nurse reeled me around back into the waiting room, but it was too late. My God, I thought, that's me in an hour. Sara was sitting there cool as a cucumber, sunk into her boredom, and she gave me an enigmatic little smile. It wasn't enough, Sara. You could have managed more.

She led me back again. My heart was hammering like you wouldn't believe. This office they plopped me in wasn't like Dr. Robert's. There weren't any tools of the trade out. Everything was hidden in panelled cabinets. I didn't see a drill or a butcher knife anywhere. It scared me more than ever, PJ. And there on the wall, on a lit board, hung my X-rays—three times larger than life. I could see the three impacted teeth, pointed like torpedoes at my other teeth, intent on ruining that thousand dollar smile. Oh PJ, there's times when I doubt everything about the way I am, the way I try to live—the purpose of life itself becomes obscured, PJ. God I wish you'd been there.

Dr. Matthews sidled in wearing a Gucci tie, Gucci shoes and a Pucci belt. At least I wasn't crying, but I was shaking like a little old dog. He took my blood pressure and told me I had blood pressure to be proud of. He pointed to my X-rays and said I'd had enormously successful orthodontics he was there to protect. He gave me a long somber gaze and asked me just how I was planning to pay for this operation.

Swiss Francs, I wanted to say, but dear God I was afraid to alienate him. "I'll pay you today," I said. So what if I had to drop out of school and go live in the gutter. You take life as you find it.

"That's a good girl," he said. I must have been desperate, because those words flooded me with gratitude. I'm a good girl, PJ, a real good girl, my oral surgeon said so. He reached in a panelled drawer and got his needle, his eight inch long needle, and that's when I started crying again. "There, there," Dr. Matthews smiled, "I think it's best if we put you under, don't you?"

"Please," I managed, and he shot his sodium pentothal into the crook of my arm. My little carcass shook and rattled. I looked him in the eye, one last imploring glance, and PJ, praise the Lord, that's the last filthy detail I remember.

I woke up an hour later, with a swollen tongue caked with blood, and the Doctor looked in the recovery room. They had me lying on a little white bed. "Doc, did you do it?" I tried to ask but the words wouldn't form. I was only a mouth now, a bloody, gummy mess of stitches with a dully pounding pain everywhere. I looked down to make sure he hadn't amputated a limb or two. Dr. Matthews gave me a sympathetic pat on the head. "I only took two out," he said, "they were so bad, I had to take out gum and bone to get at the roots."

HE ONLY TOOK TWO OUT, PJ. Luckily I was too groggy to comprehend what he was saying. When I could stand, they brought Sara in to take me home. They gave me cotton balls to soak up the blood. They gave me prescriptions for codeine and penicillin. You understand I was still far away—it was Mouth these things were happening to, poor throbbing Mouth being punished for saying all sorts of mean things in her life. I was still in that glorious sodium pentothal haze. Mouth was the only reality.

They gave Mouth a piece of literature to read and absorb: "What to expect after removal of an impacted tooth." I walked Mouth on out, rather efficiently, I thought, and you know what? They have a separate door for victims to leave by so the people in the waiting room don't panic.

For two weeks I was Mouth. Two weeks of jello and yogurt, and all-accepting codeine haze, ice packs, hot water bottles and silence. I just couldn't talk and all my friends came by and it thrilled them. I never realized before that they, too, might have something to say. In every cloud, eh PJ? I was ugly as sin, my left cheek bulging and bruised black and blue, drooling saliva and blood. Allen asked if I'd taken to kissing Mack trucks. Bertie asked if they'd used an exacto knife. I didn't dare laugh. Laughing made the stitches creak.

I felt like my mouth was public property now, a vast, mysterious, even mystic network of canals, gums, rivers and valleys. I used to put cheeses and kisses inside and never think twice about it. Now it'll never be the same. The second visit was just like the first. I became Mouth, and Mouth was supreme. I tell you, I'll always feel differently about Mouth. I've got more respect. I know Mouth's power, and Mouth's fury. I've seen it all, PJ, and once again I've survived.

MARGE
Sharon Weber

The scrawled, jittery handwriting is unrecognizable to the man. He turns it over in his hands; finding no return address, he opens it.

Dear Jim,

Why didn't you come and visit me in the hospital? I waited and waited. You never came. I wasn't contagious, you know. Were you so ashamed?

Well, you haven't asked, but the hospital was awful. I thought those were the worst 21 days of my life. How wrong I was. It's the 21 days after the hospital that have been the worst. In the hospital, you know you can't get a drink. You know it's not in your grasp. Out here, it's all around you. Signs jump out: "JB $4.98 a fifth," "Grab for all the gusto you can." Billboards show tall, cool, sweating glasses of Bloody Marys or gin and tonics, glasses that look so real you want to reach out and grab it. You want to feel it drip down your face as you pour the liquid down your parched throat.

There's no way to get around it. I can't tell anyone about this. Anyone but you, Jim, although you *did* desert me. But, dear brother, you're elected to hear me out. Ed is so busy; he has to work double shifts to pay all the bills. Kevin and Jill are so busy with their own friends. And I know I've hurt them enough. I know they probably hate me. I don't even like me, Jim. Do you? Probably not.

I hope you're not telling the rest of the family about me. I'm not proud of myself. I'm not a proud drunk. I was not a social drinker gone too far. I was a sneak drinker, Jim. Not like Grandma, running to the pantry to take a sip of cold beer on a hot day. No, I used to hide bottles in my drawers. Used to take them out after Ed and Kevin and Jill left in the morning. First it was just a sip to get the blood flowing. Pretty soon the sip lasted until after lunchtime. Then I'd stop and spend a normal evening—Ed would watch TV, Kevin and Jill would dash out to various friends. Pretty soon I'd start finding odd jobs to do in the bedroom, like cleaning out the drawers. But the only thing I'd clean out would be the bottle I'd stashed.

It wasn't long before I couldn't stop, before I couldn't hide it. They began to notice. Sometimes I just couldn't stand up. And what do you do with something that doesn't work anymore? You take it to be fixed, of course. So I was taken to the drunk-garage. And they fixed me up. Oh, they fixed me up fine. But the trouble is, I don't feel fixed. Ed thinks I'm OK, I guess. As long as I lay off the bottle, I'm good old Marge. To hell with the fact that my kids run from the house as fast as they can. Forget about how hard it is for me to wake up in the morning knowing there are no more little bottles to float me through the day. Forget that I'm pouring out my troubles to my brother, who didn't come to visit me in the hospital and who probably would like to be an only child right now.

I suppose I've taken enough time out of your busy day. Just do me a couple of favors, Jim. Have a drink on me and really enjoy it. And kiss

Elaine very passionately today. Hold her and tell her you love her and make her feel good. Then take those kids out for ice cream before they get too old and don't need you anymore.

Love always,
Marge

Books and papers were strewn about the kitchen table, and while Karen's blonde head was bent over in concentration, Jill's brunette head was up, her eyes staring straight ahead at the white refrigerator. There were little magnets shaped like fruit—a banana, an apple, a cluster of grapes—tacked in no special order on the stark white refrigerator door.

"Jill, why do we have to study all this nonsense just for one test?" Karen looked up and saw that Jill was staring straight ahead. "Hey, you're not even studying! What's wrong?"

"I know for sure." Jill pulled her eyes away from the refrigerator and looked at Karen with no expression on her face. "I know for sure that my mother is drinking again. I went home after school and before I came here—she was—I don't know, asleep or passed out, I guess—on the couch. I called to her, but she didn't wake up. At first I thought, maybe she's sick. She's been complaining about having headaches a lot lately, so I figured I'd let her sleep. When I walked into the kitchen, it was a mess. Well, like I said, I thought she had been sick, so I cleaned up. I went into the front room to collect all the glasses so I could clean up all the dishes." Jill looked down at a bare spot on the table. "There was an empty glass next to the couch. And an empty bottle. It was Smirnoff vodka." She took a deep breath. "I didn't know what to do. I wanted to run out of there. I wished that I'd never gone home. But I picked up the glass and the empty bottle and I took them back to the kitchen. I scrubbed the glass real good. I threw the bottle in the garbage can. Then I took the garbage out to the alley." She looked up at Karen. "I don't know who I was trying to cover up for—for her, for having gotten drunk again or for me, finding her like that. Anyway, I wrote her a note. Told her that I had cleaned up the kitchen and was coming here. I didn't mention the bottle."

Marge was still sitting on her bedroom floor, clutching the bottle like it was a life preserver. Her mind still told her that everything was OK.

She looked down at the miraculous bottle she held in her hands. She felt safe. Nobody knew. Nobody knew that she had a drink every now and then in the afternoons. Because she brought her own bottles of J.B., nobody found any liquor missing.

An alarm went off in her head. J.B.? She searched back in her mind. She didn't drink J.B. anymore. She was positive that she had had vodka that afternoon. Smirnoff vodka. The clear liquid in the clear bottle flashed in her mind. Yes, it *was* vodka! Marge's hands began to tremble. She hadn't drunk J.B. for months. Not since before the hospital. Then she had craved J.B., but since then, her tastes had changed. She stared blankly at the bottle shaking in her hands. This had to be an old, forgotten bottle from ages ago. Then where was that empty, clear bottle of Smirnoff's?

THE LETTER
James O. Elder

On the Sunday afternoon before the Monday morning that Maxwell
Towbridge escaped from the Kentucky State Correctional Center in Jerline,
Kentucky, he was awakened in his cell by a strange flapping sound. It
wasn't a loud flapping, nor was it a constant one, but it was loud enough
and repeated with enough regularity to gently tug the thinly laced veil of a
hot, muggy afternoon's sleep from his face. For a moment the flapping
stopped. And so did the veil; it hesitated long enough for him to see a clear vision of his brother Marvin raking clusters of dry autumn leaves, orange and
brown autumn leaves that crackled to the touch in the back yard of a mammoth white house with towering pillars surrounding it. For every two-foot
patch of land that Marvin cleared, a floating wicker basket would swoop
down and shower him with more dry leaves, and no matter how fast he
worked, the floating wicker basket always worked a bit faster. Max
couldn't tell by the twisted expression on his brother's face if he was enjoying his task or hating it. But no sooner had the flapping sound started up
again than the veil started slipping down his face again, only this time his
brother Marvin was matching the strange flapping sound stroke for stroke
with his rake. As the sweaty veil of sleep fell from his chin and slid across
his chest, a hot breeze sauntered through the barred window up over his
head from the direction of Lexington, opening his eyes to see Sleepy
Pankowitz fanning a letter across the bars of his cell.

Max eyed the thin spaghetti figure fanning the letter against his cell
through the V-shaped space of his worn, out-turned boots, which save for
the white jockey shorts, were the only clothing he wore. His T-shirt and
khakis were draped over the railing at the foot of the top bunk, where he
lay on his back with his fingers knitted into a weave and nestled up under
his head.

Sleepy glances down either side of the long, empty corridor before look
ing directly at Max with those mirthful blue eyes—blue eyes that are always
bowed at half-mast when they are not outright sequestered by narcolepsy.
Sleepy quickly glances down at the letter in his hand and then back at Max,
the quarter moon smile on his lips leaping twofold.

"Why aren't you watching the movie with the rest of the guys, Max?"
Sleepy says in that deep, hazy voice of his which never registers a decible
above a whisper, and which—even to Max—is a damn good imitation of
Lauren Bacall.

"It was too hot, too many people, and I'm tired of watching John Wayne
movies. Now cut the bullshit and tell me how much you want for the
letter."

Sleepy winces at the aggravation in Max's voice, but sensing a pinch of
curiosity, he sniffs the letter and flashes an impish smile.

"Well, Max, I'll tell you, it smells like it's worth about ten packs...but
seeing as how you put in a good word for me with Turkey the other night,
I'll let you have it for five, but that's five packs of Kools mind you; I don't
want any of those stinking Pall Malls you've been trading with the fresh

meat".

"What makes you think I'll pay you five packs of Kools for a letter that I can read for free tomorrow?"

"Well, first of all, Max, it hasn't been butchered by official hands; secondly, I'm sure it's at least three pages long; and last but not least, it's from somebody by the name of Jesse-boy, and with a name like JESSE-BOY it's just got to be hot stuff".

Max slowly swung down from his bunk like a seasoned paratrooper at a thousand feet, slid his footlocker from under the bed, and began riffling through the cupcakes, candy bars, magazines, tattered photographs, T-shirts, underwear, and his precious Lexington souvenir—which he'd ceremoniously wrapped in a white silk handkerchief—until he finally reached the cigarettes. He thrust six packs of Pall Malls at Sleepy and said, "Take it or leave it."

Sleepy immediately dropped the letter inside his shirt, spun around on his heels, snapped his chin in defiance, and said over his shoulder, "You'll get the letter tomorrow at mail call like everybody else, and don't blame me if there's nothing left but 'DEAR MAX...SINCERELY YOURS.'" And with that, Sleepy walked off down the long, empty corridor toward the lounge and John Wayne.

Max counted Sleepy's slow, methodical footsteps echoing down the steel corridor, the urge to read the uncensored letter clawing at his throat. By the time he counted to seventeen, the footsteps stopped. When he heard them start up again, he was sure they were growing louder and louder rather than more faint.

When Sleepy reached Max's cell this time, he spotted three packs of Kools wedged in between the bars; he nonchalantly picked them up and replaced them with the letter. Neither man said a word, although they both knew that Sleepy couldn't have gotten a drag off a cigarette if he'd dropped that letter back into the mail bag from where he'd stolen it the day before. Sleepy glared at Max, who was obviously feigning sleep to mask his eagerness to read the letter, and in so doing he missed seeing that gesture that Sleepy made in the air with his upturned middle finger as he turned to walk away; and because it was such a hot day, even if he'd had his eyes open, he probably wouldn't have noticed the sweat stain winding down the back of Sleepy's plaid shirt, nor would he have noticed Sleepy's mangled blond hair, that ranges in color from streaks of golden yellow to streaks of bleached auburn, as it bounced up and down in unison to his slow, methodical walk.

Maxwell held the envelope up to the light to see where it was safe to tear; he quickly ripped the end off and dumped the contents into his lap. His palms grew moist with perspiration as he unfolded the letter and began reading:

> DEAR MAX,
>   GUS IS DEAD. He got killed on 16th Street trying to stick up a store-front preacher with a toy gun. I know it sounds crazy, but it's true. He got shot four times in the chest and once in the head, and they say he still lived long enough to crawl in a hallway and die. Me and Gus never did get along,

but I figured you'd prefer to hear about him from me rather
than some stranger who didn't know him at all, or luck out
and get blown away by stumbling across it in the Jerline
Gazette or whatever the fuck y'all read down there, because
regardless of how I might have felt about him, I always
knew that you loved him like a brother....

Max's hands trembled so uncontrollably that he had to put the letter
down; the opposing corner edges where he'd gripped it were damp, warm,
and crumpled. He shut his eyes and took a long, deep breath. Then he
looked at the letter lying there on the bed beside him and slowly began
shaking his head from side to side; at that very moment he hated Sleepy's
guts for bringing him that letter. As hard as he'd fought the violence and the
nightmares of being institutionalized by fantasizing about the serenity of the
outside world, Sleepy had conspired with the prison to let the outside world
reach into his cell and violently slap him into a nightmarish stupor. He's
always thought that Gus would fade out with a needle in his arm in the
back room of some musky lit "Shooting Gallery"—and that he could
accept— but not like some mangy, suicidal dog with his tail stuck between
his legs, moping across the Dan Ryan Expressway during rush hour. He had
a sudden flash of Gus kneeling in a piss-stained hallway with buckets of
blood oozing from his mouth and nostrils; only his vision wasn't of the Gus
who was killed—the dope addict who was drooling into his breakfast the
last time he'd seen him at Nick's, and in so doing had made him feel so
embarrassed that he left the restaurant without finishing his food or saying
hello. No, not in the least. His vision was one of youthful innocence, of the
Gus who'd died so long ago that he'd forgotten he was dead—the black,
lanky kid with the nappy hair and the crooked smile, the make-believe
brother that always came through when needed to punch somebody out or
to enlighten him as to the majestic beauty of a pigeon in flight. Maxwell had
his choice of visions, and he chose. But either way, Gus was dead, and the
thought of it nauseated him. He blamed the heat for the queasy feeling in
his gut, wiped his sweaty palms off on the bed sheet, lit a cigarette, and
reluctantly picked the letter up and started reading again—and in THIS he
had no choice.

...Gus's habit had him by the balls, Max, and wouldn't let
go. He joined the "program" a couple of times, but the best
he could manage was to swap habits: a methadone habit for
a heroin habit. I rapped with him a few times since the last
time we saw him nodding in Nick's, and I swear, Max, you
wouldn't have recognized him. He had these crusty looking
scab sores all over his face and hands, and his skin was so
burnt out he'd turned ash gray. Little Mickey told me that
he'd gotten so down and out that he'd started shooting T's
and Blues and that part of his ass had fallen off—can you
imagine that—that's why he'd quit taking baths, because
whenever he'd wash with a rag, part of his flesh would peel
off. I don't know what you and the good ol' boys down
there be getting off on, but if it's them T's and Blues, Max, I

really wish you'd ice it; that shit is worse than rat poison.

Gus had gotten to the point where he looked like a winehead, dressed like a winehead, and smelled like a winehead, and even though he wasn't, you sure in the hell couldn't tell the difference by looking at him; and, Max, you know a booster can't steal shit looking like a winehead. All of the shopping mall security guards in and around Chicago knew him by sight, smell, and name; and they would snatch him every time they spotted him; and the 1st District policemen didn't even allow him downtown, day or night. Since his shabby appearance had blown his main hustle— and his habit was too wicked to handle a package—he started burglarizing apartments.

He made out O.K. at first. I mean, he was stealing shit as fast as Sears could deliver it. But once, while he was burglarizing a third-floor apartment over on Douglas, this niggah came home early from work and busted him; Gus had the man's clothes, TV, radio, and meat from the freezer all stockpiled by the front door, and was in the process of disconnecting the stereo system in the front room when he heard the jingle of door keys. Time the niggah saw his shit sitting by the door, he up'd with his piece and started shootin'. Knowing that death stood between him and the front door, Gus jumped from the third-floor window as a bullet grazed his back. Gus broke his collar bone, two fingers, and his right leg in two places; but he still managed to get away before that niggah could get downstairs and kill him. He walked with a real bad limp after that and had lost his nerve for burglarizing completely. But he still had that habit to feed. And right around then is when he started stickin' up with that toy pistol—a black, plastic, snub nose .38 they said in the papers.

Anyway, late Sunday night he spotted his mark sitting in a mint green Cadillac countin' a lump of cash. He eased up on him from the passenger side of the car and threw the toy pistol up in his face and told him to give it up. Now the preacher said that he didn't know the gun was a toy, but people on the street say otherwise. Anyway the preacher went on to say that when he'd given Gus the money that he had in his hand, Gus demanded him to give him the money that he had in his pocket and that if he didn't, he was going to "blow his fuckin face off," and that's when he reached into his suit coat pocket, pulled his gun, and shot him. Jive niggah shot him five times before he hit the sidewalk. Some people say the preacher is an ex-pimp hustling behind some bullshit religion that he invented and that he knew that Gus's gun was a toy, and that's why he went for his piece even though Gus had the drop on him; they also say that Gus never got a chance to even smell that money, let alone touch it.

Me and Joyce went to the funeral, and I swear it was the wildest thing I ever seen in my life, Max. People were screamin' and hollerin' and knockin' over benches, and ol' deacon Crawford got drunk and threw up on the podium right in the middle of his "Little Boy Lost" speech; but that's another story and I'm running out of paper. I hope those six years pass like six days. I'll be down to see you as soon as I can, and remember that "good time" is the quickest way out.
LOVE,
Jessie-Boy

P.S. CONNIE'S HOME.

How-It-Happens Instances

RATS
Mike Schwartz

There is a high, gray rippled metal fence, supported by a four-foot foundation of concrete that surrounds the limestone quarry on 29th and Poplar. The huge hole is a whopping four-city-blocks square, and at least three hundred feet deep. The air down there is often ten degrees warmer than street level, and in the winter months young kids have been known to sneak down via the long twisting road that slithers like an earthworm down along one side of the crevasse. There are narrow holes in the fence where the bolts have rusted, and you can look down at the road, and the machinery on the bottom, and it all looks like a Tonka Toy set for a small child.

On one side, there is a now useless dumping area. Useless because there was a popular idea several years ago to fill the thing up with garbage and make a park out of it. The program had to be scrapped when the rat population became such a problem that people who lived in the area became fearful for their lives. One neighborhood woman recalled an encounter with one of the larger rodents. Eyes glaring, she said, it had somehow broken into her home and was seated on her sub-pump. Butcher knife in hand, she went after it not out of bravery, but out of a mother's protective instinct for the safety of her child. The rat, upon first seeing her, just crouched slightly. She moved closer slowly. Slowly the knife raised above her head, and the rat, not more than three feet away now, just twitched his nose. Closing her eyes in anticipation of the gruesome sight of a skewered, gnawing rat, her arm stabbed downward. The rat, acting quickly, but not quickly enough, jumped out of serious harm's way. The knife, however, did manage to slice through the base of his thick tail. The woman happened to open her eyes just in time to see the rat scurry up the stairs and out the door she had left open to quickly jettison the lifeless corpse (had she killed it).

After the initial shock of the incident, she confided in her neighbors. Most of them took her rather lightly. Joking, they asked her, "Cut off her tail with a butcher knife? Did you ever see such a sight in your life?" Even her husband had asked if she would use it to make a rat tail comb. This levity did not amuse her, and not only did she refuse to speak to the neighbors for several weeks, but it was rumored that her husband slept downstairs on the pool table for more than a month after.

The garbage, of course, had to be burned. Crews of men with protective leather boots stood out in the street waiting, large cans of poison sprays in their hands, for the rats to run from the flames in packs. Some died on the way up from exhaustion and smoke inhalation. Many were burned along with the trash. It is an eerie thought that lying among the rusted tin cans with singed labels, and hard weathered chunks of cindered garbage that carpet the quarry's floor, are the ghosts of many rats.

*   *   *

There was a movie theatre located on Thirty-first and Lowe Avenue called, appropriately enough, The Lowe Theatre. It serviced mostly the younger members of the community, showing such epic films as "The Ghost and Mr. Chicken." It had no marquee or balcony (I think it had one, but I also remember hearing that it collapsed soon after the building was completed) and a filthy little lobby that smelled of dust. The candy counter was covered with streaks of tape covering the cracks in the glass, and someone was always unscrewing the salt so that the next user would dump the entire contents on his popcorn. There were only three aisles, dividing the four sections. Mostly, everyone sat in the back row center. During a Saturday matinee it was the only safe place to sit. Throughout the film, like a background sound track, one could hear the steady pink pink pink pink of the Boston Baked Beans. They were the biggest selling candy. Not because of the taste, to be sure, every one hated them, but they hurt well enough if you hit someone in the head with one.

A lot of things flew about during a show, popcorn boxes mostly, but one industrious kid snuck in a small balloon filled with black paint. As Don Knotts approached the blood covered keys of the organ which played by itself, a large black splash swept across his nose. Like a hand grenade it had been tossed on target. The house lights went on and the manager stormed into the center aisle. "Whose the god-damn painter?", he growled. Looking around, meeting everyone's eyes one at a time, he pointed back to the screen. The projector hadn't stopped and the image was hardly visible, but he black splat was as plain as day. "So you know how much that's gonna cost me? Everybody, let me see your hands." As if he were in a hold-up, the manager demonstrated. Walking up and down aisles he checked for tell-tale paint marks. There were none. "Now I'm gonna tell you. You want this place to look like a pig sty, that's how it's gonna stay. And let me tell you, if I every find out who did this I'll kick his ass from here to Chinatown." Storming out, his face contorted by anger and frustration the picture continued, and the black splotch remained until the day the board of health closed the Lowe down, and condemned it.

There was a popular joke at the time that went like this, "Going to the Lowe? Don't drop your popcorn or you'll have to sit with your feet up for the rest of the show." The reason? Rats.

Everybody knew they were there, but while no one was hurt, it was almost laughable. They'd jump along the wall from radiator to radiator, flickering shadows in the darkness. It was a game to spot one, until one hot July when someone had his leg dangling at the wrong place at the wrong time and the inevitable finally occurred. The rat bit him on the ankle, and caused a considerable amount of swelling.

Scuttlebutt had it that he had been given the series of painful shots as a precaution against rabies. The family decided to sue, but the theatre (a shaky financial establishment anyway) declared bankruptcy. The building was sold to a man interested in opening an electronics store. He had the rows of ripped leather chairs with back rests mother's warned their children not to touch, torn out, and entirely gutted the structure.

*   *   *

Rats come and rats go, but mostly they come. Where they come from is the river front. You can see them, if you go to the fishery that sits quietly on the south bank. A large bridge suspends across the river, and the rats use this to come to and fro. If you want to sneak up on a rat and surprise him, here's what you do. You go down behind the fishery, turn the headlights in your car off (don't go without a car). Pull up slowly to the edge of the water, don't get too close. Many a rat scarer has ended up in the drink for being careless. Wait awhile, until you can hear the scuttering of little feet under your car. Watch out the front window, look toward the water. When all is quiet, and the rodent population has finally turned out, suddenly TURN ON YOUR LIGHTS, AND KICK ON YOUR BRIGHTS. Man, those rats will jump out of their skins. They'll race for the waterfront and hide in the muddy weeds. Sound like fun? Try it sometime. Try it with a girl friend. Threaten to make her walk home alone if she doesn't act right to you. You never know, it might work.

*   *   *

There is a triangle of small businesses located in an otherwise unpopulated area just south of Chicago's famous Loop. The first, and largest in size of the three, is an auto graveyard. Surrounded by a warped, weather beaten fence (made of ill fitting chunks of plywood carrying the faded message "Monocko's Auto Parts) are the gutted hulls of smashed, useless cars. Grizzly reminders of fatal accidents. Up through the floors of these empty, rusted junks grow weeds, tall and straight. To the imaginative mind, they almost appear to be oversized planters.

It is no secret to the owner of this waste field that residing in great numbers on his property are large, dangerous rats. There is little he can do but acknowledge it. Rats tend to live in areas where they can move about freely, and any attempt to get rid of them will ultimately end in vain. Instead, he has learned to live with them. That is why he carries a large baseball bat, fully covered with black tape, with him whenever dismantling a part from a car. He uses it to beat hard on the frame of the car before doing work of any kind. This scares the rats away, and so far he has never been bitten, although there have been many close calls.

Once, after pounding on the dented hood of a car he needed the left front door from, he sat on the ripped interior, and began working from the inside. It was cold out, and his hands were covered with warm, bulky gloves that made it difficult to hold the screw driver. It slipped down through a hole rusted away near the brake pedal. Reaching through it, he started groping for the tool, when something began tugging at one finger on his hand. Scared and panicked, he pulled, struggling to release his hand, but the rusted tin cut through the skin along his arm, and several stitches were needed.

Later that day he returned to the car, with his bat, and a hammer. The bat, of course was used to bang away on the hood. The hammer was to pound out the hole in the floor. It took him somewhat longer with his left hand, as the stitches were in the right.

He pounded hard, orange chips flying everywhere, until his curiosity was satisfied. He had noticed small toothy indentations on the middle finger of his glove, and thought that a rat might have been what scared him. He had almost dismissed that thought, however, because a rat's teeth would have chewed right through the leather. Unless it was a small rat, or a weak one. Or a rat on the verge of death. Like the one he found, mouth gaping, on the hard ground underneath the car.

The second business of the three is a small, make-shift fruit stand, that pops up suddenly in the spring, and disappears by mid autumn. Judging from the quality of their produce, it is hard to believe they throw anything away, but it's true. Day after day the burst melons pile on top of the dark, rotted leaves of lettuce that line the bottom of the garbage cans. When these cans are full, they continue to dump on top of them, and at night the piles of edible garbage attract the rats from the auto yard across the street. As long as the rats confined their meals to the early morning hours, the owner was content to leave them alone. But one evening he accidentally left his rear door open, and rats in multitudes rushed in to gorge themselves on fresh fruit and vegetables.

Opening the stand as usual the next day, he noticed shreds of green tissue (used to wrap the pears) scattered around the floor. He checked a crate near-by, and found a rat, tail curled about its furry body, sleeping soundly. Enraged, he screamed and kicked the box over, stomping his foot through the wooden slats. The crate caught above the ankle, and he was hopping and kicking when an elderly woman walked in with the intention of buying corn. The rat scurried out through her frail, black stockinged legs, and she leaned against the frame of the doorway, mouth open in a silent scream. The owner, who as of yet did not notice her, was swinging a broom under a table yelling, "C'mon outta there you sonofabitching rats!" The old woman gasped for air, and stumbled out the door. The owner turned, and face flushed with embarrassment, he followed her out, and pretended to be sweeping. "Can I help you with anything?", he asked. "Pears are special today." She waved him away, and leaned weakly against the bus stop.

The third and most prosperous business of the three, is a full service gas station. Because of its location, right across the alley from the fruit stand, the owner of this six pump, two rack garage has had several problems with the rats. Not to mention the sour smell of rotted fruit that persisted even stronger than the fumes of gas and oil. On one of these occasions, the owner was almost convinced he had the smartest rat in the world, because for three days, it appeared he had stolen the bait without tripping the trap.

One afternoon, after making a pot of coffee, this owner reached for his box of sugar only to find it had fallen down behind a cabinet. One side of the box had been chewed through, and checking the heavy sliding door in the back by the auto racks, he saw that it had been left about an inch from the ground. Fearing the rat might still be lurking around, he went over to the metal strong box that held his most expensive tools, and produced a brown stained rat trap. Putting three nickels into his candy machine (it would jam on dimes) he bought a bag of peanuts and put one under the trigger for bait. After setting the trap, he decided to place it along the base boards of the wall near the cabinet where he'd found the box of sugar.

When closing time came, he checked the trap, and discovered the bait was gone, but the trap was still set. He touched the trigger lightly with a rag. The metal bar sprung back with a muffled snap. The trap was fine, but the rat must have managed somehow to work the peanut out. He set the trap again with another peanut and closed up for the day. Again, in the morning, the trap was set, and the bait gone. He set it once more, and it happened still again. Setting it a fourth time, he kept a watchful eye. Toward midday, he noticed the trap was engulfed by a quivering black mass of ants. Working together, they carried the peanut away, until he killed them with a huge pan of boiling water.

Another time, though, he did catch a rat in the trap. But it was so large the bar wasn't enough to kill it. He had to pick it up with a pair of long-nosed pliers, and carry it outside to a garbage can full of water. The wood on the trap made it float, and the rat had to be held under the surface for fifteen minutes before he finally died. But for every one rat killed, many more are born, and it will be some time long in the future before all of the rats are gone from this triangle of small businesses located just before the outskirts of Chicago's famous Loop.

Public rest room facilities often have an eerie institutional air about them, and the toilets at Finnigan Park were no exception. They sat, squatted like Buddhas along one side of a huge vault-like room. There were stalls separating them, one from the other. The most popular was the center. Why? Because the first stall was right next to the gym door, which was always open (ever since the Park District painted over the hinges anyway), and anyone in there suffered from a terrible lack of privacy. The third stall was pushed against the wall right underneath the windows, and since they were always broken (even though they were protected on the outside by heavy steel mesh) the black horseshoe seat was always ungodly cold. But there was another reason why the third toilet was so undesirable; directly across from it, right next to the three urinals that stood along the opposite wall and watched you side by side like brothers, was a sink with a hole in the wall near the drain pipe. At night, when the lights are off and the gym is quiet, rats in small numbers use this hole to get inside the building.

Sometimes someone thinks it's a big joke to climb up onto the urinal and unscrew the lightbulb. The park supervisor is an old crabby would-be police officer who feels that leaving the lightbulb out like that for one week is the only way to punish such lack of respect for public property, and so the washroom stays dark for seven days.

During this period, someone will inevitably have to use the Men's room for more than liquid reasons, and there he'll be seated (unless he's new in the neighborhood) within the center stall. The room is dark except for the dull gray light coming in through the window, throwing a screen-like shadow across the single step up to the urinals. Sometimes there are no activities going on, and the park is mostly soundless. At times such as these, the rats are easily fooled into thinking the building is closed.

Through the small, uneven hole in the plaster they come in, and slowly begin nosing their away around. Sitting in the third stall this person would have no idea of their presence, unless he heard them scurrying a short distance across the cement floor upon first entering the room. If this made him curious enough to look, this sink would be out of view, blocked by the plywood stall on his right. The rats would continue, the area they cover expanding as their numbers grew, until one of them got bold and stepped into the screen pattern of light. When this happens, our man in #2 would look on unbelievably as the others follow suit. His first impulse is to scream, or shriek or groan, or make some other kind of noise, any of which is equally effective, for as the rats look up and become aware of his presence, they would scatter outward toward the walls along the baseboards and make their way quickly underneath the sink, and through the hole.

In the cold winter months teenage boys sometimes break into the Park's auditorium to keep warm, and drink beer on the stage. On one such occasion the boys brought a huge bag of unshelled peanuts in with them, and as they sat in the center of the stage, surrounded on all sides by a dark red, brushed velvet curtain, they took off their coats and tossed them blindly across the hard wood floor.

While eating the peanuts a game developed. The object was to slide the shells off the stage through the gold braided fringe that ran along the bottom of the curtain. As the evening progressed into the early hours of the next day, the shells began piling up at the foot of the stage. One by one, conscious of the time, they left for home until only three were left. Of these, two were neighbors, the other owned a car and was anxious to leave. The neighbors, forming one person through similar thinking, tried pressuring the driver into staying. But he refused. "C'mon, just for five minutes." Again he said no and walked over to one side to get his coat. The neighbors looked at each other and nodded, one tackling the driver, the other grabbing for his coat. He took the car keys out from one of the many zippered pockets and jingled them. "Gee, you can't get home without your car keys." The driver shook his head and released himself from the other's clutches. "If you don't give me those fucking keys I'll kick your ass 'till both shoes are shitty." The neighbor shrugged and said, "Well, if you want 'em just go and get 'em." Throwing them over the driver's head, they hit the curtain and slid down to the edge of the stage, almost falling onto the pyramid of peanut shells. The driver walked over to pick them up, and the neighbor shouted, "Hey, don't forget you coat." It also sailed over his head, and through a narrow slit in the curtains. "You fuckers better start walking home, 'cause you're not getting a lift from me." The second neighbor, who had been giggling on the side while getting his and the other boy's coat said, "Good, we don't want to ride in your stinky car. God damn car stinks of shit so bad every time I ride in it my mother has to burn my clothes." Laughing they both climbed out the broken window they'd climbed in through, and walked out kicking in the deep snow.

Punching the curtain, the driver tried to find the break in the slit where the two sides closed in the middle. Finally he had to lift it up from the bottom, and crawl under. He looked down from the stage and saw the coat, laying crumpled on top of the mountain of shells. Suddenly, one of the crumples moved, and out from underneath came a rat, a twitching shell hanging in the mouth. He squinted and saw that around the coat were perhaps twenty or thirty more rodents feeding on salty goodies all across the floor. Fearful of rabies, he backed out quickly to the window, and ran shivering in the cold to his car.

The next morning the rats were gone, but the coat and shells remained. Upon opening for the day, the caretaker noticed the mess and brought the evidence to the supervisor. In one pocket of the coat was a wallet, and in the wallet was a driver's license with a name and address on it. The name and address of the same young man the supervisor caught looking for his coat later that day. The same one the supervisor threatened to have arrested unless he paid for the damages in full. The amount of which was equal to the price of a brand new coat.

Rats weren't the only problem to plague Finnigan Park. In truth, the building was old and outdated. A new park was designed to replace the old one. A new field house, more baseball diamonds, tennis courts, even an indoor swimming pool. The new building was built in one summer, because it was really just "assembled," like an erector set. Piece by piece the prefabricated parts were put together. Occasionally vandals would delay the progress by pouring bags of cement in the empty pool, just after a heavy rain, or by kicking down wooden frames within the hollow structure. But the workers always managed to continue.

Soon after its completion the old building was demolished. The fence around the outdoor swimming pool was uprooted and dismantled. Kids hurled junk by the armloads into the slanted floor of the huge cement hole. The rats from the building wandered aimlessly through the junk at night, always avoiding the pool to bypass it on their way to the alley. Occasionally, though, one did manage to fall in, and there was no way of getting out. The shallow end of the pool was two feet high.

The next day, the workmen would come and begin tearing the insides out after knocking over walls with a ball and chain. Old men sitting on benches watched the destruction. Sometimes they turned around and spat. The rat ran from side to side, over and over again looking for a way out. At four o'clock it finally came.

The workmen knock off around three, and most of the grammar schools in the area ring the final bell somewhere about three-fifteen. This means by three forty-five, the park is swarming with kids. By four, one of these will have noticed the rat trapped on the bottom of the pool.

Bricks certainly aren't scarce on a demolition site, and this kid would only have to walk maybe two or three feet away to gather quite an armful. By throwing them down hard on the concrete, they break into nice, easy to handle chunks. The rat is running along the sides of the pool endlessly, so the hunter would have to walk the circumference of the pool in order to get a clear shot. Arm cocked behind his head, he fires! The dull thud that echoes up says that he's missed. He tries again, and again. Soon more kids wander over to see what he's doing, and fascinated they join in the fun. Behind them, the wind blows through the trees, scattering the autumn-colored leaves across the field.

The rat darts one way, then the next. It seems to have no feet, just wheels that instinctively know when to turn. The crowd grows, and the bricks come down in a steady rain. One strikes the rat in its hind quarters, throwing it to one side. Apparently stunned, it just sits there, leaning against the side wall. One youth dashes to the side and struggles with a heavy chunk of sidewalk. Another helps him, and carrying it one on each end they swing counting. . .one. . .two. . . three. . .The huge chunk lands on the rat's head, smashing it paper thin. Most of the kids continue throwing stones. Twenty minutes later, everyone is gone.

*　　　　　*　　　　　*

Dear Ralph,
Hey did your brother tell you about Twang yet? He moved out of his house. Had a big fight with his old man and moved right out of his fucking house. I couldn't believe it when he called me over to help move his shit in. It's not a bad flat either. Well anyway, it's about what you'd expect for eighty dollars a month. But let me get right to the thing I want to tell you, you'll laugh your fat ass right off, this is Hill-larry-s.

Twang was having problems with rats, right. Well he picks this scroungy looking cat up in the alley one day to get rid of the rats. I mean, this cat was bad. He looked like the brother Morris left behind. Didn't have hardly any hair, and always kept one eye closed. Twang didn't care, though, he just named it Popeye, and fed it just enough food to keep it from starving. Said he wanted it hungry so it'd go after the rats.

Well, anyway, last week we're all over at Twang's sitting on the floor eating pizza from Rosie's and listening to the radio, when all of a sudden the cat gets up from the kitchen and walks into the bedroom. There ain't shit in there, Twang sleeps on an air mattress in his brother's sleeping bag from the army, and keeps his clothes in a cardboard steamer trunk, but still he got mad and ran in after the cat. "Lazy fucker!", yells Twang, and he kicks the cat in the head. Then he looks down and sees the air mattress is going flat. "Goddamit!" He comes out teeth gritted, but the cat has squeezed its way in between the water heater and the sink where Twang can't reach it. He starts smiling, "Here, kitty, c'mon little puss." But the cat don't move, he just kind of watches. Then Twang says, "Alright you little motherfucker. It's time for drug warfare." By this time all of us are cracking up, and Twang yells, "You think this is funny. Did you ever see a cat on acid." I guess no one had. I certainly never had. "Well just keep your eye on the bowl." He reached up into a cabinet and grabbed a yellow bowl with a picture of a cat smacking its lips on the side. "I bought this for the bastard." He shook it at all of us. "Do you think he cares, hell no." Opening a can of tuna he sang sweetly, "Nothing but the best for you today sweetheart." He forked in into the bowl, breaking the big chunks tenderly. With the pride of a chef, he mixed the acid into the food. "Here you go snuggums." The cat backed up into the wall when he put it down in front of him. Twang walked over by us and grabbed a piece of pizza. There wasn't much left, we should have got a bigger size.

The cat smelled and sniffed for a while, then he started clawing at the bowl. When he was sure it was safe, he came out a little and stuffed his face into the tuna. Twang must have not fed him for a couple of days. He gobbled it up without a single chew.

Christ, everyone felt sorry for the poor thing, but nobody wanted to go home. It was like hanging around after an accident, to get a look at the people involved, even though you know it's going to be disgusting.

Nothing happened for about half an hour, and then Twang walked over and poked it with a broom stick. The cat hunched up against the wall and swung its paw, claws out. Twang dropped the broom and jumped back, we all started laughing. It was funny, Ralph, you know what a bullshitter Twang is. His face turned red as an Indian, so he picked the broom up and threw it like a spear at the cat, but he missed and broke the valve off the water heater. Water started spilling out all over the floor and onto the cat who started RAOOUING like crazy. Cats don't like to be wet straight, let alone tripping. Twang didn't know what to do and started sweeping the water back with the broom. But the faster he swept, the more water came rushing back across his feet.

Then Twang starts giving us orders like it was our fault or something. "Get me this, you do that." Hey, fuck him. We left him sweeping the water out that double back door of his, it leads right into the garbage cans. After we left I went home. Nobody knows what happened because Twang isn't talking to any of us, but his brother told me he called the landlord who lived next door and the two of them shut the water off somehow. He also told me the cat went crazy and died, but that's probably bullshit. Anyway Twang got evicted from his flat and had to move back in with his father. So what else is new, I haven't heard from you in two months. What's the matter, you can't write?

I used to work in a grocery store, before I got fired, and let me tell you after some of the things I've seen, I'm never going to go shopping. Those people don't care about anything except the almighty buck. People are just sheep to them, to be led around by the nose via "Tonight Only" sales and whatnot. I stood directly in front of a store manager as he scooped up potato chips from the floor into the bag, stapled it together, and marked it down half price. Worse than that, somebody bought it. Come on now people, I'm all for saving money, but that is just a little too much.

The only part of my job that was any fun at all, was unloading the trucks that came in every Friday to restock the store. We'd pull the stacks of cereal, detergent, or what-have-you into the elevator and down to the store room. Then we'd set them up into a kind of garden maze. Each week the store manager would have to make his way to the office by a different combination of twists, turns, and dead ends. Once, just for fun, we didn't leave a path for his office. It took him ten minutes to find out.

But the very best part of all this was a game that, to my knowledge, is (or was) unique to our store and that is Rat Hockey™. To play Rat Hockey you must have three things. A broom, a rat, and a goal. By goal, I don't mean a set area where points must be scored (such as a net). I mean an actual goal, an ideal. Something to go after with all your heart and soul. For instance, my goal when just a beginner was to get the rat at least a foot off the ground. But I'm getting too far ahead.

Rat Hockey is not a game you can play at any time you like. No, it is only at the rat's convenience. You see rats hide under the skids that transport the stacks of cartons and only if you are lucky enough to need move one, can the sport be enjoyed. A skid, briefly, is made of three separate boards, two by four inches, lying longwise on the short side, with more thinner boards nailed on top of them to form a platform. Underneath the platform, formed by the three baseboards are two rectangular spaces, side by side. Within these spaces the rat hides.

The object used to transport skids is a two-pronged sort of thing, with rollers on the bottom and a pump handle in front. The prongs fit into the spaces, and the pump handle acts like a jack to rise the skid off the floor and move it around by the rollers. Well, when the prongs slide in, the rats slide out, and quickly grabbing a broom you swat.

Congrats to you if you hit the rat, though probably you didn't, and this is where the goal comes in. After all, no one goes out to a driving range to just . . . hit . . . the . . . ball. No! They go out to hit the big red 200-ft. marker. And the next time out the 250 and so on until they're off the property altogether. And so it must be with rats.

Therefore, your first objective must be simply to make contact. Oh don't worry, you'll know when you miss alright, and it won't be a pretty feeling. You'll hear the wisp of straw as it brushes blandly against the floor, and see the rat race to some unreachable place as if to say, "Naa, Naaaa."

Yes, it's tough at first, but only after those few solo tries will you be even near ready to play your first two-man game. But remember, you each have different goals in mind, and his might very well be to hit the rat directly into your face. Be defensive. Just because he works with you, don't make the mistake of treating this other fellow like a partner. He's not.

The ultimate goal in all of this, of course, is to kill the rat with one blow. In all of my years of rat hockey, I've never seen it done. Well, yeah, I did once. But it really shouldn't count. Because the rat landed in the middle of the bottle returns, and cut itself open on a chunk of glass trying to get away. Really it was a rat suicide. You know, "Death Before Dishonor." Rats must not be religious. After all, suicide's a sin.

Do you want to know what's funny? Those rat poison posters the city puts up in the alleys. I don't know why, but they always struck me as funny. A big rat with a black X slashed across him. When I was too young to read, I thought it was a cartoon or something. To be perfectly honest, I've never seen any rat poison in the alley, just those signs. Maybe the city uses them on rats like my uncle Louie uses his Pinkerton sticker for thieves. He has the sticker on his car that says, "THIS CAR PROTECTED BY PINKERTON." So far it's worked. His car has never been stolen, though I can't imagine why anybody would take it. Anyway, what if the city is just trying to scare the rats away? What if they're supposed to look up at the rat poison poster and say, "Hey baby, no way. I'm getting out of this alley. I don't wanna end up with no black X on top of me." What if they're just supposed to pack up and go? And what if they don't? What if they group together and take over the world? Hit us where it hurts. What if they form Kamikaze outfits that give up their lives by chewing through our electric and telephone lines? What if they weaken us by becoming violent and biting every one they see? What if they become ant-like, and walk through the streets, eating everything that stands in their way? They multiply quickly, you know; they already out-number us. What if they stand on their little rat legs and scream, "Enough!"? In that case, we would all be up the creek.

But never fear, just because I can't see the poison doesn't mean it isn't there. I know it's there, because last week my neighbor's dog ate some, and got awfully sick, almost died. Too bad though. The little prick is always getting into my garden.

HOW PEOPLE RELATE TO CANCER
Marilyn Mannisto

It was her second day working as a physician's assistant for a group of Head and Neck Cancer surgeons. The first day had been a blur of names, instructions, strange instruments, phones ringing, and a charged atmosphere of energy and importance that thoroughly captivated her.

Mr. Ricco, whom she had seated just ten minutes earlier, had removed his eye patch and was reclining in a chair facing her. A cavity was visible through an opening the size of a golfball, where his right eye formerly was. After the initial opening, it widened out to the bridge of his nose on one side and his ear on the other. It reached upwards to the middle of his forehead, downward to the lowest part of his cheekbone and backwards in depth until parallel with his ear. Unconsciously, she leaned against the door frame and placed one hand over the raging internal tide of gastric juices that she could feel pelting the lining of her stomach. She had known she would be working with severe cases of cancer, but "severe" did not adequately describe the rampaging disease that she was now face to face with.

Dr. Singer had not noticed her appearance and he and his intern continued firing questions at Mr. Ricco as they poked and pried within the cavity. "Bled lately? Still using an antiseptic solution on your packing inside this cavity? Lost any weight since last month? Is the pain better?" He was answering all their questions, but meantime he noticed that he had been observing her. When she first realized that she was being watched, and looked into this one good eye, she fancied she saw something like pity flick across it. Dr. Singer called her forward to explain what was needed.

He was using an instrument called a cauterizer which burns the skin closed to stop sites that are bleeding. It is the common instrument used in operating rooms to stop bleeding veins because it is so much quicker than suturing them closed. However, the smell is undiluted and unmistakably that of burning flesh.

She was to take a suction hose, which is similar to a tiny vacuum, and suck away the smoke caused by cauterizing the tissue inside the cavity so that Dr. Singer's view would be unobstructed and so that the smoke would not irritate Mr. Ricco's good eye.

As she leaned forward receiving her instructions she noticed that the cavity was square-shaped and filled with patches of pink subcutaneous tissue, as well as patches of grey, brown and green skin which represented healing areas. In several places bright red waterfalls of blood were oozing down and forming small lakes on the floor of the cavern.

As he began to cauterize, smoke billowed out of the cavity. It was extremely tedious work to try and capture even the majority of it. She was thankful, for this absorbed her attention and she had not time to think of her surroundings, the gaping hole in Mr. Ricco's head, or the pain that he must regularly suffer.

Suddenly a low tenor voice broke into song; "Don't let the smoke get in your eyes, don't let the moon break your heart." Mr. Ricco was singing a parody of some old broadway show song. Startled, she leaned backward to look into his face. His one blue iris flashed in the surgical light. He winked, began studying the hair on his knuckles, and continued to hum the tune and smile whenever he caught her eye.

Uncomfortable, she was pushing herself against the back of her chair as her dark-haired friend drooped further forward in his. He had one foot raised upwards onto the bar connecting the two front legs of his chair. His head was stooped towards the hand holding his cigarette positioned on his right knee. "What's the most common type of cancer? Or, no, wait a minute...what are the three most common types?" he asked. She wasn't used to statistical questions, and that is all that Pizz had been asking all evening. None of the usual things about varieties of emotion, the stages of acceptance of the disease, or different methods of treatment. It took her a while to recall exactly what the answer to his question was. "Lung, Breast, and Colon," she murmured, "but I'm not sure about the order anymore, it's probably changed since I was in school." "Lung, really?" he queried, as he put out his cigarette. She chuckled and commented on his transparency. His girlfriend Sue broke from her intense concentration on the woven rug at her feet for the first time in many minutes and smiled. Just as she was beginning to feel a bit of the lightheartedness that had characterized their greetings, Pizz said, "Well, isn't it easy to detect cancer, and don't you get symptoms early enough to be cured in most cases?"

Sue dropped her eyes to the rug again, and their friend covered a sigh and began, "Well, the severity of the symptoms varies from individual to individual. Some have a huge weight loss, coughing, night sweats, pain, etc. On the other hand another person may have a more advanced stage of disease that was only discovered on a routine chest X-ray or he may have experienced a little indigestion for enough days to make him be concerned enough to see his physician."

At the end of each couplet of question and answer, Pizz slumped a little further into his chair and the look on his face became a little more bewildered, a trifle more serious and stern. He opened his mouth to ask another question.

"No, Mike," his friend said. "I refuse to talk about this anymore. This always happens to me. Someone asks me what I do, someone else asks me a few questions, and in record time I can change a roomful of laughing, joking, happy people into depressed uncomfortable hypochondriacs who are starting to experience all the symptons we talked about, and who can see no way to prevent getting the "Dreaded Disease" themselves. From now on, I'm a secretary, or a sales clerk...anything but working in cancer research."

Mr. Brunswick was waiting for her to open up the office this morning. You could give him a 6:00 a.m. appointment and he would arrive at 5:00 a.m. He is that anxious to get his clean bill of health and continue with his life.

He had just returned from a trip to Mexico and came in with ashtrays made out of centavos for Arlene and her. A truck driver friend of his came along. He is still battling with his employers, trying to get his position back, but it seems like he had made little progress, if any. His boss believes that cancer is contagious and despite the numerous letters that Dr. Bittel has written to him, he refuses to change his unscientific position, whether because of pride or superstition. She has no idea.

Mr. Brunswick was found to have a carcinoma of his lower lip two years ago. They had to do extensive surgery around his mouth and jaw, for it was a large tumor, but now he only comes in for check-ups to make sure there is no recurrence of disease and to see the plastic surgeon who is gradually rebuilding the chin and lip into their former contours.

One day Mr. Brunswick asked her if she had ever seen how he brushed his teeth, and proceeded to pull back his bottom lip, revealing a layer of gray whiskers along its inside surface. "Isn't that something?" he asked. "They took this skin off my cheek and it doesn't know yet that it is growing inside my mouth now. But the doc said that eventually all those whiskers will drop out and it will be like my old lip was before." She asked one of the doctors about it and he verified that. She guessed the same thing happens when they take grafts from a man's chest and use the skin to repair defects in the neck, mouth or throat.

Mr. Brunswick is never shy with any of the girls in the office or the doctors. Whenever other patients begin to arrive before she has a chance to seat him inside, he will stand up in the farthest corner of the waiting room, with hat in hand, and stare down at the floor in front of him. The only time his disfigurement causes him concern is when it may make other people uncomfortable. Yet he is not offended by their inability to accept him. He knows that they cannot understand what he has gone through, or realize how happy he is to be breathing and alive, no matter what he looks like. It is sad, though, and she tries to put him into an empty room as soon as possible. He is such a large man, with a huge six-foot frame and long swinging arms, that it is impossible for him to be obscure in a small room. Once he is among people who are familiar with him, however, he relaxes completely. He has found within himself complete acceptance of his disease and his limited chances for a long life. He makes each moment count.

Although a conference was in progress, she slipped into the small auditorium and surreptitiously began to sweep the floor. She had her order and this room had to be cleaned before the medical school dean arrived for his talk at 3:00 p.m.

She paused as the speaker caught her attention and stared at the illuminated screen which held an X-ray picture of someone's lungs. She squinted up her eyes and peered hard and fast at the right lung he was pointing to, but she couldn't see anything that resembled a tumor. Yet everyone else in the room acted like it was huge and plain as day. So she took their word for it. With each second this doctor was getting more and more excited and he was trying harder and harder to appear calm. It made her suspicious that he was trying to fool all of them, that there really wasn't a mass; or at least, if there was he had something up his sleeve. He kept shifting his weight from one foot to the other, waving the pointer wildly in the air, and his face was swelling with his own anticipation.

He told how they brought this man into the hospital and cut him in half to get inside the bad lung (which is what he said is called a thoractomy). But once they got inside, all they could see was fine, healthy tissue. There wasn't anything that looked a trifle suspicious. Puzzled, they closed him up again and sent him back to his room. After he recovered a little, they sent him back down to get another X-ray. He said that this one looked exactly like the first. In fact the mass was even a little larger, which made it even more likely that this man had cancer of the lung.

He paused and looked around at the puzzled, pondering faces of his audience. A couple people came up and took a closer look at the picture but walked away, remaining convinced that there was definitely a tumor in the right lung.

She was getting more puzzled by the minute, so she set her broom down and leaned against the back wall to see if this doctor could explain why he didn't find a tumor when he kept swearing that there was one on the X-ray.

He let the suspense hang in the air a little while longer before he told how he went down to the X-ray department and talked with the technician who developed the film. Seems that the technician was puzzled; both times he had had to turn the X-ray around because it kept coming out of the machine backwards. The doctor scanned the crowd to see if anyone suspected the climax he was coming to. Then he said that this man had a congenital defect that had never been diagnosed before. His heart was on the right side of his chest. Which is why the technician had to turn around the film in order to label the right and left sides respectively and which is why, when they looked at the right lung, it was normal and healthy.

It ended up that they had to bring that poor man back to the operating room and open him up on the other side and cut that tumor out. It turned out that basically the poor guy was cut in half.

You can't blame the doctor, and not really the technician either, for who would suspect such a thing? But she swept out of that room with a grave heart. Who knows, someday she may prove to be an exception to the general rule; and those doctors in there, why they're only human and just as puzzled as she was. She thinks maybe it's not too smart to think of doctors the way she used to, that is, as knowing all the answers and being above mistakes, but you know, it sure is a much more comfortable feeling.

Mr. Pelham lay reclining in the large surgical chair. The small opening near his eye that led into his maxillary sinus uncovered and ozzing a clear, runny liquid. His face held a sickly yellow hue and his head lay enfolded in his shoulder, completely oblivious to his surroundings or his own lack of comfort.

She hadn't seen him in the office for at least three months. He had been in the hospital most of that time due to another recurrence of his cancer, more severe than before. But once she heard that he was discharged, she imagined that he was back up to par again and working at the gas station that his son had taken over. Now that she saw him, all of these illusions fled and she escaped into the back supply room to allow herself time to think about how she could support him, now that the end was evidently so near for him.

Dr. Becker called her to help him repack the sinus with clean gauze and solution. They worked quietly, without looking at each other or chatting as usual. Mr. Pelham looked quietly from one to the other as they worked. She couldn't bring herself to ask him the usual questions about his prize-winning roses or "Pappy", the Irish wolfhound he had brought in one day when no patients were scheduled so she could meet him. She narrowed her eyes as she watched the opening being filled with packing and squinted until her eyes were partly screwed shut and the tears had less chance of forming and falling and giving her emotion away.

Finally he was through packing. She quickly put a cover bandage on and ran into the supply room. She bent over the sink and laid her forehead against the soap dispenser mounted on the wall. If this is what it will be like getting to know and love these people and then helplessly sitting by and watching them die, she won't be able to take it. She can't help but get involved with them, and she can't stand to feel so helpless that she ignores them later on, at the times when they need her support the most.

Soft steps were heard in the hallway. Dr. Becker peered in at her over the swinging doors. This was his first year of practice and he realized part of what must be going through her mind. He walked in.

"What's the matter?" Without looking up, she said, "He is dying, that's obvious, what else could be the matter?"

He sighed and replied, "Yes, after that last recurrence, he has failed in every area, under every different treatment we have tried. But we have tried, Jane. There is nothing left for us to do but make him comfortable and of course support him and be cheerful and sensitive to his needs when he can't voice them. All we are doing in here now is depressing each other, while Mr. Pelham sits in the next room, and he's depressed too."

Suddenly she realized what a valuable asset some defenses were. Otherwise you didn't solve anything, you simply created more bad feelings and dismay when you could have been playing up the positive aspects of what has gone on before and what has been learned from people like Mr. Pelham. Quickly she dabbed at her eyes and plunged the instruments into the sink. Then she went into Mr. Pelham's room. "So, I bet Pappy has an easy time with you lately, I bet you've even been letting him sleep with you!" Mr. Pelham looked up and smiled with one corner of his mouth. Well, she thought, that's a start.

Three wigs of different lengths and colors were perched on top of the faceless Styrofoam heads in the medicine room. Two patients lay connected to dripping bottles of toxic drugs with small plastic basins lying next to their heads in case their nausea should become too powerful. An oncology nurse came in to check the flow rate of the drugs and pulled up a stool next to a middle-aged woman who was taking chemotherapy for the first time. "Now", she started, "you had to sign a consent form that told you what kind of side effects you might experience with the particular drugs you are taking. Right?"

"Yes," the woman whispered.

"Have you experienced any of these after your first course of drugs last week?" the nurse asked, while checking her arms and face for changes in pigment or severe symptoms of weight loss.

"Well, yes, I had a lot of nausea for the first three days, and then my hair started coming out in large clumps whenever I brush it. So, I have stopped brushing it except when it gets so tangled that I have no choice."

"Well, you will probably lose almost all of your hair while you are on this medication, but you will also probably regain most of it once your treatment is over with. In the meantime, we can supply you with the wig that most closely resembles your hair style and color. I'll leave you with these to try on over the next few minutes, and when you have chosen one, I'll make out an order for it and we'll have it for you to pick up by next week."

A frail bony man was groaning on the other side of the curtain. When she had first been seated in this large room, she had caught a glimpse of his pallid face and the beige wool blanket covering him from the waist down. She dreaded the sound of footsteps, fearing that it would be the nurse coming in to stick a needle in her arm again, but only after a dozen tries and the dumps of displaced blood and tissue were rising and swelling in a dozen spots along her arm. Perhaps it would be easier this week and they would be able to get one into her vein before long. She also knew that she now had four more days of vomiting and flu-like symptoms to cope with. And her granddaughter was coming to visit her this Sunday. Well, she would try to stay out of bed and play with her for at least a portion of the afternoon.

She witnessed an operation for the first time last week. She goes from one case to another every morning for two hours with the head anesthesiologist as part of clinical training. The first day, they saw an entire section or lobe of a man's left lung removed because of cancer.

At first she felt queasy as the surgical knife split open around an inch of yellow, bilious fatty tissue which lay on top of the ribs. An incision was made from the top of the shoulder, all the way down the man's side and inward to his backbone, so that he was for all practical purposes cut in half. Underneath, the pulsing sponge of blue and pink tissue began to expand outward, since the skin and tissue no longer held it captive inside. Toward the bottom of the lung, the tissue changed to a dark black color and little fungating portions of tissue could be seen growing in mounds and disrupting the shape of the lung.

The surgeon worked slowly, cutting a portion away from the healthy lung, stopping to tie and clip severed veins with hemostats (which are curved scissors without sharp edges that lock into the position in which you close them), using sponges of gauze to sweep up the blood that obstructed their view. All of these sponges are tossed into a special basket on the floor and it is from them that the blood loss during an operation is estimated. If it is completely soaked with blood, that equals 100 cc's of lost blood, if only partially covered, then it is 50 cc's, etc.

No one is present without rubber gloves with a fine white powder inside to keep his hands from sweating too profusely, a green elastic shower cap on his head, a green surgical cotton gown on, the common mask extending over the mouth and nose, and even paper booties which completely cover his shoes like galoshes.

The floors are rubber to prevent electrical fires, since rubber is not conductive. The lights and tile walls make the rooms seem even colder than the 60 degrees that they are kept at (to inhibit bacteria).

The surgeons, at least many of them, do joke around while they work. For someone who cuts into lungs and stomachs every day, five and six times a day, it becomes as routine as filing or correcting test papers. But you can also be sure that if an unexpected problem arises, they are giving their entire concentration to solving it before serious repercussions are felt.

The steel voice of the microphone bounced up to the ceiling, vibrated among the chandeliers, and dropped with a whisper to the floor. At the same moment the double doors at the back of the hall were opened and a small, thin man rushed forward. The hallway's breath swept up to the podium and disarranged the speaker's hair. The small man reached the stage and began to adjust his microphone, which uttered a high, shrill protest.

The woman moderator at the right hand side of the stage glanced at the middle-aged model who was frozen in her previous position during this interruption. One hand rested on her left hip while she hugged the back of her neck with the other.

Each moderator stood behind paper-flower and sash-bedecked podiums of brilliant springtime colors. These decorations lent a stale, gaudy accent to the proceedings, they were in gross contrast with the white linen table cloths, elegant wallpaper and crystal chandeliers of the banquet room.

The small woman lifted her chin to the microphone and, while on tip-toe, resumed the fashion show. "This smart three-piece suit is perfect for that special weekend getaway. Though you may spend hours on the road, you'll arrive fresh and wrinkle-free due to its permanent-press finish. Available at the Casual Corner of Sears."

The model twirled to show the front, back, and sides of her outfit. However, the spins were quite rapid and by the time the moderator finished her recital, she stood wavering with a slight attack of vertigo.

Dr. Paul, the other speaker, boomed into the speaker: "This patient had both breasts removed in 1974. Afterwards she received a year of chemotherapy utilizing a combination of three different investigational drugs. Now she is receiving no treatment whatsoever, and merely coming in for periodic checkups."

A group of the women sponsoring the show from the Ladies Club began to clap. The embarrassed model made a slight curtsy and exited quickly off-stage.

Barb and she looked at each other with rolling eyes. Who was this Dr. Paul? He represented the typical medical authority who looked upon people as being extraneous to the disease. Just the type who would never remember your name, but would read it to you off of your chart each time you came into the office.

The banquet room was crowded with tables of four, each marked with a small lamp and festooned with a floral arrangement composed of paper flowers identical to those onstage.

At an adjacent table, the administrator of the Cancer Center (which was to receive the money made from this affair) was loudly expressing her delight with the show. "Weren't the fashions lovely? The women chosen to model were terrific. I'm well acquainted with Dr. Paul; doesn't he have a striking figure?" On and on she blabbed, stifling all other conversation in a radius of five feet. Her assistant sat egging her on with monosyllabic replies and a set smile: "Oh yes, they certainly are. So true; really?" while all the time she was looking for the appropriate moment to mention her upcoming merit review and give herself a plug for a higher raise than usual. "Heaven knows I deserve it," she thought as Irene's voice droned on.

As the finale of the show approached, a man who had been hired to entertain the guests while they were served could be heard tuning up his Stradivarius violin. All eight models came out in bathing suits, surprisingly enough, and looked quite good considering that their average age was 45. At this point, Dr. Paul smiled widely and, with some feigned emotion, proclaimed these "patients" as indications of the great strides being made in the detection, treatment, and eventual cure of cancer.

D TO THE KNEE! STONE TO THE BONE!
Dino Malcolm

It was cold and a light snow was falling. Jughead and I were sipping white port and Kool-aid while we stared out the front window of the enclosed porch that was connected to Jughead's living room. About half a block away we could see four members of the Rangers approaching us. There was Hawk, a tall skinny guy with scars across his nose. Saint, a short stocky dude who walked like he had a grudge on his shoulders. Mack was the oldest and tallest and the ugliest. Also with them was Rosco-boy; he was the one who carried the pistol because he was the youngest. If any of the others carried the gun and got busted they could get time in the joint. But Rosco-boy was only twelve. Jughead and I would usually represent our club when we would see the Stones. We were both members of the East side Bostonian Pimp Disciples. Jughead was war counselor because he was known for doing crazy things. This was a perfect time to represent our club as the Blackstone Rangers came nearer to our window. We were located on the second floor, so we had a good view of the area. Across the street was the Kimbark Plaza and the Stones were trying to run it. They would be over there every night extorting money from business and customers. We finished the wine as the Rocks came nearer to the building. I cracked a window open about an inch and a half, just enough so that snow wouldn't come inside the apartment, but it was enough so that we could represent our club. The Stones were directly in front of our window and I was the first to shout out, "D's run it!" The four stopped in their tracks and then ducked behind a parked car that was covered with snow. Jughead and I ducked down under the window as one of the members looked in our direction. The Stones were confused. They didn't know whether a passing car full of D's said it or whether some of us were hiding in gangways waiting to shoot them on sight. They stayed behind the parked car as the four canvassed the area carefully. Jughead was anxious to represent us so he stood up in the window and opened it wider. This made the snow come into the house and all over me. I tried to tell him to get away from the window but it was too late. "D's thang!" "D to the knee!" "Stones ain't shit." Jughead said in a commanding voice as he beat his fist against his chest twice. This was our code. The Stones had one also, they would use one hand against their chest. All four Stones saw him and heard him. About the same time Head's mother entered the front room from the rear of the apartment. "What's all that noise, Darryl?" Darryl was Head's real name. She was a big woman who didn't take shit from anyone. She ordered us out of the living room but first commanded Jughead to close the window. I was still sitting on the floor trying to watch the Stones and Head's mother at the same time. Jug closed the window. By this time, Rosco-boy had given the gun to Hawk who was aiming it up at the window, at Head. I grabbed at Head and yelled for him to get down. Head fell to the floor at the sound of broken glass. The shot sounded like a car backfiring. Judghead's mother also fell to the floor and the room shook a little. The bullet had broken the window and left a hole the size of a silver dollar a few feet from where Head's mother was standing. Little pieces of glass mixed with snow were everywhere, all in my hair and clothes. A piece of glass was sticking out of Jughead's hand. Jughead and I crawled on the floor over to where his mother was. She was all right except for a little shock. I crawled back to the window and inched my head up to the ledge and peeked out to see if the Rangers were still there. There was no one in sight. All I could see was four sets of tracks in the freshly fallen snow. Here I was, sixteen; and getting shot at was nothing new, but I was scared. I was scared because an innocent person could have gotten shot. Me and Head knew what to expect, we have been D's for three years and before it was over we would be shot at a lot more. Maybe killed. But this was the first time we had jeopardized his mother's life; she wasn't with anybody.

Jughead moved the following week and I became a little more careful, watching my back wherever I went. Hawk and Saint got busted for a stolen car and were sent to Cook County Jail. Mack was trying to start a new club in the neighborhood. Rosco-boy got his in the back one night in front of the YMCA; he was thirteen.

The five of us were in a basement under Darryl's apartment making zip-guns. We heard that the Stones were coming down on us that night so we wanted to be prepared. We had been members of the D's now for three months and we were experts. At least we thought we were. Every time I tried to make a zip gun it would never work. Either I had too many rubber bands or the bullet was too long or short. Darryl's zip gun was made from an old Mattel derringer cap gun. Sometimes it worked and sometimes it didn't. I remember one time we put a .22 long bullet in the gun and it exploded in Darryl's hand. He had to get five stitches in the hospital. Still, he was convinced that this time it would work. Russell was looking out the basement window watching for the police. The last time we were in a basement the landlord called the cops. We barely got away that time. The basement was as long as the apartment complex. You could enter it from one door and exit from three others or vice-versa. The concrete floor was scarred up and dirty from the coal that lined the walls by the furnace. Darryl loaded his zip gun with a .22 short bullet about the same time a police car pulled up to the window. "The Man," said Russell as he ran past us and out the door. Darryl dropped the gun on the floor and it went off making a loud echo throughout the basement. Everybody split up. Darryl and I decided not to go out any doors and instead we climbed out of a window that was facing the alley. Once outside we peeked around the corner of the building and could see the cops taking Russell, who was in handcuffs, to jail. We ran around the side of the building and quickly entered a hallway that was only five feet from us. I started ringing bells until someone buzzed us in. We dashed up to the third floor and sat down on the steps. All you could hear was our heavy breathing. It was only a few minutes, but seemed like hours, when we heard someone enter the building. We don't know how he got in because no one buzzed him in. He started climbing the stairs very carefully, pausing after every few steps. Darryl and I became very quiet, we didn't move a muscle. The footsteps kept getting louder and louder until they finally stopped at the bottom of the stairway where we were sitting. The noise had belonged to the policeman who was staring at both of us. He first asked us if we lived here and when we said yes, he knocked on an apartment door near us. The woman who answered told him we didn't. He handcuffed both of us together, then took us downstairs and outside to the waiting cars. By this time three squad cars were parked in a row. Russell was inside of the first one. The other two guys that were with us sat quietly in the second car. Darryl and I were put in the last car. A policeman came out of the basement carrying Darryl's zip gun.

At the police station the arresting officers tried to blame us for the shooting of a lady a week before on Dorchester Avenue. Officer Glazier, a six-foot-four, two-hundred-fifty-pound Gang Intelligence Unit cop persuaded his fellow officers that we weren't the ones that had gone over to that area because that was the Stones' hood. Only Stones would shoot innocent people and only D's would shoot Stones. Glazier made us sign a huge wooden stick that was as big as a bat with our nicknames. He then hit each of us with it across our rumps. The stick had many names on it. Some of the names belonged to the D's and Stones and other club members. After being hit with the stick I personally couldn't sit down for two or three days. He told us he didn't want to see us again. That was the first time I saw Glazier but it wasn't the last.

There were so many members of the Blackstone Rangers and Eastside Disciples that they would use a password to keep track of each other. The password was invented because many times members would jump on each other, not knowing that both were part of the same organization. A different password would be given to members at meetings that were held every other week. Meetings were held to find out local information that happened weeks before. They were also for announcing parties, introducing new members and collecting dues. Our dues were usually fifty cents and that went for parties and refreshments, pool and ping-pong tables and sometimes guns. Many times the Stones would find out our password and we would find out theirs. A Disciple would use a Stone's password when he went into their neighborhood and vice-versa. Sometimes we would catch a Stone and give him half the password and if he gave us the other half of the password we would kick his ass. After a while this became confusing. We would jump on each other because we didn't know who was who. The passwords would consist of two-word phrases such as apple-pie, down-hill, and black-hawk. There weren't too many ways to find out a password. Either you would find out from a girl that lived in our neighborhood who dated a Ranger or you would pretend to be a member at one of the meetings. In other words, a spy. If you got caught, it would mean instant death or worse. Gene, a member of the Motown D's, attended a Ranger meeting one time and was discovered as being a spy. The Stones broke both of his arms and legs and kicked him out of a moving car. He was in the hospital for over a year.

Since the Rangers knew almost all of the D's from our end of the community, Jughead and I were chosen to attend the next Ranger meeting. The Rangers didn't know we were members of the D's because we both attended Hyde Park High School, a stronghold of the Rangers. We kept our identity hidden at school because we were the only D's there. We had to attend Hyde Park at least until the end of the semester, when we could transfer. Everybody else either dropped out, never went, or got kicked out. At school the Rangers were drafting everybody. They even had teachers in their gang. Many times I was approached by the Stones to join but I would usually talk my way out of it or agree to show up at the next meeting and didn't. This time it was different. I was going to spy for the D's. I could have gone as a spy before but I didn't want to. To be a member of both clubs was very unhealthy. I decided to go this time because I was chosen and I had decided not to go back to that school because it was becoming too dangerous. They used to call Hyde Park High School "little Vietnam" because there were shootings and killings every week.

The Rangers held their meetings at a church on 64th and Kimbark. Gang slogans and members nicknames were scribbled on every building near the church but the church was untouched. Jughead and I walked into the church and took a seat in one of the long pews near the front altar. We had decided to pretend we were joining the Cassonova Rangers because they had more members in Hyde Park than any other group. Their church was very large with its two balconies and long pews lined along the walls and the sides. All the windows were stained glass and were many different colors. I thought that the church could hold a thousand people but I soon found out that it held more. It was weird. I was diggin' being there at the same time I was scared. It was like driving a stolen car, knowing you can get caught any minute if you panic. Members started taking seats by the dozens. There was every type of Ranger there. There were Maniacs, Cassonovas, Unknowns, Four-Tray, Five-Tray, Six-Tray, Four-Corner, Imperials, Midgets, Spanish, Boss Pimps, Cobras, etc. It took thirty minutes alone for the 95th Street Gangsters to fall in. Each one of them wore a black hat with a red band. There were Stones from the West Side, Cabrini Green projects from out North, and even from Gary, Indiana. The Rangerettes, female branch of the Stones, were next to the last to come in.

These were all young women ranging in age from 12 to 25. Personally I thought that the Disciple Queens were finer than the Rangerettes. Some of the Rangers there were eye-balling Jughead and me. The main thing was not to panic. I kept telling this to myself again and again. The Main 21 were the last to come in. They were the ruling body of the Blackstone Rangers. They took their place at the altar. They consisted of leaders of each club. The only one who hadn't come in yet was the chief, Angel. He was a short ugly-looking dude in his late twenties. I really don't know how he became the chief; I guess he was one of those types of people in the right place at the right time. When he entered, everybody stopped talking. You could hear a pin drop. He was dressed in black with a black cape dragging behind on the floor. He walked over to the center of the altar, near a pulpit, and faced his nation. Everybody rose from their seats, including me and Head. "Blackstone!" Angel shouted. "BLACKSTONE!" was the response. The noise drowned out the passing el train. He waved his hand in front of him and everyone sat back down. Angel walked up to the pulpit and stood behind it. His voice was soft and light but firm. "Black P. Stone forever. I'm glad we have a full house tonight. We must always represent in strong numbers because we are mighty, we are strong, we are Blackstone Rangers. We have a lot to discuss tonight, so let's take a roll call."

A member of each club gave Angel a list of names of people who were present or absent for the meeting. I studied the faces who were captured by Angel's voice. These were some dedicated members. Angel started speaking again.

"All of you know that the police, especially the G.I.U. (Gang Intelligence Unit) are breathing down our necks everyday. At this very moment two pigs are sitting in front of the church watching our movements. We must be careful. We must watch ourselves. The G.I.U. are very tricky characters. They will pick one of us up at any time, take us to a D-hood and then drop us off. The D's and the G.I.U. are working together to try and stop us. They can't. They won't, because we are one nation, the Black P. Stone Nation."

The crowd responded with shouts of approval.

"We must watch all new members. Any one of them could be a spy or a police informer. All new members stand up and show yourselves to the Nation."

I swallowed my heart when he said that. I looked at Jughead and I thought he was about to cry. We weren't expecting this to happen. To be put on display. If anybody, anyone recognized us, or even thought for one second that we were D's, we were dead. We slowly stood up with the rest of the new members. There were forty of us scattered about the church. Angel stepped down from behind the altar. He was carrying a baseball bat in one hand. He walked over to where some other new members were standing. All eyes were on us and the others.

"Why do you want to be a member of the Nation, brother?" he said to one person who was standing. Before he could answer Angel moved on to someone else.

"What about you, do you think you're worthy enough to become a Black P. Stone?"

Before he could answer, Angel walked away again. He walked over to Jughead and myself and stared into our faces. Angel said, "Represent brothers."

Both of us hit ourselves in the chest and shouted, "Black P. Stone run it" and "Stones forever." Angel walked back up to the altar.

"That's right, Stones forever."

After ordering us to sit down, Angel started running off at the mouth about how we should catch a D and fuck him up. "Let me tell you about those D's, they're sneaky. They will sneak up on you, shoot you in the back and then represent their club. They are only a block away from here, yet we can't take over their hood. Why?" He shouted, "Why, goddammit?! We should be running this hood from State to the lake." He waved his arms back and forth and started pacing the floor taking short steps and turning quickly back and forth as if he was trapped in a small area, but he had enough room to walk a block. He focused his attention to a corner of the church where the young ladies were sitting. "They are even fucking our women, that's right!" Some of the women lowered their heads with disgrace. "Now all of you want to go out and kill all them D's right now, right?" The crowd roared with revenge. They sounded like they could kill with their bare hands. Damn! Angel quieted them down once again. "We will get those D's but we have to be slick like them. We have to out-think them. If we were to attack now most of us would get killed, go to jail or worse. Outsmart them like this whore I used to know. Let me tell you about Helen. Helen was a fine hammer from Spain. She had all the officials' noses open. Any of you niggers ever heard of Spain?" A few members raised their hands. I didn't raise mine because I didn't want this asshole asking me any questions. "Anyway she was so fine that three of the officials were always fighting over her. They would always end up kicking each other's asses. Now Helen's old man, I mean father, didn't dig this shit. These three grown ass men would come over to her crib and break up the furniture fighting over his bitch. I mean this dame was bad, she was a real brickhouse. Her father got tired of buying new furniture every week, so he called his partner who stayed in this place called Greece and told him to send his son down here (that is, Spain) for a few weeks so he could meet Helen, marry the bitch, and these fools could stop fighting over her. Now Helen didn't give two shits about the three dudes. She had her eyes set on Bladder, who was from Troy. Now Bladder was a big-time pimp in Troy and he had heard about this whore named Helen who was supposed to be so fine. When Helen and Bladder's eyes met, it was love at first sight. Now I know none of you know what love is?"

Some of the Rangers started laughing and looking over to where the girls were sitting. Angel continued, "Not that kind of love, you assholes, Black P. Stone love." They started beating their chests and hollering, "Stone love!"

The story started getting interesting and I wanted to find out what was going to happen next. I forgot that we were spies for one quick moment and saw myself being told a story that was interesting, in a church where everybody was there to hear a story and not for no fuckin' gang meeting. But my thoughts brought me back to reality every time they mentioned Blackstone.

Angel continued, "One night Helen and Bladder snuck away and they caught the first boat to Troy. Now Troy was a bad motherfuckin' city. It was surrounded by water and huge walls. These walls could be seen miles away. A lot of times other countries would try to invade their hood, but Troy was like Blackstone, kickin' ass every day. Now when the three crazy fools heard about this they stopped fighting. Everybody was pissed off because they didn't cop any of that pussy. Helen's father, his partner's son, and the three fools joined together to invade Troy and get the bitch back. Now these were some powerful people also. Helen's father was the president of Spain and the son was a strong arm man from Greece. The three fools were hit men for both of them. They got their boys together and sailed to Troy."

Angel took a small sip from a pint of wine that was hidden in the pulpit near where he was standing. "Now like I was saying before, Troy was like Las Vegas; you ever heard of Vegas?" One tall guy sitting next to me shouted, "That's where they shoot craps and don't get busted." "That's right," shouted Angel. He took one more swallow and then returned the bottle back to its hiding place.

"When they got to Troy they had to stay on the beach that was in front of the walls because everybody was locked up inside the fortress waiting for Greece and Spain to attack. The Trojans stayed behind the walls during the battle that followed. The Trojans kicked ass every day for weeks. Spain and Greece couldn't penetrate the walls. The three fools were killed and the father got shot up pretty bad. The son from Greece, whose name was Archie, kept fighting. Now this guy was bad. He had gotten shot a few times with arrows, got hit in the head with boulders and he was still walking around trying to get this bitch. I think she had a snappin' pussy.

Whatever it was, he was dedicated. He knew he couldn't be beaten by no punks. Archie would think of all kinds of ways to get into Troy. He tried to burn the walls down, but it didn't work. He even tried digging under the walls, but that's when a boulder knocked the shit out of him. One day he was sitting on one of his war ships smokin' a joint when a light bulb came on over his head. He dashed down to the captain's quarters where Helen's father was lying in bed bleeding like a fat rat. I mean blood was all over the place, all on the walls and the floor and all over him. Archie bent down near the old man's ear and, making sure he didn't touch anything, said softly two words. Anybody know what these two words were?"

A member of the Main 21 sitting a few feet behind Angel stood up and shouted "Stone Love." Everybody started laughing. Even Head and I cracked our faces a little. Angel started up again, "It wasn't Stone Love but it meant the same thing. Don't Panic!"

Head and I looked at each other suddenly. We had heard this saying just the other night. Kellog's, our War Counselor, was telling us about not panicking when the Stones was around.

Angel continued, "Archie ran off the boat and ordered the few soldiers that was left to build this huge horse, big enough for his assassins to hide in. Now the men thought he was trippin' out but they did as he said anyway. The Trojans behind the wall was checkin' out this horse. Even the bitch, Helen, had to take a break from makin' babies to steal a peek. When the horse was finished, Archie and his soldiers got on their boats and spaced. They went as far as they could, where they wouldn't be seen by the Trojans. Now the Greeks left one dude behind who claimed to be a deserter but he was really a spy. We got to watch out for these spies, especially D spies. They are tricky and we have to be up on their tricks."

I stopped thinking about the story and started thinking about our necks again. Before continuing, Angel stared out into the crowded church as if he was trying to smell out the spies, namely us.

"The spy told the Tro's that the horse was a gift from Spain and Greece and that they couldn't defeat the mighty Trojans; therefore, they built the horse to honor them. Now this is where they fucked up. Instead of checking the horse out, they started celebrating and getting drunk; they even broke down a section of the wall to bring the horse in. I mean these Trojans were partying now, they were gambling, smoking reefer, and snorting cocaine all night long. Even the guards, who were supposed to watch for invaders, stopped watching and joined in the fun. Before long all the Trojans were drunk and running around half-naked through the city. Even Helen and Bladder started making babies again. As the night went on Troy started falling asleep and this is what the Greeks were waiting on. The trap door that was on the horse's belly opened and the Greek warriors came out. They started setting fire to the city and killing the Trojans. Meanwhile, the boats started coming back toward the city. Archie killed Bladder and was about to kill Helen but when he saw that fine bitch again he couldn't do it. He took her back with him. Now this story is true and it happened a long time ago. I told it to you because I want you to watch out for those slick ass D's."

Angel started pointing. "And you Rangerettes if you are messing around with any D's, you better stop. Helen was lucky. She had someone who cared a lot about her. Now don't get me wrong, the Nation loves our sisters and we care about you…we just don't care about those D's. Are there any questions before we leave for the day and before I give you the password?"

It was a long meeting, but this was the moment we were waiting for. One young member of the Midgets, he was about ten, stood up on the pew and asked Angel a final question. His voice was soft and tiny so Angel asked everyone to be quiet. I personally was hoping he wasn't going to freak out and accuse somebody, especially us, as being D's.

"What do you have to say, little brother?" Angel asked.

"I thought Trojans was rubbers."

Everybody busted out laughing. Some of the women were trying to hide their grins behind their collars.

Angel quieted his Stones one last time. "To be good Stones you must be dedicated. Therefore, before the next meeting I want to read about three D's dead in the papers. Before we leave I want all new members to pay two dollars for dues. The password this week is BLACK-HAWK. I want everybody to use this. Don't tell the people who missed the meeting; if they don't know the password kick their ass. Remember, BLACK-HAWK. The members started leaving the church in groups. During the confusion Jughead and I slipped away. We reached the outpost in time to give everybody the new password.

Later on that night as we left the outpost a car drove past us slowly. It was full of Stones. I recognized some of the people in the car from the meeting earlier that day. The car sped off without anyone saying anything. I knew then that I had seen the last of Hyde Park High School and the Blackstone Rangers headquarters from the inside.

T-Shirt Red was the only person from our club who got killed by the Rangers. He was ambushed on a rainy Sunday night while he and Lil' Ron stood in a courtway on the corner of 51st. They were waiting for the Cottage Grove bus. Ron told us that when he stepped into the restaurant that was next to the courtway, a blue Buick pulled up to the bus stop sign and fired two shots. Ron ran back out to find T-shirt lying halfway in the courtway and halfway on the street. The blood was mixed with the rain as it moved down Red's body and into the gutter. T-Shirt Red caught both barrels in the chest. By the time the ambulance came he was dead. He was seventeen and had been one of the original Pimp-D's.

The next day the Gang Intelligence Unit came down on us as we were standing on the corner mourning our comrade's death. They were so friendly—as a matter of fact, too friendly. The Gang Intelligence Unit was part of the Chicago Police Department. They were supposed to stop the fighting between us. One of the officers was known as the Green Hornet because he drove a green unmarked police car. He offered to give Jughead, Ron, Bull and myself a lift to the outpost. The outpost was the headquarters of the east side Disciples. We dropped the Devil a few years back. Every member of the D's from the west side and east side of the city held meetings at the outpost. After meetings we would get high and party. On our way to the outpost the Green Hornet and his pal were telling us that we should do something to the Stones for killing our friend. One cop told Ron he would let him use his gun if he could because he also hated the Stones. I couldn't believe this madness. Here we are, four D's sitting in the back of a police car being driven by two Gang Intelligence Members who are supposed to be out trying to stop gang killings, and they're telling us to go get even. They dropped us off in front of the outpost and we stood outside and watched as they pulled away from the curb.

I don't know whether it was a series of gang-related incidents or one major event that changed my ideas about gangs. I probably just got tired of looking behind my back and ducking behind doors and cars every time I walked down the streets. All of this eventually added up to my leaving the D's alone. I had just turned 19 and my love for money was growing more and more. I was dressing clean every day with my tailor-made clothes and panama hats. I was getting chosen every day by the young ladies. I was even looking for a job, even though the nickle bags of reefer I was selling were keeping money in my pocket. I was buying liquor in the stores for myself and for the younger guys in the hood who couldn't cop. My political views on life were also changing. I had stopped going to the weekly meetings our club used to have and I wasn't the only one who had left the gangbanging to the youngsters. A lot of my friends had stopped going to the meetings also. I remember one time there was a bad rumor going around the neighborhood that the D's were going to come down on the people who had stopped going to meetings and that we had turned into P Stones, but it never happened. The D's weren't like the Stones. There were a lot of grown men in the Stones who took that shit seriously. I mean 29, 30 years old, still beating their chests. I remember one incident that changed my whole outlook on life. I would say, now that I think about it, it was "the icing on the cake."

It was a very hot summer day in the middle of July, and I had just come from the hospital visiting Jughead. He had gotten shot in a crossfire at the Starlite Lounge about a week before. The shooting was over whose woman was whose. We had already missed the last three meetings and we were debating on staying in the D's. The Pimps had broken up and Shylow, Mike, and Prince had joined the Woodlawn D's. They wanted Head and myself to do the same. Head was telling me he was going to pimp whores when he got out of the hospital and I was trying to boost my reefer sales. Even though we weren't representing the club, we would still hang out with people who were still known Disciples because they were still our friends.

It was so hot that day that people were walking around with their shirts off. When I saw Rat and his two henchmen walking towards me I wanted to explain to them that I was no longer a D, but it was too late. Rat was a tall skinny guy with a big Afro. He only had about three teeth in his mouth. When he was by himself he would always use "Brother" in his conversations. "How you doing, Brother?" "We've got to get together, Brother," or "Peace, Bro." When he was with his boys he was Stone to the Bone. I started to speak but Rat and his two Stones had surrounded me. "How you doing, you D?" Rat said with a smile on his face. I said, half smiling, "I ain't that shit anymore, I'm selling reefer now. Want to cop?" One of the other guys spoke. "You a D? We don't like D's. Stones run this from State to the lake." The other guy started pointing. "We ought to fuck this D up." We were standing near a row of apartment buildings and a gangway. I saw that these assholes were in the mood to fuck somebody up and I just happened to be in the wrong place at the wrong time. I sure could use a cop about now but they are never around when you need them.

I decided to make a run for it but before I could do anything they pushed me into the gangway. Rat kept his hand under his shirt as we entered the dark area. The gangway was dark as the three men shoved me against the brick wall. My knees became weak from the load they were carrying. Rat kept telling me he hated D's and I kept trying to tell him with my hands and mouth that I wasn't a D anymore. The other two men were standing at the entrance of the gangway, watching and acting very nervous. "Come on, Rat, hurry up and get this shit over with," one of them said. Rat pulled a small blue steel gun from under his shirt and jammed it into my stomach. I stopped talking. "Stones run it!" Rat said as he pulled the trigger. I tried to brace myself against the wall to catch the impact of the bullet. A lot of things flashed across my mind at that moment: how I was going to fix the flat on my mother's car; my lady would be mad at me because I wasn't going to pick her up from work; how am I going to get rid of the reefer in my pocket?

Click. Rat and his friends looked confused as Rat pulled the trigger again. Click, Click, Click. Either he forgot to load the revolver or it was jammed. I wasn't staying around to find out. I had to get the fuck out of there and right now. I made my break for the other end of the gangway. The three tried to follow me but I was too fast for them. I ran faster than I've ever run before. I leaped over a ten foot wooden fence with ease. I twisted my body through some more narrow gangways. I didn't stop until I had reached the hood where I would see somebody I knew. As I separated myself from the Stones, all I could think of was revenge. I thought about getting my pistol and calling Shylow. I was going to go up on the tray (63rd Street) and get some more D's, and then we were going to fuck up any Stone we saw.

I was supposed to be getting away from this shit. I wasn't a D anymore. I sat down on some steps to decide what my next move was going to be. I figured that even though I was scared and almost got killed, I came out of it without a scratch. I had had a lot of close calls before. So I decided to play it off as if nothing happened. I went to the liquor store and bought myself a pint of rum and a Coke. I sat in the park that was behind the shopping center and thought about what just happened and how Somebody was looking out for me.

"Do you want a hit?" asked Billy before he put the dirty needle into a vein of his right arm. The thick leather belt was wrapped tightly around his right upper arm. This forced the vein to look bigger than normal. Billy's arm already looked like a used dart board. Little black needle marks were lined up in a row over each of his veins. "That's right, I forgot you're still chipping." Billy smirked a little as he stuck the needle into his vein. I watched as the brown liquid traveled down the needle and into his arm. He threw his head back and before he could pull the needle out he had slipped into a nod. The empty needle fell to the floor, as it always did. Billy was a real, live junkie. It seemed as though everybody was. Suddenly, everybody over twenty years old was into drugs. The gangbanging had faded out. Boy, Smack, Duji, Blow, Heroin. It was like a contagious disease. Everybody was getting high off the stuff. Nodding was in. I was snorting a little but I had made a promise to myself and Head. We agreed that if we ever caught each other shooting up we would kick each other's ass. We never got our asses kicked. Billy and I had split a quarter bag of dope. He

Dino Malcolm/87

shot his and I snorted mine. I didn't get high as quick as Billy did, but I would soon have the same feeling.

The vacant apartment we got high in was known as the Shooting Gallery. This was where everybody would get high after coppin' their stuff. The Gallery was a raggedy, vacant two-room apartment across the street from the Plaza. Dirty needles, roaches and small pieces of aluminum foil could be found on the floor and between the torn cushions on the long grey couch that was the only sitting area in the room. At any given time, four to five junkies would be up there getting high or nodding out. The Gallery was reserved for "shooting members only," but since I was the reefer man at the time, I was always welcome. I used to have the best herb and I always sold healthy sacks. Billy would always shoot his dope in the washroom with the door closed because he didn't want any junkies to see how much he had. "I told you this P. Smiley always has the best." Billy was rocking back and forth while I lit up a joint. Soon the washroom was full of smoke. Billy loosened the belt and slumped down on the toilet seat, still nodding. Smiley was the man. The cops were always arresting him and taking his El Dorado away from him. Every time I would see Smiley cruising down 53rd he was in another El Dorado. Green, red, white. It didn't make a difference as long as it was a convertible hog. I started nodding when someone kicked on the door. "Hey, man, open up!" Billy had slipped into a deep nod and didn't respond to the noise. I staggered over to the door which seemed like it was miles away, yet in reality it was three feet in front of me. I unhooked the rusty latch and Alley Dog tried to force his way in.

The door would only open partially because Billy's body was leaning against it. "Hey, man, y'all some dirty dudes. Let me hit that joint." Alley Dog was known as Leech Man because he was always begging for somebody's dope. He was known to have a 150-dollar-a-day habit and supported it by ripping off apartments and stealing cars. He once stole a Continental and sold it to a pimp for 50 dollars. "Hey, man, how come you didn't save me any of that Boy?" "You ain't got no more veins to shoot it in," I said. "Shit, man, I can still shoot it in my dick." He unzipped his fly and pulled out his dick. He steped over to the sink. He tried to hide the pain on his face as he pissed into the sink. It was that strong ammonia piss, too.

It was time for me to leave. I squeezed past Alley Dog and Billy and headed for the door. Billy would be safe there because he nodded out at the same place every day. I stumbled out of the door and tried to pull myself together before venturing out into the street. If the cops saw me nodding it would mean an ass-kicking and maybe doing some time in the County Jail. I made it to the crib in one piece. I tried to catch a few nods while riding the elevator. I knew the drugs were dangerous but you couldn't get hooked by snorting. I kept thinking this to myself as I nodded out on the couch listening to "My Favorite Things" by John Coltrane.

THINGS THAT GO BUMP IN THE NIGHT...
Chris Hyatt

I was nearly thrown out of school once for ripping someone's intestines out. I was only sixteen at the time, but the event would follow me for the rest of my life.

I had been out on the football field of Hampshire High School during my lunch period filming a movie titled "Eaten Alive." It was a project for my art class, and I was using the school's video camera to shoot it.

I'd love to tell you about the plot, but I can't because the film had no plot. It was just a five-minute sketch in which my friend Dan would turn into a monster, rip open my friend Mark's stomach, and eat his intestines. I had this thing for blood and gore—it's just that in my college years I started using plots and stories, as opposed to just having gore for gore's sake. But I do miss the old days when I only worried about grossing people out.

So, being the gross-out king that I was, I was set to make this film *the* definitive vomit-in-your-seat movie. You might think it's easy to make this kind of film, but you're wrong—I go through a lot to make one. First off, there's the call I have to make to my friend John Randecker, whose dear old dad worked at Dreymiller & Krey, the local slaughterhouse. John's dad always came through for me when I needed internal organs—he'd give me all kinds of pig and cow innards. Since they were real, they looked great on film. Problem was that they smelled worse than underwear worn for one week straight by a person who never bathes. Second, I mix up a gallon of blood using Karo syrup and red food dye. I know it's a gallon because I fill one of those gallon plastic milk containers full. My dream is to make a movie (with a plot) that requires me to go through twenty gallons of blood. But for this one I only needed a gallon. What the hell, it was only five minutes long.

Once I had shot the film and started packing things up, my friend Mark decided it would be fun to walk back into the school with his guts hanging out. I thought this was a great idea, since the doors to the school were right in front of the cafeteria, and we'd have to walk through the lunchroom to come in. Dozens of lunches would be cut short at the sight of my friend coming in with his guts hanging out. The ultimate in performance art!

Mark walked in through the doors, staggering, holding his guts, Karo blood seeping out from between his fingers. The lunchroom went dead. Mark, ultimate ham that he is, fell on the floor, turned to me (I had just come in behind him), and said:

"There he is! Hyatt! He did it! He did this to me!"

Every pair of eyes in the lunchroom turned to look at me. What I saw in their eyes was not the "Oh, God, are you sick!" response that I was expecting. No, in their eyes I saw accusations of murder. They thought I had murdered my friend by disemboweling him! In their eyes I saw a cry for justice.

This is it, I thought. I've gone too far this time. There I was, standing in front of a crowd of people who were convinced that strange-o Christopher Hyatt had finally gone off the deep end and really murdered somebody. Never mind that Mark was the class clown and that this was just the type of stunt he'd pull. Luckily, after a minute or so people began to realize it was all a joke.

Mr. Dano, the vice-principal who looked like a bi-pedal bulldog, called Mark and me to his office. He said we were a couple of punks whose attitudes threatened to ruin the school, and he wanted to expel us. But it was close to the end of the school year and he was feeling generous, so we got off with the much lighter sentence of three days' suspension. So the whole ordeal left me thinking: should I have done that? I mean, today when I meet people from my high school, they give me a wide berth. Maybe certain things, like disembowling friends, should not be done.

Images of horror have found a home in the world of the movies for almost as long as the movies have been used as a storytelling tool. From the distorted world of Robert Weine's *The Cabinet of Dr. Caligari* to the slashed eyeballs and severed hands of Luis Bunuel and Salvador Dali's *Un Chien Andalou* on up to the contemporary works of such directors as Ken Russel and David Lynch, shades of the horrific exist in the most serious and artistic of films. But the genre of the horror film, lumped into a bay of critical scorn and popular ignorance, has been relegated to existence in the world of low budgets and sleazy theaters.

In 1910, Thomas Edison produced a film version of Mary Shelley's *Frankenstein* for his Black Maria Film Studios. The film starred Charles Ogle as the monster (in makeup that looks like Bisquick and wax paper). According to Carlos Clarens in his *Illustrated History of the Horror Film,* this was the first horror film ever made. Unfortunately, no prints of the film exist, and the only evidence of its existence are the budget reports in Edison's papers and a few stills of Ogle in the Bisquick makeup.

Despite the fact that the press releases put out by the Edison company assured that the more "macabre aspects" of the story had been removed, exhibitors still found the film to be very weird. Imagine sitting in the nickelodeons of the time, where the fare was one-reel comedies and Westerns, and seeing the Bisquick monster flickering up on the screen. Indeed, one can imagine a shocked audience.

"What the hell was that?" was probably the typical response, and it marked what would be the fate of horror films for years to come, little more than curiosities in the eyes of the public.

The premiere of Tod Browning's *Freaks* in 1932 is among the most infamous incidents in the annals of the horror film. It is a good case of what can happen when a film goes farther than the public is willing to accept.

Tod Browning was probably the strangest director to flourish in the old Hollywood studio system. His films were about men driven to madness; dismemberment and deformity were integral ingredients in most of his stories. His most famous work is the 1931 version of *Dracula* with Bela Lugosi, a huge financial success which laid the groundwork for *Freaks.*

Before *Dracula* was released, the Catholic Church warned Universal Studio that "There are some things that should not, for taste considerations, be put on film at all." Universal responded by playing down the fantasy element of the film in its advertisements, and calling it "the strangest love story ever made." With this gimmick, the film became Hollywood's top grossing film of the year. Indeed, the only time horror was a reputable film genre among the general public was in the early thirties. In 1932, a year after *Dracula,* the top earner was James Whale's film version of *Frankenstein.*

Reacting to big bucks, Hollywood rewarded Browning, and he became the hottest director in town. He could do almost any project he wanted, any way he wanted, and he chose to film a short story by Tod Robbins titled "Spurs." Browning seemed to have an odd attraction to Robbins's work, having already filmed a version of his novel *West of Zanzibar* starring Lon Chaney, Sr. (the "man of a thousand faces") and John Barrymore.

The story of *Freaks* concerns a traveling side show and circus that has a stable of deformed people and two star performers—Cleopatra, the trapeze artist, and Hercules, the strongman. Cleopatra and Hercules, who are lovers, learn that one of the side show performers, a dwarf named Hans, is in line to inherit a fortune and will then retire from the circus. Cleopatra seduces Hans, marries him, and then poisons him to within an inch of his life. The other people in the side show learn about this, and soon there is a massive uprising of the freaks, who kill Hercules and turn Cleopatra into the most monstrous thing ever seen.

Browning wanted his film to contain real freaks, and he cast dwarves, pinheads, hermaphrodites (half man, half woman), living torsos (people with no arms or legs), and bearded women. The result was far more intense than most people could bear. (Even I found the film very hard to stomach.)

Dracula was obviously a creature of fantasy. Other film monsters of the day, in certain shots, openly displayed zippers on their costumes. But there were no zippers on the freaks, and they were not imaginary creatures. By casting deformed humans, Browning forced the audience to identify with the freaks.

When *Freaks* premiered, women in the audience fainted, and men ran into the street in hysteria. Browning attended the premiere with the studio heads. The producers saw the people screaming, jumping up, and trampling each other to get to the exit. Browning had a lot of explaining to do. Later, a telephone caller who had just seen *Freaks* complained to Browning, "Well, I can't sleep and I'll be damned if I'm going to let you sleep either!" He telephoned Browning every fifteen minutes for the rest of the night.

But Browning was losing sleep for another reason; the studio told him that *Freaks* was not going to be released. The film was never officially banned here, but it was kept out of distribution and has only recently been released on video-tape. It *was* banned for over thirty years in the United Kingdom (the country that later gave us Sid Vicious and Boy George), and no other foreign country has prints of it. Browning, it seems, had gone just a wee bit too far.

In the seven years I've been making movies, I've recorded for posterity some things that will not get me a job directing segments for "Sesame Street": disembowelments, cannibal feasts, people puking black bile into each other's mouths while kissing, and giant lizards made up to look like dinosaurs chasing surfers down a beach are just a few. But the one thing that I just could not film, the one thing that sent me running to the hills in terror, was something I was asked to make a video of when I was seventeen.

You see, I had this reputation when I was seventeen. It was mainly because of my friend Dan saying, "This kid will shoot anything," and if something went on in front of a camera, you can bet I'd be there acting like Hitchcock, egging on the action. As a result, Dan had me doing a "favor" for one of his weird friends.

So I arrive at the house of this guy named Leo Crutch, with my video equipment in the back seat of my wretched 1967 Bonneville. He comes out dressed like an extra from *Saturday Night Fever.* Evidently he was not hip to the fact that the disco craze had gone out of style—I mean, even *Flashdance* was old hat by this time.

But Leo, all thirty-five years, six feet, one hundred and eighty pounds of him, must have thought that it was still the scene. Either that or he did too many drugs to know the difference. He had this irritating nasal voice, like a perpetual squeaky yawn that formed words. "You're here. Good, come on in and set up your camera and stuff in the bedroom. Lynn's just about ready."

This went right over my seventeen-year-old head. You see, I was going to be paid two hundred dollars for whatever it was he wanted filmed, and I was thinking about all that money.

So I walk in carrying my video equipment in the usual fashion—tape recorder strapped over my left shoulder, tripod under my right arm, and camera in my right hand. It may be a good way of describing Leo's character to add that he didn't hold the door open for me.

Once I got in the house, I was noticing how tacky it was—beer posters, a couple of neon signs (one said "The Big 'L' " and the other said "Miami Beach"), and to top it all off, Lynn. Lynn is the type of girl that you see staggering outside the bars at Clark and Division late Friday nights. The type of girl who is pretty because she spends three hours a day putting on makeup and doing her hair, and has this look in her eyes. The look that says an original, good, coherent thought has never escaped from the dark recesses of what passes for her mind. Not bad, if your tastes run in the direction of girls who owe everything to Revlon and Miss Clairol. Mine don't.

I said hello, how do you do, and walked toward the bedroom to set up when I suddenly felt an urge to stop myself. I stood there in this guy's hallway and turned around 180 degrees to face Leo and Lynn. They were right behind me, and I looked them straight in the eyes.

"Didn't Dan tell you?" Leo asked.

No, I said, Dan did not tell me a goddamn thing, and suddenly I feel really funny standing here in your house with the neon signs, beer posters, and zombie girlfriend, so I think you should tell me before I do a one-eighty and leave. (These are obviously not my exact words.)

He explained that he wanted me to videotape a sex session between him and his girl. He wanted a tape he could use as a study guide to improve his weak spots. In other words, he wanted a film version of *The Joy of Sex* directed by me, the "kid who will shoot anything."

"I'd do it myself," he said, "but I want close-ups and pans and zooms, all the Spielberg stuff." Yeah, but Spielberg doesn't direct sex scenes.

My jaw (now touching the shag carpet that lined every inch of his house) began to rattle and a bunch of, well, noises came out—stutters, whimpers. You see, at seventeen, I had never even kissed anyone, and the idea of videotaping *real sex* was not one that held a whole lot of appeal for me. For one thing, Leo and Lynn made me nauseous.

I wanted that two hundred dollars bad. I was going to be gone soon, to the wilds of Chicago to go to film school, and the money would certainly have improved things.

No, I said to myself, if I sell out at seventeen, I'll be selling out for the rest of my life. So I told Leo, flat out, I don't do pornos.

Leo looked stunned. "I thought you shot everything!"

"I thought I did too."

Leo got manic, running around flailing his arms, really pissed off. Lynn looked at me, then at Leo, and left in a huff. I followed her out the door, and Leo followed me at close range, screaming "Asshole! Fag! Wimp! What's the matter, never did anything with a *girl* before?"

I have never seen a man as angered as Mr. Leo Crutch was at that moment. Apparently no professional videotaping service would take his assignment. (Can't say I blame them.) Lynn placated him with a promise that she'd get her brother to tape doing it. He went back inside, and Lynn wrote me a check (from Leo's account) for twenty bucks.

"Don't tell anyone about this," she warned me.

No, ma'am, I never will, not in a million years.

Three horror films must be mentioned when discussing the genre's current direction; they are George Romero's *Night of the Living Dead,* Tobe Hooper's *The Texas Chainsaw Massacre,* and John Carpenter's *Halloween.* All three were low-budget films made outside of the studio system; in fact, two were not filmed in California at all. They were financially and artistically successful, and they spawned hosts of imitators.

These films break several taboos and supply large doses of violence. What separates them from their imitators, in my opinion, is that they were made by young filmmakers who loved horror films, as opposed to investment bankers who see horror as a chance to rake in big bucks.

#1

In 1967, George Romero sat in his office at Latent Image film productions with several friends, who were also Romero's business partners in the fledgling production house. The company, which specialized in making beer commercials and the occasional documentary, was doing fairly well, and Romero felt that the time had come to try his hand at doing a feature film for the theaters.

After tossing around several ideas, the group settled on an idea of Romero's titled "Night of Anubis." (Anubis is the Egyptian God of the Dead.) The story concerned the world being overrun by the souls of the dead. John Russo (then one of the partners in Latent Image and now a horror novelist) was chosen to write the script with Romero. The group sealed their contract with handshakes over the table in Romero's office.

Romero and his crew shot the film on weekends using existing locations (which is a hell of a lot cheaper than building sets) and 35mm black-and-white footage that was left over from the commercials.[1] All of the locations were within spitting distance of Pittsburgh (where the Latent Image offices were), and included a farmhouse, a cemetery, and an open field. The story was changed a little for budget reasons—the dead souls were now flesh-eating corpses revived by radiation. (This point is not definite, however, and for the most part the film presents the zombies as supernatural beings.) The title was now *Night of the Flesh Eaters.* In fact, poster art for the film exists under this title, since it was the film's name right up until its 1968 premiere.

Local talent was used both in front of and behind the camera, and all of the crew played roles (though mostly small ones) in the film. Producer Russ Streiner played Johnny, the first victim of the walking dead who later becomes a zombie himself. Director Romero played a news reporter seen over a television screen. And the film's co-producer Karl Hardman plays Frank, the thick-headed husband who insists on going down into the cellar. Also in the cast were Pittsburgh's resident horror film show host, Bill Cardille, local actor Duane Jones (who would later star in the early Seventies voodoo film *Ganja and Hess*), and Judith O'Dea.

Once the film was complete and had its premiere in Pittsburgh at the local movie palace, the Aragon, it got a new title: *Night of the Living Dead.* At first it seemed that no one outside Pittsburgh would see the film—it had trouble finding a distribution company. The main reason was the violence. Said one representative from United Artists: "I got to watching that scene where the guy [actor Duane Jones] is hitting the other guy [a zombie extra] with the tire iron over and over and thought, 'Fuck this. If you think that people will sit through this after the assassinations of Bobby Kennedy and Martin Luther King . . .' " and this was just the opinion of one of the distributors. When the film was finally released by the Walter Reade Organization, it had to deal with the critics.

They were all less than complimentary. An article in *Reader's Digest* condemned not just the film, but the Walter Reade Organization for releasing it, and then went on to attack the people who saw the film. Only Rex Reed gave it a good notice, and he became the film's chief defender over the years, until it gained its current reputation as a masterpiece in the field.

#2

It was Christmas 1972, and things were far from cheery for Tobe Hooper. Once the young ace of the Texas film community, he was now broke, having sunk all of his money into making an art film titled *Eggshells,* a hippie love story about the breakup of a commune. The film was a disaster, and Tobe had to get off his high horse and find some other way to make films. He got his idea for *The Texas Chainsaw Massacre* when he was shopping in a Montgomery Ward for gifts, and the crowd of shoppers pushed and shoved until Tobe found himself face to face with a rack of chainsaws.

"Quickest way out of here," Hooper thought to himself, "is to yank-start one of these chainsaws and cut my way through the crowd."

Hooper didn't carry out his plan (thank God!), but the image of taking a chainsaw to someone stuck, and within a few minutes "the movie was right in front of [him]." He went home, pounded out the story on his typewriter, and rounded up his crew from *Eggshells.* The money came easily; *Night of the Living Dead* was making a lot of money in midnight shows across the country, and everyone wanted to get in on that action.

So in the summer of '73, Hooper went about shooting the film that would come to be known as "The *Gone With the Wind* of meat movies." Like Romero. Hooper shot in existing locations. In the sweltering Texas sun, he had to deal with rotting animal innards (which caused everyone to toss their cookies at least once on the set) and rising tempers caused by paltry wages. (Actor Edwin Neal, who plays the hitchhiker in the film, still calls Tobe Hooper a "bastard son-of-a-bitch" in interviews.) The film was shot in a few weeks of continuous work, sometimes in 36-hour shifts. Because it was shot fast, Hooper didn't have time to shoot inserts (close-ups of the film's action—like a shot of the saw cutting someone), so he ended up shooting the death scenes in long, deep-focus takes that look like someone just turned the camera on and let it run. This gives the film a voyeuristic quality—you feel like you're just sitting there, watching these people die.

The film was released in 1974 and attracted some pretty serious critical attention for a low-budget horror film. While it did get its share of bad press (*Harper's Magazine* called it "a vile little piece of sick crap"), it got some good reviews as well. Rex Reed took to championing the film as he had *Night of the Living Dead,* but it wasn't too difficult; 1974 wasn't as socially turbulent as 1968, and the media was too busy with Watergate to bother getting down on a low-budget horror flick. (But then, one would think that 1968 should have kept the media pretty busy as well.) It's also possible that *Night of the Living Dead* served as a buffer for this film, conditioning the public.

Today, parents' groups complain that its accessibility on video makes it dangerous to small children; most of these parents have probably never seen the film.

#3

John Carpenter's *Assault on Precinct 13,* an homage to both Romero's *Night of the Living Dead* and Howard Hawks's western *Rio Bravo,* was the hit of the London Film Festival, and its success brought Carpenter's name to Irwin Yablans, who decided to distribute the film in the United States. (It was a financial failure here.) In fact, Yablans was so pleased with Carpenter's work that he approached him about doing a film titled *The Babysitter Murders.* Carpenter took the offer, and, after changing the title to *Halloween,* wrote the script with his girlfriend at the time, producer Debra Hill.

The plot was a simple one: a little boy murders his sister and spends the next decade and a half in a mental institution. He escapes, goes back to his home town (pursued by his psychiatrist), and goes about murdering young women who are babysitting in large houses. The film was shot in twenty days for peanuts: $300,000. Carpenter, a lifelong fan of horror and science fiction, intended the film to be a quality horror film. At first he seemed to have succeeded.

Unlike almost any other horror film before or since, *Halloween* was critically praised by major critics (including horror film haters Pauline Kael of the *New Yorker* and Roger Ebert of the *Chicago Sun-Times*) and did enormous amounts of business. (It is the second highest grossing film released by an independent movie company. If you're a trivia buff, you'll be interested to know that the first place holder on the list is *Dirty Dancing,* a real horror of a film if there ever was one.)

However, within a few years *Halloween* created a backlash among critics, who charged that it was the father film of the series of slasher and "let's kill the naked girls" movies—films reviled by the critics and most serious horror buffs. All kinds of misogynistic messages have been read into the film. (The main point critics and feminist writers attack is that all the girls who are killed are sexually active, and the one girl who fights back is a virgin.)[2] So *Halloween*'s day in the sun was a short one.

These three films represent, I think, the apex of the genre of horror. All of them work with taste and skill, and they are not the work of morons with cameras, as critics and parents' activist groups would have one believe.

While for the most part horror films have kept to themselves and out of direct confrontation with politics, there are the occasional few that derive their maximum suspense by milking the current political atmosphere and making social statements. In the recent film *They Live,* Republicans from space use Earth as a Third World planet, depleting our resources and enlisting the aid of humans who are willing to sell out for money (and there are plenty). But while *They Live* uses a sort of comic-book version of the world, other films are nearly immaculate in portraying reality to make the horror all the more unsettling. The finest example of this is the 1958 Don Siegel film *Invasion of the Body Snatchers.*

The premise is simple: giant pods from outer space have come down to Earth, and they contain exact replicas of every human being in the town. The replication occurs when the victim falls asleep. The conflict of the story is also simple: Do you want to be one of us or one of them?

Coming out at the height of the Red Scare and roughly around the time of the Senate inquiry into Communist activity in this country, the film hit a certain political nerve.[3] In a book on Siegel's films, author Judith M. Kass says the film is "unbelievably doom laden, from the opening encounter with the little boy to the final shot of McCarthy himself screaming 'You're next!' out on the highway to passing motorists." In the same book, Siegel himself says, "What the pod people refuse to do is look around them . . . and see what is going on. Everyone else is asleep, mentally, and as a result are easy prey."

Siegel, wanting to call the film *Sleep No More,* walked off the picture after the studio interfered with his final cut. (The studio wanted to keep the title *Invasion of the Body Snatchers,* since *The Body Snatchers* was the name of the Jack Finney novel on which the film is based.) The studio then tacked on hopeful messages at the end of the film, and shot a final scene in which the army goes out to smash the seed pods.

In certain ways, the fantasy aspect makes the film easier to swallow, contrary to the anti-Communist films of the time based on realistic drama, like *My Son John* (in which Michael Rennie plays a good kid who gets lured by the Communists and turns into a reefer-smoking homosexual who threatens the American way) and *Stakeout on 29th Street* (in which a young girl is tracked by a detective for being a suspected commie). *Invasion of the Body Snatchers* is an excellent example of a film which sums up the politics of its time.

Now I'm going to talk about a darker aspect of horror films, the possibility that people can't always distinguish fact from fantasy when they view something on a television screen or in a theater. To some people, filmed reality is more real than the reality. These people obviously have a problem. Here are a few examples:

1. After the release of the film *The Exorcist,* several thousand people ended up in psychiatrists' offices with alarming news—they were all being possessed by the devil.
2. The police are called to the site of a grisly murder. A seventeen-year-old boy has killed his grandmother and drained most of the blood from her body. "I'm a vampire," he tells them. "Without her blood, I would have died." The police find his room is full of vampire novels, comic books, and videotapes (King, 387).
3. After seeing *Psycho* on television a young boy goes into the kitchen, grabs a butcher knife, and walks into his mother's bedroom. He stabs her forty times in the torso (King, 388).
4. After seeing the ABC Movie of the Week, a group of teens pull an old woman out of her car in a shopping mall parking lot, douse her with gasoline, and light her on fire (King, 391).
5. After a viewing of *The Exorcist,* a young couple douse their three-month-old son in gasoline because it cried too much. They deduced this was because the devil was inside it (King, 389).

While these people may have gotten their ideas from movies, the movies themselves did not make them kill. Movies did not tell them that they were possessed; the people convinced themselves that such a thing was happening to them. The teenagers who burned the woman to death admitted that they did get the idea to burn her from the movie, but they also added that they probably would have killed her even if they hadn't seen the movie.

Whether or not you hold the films responsible depends on which theory on violence you agree with. The theory held by some people is that violence begets more violence, and that media violence excites people to the point of giving them an unconscious desire to emulate it. Most people have a sort of automatic shut-off for such impulses, and so we don't act on them. But people who don't have the off-switch end up carrying out these impulses. The second theory goes something like this: when we see violence (and I mean highly produced movie violence, not news footage of auto wreck victims), it acts as a catharsis, and cleanses us of the impulses we feel to create violence of our own.

Taken at face value, the examples above would tend to prove the first theory. But a case could be made for the second theory by saying that the weird urges in all these cases were so strong that the violence in the movies was not enough to satiate them. In fact, the movie violence may have taught the perpetrators how to carry out their impulses (which may explain the kids' reasoning for burning the old woman).

Either way, the people listed above were incited to some action after seeing the movies, so it is apparent that one has to be careful in creating violent works of fiction, since you never can tell who is going to watch them.

Don't take this the wrong way—I'm not implying that filmmakers (or any other creative artists, for that matter) should intentionally go out and censor themselves. Gratuitous violence (that is, violence unsupported by the plot and theme of a piece of work) is what I'm saying should be avoided.

Maybe the best way for me to say what I mean is for me not to say anything at all and leave the moral of the story to these words by the "master of the macabre" himself, the late Sir Alfred Hitchcock:

> "How do you justify the violence of the shower scene in *Psycho?*" a critic once asked Sir Alfred Hitchcock.
>
> "How do you justify the opening scene of *Hiroshima, Mon Amour?*" Hitchcock is reputed to have replied. In that opening scene, which was certainly scandalous by American standards in 1959, we see Emmanuele Riva and Eliji Okada in a naked embrace.
>
> "The opening scene was necessary to the integrity of the film," the critic answered.
>
> "So was the shower scene in *Psycho,*" Hitchcock said.
>
> (Stephen King, *Danse Macabre,* p. 392)

NOTES

[1] Although several print sources say that Romero shot *Night of the Living Dead* in 16mm, Romero himself says in Russo's *"Night of the Living Dead" Filmbook* that it was shot in 35mm. I'm inclined to take his word for it.

[2] The sequel to *Halloween,* written by Carpenter, suggests that the Jamie Lee Curtis character is actually the killer's SISTER (my caps) and that he killed the other girls in an effort to get to her. Since the sequel came out after the brouhaha over the original's supposed "sexual punishment" themes, my guess is that Carpenter is trying to make an adequate defense for himself.

[3] Apart from the timing of its release, though, I'm not sure if the film is an "anti-McCarthyist" movie (as has been often suggested), since the political views of the director, Don Siegel, are hardly left wing. Siegel, who went on to make the ultra-fascist *Dirty Harry* with Clint Eastwood, was probably trying to make his movie more of a "better dead than Red" drama.

SOURCES CONSULTED

Balun, Charles. *"The Texas Chainsaw Massacre": Horror Holocaust.* San Francisco: FantaCo Enterprises, 1986.

Clarens, Carlos. *An Illustrated History of the Horror Film.* New York: Paragon, 1967.

Fox, Jordan R. "John Carpenter: Riding High on Horror." *Cynefantastique* 10:1 (Summer 1980): 5-11, 40-44.

Kass, Judith M. "Don Siegel," in *The Hollywood Professionals,* Vol. 4. New York: A. S. Barnes, 1975.

King, Stephen. *Danse Macabre*. New York: Berkeley Books, 1981.
Rosenthal, Stuart. "Tod Browning," in *The Hollywood Professionals,* Vol. 4. New York: A. S. Barnes, 1975.
Russo, John. *The Complete "Night of the Living Dead" Filmbook*. San Francisco: FantaCo Enterprises, 1985.

KILLING
Drew Wilson

Last year I remember reading in the paper that a man jumped off the
Marina Towers, and they couldn't find his head. The interesting thing here
is that when the head and body separate, there is enough oxygen left in the
brain for 2 to 5 seconds of normal thought process. The man may have realized what he did and may have seen his body separate from his head.

WAYS THAT SEX AND KILLING ARE RELATED:

- Both have a buildup and a climax.
- When involved in either, you drop your inhibitions and facade. These acts
  reveal character.
- They have to do with emotions. They are furious, passionate, physical
  acts which release enormous tension.
- Art is based on sex and violence.
- They are characterized by the feeling of power and the urge to subdue.
- Both have a strong energy which is attractive.
- Both are spawned from love.
- Sex and killing both carry strong consequences, but with one you make
  life and with the other you take it.
- A knife and a gun are phallic; they are modeled after the penis. All three
  convey a passionate feeling of penetration.
- Both are primitive acts and are inherent in the genes of humans.

   A cop comes upon an overturned Mack truck in an isolated area up in the
woods. The truck is on fire and the driver's compartment is smashed in, like
a Coke can that somebody has stepped on. He calls on his car radio for a
fire engine. The nearest town is ten miles away. The cop jumps out of his
car when he hears a voice inside the truck, screaming in pain. The fire
sounds like a whip when it crackles. It burns all the wood parts of the truck
and, in doing so, it heats the driver's compartment. Eventually the inside
catches on fire. You could equate it with a giant saucepan or kettle being
heated over the burner of a stove. A Country and Western 8-track tape still
plays in the unharmed tape player. The cop tries yanking open the door,
but it won't budge. A welder is the only hope to get through the door.
There is a handle alongside of the door and the cop jumps up and grabs it
with one hand. He pulls himself up and tries to get a glimpse of the inside
through the shattered glass, but has to let go because the handle has burned
his hand. The screams are heard again as the driver starts to burn up slowly. First his pants leg burns, then his ankle. The fire turns it pink, then red;
then blisters form. The blisters then pop and the flame causes the ankle to
smolder and turn black. The driver is pinned in, and can only watch himself
burn as soothing Country music plays. "Can you move?!"
   "No! Shoot me! Shoot me before I burn to death!" The voice of the driver
sounds scorched, as if there were fire in his throat. The cop pulls out his gun
but won't fire. More screams and begging are heard. The cop keeps looking

down the road for the fire engine and trying to hear the sound of the siren. "I've called for a fire truck. They'll be here any second!"

"It's too late! Shoot me now! I can't stand it!" The cop is sweating and he shakes. He extends his arm with the gun at the end, and it shakes. Painful screaming is heard. The cop stands on his toes with his arm stretched over his head and points the gun in through the cracked glass. He can't see who he is about to shoot, but he is nervous and is on the verge of crying and screaming himself.

The sound of the siren is heard coming down the road. The cop stops. "I can see them. They're here!" The driver is now engulfed in flames from the neck down. Some matches that were in his shirt pocket catch on fire and flare up momentarily, then blend in with the rest of the fire. A plastic coffee cup is on fire and drips hot plastic on his chest. The whole cup falls over and lands on him. The driver screams and his scream blends in with the siren of the fire engine. The fire engine pulls up and stops. The siren has stopped. The screaming has stopped. The cop is crying.

Dear Iva,

When I talked to you on the phone, the phrase "broken heart" came up. "Broken heart" is a cliche. It is used so much it is unsatisfying and it sounds like a lie. It doesn't sound like it could be true. The phrase doesn't have the energy as the feeling it's supposed to represent does.

The feeling is really a pain that is somewhere between the forehead and waist. You can't pinpoint exactly where. You could say it was the heart, and that would be poetic, but you can't scientifically find the spot.

The pain is like a coil of barbed wire, implanted inside the chest, which moves and turns like a snake or earthworm. If you've ever baited a hook with a worm, and pierced its collar with a hook and seen it wriggle in pain and wrap around the line, then you know the movement I'm talking about. The barbed coil has an intelligence, because every time a thought of the person appears, it turns and scrapes and the barbs get caught, only to be jerked free, tearing the insides.

The coil gets bigger and bigger and longer and fatter, like a tumor. Barbs grow sharper and more numerous. It won't kill you—it wants you to suffer. It can make you kill yourself though.

It won't let you sleep at night, but sometimes you can get a few hours by vomiting or crying before lying down. Vomiting can be self-induced, crying cannot. The coil has a tendency to lock up your crying mechanism. You feel enormous pressure, as if the coil has excreted liquid waste in the form of tears, and it's stuck inside your body. But vomiting and crying only work temporarily, for a few hours sleep. And you don't want to sleep anyway because you'll just dream of the pain from the barbed coil—you've been experiencing it all day.

As the barbed coil gets fatter and you can't escape the pain, you wish you could explode your chest internally—the insides are ripped to shreds anyway. You wish you could cram a lit stick of dynamite down your throat and have it explode from the inside, which would slit the chest down the center and cause the two flaps of skin to fly open like saloon doors. You wish you could do this because it would expel the barbed coil. You know that if you had "nine lives" like a cat supposedly does, eight of them would be gone. But "nine lives" is also a cliche. You know it is not true.

Drew

We'd ride our bikes to McDonalds and when the clerk wasn't looking we would take handfuls of these red, yellow, and white, striped, plastic straws. Then we'd go to the swing-set in my friend's backyard. Underneath each swing there was a patch of dirt. This is because you would drag your feet to stop and, after repeated dragging, the grass would wear away, leaving just dirt. On this dirt you could see big black ants and little red ones. Sometimes there would be an anthill, but it would be small and would be the home of the little red ones. The big black ones always went into the grass and disappeared. Some would be carrying small twigs or a blade of grass or other dead ants. You could put your finger down in front of them and they'd crawl right over it very quickly and continue on their way. The big ones seemed mean.

We'd get some matches and light the end of the straws. When these plastic straws burned, they would emit an evil black smoke and the horrible rubber-burning smell would choke you. The end would liquify and drip, making a very bizarre and futuristic sound as the drops fell to the ground. It sounded to us like little missiles being shot from a spaceship.

We'd drip these on the ants, and they would curl up and crackle and die. Sometimes we would get just half the ant, and the other half would frantically move its legs and try to struggle away. Sometimes we would seal up an anthill by dropping many of these drops over the opening. An ant or two would come out to investigate what was happening, and we'd sizzle him up.

We stopped doing it one day because my friend accidentally dripped some on his leg while wearing shorts and got a bad burn. Nine years later, his leg still has a small burn mark.

When a chunk of sodium the size of a dime is put in a glass of water, it explodes so violently that the explosion evaporates the water and the remains of the glass can be found stuck in the wall.

You have to handle sodium with pliers, or it may react with the moisture in your hand. Sodium must be wrapped in a dry cloth or it may react with the moisture in the air. Sodium and water just do not mix.

An interesting idea would be to throw a chunk of sodium the size of a softball into the bathtub while someone is taking a bath.

Me and Rick went out into the backyard to investigate what we just heard. We approached the garbage cans. I quickly lifted off the lid and jumped back, standing on my toes to peer inside and using the lid as a shield. There was the dead catfish with its belly slit open, being eaten by maybe a hundred maggots. They looked like little white capsules that the doctor might prescribe for you. They probably had the texture of cooked macaroni noodles. They were all together in crowded clusters at different points on the catfish's body.

Rick got the rake and, extending it into the garbage can, he carefully slipped the pronged end under the catfish and slowly lifted it out. It was at this moment I thought he might fling it at me, or at least fake a fling at me, but he didn't. He was interested in it. He set it down on the grass and we stared at it in the sun.

If you looked close at the maggots, you could see thin red veins in their bodies and tiny ridges in their skin. A fly landed on me and I jumped, shooing it off. It just flew around in a circle and landed near the same spot again on my arm. I jerked my arm and kept in motion so it wouldn't land again.

Rick went in and got a can of Raid and sprayed at least half the can on them. They reacted by moving faster and faster and getting confused and bumping into each other. Some died right off, but most eventually slowed down and fell into the grass like dead weight. Rick then sprayed the inside of the garbage can.

I pushed the fish in a Jewel paper bag with a stick, drove up to the corner gas-station and threw it in their huge metal garbage bin. It was empty, and when I dropped the bag, it made a hollow eerie boom. I shut the lid and went home. The way I killed and wasted that catfish and the sight of those maggots crawling, eating, and dying made me worry that nature was going to take some sort of revenge on me.

Once I saw a film in which a man takes a fresh cut rose, dips it into a beaker which has smoke pouring from it, removes it, and hits it against the table. The rose breaks in a hundred pieces as if it were glass. The substance in which it was dipped was liquid nitrogen, which is extremely cold. It is so cold, it froze the rose throughout and made it brittle.

A perfect murder would be to get a vat of liquid nitrogen, knock a person out and lower him into the vat by rope. Lift the body out, drop it, it breaks in a million pieces, and you sweep it up and throw the bits in the garbage can.

Tom told me about this girl he met on vacation. She was about fifteen and had been hospitalized three times for attempted suicide. Every summer for the last three years she had tried and each time she had come closer to success. She said she hated the summer.

Twice it was sleeping pills, and the third time she tried to slit her wrist on the beach. She cut an opening on her left wrist with a razor blade. The skin flapped open and blood flowed. She could see the vein she had to cut in order to be successful. This was the vein that could not be repaired. She was happy for the first time because she was so near the moment. She described the vein as a long strand of cooked spaghetti, and when she tried to cut it, it wriggled off to the side. She tried to cut it again, but it wriggled off and jumped to the other side. Every time the razor would make contact with the vein, it would jump away. She gave up after a while and just stared at the vein and the blood on her wrist.

"When the blood dripped on the sand, it turned dark brown and made the sand granules stick together," she said. "Blood on the wrist feels warm. That was the last thing I remember before I woke up in a hospital. Tubes with liquids in them were coming out of my wrist. You couldn't see where they entered, because my wrist was bandaged, but I could feel the pressure and tingling, like when you step on the footpedal of a strong water bubbler, and it squirts a stream of water against the roof of your mouth."

She told Tom about this as they walked along the beach. I wanted to know why he didn't ask her about the reasons for her attempts rather than getting involved with the mechanics of taking her life. He said he would ask her next time he goes on vacation.

THE DOCK WORKERS
Ronald L. Burns

As soon as you cross the river on Harrison Street, you're aware of the Post Office. It looks like ten floors of granite and concrete stacked one on top of the other. Situated next to the river in the old industrial district on the edge of downtown, the Main Post Office is an antique among the newer glass and steel Amazons that clot the Chicago skyline. This dead, gray building—wide enough to accommodate the eight lanes of the Congress Expressway that runs underneath—is prison for some twenty thousand employees.

Its front doors have no locks, and the building never closes; but there are always the guards—the armed, blue-suited and night-sticked guards—swarming around everywhere, positioned at all the entrances, checking badges, exuding a concentration camp level of security that only the workers who slave there every day know is imagined, faked, untrue.

Workers clutter the sidewalks that surround the building, everyone (and everything) rushing to beat an ever ticking clock, the workers hustling with brown-bagged lunches swinging in hands, fresh newspapers tucked beneath armpits, stopping for a tense, hurried second at the Canteen trucks parked at the curb that serve heartburn specials and tinfoil-covered soulfood dinners, making a frantic purchase, then scurrying on toward an employees entrance, already fishing in their garments for the I.D. badge to show the guard blocking the door—and all this—the hurry and bustle, the goings and comings, the getting back from going—motivated by an agonized fear of not making it up the stairs, and then on the elevator, and then to the locker room to change, and then down the long floor, in time to punch in.

Inside, rows of fluorescent lights glare down upon a variety of aisles, the aisles snaking down a workroom floor two-and-a-half blocks long and one-block wide, among row after row upon row of wooden mail cases with men and women sitting before them, throwing mail into pigeon-hole slots. Upon, along, and down these aisles, walking or pushing or driving or leading every form of hamper or gurney or push cart capable of carrying mail, are other men and women; the walls of the workroom are marred by signs, pictures, posters, numbers, and codes advising or warning or ordering some action dealing with the handling of mail.

The security does not stop once you are inside the building; it is said that the workers are always being watched. It is from the catwalks that this spying is said to take place. The catwalks—a grim network of enclosed passageways, resembling a continuous cracker-box, tall enough for a man to stand upright in—run along the high walls and ceiling for the entire length of the building on every floor. Studded with two-way spy mirrors (so that the workers cannot tell whether they are being observed or not), the catwalks give the postal inspectors inside a peek at every nook and cranny of the building.

Then there are the conveyor belts: long ones and short ones, portable ones and stationary ones. More formidable, however, are the floor-to-floor conveyors (i.e., conveyors that carry mail to other floors and units that are hoisted along the walls, some snaking close to the ceiling beside the cat-walks, yard after yard of intersecting conveyor belts upon which trays of letters, like broken, confused freight cars, travel in never ending clanking. Under the conveyors is a battery of mechanics carrying long wooden poles like those used in the Olympic high jumps, whose sole job it is to see that these conveyors aren't jammed, which, despite this, nevertheless happens.

There is a constant cacophony of noise: the clanking of conveyors; the soft whirring of electric tractors driven by helmeted men; the rumbling of packages, boxes, and letters being dumped from cloth sacks upon belts, along with chattering workers who wait on either side to remove the pour-ing mail in proper receptacles.

The racket of moving mail, the motion of a workroom floor in full swing, was so loud that Vince wasn't sure when the fat foreman said, "All 12:01 subs, get your badge cards and report to the detail desk!"

It was more intuition than actual hearing that made Vince look up from the tray of mail he was sifting through. There was so much noise and mo-tion—the P.A. system making announcements, foremen shouting orders—that it was nearly impossible to tell when you were being addressed. "Did you say 12:01s?" he asked, continuing to pick through the tray of Montana mail, searching for states that didn't belong.

The foreman did not scowl at him, just stared tiredly as if thinking that any fool could hear above the noise. "That's what I said," he said.

Vince dropped a handful of California letters back into the Montana tray, not caring that someone else would have to pick them out all over again. He waited in line with the other subs milling about the detail desk, then plucked the yellow card reading "Howard, Vincent" from the card rack. The subs stood in the aisle, waiting. They were being reassigned again. Of course, that was always it; you never stayed in one unit too long. Just when you were getting the hang of working there, had finally solved the riddle of what the foremen expected of you, they came and moved you again, always to another floor or a different unit on the same floor, or a different assignment in the same unit—but still the change, the impermanence, the not knowing where you'd be working next.

Two or three foremen bustled about checking names and asking to see badge cards. "All right," one ordered, "fall in!"

The subs formed a ragged line and followed the foreman, the clean-shirted back; they trudged down the main aisle toward the far end of the eighth floor.

"Wonder where we goin' now...?" someone beside Vince asked. Vince looked around to see the smooth, shaved face of the well-dressed sub he had seen strolling about the floor from time to time.

"Get your coats and lunches," the foreman in the clean shirt said. "We're going across the street!"

Vince and Dresser looked at each other, then lined up at the cloak counter with their garment checks in hand.

"Across the street," the Dresser said. "What the fuck's over there?"

Vince shrugged, exchanging his check for the tattered pea-coat with the lady behind the counter. He watched the Dresser slip a tan alpaca overcoat across one arm, and again Vince felt like a bum, the alpaca smelling even more strongly of the cologne than the Dresser did.

Half of the subs piled into the elevator, a long, wide, wooden structure looking more suitable for the carrying of cattle than the shipping of humans; the others waited for the next elevator.

Vince felt the elevator's surprisingly smooth descent, knowing by smell that the Dresser was still beside him. The doors opened on the Harrison Street side in the truck terminal, a huge, roaring, lower section of the building with runways sloping up the street and circling two stories into the building's bowels, where blue and gray painted mail trucks deposited and received shipments of mail. In single file they took one of the sloping runways toward the street; from time to time, they had to press into the wall to allow the heaving, squeaking trucks to wail by with a rush of wind and speed, the motion out of all proportion to the limited closeness of the runways.

They made it out onto Harrison without being crushed by the speeding trucks; a canteen truck stood waiting, serving tinfoil-covered plates of soulfood dinners for a buck-fifty. They dodged through the steady stream of traffic crawling bumper to bumper both ways down Harrison and stopped at a long, low, red-bricked structure which sat abreast of a freight yard and beyond that, the Chicago River.

"Where in the fuck is they sending us," the Dresser moaned.

Vince didn't say anything, following the others into the long building. A sign hanging in the entrance said: R-E-A Building—Postal Annex #3.

"Big mothafucka," the Dresser says.

But Vince does not even hear him and is even only slightly more aware of someone—one of the foremen who steps forward and says, "'A' to 'H' over here! 'J' to 'P' over there! The rest of you line up against that wall."

Vince and the Dresser are in the same group. Their apparent foreman, Wilson, a smallish, nervous-acting black man, introduces himself as they punch in. The clock makes an electronic thunk when Vince jams his card in; he lays the card in Wilson's open palm and tells Wilson his name and social security number.

It's big as an airplane hangar, Vince thinks, his eyes never stopping the constant roving, the quick upward and side-to-side glances. High and wide enough for a 747 to swoop through it at high speed, without its wings scraping the sides or its fuselage kicking up sparks on the floor!

They have already walked a block, and Vince can see no end to the building, no back wall in sight. The building looks dead, as if it has not been worked in years. Dust is everywhere, on the wide sliding doors with the numbers printed above them, on the confusion of equipment—the portable conveyors, the push-trucks, and hampers that stand in the center of the floor—and especially on the floor and in the air itself. At odd intervals above the doors, small heat vents blow out a faint, nearly undetectable warmth. Their small size seems ridiculous, insane in a place of such magnitude, but the brief moment of warmth as you pass them is welcome.

Wilson begins squinting at the clipboard. He sounds off a volley of last names. "Wait at this door!" Vince gets sent to door 47.

"See ya around," the Dresser mumbles, walking off with the rest of the group.

Wilson comes back. "All right, you all know the regulations; the same rules you learned across the street apply over here." Wilson volleys off with a long list of do's and don'ts, the same crap that Vince had been hearing every day for the two weeks he'd been a Christmas sub at the USPO, hardly listening, catching only fragments like "No goddamn smoking in the work area!" and "If I catch a bottle on anybody, they'll get their ass shipped out of here quicker 'en you can say lickity-split!" and "No fuckin' off on duty. We expect an honest day's work for an honest day's pay!" and especially. "No tampering with the mail. Don't *find* anything in this here mail, and try to *find* your way out of here with it!"

But Vince isn't paying attention. He is staring at the trailer parked at his door. Both the dock door and the trailer door are open, like someone— another group like his—had been there working just before the new team came and had now vanished, gone up in a whiff of dust and cold.

"Let's see the hands of all of you that don't have gloves?" Wilson says. He makes a notation on the clipboard. "I'll be back with your gloves in a minute; then you can get to unloading the rest of that mail from the trailer."

Vince headed for the trailer as soon as Wilson walked off. He had to step up to get inside. He stopped in the mouth, sniffing, smelling dust, listening, hearing nothing.

Damn it's long, he thought; then wondered how long it would take to unload the trailer if it were stuffed full of mail. The wall of sacks, at least what he could make out of them in the dark, reminded him of some huge, irregular honeycomb made up of dingy, gray duffle bags stacked from floor to ceiling. On top of the sacks, to prevent them from being crushed, was the lighter mail: the packages and parcels, the boxes marked "Fragile" and "Handle With Care" in large red letters or with bright adhesive labels.

"Got a match?"

Vince blinked. He hadn't seen the man in the trailer until he spoke. The man rose, huge, towering, and came forward: "Got a light on you?"

"You ain't supposed to..." Vince saw that the man was at least six-five, dark-skinned, with close-cut hair.

"Fuck their rules! Got some fire or don't you?"

Vince looked back to make sure Wilson wasn't around and then flicked his disposable Cricket. The man bent forward into the flame, sucking on a filterless cigarette. The man grunted something that sounded like "thanks," then went back to where he had been, which, as Vince's eyes adjusted to the dark, he made out to be a pile of sacks dragged down and heaped in the corner to form a kind of seat.

Vince stood against the wall; he could see the cigarette's tip glow and diminish and smell the smoke. Next he heard paper rustling, something sloshing in a bottle, a cap being unscrewed, the gurgle of a swig being taken, and then the cap-rescrewing, liquor-sloshing, paper-rustling—all over again in reverse. The cigarette glowed once more and was flicked forward, landing not far from Vince's boot—not like it had been thrown to hit Vince, but like it had been flicked to fall in the exact spot it *had* fallen; like it had landed in that precise spot to intimidate Vince exactly as Vince felt intimidated now; and like the motive behind this intimidation was to make

Vince wonder, brood over whether he was really being aimed at, exactly as Vince was wondering, brooding over the queston now.

The cigarette glowed red on the floor; Vince did not step on it. The man rose again and seemed to deliberately stalk to one side of the butt, deliberately avoid smashing it out by giving the butt a wide girth.

"You new?" the stranger growled.

"Yeah!"

"They just call you in or ship you from across the street?"

"Across the street!"

The man paced the trailer back and forth, turning quick and neat in abrupt volte-faces; the boards creaked, whispered under his weight. Vince could see him good now: dressed like an ex-G.I. in the faded field jacket, the faded and patched fatigues worn ankle high but not bloused. The combat boots looked almost new; but a closer look told that it was only the shine, the spit shine given with a polish-blackened rag—augmented by saliva—viciously scrubbed again and again across the toe in the way of ex-servicemen or skilled ghetto shoe shiners. And there was that restless quality about the stranger, that nervous, fretful manner of something jailed but not yet broken, as if (the stranger) might all at once drop to all fours—suddenly naked, fur-covered—and lift his hind leg to the wall of sacks.

Vince knew that the man had never ceased to observe him, though; pacing, brooding, the man seemed not to notice him at all. Abruptly, he stopped in front of Vince, the combat-booted foot covering the cigarette butt.

"I'm Jason McBrad!" He extended his hand, then fetched it back to remove the glove before snapping the hand out again.

"Vince Howard!" They shook hands, hard, viciously, eyeballs locked, prolonging the squeeze as if with the intention of drawing blood.

"Folks call me Mac."

"You can call me Vince." Vince could see his face good now—tense, brutal—a face like misery and hard times.

Mac felt his pockets and produced the pack of Camels. "Want one?"

Vince looked back to see if Wilson had shown up yet. "What the fuck," he said, bringing out the Cricket. "Don't mind if I do!"

Out of all the things they hated, it was probably the opening of the dock-door that they hated the most:

It is the night of the blizzard. Shabbily dressed in double layers of dust-covered garments, they stand in front of door twelve; no one is talking because they all know that it is coming, that the dock-door will have to go up.

Vince and Mac sit side by side on the portable conveyor; the rest of the crew is huddled about the heat vent, heads down, hands in pockets. The huge building seems quiet, as if all of its employees—even the other crews at other doors—are observing some brief, silent moment of mourning before they begin their chores. Through the dock-door Vince can hear the rush and howl of wind; through the door's single row of windows, he can see the broad rear of the trailer they'll have to unload. He cannot see the snow yet, but he knows that it is there, the sleet raining, pelting, tumbling down in the truck yard. It is already cold enough (even with the small, ridiculously inept heat vents blowing), but he knows—they all know (even

Mac)—that when the dock-door is raised the heat will be sucked out so fast that none would swear that it was ever there.

Wilson is standing in the aisle, looking toasty in his ski-jacket and ear-muffs. Wilson cocks an eye to double-check that the push-trucks upon which the unloaded mail will go are set up and labeled properly, then makes one last note on his clip-board before giving the order:

"Let's raise those doors!"

The order was addressed to no one, no name being called—yet it is Mac who goes forward, Mac in the olive-green field jacket, with the strapped shoulders and flapped pockets, the fatigue trousers and spit-shined combat-boots, Mac who draws himself up from the conveyor—as if Wilson has singled him out, and with pointed finger and shout, ordered him alone to be the one to raise the dock-door, Mac who stalks without hesitation to the door, the combat boots treading without sound on the cement, Mac who stoops, knees bent, the door handle clenched in both hands, and Mac who then jerks to his full height, the door rattling upward with him.

The wind rushes in, sudden, cold, hissing—followed by bushel-baskets of snow: tears instantly spring into eyes, snot starts to slide, teeth chatter, clothes ruffle back. The docked mail trailer—its rear hatch closed—does not fill the dock-door completely, but leaves wide gaps on either side. And it is Mac again—Mac who seems to hear no wind, feel no cold, get no snow in his eyes—Mac already stooping again, trying to unlock the trailer's hatch. No one else has moved—not Vince, not Wilson, nor the rest of the crew. But they all watch Mac, watch him with the same dread and awe with which they watched him lift the dock-door, standing and staring as if rooted in one spot by Mac's every move, watching Mac stand suddenly and draw back a booted foot, then let the foot land twice in swift, fatal kicks.

The lock springs open; Mac shoves up the trailer's hatch and, in the same motion, takes one large step backward.

It is like watching a huge, multi-colored, multi-sized avalanche spill down from a peak only ten feet high. The mail—the packages and parcels and bundles and sacks—having shifted around and lodged against the hatch during the cross-country ride, come tumbling down in a heavy, deadly waterfall of racket and weight.

It lasts only a few seconds, the mail thudding in a heap around Mac's feet, and some even spilling off the dock into the truck yard. And it is only now that the spell seems broken, that the other subs begin to act. Before the wind-barricades can be put into place, the mail in the truck-yard must be retrieved.

Vince goes forward; he stands for a second on the dock's edge, his face bent into the cold, then he leaps down. The drift of blown snow, lodged beside the trailer and the building itself, is nearly to his knees. He loses his balance, slipping, sprawling to one knee and an elbow. He does not raise himself at once; blinking, the snow and wind howling in his face, he can see the truck yard barraged white like a milky ocean. A hand-full of docked trailers stand in a frozen line; a double set of footprints, rapidly filling with snow, make a sloppy, smeared path toward the Amtrak Freight Yards and the river beyond.

Vince takes hold of the trailer's huge back tire and pulls himself to his feet. Snow pelts his face. He sees the three fallen sacks lying like dingy blurs in a deep drift abreast of the building. He lifts them one at a time and flings them back on the dock. He tries to climb back up, but his feet won't grip the slick sides of the building, and his hands have nothing to grab a-hold to. He can see the rest of the crew scurrying about, stacking hampers three and four high to use as wind barricades. He is about to holler for someone to help him up, then he sees the spit-shined boots about face and come toward him. He does not even see the rest of Mac, only the shined combat-boots and olive-green trouser bottoms stopping in front of him: the two rough hands grip him beneath the arm-pits, and Vince is flowing smoothly upward, as if suddenly powered by propeller, able to see Mac's face now, the frozen, morbid features not even tensing with strain or effort, lifting Vince—all five-feet ten-inches of him—as if he were no more than an empty sack of mail.

"Brush yourself," Mac says, and turns to help two other subs shove the stack of hampers into the gaps on the trailer's side. Vince slaps the snow off his pants and coat; he is cold now, like he has just been dunked in a tub of icy bathwater then set in a refrigerator to dry. He sees Mac with a pile of empty mail sacks under one armpit, stooping at the hampers and plugging up the small spaces with sacks. Once the wind barricade is secure, it is time to work the mail.

Wilson gives the order: "Let's work that mail!"

The mail spilled on the floor is worked first, being dragged, pushed, and rolled onto the push-truck with the corresponding zip-code. The address labels are read quickly, just a sweeping glance at the destination—whether it be a typed label taped to a box, or a stenciled declaration on the metal plate of a sack, or the scribbled, near unreadable message in ink or magic-marker on the front of a paper wrapped parcel—there is only the sweeping glance, and that solely at the destination, none caring about its (the package's) origin, from where it came, or who from—just to get it out of their hands, immediately, and on the proper push-truck.

Once the mail on the floor is cleaned up, it is time to unload the trailer itself. And it seems crazy when you look at it, an insane thing to attempt. You stare—with the same disbelief, the same dread with which you watched the raising of the dock-door and the raising of the trailer hatch too—at the mountain of mail standing in the trailer's mouth. And you know that the mail seen is only the front, that the forty-foot trailer is crammed front to rear with tier after tier of mail.

You're freezing cold from where the snow you've fallen into has turned into water, and you want to go home, or to the break-room—or anyplace where you can warm up. But Wilson is there and you know that he won't let you. You see him standing in the aisle, the white supervisor's button gleaming on the chest of his ski-jacket; he is standing on an empty push-truck, overseeing the progress, gripping the pushtruck's rail with one hand and waving out orders with the other: "Let's work the mail. Let's make a dent in that wall!"

It is the wall of mail that he is speaking of, the mountain in the trailer's mouth. You go forward, nearly being dragged by the motion of the other subs, and begin the chore, the unloading. You watch, with a bitter, rapt sense of pleasure, as each worker contributes the tiniest dent in the wall, as gloved, near frozen fingers, clench each piece of mail and yank it out of the wall. With that same amusement, you think of each worker's hand as a tiny member of a demolition crew, or maybe one single atom of an arching, swinging wrecking ball, the hands—like the wrecking ball—stealing away piece by piece from a wall of multi-sized, multi-shaped bricks.

And you are caught up in the tide, the motion of subs, all part of a strange procession—like players in the game 'Follow the Leader'—each sub making a grim, silent circle, an endless round-trip from the trailer—loaded down with a bundle, some (the frailer workers) staggering under the burden—to the proper push-truck to deposit the mail, and finally back to the trailer for another load.

Soon the first inch of trailer floor is uncovered, and it is good to see that inch of rough, worn, work-smoothed planks, because this is nearly the only proof that you have not labored in the cold in vain, that you are progressing, that—inch by inch—you are piercing the wall. But you do not smile, your insides do not even thaw enough to be happy—because that inch does not mean that your labors are through, that inch does not mean that you can go home.

It was the night before Christmas, the coldest night of the tour. The river was an unmoving, glass-like sheet of ice. The rail yard was a dead, frozen wasteland of crisscrossing tracks with small, niggard fires burning to keep the switches and ties unfrozen. And the truck yard lay covered in a tire-streaked layer of snow. A long line of trailers stood waiting, their rear ends backed toward the dock building.

Vince scampered up the three cement steps; he flashed open his pea coat so that the dock guard could see his postal button pinned to his sweater. He hurried through the door marked "Postal Personnel Only." Wilson, the foreman, stood at the punch clock.

"Well, Mr. Howard," Wilson growled, "So nice of you to've come at last!"

"My el was late!"

Wilson paid no attention, staring at a clipboard. "All right," Wilson said, "I'm putting you on door 15 with McBrad and Mr. James. Don't you three do any fuckin' off!"

Vince started toward his assignment; at the break room he saw the foreman called Frenchman, a tall, truck driver-looking man, shushing subs away from coffee and cigarettes. "Party's over," Frenchman kept repeating, "Time to go work the mail!"

Through the window of the cloakroom, he could see the Dresser, whom everyone else called "Stino," changing from his elegant street clothes to the more refined work outfit: corduroy slacks stuffed into blood-red, elaborately embroidered, western boots; a leather flyer's jacket with straps and buckles galore; a black skull cap pulled over his ears; and the final touch—a scarlet silk scarf tied Red Baron style and flung across one shoulder.

Stino grinned and waved; he came out slipping on a pair of leather gloves. "What door you on?" Stino asked.

"15!"

"Me, too!"

Stino threw out his hand for five; they slapped palms. "Gonna be a cold motha tonight!" Stino said.

"Damn right," Vince said. "The river's froze solid; and the wind blowing off it almost knocked me on my ass when I crossed the bridge a minute ago."

They joined the migration of late stragglers heading down the floor. It wasn't *that* cold yet; the doors were still down, allowing the whiff of heat blowing from the wall vents to stay in the building. There was a slow, lazy bustling of subs gathering up equipment. Two men shouted "Beep! Beep!" as they rolled a short portable conveyor by. A lady in a dust mask veered close to Vince, pushing a stack of hampers; Stino tapped the lady on the arm and whispered something brief and lewd in her ear; she cackled, slapped his hand away, and went about her business. A group of subs, huddled about the heat vent at door 9, waved a greeting to Stino; a steady stream of push trucks, some being led, others being pushed, came from the far end of the dock.

Vince and Stino finally came to their door; most of the crew stood about the heat vent, huddled, slapping their bodies for warmth, bundled to the hilt in the same anonymous garments of yesterday. Stino bounded up to them with a loud "Howdy," sidling up to the females, grinning, joshing, talking stuff.

Mac was off to himself, sitting alone on the edge of a conveyor, silent, brooding.

Vince stopped in front of him. "Looks like it's gonna be a cold one!"

Mac didn't smile or even grunt; he just jammed out his hand for a shake. Gone was the wringing, the milking, the weighing of each other's strength that had marked that first handshake. Now it was hard, rough, meaningless.

Mac stared past him, yellow eyes aimed at Stino. "I see you got your buddy with you."

"Yeah, Wilson threw us all together tonight!"

Mac grunted—more with distaste than disgust—continuing to stare at Stino without blinking.

"You don't like the Dresser much, do you?" Vince asked.

Mac didn't even look at him; both hands were in the pockets of the fatigue jacket he always wore. One came out now to jam a Camel into the corner of his thick lips. The yellow eyes turned on Vince now, observing him with that morbid, frozen stare which Vince could not decipher as either love or hate. "Got a match...?"

Vince could see both of them with a mere shifting of his eyes—the Dresser (Stino) flirting with the Puerto Rican as she worked outside on the conveyor, and Mac standing against the wall in the back of the trailer. Vince, stooping in the trailer's mouth to lift a bundle of exhaust pipes onto the conveyor, let his eyes shift between the two—first jerking them toward Stino, then back at Mac, who had not moved yet, who pressed motionless into the wall as if he had somehow become immersed, saturated into the very wood and steel of the trailer.

Neither of the two really seemed to fit with the rest of the subs—Stino because of his flamboyant dress, his smug, suave image of class, his image of being too good to be doing this job; and Mac because of his personality, his aloofness. Yet it was hard to tell who fit the least.

Maybe it was Stino. Among the other subs Stino was like a left shoe being used as a mitten instead of the foot it was made for. And no one had said that Mac didn't like Stino, but Vince could tell, could sense that Mac hated Stino.

Maybe it was Stino's charisma that Mac hated, the way Stino had of drawing people, the way a group of subs always gathered when Stino was around. If a bunch of subs were in a huddle, talking, joshing, it was a sure thing that Stino would be in the midst of them, talking louder, joshing harder, that Red Baron scarf flung like a red rattlesnake across his shoulder. In the break room Stino was always the first at the card table, plunking his face cards down with a thunk and a snap, and shouting a hearty "Take that motha-fucka!"

Simply put: They (the subs) hung around Stino like flies on shit!

Yet Mac was different. It was not that he shunned companionship, but that he exuded a kind of ferocity—a quick, sleek, and powerful aura of violence—which made friendship with him tantamount to a snake charmer planting a kiss on the poisoned lips of his swaying cobra. Yes, it was like that with Mac; you were never sure whether he would slap your back in crude glee or break your knuckles for sneaking up on him while he slept in the trailer's back.

They were in the break room during lunch one night. It was a simple room: a few unpainted tables and benches shoved among vending machines, boasting of coffee, sweet rolls, and candies in lighted, picture-perfect advertisements posted on the machine's front.

Stino sat at a table among three other subs, playing Bid-Whist. Mac and Vince sat on a long bench against the back wall drinking coffee. Mac clenched the cup in both hands, staring off, as if seeing nothing.

The break room was the only warm place (besides the cloakroom, and the john upstairs) the subs had access to. Every time a new person came in, a blast of cold air spat into the room with them, and there was an instant protest from those already sitting down: "Close the fuckin' door!" "Slam it!" "Don't let the heat out!"

Vince unbuttoned his pea coat and stretched his legs. There was a constant ca-chang/ka-ching/thunk of subs using the vending machine—inserting money, jerking the item release lever, snatching up their purchase, then fingering the change return slot whether they had money coming back or not. The Bid-Whist players kept up a steady racket. Stino more raucous than the rest—cards snapping down, insults being passed, the dealer riffling the deck, and so on.

Vince turned to Mac. "What're you gonna do when our tour is over?"

"Nothin'."

"Nothin'...? You mean take it easy for awhile?"

"Nope! I mean just plain ole nothin'!"

Vince frowned. "Don't you work another job, or have a family—I mean, something...?"

Mac looked at him, stared with the yellow, red-rimmed eyes, not angrily, not suspiciously, but like a scholar explaining simple logic to a damn fool. "Look! I'm on aid! I live by myself! And usually I don't do nothin' much but wake up in the mornin' and go to bed at night!"

Vince stared into his cup to avoid looking at Mac. He had never heard of anyone who did *nothing*, had *nothing*, expected *nothing*, and probably, as long as he lived, would get absolutely *nothing*.

When Vince thought about it now, he knew that there had been an immediate dislike between Mac and Stino. He was working outside the trailer on the conveyor, filling in for the Puerto Rican while she took a break. Mac was standing in full view near the mouth of the trailer, a lit cigarette in one hand, a pint of gin in the other. Mac had winked at him, one slow closing of his left eye, then raised the pint in offering. Vince declined with a shake of his head. Stino stood in the main aisle at the podium-desk, writing out a handful of dispatch slips for the push trucks which were piled high with mail unloaded from the trailer. Stino showed his teeth when he spotted Mac with the booze. Stino looked both ways before abandoning the dispatch slips and easing over to the trailer. Mac leaned inside the trailer—in full view of any supervisor who happened to pass by—taking leisurely sips from the brown-bagged pint, flicking ashes from the Camel. The subs working the conveyor watched, Vince watched, as Stino stopped in front of Mac and smiled up at him. Mac took another sip from the pint, not even frowning from the taste, not even acknowledging Stino.

Stino slipped off his gloves and wiped his hands on the thighs of his corduroy slacks. "Brrrrrrr," Stino shivered, hugging himself about the shoulders, "Shit, it's cold in this dump!" Stino never looked away from the bottle in Mac's hand; Stino's head nodded up and then down in time with the raising and lowering of the pint from Mac's lips back to his side.

"Brrrrrrr!" Stino shivered again, "a hit of liquor would sure make the night pass faster!"

Mac took another hit from the pint and chased it with a pull from the Camel. He hadn't even looked down at Stino; he stared in the direction of the podium-desk where Stino had been before spotting the bottle; he stared in that direction, like he expected Stino to still be there writing the dispatch slips instead of standing below him begging.

"Hey buddy," Stino tried, "can I get a hit from your jug?"

Mac looked down at Stino then, like it was only now that he had heard Stino, or even noticed that Stino was there. Mac took a last, slow gulp from the bottle, then very deliberately turned it upside down. And even from the conveyor, Vince could see a single drop of gin form on the bottle lip, remain there a second, elongate, then plop to the floor. "Sorry," Mac said. "All gone!"

There is an hour left before check-out time. Vince leans in the trailer's mouth. He has a pile of sacks and boxes around him from where Mac had heaped them before climbing the mail wall to lie down. He does not know if Mac is asleep or not. He can hear no snoring, no stirring. But he knows that Mac is lying there flat on his back, with his fists folded across his belly and his eyes wide open.

Vince puts the mail on the conveyor slowly; he puts a sack on the moving, whirring rubber, then rests awhile; puts a box on, then rests awhile—trying to make the mail last, trying to avoid having to go back of the trailer and drag down more work.

The Old-Timer is singing again, singing the spiritual again: "...goin' to see the kings/We are goin' to see the kings..." It seems to be the only recording in the Old-Timers repertoire, and he doesn't seem to even know all the verses to this one—just repeating over and over again the same few lines, belching the words out into the cold, the dust. The Old-Timer is the only one working the conveyor; but this is not unusual, the other subs are standing under the heat vent—even the Puerto Rican—or else having slunk off to the break room to warm up. Vince eases another sack on the conveyor; he sees the Old-Timer's gnarled, scarred hands clenching, fumbling at the sack's rough burlap finish, and the hard, leathery face tensing with strain, lifting the sack's compacted weight. The shriveled body, stooping, already bent permanently into the shape and posture of a man who has labored all his life in lifting things too heavy for him, stands there indecisively with the sack weighing down on him, looking like a heathen or a slave with the splotched headrag tied crooked on his head, and then lugs the sack inch by agonized inch to a push truck and flings it.

Vince sees Stino coming from the far end of the dock; it is not so much Stino he sees, but a bright Red Baron scarf coming his way, pushing something. The Red Baron scarf stops at each door along the way, probably joshing with other subs, laughing; the Red Baron scarf pauses to converse with other subs strolling down the main aisle, probably giving someone "five" or pecking a chick on the jaw. The Red Baron scarf comes closer, pushing an empty push truck.

Vince doesn't know why, but he remembers the first night in the building, and him and Mac being shifted to the same trailer with Stino after lunch. That had been Stino's most elegant night: Stino had been throat-slashing sharp that night, dressed to murder in the ridiculously clean, tan alpaca, the coat and him smelling like a cologne counter in an expensive department store. Working in his coat, Stino, like everyone else, was lifting sacks, staggering with the weight of mail with the air of someone used to doing light work, performing the drudgery of slaves in the garb of a prince, humping in the dust, the grime, laboring, unavoidably dragging the sacks against the tan coat, smearing it, and frowning as he watched the garment, slowly, by degrees, get messy, then nasty, then filthy. Stino at first stopped every few seconds to brush the grime from the cuffs and tails; then when the smears clung to the coat so bad that the garment resembled a zebra-stripe tan and black original, he screamed out, "I don't have to take this shit! I'm self-employed!" And Vince just watched him then, not having heard about the tailoring yet, and Vince remembered Mac watching him, too, leaning back into the trailer's wall staring at Stino like it was giving him some kind of weird kick to see a goody-two-shoes like Stino get nasty like everyone else. But Vince hadn't really taken any notice of this then, only listening to Stino shouting, "I could quit this shit right now! I'm a fuckin' tailor!" And Vince just watched him rave and wondered how much the coat had cost, and whether Stino was really a tailor, and whether he had made the coat, and how much it would cost to get cleaned, and still felt like a bum in his old pea coat, when at the end of the same night, Stino, looking like a filthy prince visiting a coal mine, left the building with Vince to walk to the el together.

Never again did Stino wear the alpaca. But as he comes up to Vince now, pushing the push truck, he is still too well dressed for a sub in a dock building, too dashing in the western outfit—the leather and corduroy and Red Baron scarf.

Most nights Mac would cop a snooze about midway through the shift. Working in the back of the trailer as he usually did, where he could hardly be seen anyway (unless the light was shined inside), gave him certain advantages: He could hide out.

The tier (or mail wall) from which Mac pulled the sacks, wasn't stacked from floor to ceiling, but had a gap, a crawl-space at the top between the tier's top and the ceiling, wide enough for a man to crawl into.

Sometimes, when Vince would be yanking down pieces of mail, kinda pissed because he had to drag the mail to the conveyor himself instead of Mac throwing it to him, he'd become aware of breathing, faint but steady. Then Vince would see the slow, spaced wafts of vapor puffing out from atop the mail wall, like a small fire was smoldering. And Vince would climb up the wall and peek over the top and find Mac there on his back, gloved fists folded across his belly, eyes wide open, staring.

Other times Mac really would stalk off to the washroom. And when Mac had been gone awhile and Wilson started noticing the absence of Mac's name during the occasional spot checks, Vince would have to sneak off to fetch Mac back to the trailer. Vince would tell one of the subs to feed the conveyor for him and then take the long floor. He'd hope that he wouldn't run into Wilson now because he hadn't asked permission to leave his assignment, and he could get himself into hot water over that damn fool Mac.

At the back of the washroom, where a row of three stalls stand, only one—the middle one—has its green door closed. And Vince sees—before the bottom of the stall cuts off his view, as if the rest of Mac were decapitated—the combat boots planted squarely on the floor and a few vertical inches of green trouser bottoms. He goes into the next stall; and with a foot balanced on the toilet's porcelain rim and a hand atop the stall, he hoists himself up. He peeks over into the middle stall, looking down at Mac, who is sitting, leaned back against the septic tank in the exact posture Vince had found him atop the mail wall—gloved fists folded across belly, eyes bucked wide open, staring straight up.

"Wilson's looking for you," Vince says. There is nothing—not a flinch, not a blink. Then he shouts it, "Wilson wants you!" But the stare, frozen like that of a smelt on ice, does not waver, does not even shift. Then he hears the snoring—not loud, not deep, just the thick, scratchy sound congested lungs make. And it is the same snoring that Vince had heard from atop the mail wall, the same rasping, heaving, belch of breath Vince had mistook for normal breathing. But now, exposed in the washroom's glaring fluorescence, Vince could tell it was something more, like the slow shock a butcher at a chopping block must get when he finds out that the strange-looking, bleeding hunk of meat he has just hacked off is not the leg of lamb that he intended, but his own left hand. You refuse to believe that Mac is asleep, sound asleep with his eyes gaped open, as if he had been frozen, unthawably, in a state of hideous fright.

Mac had no respect for the rules. You'd see him in the trailer's back loafing on the job, sometimes squatting on a pile of sacks, sometimes fast asleep atop the mail wall. Sometimes he would stand in the back smoking, not even bothering to cup the butt to hide the glow or even fan the smoke, even when the rules clearly stated that smoking wasn't allowed, even when Wilson warned you time and again that you could be fired for doing it. Yet Mac seemed to smoke when he wanted to, to loaf on the job when he wanted to, to go on breaks when he wanted to, almost like he dared Wilson to protest, to try and stop him.

And there was the drinking, too, the constant, ever-present pint bottle in the pouch pocket of the field jacket, the cheap hooch that never seemed to affect him—not in slurred speech, because he spoke seldom; not in staggered walking, because his step was always crisp and neat and military, a stalking, heavy-footed gait like marching; not in weakened intelligence, because I.Q., mental agility, never seemed one of his trademarks. And strangest of all to Vince and the rest of the subs, because they all saw him drink, was that the liquor never made his breath stink, never suffocated those around him with the sweet-sweat of rot-gut gin.

There is no movement, not even a flinch under Mac's eye moves. He clutches the sack tighter. And Vince thinks he can hear them, the muffled ticking of a hundred digitals; he tries to picture them in the sack, all neat in their gift cases, glowing the time and date with electric intensity.

"How you goin' to sneak out? Somebody might see you!"

"There ain't no catwalks in this buildin'!"

"That don't mean there ain't no postal inspectors! They could be workin' right beside you! Anybody could be one! Tell 'im Stino...!"

Stino clumps down on the gum; he looks at the toe of his boot. "That's what I heard." Stino says.

"Tell 'im Stino! Tell 'im the story!"

Stino's mouth works fast on the gum; he looks nervous. "I don't know. Smart-Alecky tole—"

"I don't wanna hear no fuckin' story," Mac cut in, glaring.

"You don't have to do this," Vince tries. "You don't have to fuck up your job over some fuckin' watches...!"

"What job?" Mac says. "You saw the bulletin board today. This shit could be over in a day or two. Tonight even could be our last time!"

The Old-Timer is still humming the spiritual, moaning it, belching it out between old and cavity decayed gums. Vince sees that only he and one other worker, the Hippie, are at the belt; the rest of the crew have slipped away to get warm. There is no mail on the belt; the Hippie and Old-Timer just lean there, as if waiting for the shift to end. And Vince wonders if what he had heard about the Hippie is true, whether he really is an undercover inspector. But he does not say this to Mac now; he does not say anything.

Mac shifts the sack under one armpit and shoves out his hand. "This is it!"

They shake—no wrenching, no milking—just a shake. Stino watches them, his mouth making wet, saliva sounds on the gum. But it is as if Stino is not there; he is not being acknowledged.

Vince wants to grab Mac, restrain him, try to fling him to the trailer's floor, and hold him down until the shift is over; he wants to shout for Stino to help him, shout for the Hippie and the Old-Timer, holler for every sub in the building to come running. But he does not; he doesn't even take the gin bottle when Mac pats his pocket, pulls it out, shoves it at Vince, then sits it on the floor near Vince's foot when Vince makes no move to take it.

"Keep it," Mac says. He turns and brushes past Stino like he doesn't even know Stino is there. He does not run from the trailer, sneak, but simply walks out, hunched, the green sack under one arm. He stops in the mouth; Vince can see him framed there by the lights; Mac is not looking both ways, just standing there for a second before hopping down beside the conveyor.

Mac uses one hand to drag at the wind barricade; he does not have to pull hard. The wind seems to assist him. The barricade almost reels back on its own, the sacks used to plug up the gaps rolling to the ground. There is the rip and howl of wind; snow belts in. Mac's clothes ruffle back; his pants wave and bag. The Old-Timer stops humming to stare. The Hippie hugs himself, moving a step back from the wind and snow that now gushes in.

"Where you goin'?" the Hippie shivers. "Where you headin' with that sack?"

Mac doesn't answer; he moves the hampers aside, stepping around them, not even looking back to see if a supervisor will spot him.

The tails of the Old-Timer's head-rag flap in the wind; he stands grinning with senile ignorance; a drip of snot trickles from one nostril and hangs thick and puss-like on his mustache. He turns back to the belt and begins humming again.

For a second, Mac is standing on the edge of the dock, looking out on the rushing, whipping patterns of white; then he is gone. And Vince, not having not moved from the back of the trailer, can hear him, can hear the double-thud of combat boots as Mac leaps from the dock, his boots finding something solid even in the snow drift.

Without saying a word, Stino turns to the mail wall and begins to drag down sacks. He takes two by their drawstrings and pulls them down the planks to the conveyor, where he then dumps them. It's like Wilson had somehow come, invisible, to the trailer and ordered Stino to get to work or lose his job, because Stino humps now, pulls the sacks down and drags them to the front like Vince has never seen him do before.

Vince sits on a pile of sacks, just lets his legs buckle, and plops down, not caring if Wilson spies him sitting down on the post office's time, not caring if the parcels contained within the sack are labeled "fragile" in bold red stencil, or that his weight could crush them, ruin Christmas for some anonymous postal recipient. He picks up the pint of gin, just holds it without drinking. He hears the Old-Timer moaning spiritual, throaty, gutteral, like a Baptist choir all compressed into one. He wishes someone would shut the old man up, plant a wide palm across his mouth to stifle the moan escaping from him.

Stino is whisking past him, whisking back and forth from the mail wall to the conveyor. Stino is not even chewing the gum now, just working, tight-lipped, silent, hard—the way Mac used to work, as if Stino is now taking Mac's place.

Vince places the pint between his thighs, squeezing them on it. He teases the cap, unscrewing, then rescrewing, unscrewing, rescrewing. In his head he can see Mac, can picture him—Mac lurking about the dock in the now snow-drenched fatigue jacket; Mac ducking behind a docked trailer as a team of inspectors walk by, bent to the wind, their shoes crunching loud against snow-covered cobblestones; Mac waiting for them to pass, just crouched behind the trailer until he can't hear them anymore and then dashing out again, running, hulking, galloping a sloppy gait in snow almost to his knees, with the sack clutched to his chest like it is a sack of gold, of glistening nuggets and bullion; Mac stumbling, dodging, slipping, lurking, like he somehow expects to maneuver between or around individual snowflakes; Mac staggering toward the mute gleam of small, niggard fires burning on the Amtrak freight lines, the flaming beckoning ties that he can hardly make out through the blizzard, his breath coming fast now with excitement because he is almost there, moving like a green-jacketed shadow, an invisible man in the near dark.

And it's almost like Vince can hear the sack, too, hear it mingled with the pounding in Mac's chest, the pulsing electric ticking of digitals.

He sits there, not feeling cold or warm, not feeling anything. He hugs the pint between his thighs, fiddling with its cap; vaporized, his breath appears then disappears in front of him. He is not aware that Stino still whisks past him, that the conveyor is still whirring, or that the Old Timer is still humming—until he hears the shots. He doesn't even think that this is why he has been sitting there, that this is the sound he has been waiting for, anticipating with every nerve ending, aching for—the sound he knew would come, and would come soon—until it came.

First there is one shot, carrying loud, deafening on frigid air; and the Old-Timer pauses in his spiritual. Then there is a volley of shots; and the Old-Timer halts completely.

And Stino has heard it, too—Vince knows this—that Stino has been listening for it, too. But Stino does not stop working; he begins to labor faster, dragging the sacks down with an increased tenacity, a viciousness— just as if he were assigned, by an invisible Wilson, to fill in for Mac.

"Wonder what that was?" Vince hears someone out front ask; he is not sure whether it is the Hippie or another sub.

A few quiet minutes pass in which he is not aware of anything, and then, "Oh shit! Oh shit!" From even in the trailer Vince can tell that it is Wilson, the voice excited, dismayed. "Oh shit! That fool McBrad done ran off and got himself shot!"

His thighs scream with pain from where he's been squeezing them together too long, and he relaxes them before he remembers the pint. He hears the clap of it slamming unbroken to the planks, and realizes that he has the unscrewed cap between his fingers. With his boots and slacks splattered, he jumps to his feet. Stino stands nearby with a sack's drawstring coiled and knotted in his fist; they face each other over the pint, watching it slosh gin, seeing a pool of it run and spread on the planks, mingling dark with the dust and dirt and mashed cigarette butts, vaporizing in the cold. A gust of blizzard wind swells against the trailer, making it sway; but neither of them stoop to pick the pint up.

*   *   *

Pushed up against the windows in Stino's first camp was his big, sturdy Singer machine. The windows faced east, and from them you could see across Wells, LaSalle, and Clark, the dividing line—to the tall sweep of Gold Coast condos.

Sometimes, when Stino sat at the machine and Vince was propped up in a cushioned chair beside him, they would stare out, watching the trickle of cars glide down LaSalle, the movement of fur-coated patrons in the Jewel parking lot, and the frozen vacant lot across from the Jewel, where, around Christmas time, a hut would appear to hawk evergreen trees to the young condo dwellers.

"I'm almost there," Stino would say sometimes, defiantly, having left something unfinished at the machine to pace back and forth in the window, glaring out. "Just a few blocks away..."

And Vince would know what he meant; any fool in his right mind would know what he meant. Just a few steps away from the Coast was that stretch of rich, exclusive land bordered by Chicago Avenue to the south and North Avenue to the north, where membership-only nightclubs abounded and swank watering holes featured nude dancing, where elegant, little restaurants had French names and tie-and-jacket dress codes, where nine out of every ten apartment buildings were condos ("to keep the niggas out" someone had once told Vince), where studios started upwards at three-fifty a month and two-bedroom were shoved out of the question. The Coast was doormen and underground parking, tree-lined streets and strolling poodle and afghan owners, designer blue jeans and fluffy fur coats, whisking taxi cabs and elegant horse-drawn coaches; but more than anything, the Coast was money. Stacks and stacks and stacks of money.

But that was the view from the front windows. No one ever looked out the back; the shade always stayed half-down, and a wilting plant sat on the sill. From the back windows, through the dry, spiraling twigs of the plant and the pane-frosted gray from your own vapor you could make out the grim network of buildings called Cabrini Green: An infamous project made up of ten and fourteen story high death traps, the color of red mud baked in a kiln, and 15,000 niggas stacked one on top of the other like beady-eyed rats in cages. And on summer nights, if you were quiet and stood in the window, you could hear the gunshots, or the intermittent wailing of an ambulance racing to the scene. And you'd almost believe that you could hear the people, too—the flash and swish of a razor slashing through air, the moans of someone cut and bleeding in a stairwell, the steady thump of a man's fist slowly, methodically, pounding his wife's face.

At the Hasty Tasty Cafe at Division and Clark, Vince and Stino sat over an enormous breakfast in a rear booth beside a window frosted with cold. Vince was cutting into a fat sausage when Stino waved his fork at the blurred window. "Check out the bum on the corner!"

Vince speared the sausage with his fork before turning to the window and wiping a sloppy peephole to see out. On the corner of Clark and Division near the subway steps stood a bummy black man with his hands on his hips. Dressed in faded woolens—the trousers too long and incredibly baggy, the jacket with its collar upturned against the cold—the man surveyed the area around him.

"Looks like he crawled out from under a rock," Vince says. Stino takes a sip from his coffee but says nothing; they both watch.

On a bench not too far from the man sits a small, wiry-looking white woman. She holds a quilted blanket in her arms with a tiny infant bundled up inside. A shawl is draped across her shoulders, and she uses its material in an attempt to conceal her heavy breast as the baby sucks and paws hungrily. She stares off blankly, not watching the man, but staring at the wide field that dominates the corner, the highrise condos that loom across it, their tall frames denting the gray morning.

"That chick on the bench don't look like she belongs around here either!" Vince says.

"But look at the dude's kicks," Stino says. Vince looks; the shoes look a lot newer than anything else the man wears—big, brown half-boots, shined to a "T".

"They look like brogans to me," Vince says around a mouthful of toast and eggs.

"Naw, I think they're tap-dance shoes," Stino says; he wipes a larger peephole on the glass.

A few condo owners amble by, muffled down in their furs, blinking curiously at the misfits that have infiltrated their neighborhood. A little girl in a mink jacket pries her hand loose from her mother and points a gloved finger at the black man. As if on some cue, the man whips off his battered felt hat and sets its crown down on the pavement.

"Watch him!" Stino says tensely; they both use napkins to clear a streaky rectangle on the pane.

There is a sudden and tremulous ringing on the pavement. The Tap-Dance man has begun to dance; his big, brown shoes, steel tapped on both heel and toe, bang out a rhythm on the concrete. Strollers stop to look at this stranger pounding out a song with his feet.

Stino slaps the table once with his fist: "Told-ja!"

The Tap-Dance man's face is drawn tight, intense, and yet expressionless; his legs shuffle with an agility so synchronized, so flawlessly timed as to be startling. He does a musical jig around his hat, and like a performing figure skater, his hands rapidly change positions—now folded behind his back, then buried in his pockets, and next reaching, stretching toward the sky. And his taps continue to ring while he primps and sashays around the hat—now rapid, staccato bursts, then slow, measured rolls. His soft-shoe bounces and rings off the fronts of buildings, slams against the window where Vince and Stino watch, echoes, resounds, and then mingles with the new music from his deranged feet.

And the woman on the bench continues to feed the child beneath the shawl, her face impassive as a rock, as though she has seen this dance, heard this song much too often. She looks off at the frozen field that stretches in front of her, its hard soil ridged with tractor tracks and the fossilized imprints of footsteps.

The passengers in a closed carriage, drawn by a noble black mare, peer out in amazement at the scene; then the driver, outfitted in top hat and full turn-of-the-century livery, cracks a whip over the mare's head and steers the beast around a corner. The suited occupants of a chauffeur-driven Rolls signal their driver to slow down while they stare over up-turned noses at the dancing black horror on their thoroughfare. A few strollers who have stopped to watch begin to turn away, some of them with tight looks on their faces, as though they had seen something which they did not want to see, had become aware of some truth of which they would have prefered to remain ignorant. Some flip a few coins into the hat; others simply trudge away, sneering with disgust.

But the Tap-Dance man swirls around and around, nimble as can be, never losing his step, never missing a beat, prancing from side to side—his taps striking the pavement with a precision timed almost to the point of igniting sparks. He feints to the left and feints to the right, shuffles backwards and pivots on his heels—all with the same grace and exactness, the ingrown dexterity, doing his soft-shoe with a passion so extreme that it seems as though, if he were to falter, make even the slightest error, this fragile bit of power contained in his feet might melt away.

And the crowd continues to watch him, those who have left being quickly replaced by newcomers. And the coins are intermittently flicked into the battered hat, being pulled from velvet change purses or the silk-lined pockets of minks and sables, wolverines and chinchillas.

Then from somewhere in the crowd, hidden from view—and Vince and Stino can hear this because a blast of cold air spits into the cafe as a customer eases out the door—a muffled voice calls out:

"Dance...! Dance, nigger, dance!"

And for the first time during his performance, the Tap-Dance man's feet land one micro-second later than timed, and for an instant his grim face becomes almost imperceptibly grimmer. But his feet dance on, his heels and toes kissing the pavement with renewed vigor, as though the deranged tip-tapping of his shoes could stamp out the hostility of the slur already spoken.

Then Stino slams down his fork; eggs and sausage jump a foot off the table. And before Vince can react, Stino is up and moving for the door without even bothering to throw on his alpaca.

"Hey, where you..." But Stino is already out the door, slashing diagonally through traffic toward the opposite corner. Vince starts to rise, then plops back down; through the window he sees Stino at the fringe of the crowd, shoving to get through, squeezing his way toward the dancing man. Pale faces, above knotted ties or circled by hooded furs, whirl around at Stino's intrusion.

Vince tenses. "Stino's about to start a race riot." Vince flings on his coat, grabs Stino's alpaca, throws a ten at the cashier, and makes it out the door in time to see Stino standing beside the dancing man. Stino kneels and places something inside the hat. In his blazer, standing beside the Tap-Dance man who is also without an overcoat, Stino and the man look something alike—like two misfits who have no business being on that side of Clark.

Again Stino pushes through the crowd and makes his way toward Vince. Vince notices the woman still sitting stiffly on the bench, staring out across the bleak winter landscape. She no longer feeds the infant but rocks it slowly, cradling its small form in her arms. She doesn't seem impressed by any of this; it's like she hasn't even noticed.

He holds the alpaca out to Stino. He sees a few members of the crowd pause to glare at him and Stino as they turn toward the apartment. Vince wonders idly if the Tap-Dance man and the woman on the bench are together.

How-to-Do-It-Better

HOW TO EAT A HOSTESS HO HO BETTER
Sue Ferraro

If you crave that creamy, chocolatey snack and a tall glass of milk, search your pantry for that coveted box or package of Hostess Ho Ho's. If you are a fanatic about that chocolate-covered cake roll, most likely you will choose the box of twelve with each separate morsel wrapped in aluminum foil, although if this desire is a once-in-a-while feeling, the package of two should be sufficient to satisfy the hunger that gnaws inside. No matter which category you place yourself under, the Ho Ho hallucination may come at any time of the day or night. You may crave one as you wake at the crack of dawn, or as the bus breaks down half way to your destination. It may come at the least expected moment. Maybe in the middle of a midterm, or after two hours of a ten-hour plan trip. Or, most dreaded, as you sit cozily with your boyfriend and he turns to say something romantic. You reply uncontrollably, "I'm starved. I've got this sudden craving for a Ho Ho." The memorable moment begins.

The important thing is not that the desire hits, but how you plan to *fill* the desire. The normal way of eating a Ho Ho, I'm sorry to say, is boring. There's no other way to describe it. You go to the pantry in search of something, anything, to eat. There is a debate in your mind as to which food to pick. There are cookies, potato chips, candy, crackers, donuts and Ho Ho's. It just so happens that the Ho Ho's catch your eye.

You pick up the package or box and place it on the kitchen table. Milk goes best with chocolate cake, so you go to the cabinet and grab a glass. Looking into the refrigerator, you get the gallon of milk and pour yourself a tall, cold glass and set it next to the Ho Ho's. There's nothing else to do except start eating.

You sit down with all the necessary gear in front of you. If it's a new box, you must tear off the perforated strip that holds the box closed. If the box is already open you've saved yourself a step and a few seconds. Remove the foil-wrapped Ho Ho with the thumb and first two fingers of your right hand. In no particular manner you tear the aluminum foil from the tiny package. If you deal with the package of two, you first tear the seal off the top, put the thumb and first two fingers in the package, and pull out a Ho Ho. The twin pack is much simpler to deal with 'cause it comes already shed of its foil wrap.

Now comes the part you've been waiting for! Eating it. First clutch the cake around its middle gently, so as not to squeeze it out of shape or force it to melt in your hand. Then, start biting from either end until it has been entirely consumed. Boring...

There's no technique, it goes by so fast. It has no grace, no poetry. You can't really admit you've enjoyed it. And the chocolate melts on your fingers and the palms of your hands. Too messy.

The proper way to eat a Ho Ho demands all the grace and class of a ballet. First you must know that it's a Ho Ho that you want to eat. The feeling must be such that if you find no Ho Ho's in the pantry or cupboard, you will be willing to trudge through rain or sleet or snow or dark of night until you find the treasure at a neighborhood grocery store.

When you finally find them, you pay the cashier with the last coins in your pocket. You ask her to put it in a brown paper bag so you won't look too conspicuous. With the energy you have left you rush home, anticipating the snack to come. All the while you should be careful not to squeeze the package and bruise the delicate morsels within. When you arrive at home, you gently set the package on the table and prepare for the ritual.

First you pour yourself a tall glass of milk and bring it to the table. After sitting down, you remove the box or package from the brown bag. If you have the box to deal with, the procedure is much like the standard way. You tear the perforated strip to open the box. Then remove the individually wrapped Ho Ho from its surroundings. You do this gently so as not to crack the chocolate frosting. Then neatly remove the aluminum foil so you won't tear it. You then place the cake on a plate and proceed to deal with the foil. The best way of doing this is to smooth the foil between the first two fingers of your right hand to get out as many wrinkles as possible. Then you fold it with your thumb on one flattened end of the log and your index finger on the other end, with the bottom end (seam) closest to you. Then you sink your teeth into the chocolatey layer, no farther. Piece by piece you remove the frosting with your teeth rotating the log with every bite. Savour the taste. After all the chocolate has been removed from the surface, you must then gently hold the Ho Ho around its middle and proceed to consume the chocolate from either end. The remainder is cake and cream.

However, there remains another technique. You notice the cake can be unrolled into one flat piece smeared generously with cream. But be careful when doing so, so the cake will not crumble. After unrolling the cake you hold it unrolled with your left hand. With the index finger of your right hand you scrape the creamy, white frosting from the surface. Then you put your finger to your mouth, opening your mouth enough to allow the cream-covered finger to go in. As the final knuckle of the finger enters the mouth, close your lips around it and slip your finger out. Savour the delight in your mouth. When the taste is gone and only the memory remains, eat the cake part with your own discretion. But—enjoy, enjoy.

In this way you're not eating it, you're EATING it. You'll smile, and the process will leave you feeling good all over. You may think, "It's an awful lot to go through just to eat a Ho Ho." I guess it might be, unless you're out to enjoy even the littlest things in life. A Ho Ho is just a small part of the Land of Hostess.

LET'S SPOIL BILLBOARDS:
A HOW-TO-USE-THEM-BETTER PROPOSAL
Cary Odes

In the town where I live, there is a wooden church almost a century old, with one large steeple housing the bells that chime every Sunday. Always wearing a fresh coat of white paint, the church and the small plot of green grass on which it stands are flawlessly maintained. There is only one thing that blemishes the beautiful scene, yet it destroys the setting so completely that it practically becomes a joke. No matter from what angle the church is viewed, a large blue and white revolving Mobil sign seems to be right in front of it, as if it were advertising the church and not the gas station next door.

Driving into the city of Chicago by any of three expressways, the commuter is confronted by a giant set of neon lips proclaiming "Magikist" as if it was the Lord's writing on Mt. Sinai. Below this puckered proclamation is a constantly changing epilogue, keeping all of literate Chicagoland posted on the cost of carpet cleaning for three rooms, the price of "Sparkle," and the correct time and temperature. Our cities are full of signs that smoke cigarettes, change pictures, and run around corners. They beg us to buy, travel, rent, save, and drink alcoholic beverages. Advertisements even tell us to watch TV shows designed to get us to watch more advertisements. Out in the open countryside, signs let us know how far it is to the nearest Stuckey's, Holiday Inn, or McDonald's. It is never far enough.

The success of signs depends largely upon the ability of the human mind to do more than one thing at a time. Although a person may be driving, talking, or listening to the radio, advertisers know that a great percentage of the conscious and unconscious mind is free to receive messages on how to spend money. Another criterion for a sign's success is its ability to attract attention. This can be done, among other ways, by making it fifty feet long, red, and flashing. And so the world becomes a giant television screen of commercials, without the blessing of an off button.

Not only are the location and function of road signs obtrusive, but the messages they contain are characteristically insulting. Rarely missing from a billboard scene is a woman, in various stages of undress, finding sexual satisfaction with a muffler, bottle of scotch, or cigarette. The woman and the product form a unit; you get one when you get the other. Somehow, though, the thought of going out with a 25-foot, two dimensional beachcomber from an Air Jamaica billboard seems less than appealing.

Another common denominator of the roadsign world is the smile, the promise of happiness through consumerism. Buy and you shall know the holy bliss of this grin. Indeed the people look as if they had found God, and all it took was the right beer. It is this look of unreachable glee that lures us to the marvels of new car payments and color television sets.

But don't get me wrong. I'm not some kind of purist nut who wants to abolish all signs. Even though I know they bombard us everywhere, desecrating architectural landmarks and cluttering even the best planned boulevards, I would not tear them down. Even though it would be so relaxing without neon lightning bolts flashing for our attention, I would still leave them standing. I have a different plan.

First I will buy the Magikist sign on the Eisenhower Expressway, and convince two friends of mine to do likewise with the Kennedy and Dan Ryan signs. Then the three of us will begin to flash outlandish remarks on the lighted grid, such as:

"Margaret, I've always loved you," or,

"Carpets mowed and fertilized, 3 rooms, $25."

Along with this will be the incorrect time and temperature; 72 degrees centigrade in summer, and 0 degrees Kelvin in winter. With luck, after a month, someone will have noticed the change.

Next on my list is to change the airline billboards near O'Hare Airport into advertisements for wagon trains west. This would serve as a hint to those who settled in Chicago only because they gave up half way to the Pacific. A small percentage of the signs around town would be reserved for nothing less than my own portrait, my name clearly printed underneath but without the pushy sell-lines "Elect," "Buy," or "Watch."

Soon I should be enough of a public figure to write a book about myself. With the money from royalties and ensuing TV appearances, I will be ready for operation on a grander scale. I will buy every roadsign along the 3,000-mile length of Route 80. Each sign will be painted with consecutive frames from a first-run movie going one way, and its sequel going the other. By driving at 55 miles per hour, everyone can watch a movie as they cross the country. New York, Omaha and Cheyenne will serve as popcorn stands. The effects would be astounding. People would drive more, in spite of the rising gasoline costs, since they could save on rising movie costs. Not only would people drive more often, but they would drive farther, sometimes even farther than they had intended. Who could turn off at Indianapolis when the climax was building for Cleveland? Mystery movies would force people to drive clear to the ocean to find out who the murderer really was.

What is the purpose of this madness, you may ask.

"Jobs for sign painters!" I will reply. The real madness was allowing the things to go up in the first place. What is on the signs is only secondary.

While the crews are out painting over all the advertisements, they might as well change some direction-signs as well. Nine miles out of Portland would be an interesting place for a sign that reads:

"Miami, 5 miles."

Actually, I propose something a little more organized than that. Why not change all the signs so that no matter where in the country a person leaves from, and no matter where they want to go, the signs will direct them to one particular location. Imagine the fun of having every driver in the country winding up in Detroit. The confusion would be marvelous. Millions of automobiles would clog the entrances to the city, all the drivers expecting to be in different places. Some cars would have skis on the roof. others would have surfboards, and there they'd be, in Detroit.

Once they are in the city, one-way street signs will lure drivers down a labyrinth. No matter where they try to go, once they are caught in the maze it will guide them, draw them along its one-way net to a large park. Cars will gather there, arriving on one-way streets, all of which lead to the park, but none of which lead back out.

The possibilities at this point are endless. If I wanted money, I could open one street as an exit and charge a nickel toll. If I wanted to end pollution, I could trap all the cars until they ran out of gas. I could open up a hot dog stand, or sell soft drinks. The power of a nation would be in my hands, and I could probably find a good deal on a used Volvo.

Perhaps I am mad after all, but who can say for sure. Wouldn't it be grand! It would add flair and humor to a country which either ignores its problems or takes them too seriously. It would add spark to the lives of every traveler.

"Dear, guess what I saw on the way to work today, 'Gone With the Wind.'"

People would finally get out from in front of their TV sets and back out into the streets. Americans would be inspired to see America. Best of all, everyone would get a chance to visit Detroit.

Does this sound a bit far-fetched? I've got more down-to-earth ideas, too. Why not teach kids to read with billboards. All along school-bus routes, there could be signs with simple sentences, mathematic equations, and historical dates. If we're going to exploit our environment, we might as well make it worthwhile.

After all, advertisers will find another way to sell their products, maybe through sky writing or painting the pavement. Heaven knows we'll learn to live with it just like we live with other things today.

Perhaps, too, I'm being old-fashioned. Signs may be destined for obsolescence, along with cars and roads. People will watch ads on portable TV's and travel in personal-sized jets. No one will watch my movies on route 80 or end up in Detroit. But some day you may be able to see the fruits of my labor on a night with a full moon. Somewhere, just above the Great Crater will be a sign reading:

"Chicago, 5 miles."

DEAR HENRY
Daniel Andries

Dear Henry,

Your design plans for building a small, personal horseless transport (what did you call it, automobile?) looked very interesting. Getting rid of the horse was, in my estimation, the real stroke of genius. Horses are a pain— always wanting grain and water, crapping all over the street, getting spooked, turning carriages over, and taking off on the spur of the moment. The driver is at the mercy of that miserable beast. Horrible. My Aunt Bertha was trampled by one of the stampeding mongrels just last week. But that's another story.

Despite all these overwhelming assets, Henry, there are a number of problems with your design which negate the advantages that are inherent in the mere pondering of the idea of a horseless, self-propelled vehicle. Let me review the plans you sent us to make sure that we are both clear as to what it is specifically that I'm objecting to.

There is a basic carriage. It has a seat in the front for the driver. It has four wheels, two on each side. Behind this driver is an engine, a gas-propelled engine. Behind this first carriage is a second four-wheeled wagon so to speak. This wagon has two benches, with a total seating capacity of four people. Now, through the back of the carriage and into the bottom of the wagon sticks a rod. You call this a crankshaft. Suits me fine. To start the automobile, the driver turns a key in a lock system that starts a burst of electricity. The electricity travels down some wires to the wagon in back.

In this wagon sit four men. Each man has a metal ring strapped to his neck, and clipped to the ring are the wires. Each one of these men, as you specified in your plans, have had their heads shaved and are wearing wet packs upon their bald scalps to keep them moist. (Your studies with electricity have revealed that water is an excellent conductor.) The wire travels above the wetted cranium and back down to the other side of the metal ring. The wire is then connected in a similar manner to the other three men before it travels on back to the front of the automobile.

These four men, if we are to go by what you have written in your blueprint, Henry, are sitting back in that wagon to get the crankshaft turning. The point of the electricity? You state: A) Most importantly to give each man more energy, thereby giving a bigger and faster start to the crankshaft, and B) To wake up any of the men who may have fallen asleep back in the wagon. You go into a lengthy discussion of the utter boredom of this job which I shall not reprint here. I shall instead merely refer to it. You claim the job is dull. I'd say it's rather electrifying, but that's neither here nor there. You state often, after traveling a great distance over the plains with little to do but watch the scenery, the crankshaft men, for lack of a better title, may fall asleep. Yet they may be needed at a moment's notice to start the automobile. It would be foolish and entirely uneconomical in any sense of the word to go back and wake each one up individually. So, you suggest that by running the electricity through their bodies, you should certainly have them wide awake in little or no time at all.

Directly behind the driver, on a small wooden platform with a hole in the center of it, sits another man. The hole in the center of the platform is connected via a funnel to the engine block where the gasoline, which propels the craft, ignites, thereby getting the engine going. The man on the platform sits above the hole. He has at his disposal approximately three cans, each containing two gallons of gasoline. His job is to pour that petrochemical fuel through the hole and into the funnel to keep the engine fed with gasoline. When he has emptied the first two containers and is pouring the contents of the third into the engine, he is to yell "One gallon left." The driver, according to your plans, should then pull over into a gas station to get more gas. This part of your plan thoroughly confused me. Henry, what in God's name, may I ask you, is a gas station and where does one find one? (We were also wondering where one would keep the key to the public restroom in one of these gas stations.)

We finally get back to the front of the automobile, where the driver, who has set everything in motion, should be ready to drive the automobile. To get the thing in motion, he must first push a stick forward, which will, you say, put the automobile in gear, or, in laymen's terms, make it ready to roll. The car moves. The speed of its motion is determined by how much gasoline is being poured into the engine at any given moment by the man who's sitting behind the driver. The driver also has an apparatus strapped to his head which helps to direct the car in the direction he wishes it to go. It is a canvas strapping that goes around the back of the head. The strap is connected to a metal bar, which is finally connected, after a complicated system of hinges and rods, to the axle on which the wheels turn. All the driver has to do, one would suppose, is to turn the head in the direction one wishes to go. The car should then bear in that direction. For a turn around a corner, for instance, the driver would turn his head a full 90°.

The vehicle is now moving, heading in different directions and accelerating at the whim of the gasoline pourer. The question of how to stop this eight-wheeled, six-passengered automobile (let me take this moment to commend you on the title you chose for this contraption, Henry; self-propelled, as auto denotates, moving vehicle, as mobile so subtly suggests) remains unanswered. Let us then apply ourselves to your solution of that problem.

You have added two more people to the automobile. They are positioned one on each side of the driver. But these two men have no seats to sit on (the least of their worries). They have instead been placed on the outside of the vehicle on two long boards that run along the sides of the carriage. These boards are called (once again, may I commend you on your cleverness, Henry) running boards. They stand on these running boards, hanging on the sides of the carriage, and when they are so told by the driver, they either do one of two things to stop the automobile. They can: A) grab onto the bar that is sticking out of the side of the car and hang down to the ground, dragging their feet and legs along the road, thereby causing friction, which should slow the vehicle down and eventually stop it, or B) for quicker stops, climb to the front of the carriage and throw themselves down by the wheels.

You claim to have devised the method for merely slowing the car down by observing some young children at a playground. They were playing on one of those nauseating merry-go-rounds. To stop themselves and the playground device, they dragged their bodies along the sides of it, using the friction caused by their bodies interacting with the ground.

I like your application of the scientific method of observation in tackling the problem of stopping your invention. It shows a keen and open mind, Henry. But I believe it also reveals one of your biggest flaws. That is that your analytical mind never thought of the practicalities involved in your current design. You obviously never built and tested a model of your automobile. But we did.

Let us take first things first, Henry. The matter of the four baldheaded men in the back with wet scalps who get an electrical current sent through their bodies. There are a number of problems with this idea.

First off, when you run that electric current down that wire, into that metal ring, up over their heads, back down, into the next metal ring, and through the next man in a likewise fashion, you end up with more than a crankshaft turning at a rapid rate. You end up with four perfectly dead men. You kill them. They die. They fry right before your eyes. While this has unlimited potential in terms of family barbecues and night lighting, and while it's true that the crankshaft is sent spinning, you now have four dead people in the back of your automobile. And here in Michigan, killing people by running electrical charges through their bodies and driving them off into the countryside is definitely considered a crime that is punishable by law. As a matter of fact, Henry, we may all get to experience the feeling of electricity running through our bodies if we continue to run an automobile in this fashion.

We've tested this method for starting a car twice now, thinking that maybe the first time we'd made some technical error in setting up the apparatus. But the only mistake we made was believing in your plans and in your judgment as an inventive genius. We are now preparing eight funeral services and consoling eight widows and approximately 45 children who no longer have fathers. That's quite a responsibility, I really don't believe that this is any way to start out the Ford Motor Company.

From a pure practical standpoint, Henry, dead men in the back of the vehicle are of no use to anybody. They can never start the automobile again. In fact, they can't do much of anything again. It's truly a one-shot deal. As as for the fact that it will certainly wake them up, I believe the facts bear witness that it just might have been a little more economical to go back there and wake each one up individually. The electricity, I assure you, will put them into a state of slumber that no driver will be able to cope with.

There is next the matter of the man who sits on the platform behind the driver and pours gasoline into the engine to keep it going and to get the automobile moving faster. There is a very interesting effect that occurs whenever one pours gasoline over anything hot. It explodes. And if it does not explode, it ignites, sending flames shooting high into the sky. While one must admit that one cannot help but be fascinated and intrigued, and attracted by the sight of a 20-foot flame rising high into the night air, that is hardly the subject at hand. I will agree that you wanted the gasoline to explode, for that was the phenomenon by which you got your automobile mobile. I do, however, believe that it was your intention for the explosion to be controlled and contained within the engine block itself. This was not at all the result. The engine exploded and caught fire, burning the poor man on the platform, setting the platform on fire, setting the automobile on fire. Pieces of metal, gaskets, rings, washers, driers, whatever, went flying in every direction. It was what one would call a genuine honest-to-God mess, Henry, yes that's what it was. And Henry, I can see no redeeming social value in having pistons and gaskets and springs flying from here to there and back again. If you can come up with such a value, please contact me immediately. I'd be very interested in hearing what you'd have to say.

We now get to the steering device, which I described as being strapped to the head of the victim, I mean driver and otherwise intrepid pilot of this flaming hearse, which now carries a total of five dead bodies in it. The first time we tested the apparatus, it pulled the driver straight down and wrapped him quickly around the axle. It only took one revolution of the axle to do it. Not a very sporting way to spend a leisurely afternoon. The second time we tested the apparatus, the driver was able to remain in his seat and was not pulled down to the bottom of the vehicle. Instead, when he attempted to turn his head, he broke his neck. This second driver was luckiest of all the people who helped to test this wonderful new invention of yours. He lived. His neck is broken, he's paralyzed for life, but he lived.

There are a number of problems with this steering apparatus that have nothing to do with broken necks and twisted bodies. If, by some freak accident of nature, this contraption for steering an automobile worked with some degree of accuracy, any slight motion of the driver's head would send the vehicle swerving off in directions the driver didn't wish to go. If he turned to look back at his gasoline pourer, (say he should live too), to tell him to cut the gas, or to increase the flow, for that matter, the results would be catastrophic. The vehicle would swerve and crash. And to talk to the gasoline pourer, or even to the running board men, you have to look in their general direction and yell. The noise of the engine makes any normal communication impossible and the speed of the car in the wind also cuts down on the ability to hear while maneuvering the auto or receiving commands from the driver. Actually, I believe that the title of 'driven' would be more appropriate for him at this point in time.

We finally get to the men who stand on the running boards. The problems of scraped knees which you most likely encountered when you observed the school children at play is the least of one's worries here. By hanging from the side of the car, clinging onto a bar to stop the automobile, the men received broken hips, lacerations of the skin, slipped discs, and there was much blood and often death. When the automobile deaccelerators climbed in front of the carriage, and when they flung themselves in front of the wheels, once again, like the other parts of your automobile, it did not achieve the purpose it was designed to achieve. It merely resulted in the death of two more loyal employees, and I assure you, Henry, loyal employees will be even harder to find after this. They were crushed underneath the wheels by the sheer weight and momentum of the automobile, and they succeeded in setting the vehicle further off course and finally, onto its side. It very definitely came to a halt, but in no kind of efficient or orderly manner.

So picture, if you can, Henry, your invention. A key is turned. Four bald-headed men with 45 children between them all light up and die. The engine catches on fire and the vehicle begins to accelerate at a rapid rate. The engine blows up, giving the carriage a further boost. The wagon hits a rock and goes flying off in another direction, breaking the crankshaft. The driver turns to see what has happened and the car takes a sharp left towards a small farm house. This flaming rocket on wheels is heading towards private property now. It's heading toward Bible Belt Republicans, Henry. The two men on the running board jump off the front of the carriage; it runs over them, and still on fire mind you, turns over and rolls into the side of the house. The entire automobile blows up, and the farmer's daughter and his horses are killed. So, all totaled, first and second trial run, the death toll lies at sixteen people and one horse dead. One seriously injured.

Henry, while you claim to have been poorly educated in the humanities, and know little of literature, especially European literature, I find it hard to believe that you are not familiar with the writings of the Marquis de Sade. While you lack the erotic touch that made de Sade so fascinating, you make up for that inadequacy by the sheer force of your imagination. The only use I can see for this automobile as it now stands is that which the state would put it to. I'm sure that the Michigan State Prison Authority would see its value as a viable alternative to the electric chair. You can kill off eight at once. Due to the visual thrill involved in watching this spectacle, you could certainly bring into the State of Michigan much needed revenue by just charging 50 cents a head; 25 cents for students with IDs and senior citizens, to watch the execution. My only concern lies in the fact that the sport would die out as quickly as the condemned prisoners would.

Beyond that, I can see no practical use for this death trap of yours. The horse is beginning to sound much more attractive, and the shit on the streets is certainly preferable to dead bodies falling out of the back of the automobiles as they go rocketing off to a certain end in the corners of farmhouses, or trees, brick buildings, or even rivers, which would be preferable, for the fire would be extinguished. There is nothing safe nor sane about this invention as it now stands. In fact, I will go so far as to say that this automobile of yours is unsafe at any speed.

Let us digress for a moment, and assume, most assuredly in a state of temporary insanity, that this automobile worked in a safe and orderly fashion without threat to life and/or property. Where would one get the seven men besides the driver (who would of course be under the impression that he was driving it for pleasure) who would be needed to get the car started, control the acceleration, and stop the thing? One would have to keep a veritable army of slaves, fed, and in good health, to merely take a leisurely drive through the countryside. It would be entirely uneconomical. Furthermore, the sheer weight of all those men would make it very hard for the automobile to move at all, much less turn corners and accelerate. Assume that each man weighed 165 pounds. That would total 1320 pounds. The engine alone weighs a good 200 pounds. The car would surely be overloaded, and not only would a horse be faster, it would be entirely feasible to carry eight people in a carriage drawn by a horse. Merely add another horse. To add another engine to your automobile would require another five men at least, and hence defeat the entire purpose of using another engine.

We've carefully considered your design, as you can tell. Henry, we wish to show you that we have faith in you. I don't know why, but we do. Therefore, we've come up with a list of suggestions to improve the design of your automobile.

First off, I'd suggest destroying the concept of relying heavily on human beings to start, stop, and accelerate the car by themselves. We suggest placing a hand crank on the front of the car which would be hooked up to a spring, and when turned in a clockwise manner and released, would release the tension of the spring and start the crankshaft turning. Much safer. The gas could be held in a tank, and there could be a pump of some kind that the driver could control to oversee the flow of gasoline and hence, the speed of the car. Furthermore, the driver could have a steering device that he could operate with his hands, leaving his hand free to think, observe its surroundings, and react to the different situations it might encounter while driving. And finally, a stick on the driver's left that would be connected to stoppers, like door jambs or hard rubber bricks, would, when pulled back, engage the bricks and stop the car (by means of friction, by the way). I believe that if these suggestions are taken to heart, something can be worked out in that head of yours, Henry. We eagerly await your reply and your new set of design plans. Good luck Henry, and thank you.

Sincerely,

Chairman of the Board of Trustees
Ford Motor Company

P.S. If you're still interested in talking to the authorities about the possible use of your present design as a means of execution, that address is: Michigan State Prison Authority, Rock and Strown Toads Road, Barn Falls, Michigan. We'd also like you to know that despite threats of possible litigation against us, we are refusing to give out your first name and your address to the families of those killed while testing your design. We suggest you keep a low profile in the weeks to come, for your own well-being.

Folktales

JABBO AND THE HAIRY DEMON
Reginald Carlvin

Jabbo's daddy was a heathen and a no-good thief. He stole corn and watermelons in the dark of the moon, grew marijuana in his backyard, robbed a dead man, killed a pregnant roach, and worse than that, belched in the preacher's face at church. So everybody thought that when Jabbo's daddy died he'd never get to heaven because the Hairy Demon would surely grab him first. That must have been the way it happened, because they never found him after he fell off the ferry boat in the Mississippi River where the current flows quicker than anywhere else. They looked for him a long way down river and in the still pools between the sandbanks, but they never found Jabbo's daddy. And they heard a big man laughing across the river, and everybody said, "That's the Hairy Demon and he's the devil's right-hand man." So they stopped looking for Jabbo's daddy.

"Jabbo," his mama told him, "the Hairy demon has got yo' pappy and he's going to get you if you don't watch out."

"Yas'm," he said, "I'll look out. I'll take my hound dogs everywhere I go. The Hairy Demon can't stand no hound dog." Jabbo knew this because his mama told him. And his mama knew about things like witches, ogres, trolls, man-eating monsters, and hairy demons.

One day Jabbo took his axe and went down in the swamp and cut some poles for a hen-roost, and his hounds went with him. But they took out after a rabbit and ran it so far off, Jabbo couldn't even hear them yelp.

"Well," he said, "I hope the Hairy Demon ain't nowhere round here now." He picked up his axe to start cutting poles, but he looked up and there came the Hairy Demon through the trees grinning. He was sure ugly and his grin didn't help much. He was hairy all over. His red eyes burned like fire, and spit drooled all over his big yellow teeth.

"Don't look at me like that," said Jabbo, but the Hairy Demon kept coming towards him and grinning, so Jabbo threw down his axe and climbed up a big, 40-foot bay tree. He saw the Hairy Demon didn't have feet like a man but like a duck, and Jabbo had never seen a duck climb up a bay tree.

"What are you doing up there?" the Hairy Demon asked Jabbo when he got to the bottom of the tree.

Jabbo climbed nearly to the top of the tree and looked down. After taking one look at them big yellow teeth, he climbed straight to the top.

"Boy, how come you climbing that there tree so fast?" the Hairy Demon asked.

"My mama told me to stay away from you. What you got in that potato sack?"

"I ain't got nothing yet."

"Go on, get away from here," said Jabbo, hoping the slim tree would grow some more.

"Shut up, boy! I'm taking your ass to hell with your no-good father. The boss-man done gave me my orders!" The Hairy Demon swung Jabbo's sharp axe and wooden chips splattered everywhere. It went this way all afternoon, Jabbo hollering and the Hairy Demon chopping. He hollered till he was hoarse and the Hairy Demon was gaining on him.

"I'll come down half-way," he said, "if you'll make this bay tree a little bit taller."

"I ain't doing nothing, so you might as well come on down," said the Hairy Demon, swinging the axe.

"I bet you can't make this tree taller," said Jabbo.

"You must be crazy, come on down, boy, I've got something to show you," said the Hairy Demon.

Then they went at it again, Jabbo hollering and the Hairy Demon copping. Jabbo had just about yelled himself out when he heard his hound dogs yelping in the distance.

"Hyeaaah, dogs, hyeeah," he hollered. "Come save me from this evil old demon."

"Shut up, goddamnit! Your dogs ain't coming, I sent that rabbit here to draw 'em off."

"Hyeaah, dog," hollered Jabbo, and they both heard the hound dogs coming closer and closer. The Hairy Demon looked worried.

"Come on down, boy" he said, "and I'll teach you some magic tricks."

"Bullshit, I can learn all the magic tricks I want from my mama."

The Hairy Demon cussed and slobbered some more, but he threw the axe down and ran into the swamp.

When Jabbo got home he told his mother that the Hairy Demon had almost got him, but his dogs ran him off.

"Did he have his potato sack?"

"Yes'm."

"Next time he come after you, don't you climb no bay tree."

"Why, mama?!"

"Look, boy, don't you climb no kind of tree. Just stay on the ground and say, 'Hello, Mr. Hairy Demon,' You hear me, son?"

"No'm, I don't understand."

"He can't hurt you. There is a way to get rid of him."

"How?"

"You just do like I tell you. First walk up to him and say, 'Hello, Mr. Hairy Demon; I heard you're the best magician around here.' He'll probably say, 'I reckon I am.' Then you'll say, 'I bet you can't turn yourself into an elephant.' But remember, you kept telling him he can't and he'll finally do it. Then you say, 'I bet you can't turn yourself into a giraffe.' And he'll do it. After he does that you say, 'Anybody can turn themselves into something bigger than a man, but I bet you can't turn yourself into a frog.' When he does it, you grab him and throw him in the sack."

"It doesn't sound right," said Jabbo, "but I'll try it." So he tied up his dogs so they wouldn't scare away the Hairy Demon, and went down to the swamp again. He hadn't been there long when he looked up and there came the Hairy Demon grinning through the trees, hairy all over and his sharp teeth showing more than ever. He knew Jabbo came without his hound dogs. Jabbo nearly climbed a tree when he saw the potato sack, but he didn't.

"Hello, Mr. Hairy Demon," he said.

"Hello, Jabbo." He took the sack off his shoulder and opened it up.

"Mr. Hairy Demon, I heard you are the best magician around here."

"Damn right, I am."

"I bet you can't turn yourself into an elephant."

"That's no problem," said the Hairy Demon.

"I bet you can't do it."

So the Hairy Demon twisted around and turned himself into an elephant.

"I bet you can't turn yourself into a giraffe."

The elephant spun around and turned into a giraffe, all the time watching Jabbo to see he didn't try to run.

"Anybody can become something bigger than a man," said Jabbo, "but I bet you can't turn yourself into a frog."

The giraffe twisted around and turned into a frog and Jabbo grabbed it and threw it in the sack. Jabbo tied the sack up as tight as he could and then he threw it in the river. He went home through the swamp and when he looked up, there came the Hairy Demon grinning through the trees. Frightened, Jabbo climbed straight up the old bay tree.

"I bet you're wondering how I got out of that sack. Well, I just turned myself into the wind and blew out. Now listen up, Jabbo, I'm going to sit right here till you get hungry and fall out of that bay tree. I got you cornered, so you might as well give up.

Jabbo thought awhile. He looked at the Hairy Demon and the hound dogs tied up almost a mile away. "Well," he said, "you've outsmarted me. But I bet you can't make things disappear."

"Hell, that's what I'm good at. Look at that there bird-nest on the limb. Now look, it's gone!"

"How do I know it was there in the first place? I bet you can't make something I know is there disappear."

"Ha ha," laughed the Hairy Demon. "Look at your shirt."

Jabbo looked down and his shirt was gone, but he didn't care because that was just what he wanted the Hairy Demon to do. "That was just a plain old shirt," he said. "But I bet you can't make the rope around my breeches disappear."

"Boy, I can make all the rope in this country disappear."

"I dare you!"

The Hairy Demon became angry and stuck his prickly chest way out. He opened his mouth wide and hollered aloud, "From now on all the rope in this country has disappeared."

Jabbo reared back holding his breeches with one hand and a tree limb with the other. "Hyeaah, dog," he hollered loud enough to be heard more than a mile away. The loose dogs chased the Hairy Demon through the swamps, taking vicious bites at his hairy skin. When Jabbo and his dogs got back home, his mother asked him if he put the Hairy Demon in the potato sack.

"Yes'm, but he turned himself into the wind and blew right through the sack."

"That's bad," said his mother. "You've fooled him twice; if you fool him again he'll leave you alone. But he'll be mighty hard to fool the third time."

"I'll think of something," she said, and then she sat down by the fire and held her chin between her hands and thought real hard.

But Jabbo wasn't thinking about anything except how to keep the demon away from the house. He took his dogs and tied one at the back door and one at the front door. Then he crossed a baseball bat and an axe handle over the window and put some more wood in the fireplace.

After a little while his mother said, "Jabbo, go down to the chicken coop and get that little baby chick away from that old hen."

Jabbo went down and snatched the baby chick out of the coop and left the old hen squawking and fussing angrily. He took the baby chick to his mother and she put it in his bed.

"No, Jabbo," she said, "you go up and hide in the loft."

So he did. Before long he heard the wind whistling and the trees shaking, and then his dogs started growling. He looked out through a knothole in the planks and saw the dog at the front door looking toward the swamps, with his fur standing up and his lips drawn back in a snarl. The dog jumped and jerked but he couldn't get loose. Then suddenly, with one frenzied motion, he tore loose from the rope and ran into the swamps. Jabbo looked out another hole at the back of the loft just in time to see his other dog jerk loose and take out after some imaginary animal which the Hairy Demon had conjured up. "Aw, shit," said Jabbo. "The Hairy Demon is here for sure!"

Suddenly, he heard something with feet like a duck scrambling around on the roof. He knew it was the Hairy Demon, because he heard him damn and swear when he touched the hot chimney. The Hairy Demon jumped off the roof when he found out there was a fire in the fireplace and came up and knocked on the front door, as big as you please.

"Ma'am," he hollered, "I done come after your baby boy."

"You ain't gonna get him," Jabbo's mother hollered back.

"Give him here or I'll set your house on fire with lightning."

"I got plenty of water to put it out with."

"Give him here or I'll kill your crops, eat your animals, and take away your year's supply of ExLax."

"Hairy Demon, you wouldn't do all that. That's mighty mean."

"Sweetheart, I'm a mighty mean man, I ain't never seen a man as mean as me."

"If I give you my baby, will you get away from here?"

"I give you my word," said the Hairy Demon, so she let him in.

"He's over there in the bed," Jabbo's mother said.

The Hairy Demon came in the room grinning from ear to ear. He walked over to the bed and snatched the covers back. "Hey," he hollered, "there ain't nothing in this bed but a little baby chick!"

The Hairy Demon cursed and yelled. He stomped all over the house gritting his teeth. Then he grabbed the baby chick and tore out through the swamp, knocking down trees left and right. When the Hairy Demon left, Jabbo came down from the loft.

"Is he gone, Mama?"

"Yes, son, he's gone. He's been fooled three times."

And to this day, the Hairy Demon has never ever bothered anyone again.

THE ENCHANTED PAIL: A FOLK TALE
Laura D. Allen

Once upon a time all men pumped the water and all wives received it in silver buckets. That was the way of the world and no one ever questioned it but once.

It happened in the town of N--. A man and wife who had just recently been married had been going to the pump together nightly for a time when the wife began to find this arrangement was not suited to her. She tried to smile up sweetly at him, but the weight of the water falling into the bucket was a strain, and each night the water seemed to get heavier than it had been the night before. The man did not notice the strain in his wife's sweet face as he barely noticed his wife at those times. He was too busy pumping and meanwhile talking about himself and what a day he had had that day. In fact, it was difficult to tell who spouted more, the pump or the man.

At last, one night, the wife asked the man if she could try the pumping sometime.

"A man receive water from a woman? The world just doesn't work that way!" cried the man. "Besides," he added, "you haven't the strength. Wives weren't made for such things."

Still, that did not put an end to the issue. She brought the subject up each day over his breakfast. Then she began bringing it up over his lunch and pretty soon was bringing it up over his dinner, too, until he could not eat a meal in peace. And when she held the bucket, she no longer smiled up at him prettily. She would wince and complain or look very sullen, pouting so hard that her lower lip resembled a shelf.

One night, furiously angry with his wife for all her complaining, he pumped that silver handle for all he was worth and sent torrents of water down upon her, nearly drowning her. After that they were both quiet for days and he was more tender toward her than he had been in months.

Yet, after a time the man's wife began giving him long looks again and he guessed he knew what those were about. So, finally, the man decided he would take the issue upon himself to end and he went, secretly, to see a sorcerer.

"Use this silver pail," the sorcerer said, handing the young man an enchanted pail, "and agree to your wife's request. This will put an end to her foolish ideas and return you two to your proper state. But, mark me," he warned, "do not gaze upon your wife while she is pumping the water, or you will be undone."

The young man assured the sorcerer he would heed his warning, took the pail, and went off swinging it happily.

That night, after switching the new pail for the old, he called to his wife. "Come! Why don't you pump tonight? I am tired and fain would receive the water," he said. Scarcely able to contain her joy, she sprang up, kissed him, and grabbed hold of the handle of the enchanted pail. So, together they ran down the hill to the pump, swinging the pail between them.

A joyful and grateful wife is a beautiful and tender creature. So joyful and grateful was she that her husband almost regretted having begun the trickery that would raise her foolish hopes, then crush them. Still, he felt she had to be put in her place.

So, at the pump he took the bucket handle firmly, went down on one knee beneath the spout, and fastened his eyes on the sight of a nearby hill. Then his wife began her pumping. No sooner had a trickle come from the mouth of the faucet than did the pail flip over upside down—of its own accord—and refuse to receive the water. Instead of filling the pail, the water drummed against the bottom of it like fingers thrumming on a kitchen table.

"What's this? The bucket is perverse!" said she. "This water is surely as sweet as any you've pumped, yet the pail will not drink!"

Again she tried, putting her back and shoulders into it. This time the water gushed more strongly from the pump, but the bucket flipped up and over as before, refusing the stream a second time. This time the cold water ricocheting off the metal hit the man full in the face, just as if a cold hand had slapped him. It stung, but it was not enough to turn his head.

Finally, with a slight tremble in her voice, his wife announced she would try one last time before giving up. She was mightily determined to make a success of the situation. Well, as always, the first water from her pumping that fell upon the pail caused it to flip over. But this time the splashing water wet the man's shirt just as his wife's tears often had after she had had a trial of some sort. And the man turned away from the hill.

Who can say what tempted him to turn? Perhaps he had to see if his wife were crying or not. Perhaps the tremble in her voice moved him. Some think he wanted to steal a glance at a wife so filled with brave determination—and making such odd grunting sounds. Others have conjectured that the sun, which was setting behind the hill, might have flashed so terribly bright that he had thought only to escape its glare in turning his head. But he turned and, intentionally or not, he looked up at his wife. In that moment, he was undone.

He had never seen anyone like her. He hardly knew her as his wife. Never had she been so radiant. Never had she been so glorious. With her hair wild as fire, her cheeks aglow, and her whole body working in a rhythm, she was more beautiful than she'd ever looked when she had smiled sweetly up at him with every strand of hair neatly tucked in place. He gaped at this woman as if seeing her for the first time. He was proud of this woman for the first time, and God, this was a woman to be proud of. Ah, unfortunate man, to see the woman in your wife too late!

No sooner had he looked than did the pail drop aright to receive the water. Seeing this, the woman threw back her head with relief and joy but didn't forget the work at hand. Nearly straddling the handle, she began to ride it as though it were a silver stallion. She rode wild and free and the pail was greedy for her water. It seemed never to get its fill before its mouth gaped still wider.

All the while the avalanching water beat the pail about, the man tried to keep the thing steady. Icy torrents that missed the bucket stripped the grass from the hillside, drenched the ground, and soaked the man until he shivered cold. Finally, he let the bucket rest on his knee for support, but the pounding water drove his leg right into the mud as easily as a hammer pounds a post. That's when he tried to rise up and pull his leg free, but the pail on top of it was as big as a washtub by then and the mud was too slick and soft to give him good footing. He slipped and fell backwards into mud deep as a down bed and before he could pull himself out of it, the fast-growing bucket stretched over him like an immense tombstone. He glimpsed the stars, the bright moon, and the woman's rosy face. Then, all was darkness. The weight of the water was upon him, crushing him and pressing him deep into the suffocating mud.

Heedless of this, the woman rode on wild and free for the rest of the night. With her head tossed back laughing and her wild hair flying free, slapping her back, she rode. And all night long the icy torrents burst from the faucet with the force of water breaking through a dam. The moon and stars flickered and flashed in the quivering darkness. And the silver pail grew larger and larger until, at last, it was a silver-rimmed pond that filled the entire valley and looked, for all the world, like a large hand mirror custom-made for the sun to fix its hair in.

Finally, just at sunrise, the woman slipped off her silver steed and dropped to her knees on the shore of the silver-rimmed pond. Feeling on fire, she cupped her hands and, dipping them into the dawn-gray water, drank cold, cutting gulps. As she drank, the rising sun changed the pond to silver. In fact, some say that for a few minutes the new, still pond became a perfect mirror that the twin sisters—sun and woman—paused to gaze into. Some even say that the flushed and wild-haired twins acknowledged their mysterious kinship with a happy, giddy, almost wicked smile. But no one knows anything for sure except that the sun rose, and the woman rose too, and each began her day.

WHY SHADOWS DO NOT WALK THE EARTH ALONE
Cliff Wilkerson

Once, many years ago, when shadows were free to move about as they pleased, there was a great gathering, a convocation, of shadows. The word had gone out that all should meet at noon at the arena of the sun on the great island of Chardon and there they would discuss what future course shadow life would pursue. A great controversy had arisen between those who wished to maintain the traditional shadow's role of mimicry and those who felt shadows should take an independent role in world affairs.

At the appointed time they all gathered in a twinkling and the island was filled, shadows being that quick when they choose to be. But as everyone knows who has been out at mid-sun, shadows are invisible at that time of day. So the island indeed appeared to be deserted to the non-shadow residents living there, though it was not so. The multitude of shadows present were all quite busy organizing caucuses, discussing the issue or greeting old friends.

The meeting was called to order at 12:01 and everyone was ready; shadows organized and socialized very quickly when they chose to in those days. The chairshadow had been attached to a foreign embassy for several centuries, so that he had a fair understanding of the protocol necessary for dealing with the diverse assembly he faced. He was confident that he could lead them to a speedy and decisive closure regardless of the final outcome. In those days that quickness was possible for shadows when they so chose.

But the chairshadow had not read the signs of the time correctly. He misjudged how deeply the rift had deepened between the two factions. The debate became long and bitter, shadows in those days being capable of lengthening time interminably if they chose. But before this day all shadows had worked in concert so that quickness or slowness was possible, but with two factions pulling in opposite directions, one trying to contract time, the other stretch it, they created such a stress that time broke and stood still. But this did not happen before the sun had proceeded to late afternoon, and anyone who has been out at that time knows that shadows have grown to full dimensions by then. One need not use his imagination to know what had happened to the gathered shadows by this time. They had so expanded that they covered all the island and an adjoining continent with a dark shadowy pall that hid the sun. A great gloom fell upon this land and then in the midst of that dark shadowy gloom, time had broken and come to a standstill. A great cry went up from all living things, for in those days even the grasses in the meadow had the power of speech. Mothers began to pray and comfort their children; fathers began to exhort and comfort their wives; all vice, debauchery, and wickedness came to an end. Reprobates and sinners repented and sought forgiveness. And the way to hell emptied as those last to die dropped into the pit and there were none to take their place, for when time stopped there was no death. But, as you know, death has no time limit upon it and hell knows no measure of time but eternity. So that last reservoir of souls in hell had no respite from their tormentors. But Satan soon heard that his kingdom had ceased to grow and not being content to leave things as they were, he wrapped his cape about himself and galloped away to earth on his black steed to take measure of what had happened. He was astounded at what he beheld, shadows in conflict and humanity in concert. He had lost three generations of souls even if time were repaired immediately, for it would take him that long to corrupt the earth again. With that realization, he became enraged. His eyes began to pop out of his head and he lashed his tail with such violence that he created a whirling dust storm that raged across the land and convinced even those last few holdouts to petition for forgiveness and salvation. Then he thundered back and forth across the land gathering great masses of shadows in his taloned hand and consigning them to the pit. He ranted back and forth until not a shadow could be found and then, his anger appeased, plunged his horse over the edge and was swallowed up. Once in hell he took fire and tongs and beat the shadows into furniture for the fiery house of the damned.

And as you have probably already guessed, when the warring shadows were no more in conflict, time began again and what shadows were left crept close to whatever or whomever they could find and hoped that the devil would think them a part of the landscape or the living creatures who moved there. And since that day they have been afraid to detach themselves.

And that is why you do not see shadows wandering alone on earth today.

THE THING THAT WENT BUMP IN THE NIGHT
Jerry Oestreich

A farmer had three sons. The eldest two, handsome and clever youths, worked hard at the planting, plowing, and harvesting. The villagers would watch and say, "What fine sons! What a joy they must be to their father!"

But the youngest son was thin and weak and did not work at all. He was so dull-witted that he could not understand even the simplest of instructions. The villagers soon learned that the boy believed anything he was told, and they took great delight in spinning tales of demons who devoured unwary youths. They would watch the boy tremble at the stories and go running off to hide in the woods. Laughing, they would say, "What a stupid boy! What a burden he must be to his father!"

As time passed, the youth spent much of his time in the woods. He felt safe there and developed some truly amazing friendships with the animals. Birds would perch on his shoulders, squirrels would curl up and sleep inside his shirt, and even the shy deer would feed from his outstretched palm.

The farmer made many attempts to educate his son. He would march off to the woods and drag the unprotesting boy back home.

"Jesus," the farmer would say, "don't you know there's work to be done?"

The boy would be led to some simple task and left with stern warnings to finish as quickly as possible. When the farmer would return to see the boy still standing in the same place and the task not even begun, he would lose all patience.

"Jesus!" he would scream, "how could I have such a stupid and lazy son?!"

The oldest sons would watch their younger brother and laugh. "He shall surely starve," they would say, "because he can learn nothing at all."

The farmer, fearing that his son would indeed starve unless he could be taught a trade, redoubled his efforts. But all his attempts failed.

"Jesus!" he finally screamed one day, "you're hopeless!" And from that day on the boy was left alone and allowed to spend all his time in the woods.

It soon happened that the oldest sons thought of marriage, and they approached the prettiest and richest girls in the village and asked for their hands. But when these ladies caught sight of the younger brother they would giggle and point.

"Who is *that*?" they would ask

Embarrassed and angry, the brothers would not answer and they soon had to cease all their proposals. They decided secretly that the younger brother would have to go, and they laid their plans carefully.

One night after supper the three brothers gathered around the fire.

"Younger brother," the oldest said, "have you ever heard of the thing that goes bump in the night?"

The younger brother shook his head no, already beginning to tremble.

"Ah," the oldest said, "it's a terrible creature. A body like a hog with teeth like a lion, and eyes that burn as red as the most evil demon from hell. It has sharp, poison spikes that cover its body like armor and steel claws bigger than a bear's. It can leap a hundred feet straight up in the air and swallow an elephant with a single gulp. The only thing it can't do is open a locked door. You do keep your door locked, don't you, brother?"

"Always," the younger brother swore.

"See that you do," the older brother said, "for I heard the thing on the stairs last night. It came and scratched at my door, but I wouldn't let it in. Don't you open your door either, for if you do the thing will surely eat you."

With more stern warnings the brothers tromped off to bed.

The younger brother went up to bed, but he could not sleep. Each wing beat of a passing owl, each scratch of a foraging mouse, each croak of a bullfrog, caused him to tremble and go rigid with terror. Sometime after midnight, when the house had grown silent, he heard a bump, a creak on the stairs, and then a hair-raising scratch at his door. The door that he had so carefully locked creaked open, he heard a low growl, and an immense red eye appeared and stared back at him.

"Ahhhhh!" he screamed. Leaping from the bed, he made a running dive out the open window, crashed through the porch roof, and lay stunned on top of the remains of his father's rocking chair.

The farmer, roused by the screams and the crash, hastened down to find his son lying in a pile of busted shingles and the remains of his favorite chair.

"Jesus!" he screamed, "what the hell are you doing?"

The bewildered youth pointed up at his bedroom window and mumbled that the beast that goes bump in the night had almost got him.

"Sweet Jesus!" the farmer screamed, "how can you be so damned dumb?"

Losing all control, he grabbed his son and threw him off the porch. Pushing, punching, kicking, he chased the dull-witted boy down the road.

"Go!" the farmer said, giving his son a last push, "and for God's sake, don't come back!"

The farmer returned to his bed and the homeless boy crawled off and hid in the woods.

For the next several weeks the boy traveled through the wood and would have starved had it not been for the kindness of the animals. They brought him nuts and fruit, and they slept by him at night to keep him warm.

One day a wandering priest spotted the boy lying asleep under a tree, a chipmunk lay curled behind the boys' ear, and a row of sleeping pigeons were perched along an outstretched leg. A shaft of sunlight fell directly on the boy's face, giving him the appearance of a sleeping angel.

"Ah," thought the priest, who had wandered far in search of a holy man, "perhaps I have found what I am looking for." The priest knew that the animals of the woods are the first to recognize a holy man and honor him, so he sat down to wait until the boy had sat up.

"Where are you going, my son?," asked the priest when the boy had sat up.

"Nowhere," answered the boy.

"Ah," said the priest, who had an ear for wisdom, "and where have you been?"

The boy, who could only remember his terrible fall from his window, pointed upward.

With growing excitement the priest asked, "And what is your name?"

The boy thought long and hard before he answered.

"Well," he said at last, "when my father talked to me he always called me Jesus.

The priest fell to his knees. "But how came you here?" he asked.

"I was being chased by the thing that goes bump in the night," the boy answered, "but I escaped and hid in the woods."

"The devil," thought the priest, convinced that he'd found what he was looking for. Rising to his feet he said, "Come with me, my son, and I will clothe and feed you."

"Thank you, Father," the boy said, "Ever since my father made me leave his house and said to me 'for God's sake, don't come back,' I haven't known where to go or what to do."

The priest kissed the boy's hand and led him to his home. There he clothed and fed him and spread word throughout the land that a holy man had been found.

That Sunday people came from far and wide to see if what the priest claimed was indeed true.

The priest led the boy to the front of the huge crowd of people. "Here is the one I have told you about," he said. "Listen to his answers and judge for yourselves."

"Where are you going?" asked the priest.

"Nowhere," answered the boy and the crowd sighed, for they too had an ear for wisdom.

"Where have you been?" asked the priest.

The boy pointed toward the sky.

"Tell them your name," demanded the priest.

"My father called me Jesus," said the boy.

"Hallelujah!" shouted the congregation, but the priest held up his hand for silence.

"What are you doing here?" asked the priest.

"Running from the thing that goes bump in the night," answered the boy.

A sigh went through the crowd, for the devil was well known to them all.

"When you left your father's house, what was the last thing he said to you?" asked the priest.

"He said, 'for God's sake, don't come back.'"

The congregation shouted and danced for joy. They carried the youth through the streets on their shoulders, and for many weeks there was nothing but celebrations throughout the area. With a holy man living so nearby, the people were careful of their behavior. There was no more crime, food was given to those who needed it, and all the people were happy and content.

It wasn't long before word of the miraculous youth had spread all the way to the King's court. The King, fearing a decrease in his power, ordered the priest and the boy to appear before him.

"You say this is a holy man," said the King, when the priest and the boy were led into his court. "Prove it or both your lives will be forfeited."

The priest turned to the boy. "Where are you going?" he asked.

"Nowhere," answered the boy.

"Where have you been?" asked the priest.

The boy pointed at the sky. The priest looked at the King, but the King gave no sign that the boy's answer was anything special.

"What's your name?" asked the priest.

"My father called me Jesus," said the boy.

The King motioned for the boy to come closer. "You say your father called you Jesus?" he asked.

"Yes sir," replied the boy.

"Hmmm," said the King, impressed in spite of himself.

"What are you doing here?" asked the priest.

"Running from the thing that goes bump in the night."

"The devil," whispered the priest to the King, and the King nodded for he too was well acquainted with the devil.

"What was the last thing your father said to you when you left his house?" asked the priest.

"He said 'for God's sake don't come back,'" answered the boy.

The priest looked at the King. "Does that convince you, O King?" he asked.

"Perhaps," replied the King, "but allow me to ask a question of my own. Tell me," he said, turning to the boy, "what is the meaning of wisdom?"

The boy didn't hear the question because he was paying no attention. His eye was distracted by the rich furnishings of the King's castle, and his stomach was still puffed and swelled from the enormous breakfast he'd consumed. As it so happened, a dove that nested in the inaccessible rafters of the King's chamber caught sight of the boy and flew down to perch on his shoulder. At that moment the boy's stomach gave a surge and he gave forth an enormous belch.

The King, who was sure that any answer about wisdom would have to be incomprehensible, was overjoyed by the boy's reply. He made the boy his Prime Minister, arrayed him in rich and costly clothes, and gave him his daughter's hand in marriage. The priest was given money to build a new church and sent home. All the people in the land rejoiced.

Some years later, after the old King had died and the boy had ascended to the throne, he was traveling through the country with the Queen. They chanced to pass his old father's house, and his older brothers caught sight of him in his coach. They ran up and begged for an audience with the King.

"Younger brother," they cried when they were led into his presence, "forgive us, for we did not realize that you were such a great man."

Being King had not cured the boy of his dull-wittedness, and he did not even recognize his brothers.

"The thing that went bump in the night was all a joke," they said. "A back-scratcher was the claws you heard, an extra key undid the lock, and the red eye was a piece of red wax held in front of a candle.

When the King did not answer, the brothers fell to arguing among themselves about whose idea it had all been. Their arguing soon led to a fight.

The Queen, who had grown weary of the delay and angry at the fighting, leaned close to her husband and said, "Why not hang them? They don't appear to be Christian men."

The King motioned to his guard. "Hang them," he said, and then he commanded his coach to drive on.

The brothers were hung from the tree above their parents' grave, their houses and fields were burned, and their families were turned out to wander like animals through the woods. The King had soon forgotten all about it.

In later years the King and Queen had three fine sons, one of which was as dull-witted as his father. The King often told his sons, when they'd grown older, that he owed all his success to the thing that went bump in the night. The older, sensible sons recognized this as nonsense, but the dull-witted son was entranced by the story. When he came of age he set out in search of the thing that went bump in the night, and he never returned.

Many years later stories were being told of a holy man in the East who could talk to animals and perform miraculous deeds. Whether or not this was truly the King's lost son is not known. The older, sensible sons thought it to be nonsense, saying that their younger brother had surely gotten lost in the woods and eaten by wild animals. As for the King, he'd long ago forgotten that he ever had a third son.

WHY WE HAVE TWO NAMES
Cris Burks Lewis

In the day of the dinosaurs, all people had one name and no two people had the same name. It so happened that every time an elder died, a child was born to inherit the name that was left. All the people were friends. There was no law and no wrong, except for a lopsided mountain near Ridge Dale. Inside the mountain lived three gnomes that practiced two fiendish habits.

On New Year's Eve, they attacked any stray folks around the mountain with the Pea-hen's feathers. The Pea-hen's feathers were red and gold. Usually, they were ten inches long. Each feather had two thousand tiny fingers hidden between the barbs. When the feathers were placed against the skin, they rippled with such force that the person would crumble into laughter and die on the spot.

On Wallen-Walen night the gnomes rode through the air on burning candlesticks which dripped over the fruit trees and caused a harvest of wax fruit. So, the people turned their backs on the Lopsided Mountain.

There lived near the mountain an old biddy who had lived ten thousand years. It was said that she was the tenth woman ever born in the world. She knew all that ever had been, all that was, and all that ever will be. Since she was so wise, the gnomes did not bother her.

Now a son was born to John and Lena. But, as no man had died, the boy remained nameless. Folks would call "hey you" or "you boy". At the same time a daughter was born to Hal and Flo. They named her Cora after Flo's mother who died the moment the child had cried.

Lena waited five years but still no man died. Heartbroken and determined to give her son a name, Lena packed a basket of fruit and set out for the old biddy's cottage.

When she reached the cottage, she set the basket on the porch, fell upon her knees and cried:

> "Wise Mother of us all
> a name I seek
> for my son so small!"

The old biddy crept out of her small cottage and stood before Lena. "Get up gal, you look stupid!" she said. Lena rose

"Yore child needs a name, eh. I say, woman, go home, fer a man shall die within a year and yore child will have a name," the old biddy predicted.

But Lena cried, "Ole wise mother, dat knows all dat ever was, all dat bees, and all dat ever will be; my son needs a name now! I can't bear another day of 'hey boy' or 'you boy'; please help me!" With that speech Lena fell onto her knees sobbing.

"Get up, stupid child, I will help you!" The old biddy yanked Lena to her feet. "But you must do three favors for me.

"First, child, you must go inside de Lopsided Mountain and get me de mind of de first gnomes, as he does all de important thinkin. He keeps dis in de toe of his right shoe. De shoe is never removed from his foot as de smell will fill de mountain with a foul odor dat will knock out every living thing for five minutes.

"Next, bring me de candlesticks they ride during Wallen-Walen Night.

Dese are kept in de cupboard of de second gnome. But, de cupboard is in de room of a thousand cries. De least foreign step in de room will provoke de cries and if dey catch you inside de room your life will be smothered by their breath.

"Finally, bring me de gold tooth of de third gnome. He keeps dis tooth in a glass jar behind his bed. However, dere's a Pea-hen sitting on top of de jar. You must be careful not to touch de bird lest you crumble into laughter and die on de spot."

The old biddy sat on the top step and lit her pipe.

"Old wise mother, I will bring dese things to you," Lena declared.

"Not so fast, stupid gal!" The old biddy reached into her apron pocket and pulled out a large sack. "Inside dis sack are all de things you will need," she said as she gave it to Lena.

"Use your head and remember two things: One, don't let dem gnomes catch you stealin' lest dey kill you, and two, don't let de sun set while you are inside de mountain or you will become a gnome." With these words the old biddy rose and entered her cottage.

In four days Lena had travelled to the Lopsided Mountain. The sunlight was peeping over the horizon when Lena plopped onto the mountain's grassy banks. She emptied the contents of the sack into her lap and examined each item. There was a mirror, a vial of ants, and six orange seeds. Puzzled, she placed these items in her pocket. Stuck in the corner of the sack were two rose buds. Dew drops clung to their petals and glittered through the sack like diamonds. Carefully, Lena removed these and placed them in a separate pocket.

Lena's ears caught the grumble of the gnomes as they marched towards the mountain. Quickly, she hid in a bush nearby. The three ugly men marched past the bush and Lena fell in line behind them. She followed them around the mountain and into the secret hole hidden under a giant mushroom.

Inside the mountain they stumbled through a dark tunnel. A thousand insects buzzed in the damp muskiness. Fuzzy creatures scampered across her toes, but she did not cry out.

The gnomes entered a room with a blazing fire. Lena hunched in the darkness of the tunnel and watched as they roasted their kill of small animals and gobbled it down. They danced around the fire until their short legs began to buckle. Then, one by one, they drifted into one of the rooms directly across from the tunnel. The mountain soon shook with snores.

Lena took the rose buds from her pocket and placed one in each nostril. The air became sweet and clean. She tip-toed into their room and bent over the first gnome's foot. She held the vial against the heel of his shoe and slowly uncapped it. The ants crawled over the rim of the vial and into the shoe. After the last ant was in the shoe, Lena scurried behind the bed and crouched in the corner.

The gnome's foot began to twitch. Within seconds it convulsed violently. The gnome jerked up with a roar. Frantically, he snatched the shoe off. Immediately he passed out from the odor. A hush settled in the mountain. The gnome's snoring ceased.

Lena flew from the corner and removed the gnome's mind from the toe of his shoe. She stuffed it into the sack and wrapped it tightly so its thoughts could not escape.

Now the room with the thousand cries was directly behind the second gnome's bed. Lena rolled under his bed. She pulled out the orange seeds and flicked one into the room. The room bellowed with cries: cries of grief, joy and pain, cries of all animals—old and young. The gnomes woke. The first gnome quickly put on his shoe as the other rushed into confusion. They faced into the room of cries, but as the first gnome had lost his mind, they couldn't decide upon any action. Therefore, they returned to bed.

Lena waited ten minutes and flicked another seed into the room. Again the room wailed and the gnomes rushed about in confusion. This happened a third time, but the fourth time, only the second gnome rose. The sixth seed brought no results.

Lena rolled from underneath the bed. She entered the room of cries and rushed to the cupboard in the center of the room. Again, the room burst into tears, but the gnomes did not stir. Lena took the three big candlesticks and placed them into the sack as she held the part in which the mind lay. This prevented any knowledge from escaping.

Lena crawled under the beds until she reached the other side of the third gnome's bed. She stood and held the mirror in front of the Pea-hen. The bird, a rather vain and comical fowl, fell in love with himself. Lovesick, he fell backward with desire. Lena removed the tooth from the jar and made her way out the mountain.

When she reached the outside, the sun was sinking over the mountain. She ran to the old biddy's house, weak and still shaken by her experience.

The old biddy came onto the porch, "You done good, stupid gal!" she smiled.

Lena handed her the sack, "Ole wise mother, please, may I now have a name for my child?"

The old biddy lifted Lena, as she collapsed on the steps.

"Call him Frank, John's son," the old biddy advised.

"But there's a Frank alive and living in Canton...."

"Stupid Gal!" the old biddy shouted. "Give him two names. Frank, John-son."

Lena smiled and tears of gladness streamed down her face. She thanked the old biddy and ran home to John and Frank John-son.

And women still go through hell just to give children their father's name.

WHY EVERGREENS ARE THAT WAY
David Caddigan

Many years ago the earth was nothing more than a large grove of pines.
This forest contained every variety of pine known, such as Scotch fir,
cluster pine, Corsican pine, the great blue spruce, and the magnificent cedar
of Lebanon. The odor of this magnificent forest was like a thousand
Christmases; the strong sweet smell of pine resin permeating the air with its
sensuous fragrance. And each conical creature would point heavenward,
the glaucous, verdant foliage contrasted against the azure sky, their tops
like a thousand church steeples paying homage to their Creator.

One day in the midst of this coniferous splendor of aquamarine and
emerald, a tiny sprout burrowed its way free of the earth's impregnable
grasp. For the first few months of its existence, the other trees didn't even
notice it. After a few years, when the sprout rose to a somewhat noticeable
height, the firs began to observe that the shape was unlike any other tree in
the forest. The trunk grew straight upwards all right, but the branches stuck
out from the trunk in a very haphazard manner. The leaves were also
shaped differently. Instead of being narrow and spearlike, these were broad
and flat, with the edges curving in and out.

The pines didn't know what to make of this stranger in their midst. This
tree obviously was not a fir, and the pines didn't know whether or not they
should share their forest with it. This soon became a topic of discussions
among all the firs.

"Personally, I think it should go and find its own forest," the larch
commented. "We don't need any newcomers to disrupt our way of life."

"I agree," said the blue spruce. "This new tree is obviously different and
just doesn't belong."

"I don't think we are in any position to decide who has the right to stay
or who doesn't," spoke the cedar of Lebanon, "after all, none of us had any
say about our presence here. I think we should petition Mother Nature. She
was probably the one responsible for this new breed's presence. And if she
wants this newcomer to stay, well, I don't think anyone of us is in a
position to argue with her."

All the trees agreed with the great cedar; after all, he was the oldest and
wisest tree in the great forest. The pitch pine was delegated the
responsibility of drafting this petition, and the great cedar himself brought
it in front of Mother Nature.

"Our Great Mother," it read, "who in your infinite power gave us trees,
the cool soil to sink our roots in, the lovely blue sky to scrape our tops
against, the rain to quench our thirst, and the stars to keep the night from
seeming so empty, please, explain to us this newcomer in our midst. He is
very different from all of us. We trees were wondering if you maybe made a
slight mistake in his creation."

Mother Nature read the petition and, smiling, told the great cedar, "I was
wondering when you pines were going to notice the newcomer. And you're
right, he is different. He is called oak. You can tell that paranoid blue
spruce that he isn't going to replace any of you pine trees. I just thought
that maybe you would like some different company for a change. That

forest is immense, and there's plenty of room, so don't you pines worry. I have everything all planned out."

After his visit with Mother Nature, the great cedar explained to the firs that she wanted the pines to welcome the stranger, and treat him like one of their own. This they did. After a while, the oak was as tall and as majestic as any of the pines. His strong brown boughs reached out and up into the sky. His thick strong trunk rose straight and powerful from the earth, and his foliage—the leaves were ten inches to one foot long, and half as wide, with very deep leaves at the lower part, dilated widely at the apex, and notched. They looked like a thousand hands waving in the breeze.

Soon the oak was joined by more of his kind, and the great forest became fully integrated, being made up of various types of pines and oaks. The forest became even more beautiful, and when the wind whipped through the trees, the glaucous green foliage resembled a giant wave in the ocean, rolling back and forth, riding the current of air.

Although everything appeared serene, the pines were unhappy. At first they heeded Mother Nature's wishes, and accepted the oaks as brothers. However, this acceptance wasn't reciprocated by the oaks.

"You pines think of yourselves as being magnificent," the oaks would boast. "If that was true, then why did Mother Nature create us? We are obviously a better tree. Mother Nature was probably bored with you, so she created us, a more improved version of tree."

At first the pines ignored their boastfulness, thinking that Mother Nature was truly just, and enjoyed all of the trees equally. But the oaks became even more brazen in their self worship.

"Look at yourselves, pines! You rise straight from the ground like giant dunce caps. And that sickly smell of your resin is making us oaks nauseous."

This final mocking was the last straw. The pines gathered together and selected the cedar to be their spokesperson.

"Listen, oaks, we pines dominated this forest long before you were thought of by Mother Nature..."

Before he could finish, the oaks interrupted him with a burst of laughter. "You honestly think that we were created by the same idiot who created you? That's a laugh. We are a far superior tree than you. Our leaves are broader and greener than any pine needle. And for you to suggest that we were made by the same creator is truly hilarious." At that, the oaks again burst into laughter.

What the insubordinate oaks didn't realize was that Mother Nature was listening to their discussion.

"So I'm an idiot," she said to herself. "I must be, to create such a conceited tree as the oak. I can't very well destroy them, that would be unfair. I will, however, teach them a lesson in humility."

No sooner had she spoken, when throughout the great forest the oaks' leaves started to change into a fiery red crimson.

"This is to teach you impudent oaks a lesson," she bellowed throughout the forest. "Every year your beloved green leaves will change color, dry up, and fall off. The crimson color is to show your embarrassment for what you said about me, and when the cold north wind blows through the forest every year, you will have to face it with your branches bare."

When she finished speaking, all the oaks lost their leaves and were left to face the north wind naked. To this day, the oaks are being punished for their impudence, and that is why in the winter the oaks lose their leaves but the loyal pines remain evergreen in their majestic splendor.

WHY HOUSES HAD TO BE BUILT
Janet Marie Brown

Grandma Addie looks out the back door and hollers, "C'mon in, y'all. Y'all see it's dark out dere!"

"Aw! Granny!" says four-year-old Leslie, as she slowly makes it to the door. She does not pick her feet up; she shuffles along.

"We was havin' fun!" Joe, Leslie's cousin, wails, as he flies up the flight of gray stairs. He's carrying his red and yellow dump truck, which has dirt stains all over it.

"Always got to come in so early," says Tosha, who is five years old. She hangs her head and drags her Raggedy Ann doll by the arm. The doll is about half her size. The other eleven children, ranging from two to eleven years old, gradually file in. There are two sets of twins. Each set belongs to a different family.

It is Saturday, Grandma Addie's day to spend time with all fourteen of her grandchildren. They are divided among Grandma Addie's one son and four daughters. Grandma Addie has on her usual flowery, shapeless house dress. Her huge, dinosaur-egg-sized breasts sag down to her stomach. Neither her children nor her grandchildren would recognize her in any other type of outfit. She stopped wearing bras "a long time back," as she always says. "Better fo' chil'ren t' res' dey lil heads on," she told Valerie a couple of years ago, when the girl was six and didn't have anything better to do than watch her granny dress and come up with questions like "Granny, you didn't put on all yo' underwear! Wont me to find yo' bra?"

"I wish we could live outside," Jimmy pouts and tries to make himself cry while sitting in his chair at the long, rectangular table.

"Live outside! Boy, whut's wrong wid you? SOON as I git thu dishin' out y'all ice cream, I see ah'm gone hav'ta S'PLAIN why De Lawd made houses in de FIRS' place."

Only the sound of the wooden scoop hitting the thick glass bowls is heard, while Grandma Addie dips out the homemade strawberry ice-cream. Then she begins her story:

"One day de bear, de lion, de tiger and de snake went climbin' up de pathway to Heben. Course de bear had to carry de snake 'roun' his neck, so de snake wouldn't be gittin' in dey way, slithin' all aroun'. Dey had anuf worries crowdin' up dey brain already.

"When dey reached God's gole throne, dey all got on dey knees, tryin' t'show dat dey were sho 'nuf seer'is bout de bizness at han'. Na y'know dat de snake had ta keep hangin' roun' de bear's neck, 'cause he didn't have no knees t'be gittin down ON, no way. De lion, who was runnin' thangs said, 'Lawd, who done blessed us an'mal creeshures wid de wo-arm sun, de nice river t'drink frum, de d'lishus grass, an'...'de lion looked pass de tiger, over at de bear an' de snake, ...'doze lil bugs, lak de bees an' de worms, we are gray'ful mo' ev'ryday. But, Lawd, dem humin bein' creeshures dat You done sent down dere t'earth, well dey is gittin' on all us an'mal creeshures' nerves. Dey 'bout t'make us go deaf an' drive us crazy wid all dat hollerin' an screamin'. If dey ain't screamin' an' runnin' ev'ry time dey see us, DEN deys tho'in rocks at us. Lawd, please do sum'n 'bout 'em. Sep'rate dem frum us, befo dey make us madder!'

" 'Aw right, ma an'mal creeshures, ah'm gointer improve on de condishuns, as bes' I can.'

" 'Lawd....,' de lion looked roun' at his three friends, 'we ar much obliged t'ya.'

"Dey slid on back down t'earth. Dis trip, de snake went on down de pathway firs', 'cause he didn't have t'worry 'bout gittin' squashed, since he could slide de fas'es'.

"When dey reached de earth, de udder an'mal creeshures lak de hawse, de rab'id, de owl, de fox, de squir'l, de bir's, an' mo', was early, wait'n fo de noos on how De Lawd reactid. An' dey was joyful when dey foun' out dat he was thinkin' on id. Dey was real friskay fo' de res' of de evenin, an' dey sang when dey heard De Lawd summin de humin creeshures fo' a meetin'.

"De nex' mawin' all de humin creeshures clime'd up t'Heben. Dey hurried on up, cause de night befo' when De Lawd called down, his voice sounded seer'is an' pow'rful, not happy an' pow'rful.

"Dey all crowded 'roun de throne, an' De Lawd began t'speak: 'Ma humin creeshures, thank you all fo' not delayin'. De Lawd had to stop an' yawn. 'Sorry 'bout dat interrupshun, but yo' Lawd didn't git no sleep las' night, cause I was bizy figurin' up a idea dat'll protec' y'all frum de an'mals. I d'cided t'give ole Henry de imaginashun to bild a house. C'mon up here, close t'me, Henry, so I kin give ya de imaginashun needed,' De Lawd poin'id his scepter t'ward Henry, who was slowly makin' it thu de' op'nin dat de crowd made fo' 'im.

" 'Na, ya got de imaginashun t'bild a house. De folks won't hav'ta be scared of de an'mals no mo'.' De Lawd looks at ev'rybody, 'Y'all won't see dem so much no mo'. An' y'all two groups won't be so tem'ted t' git rid a one a nudder, as fas' as ah kin make ya. Henry gone down dere, an' take ev'rybody wid ya, so you kin tell dem what t'do 'bout bildin' houses.'

" 'Lawd...,' a big mean voice frum de crowd b'gan, 'why Henry git t' ha' de 'maginashun? Why he so spechal?'

" 'He de ol'est. He git de imaginashun. He git t'sit, while y'all work, cause he d'serve it, but MAINLY cause I say so.' De Lawd reared back on his gole'en throne, an' smiled.

"All de humin creeshures made dey way on back down t'earth. Ole Henry didn't wase no tahm fine'in him a shaday tree t'sit un'ner. Den he started giv'n dem instrucshuns lef' an' right. All de udder humins, de wimin an' de min, follow'd 'em, as fas' as dey could, too. Y'all chil'rens shoulda seen 'em gathin' up dem fallin' tree branches, stones, an rocks." Grandma Addie is standing at the head of the table, and she bends down and pretends to be holding an armful, as she stands back up.

"All de time doze an'mals was feelin' releef, cause dey knew dat prettee soon dey wouldn't hav'ta be worrin' 'bout dem humins, actin' all crazy.

"Na, as de weeks pas'd on by, de humin creeshures was still bildin on dat firs' house. Dey was havin' problems. Ya see, chil'ren, dey kept havin' t' re-bild secshuns over an' over, 'cause while dey'd be workin' on one part, a nudder part'd fall. Old Henry did de bes' he could. He didn't know nuddin' bout de equipmen' dat was needed. He didn't have de genius dat it took t'git dem houses bild right fas' an' sturdee, eidder. 'Member, na, dat De Lawd only blessed 'im wid 'maginashun t'build de houses. Dat dere 'maginashun unforchinidly didn't include bizness brilyance.

"So, bein' impashent, de lion, de tiger, an' de bear, wid de snake roun' his neck, went climbin' back up de pathway t'Heben. When dey made it t'De Lawd, dey all got on dey knees again. De lion said, 'Lawd, we an'mal creeshures really 'preechiate how You put all yo' udder duties aside an' took care of our problem wid dem humin creeshures, 'bout two months ago. But, Lawd, dey *sho* is takin' dey sweet tahm gittin' dem houses bild. Dey's still workin' on dere firs' ONE, Lawd! At dis rate id'll be years fo'dey all got a house! PLEASE, Lawd, won't You order dem t'quickin thangs up?'

"'Well, ma an'mals, dat lag-a-long pace ain't dey fault. When I try new ideas, dey hav'ta be in moshun awhile fo' I kin know de lef'outs. Ahm gointer fix de situashun, snaply.'

"'Oh, Lawd, we all thank you,' said the lion.

"As b'fo, de snake slid on down firs', and de udder three follow'd.

"An hour later, de humin' creeshures was makin' dey way up dat very same pathway, t'anser De Lawd's call. When dey was all aroun' de throne, De Lawd said, 'Na, dis meetin' was called in conecshun wid ma gif' t' Ole Henry, awhile back. I noticed dat y'all been havin some trouble gittin' dat firs' house t'gedder. I done figured out a way t'fix dat, 'cause Henry's got plen'y mo' types of houses waitin' t'be bilt.' De crowd mumbled 'thanks,' an' some of dem slapped five wid each udder." Grandma Addie holds her hand out for the quickest hand to slap it. They all reach to do it, so she gets five many times, before she continues in the Lord's calm mellow voice. "'Ah'm gointer give de smartness fo' skill. Where's Miss Milley?'" Grandma Addie explains, "Na, she was de ol'est woman, child'ren. De Lawd peered out 'mong dem, till he saw a movement. De few humins in fron' or roun' Miss Milly made way fo' her an' her cane.

"'Na, Miss Milly,' De Lawd poin'id his septer at her, 'Ya got de smartness fo' skill. Wid you an' Henry workin' t'gedder, dem houses gone be sum'n else.' De Lawd fixes his eyes on Ole Henry, who's already in de fron'. 'Henry, I wont you an' Miss Milly t' teach de younguns whut y'all know 'bout bild'in houses in y'all spare tahm, so dat when y'all come live wid me, dey can carry on.'

"'Yes, Lawd,' said Henry.

"'I will, an' thank you fo' ma smartness fo'skill, Lawd,' said Miss Milly.

"De whole crowd a humins slid on back down t'earth, an Miss Milly an' Ole Henry foun' a big shaday tree an' started givin' orders. Miss Milly had some people makin' tools, while Ole Henry had some gathin' mo' material. Id was goin' *real* smooth, so de an'mal creeshures was conten'id. Miss Milly fixed id so dat certain ones worked on only certin parts of de house, so dat after two months, dere were many houses bein' finish'd at de same tahm. Dis was t' de an'mals d'light."

Grandma Addie seems to be exhausted as she plops down in her big chair at the head of the table. "An' dat's why you chil'ren cain't live outside. De few people dat do live out dere don't have no respec', an' plus deys suf'rin, 'cause dey ain't obeyin' De Lawd's word," she explains to her fourteen grandchildren, as they sit around the table with their empty ice-cream bowls in front of them, smiling.

"So that's where houses came from!" Evelyn, who is the eleven-year-old, says. She leans back in her chair and looks amazed. She has two thick ponytails held together with yellow yarn to match her yellow shorts set. She is setting an example for the younger children, because it is her job to help them believe Grandma Addie's stories. "Henry and Milly sure did a good job, Granny. We got all kinds of houses all over!"

"Ahm glad God seperated us from those animals. They coulda killed ALL us up, by now, couldn't they Grandma?" Five-year-old Tyrail asks, as he swings his leg and hits them against the table.

"Dat's right, honey."

"Ahm glad you DID make us come in, Granny. Cause if you'd let us live out there, we'd be suf'rin' and go down to the devil, wouldn't we?" says Jimmy, who made his grandmother tell the story in the first place. He nods his head and looks serious. His fat jaws shake slightly.

Grandma Addie just smiles and Evelyn gets up to clear the table. "Y'all c'mon t'de playroom," she stands up and beckons with her arm as she talks. Marvin, the two-year-old, has fallen asleep in his nine-year-old sister Betty's arms. "Child, gimmie dat baby so I kin put him t'beddy bye." Picking up the dark-skinned, plump baby, Grandma Addie assumes a hushed, sing-song, grown-up's imitation of a baby's voice: "Dat swee-ee-tee pie ate him ice-cream, an' den got SO-O-O comfy lis'nin' to his granny's story. Dat's what happen, ain't id, honey?"

The other children quietly tiptoe through the long hall, pass their granny, who is entering the large bedroom with the heavy Marvin in her arms. His red, sock-covered feet dangle over her arms, showing that his black, high-topped baby shoes will have to be hunted up, when his mother comes. As Grandma Addie looks down lovingly at Marvin sleeping in the crib, she hears the familiar sounds of her other twelve grandbabies, playing happily in the enormous room that their parents once enjoyed.

Parodies of
Contemporary Forms

HOW FAR WOULD YOU GO?
Gary Gaines

I know you won't believe this, but I swear on my Bruce Springsteen albums that every word is true. One night I was up kind of late. I had the flu and was feeling too miserable to sleep so I was watching one of those late night/early morning flicks on one of the UHF stations. I don't remember much about the movie except that it was one of those war films with a bunch of people with English accents in it.

Well, I was fumbling around with this jigsaw puzzle and I look up and see this commercial come on. It was one of those detergent commercials. It opened up with this guy and this young housewife sitting at a table with a box of this detergent between them. On the housewife's lap is a little boy, maybe four or five years old, in a t-shirt and jeans. He had blond hair and blue eyes and was really cute and all (you know, the All-American, kid-down-the-street type). So anyway, this lady's telling the guy how much she loves the detergent and all and how it keeps little Jimmy's clothes so clean and then Jimmy pipes up and says how good his clothes smell.

Well, I just figured this was more of the usual bullshit you get from commercials and was about to go back to the puzzle when these two guys in these railroad costumes, you know, the blue and white striped coveralls and cap, come in and the guy at the table says, "Now you go with these nice men, Jimmy, and we'll see you later." So they take the little kid away.

Then the guy starts offering the housewife money for the box of detergent and she keeps turning him down. "Now come on, Mrs._____, I'll give you fifty dollars for that box of detergent." "No!" she says as she grabs the box off the table and holds it to her. Then the guy says, "Well, Mrs._____, let's see how much you really like your detergent. Why don't you just look at the monitor over there on the side?" Then they switch the picture to this railroad track and they got her little Jimmy tied to it. They go in for a close-up and there are tears running down the poor kid's face and he's struggling uselessly to get himself free. He keeps yelling, "Mommy, Mommy, Mommy..." The housewife's voice comes on and she starts consoling the kid, saying, "Don't worry, Jimmy, Mommy's here, everything's all right."

Then the picture shifts again and there's this diesel engine racing down the tracks with the detergent's logo painted across the side and the guy comes on saying, "When we see the engine go past the red marker flag, Mrs._____, you'll have fifteen seconds to decide whether to keep your detergent or save little Jimmy's life by having us switch the engine onto another track. There goes the marker flag now! What'll it be, Mrs._____?" Then it's back to a close-up of Jimmy still bawling his eyes out, repeating "Mommy, Mommy, Mommy," really quickly now in this high-pitched, sort of delirious-sounding voice as the roar of the engine gets closer. There's a little clock now in the upper right hand corner of the screen sweeping past the seconds.

They switch quickly back to the studio where you see the mother chewing on one of her fingernails with this confused look on her face, turning from monitor to detergent box and back again like she hasn't made up her mind yet. "I don't want to put any pressure on you, Mrs._____," says the guy, "but there are less than ten seconds left." The housewife gives a little nod and continues trying to decide between the boy and the box.

Now they go to this shot of the oncoming train and little Jimmy by the bottom of the screen. He seems to have quieted down or maybe the roar of the train is just drowning him out. Anyway, when the clock is down to like three seconds the guy says, "Well, Mrs.____?" "I'll keep the box!," says the housewife excitedly. It's just another second or two before the train goes screaming over the little kid, but they hold the camera on it just long enough to show little Jimmy's head tremble and roll down the side of the track bed.

Then it's back to the studio where they show the used-to-be mother holding the box of detergent with a big smile on her face, obviously feeling she's made the right decision. "Any regrets, Mrs._____?" asks the guy. "Nope!" "There you have it, friends."

The last shot is a close-up of little Jimmy's head (nose up, eyes wide open, blood trickling out of his neck) lying in the weeds next to a box of detergent, the tracks off in the distance. And the guy's voice says, "How far would you go for your detergent?"

MAGICAL MECHANICAL MACHINE
Scott Hoeppner

Are you tired of all those kitchen gadgets that fall apart as soon as the warranty expires? Were you just saying to your neighbor this morning how you wish someone would come up with one item that does the work of all the rest? We at Upchuck Productions have come up with this gadget that does the work of all the other implements and more, better. Yes, it's the Magical, Mechanical Machine, destined to become the housewife's best friend. This one machine blends, beats, brews, bakes, butters, boils, cuts, cubes, chops, chills, crushes, crumbs, cooks, cracks, creams, embalms, freezes, ferments, flakes, fertilizes, drains, dices, destroys, grinds, gels, grates, hacks, harasses, jostles, kneads, knifes, liquefies, mixes, marinates, mends, molds, mangles, mutilates, minces, manipulates, adds, substracts, multiplies, divides, purees, pastes, purifies, pulverizes, rotates, rips, slices, squeezes, squashes, simmers, stirs, saturates, scallops, stews, scrambles, tears, tosses, vegetates, whips and dials the police in case of emergencies all in the privacy of your own home. With a flick of your finger you can pulverize an entire carrot, with a flick of your carrot you can pulverize an entire finger. No food is too difficult for the *Magical Mechanical Machine*. Highly recommended for cannibals. You say you like bacon with your eggs in the morning? Not only does our machine fry the bacon, it goes out and kills the pig. Now how's that for modern convenience. Still not satisfied? You still want more? Then listen up. The many uses of our *Magical Mechanical Machine* do not stop in the kitchen. Just change the blades and it becomes a hedge trimmer. Change the blades once again and it becomes a helicopter. Our machine can teach your children ten different languages, take the dog out after dinner, tell telephone solicitors what they can do with their siding and satisfy your husband when you have a headache. This is definitely the household device that you have been waiting for all your life. Listen to the lastest sports score and the weather while you mutilate a turnip. That's right, our handy machine gives you all the scores of the important games and even places your illegal bets and stands ready to erase all records of the bets if you are raided by the police. Yes, the *Magical Mechanical Machine* polishes your silver, places rhinestones on your asparagus, wallpapers your bedroom, projects your favorite porno movies, converts into a whirlpool bath and wards off evil spirits. This is a limited time offer so don't delay, act now. To order your *Magical Mechanical Machine* send your bank account, the mortgage on your house, and your first born male child to *Magical Mechanical Machine*, Upchuck Productions, Box 1000, Boston, Massachusetts. That is *Magical Mechanical Machine*, Upchuck Productions, Box 1000, Boston, Massachusetts. After three P.M. send to Fred, 291 Ocean Drive, La Junta, Colorado. Order today so you can mangle an eggplant tomorrow.

STATION BREAK
Cloteria Easterling

......We will return to our program "Rev. Ike and Oral Roberts Heal Their Wallets" in a moment, after these commercial messages.

Friends, ELVIS is gone but not forgotten. And to give you that little piece of ELVIS we all need, *Better Homes and Gardens* is offering you a "LITTLE PIECE OF ELVIS".

That's right friends, a little piece of Elvis. This isn't a record offer, or an offer of a life-size Elvis made from four hundred thousand toothpicks, like those other companies try to sell you. I mean we will actually send you pieces of Elvis Presley.

If you send $800,000.00 plus $40.00 shipping, handling, and postage, the employees of *Better Homes and Gardens* will at midnight, sneak into Elvis' actual grave and remove pieces of bone, decayed flesh, or whatever else we find, and send it to you for our *LOW, LOW, PRICE!!!*

Be the first on your block to own Elvis. You can display him on a coffee table, in a den or to brighten up a dark space.

Just remember friends for the LOW, LOW, LOW!!!PRICE of $800,000.00 plus $40.00 shipping, handling, and postage, you too can own a "LITTLE PIECE OF ELVIS".

SEND TO:
"LITTLE PIECE OF ELVIS"
P.O. Box 149
Back Room Deal, Nevada 0000000

Or call our toll-free number: 1-800-5555555
Our operators are on the lines waiting for your calls NOW!!!!!!
Remember to send for this offer, because a little piece of Elvis will bring a little piece of happiness into your life.

FAILURE: HOW TO RECOGNIZE
AND AVOID IT IN THE RESTROOM
Mike Schwarz

Failure. I want you to remember that word, because it has been the downfall of many people. Hardworking people like yourself. Witless drones who, through their total inability to succeed, have been left by the wayside to live out dull ho-hum lives. But don't feel sorry for them. Their failure was caused by the lack of foresight. They didn't know how to compete on a higher level, a psychological level. Coming in on time for work, or always wearing a fresh suit, was their idea of impressing the boss, and it did. It told him that they were brainless idiots waiting to be punched and programmed, but not made to handle a heavy load. These people are composed of a quivering spine of foundationless goop, which softens in wallowing self-satisfaction every time the boss remembers a petty thing like their first names.

What these people didn't realize is, that through other seemingly unrelated everyday tasks, they were giving off "Failure Vibes." That is, showing their true colors in normal situations. What I have done here is to analyze these mistakes, and compile for you a list of do's and don't's. But why the restroom? Because there is absolutely no better place to impress the boss's subconscious. Remember, any moron can be on time for work, but how many of your fellow employees will know how to get promoted just by doing the right thing in the john?

I want to show you the difference between a winner and a loser; a failure and a success; a go-getter and a go-fer. The real lesson to be learned is to control those bad "vibes," and keep them from getting out. Don't be held back by what could be pushing you ahead, read on…and learn.

The first thing you should do after landing a job is familiarize yourself with the bathroom. How big is it? How many stalls? What sinks have faucets that you can turn on and off yourself instead of all that pressing? Having noted these will be to your advantage, so do it early one morning. Meeting your boss unexpectedly in a strange restroom could be a disaster.

When entering the washroom to urinate always choose the closest possible urinal. I repeat, the closest! This will show you are a no-nonsense guy. Someone who'll stick to the business at hand, and won't waste any time doing it. The unsuspecting dope who wanders down to the middle, or toward the end stall is a dead giveaway for a failure. This guy is a time waster, he's slacking. Your boss will feel his "failure vibes" a mile away, and act accordingly.

If the bottom of the urinal is surrounded by a puddle of yellow, don't despair. Most of all, don't walk away from it, use it! Withstanding this moral disgust will prove your ability to resist discouragement, to continue, no matter what the odds. The "fussbudget" who shys away from such puddles is just asking to spend the rest of his life in the mail room. He's shouting, "Hey Boss! Look at me! I'd rather have clean shoes than handle all of those big accounts."

Should someone by using the first stall (obviously he had read this before you) be firm, hold your ground. Stand directly in back of him with only an inch between you. When he backs up to leave, bump into him and give a long dirty look until he says, "Excuse me." Doing this will not only prove you have the will power to get what you want, but it also shows your ability to dominate others.

Even if the first stall is out of order, don't be deterred. Urinate right on the out-of-order sign. Make that first urinal an objective. And then do everything in your power to attain it. If you can't get that first stall, how can you hope to cinch that big deal?

Once you have the urinal, there are several methods of "Going." Two of which are most common. One way, you stand very close, the other very far away. Does this really matter? Isn't it really just up to me? No, it isn't up to you, and yes! it does really matter. The decision could be fatal, for it's times such as these that true executives are born. But which way? Let me tell the answer through a story I heard once about a situation just like this. Then you be the judge, you decide.

John and Jim were both pissing in the bathroom when the boss walked in. "Hi Jim. Hi John," the boss said. Jim was standing real close to the stall, his chest against the top. John was standing two feet away from his stall, a long yellow arch extending from his penis to the urinal. "Hi boss," they both said.

Fifteen minutes later the boss called them both into his office. He told Jim to go sharpen some pencils. Jim beamed proudly, and went on his way. When Jim had gone, the boss said to John, "John, I like you very much. I don't know what it is I like about you exactly, but it has something to do with that wonderful devil-may-care attitude of yours. Now you take Jim, he's a good, steady worker, but he's dull. There's no sense of adventure in him. He'll never go anywhere. But you, my boy, have a great future ahead of you. Back to work now." John smiled to himself. Wouldn't his young wife be proud. In the background, over the piped-in music, John could hear the hum of the electric pencil sharpener. Someday, thought John, those will be my pencils Jim is sharpening.

Yes, John, someday soon. You see, John showed just by backing away a few feet, that within his soul is the sense of adventure…when it's safe to use it. John would never do anything really risky (like climb a mountain) but he showed the boss that he would take a gamble if the odds look good. The boss, of course, recognized that and acted accordingly. Jim, on the other hand, was just reeking with insecurity. His standing so close to the urinal told the boss that he was ashamed of his misgivings, and would rather hide than improve them. When faced with an unpleasant situation Jim would run, while John would piss all over. This is the sign of a businessman.

Even though you are hidden behind closed doors most of the time, bowel movements are just as important to your career as what kind of tie you wear. When choosing a stall here, the same rules apply. Only they are often slightly more difficult to follow. Sometimes the first stall stinks like a pig pen, and the toilet is full of large unflushable feces. Remember, sticktoitiveness is the key, don't be discouraged, get that first water hole…Unless (yes, there is an exception) there happens to be a stall with no door. Then you choose that one. Don't be embarassed. When people look in at you, just smile. Why should you care. You're telling them, and everyone else, that you're not afraid to carry out the dirty work. There is no job you won't do openly. When the boss comes across something that requires the talents of a man like that, you can bet he won't be thinking of any of those laughing jack-asses.

One very important rule. Never, never smoke in the bathroom. This just shouts laziness. I recall a story of a man who was smoking in the bathroom, and the price he paid was failure.

Joe was a good worker. He never caused any trouble, and pretty much kept to himself. Joe's job was to assemble daily function sheets, make copies, and distribute them promptly to all the department heads. For the first week he did well. But there was a time bomb about to explode. Because Joe worked entirely with papers, he was forbidden to smoke and Joe was a heavy smoker. In the middle of the second week, he was weakening.

It was Wednesday, he'd just finished stapling the sheets together when suddenly, he had to move his bowels. Asking permission, he ran down the hall, and into one of the stalls. As he stared blankly ahead of him, the thought occurred. Why not have a smoke? It wasn't long before he had the cigarette lit and half gone. Just then, a pair of patent leather shoes walked into the bathroom. Joe flicked an ash on the floor. The shoes walked up to Joe's stall and stopped for a moment, then they left. Joe shrugged and flicked his cigarette into the bowl underneath him.

When Joe got back to his desk, all of his belongings had been cleared out from the drawers, and packed neatly in a cardboard box. An angry tear swelled in his eye. Looking around he saw the company manager waving him to his office. Covering the manager's two feet were the patent leather shoes.

The manager asked Joe why he had gone to the bathroom. Joe told him the truth. The manager then replied, "It shouldn't take five minutes for a healthy boy like you to have a bowel movement, but that's how long it takes to smoke a cigarette. You're a nice boy, Joe, but we simply cannot tolerate goldbricking *or* lying here. I'm going to have to let you go, Joe, and if you should ever use this place as a reference, I'm afraid I'd have to tell what's happened here today." Joe hung his head low, collected his belongings, and left the office never to work again. Are you willing to pay the same price?

Should all of the stalls be occupied, you needn't wait for the first one. Just use the handicapped stall. No one ever uses it anyway, what are you supposed to do? Right or wrong. Most definitely right! The person who shies away from relieving himself because of some stupid figure painted on the stall door, is showing a real lack of character. Also he is exhibiting fear of Rona Douglas of Eyewitness News "Seven on Your Side." The man who throws caution to the wind in exchange for "Getting the Job Done" is showing everyone his terrific sense of Get Up and Go. He knows how to weigh values, and in what order to sequence important projects.

Finally, and not least importantly, there is the business of washing hands. If at all possible, always use a sink with a faucet you yourself can turn on and off. No one looks dignified hunching over pressing and rinsing and pressing and rinsing. If there are no such faucets, make it a point to time each one. Find out which is the longest running, and use it regularly. The numbskull who wanders from sink to sink probably can't make up his mind about anything else either.

If the soap available is bar soap, don't bother using it. It's probably dirtier than you anyway. If it is pump soap, make sure the plastic bulb is full. You don't want to be seen pumping the handle and getting nothing but thousands of tiny bubbles a la Lawrence Welk. Wash the hands thoroughly, you don't really know where they've been, or at least where the people you shake hands with hands have been. Never use the hand dryer if at all possible. Again, this is just for time wasters, not for a success. If no towels are available, use toilet paper.

Now then, just to see what you've learned: what's the last thing you do on your way out of the bathroom? If you guessed "Look at My Appearance," we'll see you in 35 years getting a gold watch for being Jr. Clerk longer than anyone else. You forgot...self confidence is the code word for success. And as long as you *know* you look presentable, why bother to check...unless you like to waste time?

Failure. Still thinking of that word? Good, don't you ever forget it. And if someone ever calls it aloud, don't turn around. It only takes one wrong move like that to undo all of the brain washing you've completed. It happened to a guy I knew once. He was up for vice president of a big firm, a shoo-in to be elected, when someone called out after him, "Hey, Failure."' Well, his head turned around so fast, his neck almost snapped. The president of the company saw it and the next day the man got to his office and door was locked. All of those years of fighting, clawing his way to the top, ruined. Just like that. Damn shame, too. This damn neck of mine still hurts when it's damp out.

Other Parodies

A CAT AND A CHICK HOOKED UP
Sandra L. Crockett

This cat, after getting next to this chick was rapping for days over his love jones for her. The chick finally got her head bumped and agreed that they would shack together.

"We got to stock up on some grub before the hawk gets to cutting," the cat said, " 'cause I might get laid off from the gig again. All of the hustlers and the pimps going be recruitin' real tough 'bout now 'cause I know they need the extra dough. Little Mama, I want you to stick pretty close to the crib, or else they sho nuff will try to catch you in their trap."

So they started shacking and then they bought a whole lot of red beans and rice just in case that cat got laid off. They didn't have any room to put all of it because they only had a one room walk up. So after talking it over they decided to keep it over his partner's house who had much more room and who also happen to live over a storefront church. They also decided to wait until the shit really hit the fan before they touched it. Pretty soon, the fat cat decided to get greedy. What was once a love jones became a red beans and rice jones.

"Check this out, Mama," he said, "I got this cousin who is so old timey that she wants me to become her little baby's god-daddy. They going to have the baptism today and it's going to be at the same little storefront church. Let me deal with this and you stay put and watch the crib."

"You got it," the chick said, "Go do yo' thang. And when you are smackin' yo' jaws over all that good grub I know they going to have, think of me. At least try to sneak me a bottle of Ripple back."

But the cat was lying his fat ass off. No cousin had asked him to do nothing. He went upstairs over the church to his partner's place and cooked up a pot of red beans and rice. Then he walked the streets, cruising. He passed a bunch of buddies who were standing on the street corner shooting craps. Every time he thought of red beans and rice, his mouth watered. Deciding that it was nothing on the streets worth picking up, he eased on to the crib.

"It's about god damn time," the chick said. "I know you been doing some partyin'."

"Just a touch," the fat cat said.

"What's the name of the kid?" the chick asked.

"Sly," the cat answered with a crooked smile.

"Sly," the chick shrieked. "Well, at least it ain't the same old Tom, Dick or Harry type of name that's common yo' family."

"What's the difference?" the cat said. "It ain't no wose than Pot-Gut, yo' godbaby."

A couple of weeks went by and the cat started craving for the red beans and rice again.

"I got to bring it to you again, mama," he told the chick. "Stay here and keep yo' eyes on things 'cause another cousin asked me to be god-daddy fo'her kid. You know how jealous them bitches are of each other so you know I got to do it."

So the naive, dumb chick agreed, and the slick cat slunk along the streets until he came to the church. He went straight upstairs, cooked a pot of food and ate. Feeling like a pig he cooked some more and ate that up. Pretty soon, he found he had wiped out damn near half of it.

"What she won't know won't hurt, and there going to be more for me." He felt like he had got away with something this time. Back home, the chick asked what name this kid had been given.

"Slick," the cat said.

"Slick!" the chick yelled. "Brother, you got to be jivin'."

Now only three days passed before this cat began to want a taste of the stash.

"I know you ain't gone believe this," started the cat, "But my favorite cousin who also just dropped a load, wants me be god-daddy. And you heard that she was my favorite so it ain't no way under the sun that I can say no."

"Sly, Slick," thought the chick aloud. "With some weird names like that, you damn right I ain't gone believe this."

"Hey, lady," said the cat, "You ain't up on nothing in this world. All you do is sit here watching the boob tube day in and day out. How you 'spect you going know anything?"

So the chick picked up around the house, bored stiff. She was beginning to wonder if she had made the right decision after all. She was not a bad looking chick, she reminded herself. If this turkey didn't start acting like he had some sense, she would space.

"Well, you ain't got to worry 'bout no more brats being brought up," he said after coming back to the house. "I ain't even got no mo' cousins."

The first thing the chick wanted to know was the name.

"You ain't going to like it no better than the others," the cat said, "His name is Wicked."

"Wicked!" yelled the chick. "Get out of here, fool! I ain't never heard of such. Wicked, huh? I got a feeling that I am missing something." Scratching her head, she got undressed, cut the tube on and fell sound asleep. And the cat was right. He never was asked to be godfather any more.

When the hawk began to tear down the streets like an icy razor blade, the cat also got laid off from the gig.

"Come on, sugar," said the chick, "Go on over and get the stash. In fact I think that I'll just mosey on over there with you."

"You got it," the cat said.

So they put their stuff on and walked over to the little storefront church. They headed straight upstairs for the food.

"What the hell!" said the chick. "We been robbed! Or have we? Wait one cotton pickin' minute here. We ain't been robbed and you ain't been nobody's godfather. The Sly, Slick and the Wicked ain't nobody but you, you dirty, rotten son of a..."

"Now wait a goddamn minute here yo'self," screamed the cat. "You better shut yo' trap or I am going to give you one 'cross yo' head."

And the naive little chick, had the word "bitch" on her tongue, and it came right on out. At that point, the cat jumped on the chick, knocked her dead in her skull and brought down the final curtain. That's the way it is.

LET'S GIVE BABIES DRUGS
Paula G. Trent

See Junior over there, aisle three? Yeah, he's the two year old in the blue and red Winnie the Pooh coordinate suit staring down the pyramid of canned peas. He's wondering if he can snatch out the center can without the others falling. He's thinking about the time he saw Uncle Jake snatch the tablecloth from under the dinner setting while the setting remained on the table. Oh hell, here it comes.

Here comes the stockboy. The scene flashes a message to his brain; his brain translates the message to his heart; his heart is pumping blood profusely to his legs. He's running up the aisle full speed with his white apron flapping behind him, the heels of his shoes thudding into the hard wax of the supermarket floor. He's trying to prevent the scene about to occur: he knows he'll have to clean it up.

He's only two feet away. There's a chance he can stop the disaster ahead. Where's Mother?

She's in the next aisle, battling that gray-haired lady for the last package of crisp, green broccoli. It's a classic battle. The ol' bitch doesn't even like broccoli. Her only reason for the battle is that her hand touched the pack first reaching for the lettuce. It's how she gets her jollies, and there's Mom battling for the benefit of her hard-working bread-winner and the little bastard in the next aisle. She wants them to have a properly balanced and appetizing meal. She can only concentrate on one action at a time. She hears the stockboy's exclamation, "Oooooh, shit!"

The center can is sliding out. Look at the little jerk standing there, watching that avalanche of cans rushing down, as that spinning can on the left comes so close to giving him just what he deserves. It's too bad it missed. Damn, those cans sure are loud. That got his mother's attention. "Biiilly," she screams, as her head jerks in the direction of aisle three. She rushes over, snatches him by the hand, makes the necessary apologies, and picks up a few cans until the stockboy, weakened by defeat, says, "That's okay, ma'am. I'll do it."

The smirk on the kid's face would make the Marquis DeSade uncomfortable. The drool of elation is streaming down the left corner of his mouth; it passes his chin and dangles from the Pooh logo. Poor Mom.

The scene just described wouldn't have happened if Johnnie had been sedated before leaving the house. Just one of Mommie's five-gram Valiums would have done the trick. This is just one of the many reasons kiddies should be given drugs.

I hear all you double-standard, baby-balling hypocrites. I hear you shrieking collectively, "I'm appalled! My God, she's sick!" I know who you are. You're the ones that "kitchie, kitchie coo" into some poor infant's face until he begins to give you his point of view, then you hand him to his owner or keeper.

Hell no, I'm not sick. I'm speaking up for my pint-sized buddies. You've stood between them and pleasure long enough. You have used the pleasure principle the same way drugs are used to alter, and to retain and maintain control of the little tykes.

Mothers, how many times have you stuffed a bottle into Johnnie's mouth to pacify him when you couldn't determine why he was yelling his guts out? You wanted to hear Nina, of "All My Children," confess never-ending love to Cliff Warner after their turbulent separation. It was the quickest, most effective way to shut him up until you'd heard the smacking of lips coming from the screen.

This standard practice of shoving food into the kid satisfies his unknown desire but leads the kid down the road to a cholesterol-laden heart. That's right. In these early stages of development, you have ruined the child's natural shut-off mechanism, and food becomes the answer to most of his discomforts. That's how fat kids are made, but fat babies are cute, aren't they? When puberty strikes, they catch hell, and it's all your fault.

How many times have you held his chocolate pudding ransom in lieu of his eating those icky vegetables you wouldn't be eating if someone hadn't done the same thing to you? Of all the many varieties of veggies in the world, he has to eat the ones he doesn't like. This is nothing more than Mother's own little power trip in action.

How many times have you inflicted tiny spurts of pain to alter his behavior? To hell with "Spare the rod and spoil the child," manipulation is manipulation however it takes place. Psychologically, physically, or chemically, it's all manipulation. I say, let's use drugs. At least they're an open, honest and effective method of manipulation.

Mothers, there are many advantages to giving Johnnie drugs. Let's take the diaper/Pamper problem. You know how it seems the little tyke shits in his diapers when you're most hurried, when you're arguing with the repairman, pulling his siblings apart, or cleaning up Johnnie's latest mess. The siren goes off in its loudest pitch. It's continuous and aggravates the problem. You love Johnnie, but at that moment you just wish he'd shut the fuck up, at least until the task is done.

Well, with one lude (Quaalude to you novices and squares), Johnnie will merely sit there and trip off of the ooziness of the squishy pack in his diaper as it moves around his ass and privates. This will occupy him for about two hours. You can have Daddy's meal on the table when the key turns the lock on the front door, or finish that juicy item over the phone about the new slut on the block.

Downers are not the only drugs that hold advantages for parents. Oh no, there's more. If the kid is a finicky eater, blow a couple clouds of grass (marijuana for squares) up the tyke's nostrils. He'll go through Gerber's complete line, even the stuff he spits back at you.

If Johnnie is overweight, and you can't get him to stop sucking up everything in sight, give him a couple of reds. You'll see a slim, new kid in no time, but be careful. As soon as you notice a sufficient weight loss, start the kid on withdrawal. You don't want him speeding away to nothing.

For the times the little bastard gets bored with everything you put before him (toys, T.V., etc.) drop some purple microdot into his Similac. Microdots provide inward entertainment for days. It's economical, too. Because of the flashbacks, you'll only have to give it to him every two months. Remember to pad the crib. Some of the little brats tend to fulfill their masochistic desires while on the stuff.

These are just some of the ways drugs and babies can be combined. Pick a drug. Be creative. If you are one of those people who lack imagination and creativity is not your style, send away for my booklet, *The Creative Matching of Babies and Drugs*. Just send your name, address, and one pound of Hawaiian or Columbian marijuana to: Paula G. Trent, P.O. Box 101657.

Let's stop being hypocrites who cover our real motives with fake and phony pseudo-protectiveness. Let's alter and control behavior openly and directly. With drugs, the kid doesn't become caught in the psychological web of having to differentiate a thousand motives and emotions that cause, or are caused by, one single act. Give the kids a break. Let's be honest with them. Let 'em have drrrrruuuuuggs!

THE YEOMAN
Desiree Washington

Chaucer's Original

A Yeman hadde he, and servaunts namo
At that tyme, for him liste ryde so;
And he was clad in a cote and hood of grene;
A sheef of pecok-arwes bright and kene
Under his belt he bar ful thriftily;
(Wel coude he dresse his takel yemanly:
His arwes droped noght with feathers lowe),
And in his head he bar a mighty bowe.
A not-heed hadde he, with a broun visage.
Of wode-craft wel coude he al the usage.
Upon his arm he bar a gay bracer,
And by his syde a swerd and bokeler,
And on that other syde a gay daggere,
Harnesied wel, and sharp as point of spere;
A Christofre on his brest of silver shene.
An horn he bar, the bawdrik was of grene;
A forster was he, soothly, as I gess.

Modern English Translation

The Knight's private attendant stood next to him.
None of the other servants would ride the journey with them.
This servant wore a coat and hood of green.
His sheaf of peacock arrows were long and keen.
Under his belt was every weapon he needed.
The Yeoman's dress code he certainly heeded.
His arrows' feathers didn't droop low,
And in his hand he held a large bow.
He had a knothead, but a handsome brown face.
He was good at woodcarving, any time—any place.
He wore a large bracelet gay and wide.
His sharp buckled sword hung down by his side.
And on his other side he had a long dirk;
He had it well harnessed, so he wouldn't get hurt.
He wore a St. Christopher medal that lay on his chest.
His horn hung in a green baldric to match his coat, I guess.
More than an efficient woodsman, I could tell by his dress!

Non-standard English

The Yeoman played servant and worked as a guide,
No other lazy-ass servant would make the long ride.
This man wore a hooded coat in loathsome lime green.

His arrows had peacock feathers from some bird he'd just cleaned.
He had 'em in a sharp leather sheath that hung on his side;
This mad—bad, fad of fashion was every Yeoman's pride.
He had to jus' plucked them arrow feathers, cause they didn't wilt.
And his bow wuz a'odd oak-like timber, man, carved to the hilt!
His head was shaped like a peanut with a face colored brown.
And this guy was the best brother woodcarver in town.
He had a brass bracelet on his upper arm,
To keep that thick bow string from doin' any harm.
He shoulda been weighed down with that heavy sword and shield.
That dagger on his other side showed he's ready—for real!
He had a silver Catholic medal around his large neck.
And he had a horn in his green baldric—my man was decked!
Even though he was a stranger,
Man, you knew he had to be a Ranger.

LADEDAH
Pete Bontsema

> The trouble is, I get to feeling sorry for
> them. I mean most girls are so dumb and
> all. After you neck them for awhile, you
> can really *watch* them losing their
> brains. You take a girl when she really
> gets passionate, she just hasn't any
> brains.
> —J.D. Salinger

> Everybody's in despair
> Every girl and boy
> But when Quinn the Eskimo gets here,
> Everybody's gonna jump for joy.
> —Bob Dylan

Ladedah was fifteen the first time he got laid. There was no real passion.
Just diversion. Follow some rich bitch backta her place. Make her feel good.
Tell her shes pretty. Tell her what she wants to hear. Run your fingers thru
her crusty oversprayed hair. Ladedah didnt mind. Then hop in the sack
with her. Get between those beefy thighs and pump away. Who cares. It
was bucks. Good bucks. Pick up fifty bucks sometimes a hundred. Those
old lonely babes pay good. No one elsell fuck em. And Ladedah didn't
mind. Ladedah was the best. He was young and looked pretty and said all
the right things. They asked for him by name. He opened up a service and
took calls and sent up appointments and sent out his friends to take care of
the women. But they all complained. They all wanted Ladedah. Ladedah
was built like a man. Not like some kid. He was hung like a stud pony.
They preferred him. So Ladedah closed shop. Sent the boys home. Handled
all requests on his own. After school. Nights, Weekends. Whenever. The
demand grew and the price went up. Sorry not enough. Sorry lady. Try
someone else. No I wont do it even if you do throw in your daughter.
Click. Hangup. No time for the poor bitches. Too bad. But who has the
time? Not Ladedah. Ladedah only had time for the best for the richest cuz
he was the best. He had the biggest cock in all of Malibu. You could see it
as he walked down the beach. The girls would melt at the sight of it.
Ahhhh. Look at that hunk of pork. And theyd smile at each other and
dream and whack their legs together and Ladedah would keep walking and
the girls would lay back down depressed. They knew they couldn't afford
him. So they beatoff at night and mailed Baggies full of pubic hair to
Ladedah with their telephone numbers. But Ladedah never called. Too
busy. He went to the local housewives. The rich ones. Sometimes they were
40 sometimes 25 or less. Whoever paid the most and looked the best. And
he grinded into them in their posh suburban bedrooms and brought them to
heaven and rolled off and they fell asleep and Ladedah tiptoed out with a
hundred in his pocket. Not bad. Twenty minutes work. Ladedah bounced
from one wealthy woman to the next, sometimes not even stopping to call

his mother and tell her hed be late for dinner. Just mounting on top or laying on his back or hopping in the shower with them or standing up while they knelt. Just stepping into a bedroom and having his pants ripped off before he could set a price and the woman diving between his legs and handing him a signed blank check. Time passed—months, maybe years, who knows and the jeans and flannel shirts were gone. Just silk shirts and double knit slacks over his broad muscular shoulders and narrow tight hips. His eyes were crystal clear and fresh and his jaw lean and strong. And the posh Malibu homes became Hollywood mansions high on winding roads. And the wealthy heavy set women became even wealthier but trimmer swimming pool loungers who wore sunglasses and sipped Tom Collinses at poolside. Ladedah bounced from one deck to the next, taking calls in his Fiat convertible and sipping orange juice thru a straw while the stereo played, and leaned back in the leather seat and rode up the winding hills. What the hell. There was nothing stopping him. Take two in a day. Maybe three. A thousand a head. Get a tan while you screw. Do it on the deck then take a dip in the pool. Do it underwater. Whatthefuck. Satisfy the horny babes. Then his name grew and his body was demanded and the lazy afternoon fucks led to nightlife parties in Hollywood. From Jack Nicholsons place to Warren Beattys, with his 600 dollar white suit flashing under the dark skies as he went from one Rolls to the next. Ladedah didnt mind. He spent his days taking it easy at his own pool sipping orange juice and watching TV. Or sleeping. With an occasional afternoon fuck thrown in for fun. Then hit the town at night. Party. Sleep all day if ya want. And the names became those of the Hollywood jetset. First starting with the lonely ones. The lonely ones with lots of money. But Ladedah wasnt after money. He just had to go to the one who paid the most. Law of supply and demand. So he went to the richest ones who were sometimes the loneliest. Karen Carpenter. Sandy Duncan. Florence Henderson. He flopped from one servant filled house to the next with the California sun beating down on his face and his skin just becoming tanner and tanner. The names grew and faces became more plentiful and Ladedah had to arrange his schedule to fit between plays and movies and tapings of the Hollywood Squares. But the women made their schedules fit his. And Ladedah just smoked a joint here and there and cruised up the sunny streets to the next woman and rolled on and rolled off and maybe smoked another joint and cruised in his Fiat to the next and rolled on and rolled off over and over again. And time passed. Time always passes. And Ladedah became more famous and his name was known nationwide. And the Karen Carpenters and Sandy Duncans and Florence Hendersons became the Cheryl Tiegses and Jane Pauleys and Erica Jongs and Gracie Slicks and Phyllis Georges. It was in to screw with Ladedah. It was THE THING. It was status. You just hadnt made it until you fucked with Ladedah. You had to make appointments thru his personal secretary. You had to wait. So what if youre Jane Fonda or Princess Grace or Jacqueline Onassis? You wait. Hell get to you when he can thank you for calling. And the price goes up. Highest bidders go first. Its only fair. Unless youre a Linda Ronstadt. Yeah. Linda. That voice. That body. Let her in anytime she wants, Marion. Dont put her on the waiting list. Ill see her now. He saw them and he saw them all. Then came the publicity. The magazines. Time. Newsweek. People. Rolling Stone. Sports Illustrated. Covers of em all. That pretty face on every news rack across the country.

Around the world. Times MAN OF THE YEAR. Yeah. That was good. 12 page spread. With pics. Good copy. Ladedah won the Nobel Prize that year. They invented a special category for him. He went to Sweden to accept the award and collect the money and screwed with the Kings wife right there on the stage. He held the 83 thousand dollar check in one hand and screwed while the audience applauded like mad. He basked on the French Riviera with Princess Caroline and screwed under the strobe lights at Studio 54 with Caroline Kennedy and Bianca Jagger. Nothing was as prestigious, nothing was as IN as a fuck from Ladedah. If you hadnt made it with him you were out. You just hadnt made it. It was that simple. Then came the invitation to the White House. Big fancy dinner. A private Lear jet was sent for Ladedah and he went. What the hell figured Ladedah. Its a free dinner. Have a good time. The dinner was laid out in a huge room with oil paintings on the wall and a chandelier over the long long table. Everyone who was anyone was there. Jimmy Carter and Rosalyn and Amy and Pierre Trudeau and Margaret Trudeau and Jackie O and Woody Allen and Diane Keaton and Jerry Brown and Linda Ronstadt and Princess Grace and her husband and Warren Beatty and Julie Christie and Queen Elizabeth and Prince Charles and Anwar Sadat with some chick in a veil and John Travolta and Donny and Marie and some Senators and Congressmen with their wives. They all wore tuxedoes and long dresses and sat at the long long table under the huge chandelier and ate filet mignon and each person had about three forks and spoons and they drank wine and talked and made witty comments and Ladedah was sitting between Julie Christie and Amy Carter and Julie Christie kept handing him more filet mignon and telling him to eat up to keep his strength and she winked and squeezed his thigh and Ladedah smiled back and Amy Carter asked him if he liked carrots and he said no not really and she said me neither and turned her glum face back to her plate and the table started jiggling and the glasses clinked because someones leg was shaking under the table and it was Marie Osmond who whispered to Woody Allen that her panties were all wet from just looking at Ladedah and Woody said he knew just how she felt that he felt exactly the same way whenever he saw someone with a piece of corn stuck between their teeth too and the meal went on and the chocolate pudding was served and Princess Grace had an idea and wrote MY ROOM AT MIDNIGHT on the top of her pudding and signed it and had it passed to Ladedah and it was handed down the line to Ladedah but others got the same idea along the way and Ladedah got pudding from Jackie O and Diane Keaton and the others until he had fourteen bowls of pudding in front of him and had no choice but to eat them all and he ate every womans pudding except Amy who asked if he liked spinach and he said no and she said me neither and dug into her pudding and Ladedah ate all the pudding in front of him and felt sick as he got to the last bowl and Jimmy said lets go in the living room and have coffee and everyone got up from the table except Ladedah who was slow in rising and didnt follow the others but went out on the front porch instead to get some fresh air and the porch was white and the spotlights were bright and shining on the doors and pillars and Ladedah stepped off the porch and walked onto the lawn with the bright white house behind him and he walked into the darkness with huge evergreens on either side and way in front of him was an iron spiked fence and he was getting some air in the middle of the lawn when he heard a voice behind him and he turned and saw the silhouette of a woman on the bright porch and he squinted but couldnt tell who it was and was only able to make out a long flowing gown and some kind of hat on her head and the woman called his name and he stopped and waited as the figure came closer then became clearer under the starry summer sky and the woman stepped up close and it was Queen Elizabeth and she said hi handsome I wanted to get to you before the rest of them and without saying another word she dropped to her knees and started pulling down Ladedahs zipper and Ladedah looked around and saw nothing in the darkness but the tall evergreens and the spotlighted house way off and figured what the hell I might as well get her outta the way now and he let her get into his pants and she said he had the biggest cock in the world and she used her mouth and Ladedah reached down for her tits and pretty soon they were sprawled on the grass in the darkness and fucking like mad and Queen Elizabeth was screeching and scraping his back and she took off her crown and put it on Ladedahs head and said Im taking you back to Fuckingham Palace and Ladedah laughed but thought it was stupid and he grinded into her as he faced the grass and watched some ants carry a dead fly and then he saw a big black shoe under his nose and looked up a long grey pant leg and saw a Secret Service agent with a gun staring down at him and he was scared for a second but the agent just winked and said keep it up Ill stand guard and the agent looked away and Ladedah shrugged and figured whatthehell and he continued to pump until he felt a flashbulb pop to his left and he looked over the Queens face and saw a photographer crouched down with the White House in the background and the photographer said dont let me bother you I just wanted some pictures for the paper and Ladedah shrugged and looked at the Queen who had her eyes closed and her tongue hanging out and more flashes popped all around and Ladedah saw dozens of newsmen circled around at all angles and then a TV camera was set up to his right and Dan Rather crouched down and described the live action for the folks at home and then Dan stood up and walked around Ladedah towards the White House where Jimmy Carter and the whole party had come out to watch and they all stood behind the photographers with the glowing house in the background and answered questions with smiles and Ladedah kept pumping and the Queen moaned for more and Ladedah gave it to her and glanced around while he thrusted and he saw people by the spiked fence looking in and holding onto the bars and they were smiling and Ladedah saw the buses behind them in the street and the people were clapping and Ladedah smiled and waved and went back to screwing and Queen Elizabeth moaned louder and flashes popped and people cheered and the dinner guests watched and the Queen screamed in ecstasy and more flashes popped and the scream reached new heights and the people whistled and applauded and the Queens grip loosened on Ladedahs back and Ladedah figured shed had enough and he pulled out slow and adjusted the crown on his head and the Queen lay inert for a minute until a smile grew on her face and she sat up with a sigh and lit a cigarette and Ladedah got off his knees and stood up and pulled up his pants and people surrounded him and slapped him on the back waytago—attaboy—good job old sport—and everyone congratulated him and swarmed around him and another group formed around the Queen and slapped her on the back and suddenly Dan Rather ran from the Queen to Ladedah and asked how does it feel and

Ladedah shrugged and said it was a little tight and dry but—no no what I mean said Dan is that the Queen has just made you King and Ladedah looked over at the Queen on the lawn with her long dress over her spread legs and she was signing a piece of paper and she was smiling at Ladedah and nodding and Ladedah just looked at her and Dan Rather shook him by the arm and asked him how it felt to be the KING OF ENGLAND and Ladedah just shrugged and said whatthehell someones gotta do it and Dan Rather slapped his leg and everyone started roaring with laughter...

WAMPUM LAKE
Marie Ostarello

Jeff loved an audience. Get him in front of a crowd and he'd give em a show alright. Gave a great one Memorial Day out at Wampum Lake. Had to be a thousand or so partyin out there that day. First day of the season. People hung out blowin joints. Tossin frisbees. Flippin chicken legs on the grill. Sellin drugs or coppin drugs. A few people were freakin out on some bad shit that was goin around. Their eyes were bulgin and their mouths were droolin like dogs man. Bad trip. Unusual for Wampum. Wampum was the place to be if you wanted drugs man. Good drugs. Any kind. You could cop it out at Wampum. Cars parked next to each other in rows and set up shop. Sold outta their trunks man. Like a fuckin market. Acid. Tick. Columbian. Beans. Ludes. Whatever. People just yelled out their merchandise as the cars passed by in a procession. If they were interested, they'd stop. Check out the goods. And make their purchase. They didn't even have to leave their cars. It was a fuckin drive-in drug store man. Kept the rangers busy. Those fuckin pigs. They were at the gate hasslin people who wanted to get in. Too crowded they kept sayin. Jeff snuck in on his dirt bike from the railroad tracks behind the lake. It was hot as hell and Jeff was sweatin like a mother. He wanted to go for a swim. Signs everywhere posted no swimming allowed. But Jeff never could figure out why they had that stupid rule. It was a stupid fuck rule and it pissed him off. He swam anyway. And fuck em if they can't take a joke. Haw haw. Helbe and Gray joined him for a party out on the lake. Swam out to the middle with a six-pack a Michelob and a packa cigarettes (and if ya were cool ya called em snigs) held high up in the air. They came prepared. Balanced out in the middle of the lake on a picnic table poundin Lobes and sniggin in their skivvies. When one of em moved the table tipped and rocked and tossed, and their beers sunk and their snigs floated away. And who was the fuckhead who moved? Not me man. Oh, who the fuck gave a shit anyway. They were havin fun. A fuckin ball. No shit. The yellow ranger cars patrolled the long straight drive that ran along one side of the lake. All the cars parked along it slammed down their trunks and closed up shop until the rangers had finished their bad ass patrol. They waited for em to pass but the rangers spotted the three swimmers out on the lake. They flashed their lights and barked over the loudspeaker there's no swimming allowed, get out of the lake immediately. But Jeff thought they had alotta nerve. Who the fuck did they think they were talkin to? Don't them assholes know we own this lake? Who do they think they are tellin us what to do? They're rangers with guns Gray said. Helbe agreed. Pigs. That's what they were Jeff thought. And we're gonna show em. Haw haw. Right you guys? Don't wimp out on me now man. Let's have some fun. Okay man? Crowds gathered all along one side of the lake. Jeff looked like the MC at a circus and Helbe and Gray the clowns. Jeff swept his arm and ta dum! Helbe dove off the picnic table like a swan. Drum roll please. A sweep of the other arm and ta dum! Gray jumped and tucked into a back somersault flip. The crowds roared. Applauded. More people gathered round. Two even stopped shootin tick into their arms to catch the show. Like wow man. What's goin on? What's that guy on man? Must be some good shit. And people whistled and cheered. The pigs got pissed off and kept yellin over their loudspeaker. Young man if you get out now you will be fined but you won't be arrested. But you must get out of the lake immediately. Do you hear? Immediately. More ranger cars swarmed to the mob scene like pissed off yellow bumble bees. Helbe and Gray got scared and swam off to the back shore and escaped through the woods. Chicken shits, Jeff mumbled. Huh. Arrested. Huh. I'll show em. And now for the highlight of the show. Jeff turned his back to the crowd, slid his wears down to his ankles and mooned every last one of em. He wiggled his ass and the crowd roared and applauded and chicks whistled. One bitch with bleach blonde hair and a fringe halter top screamed let's turn it around honey, nice ass but I wanna see the prize. And another agreed and hoped it was a grand prize. Jeff turned around and faced the crowd and wrung out his wears and twirled them around his finger like a baton. The crowd cheered and clapped and Jeff bowed and laughed haw haw cuz he was havin a fuckin blast. Dancin around on that picnic table. Man from the shore he looked fluorescent. His skin was so white it glowed out there like a lightbulb. When the rangers beamed their spotlight on him (just to piss him off) the crowd started puttin on sunglasses as a joke. Jeff laughed haw haw. He was in the spotlight alright and he was havin fun. So was the crowd. Dealers took advantage of the confusion and popped open their trunks and started dealin again. Some guys taped a joint and matches onto a baseball and tossed it out to Jeff. Good catch. Good joint. Jeff toked and bowed all lit up and laughed haw haw cuz he showed em who's boss around here alright. The rangers swarmed in groups makin plans. The one with the loudspeaker kept on yellin we've got all day mister how bout you? You gotta come out sometime and we'll be here just waitin fer yer ass. But Jeff laughed haw haw. They wish they could catch me. Dumb fucks. Think they're cool cuz they got guns and loudspeakers. They're a buncha wimps man. The pigs kept on blarin when you come out, yer gonna be one sorry smart ass. The crowds booed the rangers and rocked their cars. The Fatman sat on the hood of one car and smashed the tires to the ground. The ranger beeped his horn. Get off my car you derelict. The Fatman slid off and the car bounced up and down boosh boosh boosh and the ranger behind the wheel flew up and bumped his head on the roof. Fatman. What a slob. The guy had to be 450 pounds man. Nobody messed with his ass. Not even the rangers. Shit they couldn't handcuff his hands together if they tried. His arms weren't long enough to fit around his body. The fat pig. Sold good drugs though. Stashed em between his fat sweaty rolls. He'd pull up a thick slab a fat and inside there'd be a bag a tuinals or black beauties. The pigs never found the shit. Smart dude that Fatman. He got the pigs all pissed off while they were tryin to set up their plan. They all agreed. It was gettin to be a fuckin mob scene and somethin had to be done with that idiot on the lake. They plotted. His motorcycle was clear around the lake on the back beach. There was no road that led there so if they were gonna catchim they'd have to ride over the curbs and onto the field and around the lake to the back shore. If three cars went around one way and the other three the other way, they'd have the shit before he knew what hit im. And Jeff watched the six cars as they rolled and bounced over the curbs and circled the lake. No shit he thought. They were gonna actually try an catchim. This was gonna be one helluva race. People scattered everywhere pickin up their barbecue grills and runnin out of the way. Jeff swam back to the shore like a mother. He swallowed water. It tasted like carp. The pigs were gettin closer. They were almost to his bike when he struggled onto the beach and fuck the clothes man who's got time now. Gotta show the assholes what it's really like to race. He pounced on his bike and he kickstarted it and it popped and skipped and snorted. Lezgo baby. Yeah. He flipped his wrists and roared off head on at the cars and swerved just inches from their bumpers and laughed haw haw at their confusion and outta my way mother fuckers haw haw and popped wheelies his wet hair flyin back cool like and the rangers chased after him like fuckin dildos man around the lake and into the lake and into each other and the crowds stood on cars and some climbed the trees and filled the branches way up and the trees swayed from the weight and some whipped off their clothes and went swimmin in the lake and dove off the picnic tables like swans and mooned the fuckin rangers with their white hairy asses and some threw hotdogs and squirted barbecue sauce at the rangers' windshields when they passed around the lake like cartoon racers and Jeff laughed haw haw and slapped his knee as one car plowed into a keg wham foam everywhere haw haw what a fuckin blast. A day to be remembered alright. Too bad Jeff hadda later the scene man cuz it'd be fun to hang out an see what happened but Jeff zipped off down the field and raced away down the train tracks haw haw while the pigs stopped dead at the tracks and leaned over their yellow car doors pantin and swearin as they watched him ride away.

THE ELBOWS
Bill Burck

We love the extraordinary; our appetite for it is voracious. Well, it just so happens that I have in my possession a particularly extraordinary tale. Without further ado then, here it is, the story of a rather baffling pair of elbows.

The back door slammed, the window rattling, and George Jenkins snapped awake. He was lying in bed on his back with the covers pulled up to his chin and the first thing he noticed was that he had a rock-hard boner. A boner, he thought to himself, Hmmmm.

He heard the loud clunk as his wife set her bowling bag down in the kitchen. He rolled over and propped himself up on one elbow so he could shout out to her, "Dearie, I left the change from the groceries on the kitchen table."

At the same time, he imagined the sight of her as he said it. She would be standing with her hand on the icebox handle, ready to pull it open and fetch out a can of Buckhorn, her favorite beer and thus the one they bought. She would immediately espy the two neat piles of coins, three quarters next to four pennies, sitting atop the doubled-up bills. Crisp bills. He had specifically asked the cashier for the cleanest, crispest bills in her checkout drawer and had remained politely adamant on the issue despite the young lady's gum-cracking snort of disdain. If there was one thing his wife Myrtle Jenkins, nee Morgan, despised, it was crumpled and dirty billfold currency. And George Jenkins had ironed money enough times for one lifetime in the few years he had been married.

George knew that his wife's mind would be clicking right now as she tallied up the groceries, clicking rather slowly perhaps, but clicking nonetheless. A dozen eggs, click. Laundry soap ("He better have gotten Tide like I told him and not that faggy All-Temp-A-Cheer"), click. Two sixers of Buckhorn, click. Zip-lock sandwich bags, click. A loaf of Wonder Bread, click. Sandwich meat, click. Click, click, click. Subtotal, click. Tax, click. Total, click. Then subtracting it from the twenty she'd left clipped to the fridge, click, she would arrive at a remainder of about five bucks. He heard the change jingle and her purse snap closed and the refrigerator open and shut. He knew that he had done the right thing in returning all of the change with a receipt, instead of buying a lottery ticket on number 007 as he had been sorely tempted to do.

And Myrtle Jenkins nee Morgan thought to herself as she ripped the fliptop off of a Buckhorn and raised the can to her lips, tilting back her head, "What an honest fool of a husband I have. He is so stupid. Does he think I won't find a reason to get pissed at him if he dutifully returns every piece of change to me? Very well, I'll spend this extra money on that horse in the fourth at Arlington tomorrow."

George Jenkins lay down again on his back and checked his boner tentatively with his fingers. Still there, but softening a bit, like a stick of butter starting to get warm. Hurry up, honey, he thought to himself, Come to bed quickly. You've been bowling all evening, you've had a few drinks. Come to bed and I'll sink it in you. Then he pulled out the *Playboy* magazine he kept between the mattresses on his side of the bed and opened it up to one of the pictorials. His boner perked up quite well.

"What did you bowl, honey?" he yelled out, as his eyes gulped in the lithe, white thighs of the young, raven-haired Chinese Girl named Wei Lei, who liked jogging and neato movies and who was sprawled languorously in the empty bathtub.

"Terrible! Just fucking terrible. We lost to those bozos from that Lutheran church in Berwyn. Those Nazis! I threw so many gutter balls and I could have just strangled their captain. Oh! She just sat there smiling away daintily. The whore is thin as a rail and her ball can't weigh more than a billiard ball. Goddammit, how does she throw so many strikes? Oh! I tell you, that smile, and does she think I can't see through that cheap blonde wig of hers!"

"Oh, that's too bad, my dear," George sympathized. "Come to bed why don't you?" He said it in such a way that the suggestion of a little loving was unmistakably present in his voice.

Certainly Myrtle Jenkins nee Morgan, for so she prefers to be called, discerned the meaning in her husband's voice. She crushed the aluminum can in her hand, the metal making a popping noise, then tossed it with a flick of her wrist into the garbage can. She felt a tingling in her loins, but couldn't be sure if this was a result of George's suggestion or an effect of the Buckhorn she had just guzzled. Her head was already beginning to swim a bit. Opening the refrigerator door again, she pulled out another Buckhorn for her and one for George.

George heard her footsteps coming down the hall to the bedroom. Frantically he pried up the mattress with one hand and thrust the *Playboy* under it with the other. Then, in a sudden fit of inspiration, he reached out and snatched a bottle of cologne off of his dresser. There was no time to be choosy. Unfortunately, he happened to latch onto the Lectric Shave. No matter. The top was off, Lectric Shave splashed onto his naked chest, the top back on, and the bottle slipped under the bed in less time than you can say, "The name's Bond. James Bond."

When Myrtle Jenkins nee Morgan stopped in the doorway, George was lying on his back, his hands casually cupped under his head, the blankets kicked down around his ankles to reveal his entire nakedness. He was smiling slyly and generally trying to look very rakish.

Before I continue any further with this account, I think it would only be fair to you the reader, if I take the chance now to freeze the action and provide a description of the persons and personalities of George Jenkins and wife, Myrtle Jenkins nee Morgan. Thus, when the action continues anew, your closer acquaintance with them will allow your imagination to fill in the gaps. Perhaps you can look at this exercise as comparable to the mechanics of the cartoon. A cartoon is, after all, a series of still images, which when sped past our eyes at sufficient speed, produces the illusion of fluidity and movement.

Myrtle Jenkins nee Morgan stood in the doorway, and her frame was anything but slight. Her head was large, her jaw square. Lantern-jawed, some call it. Her features were blunt. This blunt aggregation of features was also assembled in a rather blunt fashion. It was an open face, a face that readily betrayed the fact that Myrtle Jenkins nee Morgan never resorted to subtlety and didn't appreciate its use by others. "The face of a rutabaga," someone had once referred to it, and they were right.

Her shoulders were broad, and her body travelled straight down from them to the hips. Her figure didn't come even remotely close to resembling the classic hour-glass shape. If I were to compare her to an object, I would have to say that she resembled most closely a mailbox. Her legs were two pillars, firmly rooted to the ground. They seemed designed with only one attribute in mind—strength. Not some supple, Amazonian strength, mind you, but pure strength, of the tree trunk variety. It shouldn't come as a surprise then to learn that Myrtle Jenkins nee Morgan was a construction worker.

And if there is one quality which is at the heart of the type of strength to which I am referring, it is solidity. Myrtle Jenkins nee Morgan definitely had solidity as she stood in the doorway, a Buckhorn in each hand. Just look at those shoulders.

But let us turn out attention to George. We already know a few things about him. One of these is the fact that he had a boner, the size and dimensions of which we will leave to the imagination of the reader, though it did give full satisfaction to Myrtle Jenkins nee Morgan, a woman who was rather big in the womanly way. This was, however, the only big thing about George Jenkins. He was an extremely thin man. He was most commonly referred to as "George the Wimp." Luckily he was good-natured and had a pleasing face, which was rather easy to like. His only failing, if it could be called that, was his choice of James Bond as a role model. He owned all the books and made regular pilgrimages to the movies at the revival theaters. He had a pretty good idea of what it took to be a James Bond. Unfortunately, he continually ran into no end of trouble in putting this knowledge into practice. If he had the right line, his timing was off. If he got the timing right, then he delivered it weakly. And even if he got it all straight, then his physical presence simply couldn't back it up, and he was laughed at. But he wasn't discouraged by failure, because he knew that deep within him lurked a true James Bond, and someday he, George Jenkins, would become that gallant man. Meanwhile, he was a dutiful husband and worked as a lab assistant at the University of Illinois Medical School. He cleaned up the dissected corpses.

There they were. Myrtle was barely lit, a dark silhouette against the light from the hall. The shades were drawn tight on the windows. And since George could think of nothing properly James Bondish to say at the moment, he settled for, "Let's have that beer over here, honey."

Myrtle Jenkins nee Morgan tossed him his can of Buckhorn, and he caught it fumblingly with two hands. "Let's fuck," she said. Two Buckhorns spit and hissed as they were opened.

Her St. Barnabas Bombers team shirt hit the floor. Her blue, polyester pants followed immediately after. One arm curled around behind her while the other raised the Buckhorn to her lips. Her Adam's apple bounced up and down her throat. Her bra snapped open and she shrugged her way out of it. Her bosoms vibrated like twin mounds of jello as she shimmied her panties down her ample buttocks. The empty Buckhorn was crushed and landed on the heap of clothes. Not once did her eyes leave George's boner.

George swallowed hard. It wasn't the beer. For some reason, he felt the need to swallow whenever he was about to make love or whenever he was about to see two people do it in the movies.

Myrtle Jenkins nee Morgan hit the bed like a ton of bricks. She bounced over next to George, and her hand immediately sought out his boner.

"Whew!" he gasped, as her cold hand encased him.

What followed was a flurry of flailing arms and legs, as Myrtle Jenkins nee Morgan rolled atop George and clamped her mouth on his, then rolled over on her back, dragging George along with her. The bed creaked its protest as he bit her neck and placed a hand on one mound of mammary and began kneading it. All the while, Myrtle Jenkins nee Morgan's hand was working away at George's boner. She never had mastered any sort of delicate touch, and it was often the case in these instances that George felt like a stick shift. After several more position changes, which became increasingly violent and which severely tested the resiliency of the bedsprings, George ended up on top, plunging away between the gaping thighs of Myrtle Jenkins nee Morgan.

It was then that Myrtle Jenkins nee Morgan arched her spine and reached up both hands under her pillow. As her hands wormed their way under the pillow, they encountered two moist, solid lumps. Her breath caught in her throat for a moment, and George continued pumping away, oblivious to his wife's sudden distraction. Her fingers then probed about the firm objects, feeling a knobby protrusion on one side of each and two moist, fleshy ends, flat but yielding. Her eyes popped wide open and she shrieked at the top of her lungs. This quite upset George's rhythm, and he came instantly. At the same time, Myrtle Jenkins nee Morgan heaved her hips violently skyward, propelling George into the air so that he landed on his feet next to the bed, visibly shaken, his precious carnal essence spraying across the bed and fleshy belly of his wife.

It seems that Myrtle Jenkins nee Morgan had discovered a pair of elbows beneath her pillow.

She sat bolt upright, an elbow clamped in each meaty fist. "You...you ingrate!" she sputtered. "Is this your idea of romance, you ignorant chucklebutt? You cur, you Huckleberry Hound, you heretic! How many times (her voice began to rise in pitch at this point) have I told you to never—Oh! you good for nothing rapist—never, never, never-never-never bring home your work with you? Now this!" and she brandished the elbows so threateningly that George stumbled backwards and fell to the floor at the foot of the bed, quivering uncontrollably.

"B-b-but my dear, my sweet, my p-precious," he protested feebly, "I've never s-seen those elbows before in m-m-my life."

Yet even as he said this, it had a ring of falsehood about it, because a flicker of recognition had entered George's eyes and voice. Yes, indeed, there was definitely something familiar about those elbows. Myrtle Jenkins nee Morgan easily detected the hollowness of his protests.

"Hah! Never seen them before, eh? You scoundrel! You brigand! Who are you trying to kid, you oaf? Maggot, beetle, BUG! You're sick! How did I ever marry you? Answer me that." George lay silent, quivering. "I could have married dozens, scores of others. Fred Melnick! I could have married Fred Melnick, you know that? He gave me a sledgehammer on my nineteenth birthday. He's a plumber! Does he put elbows underneath his wife's pillow? Oh! You scumbag! You're a maniac, that's what you are. A regular Mr. Potatohead. I've half mind to call the police, and after them, the funny farm. Oh! I can't believe it. Wait till I tell mother. ELBOWS!"

It was then that Myrtle Jenkins nee Morgan cast her gaze at the elbows. A thin trickle of transparent red fluid had seeped from one of them and was following gravity's call down her wrist and onto her beefy forearm. Upon seeing this, she uttered a gurgling moan and fainted dead away.

As far as George Jenkins was concerned, his wife's temporary demise was a blessing straight from heaven. He peered up at her from where he lay on the carpet past the foot of the bed. So far so good, thought George Jenkins. Slowly, he rose to his feet. Yes, he must dispose of those elbows and then deny all.

What's that, honey, elbows? he would wonder innocently. Oh, you certainly must have been having some sort of nightmare. Elbows, clean-cut elbows at that? My, my, you should stop drinking those Suffering Bastards, honey. They alway do it to you.

Quickly and quietly as he could, he dressed himself, pulling an overcoat with large front pockets on over his clothes and topping himself off with a rakish, beaver fur cap. He approached his wife with great trepidation. She lay as before, like a felled buffalo, the line of cum a dry scar across her belly. What if she's been playing possum all this while, he thought to himself, just waiting for me to come close enough so she can rip out my larynx. But such was not the case, and the elbow joints were soon in his hands, wrapped separately in handkerchiefs, then each thrust deep into an overcoat pocket.

Instead of flying out the door at this point, for some strange reason he had an irresistible urge to brush his teeth. And for some even stranger reason he went ahead and brushed them.

George stepped out into the yellow glow under the front porch light. The cold snapped against his cheeks like the bite of tiny castanets. He cared not a whit if his wife awoke now. Was he not outside? Was he not a man? A free man? Was he not dressed warmly in this chill night air? He fairly danced down the front steps, turned nimbly on his heel and set off down the sidewalk with a jaunty spring in his stride. He laughed out loud for no apparent reason and adjusted his cap lower and to one side so the brim angled just above his eyes, making him look, he thought, particularly dangerous and sly.

He glanced slyly up and to his left at a streetlamp that was humming like a treeful of locusts. It blinked off all of a sudden, catching George off guard. Had he had a Walther PPK nestled securely beneath his armpit in a shoulder holster, he most assuredly would have drawn it and rolled to his left, cat-like, raised to one knee, and fired, eliminating with one shot the offending streetlamp. But there was no Walther PPK and George simply laughed out loud again, shaking his head.

Then, for some reason, George imagined a beautiful, tempestuous young woman walking toward him in a long mink coat, spike heels and nothing else. Why, no doubt she would have immediately been in his arms, trembling in anticipation of a rapturous pressing of lips and smelling faintly of brie cheese. George often fantasized about women who smelled of cheese. Musky, dark, earthy women. Brie and Jarlsberg were his favorites.

Ah yes, he thought to himself, this is good, this little walk. Damn it, I must do it more often.

George then plunged his hands deep into his overcoat pockets. Up until this point, he had felt warm and contented, but when his hands encountered the two rag-wrapped lumps in the bowels of his pockets, a wave of cold swept up his spine and most of the spring in his stride abruptly disappeared.

Before long he was standing on the corner of a busy street, Cicero Avenue. The light was green, but he didn't cross. He didn't know which way to go. He glanced uncertainly to his left, and his heart almost stopped. Coppers! A patrol car sat at the stoplight, waiting, white exhaust drifting up idly behind it.

He took a quick step forward to cross the street and then stopped in his tracks. The Don't Walk sign was flashing. He glanced furtively over at the patrol car. They were looking at him. His fingers twitched nervously on the elbows in his pockets. He thought of his hat—My God, I look like a gangster—and then tipped it back on his head so the brim pointed up into the air. He stared down at the ground and tried to whistle, but it was no good, as if he had a mouthful of crackers. He had to appear innocent, so he repeated to himself under his breath, "I am Henry Fonda, I am Henry Fonda, I am Henry Fonda."

These were certainly his last few moments as a free man—he was sure of it—and he spent them in deep thought.

Damn these elbows. Damn them to hell! What right had they to show up in my bed? Under my wife's pillow? It doesn't make sense, no matter how you look at it. Besides, it isn't even fair. The police won't understand and neither will the judge. They'll laugh at me. My wife will run away with Fred Melnick. Oh my, I'll spend the next few years in jail and lose my dear Myrtle in the bargain.

At this point George grew so furious that he almost wrenched his hands out of his pockets and hurled the accursed elbows as far away as he could. But the light had changed, and George held his breath as the patrol car drove past. It didn't stop. His breath rushed out of him, and as he watched the red taillights move away down the street, he saw several blokes come staggering out of Blarney's Tap. He recognized them. This was the last thing he needed. He turned away, hunching his shoulders and letting his head sink down between them.

The light was green again and he headed across the street. He hurried across, shuffling his feet, still hunched up, trying to look as un-George Jenkins-like as possible. All of these un-George Jenkins-like movements conspired to transform the shallow crack in the pavement, just the other side of the median strip, into a rather formidable obstacle to George's passage. In short, the tip of his right shoe struck the crack just so, and he tripped. There was only one possible course of action: to cushion his fall with his hands.

Well, it just so happens that those two most needed appendages were, at that moment, deep in George's overcoat pockets and, moreover, each had been clutching handkerchief-wrapped lumps of elbows. George yanked his hands out of his pockets to intercept the rapidly approaching ground and the confounded elbows flew through the air and skittered across the asphalt. As George fell, for some reason he found himself thinking of whipped cream topping. He struck the street hard, struck so hard in fact that the wind was knocked right out of him.

Meanwhile, the elbows had rolled to a stop. And the stoplight had changed. The cars were beginning to inch forward impatiently. George opened his eyes to take one last look at the world. The bottom half of his vision was filled with street; the top half, sparkling luxury car. In between the two, with a large radial tire several feet on either side of it, there lay a clean-cut elbow joint. Then George was on his hands and knees, coughing violently.

The car in the next lane, a yellow taxi, had been inching forward slowly, and now it stopped right next to George. The driver rolled down his window and leaned out.

"Hey Mac," he said.

George looked up and saw a fat, sack-of-potatoes face with a stubble of grey whiskers on it like a coating of dried salt. A short, fat, unlit stub of a cigar was clamped in its mouth.

A luxury car honked loudly. The distinguished woman in the passenger seat by the driver, said, "Oh my," bringing the fingertips of one hand up to cover her mouth.

The cabbie pulled his cigar out of his mouth with his hand so he could yell. "Whatsamatter wid ya, ya fuckin' handjob? Can't ya see da guy's hurt?" Then he put the stogie back in his mouth very deliberately, clamping his teeth down on it and puckering his lips around it. "Jesus Fuck-king H. Christ, that thing's bleedin' ovah dare!" And he pointed right at the elbow.

George struggled up to his feet. "What!" Huh?" he sputtered.

"Hey, Mac, is dat yer ham hock dare?"

George stared dumbly at the elbow. Hock? Ham hock? His eyes lit up. George pointed at the elbow. "That hock there? Yep, that's my hock all right. Uh-huh. That there's my hock."

Sure looks awful funny," the cabbie said uncertainly, scratching his head, "bleedin' like dat."

George nodded vigorously. "Fresh. Freshest, meatiest damn ham hock in the city of Chicago. It's one of a pair. The other one's right over there," and George pointed at the other elbow, which lay in the street in front of the taxi.

The luxury car honked again. "Aw, fuck off," the cabbie snarled. "Well listen, Mac, I got a fare waitin' fer me ovah at Midway, so I gotta run. Y'bettah pick up yer hocks dare before they ain't so fresh no more, y'know. Take care." And he zoomed off.

George did just that. Then he was on his way again, trudging down the side street. He didn't stop trudging until he came upon a sewer with mist rising up out of it. He took his hands out of his pockets quickly, as if someone might have been watching him and reading his mind. What if it were illegal? George shivered. But who would know?

He reached into his pockets and clenched the elbows in his hands. The handkerchiefs felt moist and somewhat sticky. He took a quick look up and down each street. There were no cars coming. George felt very devilish. He yanked his hands out, bent down, and then they were in, splashing hollowly down below. Gone, gone, gone into Sewer land. He spun around on his heel and headed back toward Cicero Avenue. He felt so good that he was going to go back to Blarney's to drink Buckhorns until they threw him out.

When he heard the car start up behind him, he paid it no heed. And then the loudspeaker bellowed so loudly that he jumped. "ALL RIGHT THERE,

YOU, HOLD IT!" George Jenkins nearly urinated in his pants.

His thin shoulders drooping, he stumbled timidly over to the patrol car. "Wh-what can I d-do for you, Officer," he stammered weakly.

The policeman narrowed his eyes and replied with a controlled type of vehemence, "Buddy...you can just open the back door there and get...in. You're coming with us." And his partner nodded slowly.

"B-b-b-but Officers, on wh-what charges? I d-d-d—"

The cop cut him off with a surly "GET IN!" And George scrambled to get in.

As for what happened after that, the reports are many and all conflicting, so I can't really say.

THE WIENIE
Patty McNair

I

A rather unnerving thing happened on the north side of Chicago on Monday, July Seventh. As usual, Surita Toy slept through the morning. Sometime around noon she awoke feeling an undeniable pressure inside. As she opened her mascara-caked eyes, she saw the yellowing drool and muddy makeup stains on the ratty pillowcase her face was flattened against. She needed to pee. She hoisted herself from the gritty sheets and straddled the corner of the bed. Every movement brought forth a different squeal from the rusted coils below the lumpy, smelly mattress. She opened her legs covered with black fishnet stockings—holes at the toes and knees and a gaper below the waistband—and scratched. Clawed, actually. Surita Toy raked her half painted, half peeled, spiked and broken dirty fingernails into the skin of her upper inner left thigh—right where the rash started before it traveled upward toward her navel. The desire to scratch was considerably stronger than the desire to urinate, so she succumbed to one and momentarily ignored the other.

Her itch somewhat subdued, Surita Toy slid from the beaten bed. The irritating screech of the box spring assaulted her sleep-sensitive ears like the yowl of a cat in heat. She hated this old bed. If one passed by it too closely, it creaked. Needless to say, when she had customers ("guests," as Xaviera Hen called them) the noise was similar to an el train crying around the bends of track that surround the Loop.

Surita Toy left the debris of her tiny room—the unmade cot with the over-filled ashtrays surrounding it like candles on a shrine; the torn colored hose strewn around the room in lumps that looked like neon ant hills—electric blue, goldenrod, fuschia; shoes scattered strategically like well-placed land mines waiting for a victim to stumble through in the dark; one scratched metal folding chair piled high with bras, garters, slips in desperate need of laundering; a three-drawer chest, each drawer brimming to overflow: papers, clothes, cosmetics poking out of the openings—and yanked the door closed behind her.

She headed down the long hallway past the other girls' rooms. Neat, frilly pink four-posters, streamlined hideaways, and fur-covered waterbeds could be seen through the open doorways. Surita Toy continued on to the door at the top of the stairs.

The bathroom was occupied. Surita Toy pressed her knees together and slapped her left thigh to stun the itch creeping there. Xaviera Hen (the girls called her "Mother") opened the bathroom and huffed past the other woman.

Surita Toy peed, wiped, scratched, and headed down the stairs to the kitchen. The aroma of bratwurst and sauerkraut wafted through the air. She would have preferred eggs, but Surita Toy knew better than to ask Mother Hen for breakfast when the hour called for lunch.

Xaviera Hen sat at the Formica table smoking and clucking. She did not like her girls sleeping past nine—after all, lots of guests stopped by on their way to the office each morning. Xaviera Hen sucked on her can of Old Style Light and watched Surita Toy slice open a torpedo roll for her brat.

Surita Toy felt the eyes of Mother Hen on her back as she fished in the kettle for a sausage. She wished she had changed her dress from the one she had slept in, aware of the creases and wrinkles and sweat stains circling her armpits. She tugged at her hem and jerked at the waistband of her stockings, expanding the hole across her belly.

Surita Toy dipped the aluminum tongs into the boiling water again, bobbing for a hunk of meat. Xaviera Hen sighed in exasperation. Surita Toy turned toward her as she plucked a bratwurst from the pot. She plopped the link into the roll she had prepared, keeping her eyes on Mother Hen's face. Tentatively, she pulled a chair out from under the table and sat. The springs creaked.

"Brats smell wonderful," Surita Toy cooed to warm the chill in the kitchen air. Xaviera grunted and lowered her eyes finally from those of her employee to focus on the stubbing out of her cigarette in the plastic ashtray marked "Climax Motel."

Surita Toy bit into her sandwich and came away with a mouthful of dry, slightly stale bread. Must have been a particularly short brat. She peeled back the bun and inserted her finger, pushing the swollen red tube up to the edge of the roll where she had bitten—the pattern of her teeth forming a semi-circle in the crust. Surita noticed the feel of the link under her grimy fingertips. It was not the feel of an ordinary hot dog—slippery taut skin pulled over the machine-pummeled and molded meat. The skin moved slightly as she touched it, and the insides (though firm) were not solid like those of a bratwurst. It was sort of squishy and veiny like a—

Surita Toy dropped the roll and its contents and gasped. It was not a wiener at all! It was a wienie! Indeed, it was a penis.

The appendage popped out of the bun and rolled across the table toward Mother Hen.

"What the—?" Xaviera bellowed. She jumped from her chair as she caught sight of the eyelet at the end of the wienie. Shiny strands of sauerkraut stuck to the skin in pale contrast to the deep blue veins showing through the semi-transparent, bruised-looking flesh. She hollered at Surita from the safety of the doorway that led to the stairwell.

"Now look what you've done! Wench! I have told you a million times to take it easy on the guests! Not everybody likes the rough stuff, you know. Why you . . . you . . . you tramp! I'll have you know this is a respectable establishment. I don't know why I ever hired you. Just look at you—those ripped nylons, that awful dress! I never did understand why you insist on sleeping in your clothes all the time. And that room of yours—*P.U.* Ever think of changing those sheets? At least after every tenth guest or so.

"Speaking of guests, I've about had it with the complaints, young lady. Just yesterday three gentlemen complained of teeth marks on their privates. What are you trying to do, bite it off? And you don't yank on the damn thing . . ."

Mother Hen rattled on in her rage and scolding, punctuating her remarks with indignant adjustments of her straight-seamed nylons, lacy garters and rayon lounging robe. Surita Toy was used to this barrage of insults. She tuned out the braying woman standing at the foot of the stairs and moved closer to her find lying on the plastic table top, studying the swollen purply-redness of the dink, mentally measuring the four inches from its small bulbous head to the end—the part that normally was attached to a male body. How very bizarre.

Yet, somehow very familiar.

She poked at the thing, watching it roll awkwardly over the surface of the table, trailing sauerkraut. Using her thumb and index finger, Surita pinched the skin just below the head and lifted it, as one lifts a kitten by its scruff. Surita wrapped her unmanicured fingers around the sausage. The texture in the palm of her hand, the skin still warm and somewhat sticky from the cooking water, the weight of the phallus sparked her memory. Of course. Surita Toy saw Richard Less standing over her rumpled bed, three-piece suit still intact with the exception of the open barn door where the little pony was sticking out its tiny head.

This was Richard Less's thing.

Surita Toy brought it close to her face and squinted. She had never seen one of these in such bright light before, rather ugly actually.

"How could this have happened?" wondered Surita. She was confused, alarmed. "Mr. Less is always in such a hurry, maybe he forgot to tuck before he zipped? No, it doesn't make any sense at all."

Xaviera was still ranting as she edged herself around the kitchen, feeling her way with her hands behind her back, inching along the countertops.

"You get rid of that thing now! I mean now, before the lunch hour rush starts . . . this instant!"

"I'll just take it up to my room for now," Surita offered. "I'm sure I can think of something to do with it later."

"Not on your life, sister! This is my house and I'll have no unattached members hanging around. Besides, if you stash it in your room, it's sure to get lost in all that garbage and turn up in some other guest's underwear. No, sir. You take it out of here NOW."

Surita Toy scrambled back up the stairs to her filthy room and pulled two sandals from the various piles. Luckily, they matched. She found an old McDonald's bag in one corner, dumped the remnants of a month-old Filet-o-Fish and the red cardboard french fry container on the floor, and pushed the hunk of flesh into the crumpled sack.

Surita Toy left the hotel and headed east on Division toward Lake Michigan, past Cabrini Green and all the night clubs just off State. She considered dropping the bag in one of the green dumpsters that adorned the mouths of the alleys up and down the street, but in that area there were too many starving homeless folks who pulled their meals from those cans. She could not allow Richard Less's penis to be eaten like a discarded salami by a blurry-visioned old bum.

Once down by the lake, Surita Toy thought of tossing it into the water or burying it under the sand. But at 1:00 on a sunny July afternoon, there was not even an inch of sand to be seen beneath the multitude of bronzing semi-nude bodies. And most assuredly, she would be fined if she were seen littering into the lake—there were dozens of battered white signs posted along the water that said so.

Casually (well, somewhat casually she hoped—all things considered), Surita Toy strolled back up Cedar Street toward State. The tree-lined residential block of the Gold Coast was quiet, empty of pedestrians. Surita attempted to dump the bag into one of the huge planters in front of a silvery highrise, but at that moment a snooty-looking nanny, complete with starched white cap, support hose and baby carriage, came down the marble drive and called, "Say there!" The voice was shrill, nasal, grating like a fine silver fork scraping across a Wedgewood plate. "I believe you forgot something." She pointed a white-nailed, knobby-knuckled finger at the grease-stained bag resting on a bunch of yellow snapdragons.

"Of course," Surita mumbled. "Thank you." She picked up her prize and, stuffing it into the pocket of her dress, headed to State, took a right, two blocks to Division and continued west to Clark.

But I'm afraid I haven't told you a thing about the real Surita Toy. I am so sorry. Surita Toy was an admirable girl in a number of ways.

Like most small town runaways turned hooker in the big city, Surita was a lazy young woman. How else could she stay in bed all day and make a living? Her income was mediocre at best, as were her talents, but she had a roof over her head and food in her belly—and of course, her warm if dilapidated bed. Surita Toy had her quirks, as I'm sure many in her profession did. After spending the major part of her waking hours removing her clothing, she insisted on spending her nights sleeping in her clothes: dress, hose, occasionally even her shoes. Yes, she was a slob. Not just sloppy: dirty. More often than once her more finicky customers commented on this. Particularly Richard Less. "Don't you ever bathe? I'm afraid one day I'll catch something rolling around in all this garbage. Woman, you are disgusting, are you sure you've had your shots?" Surita Toy was never amused by his banter and assured Richard Less that she was indeed disease-free. Then she would tug him toward her and dig her toenails into the flesh behind his ears, and her claws into any other area she desired.

The industrious girl entered the darkened subway stairwell and lowered herself into the blackness. The cool air from the depths of the city's transit system sent a chill up her spine, and Surita Toy jammed her fists into her dress pockets and squared her shoulders against the shiver working through her small frame. Her knuckles smashed into the bag in her pocket and as a rumble welled up beneath her feet, she came up with a plan.

Surita Toy zipped down the stairs at the Division and Clark stop, hoping to beat the train she heard as she flashed her pass at the leering man in the cubicle. Too late. She heard the thunder of the train echo somewhere far down the long dark tunnel. An old bum with rags wrapped around his ankles and feet, shorts from Bermuda, and a calf-length overcoat that had no buttons, collar, sleeves or lining, released himself from the fly of his pants and took aim. Surita Toy heard the initial splash as his stream hit the opposite wall across the tracks and then the muted piddle turn to dribble as the derelict relieved himself quickly and efficiently. She fingered the crumpled McDonald's bag in her pocket and noticed the size of her find was quite a bit smaller than that which the drunk was now stashing back in his shorts. He never seemed to notice Surita, turned his back to her, and walked further into the tunnel to find a pole to lean on.

Surita Toy felt relatively safe now. She heard another train roaring toward the platform and positioned herself close to the lip over the tracks. Putting one foot far behind the other for leverage, Surita wrestled the sack from her pocket. She leaned forward with one arm stretched out over the third rail of track, her face toward the oncoming light. The wind shifted and blew her hair back from her sweaty brow, her balance faltered slightly, and she held the bag more tightly in her outstretched hand as if to steady herself. Over the screech of train wheels on steel, Surita heard the distinct sound of heavy footfalls on the stairs behind her right shoulder. She glanced back at the "kerchunk" sounds and caught sight of a man.

"Yo, babe!" the intruder yelled. "Watch it!" He jumped toward Surita as the train rushed past the pair, crushing the paper bag that had held Richard Less's wienie under its heavy metal wheels. Surita had barely dropped the bag and pulled her arm back in time to avoid losing her right hand. She staggered back from the edge of the platform directly into the arms of the man who had called to her before.

"Just what do you think yer doin'?" The man shook Surita at arm's length. She dropped her head in cowardice and stared at his shiny black biker boots with heavy chains wrapped around them from heel to pointed toe. Neither of the two spoke for many moments until he shook her again. "Yo, babe. I'm talking to you. This is city property; just where do you come off throwing junk around like that?"

Surita timidly worked her eyes up the man's skinny legs in too-tight black denims, past the gray wool hunter's socks tucked over his pantlegs into his boots like legwarmers. She let her eyes flick over the noticeable bulge below his oversized brass belt buckle that formed the letters "R-A-M-B-O," and up to the silk-screened fist printed on the black sleeveless muscle shirt. The man had a bulging chest and strong arms and the red beret of the group "Guardian Angels." A self-appointed subway patrolman. As Surita saw it, self-appointed or not, the man was still a patrolman.

Surita reached up to his teenaged face: black, gleaming with perspiration. The young man stepped back and stood in a tense "at-ease" position, sucking in his stomach and pooching his chest out even further to demonstrate his dominance of the situation. He tapped a foot slightly, impatiently.

"Well, I'm waiting for an explanation. Can't you read? Baby, just look at that sign." He pointed a well-chewed, clean pink-nailed finger at the sign over the tracks that read "Litterers will be subject to a $50.00 fine."

Fifty dollars would take at least five guests, and Surita Toy was in no mood to give up that much hard-earned cash. She stepped closer to the Angel again and ran one of her nubby fingers along the valley that led from his belly button to his chest, tracing the fingers of the fist painted on his shirt.

"How about a free ride, fella? And I'm not talking subway . . ."

"Look, babe—whatever yer sellin', I'm not buyin'. Get it? Besides, I got three chicks of my own 'round here that keep me satisfied. I'm not lookin' for no strange . . . and you are strange! Now paws off and let's go back up into the daylight. Seems like you have some explainin' to do."

Surita swallowed hard and blanched. The two climbed the stairs into the bright sun and here the events of that steamy summer day seemed to melt into one another.

II

Richard Less slammed his palm down on the off button of the chirping alarm clock. He squinted at the digital reading in the semi-dark room. Monday, July 7, 5:30 A.M. He rubbed his hands together as he always did upon waking up, a warming motion even though he was not cold. It was a habit for which he had no explanation. He noticed the itch near his groin, the one he brought home before the weekend from that cheap brothel he visited every Friday afternoon (whether he needed it or not), and Richard Less scratched the tops of his thighs and lower abdomen with his closely-clipped, highly-buffed fingernailss. His expensive manicure did not leave enough length of nail to provide much relief to an itch, but he scraped away at his skin nonetheless.

Richard Less tossed back the butterscotch down comforter and champagne satin sheets and narrowly escaped the cloying embrace of his wife, Hope. Each morning she tried to capture him in her arms and threaten him with love-making. As usual, Richard Less was out of bed and in the chrome-adorned bathroom long before his wife had her eyes fully opened.

The room was silver and white. White fluffy 100%-cotton towels hung from chrome rods surrounding the double vanity and sunken tub. A plush white wall-to-wall pile warmed the soles of Richard Less's feet. The sliding doors that provided privacy for the bather were made of two floor-to-ceiling mirrors. The bathroom door was hung with a full-length mirror as well. Another wall of reflective glass crossed over the long vanity counter. Richard Less positioned his body to admire the reflections of reflections of his reflection. Not bad for forty-two.

The lean quadriceps bulged slightly and strained the soft material of his pant-legs. That's what five miles a day did. He leaned forward a little to examine the small balding patch at the crown of his head under the bright fluorescent tile lighting. He adjusted a curl here and there to cover the shining area. Richard Less straightened up, thrusting his chest out and shoulders back, sucked in his gut and pulled the pajama top up to expose his washboard stomach. The health spa tan accentuated the ripples achieved from hundreds of weekly sit-ups. He stepped backward in the direction of the throne and released the drawstring of his gray striped Polo pajama trousers, unaware of the slight rustling sound they made as they hit the extra-padded carpet.

He was about to sit when he noticed the bright red rash spreading there. Frantically, he drew the pajama top over his head and added it to the pile made by his pants. He moved closer to the mirror on the door. How awful. The skin appeared smooth yet bloated from the tops of his thighs to the lower abdominal muscles just below his belly button. Hip to hip, the redness stared back at Richard Less from his reflections. He turned to the mirror at his side and saw the same disgusting rash.

Richard Less fought the urge to scratch at the irritation. He moved even closer to the full-length mirror and studied the infliction for blisters, broken skin, bumps, anything one might associate with a rash of this kind in this body region. There was only redness and that relentless itch. As he studied his belly and thighs he realized that it was probably not quite as bad as it originally appeared. The severity of the rash was initially amplified by the absence of his penis.

THE ABSENCE OF HIS PENIS??!!

Richard Less reached down and groped but felt nothing except taut skin. He passed his hand from one jutting hipbone to the other and felt the flat surface.

He turned this way and that examining his reflection in the multiple mirrors and saw nothing resembling the slight protrusion he was used to seeing there on his body. Never having been a hairy man, Richard Less wished for some curls to hide the obviously empty area of flesh.

He must be dreaming, he was sure. He went to one of the white marble basins and pulled up on the silver handle marked "C." Filling the bowl, he cupped his hands into the ice-cold water and splashed his face repeatedly. He wagged his head from side to side, sending droplets across the long mirror and wet spots to the carpet, and returned to his spot amidst his reflections. Still memberless. Shaken, yet still somewhat in control, Richard wrapped a terry towel around his lean waist and tiptoed back to his room.

It is only right that I tell you something about Richard Less. Less is a yuppie, although he prefers to think of himself as an achiever. He works sixty-hour weeks to provide his family with a lifestyle that is well beyond their means. Being named E. F. Hutton's Broker of the Month five months running has given Richard Less the impression that "When R. L. talks, everybody listens." He is filled with self-importance, desire, greed and ruthlessness—all the key ingredients of a successful executive. Yet he wants more. His house is large— he wants an addition. His child gets B's—he wants A's. His wife is a size nine—she should be a five. His Mercedes is an '83—he wants an '87. You can see the pattern. And as usual, this kind of drive leads to a rather solitary life. All work and no play, as the saying goes. Although he provides a lovely house for his family, it is far short of being a home—as the three are also short of being a family.

Richard Less looked at his sleeping wife as he gently picked the blankets up off the bed. "Perhaps it fell off during the night," he thought to himself as he rubbed his hand along the cool satin of the linens. Nothing. He snuck quietly to the walk-in closet across the room and opened the door. Pulling it shut behind him, Richard turned the lock on the knob. He snapped on the overhead light and popped the lid on the hamper. Less reached into the basket and rummaged through the fabrics, feeling for a solid substance. Nothing. Frustrated, he dumped the dirty clothes onto the closet floor and, on his knees, began tossing each piece over his shoulders after sifting and shaking it, pulling pockets inside out and wringing the toes of the socks. Again, no luck.

Richard Less quietly opened the door and crept out of his bedroom and into the hallway. A small mirror hung over an antique washstand next to the bedroom door. He took the mirror from its hook and lowered it until he could see the towel around his waist in the glass. Less untucked the corner of the towel and pulled it from his middle. No change. A flat, red surface. No penis.

Sprinting to the bathroom again, Richard secured the door and picked up his pajama drawers from the heap. He jabbed his hand in through the fly and down each leg, pulling the material up to the pit of his arm until he could see his fingertips where his toes usually were. Of course, it wasn't there either.

Richard Less wound through the curves and cul-de-sacs of his comfortable little neighborhood, his eyes surveying the satellite dishes and Mexican gardeners pushing shiny new rototillers. He saw black women shaking rugs over colorful flower beds, red-brown boys skimming pools, even an East

Indian-looking fellow sloshing soapy water over a pair of Mercedes in front of a four-car garage.

Suddenly he saw a child dressed in red and green pedal full speed past him on a bright yellow dirt bike. Less was not imagining this—it was his penis.

He watched as the boy jumped a curb and went racing over the grass and between two large houses—disappearing (again) from sight. He pulled the car over and unfolded himself from the interior.

In front of one of the houses between which Less's penis had passed was a group of gardeners laughing and drinking beer. Lunch break, no doubt. Richard Less approached them.

"You guys didn't happen to see a little p—, uh, boy ride through here a little bit ago, did you?" He had started to say what he was really after, but even a friendly group of Mexican gardeners would not look favorably on a man "looking for a little prick."

"Chure, I know who you mean," said one of the men. "He's a Banger boy."

Less guffawed. "What's a Banger boy?" He wasn't sure he really wanted to know.

"Ju know, Robert Banger. The big house. On Willow. Man's got some fine bushes over there . . . I'd like to get my clippers on that hedge. Wife's not bad either. The boy, he's one of theirs. They got almost as much kids as they got money. And they got a lotta money. I seen that yellow bike out back by the patio. Take a look."

The gardener grabbed Richard Less's elbow and steered him behind the garage—Less didn't even flinch under the clammy hold of the man's soil-stained fingers. He looked to where the man extended a blackened fingertip and saw a quarter-acre patio stretched out behind a palatial pink brick quasi-mansion. And there, with skin as deep a pink as the hue of the house, was Richard's penis.

The penis careened out of the open sliding glass doors that led from the house to the patio and bounded onto the bicycle saddle with such force that Less winced—out of habit, no doubt. Across the lawns and back between the houses to the street the penis rode, and Richard Less dashed to his sports car in hot pursuit.

He followed the bike slowly and cautiously, not wanting to attract the attention of his neighbors. The pair worked their way out of the maze of the residential lanes and onto a more traversed street of apartment buildings and mini-malls. The penis turned into one of the shopping centers and headed toward the day-glow gleam of neon lights lining the window of a video arcade. The bike was anchored to the rack outside the entrance, and the appendage, dressed in red and green, spun through the revolving door.

Richard Less maneuvered his car into a spot in the crowded lot, barely missing a pre-teen punk on a skateboard, grunting an apology as the kid stuck his head in the passenger window of the car to scream an obscenity and flip Less the bird.

The temperature was somewhere in the nineties; the Mercedes was a sauna. As Less crawled out, he noticed that his jogging pants had soaked through with perspiration, and the strong scent of Cruex assaulted his senses. Less looked down at his legs and saw the pants glued to his lower half. The hollow V between his thighs looked odd to Less. He snapped the waistband of his trousers, trying to loosen the cling of the fabric from his penisless trunk—but the pants remolded themselves to his body like fly paper to an insect. He stood next to his auto and held the pants away from his waist by the elastic, forming a kangaroo-type pouch for the air to circulate through. Less bent his head low to peer into the darkness of his clothing to once again inspect the rash and the vacancy. A blast of a horn and a whiney woman's voice pulled Richard Less's face out of his lap.

"Hey, pervert! Whatsa matter, can't you find it? Geez, they oughta lock you guys up." The middle-aged fat woman in curlers and a station wagon squealed out of the lot, muttering to herself along the way.

Less turned his attention to the arcade, appropriately named the Snake Pit. He strolled toward the entry with his hands casually folded below his belly, over his groin. Once through the revolving door, he pushed past the troop surrounding the hot and heavy fooseball tournament. An unidentified flying object whizzed past his right ear, and a scrawny girl of seven or so chased after the runaway air hockey puck. Deep inside the belly of the Pit, Richard focused hard to find that familiar head amidst the swarm of faces illuminated by the eerie lights of the flashing, coin-eating machines. A pink glow blanketed the arcade, giving it a dreamlike atmosphere. Less looked up to find the source of the rose light and noticed a skylight painted a translucent peppermint shade. The sun streamed down through the painted panes and flashed off the railing surrounding the loft-like balcony that made up the second floor of the game room. Overhangs about six feet deep lined three walls of the arcade—almost halfway between floor and ceiling. Games of lasers and silver balls hugged the three walls and challenged the arcade customers. Deep mechanical voices boomed invitations to passers-by ("BLACK KNIGHT WANTS YOU . . . HO HO HO HO!") and bells and beeps beckoned. Less leaned his head back and squinted into the pinkened sunlight and spotted it. There, in front of a particularly verbal Ms. Pac Man—its round, red, shiny-bald head just high enough so it could barely see over the controls of the screen—was his penis.

Richard Less took the stairs two at a time to the little balcony. He approached the thing step by step, grateful that his penis was mesmerized by the electronic toy and grateful that the noisy whirs and clangs of the games surrounding them covered the squeak of his Reeboks on the sticky linoleum floor. He needed time to think. How would he address this thing? Less really had no idea how one speaks to children, especially when they are not one's own. But it was Richard's. Not his child, his penis—surely it must know that. He studied the squat little being from a distance of the width of two or so machines. "Short, but thick," Less thought to himself as he always had when he had studied his penis before. He noticed the folds of skin just below the fat head, over the scout's collar. As the game increased the level of excitement the thing experienced, it began to bob in place. With every point scored, the penis seemed to stand a little taller, flush a little redder. Less smiled in admiration— fine-looking specimen. Funny though, he had never noticed that pimply redness on the smooth skin before. No matter, it was still his penis.

Less cleared his throat. He was at the penis's shoulder. It jumped at the sudden human sound. The penis turned toward Less with a nasty scowl. A vein pulsed in its fleshy head. "You made me get eaten, mister."

"Uh, I'm really sorry about that, son." He reached out a hand to pat the penis in what he hoped would be a fatherly sort of way. The flesh was hot under his fingertips. The penis squirmed at the touch.

"I don't talk to strangers," it spat from its tiny purple mouth. With that, it turned its attention to the cup of soda it had balanced on the railing, guzzling the liquid and gulping noisily. Sucking up the entire contents of the cup without a pause, the penis burped loudly and flattened the paper container beneath its heel with a hollow pop that made Richard Less jump. Heads swiveled to glare at the noisy thing. Less stood by, embarrassed by the attention drawn in their direction. Immediately, he cupped his hands in a cross in front of his flat lower abdomen. He turned his back to the crowd looking up from the lower floor and moved closer to his penis. He bowed his head and lowered his voice so that only it could hear his words.

"Now, I'm not really a stranger at all, am I?"

The penis was getting antsy; sputtering, reddening. Richard Less had to try again.

"Surely you know what you are, who I am? This morning when I woke up and you were gone, well . . . of course, I was quite upset . . . I'm just glad I caught up with you again, at last."

The penis shrunk away from Less's outstretched hand. "I never saw you before, mister. I don't know what you're talkin' about this morning—I never slept with you or whatever you're tryin' to say. You got the wrong guy."

Richard was frustrated, hot, suddenly angry. "Damnit! You belong to me!" He screamed out above the ringing of bells, clattering of balls and pucks. "You were right here last night," he grabbed his empty crotch, "and I want you back here tonight, get it? Look!" He pulled the penis by the head with one hand and pulled on his waistband with the other, intending to show the penis whence it came.

The room had suddenly grown quite silent as necks craned back on the patrons of the lower floor, trying desperately to see what the commotion was. A man in a gray uniform with a patch on the shoulder with the words "Mall Security" stitched in yellow was making his way up the stairs through the crowd moving toward the second landing. "Hold it right there, buddy," the man called to Less. The penis wriggled out from Richard Less's grip.

Richard turned to the rent-a-cop. "Yer outta here, bud," the gray-suited man said as he pushed Richard Less back down the stairs and toward the revolving door. "And don't come back, y'hear? We don't like yer kind flittin' around the kiddies—got it?" The guard trapped Less into one of the compartments of the door and gave it a whirl. Richard Less tumbled onto the sidewalk. He stood and dusted himself off and momentarily inspected the tear in the knee of his pants. He walked back to the window of the arcade and looked in. The balcony was empty. His penis was gone.

Richard Less was too excited to speak for a moment. He just stood in the large foyer with his mouth open, hands hanging limply at his sides.

"I got it right here," the young black man repeated, shifting nervously from foot to foot. "I knew you'd be wanting it, so I brought it along. You know, it's kinda strange, but there was a north side hooker sorta involved with this whole case. Scummy little thing name of Surita Toy. You don't know her—no, course not, rich classy dude like you. Anyway, cops took her. Serves her right, too. I always seen her on my patrol, you know—hustlin', grabbin' at dudes. Serves her right."

The man pulled his hands from behind his back as he spoke and produced a clear plastic ziplock storage bag. Inside was a small, purply-red tube—at first glance it could have been a hot dog. But Less knew exactly what it was. He reached out and grabbed for the bag, but the younger man held it just out of his reach.

"Well, I guess I'll be givin' you your thing and head on outta here. Nice neighborhood you got here. Long way from home, though. Cost a good buck to cab it back to the city, s'pose. I better be gettin', though. Lotta studyin' to do. Tryin' to get a scholarship for college. Takes a lotta work. I sure wish I could afford to pay for it myself . . . at least some of it." The man swung the bag absently as he spoke, waving it over Less's palm.

Richard Less caught on, finally. He reached into his back pocket and pulled out his wallet. He flipped through the contents and counted two single dollar bills, one fifty, and a crisp hundred. He considered giving the guy the singles— after all, it was his property he was paying for here—but thought better of it. He looked at the plastic bag in the other's hand again, and in a sudden fit of generosity, he pulled the one hundred dollar bill from its spot in the wallet and handed it to the young man. The exchange was made and Less had possession of his penis. He thanked the other man profusely as he showed him to the door, latching it behind him as he left.

Richard Less carried his prize back to the bathroom. He began to have some doubts as he pulled it from the baggie and noticed the smooth surface of the end where it should attach to his abdomen. What if it did not go back on? What then? But of course it would go back on.

Less pulled his pants down to his knees along with his shorts. He grasped the penis in his right hand as he would when taking a leak. He pressed the end to his body and let loose his grip. Plop! It fell to the soft carpet and rolled toward the toilet. Less tried the same thing over and over, chasing his thing around the little room as it continued to fall and roll over the floor. In desperation, he opened the medicine cabinet and pulled a tube of eyelash adhesive from his wife's cosmetic kit. He slathered the ointment over his belly and tried to secure his dink there again. No luck. He only succeeded in irritating the rash that was still there.

Less stuffed the penis back into the plastic bag and went to his bedroom. He put the baggie under his pillow and laid down on the large bed. Hope walked in and sat next to her husband. She reached out to stroke his hair. Less flinched from her touch at first, but relaxed and allowed her to comfort him.

"My poor honey," Hope cooed. "Still not feeling too well, are you? Why don't you let me call Bill?"

Dr. William Howell lived next door to the Lesses. He had been the family doctor for years—since the birth of Dickie Junior. Richard had jogged with the man on many mornings, but had never seen him professionally. Richard Less had never been sick. But this was something different. Maybe a doctor would be just what he needed. Less agreed to let Hope go next door and bring the man over.

Bill came through the bedroom door in his tennis whites. Less got up from the bed and shooed his wife from the room. He locked the door behind her and went to the windows to draw the blinds. When Richard Less was sure that no one could see what was going on in his bedroom, he pulled his pillow off the bed to expose the wienie in its plastic bag.

Bill lifted the bag and shook the penis inside. "Hmmm . . ." That was all he said, "Hmmm."

Less prodded the doctor. "Well, Doc? Can you replace it for me? I woke up this morning and it was gone. Now that I have it back, it just doesn't seem to want to stick. Can you fix it?"

"Hmmm." And the doctor motioned for Richard to drop his trousers. He knelt before Less and pressed the proper end of the thing to the area below his waist. Plop! He tried again. Same thing.

"I'm sorry, Richard. It just won't go back on. My suggestion is that you just forget about it. Of course, I can replace it surgically, but I don't suggest that. You never know what could happen when one takes a knife to such a delicate area. You're better off without it. Besides, you know how much trouble a man's penis can get him into, right?" Bill laughed, trying to make light of the horrible situation. Less was not amused.

"Tell you what," Bill spoke again. "I'll buy this from you. It would help me immensely in my research . . ." Richard Less would not let Dr. Bill finish his proposition. He was not willing to give up his penis again. Less thanked the doctor for his help (or lack thereof) and asked him to find his own way out.

Less went to his paneled study just down the corridor from his bedroom. He pulled the penis from the bag and set it on top of his desk. He stared at it and tried to sort through the whole thing. He had no idea what could have happened. He thought back to the previous week. Work had gone well. That is except for the incident with Howie Long and his assistant. Less had stolen one of Howie's most lucrative clients and was in the process of milking the rich old lady for everything she had. It was a nice play for Less, everyone thought so. Except Howie. It seemed that the rich old lady was Howie's assistant's grandmother. Consequently, some very bad blood was rising between the brokers. Howie had even threatened to report Less to the proper authorities. Howie Long had promised to make Richard pay for his selfishness.

Could Howie Long have done this? Some sort of black magic, perhaps? Richard Less would not normally believe in such silliness, but now he sat at his desk in his study with his penis sitting on the desktop instead of between his legs where it belonged. Richard would believe anything.

He wrote a memo.

To: H. Long
Re: Missing Member

I would like to take this time to apologize to you, Howie, and your assistant for the unprofessional way I have handled the account we were discussing last Thursday. However, I must inform you that I do not believe that my actions warrant such extreme measures of retaliation that you may have taken. I will in the future treat this account as I would one of my own relative's accounts. All I ask in return is that you undo whatever it is you have done and allow the return of one certain member to its proper place.

Sincerely,

R. Less

The following morning, Less slipped the memo onto Long's desk. Hours later, the assistant returned with a memo from his boss.

To: R. Less
Re: Memo

Richard, I am grateful for your apology . . . and somewhat surprised. On Thursday you seemed to have no intention of changing your business habits. I am quite relieved that you have since seen the error of your ways. I will be delighted to work with you in the future. However, I do not know what member you are talking about. Is this someone from the Exchange, the Health Club, Jaycees? Please explain.

Regards,

H. Long

Richard knew that Howie was indeed sincere in his reply. He had nothing to do with the separation. But now what?

Somehow the story of a missing penis had spread across Chicago's north side. Perhaps it was Surita, or maybe the young man who had found it. Maybe Howie Long had finally deciphered Less's memo and started the rumor himself. Soon reports of sightings reached all areas. One man saw a large wienie on the bench press of his club. Another saw one leading a tour through the Museum of Science and Industry. It was widely believed that the penis hung out at Lincoln Park Zoo, and the line to the reptile house grew longer each day as rumors of its whereabouts centered on the snake pits. But it was never actually seen by anyone at all. Not anyone, that is, except Richard Less, who saw it every night as he pulled the pillow from his bed and made sure that the thing was still there, safe and sealed air-tight in its ziplock storage bag.

III

Absolute outrageousness is going on in the city. Sometimes there is no logic at all: suddenly the exact same penis that had terrorized the suburbs in a scout uniform and on the banana seat of a canary yellow dirt bike turned up, as if nothing had happened, in its usual spot, that is, about four and one half inches below Richard Less's navel.

It happened approximately July 18th. A steady chirp of a bird outside the Less bedroom window woke Hope just minutes before her husband's alarm went off. She opened her eyes to the dimness of the early morning light that filtered through the half-drawn Levolours. Through slits of eyelids, she squinted past her husband's sleeping form toward the bird on the window sill.

Hope focused on a lump in the down puff. Tentatively, she reached her hand across the bed like a whisper and pressed. She felt the solidity beneath the tentlike bump just above her husband's thighs.

Hope was still unconvinced. Moving slowly, quietly, so as not to disturb Richard's slumber, she plucked the covers from the bed and began to burrow beneath them. She tunneled stealthily toward the lump in the blackness below the bedclothes, inching her way over the width of the king-sized mattress, sliding on her belly like a snake. Mouth open, she sucked in the dead still air, breathing the scent of her husband. Polo, Cruex, and an odd smell. Hope sniffed again. Bratwurst?

Hope felt her husband's thigh against her forehead. She raised her head and shifted the blankets to let a hint of light into her tunnel. Face to face and sure at last, Hope grasped at her husband's member greedily. It barely measured the length of one of her hands from wrist to fingertip, yet she wrapped both hands around the erection. It had only been missing a few weeks, but it must have been years since Mrs. Less had last seen it.

Richard Less was awakened by a tugging below his belly. He had been sleeping flat on the extra-firm mattress; back to bed, arms at his sides, no pillows. Fearful of what he might (or might not) find this time, he opened his eyes gradually and raised his head from the sheet, skimming his gaze down the length of his body past the bundle of blankets that was his wife, to his toes jutting out of the bedclothes. He lifted the covers and peered into the blackness. There, poking through the open fly of his flannels, staring directly into his wife's eyes, was Richard Less's thing. He whooped and tossed the linens back in joy, rolled his wife over and, without stopping to pull his pajamas down, made love to her excitedly, gently, almost lovingly for the first time in years. Once satisfied (and having satisfied his wife), he leapt from his bed and strutted down the hallway to his viewing point in front of the bathroom mirrors.

In the glass on the door—his penis! Over the vanities—his penis! Multiplied by the reflections in front of the tub—his penis, penis, penis, penis! He showered and shaved hurriedly, dressed and bent to kiss his smiling, dozing wife. He left for the office.

Turning off the expressway at Division, he noticed the girls in spiked heels, neon hose, too-tight halters and nearly nonexistent minis plying their trade to the early morning commuters. Between two gray flat factory outlets peeked the dilapidated marquee advertising "Climax Motel."

Surita Toy pulled open her door at the knock and rubbed her eyes sleepily. Flakes of a week's supply of mascara freckled her cheeks.

"First things first. Have you changed your linens? Have you bathed?"

Less pushed past her into the tiny room no longer quite so cluttered. The distinct odor of Lysol stung his nostrils and seemed to waft through the air in a cloud coming from the general direction of the lumpy bed.

Through a yawn, Surita muttered, "I guarantee, I'm clean."

"You'd better be," Less said, teasing yet sincere. He pulled at his fly with a zip and pushed Surita back onto her bed, proceeding as always. Surita grabbed at the small appendage protruding from the trousers, attempting to yank him into place.

"Hey, hey, watch it!" Less shouted.

Then, with great difficulty, Surita maneuvered her hips below his and pulled on Richard's waist, aiming and missing again and again until finally, the two pressed together, all things in their proper places. In a minute, it was done.

Richard Less drove his Mercedes downtown to his office. He made a quick pass through the locker room of the health club on the main floor of the office building. There, in floor-to-ceiling mirrors, he dropped his trousers to his knees. He shuffled closer to the mirror and once again examined his found body part. Two men sauntered out of the steam room and stole curious sidelong glances at the man smiling at the reflection of his penis. Richard Less stared back at the naked men—one of whom was more than generously endowed—and looked back at his small self proudly. Having done that, he pulled himself together and rode the elevator to his office.

Before entering his suite, Richard had to make one more stop. He ran into Howie Long and his young assistant in the john. He b.s.'ed with them for quite some time, making a point of pulling himself out at the urinal and spraying his initials on the porcelain, slopping on both his highly-polished shoes, muttering under his breath, "So there, you backstabbers, you scum! I won't give up my accounts, my commissions, so there! I'll churn whenever I feel like it, whenever!" And from that moment on, Richard Less cruised around the city and suburbs, strolling through offices and health clubs at his leisure. And all his body parts stayed intact in all the right places, healthy and itch-free, as though nothing had happened, showing no hint that anything was ever amiss. And afterwards, Richard Less was seen smiling, laughing, joking . . . chasing after expensive cars, high-paying deals, and cheap hookers, and was even once observed going into Woodfield Mall to purchase a display case, although he had not been awarded any trophies or plaques.

BURTON THE FARMHAND
Heather Jones

Burton started out to be the best worker of the lot. From his very first day he would be out there slopping the hogs before I even got up. He worked steady all day, cleaning the sty, raking the pen—he would even wash the mud off the pigs before he sent them back into the shed from the yard. I thought for once I had got me a regular guy, and I pointed it out to Greene and LaPearle one day.

Greene just blinked at me like I was the sun shining straight into his face, and then shuffled off cracking his knuckles. LaPearle spat on the ground and said to me, "That right? Regular guy? Ever wonder how that guy can spend the whole goddamn day with them pigs? Go have a look at Agatha."

Well I had kind of wondered how Burton could spend *every minute* with the pigs. Sometimes when I was in the tool side of the shed and he was in the sty, I'd hear the pigs scuffing a little in the dirt, and no other noise. I just figured Burton had a real fondness for pigs and was sittin' in there keeping them calm. But after what LaPearle said I got uneasy, so I went and had a look in the sty.

Well there were the pigs, scuffing and snorting, and there was Burton sitting in the corner. Nothing looked suspicious in there. And then Agatha turned sideways and I got a glimpse of purple and blue flashing off her neck in the sunbeam that followed me in when I opened the door.

"What's that there on Agatha's neck?" I asked Burton. Well, he just looked at me, and he didn't answer. So I steps down into the sty to examine my pig. She snorted some and kicked up some dust at first because I was comin' at her too fast, but when I put my hand on her back she calmed right down. I had a look at her neck and there she had a nice neat purple and blue collar. It was wove in the way them hippies up to Goddard College always wove their belts—macarmay I think they call it. It was pretty and everything, a nice piece of handiwork, but it didn't seem right to me that a collar was on a pig.

So I turns back to Burton. He's sitting there on a bale of hay with no expression on his face, and it was then that I noticed his hands were working on some green and yellow twine. "Burton," I says, "you know, the work you did on that collar is nice—really nice. But I don't think a collar is something that belongs on a pig."

Well Burton just keeps sitting there. He didn't say nothin'. And his hands just kept going, twisting up that yellow and green twine.

"Burton," I says, and I was really trying not to sound like I was teed off. His work was nice and it was a good thought and I didn't want to hurt his feelings. On the other hand, even Greene and LaPearle answered me when I talked to them.

"Look, do you think you could take that collar off that pig?"

Finally he looked up, but his hands never stopped twisting up that twine. He kept yanking up more of it from two rolls that were laying by his foot. "Jesus," he says, and then looks like he's thinking really hard. Then he comes out with, "I don't think so."

"What are you saying?" I was raising my voice. I didn't work my ass off keeping up my own place so that the guys working for me could say, "I don't think so" when I asked 'em to do something. Greene and LaPearle had their quirks, but saying "I don't think so" wasn't one of them.

Well Burton doesn't answer my question, so I goes out to my tools and I got a file and came back with it. I got hold of the pig and cut that collar off. Burton didn't say nothin'. He just watched me, real quiet in his corner, his hands maybe going a little faster on that green and yellow twine.

Well then I felt bad. It's no habit of mine to go cutting up another man's work, even if it's got no place around a hog's neck. So I goes back out to my toolbox and got a hammer and a nail. I drove that nail in up high on the wall of the pig shed and I hung Burton's blue and purple pig collar on the nail. It looked nice there, and I was proud of myself for working out a good compromise.

Burton didn't say anything though, and so I started to get mad at myself for going out of my way to be nice. I don't even know what made me do it. When I was standing there looking at Burton's ungrateful face and watching his hands go at that twine, I promised myself I wouldn't do it again. "A collar's nothin' for a pig," I said to him. He kept twisting that twine like he was smarting off at me, so I stalked out of the shed and slammed Burton into the dark with the door.

I stood outside the shed door for a minute listening to my blood boil. But I was so surprised by Burton saying, "I don't think so" that I started to wonder if he was right and I was wrong. Maybe a macarmay collar wasn't such a bad thing. I was thinking that when I saw Greene and LaPearle sitting on the lawn having their lunch. Now I'm not one to ask another man's opinion about how to run my own place, but at that moment I didn't know what to do. I figured the best thing at that moment would be to ask some people who pretty much did what they were told. So I goes up to Greene and LaPearle and told them the story of what just happened with Burton. "So what do you think, Greene?" I says when the story's over.

Greene looks up at me from the turkey sandwich he's trying to chew up with dentures that don't quite fit. He gives a big swallow and I could see a big lump go down his neck—he had swallowed before he even half finished chewing. Then he starts shaking his head. "Nope. Nope," he says, "a collar ain't nothin' for a pig . . ."

Then La Pearle cuts him off. He spits out some seeds that he's managed to keep in his mouth from the rye bread on his peanut butter and cheddar cheese sandwich, and he says, "By Jesus, I'd fire his ass. If I was you I'd take a goddamn .22 into that shed and stalk him like he was a goddamn deer. Soon as he starts shakin' in his shoes, I'd tell him to take his goddamn pansyass collars and his smartass mouth and get off my goddamn property."

I was about to take part of LaPearle's advice—I mean I was going to go into the shed and tell Burton that he could go and work at somebody else's place, when I looked at my watch. It was one o'clock. I had to get down to the discount auto and pick up the new fan belt for the truck, and I didn't have any beer yet for after work. So I decided I'd kick Burton off my place later. I thanked Greene and LaPearle for the advice and told them to get back to work, and I got in my truck.

Well I didn't fire Burton that day. I just hung around and kept an eye on him. One thing I noticed was that he never seemed to eat. That seemed strange to me and I got suspicious. One day I watched him through the cracks in the boards of the shed. For a long time he didn't do much. He was still working at that twine, and as he worked he stared at the pigs like they were gonna bust their way out of that shed any minute.

I was starting to feel fidgety and think that I might go have a bite, when suddenly Burton stood up and headed for the door. I grabbed a rake that was lying on the ground and started raking.

Well he comes around to my side of the shed and starts rummaging in the bin where I keep the stale loaves of bread and old packages of Danishes that I use for pig slop. He doesn't say a word to me. He just fills his arms with food for the pigs and heads back into the sty.

I put the rake down and went back to staring at him through the crack between the boards. He was tearing open the loaves of bread and tossing them to the pigs. Then he sat down on his bale of hay with an aluminum tray of stale Danishes—and I'll be goddamned if he didn't start eating them! It was the saddest sight I'd seen in a long time.

Watching him eat them stale Danishes made something push against the inside of my chest. I left the shed and went into my house. I don't know what made me do it, but when I made up two tuna sandwiches with lettuce and onions for myself, I made up an extra one. After I ate mine sitting at the table and watching the stories on TV, I went back out to the shed with the extra sandwich in my hand.

Well the first thing I sees when I open the door to the sty is that Claude has a wide yellow and green collar with all these flower patterns wove into it. I was there to offer the man some food, so I bit my tongue. There was time enough to get the goddamn collar off the hog. I was thinking that maybe all that sugar and dried-out cake in the stale Danish had maybe done something to Burton's mind. Once he ate some decent food, maybe I could talk some sense into him.

So I steps past Claude trying to seem like I wasn't mad. Burton's sitting on that bale of hay in the corner, and with the door open and me being up close, I could see that his face had got as pale and dry and flaky as the frosting on them Danishes. He reminded me of one of them undersea animals you see on the science shows on TV—the kind that ain't ever seen the sun and so they don't have no color to them. His hands were as red as his face was white, and every bit as dry. And those dried-up red hands were going at some more twine. This time the twine was blue and white. God knows where he kept gettin' that stuff. He must've had a whole bag of it hid somewhere. He didn't even have the courtesy to look up at me when I came in with that sandwich, but I'd be hard pressed to say where he was looking 'cause he had this glazed look in his eye and his head was tilted to the side, like maybe he heard a mouse scuttle in on the other side of the shed.

I cleared my throat, and he looks up at me, that glazed look going from his eyes the way a cloud goes past the moon in the dark. "Burton," I says, and I cleared my throat again. Claude bumped into my leg and I got the urge to grab him by that collar and move him aside, but I didn't. That would've made the damn thing seem useful. "Burton," I says again, "I just had a couple of tuna sandwiches and there was some extra. If I put it away it would just get green, so I thought you might want it."

"Jesus . . . I don't think so."

The words were out of his mouth almost before I finished my sentence. "Of all the ungrateful . . ." I shut my mouth because he looked so pale and sick, but I was so mad I threw the tuna sandwich on the floor of the sty where Claude ate it in one swallow. I turned around to leave and there's LaPearle standing in the door. He was leaning against the jamb with a baseball cap pulled over his eyes and one big manure-covered boot crossed over the other. He was chewing on a piece of straw and slapping my file against his thigh. When he saw I was looking at him, he held the file out to me.

This was no time to be losing face in front of my other workers, and I was mad as hell. That Burton had pushed me too far. I grabbed the file from LaPearle and cut the collar off of my boar. I spun around toward Burton, and when I saw his fingers still twisting and pulling on that goddamn blue and white twine, I held the file over my head and shouted, "By Jesus, I oughta give you a goddamn clout!"

"Fire his ass," said LaPearle from behind me.

I spun around with the file still over my head. "I'll fire his ass when I'm ready," I yelled. "This is my goddamn place. And where's my goddamn tractor? Probably stuck in a goddamn rut down in the goddamn field! LaPearle, you get your ass out of here and get back to work."

"Jeez," says LaPearle. "You know, you used to be the most regular guy around here to work for until this pansyass weaver got here. I wouldn't mind takin' a .22 to his head, then see if he wouldn't pack up that goddamn twine." Then he looks at Burton and says, "Lucky for you I don't know when pansyass season is." He tossed the straw he had been chewing onto the ground and left the sty.

I was left standing in the sty with the file in one hand and the collar in the other. I was shaking all over and I felt stupid. Nothing makes me so mad as to feel stupid, so I turns to Burton and I says, "Your ass is gone. I don't want to see you around here tomorrow."

That night I could hardly sleep. I tossed and turned all night, wondering about Burton and where he would go. I thought maybe he'd go up to Goddard College, but then I thought that not even a commie liberal professor would tolerate him sittin' around saying "I don't think so" all the time and maybe weavin' collars for the squirrels.

Finally I fell asleep, and I woke up about dawn. I pulled on my dungarees and my boots, and without even tying my boots, I ran out to the shed. I turned on the light to the toolshed and opened the sty door. "I'll be goddamned," I said to the dark and the pigs. Burton was gone all right, but each of my pigs had on a nice neat collar. Agatha's was yellow, Claude's was blue, and June's was red. "That crazy sonofabitch," I muttered, and I pulled my Swiss Army knife out of my pocket, cut the collars off, and threw them into the trash in the toolshed.

As I went about my work that day, I started to feel spooked. It was like a bad dream, finding my pigs with collars on and no one around. I thought maybe I should sit up that night and watch out in case Burton came back and tried it again. But by that night when I was sitting in front of the TV with a Gennie in my hand, and my eyelids were getting heavy, I figured that them three collars had been Burton's last hurrah, and there was nothing to worry about.

No matter what I thought that night, I still woke up first thing the next morning and went out to the sty. And if I had been a little suspicious before, now I could be sure—each pig had another collar on. I don't know how Burton had gotten to making them so fast, but there they were.

I cut them off again, all the time thinking about what I should do. When

Greene and LaPearle came up to my place I told them that their job for the day was to turn over every blade of grass on the place and see if Burton wasn't hiding somewhere. Greene started rubbing his back and stooping from just the thought of all the moving around he was going to have to do. LaPearle says, "I told you you should have run that little pansyass off this place with a rifle. If you had let me talk to him, by Jesus, wouldn't he have handed over that twine with a smile on his face and taken his ass all the way to Mexico?"

I told LaPearle to shut up and start searching while I ran down to the store. When I came home from the store, I went out back to see how the search was going. And I'll be damned if Greene wasn't sitting down there against a post on the barb wire fence with his face up to the sun like he was at the friggin' beach. LaPearle was walkin' up and down along the fence with a crowbar raised above his head.

I went on down to where Greene was sitting and I called LaPearle over. "You." I nodded my head down at Greene who was cracking his scaly hairy knuckles just at the sight of me, "Get up off your ass. And you, LaPearle, you don't need a crowbar to look for a collar-weaving little shit like Burton. Gimme that crowbar."

And what does LaPearle do? Well I'll be damned if he doesn't spit on the ground and say to me, "I don't think so." Well I'll tell you, that got me into a rage. LaPearle always had his own personality and he was always a tough sonofabitch, but until that minute he always knew when to show respect. My temper was making my ears burn and pushing at my throat, just pushing me to start something, to shout at that little smartass, but something else in me told me not to start anything with a guy who had a crowbar in his hand. So I says to him quiet as I could, "LaPearle, I guess you don't hate Burton. I hear you wanna start talking just like him." Well, that hit him where it hurt. He turns bright red and hands me the crowbar. I tried to smile at him, and then calm as can be I says, "Now youse guys get to work. That little twine-turning weasel is probably hiding out in the woods somewhere. I'll just have to sit up tonight and make sure he doesn't come back."

So I sat up that night in my kitchen drinking black coffee to keep awake. I must have fallen asleep anyway, because I woke up in the morning with my head on the table. I pulled myself up and went out to the sty. By Jesus, if those hogs didn't have three new collars I'll be a sonofabitch. I cut them off, and all day I tried to think of what to do next. By sundown I had decided. When it got dark I sat down in front of the shed with the crowbar in my lap and waited.

I guess I fell asleep again, because I woke up in the morning. The crowbar was still in my lap and my hair was all soaked with dew. When I stood up all my bones cracked, and I knew how old Greene must feel. I stood outside the door to the sty for a few minutes; I just didn't want to see them hogs.

Finally I opened the door. There they were, my three hogs: Claude was wearing a fancy yellow and purple collar, Agatha had black and white wove into zig zags, and June's was light blue with a tassle. You should have heard me curse while I cut off them new collars.

My first thought was that I would have to sit in the sty with the pigs, but when I went to shave that morning I saw my face. I was as pasty white as Burton and there were black rings under my eyes that made me look like a friggin' raccoon. No bastard was going to drive me into my grave with no macarmay collars. As soon as I finished shaving I went down to my friend DeForge's farm and asked him if I could keep my pigs at his place for a while. He had a sty that he wasn't using since he had just butchered his sow, sent the boar out to stud, and sold the little ones.

He says sure and he asks me why. I couldn't tell him I had lost control of one of my hands and he was sneakin' in at night and putting collars on the pigs. I would have looked like a fool. So I tells him that my boar kicked at one of the walls and splintered it, so I thought this was a good time to pull the walls down and build a sturdier sty.

I took the pigs down to DeForge's that afternoon, and that night I finally got a good night's sleep. The next morning, I woke up with a tight feeling in my throat. I went into the bathroom, cleared my throat and spit into the toilet. That tight feeling was still there, and I realized it wasn't on the inside of my throat, it was the outside of my neck, and it felt all squeezed up. I put my hands up to my neck and I'll be damned if there wasn't somethin' wrapped around it. I looked in the mirror and there around my own friggin' neck was one of those collars of Burton's. It was wove out of so many colors I couldn't count 'em, and it made me dizzy to try.

By Jesus, I don't know if I was more mad or more scared. I tried to tell myself that I was dreaming, but when I washed my eyes out with cold water and looked in the mirror again the damn thing was still there. Well right then I went and called the police. I swallowed my pride and left the friggin' collar on so that they could see just what kind of a maniac they were dealing with.

I was glad to see it was Joe Hudson that came up to my place—at least I was glad until I saw him keep sneaking looks at my neck while he was filling out his report. Finally I told him enough was enough, and I cut the collar off with my Swiss Army knife and handed it over to him.

I figured I had done it just in time, because right then I saw LaPearle coming down the road. Well he sees the police car and Joe Hudson talking to me with his notebook in his hand, and he comes strolling over like maybe he was gonna send Joe home and take over the whole damn situation. When he gets up close, straight away he starts squinting up his eyes and looking at my neck.

"By Jesus," he says, "looks like that asshole can't tell you from a hog."

"What the hell are you talking about, LaPearle," I says, hoping he might shut up. But he doesn't; he keeps it right up. He was just about dancing up and down.

"Seems to me you got some marks on your neck. Seems to me they look a helluva lot like some hog collars I've been seein' around here lately."

"You got work to do, LaPearle," I says, and I was clenching my fists so tight my knuckles were turning white.

Right then Joe Hudson interrupts and says he'd like to go into the sty, just to see if there might be some evidence in there. LaPearle makes like he's gonna go in there with us, but I told him to head on down to the field, then me and Joe Hudson went into the sty.

Well I'll be a sonofabitch if Burton wasn't in there just like he was waiting to get caught. He was curled up sleeping on that bale of hay where he used to sit and make them collars before. The first thing that struck me was that I had never noticed how long his legs were. With him curled up like that on that bale of hay, his knees came right up under his nose. Those knees were dirty, too, like he had been crawling around in the dirt. His hair was all matted up with burrs and his lower lip stuck out in his sleep like a little kid's.

Seeing him like that I felt sorry for him again. But it was too late to do anything about that. I had already filled out the police report, and Joe Hudson was standing right behind me.

Well Joe arrested him that day, and he was tried down to Montpelier pretty soon after that. I went down and sort of stood up for him. I said he was pretty much harmless, only I didn't think he was playin' with a full deck. The judge could see that I was right, and he sent him over to Waterbury instead of to jail.

MELCHERT THE HOARKER
Lisa Yu

O.K., so I never seen anyone write a story about some hot dog makers, but what the hell? There's a first time for everything, right? Let me tell you, I've known some in my time. Stories I could tell you, 'cause I've had this little stand here for thirty and some years, seen more than my share of wackos and fruitcakes slapping the old mustard. I could write a book.

Of all the fruitcakes I guess there never was a one that could measure up to old Melchert for sheer looniness. There's a lot I can't even say about the guy's life: for instance, where he came from, his folks, his childhood, and so forth. No one knows. Like you know how most guys you work with will be flapping their jaw, going on about this and that, and pretty soon you got their whole life story? Well, not Melchert. What I seen of him myself, that's practically all I know, so it's all you're gonna get.

Guess I oughta say a word or two about myself. First thing you gotta know is I don't claim to be any rocket scientist, O.K.? I'm a lousy hot dog seller and that's O.K. with me. I got no higher ambitions. I'm perfectly content with my little stand here in the Merchandise Mart, making hot dogs like I done for thirty years. I got no plans, like some guys do, to put in a milkshake machine or soft-serve ice cream, frozen yogurt, nacho chips, or some such — you know, get a jump on the market, maybe franchise. Who needs the headache? So I do like I always done, do it well, don't go shaking up the routine for no reason. Course now my business is being squeezed out by this giant chain — the goddamn Taco Loco clowns, if you'll excuse my French. But that's all besides the point.

Before this Melchert appeared on the scene there was these three guys been working for me awhile: Askew, Weinsap, and a kid named Dwayne, except he asks can we please call him "Rasta boy" now. Whatever. Christ, it's like the United Nations in here these days, every color and faith of the rainbow represented. The old man, if he was still around, would turn over in his grave. But hey, times change, and Love Your Brother, all that, yatata yatata.

Anyways — Askew, he's an old fool like myself, sometimes moreso than others as regards the fool part. I think the what you call the deciding factor there is if he's been hitting the sauce or not. Before he gets to it he's one sharp cookie — you know, he can do the condiments and cash all at the same time. But say he's been for one of his ten-minute rest breaks — which I allow him, as required by law. You put him on that line with his hands shaking, then he tries to cut some onions but slices up his fingers instead. So now he's got all these bandaids on and they'll come off in the ketchup, full of blood and sweat — real nice for the Health Department, you know? Worst incident I ever saw was once he's running back and forth between condiments and cash, and he slaps a handful of wet sauerkraut into some customer's hand — guy's just waiting on his change, poor soul. Meantime, with the other hand he squeezes a five spot inside a bun, right between the dog and the mustard.

Like I said, sober he's real sharp, seeing as he's been doing the job since about the dawn of civilized times. Yeah, he can be a pain in the royal butt, but I keep him on, guess I'm just a sucker for my fellow man — as you'll see. Besides, if I talk to him about maybe just cutting down to them quality dry hours, he hauls out your legal such and such about age discrimination, Equal Opportunity and so on, etcetera. Well, all it takes to shut me up is lawsuit talk, and come right down to it I'd feel bad for the guy being out on the street at his age, so I'm willing to hold out till his Social Security boat comes in.

You think he's bad, though, Askew don't hold a candle for legal mumbo jumbo to this young kid name of Weinsap. He usually runs the deep fryer. He's most of the time a good kid: hard worker, keeps up a nice respectable appearance—short hair, clean shirt and all. Sure, he's got this habit of climbing up on his high horse, like he's too good to be making French fries with us. He's from one of these Highland Park families of I don't need to tell you what religious persuasion for fear of offending somebody, except to hint that it's a group inclined towards making a buck and holding onto it for dear life. See, the dogs are just a job to Weinsap, what he really is is a law student at DePaul University, and I suppose his folks made him take the job with me, elsewise he wouldn't be caught dead in the place.

The fact that he's forced to spend time working has made him curious about the legal ins and outs of the food service industry. Particularly, I seen him studying with great interest this sheet I got up on the wall—as required by law—regarding worker's comp. I think it gave him an idea, 'cause ever since then he's been a little careless about waving his strainer around so as to drop grease blobs where he's likely to step. Kid wants to fall on his ass and lay at home with a busted leg while the comp checks from yours truly roll in.

Also he'll come around complaining about stiff joints, thinks he's developing such and such syndrome, common to laborers in the meat packing industry, which leads to severe disability and has gotten certain companies in a load of hot water. So I tells him, "Kid, packin' a six-ounce dog in a bun for twenty hours a week don't exactly qualify you as a meat packer." But Christ, every week he's got a different scheme. Says he has to go home and lay down, says he's coming down with the Epstein and Barr virus, symptom of which is fatigue. He sees old Askew slicing himself up and suddenly he's afraid of catching AIDS from open wounds, so he's taken to wearing rubber gloves on the line. It don't do any good to tell him there ain't no one in Chicago likely to get intimate enough with old Askew to be swappin' the bodily fluids, AIDS-infected or no. He's got as good a chance of carrying the bug as the Pope. Mostly I ignore him, cause while he's carrying on he generally gets the work done.

Between these two characters is a kid which is a pleasure to have in my employ, thanks to his easygoing ways, never mind the fact that most of the time you don't know what in heaven's name he's talking about. He's a colored, name of Dwayne, who's as American as you or me, lives on the West Side with his folks like he done all his life, fifteen or so years. When I hired him he was like any other colored kid in his talk, and dressed regular too—you know, Nike sneakers, jeans, and L.A. Laker's jacket or what have you—a good kid not into the gangs or the crack, which is something to be thankful for. Funny thing is after a while he starts turning into a foreigner, calling me "Boss-mon," wearing sunglasses and rainbow knit caps like he's from one of them tropical islands, and says he goes by the name of "Rasta boy" now. He grows his hair like nothing I ever seen, 'cause when the colored grow their hair it comes out in these funny lumpy things that point every whicha way and don't look too clean neither. Calls them dreadlocks, to which all I got to say is the dread part I don't take issue with.

Generally Rasta boy does odd jobs: cleaning, stocking, and during lunch rush he's perfectly capable to slice the buns and load in the dogs. He's in the habit of mumbling and bobbing and singing, sometimes squeezes the buns lovingly, but he's so good-natured I get a kick out of it, no matter how loony. If I tell him he can take his break now, he smiles and without fail says, "Ja be praised." Darndest thing. I mean, Baptists is always been peculiar, but this behavior ain't even like any Baptist I ever seen. Lots of guys wouldn't put up with it, but I say, what's the matter with a positive attitude?

So that's the three of them that made up my staff—like I said, each one flakier than the last, but here comes what you might call the meat in the sandwich, top dog of the loons, and that is Melchert, which makes the other three look like the College of Cardinals. Now for some time we did O.K. with the four of us: Weinsap at the deep fryer, Rasta boy cutting and loading, Askew running your condiments, and myself packing them up, ringing the orders—and the all-important relating with customers. You know, a joke here, inquiry into the family there. We got a lot of regulars, lots of folks work in the Mart has a dog for lunch every day. We was getting busier and busier for a while there and backing up on our orders. Between Rasta boy doing his bun thing, and Askew trying to keep his condiments straight, and Weinsap going light in the head from the fluorescent lights, the dogs themselves wasn't getting cooked often enough. So we conferred heavily and I decided to run an ad in the *Trib*.

Seeing as you don't need a Doctor of Philosophy to cook hot dogs, I accepted the first applicant which didn't smell too bad or act like he never heard of the English language, and that was Melchert. I must say he made a nice appearance: quiet, clean-cut, respectful, and so forth. He really impressed me. I was tickled to hire a fine young guy like him: wouldn't have to get on his case to shave or wear a hairnet, no half-assed college student—if you'll excuse my language—who would rather be chasing the sorority girls, and I wouldn't have to worry about him stroking out or losing a finger during lunch rush.

I started him in slow, seeing as we get real busy at lunch. You throw a new guy in at condiments, he might have a nervous breakdown. I showed him just how to cut the buns and load the dogs—just so, I said. He jumped right in there, which freed Rasta boy to cook the dogs, and between which run around stocking and pouring sodas. First day he got the routine down like a pro, never once sending a bun without a dog, or vice versa, for Askew to condiment. The whole operation ran nice and smooth, no problems whatsoever. To say he didn't talk much would be what you call a understatement, but I figured he was just nervous—first day and all.

All week long, as he's cutting and loading so fast he's ahead of the game—loading dogs for customers who haven't even decided to go for lunch yet—I notice he still doesn't say word one, not unless he's spoken to, and even then just yeah or no if he can get away with it. I mean, normally we'll all give each other a hard time, just mess around like you got to when you work that close together, even if it's a bunch of guys you don't have nothing in common with. It's what you call the psychology of the workplace. Not old Melchert, though, he didn't catch on.

Like say Askew yells out to him, "Hey Melchert, let's get it in gear, we ain't got all day"—obviously sarcastical, since Melchert's already got so many buns dogged they're stacked up at the condiment station like a pyramid. We'll all laugh and say yeah, come on Melchert, but he'll just nod and proceed to cut and load even faster. Oh well. I noticed he was quick and kept his area real neat. So I look at him there, on the ball, and I look over at old Askew dribbling ketchup all over his shoes. This kid, I says to myself, may just be ready for condiments.

Next day I explained to him all about your mustards, your onions, your chili, and so forth. It's plenty more complicated than dogging, since you got to keep straight who wants what—extra ketchup, light kraut, what have you, everybody wants it different. It's easy to get mixed up. You really got to dance, yet keep a cool head at all costs. So I asked Melchert, is he sure he understands, can he handle it for one day? "Yeah," he says—in his quiet, sickly, kind of pale way—and that's all he says.

So we tried it with Askew making dogs and Rasta boy dogging buns and taking orders, and Melchert running those condiments. It's a little tough to get used to, cause usually the guy who takes the orders will hand the dog down and at the same time yell out what they want on it, and the condiment man yells back, to make sure he's got it straight. This Melchert, true to form, says nothing. Rasta boy says, for instance, "Dis one got de onions, hit got de relish, hit got de cheese, hit sure got de mustard, but mon—don't you put on dot sauerkraut," and waits for Melchert to repeat what he says, but no. He slaps it on just right, hands it to me, and on to the next one. He's an odd one, but he does his work, so I don't question.

In between busy times, when it's quieted down, a guy's got time to smoke a cigarette or whatever, Melch doesn't quit work for a minute. He cuts onions, he cleans the fryer, he sweeps up, and he wipes down every inch of counter space. I can see it bugs Weinsap, cause ain't no way you can get work-related injuries if someone's cleaning up your spills all the time.

So we proceeded thusly for several weeks, humming along happily, and it appears as if everyone's found his talent, Melchert's being that condiments and him acts like they've known each other all their lives. Then one lunch rush I notice Rasta boy piling up those dogged buns like Melchert use to do. I look over at Melchert and he's just standing there kind of licking his lips and twitching his mouth. "Melch," I says, "you're getting backed up there." He just stands, bobbing his Adam's apple.

"Mon, did you hear me?" Rasta boy taps his shoulder, and pointing at each bun in turn says, "ketchup light onions, pickles and mustard, everything no sauerkraut, plain, plain, everything hot peppers, everything no onions, you got that, mon? Are you wit me, mon?"

Then Melchert gets this real funny look on his face and holds up one finger, the other hand messing with his collar, which is buttoned all the way up as usual, and he whispers, "Excuse me." Then he makes more noise than he's ever made put together, and the way he makes it is he hoarks. Now, I don't know if you're familiar with the word "hoark," but I'm sure you know the concept, which is to make this noise in your throat where you're trying to get at some phlegm that's back there and expectorate it. A big hoark like this one is usually followed by a not exactly beautiful spit, so we all kind of stood clear of Melch, gave him some space, but he didn't spit. He sure did hoark, though. If you want to know the truth, it was downright embarrassing. You know, a shy fellow like him you gotta figure he ain't too proud about creating a crude disturbance—specially when there's a line of testy businesspersons waiting at the counter flapping their dough, jingling their change, and glaring at him impatiently. Also, it don't look good to be making these kind of noises if you're standing right over containers full of relish and mustard—I don't know, something in the aestheticals.

Anyone else done it, a wisecrack woulda been made, and I probably woulda had a sharp word or two—it just don't look good. But poor Melchert looked so sickly standing there hoarking like the Queen Mary pulling out of dock with a dead seagull stuck in its horn, tugging away at that button that quivered on his Adam's apple, with his eyes unfocused, just staring . . . Well, I was taken aback.

"Son," I says, "is you got something in your throat?"

"It's all the nitrates around here," pipes up Weinsap from over by the deep fryer, "Melch has obviously got a sensitivity. Although saying someone is sensitive to nitrates is like saying a guy doesn't take too well to having his leg sawed off — that stuff is poison to all of us. The FDA says—"

Having the instincts of a lifelong acquaintance with the hot dog industry, I see it is a time for action, not speeches. All the time we been yakking, Melch is apparently breaking the world's record time for a single hoark, which freezes him up for all action, even something as important as applying the condiments. I ask him if he's O.K., just to make sure he ain't about to keel over, and when he nods I grabs him by the shoulder and shove him out of the way, then gesture to Askew to spread out, and I and him set to work making up for Melch's lost time.

Boy, was that whole bunch of customers irritated, standing there and watching over the proceedings like a flock of buzzards. O.K., I admit it is not so nice to have to wait for your dog while it gets cold and some clown is attending to his personal habits over it, but they didn't have to get so testy with me. "Melch," I turns and says while I'm ketchuping with one hand and counting back change with the other, "why don't you step out in the alley if you is got something in your threat, hey?" 'cause he's still going at it full speed. He nods and steps back to the back area, not once breaking the flow of his solo.

Somehow we recovered and got through that lunch, though naturally I was saddened to see some folks at the back of the line got tired of waiting and cut out to get a taco. It may sound darn tolerant of me, seeing as we lost business, but I wasn't sore at old Melchert. He came back from the alley once it was quieted down, a good twenty minutes later, and took up his place on the line, looking paler than ever, and set to tidying up his area, saying not a word about the incident.

We all looked at him sort of funny but figured he was feeling humiliated about it, so we acted like nothing happened. The kid, I decided — to speak both literally and figurative — had choked. I let it slide for now, figuring maybe he was tense to reach such a position of responsibility and decision-making so early in his career. "New guy at condiments," I chided myself, "the old man woulda known better."

Rest of the week young Melchert worked hard as ever, though if anything he made less noise about it than ever. I wouldn'ta thought it was possible for a guy to act so not impressed with being alive, without moaning and griping about it. Truth is, I felt sorry for the kid, and how little fun he was having with the whole proceedings. He still handled the condiments O.K., but I was gentler with him, relieving him with old Askew when it got busy, for fear of he'd freeze up again.

So the next week on Tuesday morning we showed up ten o'clock as usual, and everywhere is boxes: on the counter, on the floor, on the chairs, and more coming in the door all the time. See, most of our deliveries come in on Tuesdays. Everybody what's there — which consists of only me and Weinsap and Melchert at this hour — kind of grabs a box and sets to putting it away somewhere: napkins in the back, buns in the cooler, what have you. That is to say, myself and Weinsap does this, while Melchert stands there with his hands in his pockets licking his lips.

I thought maybe he hadn't caught on to our little routine yet, so I told him, "Melchert, this here isn't the new office decorations, there's all kinds of crap got to be put away." Then he grabs that top collar button, whispers, "Scuse me," and proceeds to make that gorgeous noise in his throat. Once again I took cover in anticipation of expectoration, but alls he did was hoark. The pattern, I can see, is starting to be hauntingly familiar.

Since we don't open till ten-thirty, we had more freedom this go-round to kind of study and deliberate over what was going on, so the whole both of us stopped and looked at Melchert, I on his right and Weinsap on his left. Like tourists at Old Faithful, we watched that button dance on his Adam's apple while the accompanying soundtrack burst gloriously forth. He was louder and juicier sounding this time, if you know what I mean.

"Weinsap," I spoke up over the commotion, "any theories?"

"Several," he hollers. "For instance, the ventilation system in here, which dates probably from the Civil War—is, I'm certain, below code. What with all the dry air and unhealthy cooking fumes, I'm surprised more of us don't have a problem like Melchert here." Which, speaking of Melchert, he's meanwhile in full voice. "Also there's the matter of second-hand cigarette smoke, which isn't helped any by the fact of those ashtrays you lay on the counters, encouraging the public to smoke in illegal proximity with your food prep area. Of course, to digress somewhat, these old buildings have alarmingly high levels of Radon—"

"Son," I says to Melchert, "can't you maybe see your way clear to cutting it out and lift a finger to earn your minimum wage?" Harsh words, I admit, but it occurs to me this thing he does is a voluntary action, not exactly as uncontrollable as coughing or sneezing. I guess it inflamed his sensitivities though, cause he caught his breath only to let fly more violently than ever. So I quit arguing about it for now and suggested if he must do that he might step out of the way into the alley so a person can get his work done without having to detour around him all the time.

Me and Weinsap got the boxes put away while old mucus head pursued his new hobby out in the alley. It was no big deal for us: you know, not exactly assembling a atomic bomb, but a guy likes to think everybody will jump in and lend a hand. The old team spirit, see.

But boy, I watched that kid after that. I kept an eye on him, cause his actions started to ease over from a little nutty to downright loony. For instance, he don't care for eating. Everybody, I let them have a meal a shift, so when I tell 'em to take their break they can load up a dog however they like. Course it don't take long to have your fill of dogs, so guys can get pretty imaginative with their condiments. Sometimes they even bring in their own cold cuts or cheese to substitute for the old wienie.

But Melchert—and from day one this is the thing he gives me grief about—he'd nod when I told him to get some lunch, but just stand there for a few seconds, then get back to work. This got me worried 'cause often he was there from open to close, by his own choice. (He made it clear from the first he wanted to rack up those hours, and there was plenty of chance, thanks to the whole sickly crew and their health complaints.) Well, no way was I going to let one of my workers go twelve and more hours without eating, so I'd insist, "Kid, you got to eat something. Get yourself a dog!" You know what he did? He'd reach in that container of cold wet half-cooked dogs, grab one and munch it down—no bun, no nothing—with little rabbit nibbles. Well, you ain't seen nothing to put you off your food till you seen a pasty-looking guy like Melch nibbling a nude, cold, dripping dog, pale and lifeless as his own self. That's all I ever seen him eat: day after day, week in and week out.

The more I was thinking about it, the sorrier I am for him. I decided that since he worked so hard when he don't got something in his throat, I'd try to work it out and give him a chance, whereas if I gave him the boot, who knows what might happen to the poor guy? It's a cold city, especially for sensitive types like him.

Still, this little hoarking habit bugged me, and I was dying to get to the bottom of it. He was fine so long as you didn't ask him to do something outside of the normal routine, but it got so I wanted to make him do it, push him to explain hisself. So late one afternoon a few days later it's roach day, which comes once every month. I was there, Melch was there, and so was Askew and Weinsap. Rasta boy was at school. I seen the other two was busy cleaning, and even though I knew what he'd do, I says to him, "Melchert, they're going to come spray the bugs tonight. We got to cover all the food in plastic bags when we close, hey?" and reached out a roll of garbage bags to him.

"Excuse me," he says and lets fly, louder again than last time. Me, Askew and Weinsap all turned to look at him. It's hard to ignore this sort of thing.

"Son," I raised my voice, "what's the matter? You need to see a doctor?"

"If he did," offers Weinsap from back by the deep fryer, even though I didn't notice anybody is asking him, "he could hardly afford to. It's criminal that we're expected to work without a health plan, and those lethal chemicals in the cockroach spray hang in the air for days. Merely the thought of it is enough to make a person sick—"

"These kids," grumbles Askew from where he's windexing the front counter, "is not made like we was, boss. Why, I been working since practically before I could walk, nineteen and thirty—uh, forty something, I was standing out there on Wabash selling newspapers, I been working ever since, and you know—hm—did I ever take a sick day? One single sick day? Well, not many anyways, in forty and—fifty some years in the work force . . . You ain't SUPPOSE to like it—I say—"

"Melch," I stuck the bags in his face, "are you going to help us cover everything in plastic?" He shakes his head and keeps going, adding a new move where he ducks his head and stamps his feet, still tugging at that collar. "O.K., if you can't handle that, what say you take a couple fifties, run up to the currency exchange and buy some singles for the drawer?" Now he was practically coughing up a lung.

"I think this is Melchert's passive form of protest," Weinsap yells. "We deserve medical insurance, paid vacations, at the very least humane working conditions. This is no plantation and we are not slaves. We can raise our voices in protest and demand more. We're not gonna take it!"

"In the snow I worked, in the freezing rain, in the—with polio I stood out there selling papers for a penny!" Askew is holding up a finger, getting all excited in the reminiscing, jowls flapping and eyes aglow. "No sir, it ain't meant to be enjoyed—but I loved it. You know why? I knew what it's like to be alive! You work hard, you play hard, drink hard—my Lord—was that a woman . . ." and he's lost his way in some memory.

"Melchert," I leaned over and shouted in his ear, "what say you clean out and organize the walk-in?" He's practically doubled over in convulsions. "Or wash the windows, hey?" Every suggestion I make, he hoarks worse. I suddenly got this awful feeling I could kill him if I keep asking, which made me go all cold inside. I gave up. "Step out in the alley, son," I sighed and shoved him in the back. I turned to the other two to see them screaming in each other's face, loud as ever, while Melchert's sounds got fainter and farther away. Neither one was paying attention to the other.

"Organize!" Weinsap is saying, "Solidarity forever!" while Askew is gone all dreamy.

"A goddess," he repeats, "she was a goddess in that army nurses uniform — and out of it too, by God . . ." He reaches out his hand and by accident sticks it up to the wrist in a big jar of mayonnaise. I was suddenly tired of the whole bunch of them. I sent everybody home early and closed up myself. I seen by now how Melch is started to have a disruptive influence on my whole staff. Still, I let it slide.

So, in the weeks following this incident we fell into this routine where the five of us worked smooth as you like on the line. Melchert was back to cutting and loading, with Askew on condiments. Sad to see a natural like Melchert nowhere near the condiments, but it seemed he just couldn't take the pressure. He ain't exactly Mr. Personality so far as communicating goes, so Rasta boy had to take the orders and call 'em out to Askew. It was a little cockeyed, but it worked. Besides, I knew by now I had to live with it, 'cause I had this weird feeling something ugly would happen — to Melch, to myself, or to the both of us — if I ever gave him the pink slip. I paid him to do his routine work, clean everything in sight, and once a day nibble on a dog (straight up), but tried not to ask him to do any special carrying or lifting, run around the corner on an errand, or what have you. If I ever did forget and ask him, he always responded in the usual way. If there was customers around at the time, it sure was embarrassing, but we got pretty good at hustling him out of sight fast at the first rumblings. Now there's this pattern where whenever I do anything to make him hoark, the whole of my staff sets to jabbering: Askew on the Christian work ethics, Rasta boy telling everybody not to worry 'cause "every little thing gon to be all right," and Weinsap starts talking Management and Workers, apparently gets me mixed up with big shots like Lee Iacocca. So I learned to keep it zipped.

I was use to the way things were when, on Easter Sunday, I decided to drop by the stand and count out the drawer, which I hadn't got around to doing the night before. It was real nice out: the first warm spring day of the year. I'd just been to services, like I do regular, twice a year no matter what, so I was feeling all full of religion, reflecting on what a square deal it was for all of us that Jesus got to rise up and come back from the grave and all. I didn't even mind the idea of having to go by the store on a holiday when we was closed. In fact it was a real nice kind of spooky feeling to slide my key in that back door off the alley, when the whole of the Mart was deserted, everyone usually there being elsewheres, I in my Sunday best and everywhere is quiet and clean and still. It's the special kind of feeling of being in a place always full of commotion and hard work, and being the only one around. It was like the feeling of church continued. Then I come in for the shock of my life.

If you ever think there was a guy sure of being alone, it was me in that Easter Sunday Merchandise Mart. So just you imagine how spooked I was when I got in that door and stood for a minute looking over my place: the gleaming orange counters, sparkling floors, and shiny stainless steel fixtures, feeling all at peace with my life's work, when I heard footsteps in the back area. It was the sound of someone coming down the stepladder that goes to the top of the walk-in fridge. See, our paper products is kept on top of the walk-in, which stops about four feet short of the high ceiling, leaving a long low space for storage. Someone'd been up top there when I come in and was coming down now. The steps that I heard heading my way around the corner gave me a sinking feeling that I knew what was there. Sure enough, here comes Melchert, pretty as you please, with his shirt buttoned all the way up and paper hat in place, just like he's showing up for work.

"Son," I says carefully, "you know it's a holiday?" He nodded. "You know it's Easter Sunday?" He nodded again but didn't trouble hisself to explain nothing.

"Ahem," he said, and I seen he was rallying his troops, so to speak, and if I asked him anything else (like for instance to please get the hell outa my hot dog stand), he'd let loose with the usual racket. So I looked at him, quiet like, trying to figure how to say it gentle enough so as not to offend his system. Like two jungle cats we looked at each other in the half dark, myself wondering how to attack when I knew he had his counter-attack at the ready.

Then I seen the toothbrush in his hand and felt worse. It looked like he'd been living there. Remembering all the mornings I'd show up at work and he'd be already there, I wondered how long it had been going on. "This here's commercial space, Melchert. We ain't zoned for residential, so I know you can't be living here." I watched him closely. He didn't even look uncomfortable: just bored, like he'd rather if I'd just shut up. It's loony, I tell you. He made me feel like I should be sorry for bugging him with my talk. "I'm sure you is realized your mistake now, you remember it's a holiday and there ain't nothing to do here. I understand, kid, it's a mistake anyone can make. I'm just going over here to the register," I moved slowly around the counter, and he moved like my mirror, I swear, matching every step I took to keep me always directly in front of him. "I'll just go over here and count out the drawer, and I'm sure while I'm doing that you'll be getting your stuff together so's you can go ho—" That was enough said. I didn't have to tell him outright or nothing to give him reason enough to hoark. This one practically split my eardrums.

It was so quiet there before, it was like a bomb dropped in that dark old building full of polished floors and not a soul around. Even though I expected it, I was shocked. I imagined it rumbling out, beyond the glass of my stand to the giant echoey halls of the Mart, up to the top floor and out all the walls, rumbling over the river like a foghorn blast.

I decided to ignore it, figuring the kid only had so much of the stuff in him. Eventually he'd either bring it to the surface or have to stop from the strain. But Lord, you thought he was good at condiments, he was a regular genius at holding a hoark. I tried to act like nothing was up while I counted out the cash, dropped it in the safe and recorded the numbers, but I sure couldn't wait to get away from that sound and that face, pale as a frog's belly.

"Melchert," I says when I was done, "as soon as you got it out of your throat I expect you to find your way home. You ain't supposed to be here. You go home and have yourself a happy Easter. You got to get out of here, Melchert. I think you should slide your key under the door when you go, O.K.?" Which only made him go at it more than ever. I didn't want to knock myself out hollering at him, so I got the heck out of there. Truth is, it gave me the creeps.

That's when I decided to give him the boot. I mean sure, I felt bad for the guy at first—and well beyond the limits for normal human decency if you ask me. But the day a man is chased out of his own place of business by a $3.35 an hour hot dog maker is the day he's got to take control of things. "You're the boss," I says to myself as I walked over the bridge, back out in the warm spring day. "So be the boss."

I knew he wasn't there by accident, and I knew he didn't have his hand in the drawer neither. What give me the creeps about it is he was there as if it was the most natural thing in the world. I made up my mind to give him a chance, try to have some civilized human conversation, but if not—you know, if he refused as usual . . . well, I'd tell him to take some time off.

Model Tellings

NATALIE
Arlene Littleton

Natalie always wore long-sleeved shirts in public, even on torrid summer days. Her arms were continually bruised and etched from shooting up; dark blue and brown tracks dotted her forearms from the wrist to the crook of her arm. The veins in the crooks of her arms were useless; deep, gaping, black holes that needles would no longer enter. After seven years of fixing, finding decent veins (ones that would accept the penetration of the needle) was more of a problem than finding decent stuff to shoot. There was always stuff to shoot—sometimes it was good and sometimes it was bad, but it was always there. Natalie's old man had been shooting up for 20 years, since he was 18, but he never considered himself a junkie. "Junkies die before they're 25," he'd say. "I ain't never been no junkie, I got too much smarts for that shit," he'd say. And he was right; he was no ordinary junkie. Unless you saw Bruce stark naked, you'd never think he was anything other than a good-looking, healthy, clean-cut guy, but with his clothes off, you could see that just about every vein in his body had little scars above them on the skin surface. They were clean scars though, neat little scars that were barely more than discolorations of the skin. Bruce was very careful about his habit; he kept his fits sterile and only shot up stuff that he was certain about as far as quality, and after 20 years, he'd made quantity, just the right quantity, into an art; never too much or too little, always just the right amount for the type of rush he desired. Natalie was not always as careful as Bruce. She had a running prescription for antibiotics to fight off the infection of the abcesses that would crop up on her arms from an unclean point or a sloppy fix. Despite her slipshod methods, she maintained, and her habit maintained.

Natalie would go on and off heroin like an alcoholic goes on and off the wagon. She'd have binges that would last weeks, sometimes months, then she'd get clean for a while and swear to God she'd never touch the stuff again—but she always came back to it. Sometimes she'd go off cold turkey and sometimes she'd filch methadone off one of the dealers, but always something would drive her back to the real stuff—depression, a fight with Bruce, a bad day—always a different reason, but always reason enough to set her off and running to the little dresser drawer that held her fix.

When Natalie was off stuff her appetite for sex would sharpen with an intensity that sent shock tremors throughout her entire body and caused her to wonder if they weren't visible from the outside, if they didn't show up on some seismograph in some nearby lab to mystify technicians. Natalie's urges were easily satisfied, for although she was sloppy about fixing, she was fastidious in her appearance, and she had a natural sort of beauty that didn't show the wear and tear of her habit as the veins in her arms did. She had an almost childlike flirtatiousness in her personality that she was in complete control of, although she'd never tried to force or develop it. It was just there for the using; it had always been there; and it was not a big problem summoning it up when it suited her purposes. When she was off stuff, it suited her purposes to a 'T'. Sometimes she'd amaze herself at how many times she could get fucked during the course of one evening, and each fuck by a different dude at that. She had a little black book of old standbys, numbers she could call at just about any time of the day or night when the urge hit; a listing of 'stud services', so to speak. But Natalie did not confine her pursuits to the numbers in her little book; she preferred the challenge of picking up hot young boys from the neighborhood bars, sweet hunks of beef with smooth baby faces, dimples in their chins, and tight, bulging jeans. She preferred 18 to 19 year olds; they had incredible amounts of energy, and even more important, incredible endurance. They possessed the ability to fuck again and again and again, with only short breaks in between each fuck, and they were still young enough and inexperienced enough to be surprised at and to appreciate some of the finer points of sex that Natalie had picked up. At 29, she was an 'older woman' to them; it gave her a feeling of power, and them an added excitement, a learning experience, and they were ready and eager to learn. Natalie relished the surprised look in their wide young eyes when she'd give a special little twist this way or that, or tense up those experienced muscles in a circular hug that made them jump and twitch in innocent ecstasy.

The only problem with the young ones was that they didn't want to let go—wanted to see her night after night, day after day, couldn't get enough, became emotionally involved—and Natalie wanted no part of that. They were great in bed, while she needed them, but Natalie knew her need would wear off, so she made it a rule that the young ones would be only one night stands, that they would see her once and once only. Natalie never worried about running out of young ones, there was a new crop each year, a seemingly endless supply.

Once she went back to fixing, her desire shifted; not in intensity, but in object, from cock to needle, from orgasm to rush, from ejaculation to thrust of the syringe. It was all penetration after all, one not so different from the other in Natalie's mind; a man between her legs or a needle in her vein—it only depended on what mood she was in. If heroin had to be drunk from a glass like wine, Natalie never would've gotten hooked on it. The rush, the effect from the drug itself was merely the end result and not the entire reason for fixing. It was the ritual, the ritual of preparing the stuff, of drawing it up into the syringe and pushing the air out until a scarce drop appeared pearl-like on the tip of the needle; it was tapping each vein with the tips of her fingers until she found one that would allow penetration; it was the tying off of her arm with the snake-like rubber tube. But most of all, it was the prick on the skin and the slipping in of the needle, the push on the plunger of the syringe that ejaculated the liquid ecstasy into her bloodstream. The rush itself was different each time, just as each lover was different, but the needle was more reliable than the cock. It had a permanent hard-on—it never needed coaxing, failed to perform or suffered from premature ejaculation—and Natalie was in complete control of the whole affair.

RICHARD
Arlene Littleton

It never made any sense to anyone that Richard forgot to take his pills.
Every day, day after day, it was hound Richard to take those damned pills.
Notes were taped to the icebox, propped on dressers, pressed into his pillow
at night, even folded into his ironed handkerchiefs so they'd fall out when
he blew his nose. The pills were to prevent him from having epileptic
seizures, and they worked—when he took them. Sarah thought, and told
Aggie often, that the reason he didn't take them was to get attention. This
horrified Aggie, who would then say, "Why on earth would anyone want
to have a fit to get attention? The boy isn't mad, Maw." Sarah was partially
right. Richard had learned to use his illness to an advantage if it seemed
necessary. There was in Richard something macabre, something somber and
intense and death-like, and it manifested itself in odd ways. Once, while he
was hitchhiking across country, after he'd stood out on a dark stretch of
road for hours in the cold and watched the red taillights disappearing into
the distance one after another after another, he walked to the middle of the
road and lay down on his back on the asphalt, his body straight, stretched
out along the stuttering yellow line, and he waited. Three times he heard
the approach of car or truck, the squeal of brakes, felt the air become alive
on one side of his body, and three times he listened as the motor ac-
celerated, the sound zooming past him and off into the far distance. He
never opened his eyes, flinched, or uttered a sound. The asphalt seemed
alive—the vibrations and hum of traffic far off shivered through his back,
and he thought of a movie he'd seen where an Indian had pressed his ear to
the ground to listen for the sound of hoofs. The Indian was trying to find
out how far off the cowboys were, the ones who'd massacred his village and
killed his squaw and papoose. The fourth car stopped, came to a
screeching, squealing, burnt-rubber smelling stop just three feet from
Richard's head. And Richard smiled serenely, winked to himself, and
wondered what he'd order if the driver offered to take him to breakfast. As
the driver pulled him up off the pavement, Richard feigned a stupor, began
mumbling incoherently. The only words the driver could make out were
"pills" and "seizure." Richard was only seventeen at the time.

When Richard returned home from his cross-country hitchhiking expedition, Joe sat him down at the kitchen table one night, at Aggie's request, to
have a man-to-man.

"Son," Joe said, "you got to stop doin' these things that scare your
Momma so. Three full weeks she didn't know nothin' 'bout where you was
or how you was or nothin'...and you know how she worries...like to drove
me crazy the whole time, wonderin' whether you was dead or alive or layin'
up somewhere all bashed up...frettin' and pullin' her hair out wonderin' if
you was takin' your pills..."

"I took my pills."

"Well, how was she supposed to know that, Boy? Christ! I done all I
could for this family...for you people...Lord knows that for sure."

Richard looked across the table at his father's face, watched it crinkle up into its familiar etched lines and creases, listened as he ranted on and on, listened to the unvarying monologue that Joe totally directed toward absolving himself of any blame or guilt in the situation.

"I done all I could, Lord knows that."

Richard wondered how many times he'd heard those words, wondered if his father ever really believed them, wondered if he really thought they ever convinced anyone. Those words were like the peeling plaster on the walls of the apartment; when you looked at it, something in you wanted to run over and scrape it off, smooth it out, make it right, but another part said, "What's the use? What's underneath will be worse, and I'll be sorry if I do it."

"It's not your fault." Richard said sullenly to the face that was now beet-red, to the watery blue eyes that threatened at any moment to start leaking and pouring out all over the table between them.

The memory came to him then, the one that usually came in the darkness of his bedroom, in that twilight time when reality drifted in and out like a phantom, when dreams and the events of the day became fused into one fleeting mass that comforted and cushioned and delighted him. He was only two or three years old. He sat in the middle of the living room floor and he wanted his mother, wailed and cried and pleaded for his mother, but his mother did not come. His wanting was not out of pain or hunger or any need other than that of wanting to feel secure in the warmth of his mother's flesh. Two hard, hairy, freckled arms thrust down on him from above. The hands were rough on his tender skin, awkward and hesitant as they clutched him around the middle and lifted him into the air. He was cradled into an unfamiliar lap—the clothes he lay against were hard and odd smelling. His wails subsided into sniffling whines as the voice caressed and enveloped him. The voice was velvety and deep, and he felt its tremors through the rough workshirt his head lay pressed against.

"Rock-a-bye your baby...with a Dixie melody...when you croon...croon a tune...from the heart of Dixie..."

It wasn't his mother's song, and he didn't even understand the lyrics, lyrics that would come to him in the middle of the night and comfort him time and time again. The stone-like arms seemed to soften as the tune progressed, and Richard looked up for one last time at the red-haired crooner who rocked him back and forth as gently as he'd ever been rocked and whose face, calm and unlined with eyes closed, filled the empty places inside him and lulled him into the most peaceful sleep he would ever have.

"It's not your fault." Richard tried to avoid looking directly into his father's eyes, did not want to see the gratefulness he knew would be there because of his words. He heard a long sigh, a sniff, a clearing of the throat. Joe could go on.

"Your Momma wants you to join the Army. Ain't none of it my idea...I want you to know that right off...I ain't for it and I ain't agin it, but it's what your Momma wants."

"The Army?" Richard was incredulous, unprepared.

"She figures it'd be good for you...keeps talkin' about how much good the Marines seem to be doin' for Johnnie...ain't heard from that boy for three months now though, don't know how she gets the idea it's doin' him good."

Richard looked up at his father and felt the tuggings of kinship. The mention of Johnnie's name had done it, had placed them within the same realm, the realm of family, of shared memories, evasive connections, and unrelenting binding ties. The acrid odor of shared blood rose in Richard's nostrils and a bitter taste came into his mouth from somewhere deep in his throat. He bristled.

"I ain't like Johnnie!"

And Joe, completely misunderstanding him, said, "The Army don't have to know about the fits...if you take your pills you don't have no fits...the Army don't have to know."

"I'm going to bed."

Richard rose quickly to his feet and stood before his father. It was no use. If they sat and talked for the next six months, it would still be the same between them, the gap would waver at times, seem like it may come together and close, but there would always be a stream flowing in the middle that would resist the closing, would bubble up, widen and flush out, broadening the two sides until they again stood each alone, each totally separate and unable to reach the other.

Joe stared up at him with pale blue, uncomprehending eyes, but he could not stare for long because Richard's eyes had filmed over, were hard, cold, and unseeing, and Joe knew he had lost, had not done what he'd set out to do, had veered somehow from the course and there was no going back. He did not know what they wanted from him—Aggie, the kids, the boss at the yard. What they wanted, what they expected, seemed just outside his grasp—just when he thought he knew what they wanted, they turned on him and wanted something else completely different. He wanted Richard to leave the kitchen, to go off into his bedroom and to stop standing there staring at him like he was expecting something, because Joe did not know what it was he wanted.

It was Joe who lowered his eyes first. "Go on to bed then. You can talk to your Momma in the mornin'."

Richard waited a long moment, wanting a confrontation; not expecting it but wanting it; but his father did not raise his eyes and he turned from him and left the kitchen. Just before he closed his bedroom door, his father called out. "Richard! Don't forget to take your pills...your Momma left them out on the dresser for you..."

Richard looked at the two small, pink-and-white capsules that lay on top of the note that said "Please take these before you go to bed. Love Momma." He folded the four corners of the note over the two capsules, picked it up with his fingertips as though it were someone else' dirty Kleenex, and dropped it into the wastebasket.

Richard lay in bed that night thinking for a long time. He lay on his back, staring straight up at the ceiling, his hands crossed one over the other on top of his chest. He slept in that position in case he died during the night. He would not want to be found lying sprawled in an unflattering position—uncovered pajama legs jacked up to expose the dead hairy flesh of his leg, his mouth agape, dripping, his hair stuck out at crazy angles. He had no wish to actually die in his sleep, merely thought he should be prepared for the eventuality of it.

Richard thought about death a lot—ever since the streetcar accident, and that had been almost ten years ago. He'd been on his way to his grand-mother's house and suddenly the streetcar stopped dead and his head struck the back of the seat in front of him and then he didn't remember anything lucid for the next week. He didn't remember anything lucid, but he did remember things he would never tell anyone about—things that were dark and haunting, terrible and wonderful things that hung in the closet of his mind for years. He drew upon these things often, and the same types of things would come to him totally new and different each time he would "forget" to take his pills. He had to wear white bandages wrapped about his head for a month after the accident. He wore them like a badge of honor, wished they were blood-stained and tattered and awful looking. The impact of his head slamming into the hard seat jarred loose some electrical pathways, jumbled them up so that they'd skip around like crazy once in a while, and sent Richard into violent convulsive seizures. The doctors did not know this when Richard left the hospital, and so the first time it hap-pened, both Richard and his mother were totally unprepared. At first, Ag-gie thought the boy was being silly, was playing some sort of pretend game, and started to chide him for it. He was sitting at the kitchen table, eating his cereal. He was moody that morning, staring off into space as he chewed his food, not answering her when she asked him if he was full or if he wasn't going to be late for school. But it was early in the morning, and Aggie figured the boy just hadn't slept well the night before. She had her back to him, was standing at the sink doing up the dishes when she heard the low guttural moans that sounded primitive, animal-like. She turned and looked at Richard. He was standing now, gurgling noises deep in his throat, look-ing up at something she could not see with eyes opened so wide and so full of fear it sent a shudder through her. He backed away from the horror he was seeing, flinging his arms over his head, trying to cover up and fend off whatever was trying to get him.

"Richard...you stop that now...You ain't being funny in the least..."

And then it hit Aggie that Richard was not trying to be funny, that he was not able to stop. His mouth contorted and his eyes rolled back up into their sockets. His body stiffened and he fell hard to the floor. Aggie watched in horror, unable to move for what seemed a horribly long space of time. Richard was now foaming at the mouth, and his body was convuls-ing, his head snapping back and forth and his jaws snapping open and closed like a mad dog. Aggie threw herself down to his side, grabbed hold of the small body and tried to stop the violence. It ended as quickly as it had begun. Richard became suddenly limp as a rag doll in her arms, breathing loudly and rapidly, but breathing, thank God, and Aggie sat on the floor rocking him back and forth and wiping the soaking wet strands of hair back from his forehead. Richard would remember none of it, but would be con-fused and slow thinking for the next day or two. The doctors at the hospital performed all kinds of tests on Richard after that, hooking him up to machines with wires taped to his chest and his wrists and his head. And after all the tests were over, they said he had epilepsy and gave his mother a prescription for pills he was to take every day for the rest of his life.

COOL WILLIE
Ronald Booze

Cool Willie was from Philly. He was from Philly and he was COOOOL. Not cool, but COOOOL. Ice-cool, supercool, pimpin'-down-the-street-with-a-layer-of-frost-on-his-blood-red-Pierre Cardin-three-piece-suit-and-three-icicles-hangin'-off-the-superwide-brim-of-his-blood-red-Dobbs-gangster-skypiece cool. Cool Willie was from Philly, he was COOOOL, and he shot some *meeeean* pool. Tha's right. Cool Willie's game was Poison Eightball, and he kicked ass, all over town. Whenever Cool Willie pimped through the door of a pool hall in Philly, the joint went dead quiet. Tha's right, stone cold silent as the morgue at midnight, a flat, fearful quiet that froze the spectators to the walls and straightened upright every hack and hustler bent over the green felt. Yeah, they stood up, sticks in hands, palms gettin' clammy on the cheap pockmarked ash, and they smelled their own sweat, and smiled weak, cheap smiles as the screen door slam, slam, slammed closed behind the stridin' red suit. Tha's all they saw, too, a headless red crushed velvet suit, movin' through the neck-high light, pullin' wisps of the thick cloud of cigarette and cigar smoke that filled the pool hall behind him. Everybody's eyes rode those wisps, too, watchin' that suit move straight smack-dab up the middle of the hall like it was gonna walk right through the first table. But it never did. It always turned right and went around that first table, makin' its way to the middle of the hall, to the middle table. And that's when the left sleeve of that red suit would move up past the neck and out of the light, and come back into the light with that blood-red Dobb's, gently held in the long brown fingers of the sleeve's left hand, and somebody would take it and set it down on one of the other tables (after clearing the balls, of course). It would be safe there, 'cause nobody was going to shoot any pool anywhere else anyway, not while the red suit was there.

Then, quick-smooth and sudden, the right sleeve of the red suit would flash up onto the end of the table, resting a maroon alligator-skin case there (where the hell did he find a red alligator?) and then both sleeves would come up, resting the long brown fingers on top of the shiny smooth case. The fingers would rest there for a second or so, just long enough for the light to flash and flicker off the ruby pinkie ring on the left hand the diamond-in-white-gold on the middle finger of the right. Then those fingers would sliiiiiiide, slow and easy as y'please, out to the latches on the front of the case, and with one quick "click!" that filled the pool hall and made everybody jump, the latches would pop open, and the fingers would gently lift the top of the case.

Well, if any of the rookies up in the hall hadn't dropped jaw at the sight of the red suit, or the sight of the alligator case, or at the sight of the diamond-ringed, ruby-ringed brown fingers, they sure loosed them jowls when the case was opened up. There, sittin' in two grooves of the softest, plushest red velvet any earth born creature had ever laid eye or fingertip on, were two halves of deep, jet-black polished-to-a-shine-to-make-a-man-go-blind ebonite pool cue. The neck-high tablelights shot flickering sparks and streaks of yellow off the two gleaming halves, and the shadow-hidden eyes of every man in the pool-hall would run from tip to crew of the narrow tapering top half, and from butt to gold-ringed top of the lower half of what was the baddest piece of pool shootin' equipment any of them would ever lay eyes on.

Then, the red suit's right sleeve moved to the front of the jacket, where the fingers unbuttoned it, and the sleeves would both drop down and behind the suit, and somebody would slowly sliiiiide that blood-red jacket off, and *hold* it, "don't hang it, got t'keep it in sight," Cool Willie would say, and whoever was holdin' that jacket, folded neat down the middle of the back and draped on his arm, made *sure* that he was somewhere in Cool Willie's line of sight *all* night.

Then, Cool Willie would reach into the right vest pocket, and pull out a pair of red split-leather gloves (where the hell did he find a red cow?) and pull each glove on slooooooowly, carefully, lovingly, so delicate that somebody would sigh the sigh of a satisfied lover (yeah, pool players are lovers, too) at the sight of those long brown fingers sliding in. He'd flex those fingers, three times, each hand, then slowly, carefully, lovingly lift the fat bottom half of the stick from the case, hefting and admiring it in his left hand, his pencil-thin mustache just barely curling its ends upward in a smile that nobody could see in the shadows, and the pool hall was so quiet you could hear a flea fart. Then he'd take that slim, tapering top half from *its* red velvet groove, and heft it, and lift it to the light. Then he'd join the halves, and the scrsssh, scrsssh, scrsssh of the threaded peg screwing into the hole of the bottom half would fill the pool hall, and when both halves were firm together, with that thin line of gold at the joint, Cool Willie would lower the stick till it stood upright at his right, resting its rubber butt on the floor, and smile, lettin' his glossy whites shine just a line under that lip and up-edged pencil-thin, and say, softly,

"Anybody f'r a game a poison eight?"

A WOOLEN SWEATER KIND OF DAY
John McCloskey

You ride by the schoolyard and a pale freckled kid in shorts and knee-high sweat sox is shooting baskets. The air is getting crisper, it is almost fall, night is swallowing the prison gray sky. You think how you used to do that too—behind the back, between the legs—and whatever happened to the oak tree behind the basket? A shot goes in, the steel mesh net jingles—a sound, to your ears at least, better than the ka-ling of a king's ransom of Spanish doubloons. Smiling, the kid fields the ball and spins it on his finger, making like someone he's no doubt seen on television. The gesture inexplicably reminds you of bubbling champagne. The little jerk is good, he's even gifted. But mostly, he's lucky. To be 14 again, on a woolen sweater kind of afternoon in October, with the sun going down and the basket barely visible from your natural shooting range of 25 feet, and you, YOU have the ball, and a crowd to please, and presto, after defying the laws of gravity, hanging in the air for that split second beyond eternity, you snap off your jump shot—30 feet out—swish! it rips right through, you've just won the NBA Championship, the UCLA-Michigan game, the big fracas with the local rival, YOU DID IT! YOU DID IT! and now the crowd is howling, your ears are numb with the applause, the tribute of 40000 feet and hands, and you've still got a warm dinner ahead and Mannix on the TV, and tomorrow its UCLA-Michigan AGAIN. Who'll win this time, Lindsey? And then the day after that, it's GET SMART, and when will it ever end, Lindsey and why does it ever end?

THE SEARCH PARTY: A MODEL ANALOGY
James O. Elder

And the search party roared down on Nantuck County like it was the last piece of fish at a fish fry. They blocked off roads, searched cars, houses, and barns, knocked on doors, shook doorknobs, and arrested any Black man who had the cripple-dog luck of being alone without a white man in the crowd to identify him. The FBI supervised the attack from the second floor of the Jerline Courthouse. The State Police manned communications and roadblocks on all major highways within a 30 mile radius of the prison. County police set roadblocks inside the State roadblocks. And the Lexington police department conducted the air search which was to begin immediately, or—as soon as it stopped raining. Local police from neighboring townships were put in charge of the foot soldiers who were comprised of off-duty prison guards and local volunteers who had seized this rare opportunity by the throat; for it wasn't often that these robust men of Nantuck County had occasion to brandish their shotguns and rifles in such a brazen and orderly fashion; to do so while wearing the scowls and grimaces of men in defense of their womenfolk was damn near more than this over-ripe troop of boyscouts could stand.

Now in order to get a clear picture of this awesome campaign against one man's freedom we must first play a game. Imagine you are hovering 3,000 feet in the air directly over the prison from where the prisoner escaped; it's 4:30 in the afternoon; it's raining like hell; and this siren is squawking like a chorus of wounded ducks. Draw a circle around the prison and paint the inside of it black—this circle should measure a half-mile across at any two fixed points. Now line the circle with 400 men wearing either red, yellow, blue, or green ribbons around their arms; the men wearing the red ribbons should be on the north side of the black circle, the yellow south, the blue east, and the green west. Now the purpose of the ribbons are to cut down on some of the confusion that arose seven years ago when two inmates escaped from the prison and a search group got lost and drifted into the wrong area and was attacked by another search group who thought that they were the enemy and by the time buckshot quit flying through the air three members of the search party had been wounded. So it is important that the men and the ribbons are properly distributed around the circle. At no time should you have 300 men congregating on one side of the prison while there are only 100 left on the remaining three sides; nor should you have 198 men wearing red ribbons and only 2 wearing yellow. Yes, it is essential to the game that the men and the ribbons are properly distributed.

Now march off 20 miles from the black circle and draw another circle making sure to keep the black one in the middle. Mark all the highway intersections that cross this circle with an X—the X's will represent County roadblocks.

March off 10 more miles and draw yet another circle—still making sure to keep the first two in the middle—and this time mark all major highways that cross the circle with double XX's—the double XX's will represent State roadblocks.

Now if you have done this correctly we should have three circles surrounding the prison: the first one just outside the prison walls with the inside painted black; the second one 20 miles away from the prison with X's representing County roadblocks; and the third one 30 miles away from the prison with double XX's representing State roadblocks. Now this gameboard that we've just designed should resemble a Bull's eye target with the black circle surrounding the prison being the bull's eye. Now you might be saying to yourself, "Damn, that's a big target." But really it's not. It is true, however, that if you walked from one State roadblock straight across the circle to one on the other side you would have walked 60 miles and it probably would have taken you from sun-up to sun-down and you'd still have 10 miles left over for breakfast the next morning—and that's only if you're a good walker walking on a good day. My point is that the size of the target doesn't matter—it's the purpose that counts—because targets, like all game boards, are designed for the games people play on them and not the other way around. How much fun do you think it would be to play darts on a target the size of a 3-story building? Not much I'm afraid. Why, the bull's eye would have to be at least 12 feet round in circumference and a blind man can hit that with his back turned. And therefore it would just be a matter of time before the other players got bored and quit, because nobody likes to play a game where it's impossible to prove that they're better than the people they're playing against. It doesn't take any talent to shoot an arrow into a tree if that tree just happens to be a Redwood nor does it take any shrewd cunning to shoot a basketball into the Grand Canyon. Why, it's simply no fun at all to play a game if the gameboard is not designed to meet the needs of the game you choose to play. There's no challenge to doing that because you'd have to make up your own rules as you went along—and some people refer to that as CHEATING. But then, on the other hand, a target can be as big as the moon and possess all the glitter and excitement of a Salem Witch Hunt if the game is designed for a target of that size; and on occasion it has been. Why, Russia and the United States have shot men at the moon and all they wanted them to do was to land in the light, stick a flag in the ground, and bring back some rocks. But, since the moon is 238,857 miles from the Earth, that was a challenge. So when you look down at this 60 mile wide bull's eye target don't think of it as being big, just think of it as being just the right size to play this game.

Now the objective of this game is to keep the Black man in the Bull's eye. But, as we both well know, he has already escaped. So the objective now is to keep him confined to the second circle until he is caught. Now if he escapes from the second circle this same process must be repeated all over again in the third circle. But at all cost he must be captured before he breaks that third ring, because the farther he gets away from the bull's eye the less likelihood there is of him being caught, and the longer he remains at large without being caught, the greater the odds are that he'll break that third ring. So, as you can see, time is of the essence in playing this game, and with each passing second that the prisoner remains free, his chances for success increase, while the search party's chances decrease.

Remember those 400 men surrounding the Bull's eye? Well you can start fanning them out now in groups of 5's and remember that all groups must search in the areas that their colors specify: the red north, the yellow south, the blue east, and the green west.

The prison sits in the middle of an open field about a mile from the surrounding woods and as these men trudge through the rain and thick grass, mud caking up around their boots, the party atmosphere slowly evaporates and for the first time since they joined this search party they begin to realize that this is a real man that they're hunting, a real blood and bones man, a man who was tried and convicted of commiting a crime or crimes unknown and who said "Fuck the Government—I'm not going to pay," a man whose hands can hold a gun and squeeze a trigger just like theirs, a man who could be sitting in the woods watching them right now and waiting for them to get just one step closer before he squeezes off that round. And they are afraid. The closer the men get to the woods, the further away they get from each other, and when the lightning strikes, you can see all of these five man squads stop at once and when the thunder roars in you can feel their hearts stutter, and at this point little things begin to take on great significance: the rain that is falling so thick and heavy that you can hear it tap dancing on ever-widening puddles of water that lie camouflaged beneath the foot high grass; the sky that's been painted a blackish gray by a melancholy artist who felt no need to separate day from night; and the muffled squawking of the prison's siren that reverberates inside the men's heads like the echo from a nightmare that suddenly startles you awake and then dares you to fall back to sleep; and in the distance the trees and shadows are one and you know that if you enter those woods you'll never come out again. So you look around hoping someone, anyone, will call this whole thing off and tell you that it was just a game, but then they don't and you knew that they wouldn't because you know that this is not a game; it's an act of desperation by two desperate forces and you're convinced that he's more desperate than you are. And you're afraid. But once you enter the woods you're more afraid to turn around and go back than you are to keep on going, so you keep on walking clumsily along staring bug-eyed like everybody else, praying that this demonic killer is not in your area but someone else's, and you know that if you can just make it through the night you won't be back tomorrow....

Story-Told-Within-a-Story

ADAM AND EVA MAE
Reginald Carlvin

I was about halfway through my weekly haircut, bored as I don't know what, from listening to almost the entire Third Pentecostal Unitarian Church of the Resurrection deacon and usher board discuss the Bible (in between watching the ball game, and gossiping about everybody's business almost as bad as their wives, whom they were hiding out from in this barbershop) when Sweet Daddy Seeky came in. I knew things were going to pick up now.

Now Sweet Daddy Seeky is the coolest dude—correction, make that coolest dude I know, period. No party ain't hip unless he's there, no club or jook joint is really jooking unless he makes the scene. The cleanest, baddest ride, the baddest finest women, plenty of money—that's Sweet Daddy. Maybe that's why all those other dudes his age (somewhere on the other side of fifty) didn't like him. Sweet Daddy never married, saying that there were too few of him to allow one woman to have a monopoly.

Okay. So anyway, Sweet Daddy strutted in, wearing his tailor made, all red outfit, twirling his ever-present gen-u-ine solid mahogany cane, and tossed his floppy gangster-hat over on the hat rack.

"Good afternoon, gentlemen one and all," he smiled, and the six or seven deacons and ushers mumbled something in unison.

"I just came in to get my 'fro fixed up," Sweet Daddy said, gently patting his six-inch silver natural. "Don't let me interrupt your conversation."

"We were discussing the Bible," one of the deacons said like that was supposed to scare Sweet Daddy.

"One of my favorite subjects," Sweet Daddy said, heading for an empty chair. "Matter of fact, I used to teach Bible class over at Third Pentecostal until all the hypocrites joined the church. That was about the same time you came in, right Brother Dixon?"

Now Brother Dixon didn't quite know how to take that, 'cause he didn't quite know how it was intended, but I did, and it was all I could do to keep an untimely laugh from exploding from deep in my gut.

"What subject were you discussing?" Sweet Daddy asked.

"Sin," somebody offered.

"One of my favorite subjects," Sweet Daddy offered casually.

"I bet it is," an usher made the observation, and they all started snickering among themselves. Sweet Daddy ignored this.

"Everybody talks about sin," he began slowly, "but they don't really know what they talking about. As long as you follow the Golden Rule, you can't commit no sin, for example..."

"You mean to say that the original sin was not a sin," a deacon objected.

"No, no," Sweet Daddy said, "the original sin was indeed a sin," he agreed, and I was disappointed. Usually, Sweet Daddy would go off on one of his wild tangents, making up some funny ass story just to irritate them. Even if he did agree with them he would disagree just for argument's sake. I thought he had let me down until he said, "But it isn't a sin for the reason everybody thinks it is. Now I could explain what I mean, but I don't want to bore you gentlemen..." he trailed off, waiting for them to "coax" him into telling his story, which is what he had in mind all the time.

"Awright, you talked me into it," Sweet Daddy said. There was total silence in the room. Sweet Daddy had the spotlight, the floor and every ear and eye.

"As it says in Genny-sees, first chapter, first verse, in de beginning, God created the heaven and the earth, and the moon, and sun and the stars, and the plants and trees and rocks and birds, and water and fish and on the seventh day he rested. Then about Wednesday or Thursday of the next week, God made the first Afro-American."

"You mean God created Adam," someone amended.

"That's what I said," Sweet Daddy answered, "God made the first Afro-American."

"How do you know Adam was a Negro?" someone asked.

"Adam was not no 'nee-gro.' You can say Adam was a black man, an Afro-American, or that Adam was a nigger, but he wasn't no 'nee-grow'." Sweet Daddy further punctuated his statement with a wave of his cane.

"Awright then," the speaker amended himself, "How do you know Adam was black?"

"Because," Sweet Daddy said slowly, "it says, right there in Genesis, second chapter, seventh verse, 'And the Lord formed man from the dust of the ground." Now the dust of the ground is dirt, 'cause that's what the ground is made of, right? Now there's black dirt, and brown dirt, and red dirt, and even gray dirt, but did you ever see any white dirt?"

"At the beach," somebody offered, but Sweet Daddy said, "That's sand, not dirt," to no contest.

"Anyway, the Garden of Eden was in Ethiopia, and nothing but niggers live in Ethiopia."

"So anyway," Sweet Daddy continued. "God made Adam, and then he made the Garden of Eden somewhere in Ethiopia, so Adam would have a place to stay. Now Adam was a cool brother, looked kinda like my man over there," he pointed to me, and I felt honored to be included as part of Sweet Daddy's stories, "but he was kinda slow sometimes. Now since he didn't have anything else to do, God let Adam name all the animals, which is why so many of them got messed up names today. But anyway, pretty soon, Adam had named all the animals and there he was, with nothing to do all over again, nothing to do to pass the time.

"Now God sends one of His angels to look after Adam, you know, to kinda check up on him every now and then. This particular angel's official name was 'The Archangel and Guardian Spirit of the Cold Northern Wind,' but everybody called him 'Cool Breeze' for short.

"So, Cool Breeze comes hopping through the Garden, halo cocked to one side, leaning hard on his wings, dressed in his white on white tailor-made double knit robe, while Adam was having his dinner: Barbecue and Kool-Aid."

"It don't say in the Bible that Adam ate barbecue and kool-aid," some purist objected.

"I know that," Sweet Daddy smoothly said, "they only had two chapters to tell the story in, so they had to leave out a lot of the details. Now as I was saying, Cool Breeze said to Adam, 'What it is, soul-brother?' to which Adam replied, 'Ain't nothing hap'nin,' (which it wasn't). So the Angel said, 'You sho' do like yourself some bobby-q, don't cha Adam?' to which Adam replied, 'Mumrmph,' cause his mouth was full.

"Now, you know how people get lazy and go to sleep as soon they eat and Adam was no exception, so while he was asleep, Cool Breeze got an idea, which he took back to the Head Man, which was, why not make Adam a helper so he could have somebody to talk to and what all, and the Head Man said, 'Whyeth not'eth?'.

"Now here's where a lot of confusion comes in," Sweet Daddy digressed in his narrative. "Most people think that they literally mean Eve was made from one of Adam's ribs, which is illogical. You have 26 ribs in your body, 13 on each side. If one of them had been used to make the first woman, you might have thirteen on one side and twelve on the other, or thirteen on one side and fourteen on the other, but not thirteen on both sides. And even if man did originally have 27 ribs, where did that spare one go on the cage? Now that is the answer to the question." Sweet Daddy had us confused.

"Like I said before, Adam was fond of barbecue, so Cool Breeze gathered up the bones from Adam's barbecued ribs—spare ribs, get it?—and from that the first woman was made. And even today, a good woman is like a good slab of spareribs: pretty and brown on the outside, hot, juicy, tender, spicy, sweet, lots of meat on the bones, but not too much fat and gristle, well done, but not tough, and good in your mouth." Sweet Daddy was just getting warmed up now and he knew he had us going.

"So, when Adam woke up the next morning, there was Eva Mae. In the Bible, they just call here Eve, 'cause they couldn't translate the 'Mae' part into Hebrew.

"Now Eva Mae was built kinda healthy in the chest," Sweet Daddy said, indicating a good 42 inches, "and she wasn't too bad everywhere else, either. Adam liked this even though he didn't know exactly why. I told you he was kinda slow.

"So, Adam and Eva Mae lived happily in the Garden, counting animals all day and eating barbecue and drinking kool-aid (any flavor) all night, but after two weeks of this, they got bored again; after all, just how much barbecue and kool-aid can you stand?

Now one day, Eva Mae was walking through the garden when she came up on the Snake. Now, in addition to having legs in those days, they were horny bastards too, 'cause after all, what is a snake other than a long skinny psychedelic penis with teeth and tongue?" Nobody offered any comment on Sweet Daddy's observation, so he continued.

"So, the Snake would try to screw anything; in fact, the day before, he had screwed a turtle, two porcupines, and a nearsighted giraffe, and today, he was gonna try to get down on Eva Mae. His plan of attack was a good one; he knew Adam had told Eva Mae it was forbidden to eat the fruit of the Tree of Knowledge, which happened to be an apple tree. Now let me explain to you about that," Sweet Daddy digressed again.

"Like I said, Adam was a nice enough dude, but he was kinda slow sometimes. Whenever Cool Breeze came down to visit with him, Adam would take up all of his time asking dumb questions just to make conversation, since he wanted some company and didn't have nothing else to do. On the other hand, Cool Breeze did and he wasn't up for all those idle conversations. One day, while Adam was asking Cool Breeze, 'Can I eat out of this here tree?' and 'Can I eat out of that there tree?' Cool Breeze was thinking about how much he'd like to be up in heaven, playing his electric harp and drinking MAD DOG WINE and watching comets blow up lady angels' gowns, and the more he thought about it, the more bored he got listening to Adam, so he decided to put an end to all of that crap, so when Adam asked him if he could eat of the fruit of the apple tree, Cool Breeze told him 'HELL NO!'

"Why not,' Adam asked him, and Cool Breeze said that that was the Tree of Knowledge and he was forbidden to eat of its fruit, and that if he did, he'd have to leave the garden, and Adam didn't want to do that since there was no where else to go.

"Now Cool Breeze took off for heaven, leaving Adam to think abut that for a while, figuring that Adam would catch on to the joke and have a good laugh, but Adam didn't, since he didn't have the knowledge to know that he didn't have nothing to gain knowledge of. They didn't have no cars, no TV's, no atom bombs, no electricity, no modern conveniences, no money, so there wasn't anything to know about that he didn't already know about. But like I said, Adam was kinda slow, so he didn't know that he knew." Sweet Daddy smiled at us and said, "Do you all understand that," and before we could answer, he continued.

"So anyway, Adam took this seriously, and he told Eva Mae, and Mr. Snake knew this, so he was gonna have Eva Mae eat his apple, then threaten to tell Adam unless she got up off a piece. But when Eva Mae bit into the apple, it was such a change from everything else she'd been used to eating, she ran off to tell Adam before Mr. Snake could run his game down on her. Not to be outdone, Mr. Snake just shrugged and slipped off to proposition a hippopotamus.

"When Eva Mae showed the apple to Adam, the brother almost had a fit. 'Mr Snake said it was okay.' Eva Mae told him, but Adam didn't trust the Snake ever since the Snake tried to proposition him. See, in addition to being horny, the Snake was AC/DC, too.

"But Eva Mae, not to be outdone, said to Adam, 'How can you trust the Snake when you always got one hanging around you?' Adam said, 'Where?' and Eva Mae pointed between his legs and said, 'Right there.'

" 'That ain't no Snake,' Adam told her, and she said, 'Alright then, what is it?' to which Adam replied, 'I don't know,' which he didn't. Would you know even today what your di--uh, I mean penis was if nobody had told you?" Sweet Daddy asked the embarrassed deacons and ushers who were looking at one another for support.

"Well," Sweet Daddy continued, "even if Adam didn't know what it was, Eva Mae thought she did, so she said, 'It is too a snake, and looks like you gonna have two more soon, 'cause this one's got eggs.'

" ' For the last time,' Adam said exasperated, 'this ain't no Snake and these ain't no Snake eggs. If you don't believe it, come and see for yourself. And Eva Mae did.

"Now, Eva Mae had been examining Adam's Snake and snake eggs for about two or three minutes when something strange started happening. Right before their very eyes, Adam's 'Snake' started to grow—to about ten inches. Since Adam had never felt a particular part of his body get solid before he didn't know quite what to do. Did you know what to do the first time you became solid?" Sweet Daddy challenged the deacons and ushers.

"Now Adam knew that he would have to explain this to Cool Breeze, who was due to come by in a few minutes, but since he didn't know what was happening, he didn't know how to explain it, so he decided to try and hide it.

"He could have taken a cold shower, except that they didn't have any showers, so he did the next best thing, which was sticking it in a stream, but the fish thought it was just a big worm, so that didn't work.

"Next he tried to beat it down with a stick, but his 'eggs' weren't much up for that. He tried to bury it in the sand, but the only available sand was on an ant hill, so that didn't work. Finally in desperation, he got an idea.

"Now as I've said before, Adam was basically slow, but he did have his movements. He wondered how Eva Mae kept her 'snake' under control, when he suddenly realized that she didn't have a 'snake'. Instead, she had a little cave or hole of some kind. Now Adam knew that gophers lived in holes, and that rabbits lived in holes, and if Eva Mae had a hole between her legs where he had his 'snake', then that must be a 'Snake hole'. So, with a tackle Mean Joe Green would be proud of, Adam put his 'Snake' in Eva Mae's 'hole'.

"Well, needless to say, Eva Mae didn't know what was jumping off, or rather, why Adam was jumping on, so she tried to push his 'snake' out of her 'hole,' and Adam, afraid Cool Breeze would see it, tried to push it back in. This kept up for about three or four minutes, him trying to push it in and her trying to push it out; then, it seemed like he was trying to pull it out and she was trying to pull it in; and after that, they didn't really care who was pushing and who was pulling, just so long as they kept it up.

"Now about the time that Adam and Eva Mae had come to a cli—uh I mean halt, Cool Breeze came up and said, 'What do you think you're doing?' To which Adam and Eva Mae both replied, 'We don't know,' but Cool Breeze sure did, so he ran back and told the Head Man, who realized that it was too late now, since the original sin had been committed, which was a sin, but not for the reasons people think it is. He told Adam he would have to work hard all his life and Eva Mae that she would have to go through hard labor, which she would have anyway, but He just wanted to make her feel guilty, just because they had committed the original sin.

"You still haven't told us what that was," an anxious but exasperated usher quickly said.

"I'm coming to that now, no pun intended," Sweet Daddy said, slightly annoyed at being interrupted.

"After they left the garden, Adam knew Eva Mae, which is a fancy way of saying that he fu--uh, made love to her," Sweet Daddy corrected himself, "and pretty soon, they had Cain and Abel. After Cain offed Abel, Cain went out and found himself a wife and she had Ireal, who found a wife and she had Methujael, who found a wife who had Methusael, who found a wife and had Lamech, who went out and found two wives and they had Jabal and Tubalcain...Don't you see what I'm getting at?" The assembly silently and collectively shook their heads no.

"Don't you see? Eva Mae was the only woman the Bible mentions being created, yet Cain, Enoch, Ireal, Methusael, and Lamech all went out and found wives. They don't tell you where they came from, but they were there. Don't you get it? As soon as brothers and sisters found out about sex, they started fuc—uh, practicing so much, they let things get out of hand. Folks was practicing so much, 'til pretty soon brothers and sisters were being born so fast 'til they was coming out of nowhere." That was so beautiful, I wanted to applaud.

"So, Lamech and Jabal and Tubalcain, and in the meantime, Adam and Eva Mae were still at it, so they had Seth, and Seth 'begat' Enos, and Enos begat Cainan, and he begat Mahalaleel, and he begat Jared, and Jared begat Enoch, and he begat Methuselah, and he begat so many sons and daughters 'til they only mentioned Noah, since he was the only one to do something important other than beget Ham, Shem, and Josepheth.

"Pretty soon, there were black people, white people, brown people, red people, and yellow people all over the place, drinking and gambling and throwing beer cans in the Euphrates and the world was one big ghetto. Maybe that's why they say 'The World is a Ghetto,' " Sweet Daddy said reflectively.

"Anyway, the world was in such a messed-up state 'til God got mad and decided to evict all of the present tenants the hard way, and that led to the Great Flood, which a lot of people have a misunderstanding about," Sweet Daddy said, and stopped. There was an awed silence in the room as everyone waited for Sweet Daddy's next sentence.

"Well," a senior usher said timidly, "what happened next?"

"I would like to oblige you gentlemen," Sweet Daddy said apologetically, but I must go elsewhere to discuss the wages of sin." And with that, he recovered his sky and cane and joined the baddest looking hammer I'd seen in a long time who was waiting for him outside on the sidewalk, wearing an outfit that left very little to the imagination but a whole lot to the temptation. He topped his hat to us, linked arms with her, and together they walked off down the street, with, I am sure, much the same expresion that Adam and Eva Mae had the second time they practiced.

WALDEN POND
Allan Zeitlin

It was a beautiful summer evening as Connie and I stood on the edge of
Walden Pond. We were a little drunk, and right then and there we resolved to
walk around the pond three times. To my mind, it was not the appropriate
place to be toting beer cans. But still, there we were, light sweaters tied around
our waists and walking like a couple of sleepwalkers. Earlier that evening,
Connie had not been feeling well, so she dismissed her class early. An hour
later, she was standing at my front door in north Cambridge. In a little while we
were at this transcendental shrine, smelling the summer breeze and walking
through the same clearing where Thoreau once shit like a bear. The pond was
very pretty that evening. Dozens of mallards and drakes splashed through the
water, and for the first time in years, I heard the solitary hoot of an owl. Connie
pointed to the opposite bank where eleven acres of forest once belonged to
Emerson and were now covered over with thousands of cattails.

As we began our first loop around the pond, I heard another pop from one of
Connie's beer cans. "You know," she began, "my department head would go
apeshit if I discussed the real Thoreau in my classes." She paused and held the
can to her lips, and I watched as she tipped her head back. She was a very
different kind of drinker than myself, applying a deliberation and concentration
I usually save for other things. For a moment, the tilt of her head reminded me
of my grandmother when she put in eye drops. "Do you know what I mean?"

"Connie, I have no idea what you mean."

"There you go," she said, "feeling superior to me. Just because I have a
drinking problem."

I felt a little pang in my chest. "Is that what I do?"

"No," she said with a giggle.

"Are you sure?"

"I'm sure, sweetie. I just want to share with you. I speak the truth about
Thoreau. Few people do." She looked away from me, and over her shoulder I
watched a flock of pintails fly over the water.

"Finish what you start," I said.

As we walked around the pond, Connie told me about the Thoreau most
people accept as absolute truth: Thoreau, the surveyor, poet, and pencil-
maker. "It's an illusion most people feel comfortable with," she said, and went
on to give me a rundown on Thoreau's heavy drinking, how most families in
Concord hated him, and how many of those same families still hate his
memory. Then there were the dynamics of Thoreau's sexuality, an enigmatic
mystery that puzzles most scholars. "He almost certainly died a virgin,"
Connie said. Could this be true? I wondered. Mr. Robinson, my high school
English teacher, had failed to mention it.

"One time," she continued, "Margaret Fuller came out here with Whitman
for a visit. Can you imagine those three oddballs here on one day? Whitman
wore a purple waistcoast and had a bag of pecans in his pocket. Miss Fuller
had her shoes off and walked around barefoot, and all three of them were
taking nips from a big jug of elderberry wine. Over there is where they read to
each other." Connie pointed to a clearing about a hundred feet away. A wind

came up off the pond, and Connie, a little too drunk to realize it, swayed in the breeze like one of the cattails. "First, Thoreau built a fire and then read out loud from his essay on the Merrimack River. Then Margaret read a few entries from her diary. Finally, Whitman stood up, peeled off his waistcoat, and delivered a thirty-minute lecture on the Brooklyn ferry. Henry loved it and howled his approval. Then Whitman recited his poems. 'They are beautiful and odd,' Margaret told him, 'just like their author.' Thoreau took out his flute, and as the three of them sat around the fire, he played for about an hour. The jug went around a few more times. Then they all went for a hike. Henry showed them his bean field and a family of blue jays that nested nearby. Pretty soon, they were walking around the pond, just as we are now."

We were well into our second loop. I wondered if this lecture was the same she had delivered earlier that evening in class. Her need to get drunk and discuss Thoreau's wilder side was a little puzzling.

"So the three of them walked around the pond till nightfall, laughing, passing around their jug. None of them was above getting a little shit-faced now and then. Trust me, Thoreau wouldn't begrudge us our measly six-packs. The only thing he'd resent are the busloads of school kids who come here and treat this place like a church. Open another one." Complying, I brought out another can and popped its ring.

" 'There is a man in the village,' Henry told them. 'His name is Sammual Hoar. He is Concord's most prosperous citizen, a lawyer by training and a landowner by inclination. He thinks I am a drunken idler who is out to seduce his daughter. But he is only half right.' Whitman and Fuller laughed as they dragged their asses around the pond. If you think we're drunk, you should have seen them. Henry was really on a roll. 'His daughter's name is Abigail, a very pretty name. Unfortunately there is nothing else pretty about her. I am afraid she made me reconsider my views on public flogging. Her father treats me with ill will because I set fire to ten acres of woodland he was preparing to purchase. It was an accident, of course. I was quenching my thirst when the campfire got out of hand.'

" 'It could happen to anyone,' Whitman told him.

" 'My very words,' Henry replied. 'With the exception of marrying his Abigail, I will do anything to make it up to him. But he won't have any of it. Whenever I go into the village for supplies, he shuns me.'

" 'It is his own fault for having such an ugly daughter,' Margaret told him. That's the kind of babe Margaret was.

" 'Miss Fuller,' Henry said, 'I'm going to give you some advice. Consider it carefully: Stay as you are. Never change.' Then they all took their clothes off and went swimming. Afterwards, they rested on the bank. It was the last time Henry saw either of them. A couple of years later, Margaret drowned in a shipwreck off Fire Island."

As we completed our third and final loop, I thought of Fire Island in the days before cars and hot dog vendors. I thought of Emerson sending Thoreau to the island to retrieve Margaret Fuller's belongings, and how Thoreau had returned five days later, in the depths of depression. I looked up at the sky, and it had gone from blue-black to black.

"After that, he *really* didn't care what Concord's finest thought of him. He told them all to screw off," With that Connie moved down to the bank and lowered herself into the grass. Following her, I sat down on the ground next to her. "Maybe he was a drunk, so what?" Connie said. A moment later, we were both asleep.

THE HUNT
Fern Levin

On rare sunny days, the sky was that crisp unending blue that stretched out for miles and miles, interrupted only occasionally by the sound and speck of an airplane that cleaved within its cushioned texture. Those were the kind of days that the powder blue bedroom he and Nadine shared seemed acceptable to Alan.

Sitting on the bed, he watched her in mild amusement, one eye turned to the silent people on the television, who sat in buoyant nondescript chairs. She paraded around in the ridiculous starched full slip, as she hurried to the closet, pushing aside the clothes so much like she were displaying merchandise to customers, while each screech of the hanger on the closet rod grated his nerves.

He watched the reflection of the sun roll around the creases and curves as each quick movement of her arms and upper torso caused that nylon to shimmer like satin. Then he'd look past her and feel a bit of relief as the constant blue of the late morning sky seemed to take the confinement of that bedroom, and expand it so he felt like he was outside, floating instead on a cloud, and watching it all from above.

But that damn slip. It made her look like a little school girl, all leggy and vulnerable. He tried to imagine seeing her instead in a garter belt, stomping about the room in stiletto heels like some French whore, while the ever present cigarette hung from her lips. That was his fantasy; and throughout all the years he'd been with her, he knew one thing: his wife was not receptive to fantasies, at least not his fantasies.

And that damn cigarette; even though it was the smoke that brought them together in New York so many years ago. That, and her voice.

He pushed the remote control of the television, absently watching some cartoon, as he watched her put on the grey silk dress with the pearl buttons. Then he propped up his pillow. It, too, was powder blue, having one bold navy blue stripe on its side, which seemed to scream out from the monotony of that light blue room. And then he remembered that steamy little bar around 28th Street, right in the heart of New York's Garment District, where he and Jay Stevens had wound up one night after a law school exam. He was hunched over his beer while Jay eulogized the evening in his best Brooklynese.

"My god, Alan. He's just a shit professor. That exam was plain shit, and I'm going to drink myself silly, so I can forget all about the fucking tax laws of this state. Then I'm going to dream about all the rich women I could be meeting now, if I had enough money to go down to Miami Beach."

Alan was only aware of his voice dotting the air with staccato-like sounds, as it mingled with the coughing and laughter coming from various corners, as the bartender, a round man with pearlized cheeks, consistently toweled a glass. And the mirror behind him caught it all, stretching the action on and on.

And then he saw Nadine.

Her harsh laughter rose up and up, farther than any of the common neighborhood sounds of Lou Tanner's Bar and Grill, and he squinted his eyes, readjusting his glasses to focus on the woman to his left who emitted the raucous sounds.

Deliberate gusts of smoke came out of her mouth with words he could not distinguish over the voices of the crowd. She wasn't beautiful or even plainly pretty, but she had a ruthless quality that Alan immediately found exciting. And she seemed to have power over her appearance. There were people like that. They had a way about them, that even if they were ugly as sin, you looked at them, and were drawn to them, believing that somehow they were attractive. It was all in their presence, how they delivered themselves to the public. Because even a pretty face, that stands lost in its own fears and uncertainties, you quickly abandon, and move on. But Alan found it much easier to be attracted to those whose beauty eluded him. He preferred to dig for it.

So he stared. He liked the way she handled her cigarette, and found himself becoming aroused as he watched the way her two fingers tightly clasped that thin scepter between them as she mechanically moved her arm, like lever action, from the elbow joint to and from her very red lips that sucked hard on that cigarette.

"Alan, how can you just sit there, watching that stupid show? Aren't you going to work today?"

He rolled onto his side, as Lou Tanner's Bar and Grill quickly dissolved, along with the past twenty years, and he suddenly noticed the funny design on his pajama sleeve.

"Nadine, what is this?" he said, ignoring her question, as he found himself strangely annoyed.

"What is what?" she snapped, slamming a drawer shut so he actually felt it.

"This. On my pajama sleeve."

He watched her move toward him, the unlit cigarette she had just inserted into her mouth sticking to her top lip.

She looked at his sleeve, puzzled, as she moved back, her hands on her hips.

"I don't see anything."

"What the hell kind of design is this?"

"Oh Alan," she wailed through her nose and clenched cigarette teeth. "I don't have time for these games. I've got a meeting with my banker in an hour, and you're talking about ducks on your pajamas."

"Ducks!" he screamed, and he saw a flight of them scale the invisible blue sky, while she went about her morning ritual, dressing, hands thrown about the air as she searched for something, finally going to the top shelf in the closet.

"Yes, that's it. Amazing," he said. "That's the reason. This peculiar, uncomfortable feeling whenever I wear these pajamas. And you hit it right on the head. Amazing."

"What the hell are you talking about?" she said.

"Ducks. For some reason, ducks always give me this uneasiness. That's hardly normal."

This time her sharp moves softened as she turned back to see the manner in which he delivered his words, while she emptied the contents of her green Ecuadorian lizard bag onto the bed.

"I'm serious, Nadine. When was the last time you saw me eat duck?"

Her eyebrows arched as she put some loose change into her coin purse.

"Never, right?" he snapped. "And do you know why? Well, I'll tell you...because of Jimmy MacDuff, that's why."

Alan looked out into the blue sky, past the north shore suburb, even past the decade or two that had elapsed since he even thought of the little red-haired, freckle-faced boy with the three brothers who lived with their father and mother down the block from him on Brooklyn's east side. His eyes were wide and vacant, filled with the past. He scratched his head.

"Jimmy and his brothers, they used to hunt every year with their old man. He was a gruff Irish cop. He'd take them to Upstate New York, duck hunting...I'd forgotten all about it.

"I used to sit in that big white kitchen with the black pot-bellied stove. Mrs. MacDuff was moving around all the time. She never sat down. She was always cooking, cleaning, throwing pans and dishes around, or stirring something in that huge pot that was forever cooking something on the stove. Mr. McDuff would pinch her on the ass every time she passed by him.

"When was the last time you saw your father pinch your mother on her backside?"

She shrew him a look out of her switchblade eyelids. They were that quick, he thought.

"Never, right? Of course not. Because Jews are just too goddamn uptight to pinch their wife's ass in the presence of the holy children, that's why."

"What the hell are you talking about, Alan? You're sitting here reminiscing instead of going to work and I'm listening. That's even better. And I have an appointment this morning."

"Yeah, but you don't understand. Jesus Christ. Jimmy MacD. That's what we used to call him. All those kids looked exactly alike. Like one kid growing up in different stages.

"Jimmy's little brother, Timothy, looked just like Jimmy did when he was his age, and when Jimmy got older, he looked exactly like his older brother, Kevin.

"I'm sure it could have confused someone on the outside, if they didn't know. It was like a time warp with those three. And the old man...he used to have a collection of guns like you just would not believe. And not just because he was a cop, either. But there were rifles and shotguns. Revolvers, automatics. Shit, it was like a fucking arsenal in that tenement. They were under the beds, behind the couches. There was no room with the five of them, but he was weird about his guns. They were his babies. He'd make sure they were lying just so...flat, and with nothing on top of them. He was always cleaning them. Now, where the hell did I ever see guns? Pictures, that's where. And at the movies.

"Mrs. MacDuff would ignore it all. And when pistols and rifles were being draped over her crisp linen table cloth, she'd take the cloth from the sink and wipe the crumbs around it, then set a place for whoever wanted to eat.

"You should have tasted her bread. Hot. Right from the oven. I'd smear the jelly right on it and sit, listening to Mr. MacDuff's stories about how he wanted to get the hell out of Brooklyn.

"Shit, I never even thought any other place existed. My old man was working as a tailor, and my mother barely managed to make ends meet with the check he brought home each week. I was damn lucky if I got to Manhattan.

"This one day, Jimmy's pulling on the old man's sleeve and whispering loud enough for me to hear every word. He wanted me to go hunting with them. I saw that old man frown hard. It was the same look he always wore right before he'd whack Jimmy or Kevin across the side of their heads when they'd done something he didn't like. You never put words into MacD's mouth, or put him on the spot. But apparently this time it was okay, because he looked at me. I could feel his eyes, but I was still scared to look up...and then I felt him pat my head.

"Shit, his pat was like a row of bricks falling on top of it.

"Sure, why not," he said. We can take Alan duck hunting with us. It'll be good for the boy. Make a man out of you.

"Then he looked me square in the eye. 'How'd you like to try it, son? You want to go upstate with us, for some duck hunting?'

"Jesus, Nadine, all I could remember was those narrow green eyes blazing at me with ducks, while he stared into my eyes, not even moving them once. Even if I wanted to, I couldn't have backed down.

"Then Mrs. MacD asked me if I ever ate duck, and I lied. I said, yeah, once. I figured it had to be like chicken, so it wasn't all that bad."

When Alan looked up, Nadine was standing in front of him, hands resting on her hips, and her head was cocked to one side. She was listening. My god, he thought incredulously, she was actually listening.

As if injected with fuel, he continued, aware now of his heart beating, his quickened pulse, the blue out the window so perfect, he felt if he put his finger out that window it would smear onto it, and he would bring it inside that room, spreading it right over the carpeting. It was that color.

"What did my parents know about hunting? My mother went to the kosher butcher who killed the chicken for her. And that was that. Ducks? So why not? I pleaded with them. I promised I'd bring one back for dinner. They smiled and my mother, God rest her soul; she made such a face, Nadine. But my father...he just grumbled about how duck was all right if you cared for it, but he preferred chicken.

"I never even touched a gun before that day, Nadine. I swear to you. I never wanted to. I never had good aim. You know that. Christsake, even at the pinball machines, I fuck up. Shit, Lori is a better shot than I am.

"So, here we are in this magnificent country. Near water falls, mountains, streams. Everything I'd read about and seen pictures in books, and here I am, little Jewish kid from Brooklyn, out in the clean air, duck hunting.

"They even had the dog with him...what the hell was his name? Oh yeah, Crabtree. How could I ever forget that?

"We'd watch the ducks from something called a blind. That's where you sit, quietly, waiting, nestled, hidden among trees and grass. You build it yourself. You couldn't make any noise, even if you had to scratch your nose. Naturally mine itched as soon as I got there. Mr. MacD was a good shot and was quick to fire when a flock flew overhead. The first came down in the bushes and Crabtree was right there, picking up the little guy. It was all I could do to stop myself from puking my guts out right then and there. Seeing that mass of shapeless feathers, and that little white band around his neck. It looked like a deflated toy.

"And my god, he's waving it around my face; its eyes were open, and its beak looked no more dead than it did a few minutes ago. And the fucking dog was yapping his head off. And the three guys were jumping up at their father's hand like he'd reached the level of a god. And I thought to myself: This is not for me.

"I swear to God, Nadine, mountains or no mountains, if I could've run, without stopping, all the way back to Brooklyn, I would have. But how could I ever look that man in the face? Or even Jimmy?

"And I don't know how many birds they knocked off that day. I was dazed, even after they showed me how to shoot, pointed me in the direction, and taught me how to aim. I moved in, but closed my eyes when I saw the ducks, hoping I wouldn't hit anything. I could take their teasing of me being a bad shot easier than worrying about whether or not I had bagged any duck.

"We got a dozen or so, and Mr. MacDuff plucked and dressed them. Jimmy and Timmy watched; Kevin helped. I volunteered to set up the tent, make the fire. Don't laugh. I know how to build a fire.

"But the worst part was the dinner. The little leg, the greasy meat; it barely went down, let alone stay down. I must have heaved my guts up a dozen times until there was nothing left."

Nadine was standing in the doorway of the bedroom, her purse and gloves in hand.

"Are you finished?" she said.

Alan looked at her, and then down at the bed where some mangled bits of paper from a hanger lay.

"It's strange, the things we remember."

"Yes, but I have to go now. Really, I'm late."

She was frowning now, even though a small smile lingered. "I'll see you later."

She didn't wait for him to speak; in fact she didn't even give him a chance to answer, and he sat in that position for a long time looking after her, even after he heard the front door close, and the screech of her tires against the driveway.

He surprised himself, letting all that old forgotten history spill out, only to dry up as quickly as it had materialized. Ducks, he thought to himself. What the hell does she care about ducks? He gathered all the bits of shredded paper he had absently been working on in a tight wad in his palm, compacting it even more with the fist of his other hand. Then he threw that ball into the blue wastebasket that stood next to the desk.

Fingering the pattern of his pajama sleeve, he headed for the shower. He felt that peculiar anxiety lift off him, the hidden truth had materialized. He should have been happy; he should have been uplifted, relieved. But instead a darker successor to his emotions settled inside him, reaching and stretching into each shadow of his being: Betrayal.

Eulogy of a Hitherto Uncelebrated Object

THE BOOK OF MATCHES:
A CELEBRATION OF AN UNLIKELY OBJECT
Chris Sweet

Consider the most marvelous book of all, the book of matches. Matches: the name alone summons to consciousness a dream of perfection—for what *is* a match? A match, in the broadest sense, is unity within plurality, the formal cause of all philosophy, the answer to all faithful men's prayers, the impalpable palpable, and the undulating, imperturbable body of what we can know and what we cannot know; yin and yang, the marriage of light and darkness. At the mere mention of match, the mind flies to a last vision of Adam and Eve, there upon the plain under the eastern gate of Eden, fended forever from their recent seat of bliss by the fiery sworded angel, our first parents, who

> " ...hand in hand, with wandering steps and slow
> Through Eden take their solitary way."

Was there a more perfect match? Woe to the serpent! Our wandering parents walk hand in hand, yet solitary, united, yet not as once they were, but forever two singular beings.

I sing of the metaphorical match, the match of redemption through suffering. Was ever a match consummated, that was not first struck, and roughly so? All matches first must be torn out and scraped along the raw, sand-textured striking strips of this life, if they ever are to confound oblivion and *live*! One thinks of the poet who sings of his old age and failing powers as he gazes into the fading furnace of his hearth, reduced now to glowing charcoal:

> " In me thou see'st the glowing of such fire
> That on the ashes of its youth doth lie
> As the deathbed whereon it must expire,
> Consumed with that which it was nourished by."

Just so, the rough scrapes and raging fires that nourish youth do finally consume the body that delighted in them! Yet, without the first striking consummation, can one ever say, "I live"?

I sing also of the allegorical match, the match of our divine origins. For who cannot conceive a match, the ideal match, perfect in all matchness? And are not all matches manufactured in some likeness of this ideal match? Yet look deeply into the book of matches; is not each plagued by an imperfection, a falling away from the ideal? Here the cardboard was cut unevenly; there one accumulated less sulfur upon its head than the others; another stretches taller; another bears a longer, more tapered neck. Some swell to red-tipped heads, some green-tipped, some hoary white-tipped. Yet all bear the image and stamp of the one, true match. Who has not observed at first striking how the sparks leap up, the flame shoots skyward, seeking from the moment it takes life to give itself back to the splendid face of divinity? Thus are men born shining babes, trailing wreaths of cloud, as it were, that point to our diviner origin. The first sparks and burst of flame—the idealism of inspired youth—last but a second; failing to touch the sky, the match forgets what it once knew and burns steadily towards its end. At last, in old age, it shrinks, it fails, it swells, it dies; poof! Thus all transient things return to their elements.

But let us descend from these heights of Promethean Caucasus to view the match in the dimmer light of everyday, a tiny fire stick, useful in a myriad of small, human endeavors. With a match you can pick up a girl in a bar, while her "…Soule transpires/at every pore with instant fires." With a match you can find a lost contact on a dark stairwell, unfreeze a frozen car-door lock, revive the doused pilot light. Yet in this mundane fact lies a great truth concealed: just as every fiery romance is also an ordinary affair between ordinary people, so the match is at once philosophic and extraordinarily ordinary.

Let us pause and see what we can find written in the books itself. Feel its outer skin—smooth, like plastic, as though oiled. What other book has so many colors and such varied artifice upon its cover? Its variations outnumber all the species of fish in the fresh and salt pools of the globe. Yet each book of matches is the shadow of its ideal, the one book from which all others take form. At first, it appears as two flat, rectangular surfaces back to back, yet not flat against one another, but somewhat farther apart at the top edge than at the bottom, shaped like a wedge or the head of an axe, to enclose a space that is roomier in the head than at the feet. This skin of the book is called the cover, for it covers the book's contents. On the cover you see the celebrated colorations and designs which mark the species—collectors value the cover above all else, for often the sight of a rare, long-missed cover shakes free the memories of past pleasures—a trip, a dinner, or a seduction. Upon the seamless plane of the cover is laminated a band of rough, fine grit—the striking board or striking strip, a surface designed for friction, and contrasting with the oily, glossy skin of the cover itself. Its sole purpose is to create enough heat through friction with the match head to ignite the match, called *striking the match*, or *giving a light*. But let us delve deeper inside to unlock further secrets of the book.

Turning the book on its edge, you can see the inner contents; is it a mummified choir? a petrified garden of extra-terrestrial flowers? a visible catacomb of the dead? Look closely; as from one stem, four overlapping rows of stalks tipped by ovular heads rise from the blade-edge of the cover to nestle in the broad back-edge, like seeds in a seed pod. Peering into the book from the side like this, you experience the same revelation as when cutting into the guava fruit for the first time, to reveal a hive of black, umbilically tied seeds; just so the head of the matches—for that is what they are—appear umbilically tied to the center of the book, from which they radiate like the seeds of the guava-womb.

Open the book by sliding the moveable portion of the cover upward with your thumb and peeling it back. The first thing you notice is that the cover consists not of two pieces at all, but a single strip wrapped around the matches and, when closed, tucked in upon itself, so that the unresistant match heads are completely ensconsed. Not only that; the striking strip on the outside stretches along the blade-edge of the book while the heads nuzzle a safe distance away under the folds of the broad-edge; moreover, the striking strip traverses the back of the book (though, to speak rightly, the book has neither true front nor true back, for it can be read from either direction, but since it must be entered from the tucked-in side, and since our concept of "frontness" implies the gates of access, and when we show our backs it is as if to say, "Keep away, don't come near, I wish to be alone, I wish to deny you access to me," I will call the tucked in face of the book—though truly whether it has a face or not one may dispute—call this face of the book, its front) so that there is no way a striking match could pass over its unexposed brothers to ignite them and striker, in a painful and injurious conflagration.

But let us return to our investigation of the interior structure of the book. The inner surface of the cover is to the outer, as is mere paper to plastic. The surface feels less smooth, and not at all oily. The inner skin soils easily, and it cannot be cleaned, except by wearing away, through friction, as one does when erasing pencil marks from paper with a rubber eraser. Having both texture and form of paper, the inner cover of the book often serves for jotting down names and phone numbers, significant dates, poems, and messages of all sorts, for which (because of its smallness) it is often found more convenient than a journal. In this respect it contrasts with the outer cover, which will not take the inky impressions of a ball point, as though you tried to write over a grease spot or a peeled stick of margarine; press harder, you'll only crease the surface with invisible lines.

Now look at the exposed match heads from the top down and you will see four parallel rows of staggered oval heads; those four rows spring from two strips of cardboard stapled at the base, and the staggering effect results from the heads being broader, due to their accumulation of sulfur, than the stalks upon which they stand. Looking at the stalks from this vantage point, one cannot escape being reminded of broccoli, whose tiny seed heads are similarly attached by filaments to the great, muscular central stalk of the plant; the seed heads of broccoli being larger than their stems, they, too, flower out and spread themselves broadly, like these matches, although there be only twenty matches to a book but countless thousands of seed heads to a single stalk of the vegetable.

Proceed now to the great lynch-pin, the fragment of extruded steel which clawlike grips the cover and sandwiches the match stems between its circling arms, the prime principle of unity in the book; the small staple. Its arms hold everything together; take it out and the book falls apart in your hands, and no glue can replace it, no reinsertion can bring back the firm unity that was before; the process of extracting the staple may not be reversed. Taken apart, the book reveals itself as no more than a twisted particle of wire and three unmatched pieces of cardboard. Once the mathboards are out of their protective casing, they rapidly decay from moisture, friction, and bending; moreover, they become a safety hazard. Lose the cover, and you lose the best of striking surfaces, rendering your matches unusable. Better to leave the complex structure as it is, clasped in the circle of wire, tight as a loving woman's arms hold the object they love and keep it from flying apart like a universe bereft of gravity and all natural laws. In shape the staple nearly makes a full circle, but its ends stay perpetually an eighth of an inch apart, like two hands nearly touching, though they are one and the same staple. Numberless are the works of art bound by the feminine encompassing principle: to name but two, there is Lena in Faulkner's *Light in August*, and there is Molly Bloom in *Ulysses*, who begins her day with a sleep-muffled "No", and ends with "yes I said yes I will Yes." Just so, the looping staple and the book itself contain all yes and no, all birth and death, all opposites. All this you may read in the book of matches.

IN PRAISE OF THE HAMBONE
Andrew Hyzy

Some extol the sparkling but nonetheless questionable virtues of Perrier, while others revel in the bland allure of wine and cheese; less influenced by trendy middle class snobbery, I applaud the hambone.

No discussion of the hambone can be attempted without a preliminary look at the noble pig, the rightful owner of the hambone. While there are those who quite justifiably will not eat the meat of the pig for religious reasons, there are also those misdirected souls who maintain that pigs are filthy and stupid, slovenly creatures whose meat is foul and unhealthy, and whose only function should be to wallow in mud, grunting merrily all the while. These same people think nothing of eating the chicken, a repulsive cackling bird with an evil temper that feasts on grubs and worms that it finds wriggling in the dust. These confused people need only know that the pig, when given the opportunity, has proven to be among the cleanest of the barnyard animals and rejoices at the sight of mud only because it provides it with comfort from the heat, something overlooked by the Maker. I have seen pigs on farms that are not only clean, but practice a sort of housekeeping, as it were, by using only certain parts of their pen for certain functions. As for being stupid, it has been proven that the pig is highly intelligent as well as tasty, and is capable of being trained to perform chores of which humans are incapable. In France, it is the pig that is trusted to sniff out the delicate truffle, that flavorful fungus so important to the French cuisine. The pig is not lacking in other qualities either. If you would venture to ask a farmer which of his animals are the most loyal or the most valorous, he would tell you it was the pig. Trustworthy? Again, the pig. I have heard tales of palatial California residences that are guarded by pigs rather than dogs due to the pig's admirable, almost human qualities. So, to those who look down at the pig in disgust, I say Fie!! There is no more highly refined, delicious animal to be found, and the hambone is but one of the many treasures it offers.

Reckoning the average hambone to begin at the point where it starts, or opposite the point where it ends, it comprises an area of at least a square foot. The bone itself gradually tapers away to a blunt end, while the opposite end may contain a joint covered with tough gristle and flavorful fat, and, as one hambone is different from all the rest, there may be pink meat clinging to the bone depending on the attitude of he who carved the meat from the bone. If the meat has been stripped from the bone, fear not, for the bone itself is what contains the subtle flavor that lends itself so well to almost any foodstuff, and it is that flavor that makes the hambone a most desirable item. For this reason, we concern ourselves not with the appearance of the bone, as it really doesn't matter, but with its hidden, mysterious qualities.

Just as the hambone is capable of lending its flavor to other foods as an accent to their own individual taste, so it is also capable of overpowering and shadowing the other food, much as a tastelessly designed couch is able to overcome a well furnished room. For those adventurous beings who like tasteless furniture, however, this is a redeemng quality rather than a disparaging one and I mention it only as a warning for those dullards who insist upon that which is considered fashionable at the time.

The secret of the hambone lies more in its usage than anything else. As liquor can change the personality of he who drinks it, so can the hambone change the personality of the food it is teamed up with. Like liquor, the hambone can be abused, for the man who lurks in the shadows drinking his liquor from a bottle is not dissimilar to the thieving gypsy who picks the hambone up with his dirty hands and gnaws at it happily with broken,brown teeth. When properly used, however, the hambone is a delight to work with, owing mainly to its chameleon-like quality of adapting itself well to its surroundings. The ignoble peasants of Poland ungraciously fling the hambone into a seething kettle of cabbage, potatoes, and onions for a robust soup while the genteel French chef simmers it tenderly with sweet shallots and thyme, using it as a base for a rich sauce to grace his vegetables. I have been to church socials in the Midwest where I have encountered the most appealing baked beans with a most pleasant flavor, and upon asking what this heavenly taste is attributed to, I was pleasantly shocked to find that the humble hambone is the source of it. The sorrowful darkies of the South stew the hambone with collards, or mustard and turnip greens for a truly scrumptious dish that is nutritious as well, greens being high in iron; and the Germans use the hambone to make a peculiar but still tantalizing soup with sauerkraut and bay leaf. In New England, that region known for its basic yet timeless values, the hambone is revered as the *only* possible animal flavoring for split pea soup, and I have heard that in California, that diseased wasteland of decadence, the hambone is dried and pulverized, then compressed into pills that have a revitalizing effect on man's most basic urges. Countless other examples abound, but we shall not discuss them here, as they only serve to reinforce the point already made, that of the hambone's adaptability, which is like that of the esteemed cockroach who has remained virtually unchanged biologically through the centuries. This same adaptability places the hambone among the most sought after of all foodstuffs, and quite rightly so, for who among us has not embraced the hambone in one way or another? Is there anyone who has never been tempted by the aroma of a hambone wafting through the air, teasing the olfactory senses in much the same way as the sirens teased Jason and the Argonauts? I think not, and yet I find a sense of excitement in the hambone. There is still much to be discovered about it, for while I may dissect its uses, it remains a mystery still, and only time will help to elevate the hambone to its rightful place in the culinary world. Time goes on, and while we mortals pass on in the Divine scheme of the universe, the hambone will remain a treasure to be pampered and savored by those who follow. Perhaps in years to come we will see the advent of the hambone in places we are unaccustomed to. Hambone ice cream, perhaps, or hambone cake. Its limits are unreachable, as are those of the mind.

Other Stories
and Personal Essays

BROUGHT BY THE STORK
Jennifer Sheridan

"I want to be a person," whispered Ferd, the aqua green parakeet, perched behind Nora on the bedpost. Nora sat in front of her mirror applying cold cream to the skin under her eyes. She suddenly felt sick deep down in her guts. She felt as if she'd eaten bugs, worms, that they were crawling around in the slimy pit of her stomach. She felt so very nauseous. Nachos probably, ballpark nachos most likely, or artificial chocolate coating. Maybe it was just life itself that made her sick. The last thing she needed now was the bird talking, again.

"I want to be your brother."

Nora tried to ignore the bird, Ferd, who, realizing that Nora was consciously not responding, fluttered over to her shoulder in that frantic, annoying way that domesticated birds have. Due to a lifetime of six-inch flying space, their wings have somehow weakened and they are incapable of truly achieving any real velocity.

"Nora," Ferd whispered into her ear. "Nora, Nora." His breath smelled of sunflower seeds. He pecked at her neck until it was raw.

"Yes?" said Nora, knowing full well what he wanted, but not wanting to know.

"I want to be a person, person," said Ferd, stroking the side of Nora's face with one silky wing. The two looked into their reflections side by side in the mirror. Ferd wore his most insincere sincere love look, his beak dipped ever so slightly, his eyes half shut, the look that without fail wins him millet spray after millet spray. Nora looked sullen, trod upon, sad and sick and oh so tired. Her hair hung into her ashen face.

"What?" she said.

"A person, a person. Your brother," demanded the bird.

Nora knew that there was no arguing with Feathers-For-Brains. He was certainly a bird set in his ways. Another crazy idea, but, she figured, it wasn't like him to suggest something without thinking it through. Birds, by nature, aren't like that.

"No," said Nora, stomping her foot. A dull thud with her fuzzy pink slipper.

"Yes," said Ferd, "yes." And of course he is right.

Nora never could deny them anything, those darn birds, Ferd and Gus. They had two bathtubs right in their cage. They had two nests, one for each, and so many mirrors. It was outrageous. It was no wonder they were spoiled, particularly Ferd, who was younger.

What if he wanted to kill someone? Would I let him? What if he came to me with a plot to kill Charles de Gaulle or Lyndon Johnson or something, would I do it? Of course the answer is no. A bird comes to you and tries to convince you to kill someone, even someone you don't like, such as Mrs. Carlyle at the bank, the beady-eyed old snout face, she's so mean about overdrafts. He comes up with eighteen different reasons why I should do it, right down to my parents' ridiculous in-house separation and how other people would understand, what with all the stress I'm under and everything. People would be glad, actually relieved and PROUD that I had done it, killed someone nobody liked.

"Come on, Nora, Nora," he might say in that Polly-want-a-cracker voice. I taught him how to talk, for God sake! No, I know where to draw the line. Today he's requesting personhood, sure, no big deal, maybe he knows some way to pull it off, but what would be next? I don't know what he has planned. This sort of thing has happened before, for all I know. Hitler might have been a parakeet, a harmless yellow tweetie on a tiny plastic swing, until some unsuspecting moron let him try something a little different.

"What are you thinking?" says Ferd. "What are you thinking?"
"Nothing," says Nora.
"Something," says Ferd, "you think too much, too much."
"It'll never work out," says Nora, pushing her index finger under his fat belly, forcing his scaly feet onto her skin.
"No one will know, no one will know."
"I'll know."
"Please, please," says Ferd, tears in his black eyes threatening to fall down his downy face, "just for a week, O.K., a day. I want to walk about on two sturdy legs. I want to feel the wind through my hair, hair."

The transformation of Nora's brother into Ferd is quick, painless, the blink of a large, almond-shaped blue eye, the blink of a round black pin-point eye, and it is done. Her brother rolls over in his sleep, opens his eyes. He shudders, sort of ruffles himself. Nora stands in the doorway watching the event in the dim yellow light from the hallway, helpless.

No one notices but Nora and it doesn't bother her much, not much, except for a few things. Basically Leon is the same. On Saturday morning she finds him in the living room on the phone with his college girlfriend, his legs thrown over the side of the couch, as always. He is watching a rerun of a cop show, eating ice cream out of the container.
"Uh huh," he says, "that's really rotten." He laughs with his mouth open. Mint chocolate chip runs down his chin. He wipes it with the sleeve of his plaid bathrobe. When Nora sits down he takes her hand and holds it, like always. On TV a man wearing bell-bottom pants gets shot by an off-screen gun and falls into the street, clutching his heart.

What bothers me though is the look in his eyes, beady and sharp as a hawk. We are sitting in the living room and I notice that the black centers of Leon's blue eyes are bulging out against his glasses. It's got to be Ferd peering out of Leon into the world, a budgie inside a sixteen-year-old boy's body.
"Ferd," I whisper, "I know you're in there." Maybe I can scare him out somehow, shame him. This is no place for a parakeet. This is not proper behavior for a little green bird with dimples in his beak, a pet bought in the back of the five-and-dime, rescued from such a terrible existence. Have you ever been back there where they keep the birds? It's truly dreadful. And this is all the thanks I am getting here.
"What did you call me?" says Leon, leaning toward me, covering the mouthpiece on the phone, "I didn't hear you."
"Nothing," I mumble, picking a green pistachio nut in a red shell out of a silver nut bowl, "forget it."

Leon is busy picking the salted sunflower seeds out of the nut bowl and sort of clucking to himself when his father comes in wearing his black corduroy bedroom slippers and purple boxer shorts.

"Don't dig in there," he tells Leon. "You kids want to have lunch with the old man?" he whines. He always whines, he has that kind of voice.

"What's the occasion?" says Nora, crossing her ankles.

"Naw," says Leon, "not hungry."

"Come on, Junior," whines his father, "put your shoes on. We'll have a party, celebrate your mother's migraine." He disappears into the bedroom to dress.

My father always takes Leon and me out to eat when he's had a fight with Mother. Today it's German. He orders a stein of dark beer and insists I have a taste because I'm almost twenty-one. It is bitter and thick and makes me want to vomit.

"Tell me, Dad, about the day I was born," I request, wiping my mouth.

"Oh, let's see. I get it all mixed up. You were born in the morning, I think."

On TV parents know these things right off the top of their heads. Telling their kids about their births is always a warm moment right before the commercial. My father has sauerkraut in his mustache.

"Uh huh."

"One of you was late, I remember."

"Mom told me you thought I looked like your brother who died when he was a baby."

"Lewis. Yeah, well, maybe."

"She said it frightened you."

"Sorry, Honey, I don't remember."

"She said you looked like you'd seen a ghost when you came from the nursery, really pale, and you told her I looked like Lewis, the baby that died," I hear myself saying in this really breathless voice.

"What's the matter, honey," says Dad, putting down his bratwurst, "something bothering you?"

"Well, my bird got away, got out of the cage somehow," I admit, turning to Leon accusingly, like a detective in a bad movie, very melodramatic. I expect him to balk, sit up in his chair like on a perch, squawking.

"Please, Nora, one more day, one more day, one more day," he might say. "Mr. Jeffers, please, help me out, me out. Being a bird, it's a rotten life, not fit for a dog. Come on, give a fella a break, break." But he doesn't even look up, he just stares at his fingers like he's never seen them before, clicking the nails against each other.

"That's a shame, baby, really. Got out the window, did he?" says Dad.

"No," I mumble, looking at my plate, "not out the window."

After lunch Nora stands in the doorway of the sun porch watching Gus, her remaining parakeet, swinging on her perch, all alone in that huge cage. Nora's father'd given her the cage after a student named Emily had given him two cooing orange lovebirds and a birthday card he wouldn't let her read. They had died when he left them on the air-conditioning vent over night.

"Don't you think they'll be cold there, Daddy?" Nora'd asked.

"No," he said, lighting a cigar. "They'll be fine." Nora found them feet up the next morning, frozen stiff. Their little orange feathers fluttered in the breeze the air conditioner provided. He didn't believe in keeping animals in cages after that.

She watches Gus sitting there alone and thinks how lonely the bird looks, how sad. She feels it in her skin; it prickles against her like a flame. Sometimes Nora can sense things like a psychic or something. Nora watches Gus swinging back and forth, talking to herself. She doesn't even know Nora is there.

"Hello," she squawks; "hello," she answers. "Birdy birdy birdy!" Gus is pissed. She is terrified to be alone. She wishes she were dead. Nora can relate to birds somehow, birds especially. Last summer in a hotel room over Paris, Nora saw a pigeon walking through a concrete square. Suddenly it got this look on its face like it had just remembered something, some bird thing. Nora wondered at the time whether birds remember things that people cannot, prehistoric things, things that happened some time before there was anything but total darkness.

She turned to her brother Leon that afternoon in Paris, woke him up, and asked him a philosophic question about pigeons. Leon rejected it; he swore at Nora and rolled over.

"Do you think if you took a pigeon out of Central Park and dropped it in the center of Paris that it would be homesick for its own statues?"

Nora had to ask a few times.

"No!" he shouted, pounding his fists into the blankets. "No. Now shut up, would you?"

Leon doesn't like birds, never did. And now this has happened to him.

Leon is watching high school basketball on TV when Nora comes in from the sun porch. She knows she looks strung out, tired. She knows he can't help noticing the dark circles under her eyes. She can feel them. He looks up at her. She's been acting strangely all day, that's what he must be thinking, so it is probably best to just ignore her. She crosses the room, blocking his view of the TV.

"What?" he asks.

"It's Gus," she sighs, throwing herself into a chair.

"Uh-huh."

Nora had a boyfriend last year, that's what he's thinking. He was a lawyer, or a law student, or something. He worked part-time in a Pizza Hut. Charles. Charles played the guitar, sang folk songs mostly, and ate a lot of popcorn. Nora knows that Leon thought he was a big jerk, a hippie Pat Boone type, too nice. Charles said "yah mon," a lot. Still, he was someone. Leon can tell that Nora is lonely. What is wrong with Nora, that's what he's wondering. She isn't sure herself.

"She just sits on her swing in there, talking to herself."

"What?"

"Gus," mumbles Nora.

"Oh, Nora."

"'Oh, Nora' what?" she snaps.

What does she want from him? She can see the question in his face. Her damn bird got out or something, Maybe it died and the other one ate it. Maybe the other one feels guilty. Gerbils eat each other when they die. He's thinking, Nora looks like she's going to cry. She looks like she is going to come over to him and throw herself on his neck and burst into tears. All over a ten-fucking-dollar parakeet. Replaceable. Still she's his sister and all. Nora knows that Leon truly hates to see her so bad off. He even has to turn his head away. Maybe his eyes have started stinging. It's just that she looks so frail. Why is she holding herself so stiff, that's what he must be wondering. She's so goddamn skinny. He can see her hipbones sticking out. She looks as if she might just break.

"'Oh, Nora' what? What do you mean?" she squeaks.

"Oh, nothing," Leon says, but she's already turned and slinking away toward her bedroom.

"Wake up, I said. Damn it, *wake up."*

Leon stood beside Nora's bed, digging his fingers into her skin, bruising it. The purple already rising on her shoulder. She saw his nails, talons that he refused to cut, before she could register his face. The nails were thick and yellow at the ends.

"What?"

"Your bird. I saw your bird."

Some kind of trick? A shifty bird trick, maybe, but Nora decided to play along, see where it would take her.

"Where?" Nora sat up, put her hands over her eyes. She felt as if her skin had been peeled away and what was left was small, pale and unprotected, shivering under the thin blanket. Through her hands everything looked orange. It scared her.

Dropping her hands she saw Leon pacing back and forth at the foot of her bed, his hands clasped behind his back. He squinted in concentration, taking tiny, deliberate steps. Nora waited, swallowing. She yanked sharply at her hair to wake herself up. She felt the sting on her scalp.

"In the park!" Leon stopped, threw his hands into the air, fingers spread. "Do you know where parakeets go? Have you ever seen them in the dead trees outside the grade school?"

She didn't know.

"Well, they're famous." He sounded exasperated. "There are hundreds of them, in the park." Nora just stared at him, looking for Ferd in the way he shook his head from side to side. "And I think I saw your goddamn bird there just now." Maybe it was Ferd, now she wasn't sure. She tried to see his eyes, she'd be sure then, the way they bulged, but he'd turned away. "So put on your pants and let's go get it!"

It was the middle of the night.

"In the morning . . ."

"NOW!" He stomped his foot. "You can't just sleep all the time." His voice sounded frightened.

Outside the sun is shining.

"What time is it?" I ask. Leon is ahead, almost running. He slows down and reaches for my hand. We have to hurry I guess.

"Never mind," he says. It surprises me to see the sun reflecting off the snow.

"What time is it?"

"Three P.M." Leon says. He takes my hand, like always. "But never mind that," he says. I have to jog to keep up with him. He squeezes my fingers and pulls me along. I won't make it if he doesn't pull me. I feel so weak.

In the park we stop under a dead tree. He points across the snow-covered grass to another tree several yards away.

"See," he whispers, "there they are." I don't see anything at first, but when I squint I can just make out some colors moving on the colorless ground.

Birds. Budgies.

I pull Leon closer, tiptoeing.

"No," he whispers.

"Yes," I whisper back. We get about ten feet away when he makes me stop.

"You'll scare 'em," he warns. He knows this.

They look cold, skinny, weather-beaten. They remind me of the birds in the back of the Woolworth's. There are about sixty of them, all gathered together around two empty potato chip bags and a Twinkee wrapper. Pale blue, pale green, pale yellow, parakeet colors, all mixed together. They stand out against the gray snow and brown grass, and they make little cooing noises.

"Is it there?" whispers Leon. "Do you see it?"

"What?" I whisper. I've never seen anything like this before. A flock of parakeets. Urban lions over a kill, something like that.

"Your bird," hisses Leon, digging his fingers into my jacket sleeve.

Would I recognize Ferd in the pile, in all the confusion? After all this time (how long has it been, only a day?), would I even know what he looks like?

There is one green bird standing to the side, but I'm pretty sure it isn't Ferd. It's too skinny for one thing, too haggard looking. It looks like a concentration camp bird, all feathers and bones. It looks like it's going to die.

"Maybe that one," I say out loud, pointing. The bird looks up, tilts its head. He does not recognize me, but that's to be expected. I don't know him from Adam either.

"Okay," says Leon. He drops my hand and creeps slowly slowly toward the birds, making little clucking noises, rubbing his fingers together as if he has a treat. His fingers look white and scaly outside his glove. The birds look up with interest, walking awkwardly out of his reach. He gets within lunging distance of the green one. The bird looks right at him.

"This one?" hisses Leon. I nod. Leon stands very still until the bird dips his beak toward the ground, then he dives for it. The flock rises without a squawk. There is only a gentle flutter of pale wings that disappears into the empty trees. In my bones I feel all those birds settling on branches, folding their wings neatly under them.

"Come on," calls Leon, racing past me and we run back across the grass, up the block to our house. Leon is beaming in the living room, breathing hard. His hands are cupped.

"Got it!" he says.

I open the little cage door and he pushes the bird through it. It falls in, confused, flutters over to a corner. It is skinny beyond belief, skinnier than it seemed in the park. I have never seen this bird before. It isn't Ferd. I'm sure now.

"Thanks, Leon," I hear my voice saying over and over again, "thanks, thanks a million."

"Mom, Dad, I found Nora's bird," he calls, walking through the French doors into the living room as if everything is so easily rectified.

Nora was drinking a glass of lukewarm water at the kitchen sink around ten-thirty that night, looking out at the back yard through the bottom of the glass. Waves washed over the floodlighted dead trees and grass on identical lawns all up and down the block. Nora's mother shuffled in behind her. She knew it was her mother because she heard the sighing. For Nora's mother every breath is a heavy sigh.

"Hi Mom."

"Hiya kiddo," she wheezed, throwing herself into a kitchen chair. Nora heard the metal creak. She heard the air going out of the plastic seat under her mother's weight. Her mother struck a match. Nora refilled her glass, looking out over the world through tap water, smelling the sulfur. Her mother smokes Chesterfields.

Her sighs fell into sync with Nora's breathing until Nora felt them rising and falling in her own lungs.

"Tell me more about when I was a baby," said Nora, sitting down at the table.

"Oh, please, sweetie, I'm not feeling up to it."

"Come on," Nora coaxed. She heard the voice of Ferd in her own voice, seductive, eager, a little desperate. Did she learn that tone from him or vice versa? She walked her fingertips up her mother's rubbery arm. They both felt the fine yellow hairs stand on end.

"That tickles," her mother growled, pulling her arm away.

"What was I like?"

Nora wanted to know what she was like before she remembered anything. They say that the first six months of a person's life are so crucial, but nobody remembers what it feels like, being born.

"You had terrible diaper rash," Nora's mother finally offered, taking a deep drag on her cigarette.

"I did?"

"Oh God, yes," her mother exhaled. "You bled and cracked, your skin peeled. It was awful."

"Uh-huh."

"I tried everything, salves and ointments, those little medicated towelettes, every brand available. Nothing helped." Her mother stared over Nora's shoulder towards the wall. "I knew it must have hurt like anything, although you didn't cry much. You whimpered sometimes, and you wouldn't breast-feed. I remember holding your little butt against my cheek. It was so soft and helpless. I cried and cried because you wouldn't cry. You were such a little baby, but very brave."

"Oh, Mom, it's okay," Nora comforted, trying to take her hand. Her mother pulled away. "I don't even remember it." Her mother sniffled, wiped her nose on the heel of her hand and took another drag on the cigarette.

"God, my head is pounding," she said, standing up, "I'm just not up to this right now, honey." Nora took another drink of water, looking out at her mother's face through the bottom of the glass. It was distorted, which was only a relief. To see things clearly was too hard.

"Good night, Mom," Nora heard herself saying, "good night goodnight goodnightgoodnightgood." She touched her mother's cheek with her lips. The skin on her face felt cool, as cool and tranquil as glass about to shatter.

Nora sat alone in the kitchen, the sun setting a glowing lavender. She strained to feel terrible diaper rash again. She longed for her whole life to come crashing back to her, everything she'd ever forgotten, but nothing at all would come.

In a dream Nora stands in Leon's bedroom. Everything is in its proper place. The high school basketball pennants are hanging on the wall. There is a mostly nude girl on an outdated calendar above his single bed. The only thing wrong is the smell. Leon's room smells like a jungle would smell, if she'd ever smelled one, moist and hot, heavy with steam. She hears vague echoes of animal screeches, monkeys and huge birds in the half darkness. Does Nora see Leon sitting in a tree above his desk? Could he have feathers, huge greenish wings? Her brother definitely seems to have a bird body. Laughing a mechanical bird laugh, he wipes one eye with the tip of his wing and sighs.

"Poor Nora," he says, "She never did understand—basketball at all."

Nora moves her lips, but no sounds come forth. Her lips taste bitter, salty, dry. The inside of her mouth is grainy, like a pit of wet sand. Her arms are immobile at her sides and she shivers, helpless, angry, terrified. God, what is this, a dream? If so, Nora wants to wake up now. Leon is laughing with hatred. He stretches his yellow talons toward her in a green jungle light.

"Poor Nora," says the voice of Ferd, the bird, booming in her hears, "poor Nora poor Nora poornorapoornorapooor." The jungle sounds get louder, taking over the whole room. Nora feels the moisture of the jungle seeping through the carpet, covering her bare feet. She feels the low growl of a powerful animal, a massive jungle beast, something large and taut, rising through the grass. She feel the vibrations through her ankles, coming closer.

"Help me, Leon." She hears her voice echoing. "I need my goddamn bird back!"

The jungle walls emanate the feeling of no. No, you can't have that.

*   *   *

It is really night now. Everyone else in the house is asleep. I creep through the dark house, past each room, making sure. My mother is in the master bedroom, Dad, as usual now, sleeps on a cot in the kitchen. Leon is asleep in his bed. I lean over my brother's body, feeling his breath on my lips, my nose. I peel one eye open, hoping to find Ferd, the wayward bird, inside there, awake, waiting for me. Ferd would have heard me coming. He would be ready for me. It had been a whole day now. The deal had been for one day. Unless he'd changed his mind. I'm not quite sure how these things work exactly, having never before been involved in, what would you call it, an exchange, such as this.

I can't see him, not right away.

"Ferd," I call, low, gentle. Maybe he is sleeping after all. Leon's breathing is even, calm. I watch him sleep for awhile. I do love my brother. How could I have let this happen? Everything has gotten so out of control. I think about Ferd, who has always been a rather unpleasant little creature. He chased Gus around the cage, trying to mount her constantly, cackling, pulling out her tail feathers with his beak. He took bedding from her nest when she was eating. Now that I'm thinking of it, Gus had complained to me many times about these things.

Maybe I should cover his nose and mouth with a goose-down pillow. Wouldn't that be something? I would feel them rock and buck underneath until the body stopped and everything would be so still, so silent. I would remove the pillow gently, so gently, and look into Leon's teenage face, bluish in the pink glow of his night light. I could close his gaping blue eyes, no longer bulging black at the very center. Maybe I should just do that and see what happens. I do have some control here after all. The thought of it makes me feel worlds better.

I am paralyzed, can't make a decision. I return to the hallway, moving slowly toward the sun porch.

I opened the window and put the birds out. Gus and the stranger, the substitute for Ferd, who won't come back, who refused to listen to me anymore. The bodies hesitated, knowing with raw, vacant instinct that the night would last for several hours yet, that soon the frost that has temporarily waned would return in full force, cold, frozen, and so dark. They knew that everything out there was dead and would stay dead for several months more. There was nothing for them to eat. They might not last the winter. But I gave each little feathered rump a shove. They fluttered once and disappeared into the dark.

The closed window pane reflected my own face as I shut the window. Hard as I try I still don't remember any diaper rash. I don't remember any pain.

SISTER KATIE
Doris Jorden

The Prayer

It was said time after time that when it rained and the sun still shone brightly in the sky the devil was beating his wife. But there was no explanation known for a hail storm that suddenly descended on the town, carrying balls of ice the size of hen eggs on its crest—ice that was equally distributed and had enough force to smash window panes, burn and break the naked skin, and strike hearts with dread of the unexpected. Open doors slammed, windows snapped and screeched, and people who only moments ago casually strolled up and down the streets now desperately sought shelter of any kind. It appeared that no explanation was necessary, for in a few seconds the streets were clear, except for a black sedan that cruised down Main Street and came to a halt in front of Rosie's Cafe.

A man in uniform, as sleek as the expensive automobile, emerged and, like a trained soldier unaffected by the storm, went about his work. He came for Katie. Those were his instructions and he carried them out diligently. He was not a man to be put off. She had no choice but to go with him. Even her employer Rosie insisted that she leave. And so, still garbed in the white kitchen apron, she was escorted to the car and driven to the rambling split-level house on the hill to pray for a man that she had had dealings with two times before—each time when he was on his deathbed.

Henderson Townsend—king of Jason County, builder of its schools, churches, and movie houses, owner of most of all the land thereabouts, and supplier of jobs throughout the town—lay in his giant, four-poster, wooden bed, fighting for his life. His loving and faithful wife of thirty-five years, Clara, was at his side, and his two children, Junior and Delli, stood just outside of the master bedroom in the hall, their eyes wide. Delli's were struck with petrified terror over the possible loss of her father, while Junior's were filled with conspicuous anticipation of stepping into his daddy's big shoes. Katie hurried past the two of them huddled together in the hallway and stepped into the bedroom, where the frail, grey-haired man lay wasted down to the bone.

The room was like a crypt, air-tight, and the smell of death pierced Katie's nostrils, biting into her flesh. The only thing needed now was a corpse, but the people gathered had no intentions of giving up. She removed her apron and laid it on the chair near the bed, her eyes focused hard on the frame that lay shaking under piles of heavy quilts. A flicker of light registered in his eyes, a light that soon turned to hope, and he immediately felt stronger in her presence. The shaking ceased. Perhaps a sign, perhaps not, but one thing she knew was that though this room might have the appearance of a crypt, it most definitely was not one; it was a battleground for life. It didn't matter if they all were strangers, for all they really knew about each other were names and needs which were all very similar—needs so similar it wasn't necessary to discuss them. They all understood that they were gathered to fight for life until Townsend had drawn his last breath or had risen from the bed on his own. The room itself echoed these sentiments. Bottles of medicine lined the high-priced bed stand. Heating pads and numerous, exquisitely designed quilts (probably from Europe) lay on the floor near the bed for extra warmth, should they be needed, along with a humidifier and other apparatus to assist in breathing, and needles filled with clear liquid solutions to kill the pain that constantly racked the frail shell of a body. And even though rales thundered throughout the room loud enough to be heard without the use of a stethoscope, blood still pumped through the old man's veins, and breath, though shallow, could be heard. And now hope had penetrated the brain, hope that led to faith, perhaps only the faith of a mustard seed, but faith nonetheless; and she had seen faith rescue many from the pits of hell and the jaws of death; and he had seen death.

Their eyes met and, as if their souls touched, Katie laid her hand on his burning forehead, and he accepted its coolness with gratitude and hunger, like a nursing babe accepting his mother's warm breast. Katie's breast rose and fell, and in the bright light she resembled a child who awaits permission to speak. She closed her eyes, and time stood still as she sought the courage to begin.

"Father, this is your faithful and devoted servant Katie calling on you this dark Monday afternoon...I wouldn't interrupt you while you is about your work except it's a matter of life or death, and you said anyone, no matter how small they think they might be, you said that all they had to do was to call on you in their hour of need. You said that it didn't matter what time of night or day it might be, all they had to do was call on you, and you would be there beside them. I know I don't have to tell you who I am, 'cause my credentials have already been put in my file in heaven.

"I know it ain't no surprise to you, the reason I'm here calling on you. I know I don't have to tell you the reason. So I'm just down here begging you to consider this plea for this man in Jesus' name, 'cause I know you have always been partial where he was concerned. I know, before his coming home to be on high with you, he told his disciples that the only way to the Father was through him. So I know that even if you turn a deaf ear to my request, if I call on Jesus long and hard enough, you will at least listen for his sake—this I know.

"So I ask you in the name of JESUS to hear me out. I'm asking you to consider this poor soul whose flesh now defies him and feeds upon his body. I'm asking you to consider this man called Henderson Townsend: a man whose committments have been many to this town; a man who has given much to this town; a man who practically built this town with his bare hands; a man whose education was wide; and yet a man who still doubts the workings of the Lord, though he has known only your goodness; a man bestowed with many gifts and advantages; a man graced with humility from his wife and love from his fellow men—and still, a man who was not satisfied. I'm asking you to consider his wife and children who needs him. I'm asking you to consider this here town and poor folks in it that needs him, the Negroes and the whites. I'm asking you to consider the hospital being built up the road and the part that Townsend took in getting it started. Lord, I'm asking you to give him one more chance, a chance to redeem himself in your eyes. I ask you to consider the shell of the man lying over yonder and spare him. I ask you this in Jesus' name, the Holy Ghost, and the Fire, amen." The old man, blind with fever, tossed back the many quilts from his shell of a body and rose from the center of the huge bed. He got down on his shaking knees, holding dearly onto the side of the bed, and opened his mouth from which came guttural sounds resembling the voices of lower animals and then, quite clearly and unmistakably, the howl of a wolf. The hair on the back of Katie's neck rose, and she yelled, "Get thee behind me, Satan! There ain't room for you here in this house! Leave in the name of JESUS!" Her voice trembled but she was not afraid. Townsend crawled on his knees until he reached his wife, his mouth continually working up and down as though to say something urgent. No sound was audible. His eyes disappeared into the back of his head, his frail body arched and spilled out onto the carpet. It was over. He was dead. The two women stared at each other long and hard for a few seconds, neither saying a word. They both understood the meaning of death, specifically the meaning of this man's death.

The Restaurant

If old man Townsend hadn't died earlier, it would have been the usual routine Monday—people coming in for the Blue Plate Special or whatever their particular desires might be. But Townsend's death had filled the town with dread of the expected, anxiety over the unexpected, and the excitement that normally follows the shock of realizing that no one lives forever. Off and on all afternoon, Rosie, caught up in the excitement, had been giving a blow by blow account of the events leading up to his death—her own version, of course. The only thing she knew for sure was that he had died, for it was against Katie's principles to discuss how and in what way the departed met his maker. She was a missionary of God, and that placed her above common gossip. How would it look, a missionary of God using the afflictions of the sick and the dead to call attention to herself? It would be much worse than the funeral director who discusses with his friends the condition that some poor soul's feet were in when he went to claim the body. And even though she had held fast to her principles, every now and then Rosie's crisp voice would rise above the usual chatter and the song on the jukebox and she would hear, "Yes, it's true, died this afternoon...Is Hell got fire, and Heaven got angels?...Sure I know what I'm talking about. I ought to, since it was me personally who sent Katie up to the house to pray for him.... Around one-thirty and, well, you know that's my busiest time of day, but I told her to go. Hell, if it had been me, I would want somebody to be at my side. So, by God, I sent her, and that's all to it." A coldness enveloped Katie's body every time she heard Rosie repeat this story, for Rosie had not been there, had not seen the misery and the false hope in the old man's eyes, had not seen Clara's face filled with indecision as to what steps should be taken. Katie thought to herself, one more hour of this and someone would have to come and pray for her, for she would surely lose her temper, and that would be not only a disaster to the one nearest her tongue, but also a sin. It was only the slackening in the orders that put her in a better frame of mind. She could now start the preparation of the apple pies for tomorrow's special, a chore that required her undivided attention, a chore she welcomed, for this occupation had always placed her outside of the realm of Rosie's sharp, droning voice.

Big Jim Davis, prosecuting attorney of Jason County, pushed through the door at seven o'clock exactly, his usual time. He headed for the corner table by the window, his usual spot, after making it known to the public he wanted to be alone—the noncommittal gestures, a not too friendly wave suggesting tiredness, an almost cordial greeting, a half-smile masked with sternness and authority, a guise he had mastered well the past three years. He sat waiting, but not long, for his usual meal: a huge hamburger burnt on the edges and raw in the middle, mashed potatoes loaded with dark brown gravy, four slices of whole wheat bread toasted, and plenty of creamy butter. But most of all, his favorite dessert, a slug of apple pie.

"Evening, Jim, what will it be?" Rosie asked, not giving his seat a chance to get warm from his tall frame.

"The usual, Rosie, only have Katie serve me tonight; it's important that I talk to her," he said, smiling over even teeth that spoke with kindness and yet with authority. A quick scan of the crowded dining area gave Rosie reason to wonder if this was the proper time for Katie to be up front, even though her skin was almost as white as the blue-blooded white folks that sat around, eating and chatting. Young Roy Larkin and his rowdy bunch, a bunch known to try almost anything, just as long as it was wild and went against all virtuous principles, sat at the lunch counter. The Reverend Augustus Mack, minister of the Baptist Church and several dignified church members, a bunch known for setting standards for others to follow, occupied the center table. And the very wealthy Richards from over Kenawana Bank, a bunch known for opening and closing doors of finance, sat at the long table on the left. And the door steadily opened and closed with people coming and going—people that kept Rosie's place open. "It's all right," he whispered softly, reading her mind. "Just let it be heard that I have to see her. I guarantee there will be no trouble."

She whirled on her heels away from the table, both hands jammed down into the pockets of the white uniform, her red hair bouncing with each step as she headed through the swinging door leading into the kitchen. The two women looked up in unison, waiting for the figure to issue some particular instructions as she had done in the past. "Katie, get Big Jim something to eat and carry it out to him. He wants to talk to you about something," Rosie said, her brow knitted in a frown.

"Talk to me 'bout what, Miss Rosie?" Katie asked, a feeling of dread forming in her stomach. Her mind raced ahead, focusing instantly on her husband Jab. She wondered if the law was after him again.

"I don't know, Katie, but he's waiting," Rosie said impatiently.

Calmly she reached for the platter and, facing Rosie, Katie asked, "He want the usual?"

"Yes, the usual." Rosie turned her attention to Alice. "You're gonna have to work the orders by yourself for a spell."

"You sho is the center of activity today, Katie," Alice chirped as soon as Rosie's head had cleared the door. "First, being called up on the hill to pray for Townsend, but that was expected, since you prayed for him last year on his deathbed, and the year before, and he had been walking around ever since. That is, up until a couple weeks ago when he got so sick all a sudden. And now the proscuter wants to talk with you. What you reckon he wants with you? I bet you it's something to do with your old man, Jab. What else could it be?" Alice rattled on and on, while Katie grilled the special hamburger and piled the beige platter with mounds of potatoes and gravy. Katie didn't answer. How could she, when the words Alice spoke so freely had been her same first gut reaction? She changed the stained apron for a fresh one, folded it in half, and tied it neatly around her slim waist, then re-arranged her hair net. For everything had to be just right when she stepped outside the cubicle to the other side of that swinging door, the door that led to another world, a world in which she was not familiar, a world for folks, white folks, who were friendly to her in their homes but would just as soon pass her by without speaking on the streets. She was expected, and every minute she lingered, she kept him waiting. She took a deep breath and pushed through the swinging door, her heart in her throat. The roar of the music, the clatter of kitchenware, and the familiar sounds of voices filling the air all ceased in one split second. The hush was deafening. All heads turned in her direction, some immediatley, some a bit slower, some just to see what everyone else was looking at so oddly, and some in jest. In that split second, one hundred eyes focused spontaneously on her small frame—eyes that burned through her clothing, eyes set deep into hollow faces with twisted mouths and deep furrowing scowls etched across their brows, eyes that would haunt her forever. The only honest face filled with contempt was that of Reverend Mack, who didn't bite his tongue when it came to religion. He simply hated her religion, often came right out and said, "Sanctified folks are heathens." His glare she understood, for they were old enemies, and she welcomed it as an honest dispute. She realized that his stare today was mostly because Townsend, at the hour of his death, had sent for her and not for him. She pasted a smile on her trembling lips and forced her unwilling legs to move toward the table, a table that stood miles away and yet only a few feet from her. The eyes burned through her back, and she suddenly felt like buckets of lice had been spilled down the back of her dress, as she placed the food on Big Jim's table.

Scowling, young Larkin rose and yelled "What's that nig—" Before he could finish the sentence, Rosie had pushed him down on the stool so hard he almost lost his balance.

"Just shut your mouth, Roy Larkin, and don't you go nowhere," she hissed. "Now, Big Jim sent for Katie, and what Big Jim wants, he gits. Stop acting like a green tomato, 'cause you was born and raised right here and you know darn well when Big Jim is on a case, he as soon as go up your daddy's crack if he had to," Rosie said.

Slowly the noise resumed, the clattering of knives and forks and casual talk, and Katie relaxed somewhat, but not completely, for the reason she had been summoned hadn't yet been aired. Uncomfortable, she faced the white man, not much older than her thirty-five years, his large hands busy cutting into the meat, a man known for getting his man, woman, or child, and sending them off to faraway places that left scars of indifference stamped on their souls forever. But she remembered the Jim who played games with her, who was like a brother to her, until his mama, Cherokee, ordered him to stop playing with that nigger. She remembered it well, for that was the day when she realized that her pappy was white and her mammie was black. Before Cherokee's outburst, she hadn't noticed the difference; they were just Mammie and Pappy. She said a silent prayer.

Big Jim took two spoonfuls of potatoes, pulled a long white envelope from his pocket, and laid it on the table facing Katie.

"You read, don't you, Katie?" he asked.

"Some," she replied, stunned. Her first thought was why would one of the busiest men in town call her away from her work to ask her a silly question like that. Instantly her guard went up, although she didn't know why. As far as she was concerned, most white folks were foolish. Plain downright foolish. Didn't want Negroes eating with them, but it was fine for them to cook their food and tend their young. Didn't want them to come in the same door as they did, but would traipse in behind them, no matter where they went, like a small lap dog. But not this man, not Jim Davis. He didn't ever give a damn, nor would he ever care about who sat at what table or who didn't, or what door who walked through, or who cleaned his house. The only thing that concerned him deeply was a case, and even that didn't matter to him as long as he got his hands on who did it, and he usually succeded in that. He swallowed a mouthful and said, "Katie, do me a favor and read the name on that there envelope."

She picked up the envelope carefully, like she expected it to snap shut upon her fingers like a mouse trap. "Mr. Jim Davis," she stammered.

"No, Katie, I mean the name at the top."

"Mr. Henderson Townsend," she replied over the lump in her throat.

"Now, Katie," he said, staring into her eyes. "It is my understanding that you was over to the house today, that you was there when he died. Is this true?"

"Yes, I was there up until he died."

"Well, while you was over there, did you happen to see this envelope?"

"No, I weren't concerned with nobody's mail, only Mr. Townsend."

"I see," he stammered. "Did he tell you anything that maybe might seem kind of strange to you or perhaps something to tell me?"

"No, he didn't say nothing to nobody while I was there."

"Well, did he try to say anything?"

"Seems like he was trying to say something, but he only worked his mouth up and down. No words came out."

"You mean he was trying to say something, but couldn't?"

"I can't swear to that, but it sure seemed like he wanted to say something, only..."

"Only what, Katie?"

"Only nothing came out of his mouth, except..." She stopped, leaving the sentence hanging. Wringing her hands, she was afraid to go on, not because she thought he wouldn't believe her—everyone knew her word was like the Good Book—but afraid of how her answer might appear to be the ramblings of a person filled with demons.

"Except what." He stopped chewing and stared long into her face.

"A wolf howl was the only sound that came from his mouth."

The spoon fell to the plate. "What?"

"A wolf howl," she repeated softly, for everyone in the cafe had turned around to investigate his outburst.

"Did I hear you correctly? A wolf howl?"

"Yes."

"Are you sure?"

"I'm a woman born and raised in the country all my life. You know that to be a fact, since you stayed across the road, and I definitely know a wolf howl when I hear one."

"Katie, I believe you, but only because it's you telling me this and not someone else. A wolf howl, well I'll be damned! No wonder Clara and

Junior looked so blank." Shaking his head in disbelief, Big Jim said, "Do you want to know what's in this envelope?"

"Why should I? It ain't addressed to me."

"But it's about you, Katie," he said, pushing the plate to the side and opening the letter. "It's a provision that Townsend had put in his will that you get some money, quite a bit of money, I might add."

"Me?" Her hands automatically went to her throat. "Why in heaven's name me, why?"

"I thought you might know. That's one of the reasons I asked to see you; the other is that I am now on this case, Katie. It appears that Townsend might not have died, well...naturally."

"And you come running directly here to question me! Well, it ain't natural that the man ain't even in the ground, and you is traipsing about in his papers, the ones about his money. That ain't natural either."

"I came here because I thought you could tell me something, not to accuse you. And as far as the will being opened, that was the family's decision, not mine."

"Family, my eye! You mean Junior, don't you?"

"Yes, as a matter of fact, yes. And you can be sure he'll fight you every inch of the way about that money."

"He won't have to fight me, 'cause I'll simply refuse it. I don't want no part of money tainted with sweat and blood."

"You can't refuse it, Katie."

"And just why not?" she asked stubbornly.

"'Cause it ain't for you, it's for your daughter, Margaret, to use for her education, and only she can refuse it. So be there at the house Friday, when the will is read. If you don't have a way, I'll pick you up."

"I reckon I can afford a cab, but we ain't taking no money, and that's final. I'll go back to work now, if you is finished. Alice is by herself." She rose from the table, leaving the dirty plate, and hurried as fast as she could through the swinging door. Her body was alive with fear that ran up and down her spine like white, smoldering heat. She knew in her heart that, no matter what she said and no matter how harshly she spoke, Margaret would fight her tooth and nail over the money and would bring forth all reasonable arguments as to why they should keep the money. She would probably stomp her feet, and yell, and afterwards begin to quote the great philosophers.

Katie's heart was breaking 'cause she knew no matter what she said or threatened to do, Margaret would not give in. And what frightened her more than that knowledge was that Margaret was still young and unafraid. She had never seen a lynching like Katie had. Margaret had never even known about how they came in the night for Jab and beat him with tire irons into unconsciousness. Margaret had never met fear on a lonely road, that hot fear that makes your insides bubble and choke. But most of all, Katie never wanted Margaret to be afraid, for she remembered how it felt to be whole, defiant, and sure of yourself. Katie, in agony, held her hand to the ceiling, closing her fingers one by one until she had formed a fist, and holding it like she had the Almighty by the collar, cried out softly, "Father this is your servant, Katie." And as though a giant ruler swung through the clouds and suddenly rapped her across her knuckles, her fingers flew open, and she waved her hand in the air and whispered, "Let your will be done."

The Confrontation

She had fasted and prayed to the Almighty two days straight and as yet
had not received any sign that would put her mind to rest. One thing she
was certain of now was that she could no longer delay talking to Margaret.
The time had come for her to act; she could wait no longer. Come
tomorrow, the will would be read, and she and Margaret were expected to
be there at the reading. She decided it was best to get it over and done with.
She had to make Margaret understand the many, many reasons why they
could not accept that money. She walked to the middle bedroom and
peered into the semi-dark room until her eyes adjusted and she located the
hump under the covers near the far edge of the bed. She walked to the side
of the bed, sat down on the edge, and gently shook Margaret on the
shoulder. "Wake up, child, the birds is singing, the sun is gonna be up and
raring to go soon, and you will still be here in the bed with your head
buried under the covers," Katie said, hoping to start the morning as they
always did.

"What time is it?" the sleepy Margaret inquired, and stirred from under
the cover, exposing her bare shoulder. Her eyes focused on the gown at the
foot of the bed, and instantly she was wide awake. Damn, she thought, and
avoided looking her mother in the face as she pulled the covers tightly
around her neck.

"Eight o'clock," Katie answered dryly.

"Eight o'clock? But you're supposed to be at work," Margaret declared.

"I told Miss Rosie last night I had to see to some important business and
that I would be late," Katie answered.

"Miss Rosie, Miss Rosie," Margaret mimicked her, sleep still in her
throat. "Why do you call her "Miss"? She's the same age as you."

"Let's not start that same old mess this morning," Katie snapped. "Get
dressed while I start the breakfast. We've got some important business to
discuss." Katie realized this would be much harder than she had earlier
imagined—much harder.

"Why do I have to dress to talk, Mama? And what in the world could be
so important that you had to be late for work? I can't ever remember you
being late for work. Must be something special happening at the church, or
Jab is in trouble again. Where is he anyway?"

"What we got to talk about ain't got nothing to do with Jab. He's gone
out on Homer Eddie's truck to pick cotton. What I got to talk about is
strictly between me and you. You understand me?" Katie said, resigning
herself to the confines of the small bedroom and the semi-darkness.

"Well, what in the world is it?" Margaret asked impatiently, while she
pushed the nightgown with her foot until it fell to the floor on the side of
the bed by the wall, then propped herself up in a sitting position, clutching
the sheet to her throat.

"Well," Katie stammered, "you remember the other night I told you that I
went to pray for old man Townsend the other day when he passed."

"He didn't pass, Mama. He died. Is the word so hard to say? He died."

"Margaret Younger, sometimes you make me want to glue your mouth
shut and let it stay that way for the rest of your born days," Katie said,
exasperated.

I'm sorry, Mama. I promise to listen without any more interruption. Tell me what it is that is so important." Amusement danced in her dark brown eyes.

"Well, as I was saying, I told you about his dying, but what I didn't tell you was later that evening Big Jim came to the cafe and told me that Townsend had left some money to us in his will."

"Us?" she yelled, the cover almost falling away. "By *us*, do you mean me and you Mama? That's our dream come true. How much did he leave us, how much?"

"Hush now, ain't no need telling the whole town about it, and besides, I don't know how much. Big Jim didn't say, just that it was quite a bit. But since we ain't gonna accept it, don't matter how much it is."

"What!?" She sat up straight in the bed. She could feel the air on her naked back, but that was not important to her now. It didn't matter to her now if the whole sheet fell off. "We're not going to accept this money? Am I hearing you right?"

"That's right, we ain't gonna accept it even if it is for your education, and that's a mighty important issue in this house. But not even for that will we take this money, tainted with the sweat and blood of others, to get ahead. No sir, never."

"Mama, you mean the money is for my college education. Do you realize how much money that is? Why, we could pay off a lot of bills, and with the scholarship I won, we wouldn't have to worry about where the next penny would be coming from. I could really apply myself in school; I could do well. I could become the teacher that I've dreamed about since I was just a little girl. What are you saying we won't take the money? My God, why not?"

"Now, don't go using the Lord's name in vain," Katie said softly. "Now surely you don't for one minute think them white folks gonna let us just walk up and take all that money and not have nothing to say about it?"

"What do you mean, Mama?"

"First of all, child, Junior is gonna fight us about that money, and I don't have to tell you how Junior fights. The whole town knows that, child. Then, if by some miracle we win him over and get the money, where we gonna put it? The bank of Jason County certainly ain't gonna go against one of its most important customers like Junior. They just won't accept the money, and we sho can't keep it here in the house, now can we?"

"But, Mama, we can move to another city, we can do that."

"Ain't nothing or nobody gonna make me move off my pappy's land, and that's that!"

"Mama, Junior Townsend ain't nothing but another redneck hillbilly, nothing to be afraid of. He's just a spoiled child, and I don't believe the bank will turn down money just for his sake. I just wish he would try to do something to me or you. I just wish he would."

"What you gonna do, child? Whip him with his daddy's strap?"

"No, Mama, but I won't let him take nothing from me just because he's white and greedy after money. I won't let him do that!"

"Sure, you ain't afraid, not now, 'cause you is sitting in the comfort of your home, and your mama is close by your side. But what happens when you meet Junior's ruffians on a dark road one night. What then, child?"

"I'm not afraid. It's you, you're the one who's afraid," Margaret stated arrogantly.

"Yes, Ma'am, you is right, 'cause I'm scared down to my bones, 'cause I knows these people much better than you. Somebody gotta be scared," Katie snapped, and directed her gaze out the window. "You see, I've got sense enough to be scared, but you, Margaret, sometimes you reminds me of one of them incubated chickens that stands out in the rain hollering, when all he gots to do is walk inside the coop. But no, he stands there hollering until he drowns, 'cause he ain't got sense enough to go in out of the rain, 'cause he don't have no knowledge of death."

"But what is a person to do?" Margaret asked, shaken by the fire in the older woman's eyes. "Are you supposed to let anyone take what belongs to you and do nothing about it?"

"Well," Katie said, "just what is yours in the first place? Certainly not that money, 'cause that belongs to other Negroes that sweated and was deprived of many things so that Townsend earned all the money. I say first you got to know what is yours, and if you knows that, then maybe the fight is worth the bloodbath."

"I don't understand you, Mama. That's one of the reasons we should take the money. You said yourself it belongs to other Negroes. Then we should be the ones to use the money to better ourselves, not Junior."

"That may be true. Maybe we have more right to it, but that don't mean we should take it. We is supposed to earn our way in this world. You always feel better about something when you done sweated for it than when it was handed to you on a platter."

"Well, if you have already made up your mind we are not to take the money, why are you discussing it with me?"

"Because," Katie stammered, clutching her dress collar tightly, "the way I understand it is that I'm guardian over the money, but only you can refuse it."

"You mean you don't have any say-so over the money at all?"

"No, I don't mean that, 'cause I *have* got say-so and always will have over whatever you do!"

"But you can't refuse the money without my being there, without me actually saying I don't want the money, is that right?"

"That's what Big Jim said," Katie conceded, her jaw set firm.

"Mama," Margaret said quietly, almost in a whisper, her feet dangling from the side of the bed, the sheet clasped between her hands at her throat, "listen for a minute and don't interrupt. We can use that money, and you know it. Just look at this place. This house is in need of many repairs, things we've been wanting to do for years. But most of all, look at me sitting here, holding a sheet to my neck so as not to expose my naked flesh to the woman that bore me into the world. Just look at me, Mama. Take a good look at this person sitting here. Take a good look at this girl who has spent all her life with you, all eighteen years. Well, this girl wants very badly to become a teacher, something not new to you. This is something we have talked about for years. It is also something that you wanted, too; you've been behind me all the way on this. It was always understood between us that that is what I would be, if in any way possible. Now, the way has been opened for us without all the hardships we had anticipated: the extra jobs, the installment tuition, not knowing if we would be able to pay the next payment, and, if so, how or when. Perhaps the money is the product of ill-gotten gains, but if we take that money and put it to good use, like my education and a few things you need for this house, what harm can it do? With my education I'll be able to teach many Negro children, pull them along so they won't stand in the darkness of illiteracy like most do for the rest of their lives. I've never went against your word, but I'm begging you, Mama, don't make me do this, don't make me turn down this money, the answer to my dream, I beg you." There was a look of helplessness on her face, as stark naked as her body under the sheet.

The time had come to end this discussion and Katie's heart was heavy and sad. The only child she bore sat before her, pleading for a future that she deserved. The right to go out and become her own woman was all she asked. She stared and said nothing. The sight of old Boswell's body lying on the bank of the levee full of bullets crossed her mind, and she knew she had to refuse. It was as simple as that. She had to refuse. "Say no more about it, child, we will not take the money, and that is final," she said finally. She stared hard into Margaret's eyes and turned her head away quickly to avoid the disappointment in Margaret's eyes. Margaret's face darkened with anger, her mouth opened in surprise, and her nostrils flared. She dropped back heavily on the bed and stared at the dingy yellow ceiling, defeated. Katie watched the young girl who reminded her of someone in her past. She stood in the familiar surroundings of her home, and yet in another time. Before her, the face of a young white man. His name she did not know, but his face she would remember forever. He and several other white men stole onto their land in the early morning and set fire to their barn. She was ten years old. She supposed he considered himself a true blue blood, righteous in his act to rid the earth of heathens—the scum of the earth, the niggers, and the folks that stood by them as well. He sat proudly on his horse bareback and in one swift motion bent down, swooped her up in his arms, and tossed her across the wire fence. She fell flat on her face, unharmed, with only the wind knocked out of her, but she couldn't get up, no matter how hard she tried. She lay there and watched her pappy, who walked up to the young man on the horse and said not a word. He stood for a moment staring at the young man and then, as though he were a scientist, he calculated an exact spot and smacked the horse in the temple with a mighty blow. The horse's legs trembled under the pressure, and it crumbled to its knees, spilling the young man in a wide-legged position right into her pappy's hands. He grabbed the young man by the collar and shook him. He shook him until his teeth clattered like a man having seizures. He shook him until the light in his dark blue eyes turned to a golden amber. He shook him until he finally tired, and he set him firmly on the ground again with orders to "Get me my gal and be damn quick about it." The young man scooped Katie up from the yard and placed her gently into her daddy's big white arms.

She stared at Margaret and realized that one day someone would shake up her world, much in the same way as the young white boy who rode into their lives that morning. She walked from the room, leaving Margaret lying on the bed. She walked back to her room to prepare for work, but caught a glimpse of the morning sky from the back door and went out and sat on the steps. With the warm sun bathing her skin, she suddenly felt like a child again. She wondered if she had made the right decision. Outside, everything seemed so calm, as though what had happened between her and Margaret inside the house had gone unnoticed. She needed someone to tell her she had done the right thing, and yet she knew there was no one she could discuss it with other than Charlie, and he was out and about already. She suddenly felt like the small child lying on the other side of the fence, and she laid her head in her hands and cried out, "Pappy."

RIDERS ON THE STORM
Pete Bontsema

To add insult to injury, Dean had no idea where they were going. Tim had lured him out here with coaxes of "C'mon, just go. You won't be sorry. Yer gonna have the greatest time of your life, but if I tell you about it, it'll ruin it. So just go, OK?" And Dean, sucker that he was, had gone.

They continued down the dark, snow-packed street, with the cozy houses all around them with frosted windows and bright lights and smoke rising from chimneys and heat ducts. The streets were empty, and the sky, which had been cloudy for the past day or so, full of snow that fell slow and gentle, was now void of all obstructions, clear and black and virtually starless.

"All right," he said, "before we go any further, tell me where we're going."

"Just wait, OK? The river's right there. Just walk a little farther and then I'll tell ya. If I told you now, you'd be sorry. It'd ruin everything later."

Dean nodded. All right, all right. Sometimes you trust people in matters like this and sometimes you don't. This, as far as Dean was concerned, was Tim's last chance. They were too close to release to be taking chances like this. It was already about seven-thirty; they'd never make it back to the hospital by nine. And that meant coming through the emergency entrance which meant that they would get in trouble when some nurse called upstairs. This better be worth it.

They jumped off the limb and took two long strides on the side of a brush-cluttered hill. And then they were on the river.

"This is perfect," Tim said. "You can't do what we're doing unless this ice is super hard. We came out here once and it was hard enough to walk on, but there was water on top and we got our feet soaked. That's why you don't want to get wet. But we're OK tonight. This should be perfect."

They walked to the west and the trees around them got thicker as the houses fell behind them. There were no houses out here, only this valley of iced river set between the trees. Up ahead, in the distance, was an archway, the grey stone outline of a tunnel, with a circle of darkness in the center. And above it were cars, dozens of cars, going north and south, crossing over the tunnel. Dean watched the cars, turned his head from side to side, and slid along on the ice, studying. Tim looked over at him with a smile.

"Figure it out yet?" he asked.

"Is that the Tri-State?" Dean asked, pointing.

Tim nodded. "Very good, very good."

"And so where does this river go?"

"You'll see."

Dean felt better, though still confused. At least he had found a road he knew. But he was confused as to how far south they were. The ride in the cab had been lost to stoned-out sightseeing and he had lost track of exactly where they were. But then he was given a hint. Planes were visible in the distance, taking off to the west, going away from him, so far away that they were just strings of colored lights. And the Tri-State was humped in front of them, mounded high and blocking their view. "O'Hare?" Dean asked himself. It couldn't be. "I know we're too far south for that."

They walked on, and the cars on the Tri-State flew past overhead, their headlights flashing over Tim and Dean's heads. They came to the mouth of the tunnel and peered into the round tube of pure black, smelling like soggy weeds and dirt, even in this frozen environment.

"Because you were such a good guesser," Tim said, digging into his coat pocket and twisting himself to shine more light on his hands, "you will be rewarded with a joint." He stepped boldly into the tunnel, splaying his feet wide, reaching up to the cold cement walls, penguin-walking to the inner depths. "There's usually water here that isn't frozen," he told Dean. "Just try to straddle it."

Dean followed, thinking, Jesus Christ, what the hell am I doing? He wanted out, but there was no temptation to go back. His curiosity had been aroused. And the lure of the joint made all ideas seem acceptable. Tim led them to the halfway point and leaned on the south wall while Dean leaned back on the north. The roar of cars could be heard overhead and both of them turned their faces to the arched ceiling, with Tim basking in the excitement—"Shit man, those cars are only about four feet up there!"—and Dean checking for cracks and faults in the construction. Tim lit the joint in the airless dank tunnel and passed it to Dean. He pointed toward the ends of the tunnel.

"See? You can see out either end from here."

And you could, but there wasn't much to see. The river behind them was merely a fleck of reflected streetlight shining on the ice, and the other side only revealed a drop-off that led to more snow and trees.

"This is where we would always party before going on," Tim said, tilting his capped head back to the wall. "Shit, I wish we had some beer now. Man, we'd sit here and drink a twelve-pack and then you wouldn't feel a thing. You wouldn't even know it was cold out. And the only time you can ever come out here is when it's cold like this. That's the only time you can be sure that the river'll be frozen the whole way." He took another hit off the joint and Dean listened. Tim already had hinted that there was more river-walking to be done and Dean was hoping he'd let slip their destination. "We came out here one year, when I was a freshman, and this kid I know went through a soft patch of ice and his shoe got stuck in the mud because it isn't all that deep." Tim started to laugh, passing the joint back to Dean, "And it got stuck in the mud—right up there outside this tunnel—and it just got sucked under. We had to reach in and undo his laces and pull his foot out and leave the boot there." He tilted back on the wall, laughed to the ceiling and let the sound echo through the tunnel, jiggling his leg nervously, shaking the calf muscle. "We had to carry him back home. What a fuckin' pain in the ass!"

All this was just music to Dean's ears and he smoked on and tried not to picture his own shoe getting stuck in the mud. By this time he was all wild-eyed anyway and there was nothing to calm either of them down.

"But we don't need to worry about that tonight," Tim went on, "because this ice is Class-A hard, man, like a rock. We're better off out there than we are in tunnels tonight." He pushed off the wall. "Let's go."

They continued forth, straddling the ice trail at the bottom of the tunnel, not wanting to walk on it and break it up and let the water flow. Dean held the joint for a few extra nerve-building hits and followed Tim.

Then they came to the end of the tunnel and stood at the mouth, and this is where the world opened up to Dean. The Tri-State was still over their heads, with a few Sunday night drivers still going by, and in front of them was a hundred-yard patch of barren trees, black-limbed, sickly-looking things that seemed lonely in the snow and night. The trees stood in a small triangular patch, a tiny leftover sanctuary of nature squashed between the onslaught of roads and highways and industrialization. And there, off past the trees, a mile or more in the distance, was O'Hare Airport. The tower stood bleakly gold above the terminals in the clear night, and planes rolled along the runways, cruising slowly, positioning themselves for clearance, then making the long build-up of momentum and finally sailing up into the sky.

"*Now* do you know where you are?" Tim asked.

Dean nodded. "Now what?"

"Now we go down here."

Tim slithered down a snowy hill, down to where the river continued, down to the snow. Dean followed, holding to the hill itself, slipping along. They walked on more ice, along the river, through this small area of trees, with the Tri-State behind them and another busy road up ahead, and another tunnel.

"That's Mannheim Road," Tim said. "We have to go under it, too. And that one is tougher."

Dean gazed all around, watching the cars to the rear, watching them disappear out of sight down the way, looking toward O'Hare which was right there, but still a long ways off. He shook his head and wondered how Tim ever found things like this, how he had ever ventured out here in the first place. They came to Mannheim Road, with a lesser flow of traffic overhead, and another tunnel in front of them. And this one presented an entrance covered with metal bars, meshed across the front to prevent people like Tim from continuing.

"Now we need a big rock," Tim said, and immediately he set to searching the grassy area of snow, up by the trunks of trees around the river. "We left one here last winter. I wonder if it's still around?" He kicked at the snow and Dean did the same, scouring the river's edge, dragging a toe along the bank, looking for a big rock and not knowing why.

"How about this one?" Dean asked, tearing a basketball-sized rock from its moorings at the water's edge, sliding it out with a long fling of his leg while still keeping his hands in his pockets.

"Perfect," Tim said, bounding back to the ice and skating across. He kick-pushed the rock to the tunnel mouth. "Now we gotta pull that screen forward, get the rock in, and climb through." He smiled innocently at Dean. "OK?"

Dean didn't bother to answer. Bending over, he latches onto the thick metal mesh and pulls it back with all his strength, straining with the effort, slipping on the ice. Tim shoves the boulder into position, leaving an opening just barely wide enough as Dean lets the mesh settle down. He crouches down, presses his back to the tunnel, facing the iron screen, and wriggles inward and upward, squirming his body through, sucking in his gut so his coat won't rip. "This is even more fun going out," he says from behind the mesh, and his legs squirt up behind him. Dean imitates the method, struggling through, and Tim tries to push the metal out for more ease, but it won't go. Dean comes up and they are in another tunnel, under

Mannheim Road, and again the cars are only a few feet overhead, speeding by at forty-five with a rumble that shakes the tube.

"Now out the other side," Tim says, and they're moving quicker now, fighting the clock and the cold, waddling over the mess of old cans and discarded paper that is frozen into the rivulet of water.

And when you come to the end of this tunnel, there is nothing except the wide expanses of O'Hare Airport. Tim stood in the opening, with a hand raised to the tunnel roof, looking out of the enclosed darkness to the broad field of snow-covered grass and cleared runways. Dean came to the end, crouched in the opening, and scanned the horizon, watching the planes take off not more than two hundred yards in the distance. A 747 started from the far right, blinking its lights, whining its engines, then rolling, rolling, slowly gathering speed, crossing in front of the tunnel's view, then lifting its nose, aiming to the sky and taking off with a loud clatter and the monumental roar of engines. Dean's face hung open at eyes and mouth and his view shifted like a cat watching a horsefly, drifting around with an unknown purpose. All those times of going to O'Hare to watch the planes take off and land and never, never seeing it from this position. If this was all they came for, he would return a happier man, with a wider knowledge of things in general. But Tim had other ideas.

"OK," Tim said from his stance at the tunnel's mouth, "now things get trickier. We keep going on this river until we get out there."

Dean looked at the river but had no idea what "out there" meant. But he had come this far and there was no sense turning back.

"You have to keep low because they have this ground radar that looks out for things like trucks and little planes and it'll pick up a person if you get in range. But we're safe because the river is sunk down like that, so it should go right over us. Just follow me and do what I do."

And Dean did. They crouch for fifty feet of river and climb under a chain-link fence that surrounds the airport. This is their most vulnerable position, with Mannheim Road right behind them, and Irving Park just to the south, and all of O'Hare ahead of them. The fence has been cut many times, and they slip through easy and continue in a crouch down the river, hidden by the snowy banks on either side. Dean stares at Tim's ass, keeping his back below the level of the land, his heart beating like mad, his lungs tight. Tim breathes in pounding bursts, chugging, setting the pace, picking up the action, saying little, moving, moving. The river ends at yet another tunnel. "This is the last one, I swear to God," Tim says as they rest breathless just outside. "But it's also the worst. Just squat like hell and run. I hate this fuckin' tunnel myself," he informs Dean, "but it's the only way through." His breath goes up in clouds and Dean wants to go back. His feet have been hitting the ice like rocks, feeling like ice themselves, and his nose is as brittle and red as his ears. "Let's go," Tim says.

They go single file one more time, severely crouched, brushing their arms along the cement floor, moving like chimpanzees, and Tim yelps all the way through, "Goddam fuckin' shit-ass tunnel, I wish I had a fuckin' flashlight." This tunnel is pitch black, darker than the others, smaller, more hunched, and when they get to the middle, Dean cannot see Tim though he is two feet ahead, and he cannot see light at either end. The only thing carrying them is Tim's frightened, but near joyous, screams and curses at the tunnel. Dean brings up the rear, frozen from head to toe but coldest in his back, right between the shoulder blades where the fear hits him, and he expects, at any moment, to feel the hand of some security cop. They come to the end of the tunnel and Tim sits down, his forehead sweating from the run, hot under the wool cap. Dean steps to the tunnel mouth and peers out.

"I should've told you before we started," Tim says between breaths, "that this tunnel sometimes floods. You can never be sure what'll happen."

Dean gives Tim a "thanks a lot" and stares out at a frozen body of water, not very large, but a full lake, with high banks visible all around. "What is this?" he asks.

"Lake O'Hare. This is where they ditch planes if they have to. Like if it's a crash landing and they know it's gonna burn, they try to slide them over here. It's also where they dug out all the stuff to build around here."

Dean nodded. He remembered seeing the lake on street maps. "So now where do we go?"

"Look over your head," Tim said.

Dean leans farther out and twists his neck to see above the tunnel entrance and sees a short metal ladder drilled into the cement face, going up to the level of land. "Up?" he asks, and at that moment, with no warning, the tunnel racks from side to side, shaking and vibrating, and Dean presses his hands to the wall and eases into a crouch, while Tim sits with legs outstretched and eyes closed, smiling at the earthquake rumblings.

"I also shoulda told you," he says slowly, "that we're right below a runway right now."

Dean whips his head outside as the tunnel quiets and sees the tail end of a jet being dragged to the sky. "What the fuck are we doing, Tim?" he shouts, sick and tired of the mystery of the night. "What are we doing out here?"

Dean is honestly mad but Tim just laughs, like he was waiting for this all along.

"I told you this would be the night of your life. And you're almost there, so don't go asking questions now."

"Well, I hate to tell you this, but I'm not going any farther until you tell me what we're doing."

The tunnel goes quiet and all that passes between the two adventurers are clouds of thin breaths. Dean sits down and rubs his head, whipping his head from one side to the other, looking at the black of tunnel to one side and the frozen lake to the other.

"Do you realize how much trouble we're gonna be in? Huh? Do you? Do you ever think of those things? We're gonna be so fuckin' late when we get back. How are we gonna get back anyway?"

Tim shrugged. "Call a cab, I guess."

"You know something?" Dean asks. "You're a fuckin' idiot. Why you brought me here is beyond me, but whatever it is, it isn't worth it."

Tim doesn't even try to raise his head to look at Dean. He just nods to his lap. "Oh, it's worth it. Believe me." But then, just in case it might not be convincing enough, Tim looks up at Dean with an apologetic face and offers another temptation. "You wanna do another line?"

Dean's jaw drops and his head juts toward Tim. "You brought the coke out here?"

Tim nods sheepishly.

"You *are* an idiot. You know that's my coke too. What if you lost it, or got it wet? And how can we do it here? One gust of wind and it's gone."

"We'll do it back there," Tim says, pointing back up the tunnel. "If you'll hold the lighter, I can cut it up."

Dean looks into the blackness, shakes his head and actually begins to smile. There is no discouraging Tim, no stopping him from the things he wants. It's like he goes through life with blinders, satisfying only his selfish needs and not caring about anything else.

"All right," Dean says, figuring if they're going to be put away for life, they might as well go out in style.

They crawl twenty yards back up the tunnel. Dean blocks off the near end of the tunnel with his back and Tim faces him, hindering any breezes that might come from that way. The cement is hard and cold and digs at their knees. Tim sets the small pocket mirror on the ice, choosing a dry spot, and pulls the Snow Seal packet from his pocket. Dean leans on his elbows and guns the butane lighter at a steady strong flame, shedding just enough golden light to show their faces, the mirror and the pile of white that Tim dumps out. He cuts two, quick, healthy lines, snorts one up in an instant, then hands the taped-up dollar bill to Dean. There's an instant of darkness as the lighter changes hands, and then more golden light, and Dean tilts down, anxious for something to obliterate the mixed feelings he has toward Tim; he wants something that will create only good feelings for this closest of friends.

After the lines, they pack up and sniff their way back to the tunnel exit, revitalized in their search, moving through the dark and cold, snorting over and over to push the coke back, looking for a quick high.

"OK," Tim says, "now I have to tell you what happens."

But before he can, the tunnel begins rumbling and shaking, and the noise makes both of them hold their ears as another plane shoots off the runway. Tim lets the noise fade, then uncovers his ears.

"OK, now we go up the ladder and onto the grass. Or snow. And now your shoes are gonna get wet, but don't worry about it because this is it. As soon as we get out there..." he says, hanging in the round doorway, not yet setting foot on the lake, looking back at Dean's eager and listening face. "Well, on second thought," he says with a laugh, "just come on. Just do what I do. If one of us dies, we both die."

And that sounded all right with Dean. Tim tips backwards out the tunnel and grabs the bottom rung of the ladder, pulling himself up, and Dean watches the head, body, and legs disappear from inside. He follows, staying close behind, not wanting to get deserted. He lays his gloves on the rungs and moves quickly to the top where Tim waits, crouched low, looking into the distance. Dean comes over the top and crouches beside Tim.

And there, right in front of them, not more than thirty yards away, are the bright white lights that line the runway. They are near the south tip of this runway, the one that sends planes zooming out over Irving Park Road, about two hundred yards from the fence that borders the property, where cars roll by in the dark, where couples will sometimes stop and park and neck while the planes rip overhead and shake their cars. Dean's heart pounds and his mouth is dry. Tim stuffs a handful of snow into his mouth, brushes his hand on his pant leg, and points up the runway. A plane taxis into position more than a half mile away.

"See that plane," Tim says, his words excited and rushed, and Dean nods, waiting for more. But it doesn't come. Tim points the other way, toward the opposite end of the runway. "Let's go over there."

He crouch-runs to a spot he knows well, a place he's been before. It's a spot about forty feet off the side of the runway, away from the lights, in a slight depression of darkness. Dean follows, crouching behind, and spinning around like Tim when he gets to the sunken spot. They both look up the runway, breathless and anticipating.

"What the fuck are we doing?" Dean asks. He looks into Tim's dilated eyes; he has the look of someone about to tackle an airplane.

"Wait," he says in a whisper, "just wait."

Dean waits and they crouch in the snow that fills their shoes, staring up the runway at the big plane which turns and whines and finally positions itself at the far end, aiming their way. And then it starts up, starts rolling.

"OK," Tim says, "get down," and he rolls onto his back, spreading his arms and legs out like he's going to make a snow angel. "Like this," he adds. "And dig your fingers into the ground if you can. Just hold on." The plane gets louder already and he shouts to be heard. Dean lies beside him, on the outside, farther away from the runway, and they both are spread-eagled in the snow, with their inside hands nearly touching. "Turn your head to one side, like this. Watch the runway; it's great. But close your eyes in a second." Dean does as he is told, obeying blindly, having no other choice. He turns his head, gazes at the back of Tim's head, and as the plane gets closer, the ground begins to shake.

The 747 tears past, with its long wings nearly over the boys' heads, and the power from the engines lifts their heads off the ground and slams them back down. They grip into the frozen mud harder, as hard as they can, but their bodies still slip on the wetness. The nose of the plane goes up and it gets airborne, and the landing gear begins to rise, and then, in a delayed effect from the engine thrust, comes the moment Tim has brought Dean here for. The snow swirls all around them, starting from behind their heads, then sweeping over them, and the backlash from the rising plane sends snow up from their feet, covering them, burying them under six inches of powder, swirling and scraping over them in icy particles, then subsiding into calm rest, leaving them buried side by side.

Dean waits only a moment in his snow-made grave before popping up to see if he is still alive. He gasps for air and watches the plane go up and away, out of sight. Tim does not come up. Dean slaps the ground next to him, digging for Tim's body and finally uncovering him. He comes up with a smile and leaves his face plastered with snow, then brushes it off.

"So," he says, smiling cocksuredly, "how was it for you?"

Dean laughs and shakes his head. "I don't fuckin' believe it. This is the stupidest thing I've done in my life." His face hurts and his body is cold, but he is all too full of excitement and the thrill of survival to feel it. And the dope and coke haven't hurt any.

"Yes, but did you come in your pants? I know I'm all sticky. But a lot of first-timers just shit in their pants. What'd you do?"

"Neither."

Tim fell back in the snow and stared at the black sky, the wide horizon that can only be found out at O'Hare where there is enough open space to free your mind. He spread his arms out and rolled them in the snow, dreaming to the sky.

"Christ," he said, "I'd love to latch onto the landing gear of one of those things and just hang on and then let go way over there by the water tower and just fall to the ground." He suddenly turned over and looked up the runway. "Let's do one more, then go."

Dean agreed. And again they dug into the snow and mud and averted their faces toward the runway. This time Tim told Dean to watch as the plane rolled closer and he did and it was an incredible sight, seeing the United jet rolling at you, so close that you'd swear it was coming right for you. And then you close your eyes and the wings go overhead and the ground shakes and you grit your teeth and fight from sliding away, and then there's that infinitesimal delay, and then comes the snow. The particles hit with a force that hurts, like millions of tiny ice balls, but you're so tensed that you feel nothing. And then it all settles, and you lie there, covered from head to toe, indistinguishable from the terrain, not looking like a mound of fresh white dirt of a grave, but just a natural swell in the contour, just a part of the earth. And you awake from that like you've been gone for a million years, and your head rings with the sound of the engines, and you feel exhilarated.

The reverse trip through the tunnels was a pleasure, with both Tim and Dean talking excitedly, feeling strong and indestructible. But that pumped-up feeling didn't last forever, and when they came back to the street where they had been dropped off, they were feeling nothing but cold. They trudged along the dark street, smoking a joint and thinking about the hospital. It was past nine; they would have to use the emergency entrance. And that ruined everything, so they didn't talk about it. They stopped at a pizza parlor which was closed and called a cab from the pay phone, waiting in the cold, huddled against the wall. The cab came and Tim threw open the front door and said, "Mind if we ride up front? We're freezing." The cabbie said OK and added that they didn't look too good, but neither Tim nor Dean gave it a second thought, happy only to have a strong heater blowing at their feet. They bent forward and cupped their bare hands to the heat.

"You know," Tim said as they rode, "usually when we do that we wear snowmobile suits. And face masks." He smiled at the words that kept coming. "And we wear ski goggles and long underwear and we bring flashlights. I don't know why I let you talk me into going out there."

The cabbie looked over at them. "You boys been ice fishing or what?"

"Sort of," Tim answered, tipping his hands and bouncing the hot air to his face. "I think my feet may be frostbitten. How 'bout taking us to the hospital, huh? Our Sainted Lady. You know where that is?"

The driver did.

"Just take us to the emergency entrance. We gotta get in quick."

It was all a joke of course. And they went in the emergency entrance and tried to pass unnoticed to the doors that led to the hallway that led to the lobby that led to freedom. If they could get through there, they would be on the elevator and then they could slip back onto the unit. But no such luck. A nurse stops them in the waiting room.

"Can I help you, boys?" she says, looking up at them with an expression of servitude. She's a short woman, grey and in her sixties, with glasses, wearing the white dress and hat of such nurses.

Dean takes it from here. "We're from the ninth floor. We're coming back late from a weekend pass. Car trouble. Couldn't get it started."

The words go past her. She stares at their faces, moves closer, then reaches up and touches Tim. "Why, you're bleeding!" she says, pulling her fingertips away and showing a trace of red.

Tim reaches up and feels himself, and Dean, who had been concentrating on the hallways and not Tim, takes his first look too. There are tiny, miniscule slicings on his cheeks which show blood.

"And you're bleeding too, young man," the nurse says to Dean. "What have you been doing?"

Dean feels his face, sees the blood, and he and Tim look at each other, thinking, thinking. It was the airplanes that did it, of course. The blowing of snow and ice left their mark on their faces, and the cold kept the cuts frozen and contained. But the heat of the taxi and the warmth of the hospital have loosened the blood and it seeps out. They stand there in the carpeted waiting room with people staring at them, sitting in chairs and eavesdropping.

"It was real windy out," Tim says, "and we had to walk here. I guess that's what did it."

"I guess so," the nurse says, and she grabs Dean's wrist. "Come here, both of you."

They sense trouble, but it doesn't pan out. She takes them back to the examining area and goes to a rolling tray full of syringes and cotton and supplies. She dabs at their faces with cotton balls of alcohol, and they cringe at the sting, pushing her hand away. "Now, now, cut that out," she says to Tim, and he laughs at her and grimaces at her care. "I think you'll be all right," she says, "but you shouldn't be out walking when it's that windy. Is it still bad out?"

"No, I think it's settled down now," Tim tells her.

"Well, I hope so, because I go home soon, and I wouldn't want to get caught in it."

After her inspection is completed, they all go to the Nurses' Station and she gets on the phone, calling up to the ninth floor. She gives them the names, and Dean and Tim watch her face during the pause, trying to guess what is being said at the other end. But the call is quick and there's no exchange, no expression to guess at.

"OK, boys," she says, hanging up the phone, "you can go up now. You know how to get there from here?"

Tim doesn't, but Dean does, claims he remembers it from when he was originally wheeled in, a time when he was comatose. It seems unlikely, but he picks a flawless route to the elevator.

"Whadda ya think they'll do to us?" Tim asks, finally seeing the consequences of the evening.

"I don't know," Dean says, and he leans on the wall and looks at the floor, feeling his face, and his toes are just beginning to feel truly warm.

They get off and come around the corner, and Clara waits at the door.

"Out on pass, huh?" she says humorlessly. "I didn't think you guys went home on weekends. Have you started issuing your own passes?"

It was too late to fight or lie. "Sorry," Dean said, "we just had to get out."

Clara crossed her arms and walked them inside. "Well, you're on your own for now. But this will go on your record and it won't look good. I'm sure your doctor—among others—will talk to you in the morning."

Yeah, yeah, yeah. Just let us get in a hot shower and to bed. They listened politely and didn't sass back, just tried to look hurt and remorseful. Then they did get those hot showers and they lay in bed talking, staying out of the Day Room even though it was only about 10:30 and people were crowded out there, trading stories about the weekend, proud of how well the homelife was beginning to look, anticipating with happiness how they would make their return and readjustment. But Tim and Dean figured it was best to keep a low profile, so they stayed in the room and finally, exhausted, fell asleep about eleven.

When they woke up the next morning, both their faces were swollen and red. Dean's cheeks were puffed out and delicate to the touch, hurting so bad that he could hardly chew. But Tim's eyes were nearly swollen shut and he went through the morning with only a thin slit to peer through, spending a lot of time in the bathroom going, "Why is this happening? I don't get it," then bursting out to see if Dean was afflicted in the same way, and Dean just sat on the edge of his bed saying, "I can't feel my lips," pressing his fingers there over and over and drinking through a straw.

VIOLET RIBBON
Rochelle Knight

In the life of a black girl-child there come a time for ribbons.

It was lying on the ground by a bush—violet, shiny, and like new, stirring with the breeze, then falling still in soft, billowing ripples. Then the wind blew again, and it straightened itself out and threatened to fly away—a violet butterfly—but it caught on a twig, and settling with the wind, gathered upon itself, like mint ribbon candy at Christmas.

It was the kind that Valerie always wanted for her hair, and she plucked it carefully from the twig, so as not to tear it; and looking about to see who watched her, she folded it into the apron pocket of her dress and patted the pocket gently. She wondered how it came there, to the vacant lot, overgrown with wildflowers, weeds, and tangled brush—and from where did it come, and why. It didn't belong among the thorns and dirt and ants and worms, with dented cans and gum wrappers and splintered glass and trash.

The Terrell family lived in the big house across the street, and perhaps it had blown from Imogene's bedroom window, while she was standing in front of her mirror, tying colorful bows onto her thick, long, black braids. She always wore ribbons of colors and blouses with ruffles and black, shiny shoes with soles that never flapped. Or she had probably laid all of her pretty dresses and blouses out on her bed and was deciding, with her finger to her chin, which one to wear with which ribbon, when it lifted up in the breeze and floated out of the window.

Valerie had long braids. They were not as long and thick and shiny as Imogene's. And she'd had ribbons, mostly white ones and red ones and even once a yellow one, but she'd washed and ironed them again and again until they were threadbare and the delicate fabric was faded and snagged.

Valerie headed for the store, passing Sammy Colemen, shooting marbles in front of his tiny, weather-beaten house. She stood back and watched in silence. He wore Osh-B-Gosh cover-alls and was bent on one knee in the dirt. He flicked a large, clear marble with his thumb, kicking up the dirt beneath it—the cat's-eye boulder sped to a small cluster of marbles four feet away, struck with a loud solid thap! dispersing them in a rainbow of colors. He didn't look up, but scrambled up to collect his marbles, slapping his thigh, as dust rose from his cover-alls. She turned the corner and halfway down the block was a rectangular sign that read in faded red letters "HOFFSTATDER'S" over the door of the store owned by Hedwig and Herman Hoffstatder. It was called H&H. Given the tendency of the populace of the neighborhood to shorten any words that were foreign, too lengthy, or too troublesome to pronounce, coupled with the fact that all children were to address all adults by their last names and with the handles of Mr. and Mrs., they simply called it H&H. As Valerie approached the store, she patted her pocket once again, stepped on the flat cement block with her dusty shoes, and pushed the door open with her elbow. A cow-bell jangled harshly over the door, and Mrs. Hoffstatder's face, soft and white, rose from behind the counter, where she'd been sitting on a plumped-up sofa pillow, and her heavy body followed reluctantly. Her jaws were pleasantly puffed, until she saw it was only Valerie, for Mrs. Hoffstatder never smiled at her non-adult customers unless they were accompanied by their mamas, and she never waited on the black men unless Mr. Hoffstatder was absolutely incapacitated. She'd set a smile in her face for the neighborhood women, who came with colorful bandannas wrapped around their heads and in their cotton dresses, some followed by a brood of children, in an array of brown tones, who yanked on their mothers' skirt-tails and whined, "Mama, can I hav'va penny? Pleazz...Mama, just one penny," "Me too...me too." But she had been known to shoo the same kids out of the door with a broom when they were alone, mumbling to herself, "Schwarze...dunkel finster...schwarze." The children fled from the fierce look in her eyes and the transformed face, creased with deep lines.

"Vaht did your mother vahnt now, Valerie?" Hedwig Hoffstatder questioned sternly, placing her amazingly small hands palms down with the fingers spread flat on the counter, and slumping her shoulders, resigning herself to patience, while looking down on Valerie.

"My mama want...my...my mama want," Valerie stammered, groping in her pocket for the change and feeling a brief fright at the thought of having lost it, and then calculating how she could save herself a penny for candy. "She want nineteen cents' worth of salt pork." Mrs. Hoffstatder didn't move.

"Yuh sure she don't vahnt twenty cent?" Valerie kept her head down and her hands in her pockets, one of them fingering, with the back of her knuckles, the silky ribbon.

"She want nineteen cents' worth," Valerie said stubbornly, now looking up at her. Mrs. Hoffstatder pushed herself from the counter and went into the shadows at the back of the store, where a small meat showcase displayed, through shiny glass, a roll each of bologna, salami, and cheese; a row of pink, fat-laced pork chops; two rows of fresh, whole, yellow chickens, sprinkled with chipped ice; several rows of smoked bacon, rib-tips, and fresh ham-hocks; and from the last row she reached in and pulled out a large slab of salted pork and laid it on a butcher-block table. Taking a gleaming twelve-inch butcher's knife, she measured and sliced off a small piece of fat, streaked with lean, and laid it on the scale. When the needle point settled, she removed the rectangle of pork, sliced off three-quarters of an inch, ripped off a measured piece of brown paper from a roll suspended over the butcher's table, and wrapped it tightly.

Valerie had stood in the U-shaped space of the store, right next to the counter that held the candies in huge glass jars with white caps. The counter to the back of her was one where only grown-folks stood. On the shelving behind it were dark, wrapped packages and bottles with crossbones, items for old people and sick people, and things whose names were written on notes, folded tightly, when kids were sent to the store to purchase them. Valerie faced the candy jars, in a quandary over how to spend her penny. Mary Janes? Bazooka bubble gum? Or a Tootsie-Pop? She watched a fruit fly make a speedy trip, darting in and out of the potatoes, onions, turnips, and rutabagas in the bins just below the candy counter, then zoom past her nose, and, by an irregular course, make its way back to the brightness of the front window of the store, where apples and oranges and a few overrripe bananas lay sunning on gray cardboard trays. Somewhere between the chop-chop of the knife as it hit the wood, and the rip and crackle of the paper, and fruit fly, and the Mary Janes, it came to her—not a thought, but an image. It was a butterfly, a butterfly metamorphosed into a violet ribbon just to please her—just to please HER. A smile spread across her face as she realized Mrs. Hoffstatder was standing before her. She handed her two nickles and a dime and turned, leaving the store quickly with the image in her head, forgetting the Mary Janes. Mrs. Hoffstatder held the sweaty coins in her hand, watching Valerie's back, until the cowbell clanged over the door, then threw them into the cash register with a shake of her head and returned to her sofa pillow.

She put the ribbon in the right-hand corner of her drawer. Hers was the second from the bottom of a five-drawer, green-painted chest that she and her sisters shared. It lay alongside her other treasures: a pearl-studded hair comb with several of the yellowed beads missing; a pair of white garters that she was saving for the day when her mama said she could wear nylon stockings; a green rubber snake she'd kept over the years and pulled out on occasion to alarm her sisters; a flattened-out, pink cloth rose she'd taken off a now discarded dress; a small picture, now cracking and fading, of Bobby Williams, her fourth-grade first love. It lay face down in the bottom of the drawer. She hardly ever looked at it. His wide, thin lips stretching across his smooth face and his doleful eyes reminded her of the way he used to look at her. It made her feel sad and quivery inside, and she kept it because it made her feel. The ribbon lay beneath her neatly balled socks, her two white under-slips, three pairs of panties, and her other bra, which she kept on top. She hadn't wanted to wear a bra, but Jolena had insisted. It was like a harness to her free spirit, but it did keep her tender and swelling, lemon-sized breasts from bouncing and throbbing with pain when she ran.

She planned to wear the ribbon on her twelfth birthday. It was only one week away. But something happened which made her forget the ribbon for a long time. On her birthday Jolena called her into the big open kitchen, where the back door stood open and a warm breeze swept through the house, stirring every curtain, doily, and bedspread fringe, lifting up the dust from the furniture and carrying it out the opened window. She was sitting at the long kitchen table, in the center of the room, snapping green beans and pitching them into a white plastic bowl on the table.

"Sit down, punkin," Jolena said, cheerfully, nodding at a chair across from her, still snapping the beans. It had been a long time since her mama called her "punkin," and Valerie slid into the chair, feeling a closeness toward her mama she hadn't felt for just as long.

"You twelve today? How you feel?" Jolena looked at her, smiling, her hands still busy. Their eyes met and locked in a moment of single-minded harmony, which made Val uncomfortable, though it felt good and warm to her inside. She reached across the table and, taking a long green bean, snapped it into three even pieces and threw them in the bowl. Jolena's eyes held hers and she couldn't look away.

"I feel the same," she finally answered, dropping her eyes bashfully, smiling and fidgeting on her chair. Somehow, she always felt like crying whenever she and her mama talked seriously, when she was out of the group and alone with her.

"Well," Jolena said, "maybe you'd feel a little different if you wore yo nylon stockin's to church on Sunday."

As in listening to the lyrics of a song in which only certain words ring clear, Valerie had only heard the words "nylon stockings," when she suddenly jumped up from the chair, knocking it over, picked it up, and made her way to the other side of the table, where she squeezed her mama's head to her stomach.

"Oooh, thanks, Mama, thanks," she groaned, laying her cheek on top of Jolena's soft hair and smelling the Royal Crown Pomade. When she loosened her grip, Jolena let out a sigh, then added sternly, "Just on Sunday now. Just on Sunday." Valerie was about to to dash out of the kitchen when Jolena's voice stopped her. "And you can git yo' hair hot-curled today. Becky'll do it for ya."

Val started jumping up and down, kicked over the yellow plastic garden pail at Jolena's feet, the one that had held the fresh beans, scrambled to her knees, scraping them from the floor with her cupped hands, then stood and jumped again. When she stopped, she was standing to the side of Jolena with her hands clasped before her, as if she were about to pray.

"This is the best birthday I ever had," she said softly, looking again for her mama's eyes, but Jolena had now turned her head and resumed her bean snapping.

"Yeah, punkin," she said, without turning her head, "I know." When Valerie reached the threshold of the door that led to the girls' bedroom, but which really should have been the dining room, she stopped, turned, and asked, "Where's Becky?" Jolena chuckled, reached into her pocket, and pulling out two shiny quarters, laid them carefully on the orange vinyl tablecloth, as if the coins were gold.

"Go git yo' stockin's. Becky'll be back befoe the day's over."

When Valerie rounded the side of the house on her way to the store, she heard her mama's singing floating out of the kitchen window.

When we all see Jesus, we will sing and shout victory. It was clear and soft and sweet.

Valerie sat in the choir loft on Sundays, barely able to concentrate on anything more than the curls that bounced about her shoulders, the sheer stockings that hugged her slim legs, and meeting Johnny Lee down at Lea Point after service. She was now fourteen. The newness of the curls and stockings had worn off, and an aura of femininity now enveloped her like a new skin, one which she wore as confidently as she'd worn the old one. From the loft, she saw the ritual which had occurred every Sunday since she could remember in a different light, as if it were a scene of a play being rehearsed again and again. Missionary Barner, the epitome of sanctification, dressed in white, with a white, lacy handkerchief tucked around her neck, her dark brown face like an eruption, opened the service with a song, "So Glad I'm Here." The organist raced down the keyboard, searching for the off-key note, as the congregation joined in clapping their hands and beating their tambourines. Her father, Reverend Clyde Mays, who sat below and to the right of the choir in one of a row of seats reserved for the ministers, raised his bent head from meditating and called out, "Sing, church, sing!" then dropped it again. And Deacon Dunn prayed a long prayer, while young mothers jiggled restless babies on their laps and drowsy children slid into the corner of the pews for a nap. Then the organist struck a chord, giving the signal, and the choir rose in unison, just as they'd practiced it, as the late-comers filed in. Always among them was the Ambrose family. Sister Ambrose came straight to the front, pulling her two young daughters behind her, with a self-conscious bow of her head and an apologizing finger held up. Mr. Ambrose (though he came to church, he had not joined) sat near the back and usually on the side of the church facing the choir, where he stared at Valerie throughout the service. He was a handsome man, with gray transparent eyes and curly black hair. It had been commented that he looked like a darker Clark Gable. Those eyes always found hers through some small space between the angle of heads and held them against her will. They penetrated her, undressed her, sent shivers over her, and made the seat of her underpants wet. And while it made her tingle with excitement, it also frightened her. She would snatch her eyes from his and turn to stare out the choir window, down the grassy hill, counting the small white houses that sat below and naming the families who lived in them. And maybe if Valerie had not sung alto and sat in the back row, Jolena would have seen her twist her handkerchief so tight that it balled into knots, and how she uncrossed and recrossed her ankles, and figeted on her seat. Val would direct her thoughts to Johnny Lee—walking together, hand in hand, over the grassy slopes at Lea Point and sometimes running, him chasing her and catching her, pinning her to the ground. And her pleading with her eyes and sometimes her voice, "Please let me up. Not now, not yet." For she had heard often enough that "a man jes' wont one thang from you, girl, then he don't won'cha no mo'." And if there was anything in the world she wanted, it was for Johnny Lee to want her forever. And she knew if she was ever gonna do that "frightening thing," it would be with Johnny Lee. He was five inches taller and three grades her senior, brown and strong, and when he rolled from her onto the ground, grasping his crotch, his groan was filled with pain, and she felt his pain in her. It cut off her speech, but she had to wait. Johnny Lee had to want her forever.

Valerie, daydreaming, usually missed the organ cue and jumped up after the others were already standing. The organ played the introduction, Lola Bellsworth tuned her voice, and the choir harmonized their voices to back her up. Then Lola bellowed out a song in a vibrating soprano voice with such soul and fervor that it brought the congregation to their feet every time, clappin' and praisin' to God, some with their hands thrown up and tears streaming down their faces, and others shoutin' and shifting the pews about. And when Lola sat down, she trembled and spoke in tongues, while deacons repositioned the pews and the sisters retrieved hats and pocketbooks, shouting "Thank you, Jesus" and "Praise the Lord" and "Halle-lu-jah." Reverend Mays stood quietly at the podium with his arms stretched over his congregation. And when the dust and bodies cleared and the sisters dabbed at their perspiration, fanning themselves with cardboard fans, those eyes found hers again, and all through her father's long sermon she struggled to avoid them.

After church, when the congregation mingled, Mr. Ambrose found her, appearing out of nowhere, and pressed money into her hand or slipped it into her pocket, sometimes as much as twenty dollars. It stunned her each time. It was as though something were being stolen from her instead of given to her, and she wanted to expose him, but she felt she would only expose herself.

She kept all of the money tied in a blue kerchief, tucked in her drawer, behind and beneath the comb, the picture, the green rubber snake, the pink faded rose, and the violet ribbons.

Johnny Lee joined the army and was going to leave right after graduation. Val heard it through the grapevine: Johnny Lee told Rob; Rob told Duck; Duck told his sister Teena; and Teena, Val's best friend, told her. She'd gone to the Point two Sundays in a row and he hadn't met her. And on the third Sunday, when the members were spilling out of cars and panting up the hill for morning service, Teena came running up the hill out of breath, her big eyes flashing. "He won'cha ta meet him today," she whispered, looking around to be sure nobody else heard. Val's heart flipped. She wanted to laugh and cry, but instead she stood very still, questioning the eyes of Teena, who stood on the step below her in front of the church, looking up at her anxiously. Teena, who usually sat in the second row of the choir, sat in the back row with Val, nudging her to stand and sit and signing extra loud to make up for Val's hardly audible voice. Val was in a daze. She'd already asked herself all of the questions. "Why didn't he tell me?" "Why is he doin' this?" "What am I gone do now?" And now her thoughts were suspended, with no more questions and no answers, and she hung in mid-air, like her thoughts, waiting only to hear from him words that would plant her feet back on the ground. She felt Teena's elbow nudge her and her hand touch hers, but she felt, heard, and saw nothing else. And as soon as service was over, she dashed into the parsonage and changed her shoes.

When she came out of the bedroom into the living room, her mama and Sister Barner were talking in the dim, cool room. Sister Barner sat on the piano bench and Jolena stood alongside the piano, leaning on one elbow. Valerie walked up and blurted out, "Mama, I'm goin' for a walk." Jolena cut her eyes at her and Sister Barner's head jerked up. It was then that she realized she had interrupted. But before she could apologize, Jolena said, still eyeing her cooly, "I want you ta go ta the store b'fore it close. Git some sweet potatoes. The money's on the kitchen table.

"Why cain't Becky or Jesse go?" Valerie snapped back, emphatically placing one fist on her hip. And before she could catch her breath from the outburst, Jolena's hand flew across the piano and slapped her across the cheek. The delicate brown hand that struck her lay trembling on the shiny mahogany, as Valerie stood glaring into her mama's angry eyes, her mouth fixed in an O and her hand pressed against her burning cheek. She felt her body grow rigid with indignation. She was aware of Sister Barner, her hands folded on her lap, casting a righteous look back and forth at them. Val didn't move—of that she was sure—but somehow, even with her back to the bedroom, she saw herself standing at the threshold of the bedroom door with tears in her eyes, screaming, "I hate you, Mama! I hate you!" And then, and only then could she move. Thinking then that her mama heard her, she ran from the room, through the bedroom and into the kitchen, where she grabbed the money from the table and went out the back door. She saw Jesse standing in the backyard talking with a cluster of girls under a tree. She pulled her to the side and promised her a dollar if she went to the store. Through a blur of tears, she saw Mr. Ambrose looking at her, and she took off down the hill, her blue Sunday dress blowing in the wind.

ON THE WARD
Richard Cantrall

The first day on the ward, Red and Squeeky wheel me up to the desk. there's this big woman standing there, peering down at a chart through these thick glasses. She's a brown bar. Lieutenant Twixton they call her. She's got kinda stringy hair, thick glasses, and she wears these starched whites. They's so stiff that they rustle when she walks. Shoulda been a librarian. Nice ass, though.

Anyways, Squeeky asks where he should put us. She doesn't say a word, doesn't even look up, just keeps staring at the chart through them thick glasses and points down the hall at a couple of beds. They put me in this regular hospital bed, only it's painted that shitty, Army OD green. Baker—you know, the guy staring at the ceiling in the ambulance—they put him in this weird contraption. They call it a circ-electric bed. It's just a thin mattress with these metal bars going all the way around them in a circle. They got all the quads in them. Baker, you see, is a quad. Can't move. Can't do nothing. He just lies in his circ-electric all day, staring at the ceiling, without moving. You can't do that for long before your ass starts to fall off. Skin just sluffs away. So they put the quads in these circ-electrics, and when they want to turn them, they just push a button and the whole damn thing turns around. Does a complete 360-turn at the touch of a button. Amazing.

This place is something else. Not like any hospital room I've ever been inside, leastwise not this side of the Pacific. Most of them's just tiny boxes of rooms with three or four guys squeezed in it. But not this place. It's big, like a basketball court or a banquet hall at some Elks Club convention, and it's filled with beds. Must be twenty beds on this side of the ward. Most of 'em's occupied and occupied with cripples. All of them's cripples.

God, there's lotsa windows in this place. The whole east wall is just windows. They go almost to the ceiling. Nothing to see outside of them. Just an empty street, grass lawn, and the trainee's barracks—more dirty yellow buildings. Seems like the Army's got lots of dirty yellow buildings. Squeeky tells me there's a lounge they got in this one, all set up in one end of those barracks. And they got a pool table and a color TV. One of these days I'm going to get out of this bed and go down there and have me a beer, have me a beer and play pool and watch TV. Even if they got to carry me down there, I'm going to have me a beer.

There's an artillery range just down the road from us. None of us cripples ever saw it. But every afternoon you can hear the Big Boys doing their thing. Whole fucking building shakes. Them Cherries just can't wait to see some action. Crazy motherfuckers. First time I heard them, thought I was back in Nam. Musta been dozing, when all of a sudden I hears these 106s. Jesus! Would've jumped a mile, if I could've. Baker, he starts wailing and screaming at the top of his lungs—wailing and screaming like some goddamn banshee. Jesus, that guy's crazy. Anyways, I was shivering and shaking for the rest of the afternoon—leastwise, until lunch.

They sure feed you here. No more beans and motherfuckers. Real food and lots of it. They practically shovel it down your throat. Lots of shit on the shingle, bacon, eggs, potatoes, toast with buckets of jam, tons of coffee for breakfast, soups, chicken, turkey, desserts for lunch, steak for dinner. Musta gained ten pounds my first week. What a life. Almost enough to make you forget. Almost.

Red and Squeeky wheeled Mitchell up to the desk. It was his first day on the ward. Lieutenant Twixton was on duty that day. She didn't pay any attention when they came into the ward. She just stood there, peering through thick glasses down her nose at a chart. She looked just like a librarian standing there in her starched whites, all prim and proper, with her stringy brown hair that hung over those thick glasses, peering down at that chart, engrossed in it like it was *War and Peace.* Red didn't stop at the desk. He just kept pushing Baker on his gurney into the ward. But Squeeky had stopped in front of the desk and, holding tight to the handgrips of Mitchell's wheelchair, he asked, "Where we put them?" Lieutenant Twixton pointed down the hallway at an empty bed, never looking up. Squeeky wheeled Mitchell into the ward and up to a green, metal-framed bed. Then, reaching under Mitchell's arms, he pulled up and pivoted on one foot toward the bed, setting Mitchell down on the edge. Then he grabbed his feet and twisted them up onto the bed. He turned the cover over Mitchell and then joined Red at a circular, chrome-framed apparatus, a thin mattress surrounded by a circular, chrome frame. It was Baker's bed, a circ-electric bed. They loosened the sheet on the gurney and lifted Baker with it, Red grabbing him under the shoulders, and Squeeky grabbing him under the buttocks. They lifted him to the edge of the circ. Then Squeeky ran around to the other side and pulled Baker to the center of the mattress with the sheet. Red noticed the red, festering sores on Baker's buttocks. "Well, you won't have to worry about that no more with this new toy," he said, pointing to a small metal box attached to the circ by a wire. "We just press the button and the bed turns around. You can go all the way around in a circle, just like a ferris wheel. Only it's a free ride." Baker said nothing; he just stared at the ceiling. Mitchell looked across the ward. It was a big ward filled with beds. Paraplegics and quadraplegics lay in the beds, lay motionless in the beds, staring out of the windows. Windows, the first thing Mitchell noticed—they lined the east wall, stretching almost from floor to ceiling, big windows looking out on the street, looking out at nothing but barracks, dirty, yellow barracks. Squeeky watched him looking out the window. "Sarge, there's a lounge in them barracks. They got beer and a pool table and a color TV. One of these days, you and me, we're going down there to have a beer, shoot some pool, and watch TV. Even if I got to carry you, we're having us a beer."

Mitchell leaned back in his bed, put his hands under his head and closed his eyes. Just then there was a loud boom-boom-boom, and the building shook. His eyes flew open, and he began to shake. "Take it easy," said Squeeky. "It's only the artillery range down the road. 106s." Mitchell scowled. "I know what they are." And then Baker began shrieking, crying out with a high-pitched, long, loud moan. "Fuckin' pogue," Mitchell muttered under his breath.

Mitchell didn't stop shaking until lunchtime. Red and Squeeky wheeled in a big, square, aluminum box. They opened two doors in the middle of the cart and began sliding out trays. Squeeky brought one over to

Mitchell. He set it down on the bedside table and lifted a metal plate cover. "Here you go, Sarge," said Squeeky. "No more beans and motherfuckers." Steam rose in the air. Mitchell almost smiled.

It was gettin' pretty boring sittin' here every day, just sittin', until that day they brought Mitchell onto the ward. You just sit here all day staring out these windows. We got these tall windows all along the wall. Go almost to the ceiling. All these goddamn windows and we got nothing to see out there, just the street and these fuckin' pogues' barracks. I get tired of just sittin'. I was sittin' chowing down on some S.O.S. Pretty good chow they got here. Better than beans and motherfuckers. I was just chowing down, when I hears this noise. It's Red and Squeeky, and they got this guy on a gurney, name a Baker, and he's screaming his fool head off. I can't stand these crybabies. And next to him in a chair they got Mitchell. Big guy, broad shoulders, holding a cigar box and a green beret in his lap, staring out with these big eyes, smoldering eyes, eyes that could burn you if you got too close. And he's lookin' at Twixton with those eyes.

She didn't notice. Got her face buried in them charts. Always got her face buried in them charts like a goddamn librarian. Looks like one too with them big, thick glasses and that stringy hair, frayed at the edges. Fuckin' brown bar. Squeeky asks her where to put these two guys, and she doesn't even look up, just points down the hall at the beds. But Mitchell, he's lookin' all right. They wheel him in and he keeps looking back at Twixton's ass. Smacks his lips, then gives me a pat on the shoulder as he goes by. "How ya doing, old-timer?" he says. Old timer—I ain't no older than him. He winks and gives a quick smile. Smiles—can you imagine that? Nothing to smile about on this ward. But Mitchell, he ain't like the other paras. No, he's different. The way he moves, the way he talks, you'd think he was a regular guy, not a para at all.

They brought him up to the bed right next to mine, a regular bed, just like the rest of us para's. The other guy was a quad. Took him to a circ-electric, this hunk of metal with a mattress in between it. Looks like some kinda round jungle gym like we used to climb on when we were kids. Yeh, it's a goddamn jungle gym, only you don't climb it. You just lie there, and every once in a while the medics come over and push a button, and you turn around in a circle. They say it's to stop bedsores, but I think they just want the guys to feel like they're still alive, like they can move.

This Baker guy is still moaning when they put him in the circ-electric Twixton brings him a hypo, jabs him in the ass, and he quiets down real quick. Don't know what they got in there, but he's sure hooked. Mitchell, they put him in his bed and right away he says, "Got any beer?" Squeeky says there's a lounge in the barracks across the street. "Well, go get me a beer," says Mitchell, "and one for the old-timer," he says, pointing at me. "Get one for Baker, too." Yeh, Mitchell sure ain't no ordinary para. He's different. Funny though. He makes you feel like you can be different, too. Or maybe not different, but a regular guy.

Baker, he never did say much. Just lay in his circ-electric starin' at the ceiling. He was an older guy, twenty-five or twenty-six, blond, thin mustache, blue eyes, kinda vacant, starin' out, lookin' at nuthin'. No,

Baker he didn't say much, just lay there a moanin' and a wailin' until Twixton would bring him his Demerol.

Wife visited him a lot. She didn't say much either. Just sit next to him, holdin' his hand. Small, kinda mousey woman, faded brown hair. Janey's her name. Just sit next to him holdin' his hand. Come in at lunchtime. Feed him. Shovel a fork full of food into his mouth. He'd dribble it. Food runnin' down his chin, coverin' his bedsheets. She'd just go on shovelin' it, never sayin' a word. Sometimes he'd start swearin' at her. "Fuckin' bitch. Why don't you just leave me alone," he'd say. And she'd go on feedin' him, not sayin' a word, just shovelin' the food in his mouth. Hour or two later, he'd start the moaning. Shot would be late and he'd start wailin' and moanin'. That's when she'd leave. Never stayed round to see Twixton stick him.

Changed after Mitchell came on the ward. The first day he was here, right after she left, Mitchell, he wheels over to Baker. "Hey, pogue, who the fuck you think you are?" He always called him pogue. Told Baker he didn't deserve a good woman like that and how he better start treatin' her with some respect. Baker didn't say nuthin'. Just started cryin'. Big sobs. Never swore at her after that.

Mitchell, he was the only guy who'd talk to Baker. Rest of us, stayed away. He gave me the heebie-jeebies. Them moans, just sent a chill down my back. Didn't want him around, but never said nuthin'. I mean the guy is a quad, and I kinda figure those guys is entitled to their moans and groans. Fuckin' bleedin'-heart. You'd think a para would a know'd better. But me, I'm a fuckin' bleedin'-heart. Wouldn't say nuthin', even though I wish Baker was someplace else with his moans. But not Mitchell. He don't think like that. Hears them moans and he shouts out, "Hey, pogue, shut the fuck up." Pogue, he calls him. Jesus! Baker, he's got the Silver Star just like Mitchell. Squad got bushwhacked on patrol. Saved the whole lot of 'em. Served twenty-one months in Nam before he got hit. Crazy fucker re-upped. Re-upped and he's got a wife and two kids at home. But whenever he wails and moans, Mitchell calls him pogue. Seems to quiet him down.

Baker, he's got a new navel. Right on his side he's got a new navel with a colostomy bag tied to it. Little plastic bag attached to a hole in his stomach. Little plastic bag filled with shit. Stinks. This bag, it would fill up with shit every day. Twixton would come in to take it off and it would stink. Once Red was turnin' him. Pressed the button, bed turned, and the bag got caught in the bars. Tore it right off. Shit flyin' everywhere. I couldn't stand the smell. Right away Baker, he starts wailin'. Mitchell, he wheels over. Don't call him pogue, though. Got a carton a cigarettes with him. Pulls out a pack, rips it open, offers one to Baker. Baker shakes his head. Mitchell shrugs his shoulders and starts to wheel away. Leaves a pack on the bedside stand.

"Don't go," wails Baker. So Mitchell, he stays. Parks his chair alongside Baker's circ. Smokes his Kools. Don't say nuthin', just sits there smokin' his Kools. Seems to quiet him down. Finally Baker, he says, "Open the drawer for me." Nods toward his bedside stand. Mitchell wheels over, pulls open the drawer, and there's a pack a letters bundled together and tied with a ribbon. "Read me the top one," says Baker. It's in this blue envelope. Some mud smudges all around the edges. Mitchell pulls it out a the pack and opens it. Then he begins to read:

Dear Ken,

When are you coming home? Everybody's anxious to see you. Dad's been busy in the store. He had a good year. Maybe saved enough to go on that vacation he and Mom's always talking about. Had a nice garden this year. Nice, plump, juicy tomatoes—the kind you always liked. Remember when you used to pull them off the vine. "Just right," you'd say, and then you'd pull out your pocketknife and slice them, pour a little salt over the slices, and pop them in your mouth. I'm saving a whole bushel of them just for when you get home. We're all so excited about you coming home, especially little Billy. We just had a birthday party for Billy. He's three now. Hard to believe it's been that long. The kids are getting so big.

   Ken, I miss you so. What day are you coming home? Dad wants to take some time off work so he and Mom can fly out there to the West Coast when you come in. Oh, I can't wait to hold you in my arms. We've got a big turkey dinner planned for you and Mom's cooking her sweet potatoes and some rhubarb pie, and they got dances every weekend now at Hank's Place. We'll have a wonderful time the day you come home. Hope it's soon. I miss you so.

Love you,
Janey

Mitchell set the letter aside. Baker just lay there real quiet. And then his head began to shake like he had palsy or somethin'. Shook for a full minute. And then a tear fell down his cheek. Just one tear. He turned his head away. Mitchell didn't say nuthin'. Just pulled Baker's cover up. Pulled it up to his neck and then wheeled away.

On Wednesdays, they always took us out to Sally's Place. That's what we called it: Sally's Place. Red and Squeeky, they'd wheel a couple a us paras out a the ward, up another corridor, just kept wheelin' till we got to these wide swingin' doors. Push us through and there's this big, Olympic-sized pool with a green skylight thirty feet above. That's Sally's Place. Sally's the physical therapist. Lieutenant Sally Foley. Good lookin' woman. Tall, blond, well endowed. Got this low voice, kinda sultry, some kinda accent, Georgia, I think. And she's got these eyes, dark brown and deep. I mean deep. You stare into those eyes a while and, well, she just makes you tingly all over, tingly, even in these useless lumps they call legs. Sally, she's got thin wrists, but she's strong. She eases you into that pool like you was a baby, 'stead of a two hundred-pound hunk of meat. You feel good around her. Know she can handle you in the water.
   Strange how in the pool you feel different. Got that green light filterin' through the roof, and it's kinda hot and steamy, and they lower you down into the water. Water's nice and warm. It's a different feelin' than being in the chair. Don't feel quite so helpless. You can move around, even with them dead limbs trailin' 'long behind you.

It takes a while to get used to the pool. When Sally first took me in the pool, I don't mind tellin' you, I was scared. Scared I wouldn't be able to keep my head above water, scared I'd drown, scared of my own helplessness. With most guys it's like that. But not with Mitchell. No. First day he goes in the pool, doesn't wait for Sally to hold him up. No, he just swims across that pool, all the way across, just glides across like a shark, real smooth-like. Back and forth. Musta done twenty laps. I think he was showin' off for Sally. She took note, that's for sure, she took note. Mitchell say's he's gonna swim the English Channel some day. I believe him.

One day Mitchell and Sally, they was in the corner of the pool whisperin', talkin' 'bout somethin'. I didn't know what, until the next week when Sally comes into the ward with Red and Squeeky. Red comes over to me and grabs the handles of my chair. Squeeky grabs Mitchell's chair. "Time for PT," he says. Start to wheel us out the door. Squeeky wheels Mitchell past Markson. "Stop," says Mitchell. Gets this big grin on his face. Nods over at Markson and says, "Let's take the kid with us."

"You know we can't do that," says Squeeky.

"Ah, sure you can." says Mitchell. "Twixton's not here. What she don't know won't hurt." Then he waves to Markson. "Hey, kid. Wanta go for a ride?"

Markson smiles and says, "Sure. Sure thing, Sarge."

Sally was standin' there by the doorway with her arms crossed, takin' it all in. Squeeky looks up at her. She nods. Squeeky grins. "All right, Mitchell," he says. So Red and him, they pull a gurney out of the corner and roll it over to Markson. Roll him over and strap him in. Red took Markson, Squeeky pushed my chair, and Mitchell, he wheeled himself. Sally followed us. We wheeled on down the corridor and up the hall till we got to them swingin' doors. Got a big sign over it: POOL. Never paid no attention to it before. But Markson, he notices it right away. Looks up at the sign and his eyes, they get big as saucers. Looks kinda panicky. "No. No. I don't want to go in there," he says in this pitiful voice. Mitchell wheels over to him and puts his hand on his shoulder. "It's all right, kid. It's all right. You don't gotta. Just wanted you to come along and watch. Make me feel real good to know you was watching." What could he say? Markson nodded his head.

Red and Squeeky help us into the water. Hold you under the arms and just slide you in the water. We just float for a while, lyin' on our backs looking up at that green skylight. Sally's holdin' me up at the side. And then Mitchell, he starts glidin' across the pool. Goin' from one end to the other, goin' across again and again. Markson, he just stares, lookin' real intent. Mitchell keeps glidin' back and forth. I'm at the side just bobbin' up and down. Finally, Mitchell, he stops and then he swims over to the side. Looks up at Markson. "How'd you like to try." Markson gets this wild look like he was afraid we was gonna pull him in or some big wave's gonna reach up and grab him, sweep him in the pool, and drown him. Mitchell nods toward the hoist. This swing-like arrangement hanging from a pulley. "No! No-ooo!" he shrieks.

"Kid, we're gonna be right here, right with you," says Mitchell. "Be right here by your side. Sally here, she's got strong arms. And look." He pointed up to a padded, black leather pad hangin' from a hoist. "That'll keep you afloat."

Markson calmed down after that. Still looked kinda shaky. Face all white. But Mitchell kept it up. "Come on in," he says. "Come on in." And finally Markson nods his head. Woulda never believed he'd do it, but there's Red and Squeeky helping Sally tie the pad around his waist. They lift him up and then down into the water. Red holds on to the rope and they slowly lower him into the water. Sally and Mitchell and me, we was all around him, and then Sally starts glidin' him through the water. Mitchell swims at his side. I kinda dog-paddled along. The hoist is a creakin' and whirin' with the motion.

Markson's a little shaky for a while, but then he gets this grin on his face like he died, gone to heaven, and found all the pussy there he could eat. First time I seen him with that grin. There's Markson floatin' along with this big grin on his face and he shouts, "I'm moving. I'm really moving." Kid really took to that water. Never seen no quad in the water before, but the kid, he really took to it.

THE TUPPERWARE LADY
Renée Hansen

The Tupperware lady came regular that summer, just about every Monday, with her two tattered shopping bags filled with Tupperware samples, which she let rest on the seat next to her. As soon as her car elbowed round the corner of Laurel Road, there were children leafed around it. Some had come in excitement over the car. It was huge, green, in the shape of a small tank. Those children would hold their palms flat to its sides or let their fingers dance over the hot chrome bumper. Others came thinking of the mints they would get from the Tupperware lady, and they would walk along the side of the car eyeing that small, pink Tupperware dish which was glued to the front dash. The dish was always full with cellophane-wrapped candies. The children knew how to get them. They knew if they snaked along the sides of the car, if they smiled and asked, "Can I come for a ride, please, can I come for a ride?" that the Tupperware lady would begin to brake more and nervously reach her fist into the bowl. Then a small, flappy arm would extend itself out the window and, when she opened her fists, peppermints would drop out into whoever's hand happened to be there. By the time she reached her first stop, which was always the Alexander home, most of the children had fallen away from the car and sat at the side of the road in driveways and just inside breezeway doors, their cheeks stretched with peppermints.

There was a "lady's" attraction between Gloria and the Tupperware lady, and no one could quite explain what it was. They only knew that the Tupperware lady swished her gray skirt more and took more pauses as she walked up the drive. "Your willow," she would say when she reached the patio (and she would say this whether Gloria was there to hear it or not), "your willow," she would shake her head, her jowls flapping like sails set free in the wind, "it just takes my breath away."

You might think it was odd that she would always choose Gloria's home to go to first; except that then you might think twice on it and conclude that Gloria's home *was* strategically situated in the middle of the block and that Gloria's schedule was always more "open" than the other women's; and lastly you would reason that it was Gloria who always had something to buy. Still, after all this reasoning, you could not deny the fact that there was something odd about the Tupperware lady. It was even more disturbing when she finally came to knock at *your* door. You would ask her to come in and sit down in your kitchen, and she would say, "Thank you, I'll have only one cup," before you had ever offered her anything. You would tell her your dog just had a litter of pups, and she would lift her hand to her cleavage and say, "How wonderful...and I suppose they're all suckling away right now. Just suckle, suckle, suckle..." And there she would be, at your table, smiling, her lips so tightly pressed and copper-colored that you want to press a shiny penny right over them to see if it makes the same color and form. She'll keep asking, "So how are you, how are you?" And after a few visits you might let on that your great-uncle has passed away. And she'll shake her head, her cheeks will flap back and forth as if in the wind, and no one will look more genuinely sorry than the Tupperware lady, which will necessitate your telling her more about your great-uncle. Then one day you'll realize you don't know one thing about the lady, and she knows, criminally, so much about you. One day you'll realize that there is something about her appearance that has nagged you all along, and eventually, for lack of a better find, you will pinpoint this nagging thing to her hair. She has a built-up net of hair. On the inside of this net are tufts and tufts of knotted, gray hair, and on the outside she has a flat, thin layer of strands combed up around it. On the inside she has stuck three black hairpins, and these can only be seen by peering through from the outside. And then one day you will greet her at your door and, though she is out of breath from having walked up your drive, all you can say is, "No thanks, no Tupperware today."

But all this never happened at the Alexander house; at Gloria's, things were different. Hours before the Tupperware lady came, the house got a "good straightening," as Gloria put it. The pillows were replumped, then set down at a precise diagonal, where the back of the sofa met the arms of the sofa. The rug was brushed up with the carpet sweeper, and every surface in the house got a thorough "going over." She even wiped the water drops out of the bathroom basin so that water spots wouldn't form. By the time Gloria reached the kitchen and started wiping down the cabinets, her children knew it was time to go outside. Being in the house during a visit from the Tupperware lady was forbidden.

Randi could never understand this, since her mother had always insisted she stay for other demonstrations. The Fuller brush man would bring suitcases full of brushes—short-bristled ones for shoes and longer-bristled brushes for upholstery. The Fuller brush man brought waxes and creams and cleaners, each one of which Gloria would smell and then hold out so that Randi could smell it also. And if they opened the jar up three and four times again, the Fuller brush man knew he had a sale. He would smile his twenty-nine-year-old, broad, college town smile, with a certain ruddiness at the center of his lips and, at the corners, a barely perceptible white-pink. He would look down to his brown wing tips and think to himself that they hadn't been such a bad purchase after all. Long after the Fuller brush man had left, there was the smell of mink oil and leather cleaner heavy in the kitchen.

It was a majestic sight to see the Tupperware lady sitting there in Gloria's kitchen, her breasts pointed out firmly in front of her. The bottoms of these great cornucopias rested just a bit on the folds of her stomach. Through the window beyond her there was a gulf of green grass and that one large willow.

"Hellow, hellow, hellow, my dear. Good to see you my dear." This was repeated several times as she settled herself into the wooden armchair set at the window next to the pink kitchen table. Her body expanded into every available inch of surface. "I can only stay for a cup," she said, and then Gloria went to the counter and poured her a cup of coffee. She held the cup beneath her nose. She breathed in deeply, her small nostrils quivered.

"I'm glad you could come by," Gloria said, as if there had never been this long-standing appointment with the Tupperware lady on Monday afternoons.

"Thank you, and you look so fresh today. Just as fresh as a daisy." She would always say this. Today she could tell that Gloria had once again been hacking away at her hair with the scissors. She reached across the table and clasped her hands on top of Gloria's hand. Gloria had just lotioned them. The Tupperware lady felt the lightness, the wetness of Gloria's hand—a newborn wetness, slightly damp, slightly cold. She wanted to feel Gloria's hands warm before she let go of them, but then Gloria withdrew her hand, and the veins running up her shoulder tightened as she did it, as if the hand had been buried.

The Tupperware lady took a sip of coffee and set the cup aside. "Well, you look fresh and pink," she began again. "And how is that new lettuce crisper working out? There's a new attachment for it. I'll have to show you later. A plastic handle. Slips right on. For going on picnics or outings and things." Mrs. Brokaw was a kindergarten teacher during the winter months and sold Tupperware in the school break. All the light, soothing phrases she used during the kindergarten year were coming across the kitchen table.

"I just have to take off one little shoe before we start," Mrs. Brokaw said. She folded her large body in half so that she looked like a dollop of dough left there in the chair. "That bone of mine must be pressing up against the top again." She had said this nearly every day of the kindergarten year. "The wee little bone," she called it, "making trouble for me again." She had a small hump, colored black and blue, which stuck out at the top of her big toe. In class she wore shoes with solid bases and thick leather. "To stop the hump," she explained to the children, though when she removed the one shoe, the hump was always there. Still, she wore the shoes, until one day her feet began to swell right out of them. They expanded like flour until the edges of her shoes were rimmed in skin, and when, at midday, she took the shoes off, there would be a deep C-shaped indentation in her foot from where the mouth of the shoe had been and another C-shaped ridge from where the tongue flap had pressed. It looked like six pencil erasers had been embedded right there in her feet, but it was only the six holes where the eyelets had been.

Mrs. Brokaw released a loud "Ahhhhh" after the shoes were off, the same "Ahhhhh" heard every day in class.

"You know, Gloria," she said, "I noticed how well your peonies have taken. It's lovely work, dear, splendid. You should be proud of yourself."

"How are Ed and the children?" Mrs. Brokaw asked, her tiny, blue eyes looking right into Gloria's.

Gloria pushed the hair back from her face, thought to herself that she would let it grow out. "Ed and the children," she said. "Ed and the children. How are they? Did you ask how they were? Fine, I guess. Fine."

"Well then," Mrs. Brokaw said, not even leaving room for a pause, "How are you?"

"Me?" Gloria said, putting both hands at the sides of the table and beginning to inch them back and forth. "I am frustrated with the damn painters. They've been her six times and they still can't get the color on that wall right. Custom painters they call themselves. This house," she continued, "is just never going to be finished. I told Ed we should move to a place that is done, finished, and complete."

Well everyone gets upset over the house now and then," Mrs. Brokaw said.

"Ed thinks I'm crazy."

"Nonsense," Mrs. Brokaw said.

"I mean about wanting to move all of a sudden."

"More nonsense," Mrs. Brokaw said, waving one hand in the air and picking up her cup to sip. Then she reached into her purse, drew out a tissue and blew her nose. "Nonsense if I ever heard it," she said again, as she finished wiping her nose. "Everyone moves at some point in their lives," she continued, then tucked the tissue inside her purse and snapped it firmly shut.

"Even the children are beginning to think I'm crazy. He pits them against me sometimes."

"Well, it's hard being with the children all day," Mrs. Brokaw said.

"Damn right it's hard." Gloria said. "And then he comes home and he pits them against me. He looks at his potato soup the other day and says, 'What is this stuff, Glor?' 'Potato soup,' I say. Then he plops his spoon in it just to be funny, just to get a laugh from the kids, because the soup flew out at the edges. 'God,' he says, 'it looks like someone took a weak shit. This doesn't look like the potato soup you usually make.' 'It's the same soup,' I said. 'Naw,' he says, 'you did something different. You cheated and you just don't want to tell us.' I was getting so mad by that time I said, 'Stop playing with it, Ed; if you don't want it, don't eat it.' Then Randi chimes in, 'Do I have to eat it?' Then Gary and their father look at me, and he says, 'You're not going to make them eat it, are you, Glor?' Of course I was going to make them eat it. They had eaten that soup all their lives—the same soup. I spent an afternoon making it and I'd be damned if no one was going to eat it. Then the kids start whining more, and Ed turns to them and he says, 'I'm sorry, kids, but your mother says you have to eat it.' And you see, you see how he does it. He wants to come home every night and be the big hero for them. Save the kids from their mother. And you know what kind of ideas that gives them? They hate me. They all hate me. And I'm beginning to hate them. You know what I did? I just took that whole vat of soup and dumped it down the drain, right then and there. And he says to me, in front of the kids now, of course, he says, 'Awww Christ, Glor, you didn't have to do that. I think you're nuts, you know that? Someone would have ate it. We could have given it to the dog, for Christ's sake.' Then they all started laughing. And Ed still had his bowl of soup in front of him and, just to be funny, he started calling, 'Here, King. Here, King. Come and get your supper.' And King never came. And they all kept laughing, so I just left. I took a drive. I just had to get out of there. But we're strangers. You see what I mean?"

"Nonsense," Mrs. Brokaw said, "I had both your children in kindergarten and they both think the world of you. Why almost everything they made, they made for their mother."

"No," Gloria said, shaking her head, pushing back the blunt ends of her hair, "No, I don't think it's as good, as easy as that."

"Then you have to work on it, dear."

"They hate me."

"Nonsense," Mrs. Brokaw said, and she pinned her shoulders back to the chair so that her breasts were hoisted a bit off her stomach, and she looked her most majestic. "Sheer nonsense!" bringing her gray eyebrows so close together that you could see them below the frames of her glasses.

"Things have got to change," Gloria said.

"That's right," Mrs. Brokaw said.

"It won't be easy."

"Why do you say that?"

"Because," Gloria said, "because I told Gary he couldn't build a fort in the backyard. I don't know why I told him that. There's plenty of room back there. I just don't want a fort in *my* yard. Is that too much to ask? It's my yard too, and I don't want a fort." She began running her thumbnail down the middle crack of the table until small shavings of dirt began to corkscrew out. "Well, I'm sorry but that's just the way I feel about it," she said looking at the thin swirls of dirt forming on the shiny surface of her pink table. "And Randi," she continued, "I was so mad at her the other day. I was so mad I couldn't see straight. I wanted to take her shopping, and she wouldn't put on the new sweater her grandmother had just bought her. There was just no way I could get her out the door with that sweater, so I took her by the wrist and dug my nails in. God, I was so mad at her, she has scratch marks three inches long. Oh, I don't know," Gloria said, lifting her nails out of the crack for a moment, examining beneath them, and then digging them back in. "I just don't want them in front of me sometimes. I just don't. And that is that. And there's nothing I can do about it. Nothing."

Mrs. Brokaw rubbed one hand in a circular motion over the table. "Just give it time, dear. Everything takes time."

"Do you know what I want?" said Gloria. "It's so simple. I want the painters to come in here and for once get the right damn color on the wall, and then this house will be finished, done, complete. And then I want to move. I told Ed there were just no two ways about it. We are moving this fall."

"I'm sure it will be for the best," Mrs. Brokaw said. "It seems to be what you need." Her small blue eyes blinked, and her hand dropped down to the handle of her Tupperware shopping bag, which, they both knew, meant that Mrs. Brokaw had been there nearly an hour and that now it was time for business.

"Even if it's not for the best, we're moving anyway," and then she removed her hand from the center crack, examining her nails once again, and began to snag an uneven one with her teeth.

Mrs. Brokaw lifted the two worn shopping bags onto the kitchen table. Among other things that day, Gloria bought two square Tupperware containers, (having purchased all the round bowls and containers, she thought it was best to start assembling a collection of square molds). Immediately, she placed them among the others along the bottom row of her cabinets. Mrs. Brokaw stood over her and pointed out how they packed and stacked better.

After Mrs. Brokaw had said her last good-by and "take care, dear," to Gloria, she would stand there on the patio, in the silence of a suburban summer day, just slowly breathing in and out. Her bosoms were first hoisted up a bit and then let down a bit. It was as if she were practiced in a breathing technique that was especially beneficial to her breasts. For the first time, you could see that she had a thin, patent leather belt around her waist. Then she would practically march down those few steps from patio to lawn, swinging her beaten shopping bags high out in front of her. And the last thing that struck everyone as odd between Mrs. Brokaw and Gloria was that Mrs. Brokaw should look so happy, as if she had just heard of a new birth and were ready to take off skipping every time she emerged from Gloria's kitchen.

FOLLOW THE SIGNS
Lilli-Simone Langer

From the back seat I watched as my cab surged forward, then slowed down. I was breathing through my mouth to avoid the dry, dusty odor, like yards and yards of carpeting in desperate need of vacuuming. We were gradually catching up to the car with the dome light on, a faint glow just ahead, hugging the far right lane.

It was an invitation away from the dark streets and building after building with faraway windows lit. That one car with its light on equaled a neighbor's house with a bedroom window shade absently left up, or a public scene when emotions suddenly flare up and out of control. A sliver of privacy is exposed, laid out before you, or driving alongside in the next lane.

My cab was soon a few feet ahead of her car. My window was aligned with hers. There was a moment when both vehicles traveled at exactly the same speed and it felt as if neither of us was moving at all. And that was when I looked over.

The woman was driving and curling her lashes at the same time.

I watched her as easily as if I were just glancing over from a neighboring sink in a public bathroom. She checked the road and then shifted her attention to the rearview mirror and clamped the curler around a row of lashes. My cab began to steadily pick up speed. I twisted around and watched her, barely keeping up with traffic, driving with one hand balanced against her cheek, squeezing the scissor-shaped handle.

She began to fade back and the faint glow from her car soon disappeared and there were only headlights behind me.

I tried to come up with a reason to curl your lashes at 45 MPH.

I could remember a commercial for a car with such a steady ride that a man cut a diamond inside, but he was in the back seat and someone else did the driving.

My cab began what used to be the first wide curve of an "S" before years of renovation made it into a safer "C."

"A cabbie died there today," said the driver. I looked up past a rolled-up sleeve and a tanned arm, backlit from the meter's red glowing numbers, to the tip of his finger which was pointing directly to something beyond the windshield. But because we were driving along the curve, the aim of his finger drew a line across an office building, followed by what I thought was a Polish embassy. Both looked dark and hollow.

"One of our drivers," he said, "was just driving along slowly, and they drop concrete from a construction site. Killed," and his hand tossed something invisible away and then returned to the wheel. If there was a construction site nearby, I couldn't find it. I knew that I was supposed to say something. I offered what seemed appropriate.

"How terrible," I said, and then added "Really, that's just terrible." He didn't reply. Then, while thinking about it, I added, "It's luck. Or bad luck and good luck. Or maybe just fate? If he had only missed one green light that he made that day—" and then stopped because maybe I shouldn't have said that. Again it was silent. The cab raced along. I watched as we flew through a yellow light. I wondered if we were both thinking the same thing, that that could've been our "one light." Were we lucky to have made it? Would it have been better if we'd missed it? If every second had the potential to completely alter your life, then making a yellow light or having one more cup of coffee or the difference between getting up when the alarm went off or hitting the snooze bar and sleeping for five more minutes could decide your destiny.

The concept was overwhelming.

I tried to put that whole fate issue out of my mind. I told myself that I should be thinking about Margie. She was the reason that I was in the cab, going to my mother's house.

At the time it meant nothing. I was only a child. I was sitting at the kitchen table with my sister Margie. We were eating breakfast. Cereal. We would pour on the milk and then add extra sugar and then wait a while. We liked it really soggy. We were wearing pajamas, bright cotton shirts with matching pants which had feet attached, a kind of built-in sock with a plastic sole which added traction but was hot to wear. It was sunny out. My mother was just a shadow at the sink with her back facing us, and Margie asked, out loud, to anyone who would listen, "What if the numbers won't go away?" I laughed because I didn't understand and soon Margie was laughing too and my mother probably frowned to the wallpaper above the sink, ribbon-tied clusters of violets, forever on the verge of blooming. She had a habit of looking off in the distance, angrily. You would have thought that she hated the walls of our house if you had seen the way that she glared at them.

Then there was one autumn when every day Margie insisted on wearing the same sweater. It was a big, thick, golden yellow knit. It gradually became stretched and stained but still Margie was so determined. My mother was constantly trying to reason with her, always pitching and promoting all of Margie's other sweaters. And then, one day, Margie awoke to find her yellow sweater gone and she was given a story about how it was tired of being worn and had left, and Margie went to her room and could be heard crying from every corner of the house, screaming and sobbing, until the doorbell rang and Margie, as she was instructed, answered it and found that the sweater, in a heap on the welcome mat, had decided to return.

The question about the numbers and the sweater is all that I can remember. Until the big storm. The snow just kept falling until the city stopped beneath it. The only movement in the streets were kids. Hip high in snow, they pushed against it to create trenches and then dragged their sleds behind. If you were alive that winter, you have a story. Everyone does. Here's mine. While helping a man push a car out of the snow, my father had a heart attack and died. I was eight and my sister was twelve. And that was when the threes arrived. Like after a bite of food Margie HAD to tap her fork to her plate three times. My mother complained about the noise and Margie changed it to take a bite, put your fork down, and tap with your finger on the table three times. And at the end of every block we had to pause because Margie HAD to tap her toe to the cement three times. And before long, she was doing it all in threes, washing her hands, twirling in the yard. And then the threes took over. She HAD to blink her eyes three times between words spoken, taking forever to spit out a sentence, her face all aflutter with movement. And when it got really bad, when something upset her, there were thirty-threes if the threes didn't help, taking hours to walk, or read, or chew, always stopping to count because she HAD to. My mother, sure that Margie was misbehaving, doing it just for attention, would reach the point of screaming, "Do you have to do that?" and Margie would answer with a frightened, quiet, "Yes."

The cab was approaching my mother's house. I slid along the seat, to get out of the door nearest the walk and made a mental note of the quirk. Because I didn't get in and out through the same door, it would stick with me, nag at me a little. Sometime in the future, I would have to reverse it, getting into the back of a cab through the driver's side and getting out through the other door. It would have to be done to return the symmetry. It made sense. I thought of the pattern as beads on a strand. If you started with a red bead, the break in the ritual, you could follow with black, white, black, white beads, back on schedule, getting in and out of that same door, for as long as you liked, but only if you eventually added and ended with another red bead, reversing the quirk, re-establishing a pattern.

The cab driver was looking for the address and I instructed him to stop at the one that was lit up. Practically every room contained a burning bulb and the house was so bright that it almost blazed. This was supposed to set a shining example of a house full of people to all potential robbers. It was one of my mother's habits. If she had been home, a single light would have followed her from room to room.

As always, I was surprised when the key fit into the lock; this hasn't felt like my house for many years.

The kitchen was, and always will be, spotless. My mother is like that, forever with a wet rag in one hand. I remember once, early on when Margie started to lose control, and the numbers were gaining ground, I thought of something that my mother had mentioned. She had said that when she first married my father she couldn't believe how often he showered. She used to tease him about it. It was a game that they played. It stuck with me. Then it bothered me.

One day, while watching my mother clean the dust from a crack between the refrigerator and a cabinet, I asked her about it. I never mentioned Margie, but she knew what I was getting at. She exploded.

"There was nothing wrong with your father!" she screamed, without ever turning to face me, still stabbing at that crack using one of her large, wet rags, wrapped around a yard stick.

I turned on the kitchen television and watched to see if the news would mention the cabbie that had been killed. The anchorwoman relayed much the same information as my driver. Then the screen showed the cab. I was surprised. There was nothing more than a wide, circular dent in the roof. When the camera peered inside there was no blood, only bits of concrete covering the upholstery and the dash. One of those wooden beaded seat covers was hanging off to the side, but still anchored to the headrest.

I thought about how it must have been a sign of something. A woman primping and driving at the same time. A huge mass of concrete dropped from a construction site, killing someone. One accident foolishly waiting to happen. Another one, a job well done.

I find signs in the most unexpected places. A scrap of newspaper being blown along the sidewalk is usually chased, caught, and read, sometimes saved. Once, while I was watching television and aimlessly flipping channels, the announcer for a bowling match suddenly said, "You can't let what you've done in the past affect your next shot. It's gone. It's finished." That was profound, really, so profound that I wrote it down. Then, leaning in and listening, I waited, hoping that the announcer would offer some more profound advice. He didn't. Just a lot of talk about how balls react and some very important spot called "the heart of the pins," which didn't mean anything, I was sure of it because I really thought about it. Still, that first thing that he said must've been a sign of something.

I once saw a movie with a female character who was always finding playing cards, single ones, and they were really good signs because they were incredibly obvious and ALWAYS foreshadowed what was about to happen.

There is a man who almost every evening walks down my street singing deep, operatic scales. But the other night he walked by singing "The Star-Spangled Banner." Then, later that night, on my way to the drugstore I passed a parking lot where the restricting wood beam at the entrance had a little American flag, on a thin stick, stuck to the very tip of the arm.

That was certainly a sign, but not like the Hollywood version where a girl finds a jack of hearts and then meets a really great guy. This was a sign like the dangerous woman driving and the concrete falling, because I'm not sure what it meant.

Earlier today my mother called and sighed and spoke as if she was talking to no one in particular. Thinking out loud, she said, "Margie's back in the hospital."

Her words broke the predictable beat from my kitchen faucet, dripping for days, still tapping at the porcelain as my mother droned on.

"They think that she'll stay awhile," she said, and then sighed again.

I have a big old vinyl chair which really belongs in my living room, and I'll slide it in there whenever I have guests, but most of the time it better serves me in my kitchen. The chair is the place where I rest all of the things filling my arms when I enter the apartment, things that would normally be placed on a kitchen counter, something my kitchen is without.

As I listened to my mother talk I had to sit balanced on the very edge of that chair's cushion. There was a stack of things that I'd been meaning to sort through, throw out, or put away that was taking up most of the seat. But so much time had passed that it was starting to seem as if that pile of stuff was exactly where it belonged; it had begun to feel perfectly natural for me to share the chair with it. And then my mother called and suddenly the dripping water was too loud and the chair felt cramped and I thought about pushing myself backwards, sliding my butt easily over the junk mail, smothering the glossy sheets of colorful ads, and continuing backwards until I crushed a box of new light bulbs between my back and the chair, pressing hard to ensure that the shards of glass would slice past my shirt and enter my skin. I would welcome the pain and sit bleeding in the kitchen.

"I just had to," she explained. "Margie wouldn't leave her apartment."

"Uh huh," I answered, with my bare feet pressed to the linoleum and I started to push with my legs, but my thighs refused to budge from the vinyl.

"The doctor said," she continued, and the entire chair started to inch slowly backwards across the floor, until it hit the wall behind me strong and solid.

My mother had let go of something. The realization suddenly swam around my kitchen, out of control, a spiraling wave without hope, fueled by fear, terror rushing through it. It felt as if the panic had pressed a thin filmy fog against the window pane, or brushed past the stove's pilot light, threatening to push the flame free, leaving the jet to fill the room with gas. The water started to drip faster, beating down into the sink, the noise drowning out my mother, and with my chair against the wall I could surely crush those bulbs if I kept pressing backwards. I didn't know if my voice was calm or if I screamed above it all and asked, "Do you want me to come over?" and heard only part of her answer, "No, I'm going to"—and not able to listen anymore. I told her that I had to go or needed to go and hung up.

And then it happened. The answer came. It seemed so simple. All at once. I was no longer Margie's little sister. I would be the person to worry when she wasn't well, to hope that she would get better, and I would believe that it would happen. I would take all responsibility into my arms and cradle it.

The kitchen settled. The faucet gained control and returned to a slow, barely audible drip. The window cleared up and the room was bright once again. That was when I knew that I had to go to my mother's house. There I could take care of everything.

Margie has been in the hospital before. It has been several years since I've had to visit her there. I remember the psychiatric ward, housed in the oldest building, the center of the large cluster which constitutes a teaching hospital. There was a time when that one old building was the entire hospital by itself. It is the point from which those towering new buildings spread.

We met in a reception area, a large, dark arrangement which could've been the lobby of an old hotel if Margie hadn't been wearing a gray, formless patient's smock. She looked incredibly thin. Deep creases in the material seemed almost able to meet each other, as if there were no Margie in between.

As we walked I watched her profile. Her nose was my father's, always had been. It ended with the sharpest point and added a serious tone to what was otherwise a baby-face.

Everything seemed all right when we were seated in the cafeteria. Sure, Margie was doing something with her legs, some counting under the table and her upper body swung a little as a result, but she seemed otherwise in control. We were both drinking coffee when Margie mentioned the numbers. I never asked her about it, it was my way of telling her that I would accept it, that it didn't matter to me. But there in the hospital's cafeteria, Margie suddenly started laughing and when I asked her why she said, "I was laughing about something I used to have to do with stairs."

"Do with them?"

"Count them," she said with her head, neck, and shoulders rocking; the motion was child-like but the rhythm was mature and precise. And she explained, "I used to have to count the number of stairs to a flight and they would have to end in an odd number." I suddenly remembered a much younger Margie making a kind of hop step up a pretend stair at the very top of a flight. I realized that she'd been counting, ending with an even number, and then adding one. Margie continued talking, still amused, telling me about how the totals for the flights she climbed often were memorized. She mentioned our school, the library, a building with our doctor's office inside. There was a time when she knew the totals for what sounded like dozens of flights. And she said that she was constantly comparing the totals of the different staircases, looking for something, some correlation. I wondered if she meant a sign. Then I watched as she suddenly stopped laughing, and for a moment her mouth was set absolutely tight, and then she explained that there was one stair-way, the front stairs inside of our house, that for some reason she'd decided that she couldn't or shouldn't count. So she never did.

"But it wasn't easy," she told me, leaning closer and lowering her voice. "I was so used to counting stairs that whenever I took those front ones I would have to force random numbers through my head, I'd think twenty-three, one, five, sixteen, eight, twelve." I wanted to laugh. It could've been funny if she hadn't explained it so slowly and carefully. There was something absolutely and utterly important that I was supposed to understand.

And now I've realized what it was. She was telling me that she wanted to know. A part of her needed to count those stairs, but couldn't. She had to know the total, but was frightened.

That's why I've come to this house. Because after my mother called, and I realized that she'd given up on Margie, all that came to my mind were those stairs. Margie had been in control then. It didn't matter that she had to count them, and sometimes add to them, because she could get past them. And then there was that one flight, and how she couldn't, and then our dad died, and the decline followed.

I look up to the same wallpaper that still covers my mother's kitchen walls. These violet buds have been waiting since the first time Margie mentioned the numbers. There is a sense of closure now. It is as if I'm about to make these printed flowers bloom.

Leaving the kitchen and moving to the hall takes a moment. It's starting to come together now. I control what I can, and follow the signs when they appear. It is as if Margie got stuck on this staircase, and I'm about to push her past it. I face the tall carpeted flight, noticing the dirty tread marks up the center, thinking that it could be more than just a sign of age. It could be a sort of path, my path to the landing where I will turn and continue climbing. From there the top of the flight will be before me.

I know that I will never feel this sure of anything, ever again.

Without hesitation, this first step is one, then two, three . . .

DISAPPEAR
Eduardo Cruz Eusebio

When Sam was born he was chubby and fat, with slits for eyes. We called him Baby Buddha. But as he grew older, he began to appear less and less Asian. His hair grew curly and brown with red highlights, like his mother's. He actually had a bridge on his nose, something I didn't enjoy until I reached my teens. His face grew longer and eyes wider.

We're driving out to the country for the weekend on the highway out of Chicago, heading west into the fields of northern Illinois. All summer the sun has been punishing us, boiling the air. We're sealed in our car, with air conditioning keeping the sun at bay. We're going to visit Kate's grandparents, to collect their family histories. This weekend we're talking to her mother's side.

"Dee, they aren't getting any younger," Kate said over supper on Wednesday, "and when they're gone, well, you know."

"Then it's all gone," I said, thinking about my history and how I'd had to search through cold books, and had never known my uncles and aunts, much less grandparents.

"So, let's go this weekend."

"Yeah," I said, feeling a tinge of bitterness, "it'll be interesting."

So we're driving out. Cars are becoming sparser, and suburban sprawl has surrendered to advancing grids of soybean and corn. Kate sits in the back seat with Sam, our two-year-old. He hates sitting in his car seat, so Kate usually plays games with him to entertain. I twist the rear view so I can watch her. Sam's sleeping now with his thumb stuck loosely in his mouth, his tattered blanket nestled beneath his cheek. Kate smiles as she watches him sleeping. And I imagine she used to watch me the same way, before we both got tired all the time with working and writing and going to graduate school and everything. She turns and catches me watching her. She wrinkles her nose and makes a little pig snort. She's still so beautiful, with her curly and unruly brown hair, and blue, blue eyes, but so embarrassed when I look at her. She still imagines herself a chubby, dumpy farm girl with cropped hair and overalls.

"What's up, Dee?" she says.

"Guess," I say lewdly.

"I bet it is," she says as she punches the back of my shoulder.

Lewdness is my role in this marriage. I've refined it. We have routines.

"I've got somethin for ya," I say, "and I think you're gonna like it."

"Says you," she answers smugly.

"White woman, you're gonna pay and pay again for that remark."

"Says who?"

"Says this yellow man, that's who!"

"Wait a minute," she mutters in disgust, "are you telling me you're an Asian?"

"Yes, quite yella."

"Eeeww, and we've had children together?"

"That's what us Asians are best at, White woman," I proclaim. "You do want to have ten more, don't you?"

Kate turns to our sleeping son and strokes his head. "Look at him, David," she says.

I look at the boy dozens of people, even strangers, have complimented us on. They compliment us as if his cuteness, or handsomeness, or exoticness, or brightness and laughter were caused by us. As if Kate and I planned it all along when we met in college. As if we'd whispered to each other in that experimental film class, huddled close in the darkness of that cramped room, a grainy film flickering on the wall, our faces inches apart, "Let's mate and have a pleasant and good-looking child. Let's mingle gene pools. Let's do IT for the children."

I look at Sam in the rear view. In some inexplicable way, he's the most beautiful thing I've ever seen. "We should have more," Kate whispers, "shouldn't we, David?"

"Yeah," I say, "let's." I wonder if our other kids would look like Sam. Then I wonder what his children would look like, and if he'd marry an Asian girl, unlike his father. Would he even consider it—this American boy?

I turn off the highway and onto two lane blacktop. We have an hour left to drive. We pass quiet silo towns connected by railroad tracks, farmhouses alone and silent in fields of green corn, and then we switch to rumbling, dusty, gravel roads. I drive by sight; the route exists beyond mere memory. I know the roads by feel. They are smooth and rattling, with curves I can seize at full speed and others I have to slow down for. They have no names, unless N5232 and E3056 are names one gives to roads instead of Elm or Glenwood or Liberty.

I turn left after we pass a house that has been unfinished for at least two years. Today it sports new siding, and sprouting grass is beginning to green the yard. I choose the right fork when we come to the line of trees that hide a row of plantation style homes . . .

I think about Sam and future kids and progeny, about parents and ancestors. I wonder about my mother and her visions. Did she see visions of the past or future? Was it some sort of ancestral memory?

She never shared them with anyone. Often I'd find her alone, in the kitchen, staring into space, shaking and sweating, with tears rolling down her porcelain face. When I was young, I'd ask her what was the matter, I'd tug her legs and pull on her skirt until she cleared her head and finally saw me, and kneeled down to comfort and hold me.

As I grew older, I stopped shaking her, and began to just watch. I'd sit in a chair and witness her head turning slowly as the visions moved across her sight. I'd eat a cookie as I'd watch her look at a place that wasn't there and make sharp movements with her arms that looked like warnings, pleadings, praying and frozen death. Then the sight would leave her. And she'd gaze at me, with her shining, black hair falling straight to her shoulders, and her wide, delicate face exhausted beneath the glistening sweat. She'd peer at me with her almond, Asian eyes and I'd know better than to ask her why.

It wasn't until years later, after I graduated from college, that I began to have visions of my own. These sights were not like my mother's. They didn't take over my being, and force me to watch them played out. They were sights that, more often, came to me like vivid dreams, directly from my overindulged imagination. They were sights I'd acquired from my grandfather's journal, which was passed to me when he died. I hardly knew him, and only met him once after my family moved to America when I was two. But I acquired the journal because I was known as the writer of the family. The expectation was that I should, ten thousand miles away from the Philippines, fill out the family histories.

I sat on my dorm room bed and plodded through the journal. I was a senior at the time and had acquired it a full year before, but never had time to read it.

Kate had deserted me for the weekend, visiting her sister in Iowa. My fellow droogs cavorted across the border in Madison, Wisconsin, nurturing their lost childhoods. They claimed that U. of Wisconsin women were more cosmopolitan in the ways of unfettered love, and that another weekend in our provincial college town would force them to consider transferring to a Big Ten school, where the classes were easy and the women plentiful. Or was that the other way around? Being Kate's dutiful fiance, I declined to debauch with them.

All in all, these circumstances added up to one brutal fact. I was alone for the weekend. Horribly alone. Unable to bring myself to study for classes, I finally reached for the journal. Fortunately, it was written in English. Unfortunately, it was dull, filled with facts and reportage one usually finds in government documents and family histories. But one instance caught me. When telling about his father, my grandfather wrote, "Lapu Isidro had many large scars on his body and a withered right hand. When he was a boy, the American soldiers came in their train. They destroyed his village (1899). . ."

I had no idea what the entry was about. Those short sentences were all he wrote, as if destruction were an ordinary occurrence, like a birthday, baptism, or wedding. The entry drove me to the college library, trying to fill in the missing pieces.

Standing between quiet walls of books, I discovered a forgotten war called the Filipino-American war. I read of betrayal and butchery on both sides, of guerrilla warfare and reprisals. On that first day, I didn't find what I was searching for. The remainder of that year, I continued hunting through the various libraries and used book stores in town. My search wasn't obsessive, but it was something I felt I had no choice in. I had to fill in the histories.

It wasn't until after graduation and marriage, a move to another state and town, and my entry in the world of plodding work, that I uncovered a young American soldier's account of actions taken along the coastal provinces north of Manila. It was in a book I found in a dusty, used book store. I stood there among the dark shelves, reading the passages. I didn't want to believe them.

"December 9, 1899: A scouting party led by Lt. Andrew Bingham of our 31st Kansas Volunteers was butchered. The bodies were mutilated by bolo cuts. Penises were removed and stuffed into mouths. The head of Lt. Bingham was discovered wrapped in cloth and burning. Thadius, I am probably growing hard-hearted, for I am in my glory when I can sight my gun on some dark skin and pull the trigger. This land will be the death of my soul. These men are not men to me, Thadius. They are dark skinned niggers and black rabbits. We do not kill men. We go on goo-goo hunts. This land consumes me. I long to be home with you and Mother and Father, once again.

"December 11, 1899: We boarded a train carrying our company to the area where the scouting party was found. We were led by Major Frederick Noonan. We rode north in the dark morning. . . . "

I look in the rear view. Kate is asleep, her head resting on Sam's car seat. They have the same open mouthed expression. And I wonder if Sam will keep anything of mine, if he will have my snorting laugh, or my way of sauntering when I walk, or my midwestern drawl. Every day he looks more and more like Kate. It's not his fault. It's the way things have to be. I turn the rear view so I see the road pulling away behind us. I think of the visions I began to see after I found the histories, and I wonder what was worse: the visions my mother suffered through, or the ones I gave myself.

Eduardo Cruz Eusebio/329

Now the visions come to me: when standing alone in front of the bathroom mirror, scrubbing my Asian face that doesn't quite match the midwestern white boy I am inside; when sitting, slouched on the swaying and crowded morning train, feeling my Asianness surrounding me, a wall made of stereotypes of what I am and what I believe and what I'm supposed to look, sound, and smell like; when I stand in the darkness of my bedroom, naked, listening to the rustle of my wife and two- year-old son, as they roll, tasting their mouths in their sleep as I stare out the window at the glowing street lights and cars; and when I'm driving in a quiet car, along roads I know like the features of Sam's little face, or the slow, soft curve of Kate's back. I open my eyes, and see what Grandfather wrote about.

It's 1899, and the military train coughs slowly through the clear, moonlit night. It creeps toward the thatched coastal village, which is raised on stilts along both sides of the track. The train never stops here, but the village exists in the hope that it someday will. The fertile sea shimmers in the near distance, carrying the smell of fish and salt through the tropical air. Low, rounded mountains balance the sea on the other side. Clouds of engine steam dissipate quickly in the humidity, as the train pushes closer to the sleeping village of my great-grandfather, Lapu Isidro.

With his parents and sisters, Lapu sleeps in their house on stilts. The night is warm. They rest without sheets on mats of reed, huddled beneath clouds of pale mosquito netting that hang from the ceiling. Beneath the bamboo floor the pigs grunt and complain in their pen. Lapu is ten, skinny, barefoot, deeply tanned, and he wears threadbare shorts and a shirt. He is a Catholic, and on Sundays his wardrobe sees the addition of a clean, bleached shirt made of softened burlap and a pair of battered shoes that overwhelm his small feet. His family, for as far back as they can remember, for centuries, has attended Sunday service in the Spanish church in the next village. But now, the Spanish have been driven away by the Revolution. Only the Filipino priests remain. The Americans have picked up the scraps.

Lapu's family, alongside others, farms rice in ponds full of silt and mud. Lapu spends the day, knee deep in water, bent over, planting young rice seedlings as the tropical sun beats through his reed hat, making him light-headed. He spins the hand crank that supplies the ponds with fresh water from the nearby stream, pumping his skinny arms in dizzy circles.

But tonight Lapu sleeps, and in his dream he fishes the quiet river mouth with his smiling father. As they haul the sticky nets into the canoe and toss the wriggling fish in a pile at the end of the boat, they pity the servile rice growers, the slaves of the earth and seasons. In his dream, Lapu is a bare-chested fisher-man, and the river and sea give him food and freedom. He admires his father's new, muscled back, not bent from years in the rice fields. His father stands suddenly, his long, black hair thrown back, as he drops the last of the netting into the boat. He smiles at Lapu, then dives powerfully into the water. Lapu scans the river for his father of dream, but cannot see him. Lapu waits, but he doesn't surface. The sky gushes dark, filled with greenish and purple clouds, and winds howl from nowhere. Still his father doesn't surface.

"Tatay! Tatay!" Lapu shouts.

Crimson lightning shatters the dream sky.

The military train shrieks to a stop outside the village, and ten American soldiers leap off a barricaded flatbed in front of the engine. Five advance toward one side of the village and five to the other. They are dressed in rumpled, dark blue shirts and khaki pants, waists encircled by ammunition belts. They sport cowboy hats dark with bands of sweat, and coarse beards and mustaches. Leading each group, a soldier marches, holding aloft a torch that flames yellow and orange. On either side, moving in a line forming a V, soldiers grip their bayonetted rifles at the ready. They hunch slightly as they scan the dark village and trees for snipers or waiting bolomen. Aguinaldo's nigger bandits fight dirty. They will not be civilized. They ambush and butcher American troops, then disappear into jungle, mountains, and villages. They revolt. They won't stand still to be shot. The soldiers reach the first stilted huts, they halt, glance about suspiciously, then peer back at the train.

In his dream, Lapu shouts and cries into the boiling water that has swallowed his father. A heavy rain has opened the sky and pelts him with large drops. Lapu stands as the winds buffet the boat, ready to leap in and join his father. Shocked, Lapu falls to a sitting position as his father's head bobs to the surface beside the boat. His father is smiling slyly as the waves toss him up and down. His black hair is plastered to his dark face and wide nose. "Why are you crying?"

"Tatay, I thought you were dead."

His father laughs, "Lapu, you were named for a brave chief, the man who killed Magellan, and drove the Spanish away."

The boy cries.

The rain circles his father. "Where is your courage, Lapu? Where is your courage to command the water, wind, and sky?"

A gunshot splinters the still night. Lapu sits up quickly, and through the pale netting recognizes his father standing by the window. This is his real father, gaunt and tenuous, making unsure jerky movements. This is not the muscled father of his dream. Lapu shivers and wonders if the explosion was real.

At the edge of the village, a young man named Rosendo sits slumped against a pole that supports his family's thatched hut. His eyes stare blankly at the soldiers, his mouth open in surprise. The top of his head is shattered and gaping at the sky. Behind him, in the pen beneath the house, his family's pigs shriek in fear at the smell of blood. A skinny volunteer named Will stands close, his inexperienced rifle raised, still locked in his grip. Chubby Perley steps forward and knocks Rosendo over with a kick, "Nigga boy," he slurs, "you one lucky goo-goo." Rosendo's pale and crimson brain tips from his skull into the dirt. Chubby Perley pulls Will back as a command is shouted from the train.

On both sides of the track the soldiers withdraw a few paces and kneel, rifles pointing outward, waiting nervously, forming a protective circle around the soldiers carrying the torches.

On the flatbed, Major Frederick Noonan appears in the lamplight. His blue uniform is dark and immaculate. He raises his gloved hand and behind him soldiers scamper about fire-fighting equipment, twisting the coupling on hoses, tapping the gauges on tanks of kerosene that once held water. The circles of soldiers move to the first huts. The two men with torches stretch their flames to ignite the dark, thatch walls. Flames sputter, then flare with loud exhalations. On both sides of the track, Holmes and Frank grin as they spread the flames, their faces bright and touched by the dancing light and heat. Another shouted command from the flatbed, and they drop the torches. The volunteers quickly retreat to the tracks where they wait alongside the train.

Major Noonan moves to the front of the flatbed, as Rosendo's frightened and confused parents begin crawling down the ladder from their burning home. Noonan stands on the sandbags, and takes off his blue, piped hat.

"31st Kansas volunteers!" he shouts.

"Sir!" the troops answer.

"Civilize the niggers!"

The bristling fire hoses send bursts of kerosene into the flames along both sides of the track, quickly spreading the blaze from hut to hut. Rosendo's parents are ripped in half by rifle and machine-gun fire, as they stumble toward the train. Other villagers begin to pour from their homes, some writhing in flames, some screaming from fiery doorways and windows, or falling bloody and punctured from ladders. The acrid, sharp, choking smell of burning thatch and flesh and powder and the drunken fumes of kerosene soak the air, as black smoke rises high above the village and is carried out to sea. The popping, and the rasping of weapons. The acrid and salty scent of thick and flowing blood. Half the village roars in flame.

From beneath the fiery collapse of her home, Theresita emerges scorched and staggering, her clothes and long black hair burned away, her skin oozing, one breast ripped away by a burning timber. She moves through the smoke toward the soldiers, like an apparition. Their white faces and uniforms are familiar to her. She has sold fruits to them in the next village, and they have often flirted with her, rubbing their rough faces against her hands, giving her trinkets and strange fish from cans. Perhaps they will stop the fires, stop the end of the world.

George races down the track with a whoop, in pursuit of running Emilio. He passes Theresita, who crumples an instant later. A shot from the flatbed brings Emilio down, and George rushes forward, sinking his bayonet into Emilio's naked stomach. The blade makes a slurping sound as if it were being pushed into a sack full of water, and the Filipino's eyes and tongue protrude from his head. The volunteer jerks his blade out and begins to methodically fire round after round into the dying man's body, raising his rifle to his cheek each time.

As Lapu stares at the ceiling, wondering about the peculiar smells and sounds of this strange dream, the walls and roof flame suddenly, burning yellow and white, as bright as day. In the window, his father lurches backward with a bright crimson and toothy hole where his face was. Lapu's four-year-old sisters hiccup in fear as they try to tear their way through mosquito netting. His mother clutches at the girls, her eyes round with fear and her mouth gaping, as pieces of burning roof begin to float down, drizzling like rain. Then the floor opens to swallow her, his father, and hiccuping sisters. They are heaved upward, then disappear. Lapu crawls to the hole, looking for them as the rain of fire broils patches of sticky red and white blisters into his back. The bamboo gives way beneath him and he falls, landing heavily in burning debris. Before he succumbs to oblivion he lifts his frozen right hand, and in the dancing flames sees a thick bamboo stake driven through the palm. I'm dreaming, he tells himself. But inches away he smells the choke of burning of flesh. —And he cannot tell if it's pig or sibling or mother and father. It's so hard to tell. In war, it's so hard to tell.

"Don't crash, Dee" Kate says as she squeezes between the bucket seats on her way to the passenger side. I notice we're near her grandparents' house. My mind feels muddy and slow. But as my role requires, I have my right hand waiting to cup her buns when she sits. She's wearing a miniskirt today, so the effect is more apparent. She pinches my arm. "Lech!" she exclaims, "I'm just a piece of meat to you!"

"Yeah," I say, "white meat."

Kate turns up the air conditioner, chilling our naked legs. Visions and smells of burning thatch reverberate in tiny waves through my mind, dissipating. Clouds of hot summer dust hide the road behind us. Then we're there. At a small, white farmhouse nestled in a pocket of fields tall with emerald corn and bushy soybean.

Grandpa Sanderson stands in the front yard. I wave at him and wonder how he can stand the heat. I recall that he's probably spent most of his life outdoors —farming, fishing, and hunting down in the woods across the fields. I know more about him than all my grandparents combined. He's peering up into the sprawling oak that covers the lawn. He's covered with mottled patches from the leaves blocking the hot sun. His face rests in darkness. A shoulder and kneecap and foot are lighted by patches of sunlight. He finally lowers his gaze and waves at us, smiling. I know he'd seen the dust from our car, rising in the sky two miles away. He'd probably seen it from his rocker on the porch and was now acting like he'd been standing in his yard, gazing at branches in the oak all afternoon long. Acting like he wasn't excitedly looking forward to seeing his granddaughter, and great-grandson, and possibly even Kate's husband and Sam's father.

He takes his time, walking to the gravel drive, hunched over and plodding with long steps like a camel. His perpetual, faded overalls hang rumpled and stiff over his gray, formerly white, T-shirt. He's grinning. The huge gaps in his tobacco-chewing teeth are as dark as Halloween putty.

In the back of the car, still restrained in his seat, Sam slaps his palm on the window, squealing frantically, reedy and high. "Gampa, Gampa!" though the man is really his great-grandfather.

I reach back and spring Sam from his car seat. He immediately jumps to the floorboard and waits impatiently by the door, grinning at the man. Kate twists the rear view and touches her hair. She opens her door, sticks her tanned legs out, then leans back in to check her lipstick. The heat rushes in, and Grandpa Sanderson knocks on my window. I open my door and he has to step back a pace. The dusty sweetness of a freshly mowed lawn fills the air. Stepping out I glance up at him, see his smiling blue eyes, then look at the wall of corn fencing in the far side of the yard. In the country, glancing is all right; staring someone in the eye for too long is rude.

"You gonna let my great-granson on outta there?" His voice is almost as high, reedy and jumbled as Sam's. There's a sweet and sour tobacco smell about him.

I take the rough and calloused hand he offers and squeeze it. "Only if yer thinkin a keepin him," I drawl, unconsciously pulling out my old, central Illinois slur. I open Sam's door and he jumps into Grampa's arms, then ignores him. He shoves his thumb in his mouth and looks everywhere but at the man cuddling him and smooching at his cheeks. Two-year-olds are like that. At least Sam is.

"Yer jus an onry little theng aren'cha?" Grandpa wheezes, lifting Sam above him.

Kate walks around the car. "Not as onry as an old man I know." She hugs the both of them, pecking a kiss on Grandpa's wrinkled, pale cheek.

I shove my hands deep into pockets, and force a chuckle. "Hmm," I grunt, for want of a better expression. Then I wonder, again, how he can stay so pale and unburned while spending most of his time outside.

When Kate and I were first dating, I couldn't understand a thing the old man said. It's not much better now. I'd attend family gatherings and recline in his warm, plaid living room with the rest of the men, on the couch, talking about "man" stuff: farming, cars, and all the American sports based on balls and running. The women would be clattering about the kitchen and dining room, chattering high and laughing, having much more fun. And Grandpa Sanderson would lean over and talk to me with his friendly, airy speech, sounding like oxygen was whooshing out of the balloons of his lungs. I'd nod and smile. Me, the foreigner, the Asian, probably the only Asian he'd ever talked to, pretending I understood perfectly.

He could have been asking me if I really ate dogs, and if I'd seen his missing coon dog, Socrates. That dog could climb trees. Smart too.

I'd nod. Smile. Yep, good tasting dog. Damn good dog!

He could have been asking me if I was going to make his granddaughter and great-grandchildren eat dogs.

Sure. Yeah. Can't beat it.

Grandpa Sanderson plops Sam on the ground. "Ya likin Chicago, then?" he says to me. I let his words sink in for a minute. It's the only way I can understand them. My subconscious is smarter than my conscious when it comes to translating his wheeze.

"Yeah, I'm liking it. Feel pretty comfortable there." I look at him, making sure I'm on the right track.

He nods and kicks a bug off his work boot.

"All kinds of Asians in Chicago," I add.

Kate strokes Sam's hair. Sam prances in place, sticking his tongue out at us. "Dee, you don't even know any Asians," Kate teases.

"Yeah, but I could if I wanted to. Wait a minute, I know an Asian at grad school. She's, I think a—"

"Ain't never bin ta Chicago. Seen Chicago on TV," Grandpa says.

"It's nice," I say. "Lots to do."

Grandpa tugs on Kate's miniskirt and she pulls away laughing. "Where's the rest a yer skirt girl? Someone done cut off the bottom off yer skirt."

Grandma Sanderson pushes open the screen door. Every time I see her, she seems to be getting shorter and happier, if that's possible. "Come on up here and give yer Gramma a kiss, Kate" she calls. "Hi, David. Sam, can you give Gramma a kiss?"

For the next couple hours we sweat in the living room. The window fan blows hot afternoon air on us. The whirling air smells like sour tobacco juice and dust. We sweat and talk. Kate and I sit on the plaid sofa, behind a low coffee table covered with boxes of old papers and photos. The grandparents rock in lounge chairs on both sides of the room. Now and then Grandpa leans over and spits brown saliva into a white plastic cup. The cup sits on a spattered newspaper on the brown carpet. They talk, and Kate and I ask questions as Sam amuses himself with dusty old toys and a speckled, arthritic coon dog too achy and crying to chase him. The tape recorder spins. I jot notes on a pad of yellow legal paper, feeling like a historian. We pore over a yellowing sketch of a family tree tagged with names as leaves. The tree is shaped like the oak outside, wide and plump. I wonder what my family tree would be shaped like.

"When were you born? What was your father's full name? Your grandfather's occupation? What's your earliest memory? Your memory of an event with your mother? Your father? Your siblings? What was the effect of the first world war on the family? WW II? What was the feeling about Germans? About Japanese?

When did your family acquire a car? Electric lights? How long did you use an outhouse? How many head of cattle did your father own? Horses? Buggies? How did you keep food fresh before refrigeration?" We record. We flip the tape over when it runs out.

We examine photographs. Some people wave and grin, others stare blankly. One man stands in a studio, dressed in full Civil War uniform. Others are dressed in the uniforms of other wars.—WWI and II, and Korea and Vietnam. There's one smiling young man who wears a slouchy uniform, boots and a cowboy hat. At his side is a large caliber rifle. The uniform of a volunteer. I flip it over. There's no date and no name, but it has the look of a photo taken around the turn of the century. Could be an Indian fighter, I say to myself. Wounded Knee happened in 1890. Could be the Spanish-American war. Could be . . .

"Who's this?" I finally ask.

Kate glances at the photo, then looks at me sharply. She doesn't say anything. She's heard me complain before, about a forgotten war, and the forgotten deaths of hundreds of thousands of Filipinos, of ruined crops and starvation, and imperialism, and the betrayal of a sovereign nation. About the deaths of certain Filipinos. Deaths close to home. I'd read her the excerpts from my grandfather's journal, shown her pictures out of books of young Americans dressed like cowboys, holding rifles in the Philippines.

Kate stares at the side of my face and takes the photo. She hands the photo to Grandma who frowns squinting at it. "I can't—I don't recognize him, Kate. You try, Dad. Must be your side."

Kate walks the photo across the room and sits on the armrest of Grandpa Sanderson's lounger. He looks closely at it, then back at me. "Nope," he says. Then he swats at Kate's rear as she walks back to the sofa.

Kate laughs. "He's always been annoying us, ever since we were little. Whenever we'd walk by his chair he'd jab at us. Ornery old man." Kate sits, holding the photo between her bare legs. "He can't let a kid go by his chair unteased."

I'd seen him poking and teasing all his grandchildren and great-grandchildren a dozen times. It didn't matter how old they were. From two to thirty, all were open game. Kate didn't need to explain it to me. I'd seen it. It didn't need explaining. I pick up another photo, one of an old ocean liner. In the corner of my eye, I see Kate quietly bury the unidentified soldier beneath a pile of yellowed correspondence.

Grandpa Sanderson and I stand in the garden out back. The sun is low and orange. The oppressive heat has finally released its hold. A slight breeze rustles the corn in the bordering fields. The leaves of the sweet corn in the garden mimic the sound. Grandpa stoops in the dark earth a few feet away, pulling up a few small carrots. The garden smells like liquid flowers and fertility—like Kate used to smell before we got used to each other.

When we were first married, I could have identified her while blindfolded and from three feet away. She smelled like richness and earth, and soap and sex. When we couldn't see each other, I used to take a shirt she'd worn and sniff at it before going to sleep at night. It was almost as if she were there. She'd do the same. I remember her saying to me, "You smell like someone I'd marry."

And I'd bury my nose in her shoulder and murmur, "You smell as fertile as the Tennessee Valley."

She'd push me away. "Let's hope not, Dee. Fertility is, well you know . . . dangerous."

Grandpa Sanderson holds a bunch of carrots up to me. "Come on, won't bite cha."

I take them by the bushy green, holding them away. They are wide and squat carrots, like nothing I'd seen in the grocery. Grandpa keeps pulling bunches out and handing them back to me. "Got enough em there, Dave?"

I heft them. "Yeah, sure, I think."

Grandpa Sanderson pushes himself up from the ground and slowly creaks to his feet. "Cabbage ready. Like cabbage? Nice stew." He steps over a few rows and pulls a large pocket knife out of his overalls. "Which one ya want?"

"I don't know how to cook cabbage," I say, following him.

He kneels, wheezing over his shoulder, "Boil the sucker up, jus boil it er fry it with some pork fat." He pushes the plant's dark outer leaves away and hacks at the stem of the pale cabbage head with his knife. Rising, he quickly tosses the head at me. I drop the carrots and catch it. It oozes with liquid, soaking the front of my shirt.

A giggle escapes me. "This sucker's heavy."

"Better'n the store-bought garbage," he says, grinning with his shattered teeth. He spits a stream of juice between the rows.

And for some reason, standing there holding the head of cabbage in my arms, I start speculating that the size and weight of it would probably be close to a human's. I blurt without thinking. "You knew the soldier in that picture didn't you?"

He glances down at me then looks out at the corn and darkening sun. "Farming was never good enough fer my uncle. Wanted to see the world. Joined up. Died over there."

"Where?"

"Where you from," he says as he turns and walks to the house. I watch his long, field-eating strides, feeling a lump coming to my throat. Nearing the back door, he points at a metal bucket filled with water. "Wash the carrots in that. Don't need ta wash no cabbage."

"Thanks," I manage to call, before the screen door closes behind him.

Then the cabbage feels like a baby in my arms. A head, then a baby, then a head again. I drop it, and stand there in the garden. In the cooling dusk, I can hear murmuring through the open windows. I can hear the high laughter of Sam as somebody picks him up and tickles him. I hear Grandma Sanderson's high, crackling giggle. I hear Kate's cheerful scolding. And I feel like I'm part of it all. Like there's this quiet voice saying, "You belong here, to somebody, to us." And I want it. I want it more than anything. To finally belong and stop caring about being Asian and different. Then I see my mother, standing in her kitchen, crying, watching visions cross her sight. And I know what shook her. It wasn't her own memories of the Japanese and World War II. She had strength enough to handle that. It was the memories she was born with. The ancestral memories.

She saw the family murdered in burning houses and open fields. She saw no escape and no forgiveness, but that was all. That was as far as her vision could take her.

I see something gentle and relentless, soft and slow and sure. Beyond visions, and resting in certainty. I am the new addition in a long line of good country folk. My Asianness will be added in, then subtracted and subtracted, until this new land accepts me by making me slowly, comfortably, disappear.

MY JOB
Don Gennaro De Grazia

There're folks like Steven that'll tell me that all the trouble I got into was 'cause I'm poor, and I take exception to that. 'Cause friend, I'll tell ya, you can say it's 'cause I'm stupid, or 'cause I let a girl get the best of me, but being poor, see, being poor allows a man a certain amount of freedoms, so long's he's got himself a job.

I've had lots of jobs in and around DeKalb, but the best one would have to be being night manager of Fran's Do-Nut Shop. Fran's is right on Central Street, not by the University, but down more by the lumber yard and the Del Monte cannery. I say "night manager" 'cause, besides Steven—this ol' black guy who stays in back all night and bakes, an' washes dishes—there was never anyone else around, so I took to calling myself the boss. And it's kind of funny that it was at Fran's—best job I ever had—that I got into all this trouble.

I'd come into work early one night to see Dina, who, I guess you'd say, was the day manager. She was also my girl at the time. Anyway, I come in the back way, an' when Steven sees me he's got this look on his face like my ol' bloodhound Andy gets when I catch him taking a shit on the rug. So I ask him what's up, and he just nods towards the front, which ain't nothing more'n a glass counter and a few round tables and stools. So I go up there and what do I see but Dina sitting her little ass on the lap of some big guy with a Johnson's Motors sweatshirt on, feeding him a vanilla eclair.

Now, I knowed what was up. Those Johnson guys make six dollars an hour to start, compared to what I make, which I ain't even gonna say. And they get weekend nights and holidays off too, unlike myself. So I just looked at 'em until the guy said what're you lookin' at? and I said nothin', 'n' Dina giggled while I walked in the back to get my apron. When I came back out they were gone, and I spent the rest of the night getting madder and sadder and spilling coffee all over myself on top of it all.

It ain't that Dina was all that great—sorta pretty, that's all—but it was just that she was only the third girlfriend I ever had. And the first one was when I was in second grade so that don't count. And the middle one, well, that was Tracy which you better not get me started on. Just that she and I was voted king and queen at DeKalb's homecoming not five years ago. Now, you look at me and you know I wasn't voted king 'cause I'm so goddamned pretty. It was because she and I dated all through high school and were gonna get married just as soon as she got through going to college to be a teacher, an' I maybe got my long distance trucker's license. But the first time I went down to visit her at school she was wearing this sorority shirt with these Latin letters sewn on it and acting real strange. She sure looked pretty though. And I swear to god when she told me she wanted to start seeing other people I busted out crying. Just sat there in her dorm room and busted out crying so loud she started to get embarrassed, and finally called campus security who came and escorted me out to my truck. This was the same truck I got now, 'cept without the gunrack and the mudflap decals and the rollbar.

So that's why I joined the Navy. Tried to join the Foreign Legion but that shit didn't ever exist I don't think. When I got out I came back to DeKalb, and heard Tracy'd dropped out of school and got married somewhere, I don't know. That's when I got the job from Fran. Fran's this old lady who I'd say owns half of DeKalb.

Came here from down South I heard, and pissed all the DeKalb women off by sleeping with their husbands, and pissed all the men off by buying up all the businesses around here. So I was a little bit scared when I went into the gun shop to see her about a job. She wasn't too mean, just real silver haired, and serious. And she told me I couldn't work at the gun shop, but I could at the Do-Nut Shop if I wanted to. So I did, and that's where I met Dina.

Now I knew from the start that Dina was just a little jerk, but I'd just spent four years kinda thinking I'd be coming back to Tracy. And when I finally realized that just weren't ever gonna happen, I'll bet I felt lonelier than I thought was possible. And for all her faults, Dina was as pretty as a flower. But damn if she didn't go and spend all of my money. I had quite a bit saved up from the Navy, but it came and went just like breath on a mirror. Dina'd need all these things, that's all I knew them as—things, and she was always wanting to go out. There aren't many places to go in DeKalb, but there's the Egyptian Theater, which is this little art movie house and that's where we'd go. Sometimes I couldn't go so I'd just give her the money.

But finally, when the last of that money was just about spent, I started to say no to certain things. Like she wanted to go see this comedian from New York one night, the kind you'd see on that Davis Letterman's show. I told her I could tell her exactly the same jokes he'd tell her, for free. Like, it's stupid that they make breath mints for dogs, 'cause they're always sniffin' each other anyway, and drinking out of the toilet. Or, it's stupid that they have labels on mattresses saying you'd better not take them off, 'cause who's gonna know the difference if you do? But I guess I don't have a big long nose or a New York accent, so I ain't funny.

But when she wanted to go see this string quartet do Jimi Hendrix songs, I said hell no, not when I'm still saving up for that rollbar, and that was it—the next day she was wiggling around in that Johnson Motor's guy's lap, feeding him a doughnut, and laughing at me.

I told myself it was just as well, but I won't deny I felt like crying again. She'd once told me how, when she got to be a famous actress or clothes designer someday, she'd buy the Do-Nut Shop from Fran, and make me the president of it. And I knew it was all her baloney, but it was sweet to hear it anyways.

But I'll tell you something, after I got off of work that night, I just laid on my back and stared at the ceiling and got madder and madder. By the time the sun came up I was so mad I had to put my jeans and boots on and go outside and walk. I walked all around town—past the feedstore, down through the college campus, and up by the post office. When I passed the library, I saw a sign in the window that said "Art Show," so I walked right in. I was gonna buy the biggest piece of art I could still afford, and take it into the shop, and smash it right in front of Dina. But the little old lady running the thing told me it was not a sale, but a show. She said I couldn't buy anything, but I could look around. So I did, and all the stuff looked so ridiculous I got even madder, and I went up to the little ole lady—Frieda was her name—and asked her if I could enter some of my own art, and she said yes, and that, my good buddy, is how I got myself in all this trouble.

I went and tore three pictures out of different books and magazines and pasted them into a triangle. The first picture showed old James Cagney reaching over the breakfast table and shoving half a grapefruit into this lady's face. The second one was this old trailer photo for the movie "Kiss Me Kate" that showed a full grown woman, turned over some guy's knee and getting spanked. And the third one (and this is the one I'd say got me in the most trouble) was from this porno magazine and it was of this lady who was all tied up, and, I guess you'd say, naked. Underneath it all I wrote "What is the proper way to deal with a no-good woman?" and left a little note-pad for folks to write suggestions on.

Well, Frieda didn't like my art one bit, but she hung it up anyways, and I went to work, feeling a whole lot better. I told Steven about it, and he just shook his head like he'd always knowed I was a fool, but didn't know till just then that I was an idiot.

The next day I went past the library and there was a hundred people at least standing outside listening to some guy who said he was from a student group at the University called the John Lennon Organization. He was all pissed off about my art and said I ought to be arrested for subug-jating woman. Next up was this girl in army boots who said it was time for all women to join together and stop being treated like some sort of objects. I'd say she herself looked less like a woman than she did some sort of object—a fireplug maybe. Then this lady professor got up and said what I'd done weren't art at all, but trash—dangerous trash. And she was followed by my old preacher who said my art was immoral and all that, 'specially the naked lady, and finally some hippie couple got up and sang "Michael rowed the boat ashore." And then the girl in the boots jumped up and said she was going in to take my piece down and the whole crowd said "Yeah!" and started stampeding towards the door. Then just as they reached the steps, old Frieda came outside with Sheriff Boone and said to hold it right there. They tried to argue but Frieda just told them to shut up. Then I went up and stood next to them and said "Yeah, you all just shut up." And then the sheriff said for me to shut up, and some other girl in boots ran up and threw a jar of pig's blood in my face.

"Honey," I said, trying to act like it didn't bother me at all, "I was born and raised on a hawg farm. Mm-mmm," I said, licking some of it off my cheek, "Mother's milk."

But I was just bluffing. I was born and raised on a dog farm, puppy mill, whatever. And the sight of blood made me want to fall over and pass out. And the sight of all those people shaking their fists at me and all, made me want to fall over and plain die.

Afterwards the sheriff drove me to the Do-Nut Shop and told me he might be back later to book me on a pornography charge. Then he just shook his head and said he didn't want to be around when Fran found out about this. I'd forgotten all about her.

When I punched in, Dina was smirking and knowing my ass was fired just as soon as Fran found out. And Steven was acting like he wasn't talking to me. Oh yeah, I forgot to tell you, that picture of the naked lady all tied up was of a black woman, and so all sorts of minority groups hated me now. But when I told Steven to quit acting so high and mighty—that I'd ripped that picture out of one of his dog-eared copies of *Players* magazine I'd found stashed away underneath the sink, he couldn't very well stay mad at me. But all he would talk about was how I was a goner soon as Fran found out.

So I got to thinking, I had to work terrible hours at the place, for terrible pay, but it was really the only place I'd ever felt comfortable. And now I was going to lose it all. I looked up front at Dina, and thought of Tracy. They'd really done me in. Made me cry, took my money, and now they'd taken my job. My good old job. I'd never get that rollbar now. Then, all at once, Fran came in looking silver haired and stern as ever. And I swear to god just as she came in, the phone rang and she picked it up. I knew by the way she was looking at me that it was one of them woman's organizations. She just kept nodding and saying "Oh, how terrible." Then I knew they were getting down to the nitty-gritty and that they were demanding that she fire me. She hesitated a little bit and then they must have let loose with both barrels because she started saying "I firmly agree but . . ." and "Right, but . . ." "Uh huh, uh huh." Then, all of a sudden, she goes, "You find somebody'll come in here an' work seven nights a week, Thanksgiving, Christmas, and Easter, and all for shit wages, and then I'll fire him. Until then, fuck you!" and slammed the phone down and left.

Now I still got this job, and I got that rollbar a long time ago, and you see what I mean now, right? Being poor allows a man certain special freedoms that he wouldn't otherwise have. That is, just so long's he's got himself a job.

MR. NOBODY
Adrienne Clasky

Mr. Nobody lived in the broad, blank wall above Amanda's bed. Or rather, he stayed there.

"It's my hotel," he'd say, and grin.

He was tall, taller even than Uncle Sammie. And he was Aryan. Amanda knew this positively though she didn't know what Aryan meant, except that she heard it around the apartment a lot and it had something to do with tricky people.

Mr. Nobody was totally bald, his skin was translucent, faintly pink and slick, covered with something shiny and wet that made Amanda think of mucus, but it wasn't green. And if he touched your forehead, you'd turn into slime, so she never let him touch her, though he often wanted to, curling up in the wall and setting his pointy chin on his slick shoulder, saying, "Oh, c'mon, *come awn*! Amanda Polanda."

His tongue was grey-blue and almost see-through but not like that ashtray in which Gramma kept toothpicks in the front room. The tip of it was always darting out the corners of his mouth when she would tell him stories or try to find out about him, because he would tell her nothing.

"What do you *want*?" she would sometimes ask him in the cornflower blue of early morning.

His tongue would dart, but he would not answer.

Once she asked him about Giggi and Gagga, her other imaginary friends, whom she could not remember, whom her adults were always asking about.

"They left," he said and clapped his feet over his ears.

"You made them leave."

"I didn't make them do anything. They just left. Bought a condominium across the street. Don't like me. Nobody likes me. I'm Mr. Nobody." And he began licking between his toes.

He kept her up nights with his whining.

"Don't go to sleep dandy Mandy! Talk to me. I'm *looonely*!" And he'd twist himself up like a pretzel.

And Amanda, sitting crosslegged on her bed, looking up at him from under the hood she'd made out of her icy-blue blanket, tried to reason with him:

"You have to go to sleep. You have to get all rested, else you'll spoil your whole day tomorrow."

"Ooooh," he let out a whine, a thin horrible sound that made her remember something from when she was four, something that maybe really happened or maybe was a dream because it was queer and slow like a dream.

Suddenly she's standing in the shadowy hall that's really a hall where all doors open off of. The quiet blows hard in her ears. Her grandparents' door is closed. Her momma's door is open—a rectangle darker than shadows. Her feet become cold on the tiles; she huddles them together. The whining starts again, long and twisty like wire. She is pulled by the stomach on through the kitchen; her feet slap-slap across the tiles. The grey carpet hushes her feet. The whining stops.

In the living room the dark seems thick like fog, but after a minute it clears away. Her mother, facing her, is across the room, squatting like a frog under the windows. The beige curtains fall like magic hair over her shoulders. Her eyes are wide.

The whining starts again.

Her mother's eyelids sink closed. Her face goes still as rock.

Amanda thinks, "What a crazy place for sleeping." The whining distracts her. It comes through the window. Amanda pads over to the windows, hands paddling through layers of curtains, parting them.

The whining stops again.

Amanda touches her nose to the cold glass and sucks in her breath and holds it.

A man (she pretends he is a stranger and not her father) stands under the white shower of light from a street lamp, very straight and directly in front of the pole which seems to stick out the top of his head and between his legs so he is like a human popsicle. And he is melting; his roly-poly cheeks are shiny-wet. His eyes are squinted into slots like those on a piggy-bank's back. She wonders if he's waiting for someone to come by and drop coins in. Out of his mouth sticks a fat dead cigar. He curls his lips back away from it and the whining starts. The cigar trembles.

Amanda begins yelling, "Stop it, you old popsicle man! Stop it right now! Go away and stay away. No pennies for you here, you piggy-bank, you popsicle!"

There are sudden hands on her shoulders and she's falling backwards. She's sitting on her mother's thighs, her mother's body wrapped all around her, her mother breathing heat on to her scalp...

Amanda fisted her hand into her cheek and hissed up at Mr. Nobody, "Stop it! Stop that whining right now!"

But he wouldn't stop. He popped out of the pretzel, slapping loud and wet against the walls of his place. He stretched out wormy and writhed and whined.

"Stop it! I have to sleep! I'm going away!"

Holding her blanket together at her chest she stood and walked to the edge of her bed, her hood slipping down her fuzzy head. She crawled onto the dresser and curled up in the middle of it where he could not see her.

He went on calling to her for a while, "Randy! Handy Mandy!"

"I'm going to ignore you," she said to Nobody, "If I ignore you, you'll get bored and go to sleep."

There was a long sigh and then just the even breathing of silence. Something uncurled in her stomach.

The relatives and neighbors all sat around the kitchen table after supper, except for the grandmother, who stood between the grandfather and Uncle Ben, the silvery coffee pot shining between her hands. A conveyor belt was started; cups shaped like bluebells were passed around the table, pausing under the coffee pot and its black waterfall of coffee.

Amanda sat cross-legged on the floor in the corner between stove and sink, playing with her Barbie dolls. She had three of them. Two were new: Barbie with a bubble hairdo like Gramma's and Ken, so blond he was almost bald. The old Barbie was dark-haired, but Amanda had chewed most of her hair off, leaving only patches above each ear. She looked very odd, like a middle-aged man with boobies.

Amanda grabbed the dolls by their necks and pressed their three faces together at the mouths, whispering, "Smoochy smooch-smooch, kissy kiss smooch..."

The adults above her talked fast and all in a scramble. Occasionally an odd phrase would peal louder, clear, would hang near the ceiling with the smoke, drifting.

"Where's Hazel tonight?"

"Hazel sure came in late last night, didn't she? The sky was already blue when I heard her heels clicking up the walk."

"Ahhh, that's the life, the life of a single girl..."

Amanda separated old balding Barbie from the other two and stood her against the cabinet to watch. The new Barbies went wild, their bodies waving through the air.

"Kissy kiss-kiss, smoochy kissy-kiss."

Something hissed, mean and scary, overhead. Amanda looked up. The outer ring of the burning-white ceiling light had gone blank and grey, and a thin smoke snake curled away from the connecting bolt. Amanda pulled the Barbies into a bouquet, holding them at the ankles.

Then the other, inner ring made a clicking sound and started flickering, and the whole room seemed to be fluttering with the grey shadows of a thousand ugly moths.

"Up, there goes the light."

"Oh, goshdarnit, Al, what're we gonna do?"

"Relax, relax. We got plenty of good use out of it, ten years."

"But what about tonight?"

Amanda heard tight wires in her grandmother's voice; Gramma was scared of dark, of fire. There was the faint bitter smell of something burning that's not supposed to.

The back door blew in and Amanda's mother moved so fast through the hall she was just a blur across the wide doorway of the kitchen. She went into her parents' room.

There was a pause of silence. The moth shadows fluttered over everything. Then the voices of the Adults, like hammers:

"Oh, who was that?"

"Was that Hazel?"

"So she doesn't even stop and say hello?"

"This I'd expect from her brother Sammie, but not from our Hazel."

Amanda saw the grandmother, her face pinched towards her mouth, look down into the grandfather's face, which was calm as granite, like always. The grandmother got up and moved around the corner into her bedroom. The grandfather pulled in closer to the table, his chair's legs screeching across the tile.

"Uh-oh," Amanda thought and popped the Ken doll's head into her mouth. "He's gonna get it now." She waited for Gramma to run out and yell at him for scraping her good floor.

The grandmother did not.

The grandfather folded his hands on the table and cleared his throat and began to talk, "Hey, Rey. I saw old Mrs. Magilicotty last week. She looks terrific, still walking around and everything."

His voice boomed on, and Amanda sat very still in the corner, sucking

Ken's head. Her grandfather never talked.

This was scary, people doing things they never did or not doing things they always did. And all because of that crazy stupid light. She would find her grandmother; she would tell her how Grampa had ruined her good floor. She popped Ken's head out of her mouth and skated in her fuzzy slippers across the tiles to her grandparents' room.

Hazel sat in a fuzzy circle of orange light on just a little piece of the wide, icy-blue bed, up near the pale headboard, her body curled toward the lamp as if she were leaning into a fire for warmth. Her face was crumpled behind her hand. Her hair was beginning to feather out of the sleek French roll it had been combed into earlier that evening. She was beautiful. She wore black wool.

"Oh, Honey, calm yourself." The grandmother hovered in front of her, hands fluttering around Hazel's head but not touching.

Hazel started talking, her voice sounding like someone was squeezing it.

"He was there at the restaurant, I tell you; he was there when we got there!"

"But how, how could he know where Roger was taking you? It must be just a coincidence."

Amanda stayed by the door, one hand holding the doorknob cold at her back, the other holding the bouquet of dolls up under her nose.

"No, Mother, it was *not* a coincidence! The minute we walked in, the headwaiter was all over us with compliments and gleaming teeth. 'So nice to see you both,' he says. 'We've been waiting for you!' Morry must've slipped him a ten at least. That bastard."

"But, Honey, waiters in nice restaurants are always like that."

"That's what we thought at first. But he took us right to Morry's table."

"Well, Honey, you didn't have to go to him. You don't have to let him get his own way."

"Oh, Christ, Mother, we didn't know what was going on. We thought it was the reservation." Hazel sniffled furiously and wiped her palm up her face, setting it on top of her head.

"Oh, God, Mother, he'd had it set for three with champagne and real crystal and one lovely lone candle. That bastard. I love white candles. I told him once, just before we were married, that I didn't care if we ate off plastic plates as long as we had white candles."

"So did you give him what for? I would've given him a good k'nock."

"No, Mother, I just looked at him sitting there behind his belly, grinning behind his cigar, and I knew I was furious but I just couldn't *feel* it. Maybe if he had said something. But he just...grinned."

"What about Roger? I bet he had something to say."

"Yes, aha, Roger. He was like a machine gun gone crazy: 'Buster! You better cut this out, Buster! You better leave her alone, fat man!' He was shouting and pounding his fist into the table, rattling everything..."

"I bet Morry said something then, I bet that stopped him grinning."

"No, Mother, his face did not move—like it was carved—only tears started rolling out his black slit eyes. After a minute his fat gold cheeks were shiny and tears were dropping off his chin, but his grin did not loosen. Roger shut up then. It was probably the only thing could've shut him up. He had my elbow and was steering me out of there, but my heel snagged on the carpet. I turned to free it, and back at the table Morry was just leaning forward, plunging the end of that cigar into the flame, which flared. He sat back behind a ball of smoke which swirled round and round...that bastard." Hazel made a fist and rubbed her eye with it.

"And you were dressed up so nice, too." The grandmother smoothed the reddish hair back off Hazel's forehead.

Amanda began to creep forward.

"I swear that's the only time I ever saw him light a cigar. He always just sucks them until the end gets soggy and yellow juice dribbles out the corners of his mouth."

"I know, Honey. Shshsh..."

"Bastard."

"I know. Why don't you lie down here awhile and rest?"

Amanda pressed against her mother's wool-covered thigh. It was hard as filled plastic, like a giant Barbie's leg.

The two women noticed her in unison. The grandmother fluttered a hand to Amanda's head. Hazel glanced around her hand, then cringed toward the lamp, thinking, "Oh my baby shouldn't see me like this. A baby shouldn't see her mother crying."

Amanda began to pet her mother's thigh. "What's wrong, Hazel?"

"Ssht." The grandmother pressed Amanda's head. "Don't call your mother Hazel. She's your mother! Children call their mothers Mother."

Amanda tilted her head, trying to peek under Hazel's hand. "What's wrong?"

"It's just a headache," Hazel spoke into her wet palm, fuzzing her voice.

DEDE AND ME
Herman Bingham

DeDe lived with just his mom in a small, silver trailer in a trailer court
we used to call "Frog Town" because there was a huge, four-foot statue of
a green frog at the entrance of the court. The giant frog sat in between
homemade signs that said "IN ONLY" and "OUT ONLY" and DeDe used
to joke that the signs were mainly for his Mom.

I didn't know DeDe too well from in school. He was in the dumb class
even though he wasn't really that stupid; he was smart in his own way.
But most of the Frog Town kids were in the dumb class and so was
DeDe. I was in the smart class, so we never had anything but gym
together, and I never had gym because of my asthma. But DeDe and I
would get together after school a lot, when a lot of the other kids went to
catechism, and we would play on the black-top or smash windows or
chase the littler kids or walk to my house and talk. One time we snuck
into the fireworks factory, and on the way out I cut my ankle real bad on
the barbed wire. DeDe knew all about wrapping it up right, and he
carried me nearly all the way to my house after I couldn't hop anymore.
He even helped me make up a lie to tell my folks.

One day it had just started to rain when we climbed into the school
bus. It was the first day it hadn't rained, but once it got cooler, when the
sun was going down, the rain started. I was mad. I folded my arms over
my briefcase and kicked the quilted aluminum back of the seat in front of
me. I didn't have my hat, I didn't have my raincoat or my rubbers, and
every time it rained I got sick. I prayed that it would stop raining before
we got to Frog Town and that Mrs. Bowers had made a good dinner with
meat and vegetables. I had missed enough school as it was. DeDe wasn't
even sitting with me. He was in the back seat, facing the girl he had been
talking with since after school, the one who made us miss the first bus,
the bus we could have got on before it started raining. I turned around
every once in a while and glared at him, but he wasn't looking at me. He
was too busy joking with her. Every time I looked, he was pointing to a
different part of her body; once I saw him pointing at her knees, another
time he was pointing at her neck and who knows what else when I wasn't
looking. She got off, twiddled her fingers "bye" to him from the sidewalk,
and we drove away. Finally DeDe sat down with me.

I asked him what that was all about and told him I was mad because
we missed the bus, where we could've been dry, and now I was probably
going to get sick, and my parents would never let me go over to his
trailer again. DeDe just told me, "Don't get sick," and said it was
important that he talked with her. I wanted to know what was so
important, and he told me he wanted to know if she had any hair yet and
if she was going to show him. I didn't understand what he was talking
about. He just said it wasn't important to me but it was important to him
and we should just leave it at that until later. I said I was still mad, and
he said I'd get over it.

There wasn't any corner to drop us off at the trailer courts, so the bus
just dropped us off in the mud. When I got out, I stepped in some soft
tire tracks and slipped. I lost my balance but didn't fall. DeDe caught me.

But my briefcase went flying and landed flat in a puddle, and the mud cupped over the side of my shoe and slithered down inside. I started crying. DeDe laughed. He asked me, "You still cry?" and that made me feel worse, but I stopped anyway and rubbed my face with the cuff of my windbreaker. The orange bus popped and drove away. I turned around and watched it, feeling very alone, more alone then I ever felt, even when my parents spent all that time with my grandmother when she first went into the hospital. Everything was so strange. I had only seen Frog Town from the street, driving past. Now there it was in all its gloom: the chipped, green frog, nearly as tall as I was; the sour, gray stones; no grass; the cardboard cartons of gardens; old, dilapidated cars; and millions of bicycles and bicycle parts—handlebars, grips with and without streamers, wheels without all the spokes, broken chains, every color fender you could think of, and bent-up forks. DeDe picked out my briefcase from the puddle and wiped if off on the stones. The leather got scratched and ruined. I didn't even want it anymore. Rain rolled down my face to my shakey chin. I wanted to go home.

DeDe handed me my case and kicked a big piece of cardboard, a flattened box, over the wettest groove of mud so we could get across. As soon as we stepped on it, water came over the sides and drowned our shoes. I hopped off the box and landed in some medium softish mud that sucked my shoe off my foot. DeDe laughed, stopped when he looked at me, and plucked the loafer out of the mud. "Don't scrape it off!" I shouted. "I'll wear it like that." But the shoe was real heavy.

We half-ran past the four-foot frog and the "IN/OUT" signs, and that's when DeDe joked that they were mostly for his mom. I didn't get it and didn't care. I could already feel the beginnings of a sore throat and wanted to get into his trailer, take off my clothes, and get dry. Then I thought, Great, I bet they don't even have a drier in that crummy little shoebox that they live in. Then I felt bad because I knew DeDe didn't have a father and I shouldn't be mad at him for things he didn't have. I thanked God that I had all the things I had: a mom and dad; grandparents; and a warm, dry bed. We scuttled to his silver trailer-home and huddled by the door, under the small awning.

DeDe tried the door but it was locked. I told him to use his key but he said he didn't have any key. His mom was always at home when he got home. "In fact..." DeDe put his fist over his mouth. I saw little whiffs of mist coming from my mouth and I started jittering up and down. DeDe curled his index finger back and forth in one of his secret "come here" type gestures. He tiptoed around the trailer and I followed him without enthusiasm. The rain was getting in my jacket and seeping down my shirt. DeDe propped himself up on a couple of large tanks at the end of the trailer and peeked into a window with nearly closed curtains. His feet were off the ground and he was leaning forward like a gymnast with his arms locked straight. They were shaking. He jumped down and whispered, "Come here," and bunched up his eyebrows and tilted his head like you do when you're serious about wanting someone to come. He laced his fingers and curled his shoulders down for me to put my foot in his hands. He always had to help me like that to get over fences. He'd boost me up and make me spread his shirt or jacket over the barbed wire. Then I'd sit there until he climbed over to the other side and helped me down. Except that one time I was mad and had to do everything myself, because I didn't want any of his help, and gashed up my ankle falling over that barbed wire. This time he just wanted to boost me up onto the tanks so I could look inside. I thought he was going to show me how to break into his house, like the time I showed him how to break into my house. So he lifted me onto the tanks and I knelt on the top of the lower one and sat back on my heels. DeDe kept one hand on my back and moved beside the tanks, facing me, his back to the trailer, and asked me what I saw. I looked at him and he smiled. He could really smile like a million dollars. I kind of smiled and bent down to peep inside the little triangle not covered up by the curtains.

"What do you see?" he whispered.

I could see all the way to the other end of the trailer because it wasn't very long or very wide.

"I see a rocking chair." I was whispering back even though I didn't know why. I was just whispering because he was.

"What else?"

"I see a little table with a vase on it. Is that your kitchen table?"

"That's the *only* table. Forget that stuff. What do you see up by the window? Like right on the other side?"

I had to press my forehead into the glass and close one eye. I cupped one hand over my open eye and screwed it around the dark triangle. Just below the window, just inside, what I had been missing all along, in plain sight, was a couple, a man and a woman or girl, naked, with the fat, pimple-backed man heaving and rocking over the young girl whose eyes were squeezed shut and whose mouth was open and round, opening wider and then dilating smaller again and round. I thought, Wow, this is great. I wiped the dripping rain from the window and looked even harder. So that's what they're talking about. I turned to DeDe. "They're fucking, right?" He said, "Sshhh. Right." Wow. I giggled and put my ear to the wet window. I heard moaning and yelling. I looked back inside the little room. The curtains, flimsy as they were, let in a red light that bathed the two of their bodies. The young girl was bucking up and down and scratching long dark lines into the fat man's behind. Her nails were long and unpainted. I stared with more excited curiosity. One of my brother's friends once showed me a magazine of some people playing volleyball without any clothes on. There were other pictures of people lying naked by a pool and everyone seemed very comfortable and friendly. I told my parents and they yelled at my brother and called up the kid's folks, and after that I was more and more curious as to what the big deal about being naked was. I asked my brother but he wouldn't tell me because he didn't want to get in trouble. Another kid from school brought some cards with animals on top of each other with long, long penises disappearing into other animals. DeDe told me that was called fucking and that everybody does it once they're old enough to have jobs. Everybody does it after they come home from work or else when there's nothing to watch on TV. I told him that I didn't think my parents did it, because if they did, I would definitely have seen something like that; and he said my parents didn't *have* to do it, because they were married.

I watched the fat man collapse on top of the girl. All I could see was his back and her knees cocked over his hips. He joggled a couple times.

The girl was saying something with long, puckered lips while she drew the man's face into her neck. He kissed up and down her shoulder. She ran her nails lightly all over his back, sometimes dragging a nail on a pimple.

I stared a little while longer. DeDe asked, "Are they through?" I said, "I guess so, they stopped." "OK," he said, "get down."

I turned around and sat on the top of the tank. DeDe helped me down. Suddenly I realized I was drenched, but it didn't register too deep. I was in a kind of shock. I finally knew what the guys were talking about. I could tell them I had seen it and I knew none of them had ever really seen it. I was really happy.

We sloshed around to the side door under the awning. It was too late to care about being wet and cold. DeDe held his fist before knocking on the door.

"Any questions?"

"No. Just now I know what it is."

"Aren't you even curious about who that was?"

"I don't know. I didn't think about it. I guess you must know them."

"Naw. I don't know who the guy is."

"No? Then what're they doing in there?"

"They're fucking. The woman's my mom."

I wanted to shout. I looked at DeDe but he didn't look any different. He had known what was inside; he had boosted me up on the tanks; he had asked me what I saw! I felt scared. My insides burst and I remembered every detail, every pimple on the back, every scratch, every shove. The girl was too young to be his mom, but I had never thought at all that they were people he knew. But they had to be. He had to know them. They were in his house. I hadn't thought of that at all, and all the pictures of what I had just seen raced through my mind like a runaway movie. I smiled, scared.

"Who are they really?"

"I told you. I don't know who the guy is."

He knocked on the door.

DeDe always joked with me. I tried to figure out who the girl could be. He didn't have any sisters, which was good, because I would have hated to think he would let me watch his sister doing that with someone. The man's penis was very big and must have hurt her when it disappeared inside her. It looked like it hurt. Her face was all twisted and she was scratching him. Why do people have to do that? What does that have to do with work? And I thought, if I have to hurt someone like that just because I'm not married, I'm going to get married as soon as I can. The more I thought about it, the more scared I got.

He knocked again. The door sounded like a snare drum. The girl called out, "Just a minute," and then, "Who is it?" DeDe just knocked again. The inside door opened. DeDe opened his door and stepped up to walk in. He looked at the girl and then down at me.

"Gerry, this is my mom. Mom, this is Gerry." He squeezed past her. She looked at her hand and wiped it on her dress over her hip and offered it to me.

"So pleased to meet you, Gerry. You one of DeDe's friends? DeDe doesn't bring many of his friends over. You must be his *best* friend. C'mon in and get out of the rain, get out of those clothes. I'll just put them in the oven for a little bit and dry them off." Without a breath she turned full circle to find DeDe. "You just getting home from school now? Aren't you a little late? I was just telling *my* friend I was going to get worried if you didn't show up pretty soon. And it's still raining. Dave? David? Are you going to be in there long? I really need to use the facilities." She winked at me as if we had a secret. I just stared at her. "Now, you two better get out of those clothes before you catch cold or something worse. Wouldn't that be something if people started saying every time one of DeDe's friends came to visit they caught a cold?"

DeDe slammed his fist against the bathroom door a few times. The fat man yelled, "Hey!"

"His name's Dave? Hey, Dave! Next time you fuck my mom, don't be leaving your dirty rubbers on the floor by the bed, you asshole!" DeDe's mom gasped. Her hands went to her mouth. "What are you—"

"Shut up, you whore." DeDe was shouting. I shivered by the little table with the vase. "Hey, c'mon, Dave. Let us see your fat face. We could only see your ass from the window." DeDe's mom gasped again. She moaned.

"Not now, DeDe. Not in front of your friend."

DeDe just kept banging on the door, screaming. From inside, the fat man shouted, "Show some respect for your mother."

DeDe grabbed his own elbows and threw his shoulder again and again into the bathroom door. His mom took her hands from her face and stepped quickly to DeDe.

"No! DeDe! NO! We can't afford another door. PLEASE!"

I couldn't breathe. I couldn't move. It was like a dream in which something terrible is happening, but you can't move, you can't save yourself. DeDe had kicked down the door but the man kept pressing it flat between them as a shield. DeDe tried shoving it to one side and then the other, but the little bathroom was too small and the door stayed between them.

The fat man shouted, "I don't want to HURT him, I don't want to HURT him," and DeDe kept screaming over and over, "I'm going to KILL you, you fat ugly son-of-a-bitch." DeDe's mom was caught in the narrow hall, yelling at him, with her long, white arms wrapped around his head, trying to pull him away, kicking him. I started to scream in short bursts and DeDe looked up at me through his mom's arms and wrenched himself free, shoving the bathroom door in one last time. His mom started crying. I stopped. She was shaking and crying and wiping the blood off her knuckles. The bathroom door didn't move. DeDe gave me that look and tilted his head and said, "Let's go. You don't deserve this. We'll call your mom."

He walked ahead of me in a straight line, not even avoiding the puddles. I stayed behind, taking shorter steps, trying to walk around most of the water. I still hadn't time to catch my breath and every few steps I thought I was going to cry again. I took deep breaths and held my hands over my chest. DeDe just kept walking, marching, with his neck buried deep in his shoulders. He was leaning forward and his hands were shoved inside the pockets of his windbreaker.

He didn't even stop or slow down when he got to the phone booth. He threw open the door and the whole glass room shook. One hand picked up the receiver while the other slipped in the dime. He dialed, waited, and was done and out before I even got there. I could see his fists inside the pockets of his jacket. He paced nervously and wouldn't look at me or his trailer. The sun was almost down and the sky—except for the red horizon to the west and the dark violet horizon to the east—was a uniform gray rain cloud. DeDe pressed his fists down into his jacket hard, so hard he almost straightened out his arms. When he stopped and the jacket slid back onto his shoulders, I could see the blue indentation made from his collar pressing so hard on the back of his neck. He jittered and paced, looking all around, everywhere. "Your mom said she'll be right here," he told me. Then after a while he said, "Now you get the idea."

TRAIN RIDE WITH AN EX-CON
Janet Marie Brown

The A train came roaring down the tracks from the Monroe station and squealed to a stop at the Jackson subway. As I headed for one of the doors, a man mumbled something. I saw him from the corner of my eye, but I didn't acknowledge him, because I wasn't sure he was addressing me. I thought someone else would answer him. Then he said louder, this time definitely talking to me, "Does this train go to Sixty-third?"

"Sixty-third and what?" I asked, concentrating on boarding the train. "Ashland."

"Yes." By this time, I was stepping through the door. I still hadn't really seen him, only looked at him. Expertly, my eyes took in the space of the train. I observed that all the seats facing frontwards were at least partially filled, so I picked an empty seat facing backwards, instead of sharing one of the others. I was hoping he wouldn't sit next to me, but he did. He rattled a lot of packages. I'd seen a pair of black boots sticking out of one of them. On the bar in front of us he hung some clothing of red material, covered in plastic. A yellow cleaning ticket was attached to the plastic by one staple. It flapped around, and I doubted that it would stay on until he got home. I stared straight ahead, pretending not to notice him, and I prayed that he wasn't going to badger me to buy some of his junk. I took a sneaky peek at him. He was dark, almost black. His mustache was thick and black, but his beard was sort of flat. He sported a long, black reefer coat, the kind that looks tailor-made and has a deep V-neck. There were tiny balls of lint and strands of thread clinging to the wool. And then, from the corner of my eye, I saw him bend and reach into the white, plastic shopping bag between his feet. Here it comes, a thief's sales pitch. Hell, naw, I don't want no shoes, boots, jewelry or whatever, I thought, as I looked straight ahead. It would've been goofy to look out the window, because we were still in the subway. I would've just seen my own face and my burgundy coat, because the wall beyond the window was black.

"What size do dese look like to you," he said, releasing bad cigarette and stale reefer breath and leaning over a little. I turned to see a full view of the black boots I'd spotted earlier. He held the women's dress boots together in one hand, and I could tell they would stop at the calf. I took one into my hand, aware that the material felt like it looked—shiny and slippery. I wear a size seven, and it looked too little for me. So I told him it was probably a six, but I wanted proof. I studied the sole, searching for an engraved number, but had no luck. Then I peered inside and found a tag, revealing the number 6½. I showed it to him.

"I think dey'll fit her," he said, and being polite, I kept facing him, despite his BREATH. He'd said *her*! I was relieved to find out these were meant for someone and not for sale.

"Does she have a size-six foot?"

"Yeah, she got dem small feet—REAL little feet."

"Well, they'll probably fit then."

"Yeah, cuz in boots she wear a six-and-a-half or seven, but in shoes, she can jest wear a six. I think dey'll fit. Dey look like her foot," he said, inspecting the boot in his hand. I handed him the boot back, and he gave them both another look before setting them back in the bag. As he did this, I looked out the window, as if to end the conversation. It felt good to be away from that BREATH. He got quiet too. The train whistled and rocked, and the beige project buildings, not the el, seemed to be moving in the dusk. I looked over at the tired, middle-aged, working class people in front of us, facing us. I knew all of them had been staring, listening, and thinking either that I shouldn't be talking to him or that I was naive and "Shame on him."

He made a movement, and my eyes spontaneously went from the people to the man by my side. I casually watched him pick up the badly torn Carson's bag that was taking up some of the aisle. Producing a huge, red, valentine heart-shaped box of candy with a pink, plastic rosebud in the center, he said, "I got her dis cuz I forgot to git her something for Valentine's Day."

"Ooh, that's pretty. She'll really be surprised. You must've been in a good mood today," I said, holding my breath in preparation for the odor of his.

"Dis was on sale," he said, and I thought, "well, hell, Valentine's Day WAS a week and a half ago." But I just smiled. He folded the torn bag over the valentine and set it down beside him. Then he bent down and started digging under the women's boots in the shopping bag. Out came a gigantic brown and tan cowboy boot. It seemed freakish compared to the dainty black ones I'd just seen. It looked like something Paul Bunyan would wear.

"I got me dese."

They really looked hideous to me, but I said, "Those look nice too." I must've said it shakily, because he said "huh?" I repeated myself more firmly the next time. He put them back in the bag, making sure her boots were on top. He sat back, only to start rummaging in his coat pocket closest to me. I was ready to be left to my thoughts, even though I'd adjusted my senses to his BREATH. So once again I turned toward the window and studied the backyards of the three-flat buildings. Since it was getting dark, I couldn't make out some of the signs of poverty, which were clear in the daylight, such as piled garbage in cans, on porches, on steps, in grassless yards, and the broken windows with paper stuffed in the holes or taped over them.

Then I blocked the buildings out so I could see his reflection. He was fidgeting. I saw a wad of gold chains with price tags looped around them. Taking a quick glance to my right, I saw that he had a lot of chain bracelets in a tangled chaos. One price tag had a six and some zeros, so I figured it was six dollars. To myself I said, "Umhm, I was right. He DOES want to sell me something." I hoped he wouldn't get loud when I turned him down. "He'll probably get up and ask everybody on the car." He kept working at the knots, and I turned back to the window. I pictured Jay's handsome face with those pretty deep eyes and thought about how tomorrow I'd give him a long kiss before stopping to speak or even look at him.

The man snapped me out of my daydream by nudging my arm and asking, "Can you read dat and tell me if it says fourteen carat." I took the bracelet and squinted at the familiar hook, but I couldn't make out *14 kt* or anything else. The scrawling was probably designed to fake out a person who doesn't know any better. I immediately noticed that he'd removed the price tag.

"No, it doesn't say fourteen carat," I said, handing it back.

"It's real gold, though," he said. I thought he was trying to convince me so that I'd buy it. But then he picked up the torn Carson's bag and made that rattling paper noise until he had uncovered his valentine's box. He put the bracelet inside. The pieces of chocolate were shielded by a cellophane covering. I was puzzled because he didn't try to sell me one. "Monique [he probably meant Monet] makes good gold. It don't ever tarnish."

Realizing it was a good imitation, I didn't explain that gold-colored costume jewelry wasn't real, and she still better not take a bath in it.

"You know I'm jest being nice to her. She ain't ma woman. We're just frien's. She was good to me when I was in de joint. She came to visit me, an' you know I jest wanna show ma gratefulness. I'm on ma feet now, so it's my turn. She WAS ma woman, though, fo' I went to de joint. But you know, things change. I'll do anything fo' her, too."

I nodded and commented, "That's nice" or "Right" now and then. I showed no reaction to his confession that he'd been in "de joint." I was really interested, and it must've shown, because he continued to tell me more, and I didn't smell his BREATH much anymore.

"You know people get the wrong impression when you say you been in de joint. Dey think you ain't no good. But I jest wanna have something outta life. Yeah, I sell me some lil' drugs. I want things.

"I was in dere fo three years, but I'm on de right track now. Dey got me on attempted murder. Dis motherfucker was stickin' me up with a knife, so I shot him. I'll do de same thing again if somebody tries to take ma shit from me."

I pictured him dressed in a leather jacket and jeans, standing on a corner one night. A man, much skinnier than him, comes up and tries to act casual by feeling his worn, faded blue jean jacket and then his windowpane-stitched, elephant-leg jeans pockets, as if only looking for a match for the cigarette hanging from his chapped lips. When he's sure Flatbeard is the only one around for a couple of blocks, he pulls out a switchblade. The blade is gleaming. "Gimmie yo' wallet, asshole," he drools, and gestures with his free hand. Flatbeard reaches in his jacket's inside pocket, and before he brings his hand out good, he's shooting a pistol that's so little it looks like a toy. The first shot puts a hole in the man's stomach, and his eyes bulge from the surprise. As the robber throws his hands up in the air, blood spurts out to form a stain on his blue jean jacket, and then a bullet gets his neck, and the last one gets his forehead. Flatbeard smiles and says, "Motherfucker," while the robber's body flinches on the glass-speckled sidewalk.

"Wasn't that self defense?" I asked, wondering if it happened anything like I pictured it and wondering if he was telling the truth.

"YEAH."

"They didn't believe he was robbing you?"

"Yeah, they knew it, but dey said I shot him. See, dey was wondering how I had so much and didn't work. I jest know how to make my big bucks. I was born with de gift. Dat's all right, I'm ready fo' dey asses now, but I ain't gonna let dem catch me no more.... I'm a good person, I jest want so much fo' I die."

I wanted to discourage him, but I knew it'd sound stupid for me to say, "You should do what you know is right; that way nobody will be looking for you. Since you have a record, they are expecting you to break the law and come visit "de joint" again. So fool them. You can out-slick them by being law-abiding." I just kept my mouth shut, though.

"You a nice woman. You got a husband?"

"No, but I'm engaged." I lied to insure that he wouldn't be tempted to request my phone number.

"Well, I hope he don't mess up, 'cause he'll be sorry."

"Thank you," I said, rising to get off. He told me his name (but I can't remember it), and I told him mine—Sandra, the name of my best friend.

"It was nice talking to you," he said, as I stepped over his pile of packages.

"You too," I said truthfully. "Have a nice evening, and I hope those boots fit her."

After a long pause and right when the doors slipped open, letting the wind blow at me, he said, "Thank you." I could tell by the soft look on his hard, flat-beard face that he was really thanking me.

BULIMIA
Rochelle Weber

Every Monday, Wednesday and Saturday, Susan entered the ladies' room at Marshall Field, trying not to look as furtive as she felt. The ladies' room was long and narrow, with walls painted an institutional pink and a faint smell of urine and pine-scented disinfectant in the air.

A slender woman in her mid-twenties, platinum blonde hair fashionably cut, Susan always carried two pink boxes from Heinemann's Bakery, tied closely with string.

She glanced around the room and busied herself at the mirror until a customer left the third stall, washed her hands, and walked out. At last, Susan was alone. She chose a stall in the center of the room, entered and locked the door. After hanging her purse on the coat hook, she removed her sweater and hung it over her purse. Sitting carefully on the toilet, she slowly and quietly pulled the string off of the first box. The grating of the string seemed immensely loud in the small, echoing space. She paused as the smell hit her—the rich, lush, brown smell of freshly baked chocolate cream pie.

She daintily lifted a curl of chocolate from the fluffy, white, whipped cream top and dipped it (as you would a potato chip) through the cream, into the still-warm chocolate filling. She sighed as her mouth filled with the velvety-smooth, rich-tasting pudding mingled with the cool, milky taste of the whipped cream. Susan used the chocolate curl as a scoop until it began to melt between her fingers, then ate it and selected another one.

The chocolate curls worked as utensils, until she had eaten all of them. With only half of the pie gone, Susan resorted to finishing with her fingers. She ate frantically but carefully, trying to be as quiet as possible and trying not to make a mess. She leaned over the pie on her lap to keep from getting chocolate on her blouse. The minute she heard the door swing open and the murmur of voices in the store, she stopped eating and sat frozen, holding the creamy chocolate pudding in her mouth, waiting for the other customers to leave.

Eating the crust was always difficult. She was careful not to drop any crumbs on the floor or on herself. It was very important that no one see her or hear her eating. She couldn't leave any evidence at all—no stains or crumbs on her clothing.

She ate both pies as quickly as she could. Finally finished, Susan closed the boxes and carefully retied the strings so that it would look as though she simply had taken two pies into the ladies' room and brought two pies back out again. She couldn't let anyone suspect that the boxes were empty.

This was always the hardest part. Susan sat still and listened for a minute; hearing no sounds, she bent down and checked under the stalls for other feet. Satisfied that she was completely alone, Susan removed her blouse and hung it over her sweater and purse. Then, kneeling before the toilet, she held her hair back with her left hand and stuck the index finger of her right hand down her throat. She wiggled her finger around until she began to gag and finally vomit.

Having eaten the pies as quickly as she could, Susan hadn't given them a chance to begin to be digested. They weren't yet mixed with the acids in her stomach and hadn't started to curdle. They tasted and felt just as good coming up as they had going down.

When the spasms stopped, Susan flushed the toilet, put her blouse on, and left the small cubicle to rinse her mouth. Although the pie hadn't mixed with her stomach acid, there was still enough acid coming up at the end to cause tooth decay. She then sprayed her mouth with Binaca. Susan went through almost as much Binaca as pie, because she was afraid someone might smell something unusual on her breath—traces of the chocolate or of the acid.

After retrieving her cashmere sweater and purse from the hook, she combed her hair and fixed her lipstick before leaving the ladies' room. She always carried the empty pie boxes out of the store and down the street for several blocks, tossing them into a trash basket in a quiet area. Temporarily sated, she would turn toward home.

STOPPING AT BALISTRARI'S
Arnie Raiff

The truck rattled and sputtered its black smoke as it bumped along down the middle of Harrison Street along the old streetcar tracks in the center of the cobblestones, the rails a thin gray parallel line of metal. There was no streetcar clanging down the street. Ben pulled alongside one of the new diesel buses and leaned past David to gaze at it. They were stopped at Kedzie Boulevard. Ben looked the bus over from front to back as if he were studying it. He read the advertisement along its side. It showed a young woman in a sleeveless blue dress tilting her head back and taking a long cool drink of Coca-Cola; her blond hair was caught in the wind. Bright, red Coca-Cola circles were on either side of her and underneath the words: "Things go better with Coke." Ben pulled himself upright behind the steering wheel and turned to David with a smile: "Like to have one of those drinks when we get to Balistrari's Grocery, David?" David smiled back at his father and he could feel the muscles in his arms tighten and that feeling of being high up fill him again with a giddy delight. He puffed out his chest and smiled back at his father and he felt warm inside again like it was a special day. He sat very still now with his hands tucked underneath his legs against the black plastic seat. The flies buzzed around him but he didn't move. And the truck percolated at the stop but the thought of a cool Coca-Cola at the next grocery stop made him want to be very still and hopeful.

Ben pulled the truck across Kedzie Boulevard in front of the diesel bus, crossing the intersection ahead of it and its foul-smelling smoke. A trolley bus stood at the cross street with hard strands of coiled wire caught in a cable high above near the lamp posts. The coiled wire was caught on rollers and moved with the bus as it glided to a stop next to the curb. And as the passengers boarded and left the bus, David watched them as if he were watching a movie. They had a dreamy, hot, steamy appearance in the bright sunshine.

Squeaking, the truck rumbled over the old streetcar tracks towards Lawndale Avenue, where the Balistrari Grocery Store stood on the corner, tucked into the side of a massive yellow-brick building. Ben knew when he made his first stop that he had to convince Balistrari that the new frozen products were worth stocking. For Ben, the sales part of the job was a promotion. This promotion was the first step, he thought. Fifteen years on the trucks was more than enough. Strikes, low pay, and the back-breaking work was finally too much for him at forty-six. Next year, he wanted out. He wanted off the trucks for good and to work from behind the steering wheel of a company car—those sleek new Ford sedans. And he'd be wearing a suit instead of the thick cotton freezer coat. Two years ago, he had been caught between two trucks and had broken both legs. They still ached every time he walked or climbed in and out of the cab. Next year no more trucks, he thought to himself again.

He looked over at his son, who was hanging out of the window and waving his arm out the side of the truck. "Get in here. You want your arm cut off?" And David pulled himself inside, quickly putting his hands under his legs like before. For a moment he'd been lost in the breeze as the truck rolled along.

Ben jerked the truck to a stop and rolled it in next to the curb in front of

Balistrari's. He took his metal clipboard from the seat and jammed open the door, which squealed on its hinges. He pulled his 5 foot, 10 inch frame down, hitting the running board with his left workshoe while David clambered out the other side. The brightness of the sun made Ben squint as he crossed in front of the truck and then moved along its side to the back doors.

He stood behind the truck, checking the items he'd try to sell to Sam Balistrari. He glided his pencil along the page and made a few checks next to some. David stood next to his father with growing impatience. He could feel the heat seep into him. When the truck was moving there was some excitement, but he couldn't stand still. He bounced on his toes, pressing his hands inside his jeans pockets. He hoped his father would suddenly swing the metal doors open to the freezer so he could jump inside and get out of the heat. He flexed his muscles like he was in front of a mirror and he was a strongman. He'd show his father how strong he was. Ben looked at him with a smile: "Come on, strongman, let's check out the stock. I'll introduce you to Sam." And Ben laughed to himself because the pleasure of having David with him was coming back, making the day special to him too. A wave of giddiness caught him as he swung his arm around David's shoulder and drew him towards the grocery store.

Balistrari's Grocery Store smelled of oldness. Dust-laden boxes of Cheerios and Wheaties, stacked almost to the ceiling, stood side by side. Next to them were yellow boxes of Arm and Hammer baking soda and baking powder, also mounting to the ceiling. Then more boxes. Boxes of Oxydal detergent in rainbow colors and bright orange boxes of Tide and the white fronts of Ivory Flakes with a cherubic baby's face on the blue and white front cover. All dust-covered, dulling their colors. Next to them hung a wooden pole with metal pinchers at the top end. Balistrari, a small chubby man, used the pinchers to grab the boxes off the top.

The other smells of cheese and Italian meats greeted the boy and his father as the door, chiming open, announced their presence.

Balistrari stood behind a white marble-hard counter where he was intently marking with the stub of a pencil a brown paper bag that lay flat on the counter. An elderly woman stood looking down at the pencil scratching out the numbers, watching him mark the numbers to make sure he wasn't making mistakes. She looked over her spectacles that she wore low on her nose. She had on a clean, faded green cotton dress with large white flowers printed on it. Her black shoes were laced to the top, the heels thick and elevated. The shoes looked like men's shoes. She wore silk stockings that were rolled down to her ankles. The dress hung down just above the rolled-down stockings. Balistrari, just finishing up his addition, wore a butcher's apron over his shirt and pants.

"Do you want me to put your groceries in the paper bag, Mrs. Batko, or should I just put them into your shopping bag?" He pointed to the blue cloth bag that she held at her side.

"Put them in the brown bag first. I use it for garbage." And then she pointed, impatiently wagging her fingers at the bag on the counter.

"Fine, fine, Mrs. Batko." His voice was louder than necessary. "You're sure you wouldn't like to try the new frozen orange juice?" He looked at Ben, who stood next to the ice cream freezer. "Special price just for you—thirty-nine cents. You tell me if it doesn't taste just as good as fresh squeezed." He was already putting the Ivory Flakes and the bottle of milk into the brown bag with the baked beans and the cans of peas and corn.

"No, no, my husband says it tastes like chemicals. You sold me it last week." She shook her head and then added, "What, you can't get anyone to try it, Mr. Balistrari? Your wife doesn't like squeezing oranges?"

Balistrari smiled at her. "My wife loves the stuff. I drink it every morning. Better than fresh. Better than squeezing! You squeeze and only a drop comes out. Your husband shouldn't be so finicky." He finished putting in a small bag of oranges and asked her to hand him the cloth shopping bag. "Last chance. One can could last you a whole week."

She handed him the bag and smiled. "Okay, okay, give me a can but if he don't drink it, it's the last time. Maybe he'll get used to the taste. A whole week, tch, tch, tch. Go on before I change my mind."

Balistrari walked from behind the counter to the ice cream freezer and brought her back a can. "You owe me four dollars and twenty-nine cents." She handed him a five dollar bill. While he rang up her sale, she looped the cloth bag around her pale arm and let it hang there. He handed her the change and she put the loose coins in a small change purse and stuck that in her bag as well. "Remember, tell Max not to be so particular. Have a nice day, Mrs. Batko."

She smiled. "Good morning, Mr. Balistrari."

When she turned towards the door, she noticed Ben and his son standing near the ice cream freezer. Without paying any attention she swept past them, holding her bag tightly against her dress. Ben watched her leave the store. He was mildly pleased that she took the orange juice and he wondered if he could sell Balistrari the latest frozen foods on the market. The door chimed when it opened and closed. The heat from outside wafted into the damp grocery store. Ben went up to the counter while David looked eagerly at the baseball cards, bubble gum and candy stacked behind a glass case next to the counter. He was thirsty. He moved down the aisle to where he could see the heads of Pepsi-Cola bottles and Coke bottles and K-O pop and Orange Crush.

"Good to see her take that orange juice, Sam. But you can't beat fresh squeezed, we all know that. I thought she might not take it. That stuff'll sell, you'll see." Ben could hear himself talk and he hated the sound of his own voice. The sound reverberated inside of him but he knew he'd get used to this selling stuff. He had to get used to it. He couldn't work the truck anymore. "How's sales on the orange juice anyway? How's the peas selling?"

Balistrari came from behind the counter and walked over to the freezer and opened the top. "Come here and look for yourself."

Ben walked over, his clipboard against his chest, and peered down into the dark freezer. Twelve bright orange cans sat one on top of the other in stacks of six. He looked at his clipboard. He had given Balistrari twenty cans two weeks ago. "So you sold eight. That ain't too bad. I'll replace the eight. How'd the peas sell?" Balistrari flipped open another compartment. Only two cans of Birdseye green peas lay at the bottom. "Great," Ben said and winced and looked at his clipboard again. "I gave you twenty-four of those. How about another case? I got something new for you."

Balistrari flipped the freezer lid shut. "A case sounds good but that orange juice. I don't know. Maybe next time. Maybe after I sell out what I got. What's new?"

Ben walked back to the counter with Balistrari and laid his clipboard down. "Sam, the vegetables could sell good. I got green beans and corn. No salt to preserve them. Healthier, Sam. How about a case of each? First case be a little cheaper, you know."

Sam Balistrari liked Ben. He'd known him for years and he'd been using Beatrice products all that time. He always liked to make Ben's job a little easier because over the years Ben took back damaged products with no questions asked. It was a business relationship built on trust. So while Sam studied how he'd make room for the new frozen foods, he stared at the boy who hovered around the soda cooler. "Ben, you never introduced me to the boy."

Ben looked over at David standing by the cooler. "Sam, that's my son David; okay if he takes a pop?"

Sam touched his chin like he was thinking it over, but he was actually thinking about what to say to the boy. He finally walked over to the cooler, leaving Ben back at the counter. The smell of cool, stagnant water came up to him while he stood next to the boy. "So you're Ben's helper today, hey?" And Sam extended his hand to the boy. David took his hand tentatively, shyly, and tried to look around the heavy-set man to his father. "What kind of pop you want?"

David tried to look around Sam again but his vision was blocked. "Pepsi, if it's okay?"

Sam reached in the cooler, took a blue and red Pepsi and popped off the metal top on the opener at the side of the cooler. He handed it to David and walked back to Ben, who was checking his order. "I'll take those cases from you. I'll have to make room for 'em in the freezer but if I can sell those frozen peas I guess I can sell frozen corn and frozen green beans. Give me the two cases and another case of peas but none of that damn orange juice. Maybe this winter when oranges are scarce the stuff'll sell but I gotta have room for ice cream in this heat."

David stood by the cooler, slowly sipping his pop and watching the men, who stood down the aisle. The door suddenly swung open, sending off another peal of chimes.

A black man and his son came into the store looking around as if it were their first time. The man, dressed in overalls, wore a cap with the visor pulled down shadowing his eyes. His boy, who held his hand, was dressed much like David, with sneakers, jeans and a white T-shirt. They walked slowly down the aisle towards the counter where Ben and Sam stood going over the order. Sam was behind the counter making out a slip to give to Ben and Ben was marking his price sheet, about to hand it back to Sam, when the boy and his father reached the counter. The boy broke away from his father and walked sullenly down along where the glass case held the candy, baseball cards and bubble gum. When he got to the end of the case, he looked up and saw David, who was sipping his pop and staring at him. Their eyes met momentarily and then they both looked away from each other. They looked down at their gym shoes as if they had suddenly been embarrassed by an unwanted intimacy.

Sam raised his head to look at the black man, who removed his cap and was about to speak when Sam interrupted. His voice was thick, harsh and low and it seemed to hiss through the dark grocery store. "What's your business here?"

The man held his cap in both hands and twisted it and turned it around in his hands. "There's that sign outside," the man said.

Sam turned to Ben and looked at him as if they shared a secret. Ben stood there next to the black man holding his pencil poised at the sheet. "What sign?" Sam shot back.

The man kept turning the cap in his hands and there were specks of dried yellow paint on his hands and you could see the paint clearly as he turned the cap. "That sign about needing somebody to deliver groceries in the neighborhood. I ain't had regular work in a long time. Me and my son there could share the work." He turned his whole body so he was looking at his son while he finished his sentence.

Sam shot a look over at the boy, who looked down at the bottles of soda as if he wanted to ask about them. He sweated profusely and looked at David, who suddenly stopped drinking and held the bottle at his side trying to hide it. Sam kept looking at the boy standing next to the cooler. "Hey, get away from there, boy. You come over here where I can see you. Been lots a kids coming in here and taking pops without paying for them." He turned to Ben when he said this.

The boy shuffled over to stand next to his father. "You don't have any reason to talk to the boy that way. He don't want to take nothing from you, mister," the black man said.

Sam looked back at the man. "Don't tell me how to run my store. I been in business almost twenty-five years. Nobody ever come in here to tell me how to run my business and nobody's gonna start telling me how to run it now."

The man shifted the hat around and around in his paint-splattered hands. "About that job," he asked.

Sam leaned down on the counter now with the palms of both hands, his arms stiff, and looked down at the boy. "What job? That job got filled yesterday. Yep, I got a little kid in the neighborhood to run those groceries for me. Musta forgot to take the sign down. There ain't no job and if you ain't gonna be buying anything you can see I got business to take care of here." Sam turned to Ben. "I'll take those cases." And he handed Ben a slip of paper.

David held the pop by the neck at his side. The man put his cap on his head tightly, so it shadowed his face again. When he put his hands to his sides they were balled up in fists. Ben could see the fists from his side of the counter and David could see them from where he stood, but Sam had turned his back to the man and was putting away the price list Ben had handed him. When he turned around again, the man turned as well and took his son's hand and walked down the aisle towards the door. "There's nothing good for us here, son." The door chimed when he opened it, and it closed after he and his son had gone out.

Sam's heavy face was red with anger. "Damn it, Ben, this neighborhood's no good, I'm telling you. No damn good. If I don't get outta here soon. . . ." Sam folded his arms against his chest. "That must be the tenth fella that's come in here for that job since I put up that sign yesterday."

Ben said nothing and he was about to start for the door to fill Sam's order. But he couldn't help asking. "You mean that job's still open?"

Sam looked at Ben and chuckled under his breath. "Of course it's open. You think I'd hire a damn nigger to work here? Why, those good for nothings steal everything I own."

Ben said nothing. He looked at the floor. He had to do business with Sam and he knew it. And David watched, still holding the bottle next to his side. "What's he gonna do?" he wondered to himself. Ben stood there and took a breath and looked back into Sam's eyes. Sam stared back insolently as if to dare Ben to challenge him. And Ben whispered almost under his breath, "The neighborhood *is* changing, Sam."

"What?" Sam shot back the question.

And Ben, holding the clipboard at his side, said again, "The neighborhood *is* changing, Sam." But Ben's voice was unnaturally loud.

"You're damn right it's changing," Sam affirmed. "And those people don't belong where they ain't wanted."

It was another challenge to Ben. Ben looked around uncomfortably and saw David dumbly holding the soda at his side. "David, finish up that pop; we gotta get those cases outta the truck." David balked. He stared down at his hand as if frozen to the spot. "Damn it, David, I said finish that soda now. We've got deliveries to make."

And David, shocked into action, drank the soda down in a gulp, though he wasn't thirsty. He drank it down, put the empty bottle next to the cooler and followed his father to the door where the chimes rang when Ben opened the door. Ben waited there for David to join him, holding the door open. And as David walked down the aisle to reach his father, he realized that the day had suddenly lost some of the magic he had hoped for. The heat from outside smothered his breath and he felt blinded by the sun's sudden glare when he met his father at the door. The chimes rang again as the door closed behind them.

VAMPIRES
Wanda Welch

When our cousins Bubbie and Junebug came into our lives, my sisters and I were pretty excited. For one thing, it was the first time we ever met them. Nobody ever talked about them, at least not by name, and another thing is we ain't never known anybody that was a truck driver.

I mean, it all happened so fast. One minute me, Mama, Williemae, and Peg, we were all sitting on the front porch, talking about the neighborhood gossip, when this big ol' truck—I think it's called an 18-wheeler, Junebug told me, but I forget—anyway, this truck comes roaring and stirring up dust all over the place, looking like it had just appeared from out of the ground, from the dust itself, instead of from up the road.

Well, this truck stops right in front of our house. By the time the dust had cleared, and by the time we'd all stopped choking and strangling from it and getting it out of our hair, there standing before us was Junebug and Bubbie. The first thing I thought was how much they looked like Laurel and Hardy. Junebug was so tall, and Bubbie was so fat and short, until I reckon that's what most people would think the second they set eyes on them. The clothes that they were wearing didn't make their appearance seem any less funny. They had on some blue-jean farmer overalls and T-shirts that they wore underneath, some brown-looking pointy-toe cowboy boots, and New York Yankees baseball caps. They both had that same squared-off chin, pouty bottom lips, and high cheekbones that ran in my family, only it was put on two differently shaped faces, Bubbie's round one and Junebug's narrow one.

While we all stood on the porch watching them, they walked up to the house and onto the porch, and grabbed Mama around her round shoulders and waist and hugged her, laughing and heehawing all the while.

What Mama was saying with her lips and saying with her body was two different things. She was saying, "Why Bubbie, Junebug, it's good to see y'all," but Mama's body had stiffened like a tree. I thought it was kind of strange and wondered if anybody else had noticed it, but nobody seemed to. "What y'all doing down this way?" she asked. It should have been a question full of happiness and surprise, and it was full of surprise, but not happiness, it was more like fear and suspicion.

Mama's questions were lost among the questions that we had with these new-found relatives. There we were, me at age sixteen, Williemae, seventeen, and Peg, fourteen, and we'd never left Baton Rouge, not once. We'd never even been to the Mardi Gras, but our cousins had been to Chicago, New York, California, and other big cities, so we talked about all those places and their family in Arkansas, which is where they were from. This went on way past dinner time, late into the night.

After everybody had talked themselves out, we all just sat there on the porch looking at each other and the stars and listening to the insects and the creaking of the wood underneath that ol' rocking chair of Mama's.

Mama sat in her chair, rocking and looking at the sky as if she was praying. Bubbie spoke up, "Well, Aintee Viola, me and Junebug . . . see, we was hoping to stay here a spell, if you don't mind."

There was a silence that covered the noises of the night as we all waited for Mama to answer. She flicked a strand of graying hair out of her face with her round fat fingers, and I saw just how much she looked like a combination of the two men. Her long face looking like Junebug's and her body favored Bubbie's. Peg began to jump up and down and held her hands together, silently pleading for Mama to say yes. Mama turned around, startled-like, as if she had just heard Bubbie ask her the question that felt like he had asked her ages ago, or so it seem like to me. "I don't know where my manners are. Come on in the house and I'll get y'all something to eat and get y'all settled."

We all jumped up and started squealing and laughing, then we all went into the house, and while Mama was fixing dinner, me, Williemae, and Peg went to the bedroom we all shared and fixed it up so that our cousins would be comfortable for the night, and then we went and ate dinner.

Once we got Junebug and Bubbie settled in our room, me and Williemae changed into our nightclothes and headed for the living room sofa and love seat, trying to race to the sofa, because the love seat was too short and made for an uncomfortable sleep. Mama stopped us and told us to go to her room, because we would be sleeping with her and Peg in her bedroom. We didn't ask any questions, we did what we were told, because to ask questions or dispute her word would end up with us getting a good whipping.

Williemae plopped on the bed besides Peg, scooted her over with her behind, and grumbled, "I don't see how all of us are going to sleep in this bed. Mama's be-hind is too big, and Peg, your elbows are too pointed, and you just going to be pushing them into our sides all night." She puffed up her cheeks and pushed her lips out and hung her head down so that her long neck looked as if it was bent. Her hair was rolled in homemade rollers that she made by tearing strips from a brown paper bag, and they just flopped all over her head as she hung her head down, making her look like a big clumsy bird. Peg laughed and I joined her, not just laughing at Williemae, but at Peg and myself as well. We all looked like clowns. Peg had fell out the bed laughing, and the old gown of Mama's flopped and fell behind her. Her body was lost in it. All of us sat on the bed dressed in Mama's gowns, and I guess the presence of our cousins brought out the giddiness in me. Williemae tried to stop us from laughing and covered both our mouths with her hands, holding on until our eyes looked like they would pop out, and we burst out laughing in her hands. She wiped her hands on our clothes, implying that we had spit in them, and I pushed her, making her rollers shake back and forth on her head, and making us laugh again, until Mama came into the room. Then we quieted down as she sat on the bed.

"How come we all gotta sleep in here? Can't me and Ruthie sleep out in the living room? Peg can sleep with you, Mama," Williemae asked.

Mama looked at all of us, eyes wide with fear, and whispered, "I want all of us to stay together for as long as *they* stay in this house." We didn't need to ask who the "they" were, we knew she was talking about Junebug and Bubbie. "They vampires and they'll suck your blood out of you as sure as I live and breathe." Peg started to giggle, but Mama cut her off, "This ain't no joke. Remember when I use to tell y'all if you didn't be good, I would get some vampires to get you?" She didn't wait for our answer, for she knew we remembered. "Well, that's them."

"How you know that they're vampires?" I asked, unconvinced.

Mama shrugged. "They were born that way," she said matter of factly.

"What are we gonna do?" Williemae asked.

Peg cried, "Make them leave!"

"You better hush your mouth, before they hear you." Peg covered her mouth with her hands. "I can't just make them leave, they might get mad and kill us all."

"Ain't that what they're here for in the first place?" Williemae asked.

"I believe so," Mama answered.

"I'm scared!" Peg started crying.

"I don't believe it," I said.

Well, I was just too stubborn to believe them. I'm just the type of person that if you tell me you love me, I'd be inclined to ask why, how much, and how long. Besides, vampires are not real. So, about the third day of their visit, I was sitting on the porch with them listening to the crazy things that happened on their travels, and some of their dirty jokes and stuff, when I just came out and asked them, "Y'all really vampires?" There was a heavy silence, before June-bug took his hands out of his pockets and answered, "Yep."

"Well, I don't believe you," I said.

"Well, we are," Bubbie said.

"Y'all lying. Where's your vampire teeth then, huh?" I challenged them.

Bubbie got up from Mama's old rocking chair and walked toward me, until he stood in front of me, face to face, as short as he was, and said, "You're a nosy girl and I don't like nosy girls."

"And you are a liar," I said to him as he walked away, while Junebug sat on the porch stairs studying the boards. Finally, he looked up at me and said, "Ruthie, you just don't understand." Then he stood, ready to walk into the house. Before he left me alone to think, he stopped and said, "One word of advice to you, you're a young girl . . . no, a young woman. If you want to stay that way, don't go getting Bubbie all mad and fussed up, and doing anything stupid."

Later on that day, while Junebug and Bubbie was in the living room watching TV, we all went into the kitchen to prepare dinner. Williemae was crying silently to herself, tears streaming endlessly onto the fish that she was scaling, as her hands worked fast and thoroughly. Her left hand held the tail of the fish, while the right one held the semi-sharp knife that sliced the scales off the fish from tail to head, stopping only to turn the fish over or to get another one and start again.

I sat at the opposite end of the table, picking chitlins, watching her and Mama who was picking and cleaning greens, while Peg, who sat across from Mama, sat sniffing, and wiping away her tears before they could roll down her face. We didn't pay any attention to each other. We were lost in our thoughts, thinking about Junebug and Bubbie.

We had decided to kill them. Well, Mama had decided it for us. I still didn't believe it, any of it, not about the vampire stuff, or that we had plotted the death of our cousins. It was like a bad dream. What if we'd killed them, and they were lying? Then we'd have killed two innocent people. Besides, they were family and a person just don't kill their kinfolk. That's what I tried to tell Mama, who was set in her ways and wouldn't listen.

Mama had walked over to the sink, picked out the sharpest and biggest butcher knife, set it in her lap, and went back to cleaning her greens, just before Junebug and Bubbie walked into the kitchen, letting the fresh air mix in with the stink of the fish and the chitlins. "Just come to see how that food is coming along," Bubbie said. He pinched a big chunk of Peg's chin, laughing at her as she squirmed under his touch. "Y'all don't need any help, do you?" he asked.

Poor Peg, and Williemae too, they had taken this all too hard. These last couple of days, both their little round fat faces had sunken in and lost the healthy look that they usually had, and their eyes had sunken in too, making them look like maybe Junebug and Bubbie had bit them and made them into the walking dead. Seeing Bubbie pinch Peg, terrorize her, made me pity her and made me want to see Bubbie dead for what he was doing to my sisters.

"As a matter of fact, I need my towel," I heard Mama answer Bubbie. "Junebug, would you run into my room and get it for me? It's the yellow one with the flowers on it."

"O.K.," Junebug said as he left out of the kitchen.

"And Bubbie, would you hand me that salt over there on the sink?"

He turned to get the salt, and when he turned around, Mama was standing before him, knife in hand. She stabbed him, right in the heart. Bubbie fell to the floor, hitting his head on the sink on his way down.

Mama took the knife out of him and said, "One down and one more to go." She stood behind the kitchen door poised and waiting for Junebug.

I couldn't believe it, I ain't never saw a person kill another person before, not in real life. Then the kitchen door opened and Junebug walked in, "I couldn't find . . ." Mama got him in the heart too, but he didn't fall down and die like Bubbie, he just pulled the knife out and said, "Aintee Viola, why you want to go and do that?" Then he dropped the knife to the floor.

Peg and Williemae started screaming like they had finally crossed over and it was looney-bin time for them, while Mama bent away from the whole scene, hands covering her face, waiting for her end, like a child waiting to be hit that once-too-many time for nothing or something they did or didn't do. Mama knew what she had done, and was waiting for her fate. I just stood there, too surprised to summon any words out of my mouth.

Junebug bent over Bubbie and picked up the big mass of weight that was his brother and held him like a baby, with such ease. "If you want to know, you didn't kill him. You probably just knocked him out for a good while. Bubbie got more fat around his heart than he got around his head. He must have hit his head on something. I'll go put him to bed and we'll be out of here tomorrow." As he walked out of the kitchen, all my mind could register was, all I could say was, "Junebug, you really are one."

He stopped and sighed a tired sigh and looked at us all, at Peg and Williemae who had stopped screaming and were huddled up close to Mama, and at me. "You just don't understand. Vampires don't kill their kin. Not our own kin. We don't just go around biting and sucking people's blood. It just don't happen like that." Then he walked away with Bubbie.

We didn't finish preparing dinner, nobody had the stomach to eat. We didn't sleep either. It was just too much excitement for one day, so I went for a walk to try to think some sense into this confusion.

When I came back, Junebug was sitting on the porch in Mama's rocking chair. "Bubbie is still out. He's going to have a real bad headache when he wakes up."

"I guess so," I answered, then said, "I still can't believe it."

I stood there, still confused as ever, when Junebug came over, put his arm around me, and kissed me. I stiffened up, but he kept his arm around me, and kissed me, first on the forehead, then on the lips, then on each cheek. When I felt something on my neck, I yelled, "Ow!" and slapped him in the face as I pulled away.

"What did you do that for?" he asked, as he rubbed his cheek.

I backed away. "You tried to bite me!"

Junebug stepped closer, but again, I backed away.

"You don't understand," he said. "There are reasons for everything. You have this picture in your head what a vampire is, but it's not right. A person who gets bitten by a vampire isn't always a victim. I don't bite just anybody. I would kill an old person. Somebody like that, that their time has come for them, or someone who is already dead inside. You know the kind, the kind of person who is cold at heart and doesn't know what life is, or how to live. Then there are people like you, Ruthie, somebody who knows how to live, who has a life ahead of themself. If I were to bite you, it wouldn't be to kill you, it would be to give you life, more life. You could live forever. You are family, I wouldn't do anything that would actually hurt you."

"You're a damn vampire, a bloodsucking animal, and you tried to kill me!" I was hysterical, as I stood holding my neck.

"One day, it'll come to you, and you'll understand," he said as he turned away. He sat in the rocking chair and acted as if I was never there.

I ran into the house and jumped into the bed with my sisters and Mama. The next morning Junebug and Bubbie were gone, and not a trace of them was left, almost as if it were all a dream.

Meanwhile, I'm still waiting for something to happen. I'm still waiting for some fangs to grow, and to get the hankering for some blood. The other day I chased the neighbor's cat, and when I caught him, I set out to try to bite him and suck the blood out of him, but I couldn't get up the nerve to do it. I guess you have to have a craving for it, to do that. I do have a craving for something —it's more like a desire, though—to become a truck driver and travel all over the world, to rise from nowhere and somewhere, out from the dust. I don't know if I am one, but still I wonder.

PAPA BILLY D
Reginald Carlvin

The first time I can remember seeing Papa Billy D he was sitting in a rocking chair scratching his groin. I must have seen him before because he was my grandfather, but the first vivid recollection I have of him is on that hot, tropical morning when, sitting in his long red underpants and propped up on his two white cushions, he simultaneously rocked and scratched.

He was a tall, Black man whom age had not withered. His eyes were still clear, his voice still boomed, and he freely used his hands to massage the behinds of young girls who from time to time came to collect money for church functions or to run errands for my grandmother. I never knew his age because his vanity made him dye his hair and tell his friends that "if you can get it up, age don't mean a damn thing," but since my grandmother freely admitted to being "over seventy and grateful to God," I always thought of Papa D as a horny seventy-year-old lecher.

One July morning when I was thirteen, I walked over to his crumbling brick house to carry some cough medicine for him. He sat on the front porch drinking rum punches from a clay goblet and chasing them down with ninety-nine proof white Sunset rum. As I walked up the shaky steps, he shouted:

"Hey, boy, come here and drink one with me."

"Good morning, Papa D," I said. "I brought you some cough medicine."

"Carry it back to your mother and tell her I've got the best goddamned cough medicine devised by God or man," he said as he licked the syrupy brown liquid from the corners of his mouth.

"OK, Papa D," I said, backing away from this old man who everyone said was disgracing our family. "OK. I'll tell her."

"Boy, sit down. Stop being such a go-to-church-on-Sunday-all-day fool and let's talk."

I sat. In my childhood world, when children were spoken to, they listened; when they were flogged, they cried. There were no rights, no discussions, no arguments. Childhood was simply a tribulation to get over.

"How old are you, boy?"

"Thirteen, Papa D."

"You getting any yet?"

"Any what, Papa D.?"

"Getting any. You know what I mean. Don't pretend you don't know what I mean." I remained silent although my toes were beating an insane rhythm in my shoes. I scratched my nose, looked at a three-legged dog hopping along the glass-bombarded street and prayed that this old man would leave me alone.

"You lost your tongue, I see."

"Papa D," I said, desperate now and lying as fast as the lies could tumble out. "I promised my mother I'd carry some 'porking' beans and salt-fish cakes to crazy Miss Maude at Billings Hospital."

"Crazy Maude just passed this way half an hour ago, and she was pulling her hair and exposing half her fat ass to the wind. The bitch probably is sitting up in Woodlawn Liquors right now, downing a fifth of Mad Dog

Wine. So I don't see how she could still be in the hospital."

I ignored him. I simply plunged ahead. "Then after that Mabel Grey wants me to do something for her."

"Go on. Get out of here," he said. His voice boomed. The scorn was like a whiplash cutting through the tropical city heat. "You're nothing but a pious little shit. If I can't talk man to man with you, what's the use of having you around."

I took him at his word, jumped up and raced through the heat to tell my mother of this latest outrage. She smiled, rubbed my head and said, "Don't pay too much attention to him. It's his age catching up with him."

The next morning was the beginning of the two-day carnival festival when almost everyone in the Woodlawn community put on costumes and danced in the potholed streets. These festivals were sponsored every year by the City of Chicago in conjunction with the United States Government. Summer festivals were held in every major city in the United States. I asked my mother why did they have a festival every summer in our neighborhood?

"The rich businessmen plan parties for us so they can cool us niggers, Puerto Ricans and poor Whites off, to keep us from joining together and taking over." She said this so matter-of-factly as she bit into a hot piece of bacon.

"Take over what, Mama?!" I asked curiously.

"Never you mind, boy." She laughed as she shooed me away.

My grandmother would have nothing to do with these celebrations that she regarded as essentially "heathen." But Papa D, sick or not, never missed a chance to get into the streets, for on the pretext of dancing he could get to feel up the girls who were young enough to be his granddaughters. My grandmother, chagrined at first at the spectacle of her husband with these young women, grew tolerant as she grew older, but her lips remained touched with chronic melancholia. Once she could not resist telling him, "You're nothing but a fox-trot man trying to dance these new dances that are too fast for an old man like you." And I, unfortunately present, was pulled by my ear and forced to listen to my grandfather's tirade against his wife.

"Look, boy," he said. "Look at your grandmother. She has no ass. Now what's a woman without an ass?"

Grandmother walked out of the room, ran down the steps and held onto the big red oak tree that she had planted on the second day of their marriage. She crossed and recrossed herself, and her lips made quivering sounds that from my distance I could not hear. After a while I said, "Papa D, that was not nice. Look what you did to Grandma."

"What do you know about nice?," he shouted. "She thinks because I have grown children I should be pickling my dick. It's not that I want to touch her, mind you. She looks like a shriveled-up prune and I like watermelon. As a Black woman she should have some sense. She should let me have my fun. What harm am I doing?"

He was silent. I looked at him and then looked at Grandma still crossing herself under that red oak tree. Suddenly Papa D burst out, "Why does she have to wear white high-heeled shoes every time she goes out of this house? Why does she have to wear gloves to go to the market? Why? You tell me why? Why can't she be like everybody else?" Then he slammed the door and disappeared.

I waited until Grandma was through with her incantations, and then I ran up to her and held her hand. She was a woman who had allowed life to rest lightly upon her so that, although the curves had gone from her body, her face was almost free of lines. She had been a beauty once, and she knew it. Even though the years with my grandfather had challenged her patience, she had vowed her devotion to him at her marriage ceremony, and he remained the focus of her world.

"I wish you and Papa D got along," I said.

She looked at me, screwed up her lips and said, "We get along, young man. We've known each other for over fifty years. How can you say such a silly thing? Of course we get along."

"Then why do you argue so much?"

"Arguments are God's way of reaffirming a man's tie to a woman. That's all they are."

"He says you dress up too much."

"What do you see in this neighborhood except run-down buildings and people getting robbed? What do you smell but those old stinky winos standing on the corner? So I wear four kinds of perfume. So I wear white gloves everywhere. What crime is there is looking your best in front of your God?"

"No crime, Grandma."

"You see, you've got to have standards. And your grandfather and I argue because he has none. After all these years he can't understand that even if God makes no distinctions among people, man does. Man does, son."

I didn't quite understand what she was saying, and although I wanted to hear more about the ways of old people, I thought it best to feign disinterest, for the drums were already beginning to beat all over the neighborhood, and the days and nights of laughter were at hand. The first day of celebration I went to join the dancers in the streets, and it was good to look at those black bodies glistening from the sun and from cheap sequins. My friends were at the head of a line of young dancers who moved with assurance that their bodies would always remain intact. Their feet jumped to the calypso music while the women sang:

> "My lover lost
> Find him.
> O! Where is he?
> Find him
> In somebody's panty
> Find him
> O! Can that be?
> Find him.

The feeling was tropical, almost like living on an island. And as I saw them and smelled the summer sweat, the early morning dampness, as I saw the flamboyance and the abandon of the people I loved, I raced to the front of the band headed for Washington Park, and I closed my eyes as the drums made my body move.

We did not hear from Papa D until late that night when he was brought home by Dora Stephens, a nineteen-year-old fox who people said had the largest feet in the neighborhood. My grandmother was looking out the window and so she saw them when they were about fifty yards from the house. She hurried into her bedroom, put on her white gloves and went to meet the revelers at the door.

"Please put him on the living room couch," she said to Dora Stephens. "He must have had a hard day."

"Hard is right," Dora Stephens said. "I told him to take it light but he wouldn't listen. Maybe you should rub him down with some bay rum and give him some iron tablets."

"Thank you for your advice, Miss Stephens. I don't think we need it in this household."

"Just trying to help, ma'am."

"I'm sure," Grandmother said.

As Dora Stephens started to leave the room, Papa D opened his red eyes and said, "Watermelon. Hey, sweet, sweet watermelon." She stopped, winked at my grandfather, tried to hold her costume in place (she was dressed as a bunch of ripe bananas), smiled sweetly at my grandmother and walked out of the house. Grandma added a new score on her sheet of bitterness. But she merely handed my grandfather the bay rum and put a blanket over his body.

"Woman," he shouted. "Get this goddamn shroud offa me. I ain't dead yet; I'm as good as they come." Then he stumbled off the couch and went to sit in his rocking chair on the front porch as mosquitoes and lightning bugs made their own special music around his ears.

The next morning Papa D did not feel well. He coughed incessantly and was forced to wear red flannel drawers even though the material itched him. I had gone to see him early that morning, and I heard him talking to himself. When I asked him about this, he merely said, "I'm retracing my memories, boy. That's all I'm doing. I'm dredging up the good past." My grandmother rubbed his chest with hot, white soft grease and nutmeg, but he continued to have his coughing spells. At midday he announced that this year he would be dancing, "as usual, in front of the bands."

And my grandmother, accustomed to losing her wars with him, sighed deeply. Then with a bitterness I did not know she possessed, she said coldly: "There's no fool like an old fool. There's no turning back of sour milk."

Grandfather ignored her, and at three o'clock he put on his costume. (This year he was dressed as a billy goat.) He went into the streets that were crowded with masqueraders, and I watched him from the corner as he moved haltingly to the head of the band, his face imbedded with smiles, his head nodding greetings to his laughing cronies. This was his day, and he wanted everyone to know that he was as he always was, that no cough could keep him locked up in some crumbling brick house away from the sounds, smells and people that he loved.

The band started, and Papa D stretched out his hands, threw his head back and began to dance in the afternoon sun. He locked arms with a pretty girl who was dressed as a mermaid but whose scales had already begun to come off. "GO! SISTER GO!" shouted Papa D as he whirled her around, and the girl, becoming suddenly everyone's center of attention, began to jump up and down, her fish scales writhing frantically. Her eyes were closed, her lips open as she let the music wash over her. Papa D's smile spread across his face like lightning in the sky as his colleagues' voices, raised in admiration of him, grew louder. He moved his hips, licked his lips and waved his red bandanna in the air. I watched it all from my corner, and as the band moved away, I heard my grandfather's deep bass voice, towering above the rest, sing:

> "There's a little chocolate gal next to me
> Prettiest little woman that you ever did see..."

That was the last time any of us saw Papa Billy D alive. Chicago Park District workers who went to the park in the early morning to drink wine and pretend to clean up the park found him dead and naked near the lagoon. The autopsy reported that he died of natural causes, but it did not take us long to find out that he had taken the big-footed woman, Dora Stephens, to the park that festival night. My grandfather was an actor of sorts, and so I imagine that his face, on the moss covered ground near the lagoon, must have shown all the torment and ecstacy of his role, for he was about to prove to himself that he could still make a young woman's juices flow. We put the pieces together after Dora Stephens, unable to contain her silent terror, told her friends of that warm night when my grandfather coughed his life away while hanging limply on top of her. She said that she had tried to get him to stop but that he had insisted that he could go on. His urgency had frightened her and she abandoned him. I did not understand it all then, but now, with a little pride, I see this wild old man facing his death and floating with elation while letting the dreams of youth escape into the woman buckling between his thighs.

When my grandmother found out the true story of Papa D's death, she took an axe and cut down the red oak tree that she had planted on the second day of their marriage. Then she brought all of his clothes into the yard, sprinkled them with gasoline and before she lit the match, screamed into the bluish night:

"No standards. You never had any standards, Papa D. You died the death of a fool because you loved the sweetness between a woman's thighs more than you loved your life. May God let your whoring soul rot in hell!"

She stared at the fire with dry eyes and did not glance at the neighbors who peeped from behind their cotton curtains at this most gentle woman who was raising her voice for the first time in public against the only man in her life. She sat in the backyard all evening as the glow from the fire gradually died down, and we could no longer see her bright brown eyes. We sat on the wooden steps of the home, some twenty yards away from her, and we were afraid to comfort her since all she needed was the comfort that she found in herself. When the fire went out, she scooped up the ashes, put them in a large brown apple butter jar that she brought into the house. She placed the jar on her dressing table, took her wedding photograph out of the album and placed it next to the jar. Then, humming softly, she walked around her house, turning off the lights. And without saying anything, she closed her bedroom door and went to bed.

CLAUS AND GLORIA
Gary Johnson

CLAUS: 1

The doorbell rang with an insistent plea: one, two, three short bursts, then a long haul. "Claus, get some pants on!" Gloria said in a hurry while she rushed past him to the front door. Claus jumped up, banged his knee on the coffee table and retreated to the bedroom hobbling and cussing.

He had had too much beer the night before and slept most of the afternoon. Now early evening didn't present him with any pleasant feelings in his stomach. "The in-laws," he muttered to himself while pulling on a pair of trousers. "Grandma! Grandpa!" he heard through the closed door. "And the kids," he muttered as he slipped on a pair of dress shoes. He stood for a moment at the door, motionless, hand on the knob, listening to the conversation going on in the living room.

"Gloria, it looks so nice, it's so modern," her mother said excitedly.

"Claus finished it Friday night, well, except for the rug. We did that yesterday," Gloria said.

Claus entered the brightly lit room, his hands bulging his pockets at his sides.

"Hello, Claus," the in-laws said in unison. A stupid smile formed on his face. He knew it was a stupid smile, mechanical.

"I bet this remodeling cost you a pretty penny," the father interjected.

"Well..."

"And I bet you saved a lot doing it yourself."

"Yeah..."

"Where'd you get the ideas?"

Claus was steaming already. It was hard getting in a word when Gloria's father was present. The last time they visited, Gloria asked Claus why he was so quiet. "You didn't say three words all night," she said in her biting way. Again he said nothing.

"Here," Claus said quickly. "I got some of the ideas from this magazine." He flipped it towards the father-in-law, the pages fluttering color in the air like a wounded bird, then he turned and left the room to find refuge in the john.

The kids raced around the house in their excitement like wild dogs, Karen with her Sunday shoes, hard heels, and Jimmy with the new cowboy boots Grandma gave him for his birthday. Claus listened to the frolicking from the bathroom, sitting hunched over on the closed stool. He felt a tenseness in his chest that he could not explain but figured it was the company that produced the pressure. He looked around and noticed a pair of Gloria's blue fuzzy slippers lying on the dusty weight scale next to the white tub. On the ridge on the tub, in the corner next to the dried, twisted washrag, were little wafers of soap of various sizes and colors, blue, white, pink, and yellow, by-products of many baths, that Gloria would melt down into something useable—a big bar of twisting, swirling colors looking somewhat electric or surreal. And above, hanging on a towel rack inside the tub, were a pair of Gloria's panty hose that permeated the immediate area with the sour smell of body odor, almost unbearable if one were lying beneath them in a hot tub of steaming water. And on the windowsill sat a dusty, plastic flower of red jutting out of a pot of the same color with little windows that released a rose fragrance. But the deodorizing gel had long been eaten away by stale air and the hot sun rushing through the etchings of the translucent window. Footsteps approached the door and he turned to encounter his tired face and heavy lids, and reached back to flush the toilet to give him more time. The sound filled the room—the gurgle and rush of the water and then the hissing of the plumbing.

When his father would come home late, smelling of whiskey and ranting about the factory, little Claus would steal away to the bathroom and lock the door with a skeleton key that hung up high on the woodwork. From his retreat he could hear the yelling, the violence of objects being thrown against the walls and onto the floor. His father's voice was all that could be heard, for his mother knew her place and just stood by the stove, her back to him, silently minding the simmering stew or homemade soup. Claus heard the anger, smelled the salty air of dinner, felt the pain.

He felt as if it were his fault, as if he had done something to ignite his father's anger. Huddled in the cold darkness of the john, he would sit doubled over on the closed stool and rock back and forth. Light from the streetlights crept into the tiny room by way of the window above the tub, and a thin slice spilled onto the cold, tiled floor from under the door. He watched the floor intently, waiting for the shadow of his father's feet, and when he spotted them, he would then pull the chain and quickly open the door.

"Goddamn kid's taken a shit in the dark again!" his father would yell, and his big, chapped hand would slide along the wall until it found the switch. And when the light splashed onto the yellowed tiles and the checkered floor of black and white, his son would be gone. "Goddamn kid!"

And Claus would be at the stove huddled close to his mother's breast; the two of them standing there silently, arms around each other. Claus could smell her warmth, a light, powdery scent, he thought, and he smelled the brewing coffee and the browning meat and fresh vegetables, and he felt the heat of the stove radiating out and caressing his skin and the warm glow of his mother's body going much deeper to a place he had not yet discovered, and he felt safe.

But the chain was pulled again, and that sound of the door flying open and hitting knob against wall with a violent boom sent a shiver up his spine, and his eyes would go wide, and a pleading look enveloped his tiny, soft face. His mother could do nothing for those sad eyes of terror. Claus would scamper away and up the back stairs just ahead of his father's heavy footsteps entering the kitchen. And his mother would turn toward the stove with watery eyes. Claus never saw her cry.

The same meal would find its way to the table the following evening because his father said he was not in the mood for food. Then he would stomp out into the night to find solace at the local pub at the end of the block.

Claus would be asleep under layers of blankets in the upstairs bedroom when his father returned usually in a somewhat better mood. The screeching of his father's fiddle would wake him, slowly at first, and then, as if someone were violently shaking the bed, Claus would jolt awake, wide-eyed and scared. He hoped his father would not ascend the stairs to come into his room and terrorize him. He would lie awake to keep guard and follow the squeaking sound of drunken music that paraded back and forth under him. From the kitchen to the living room, around through the hallway past the piano, through the dining room, Claus could see in his mind's eye his father stumbling over chairs, rearranging tables and other pieces of furniture that got in the way of his benumbed hips. Then all would stop, and the john would flush, and the singing pipes would signal the end of another night of terror. Claus would try to sleep but would never accomplish the task until the sun lit the horizon, and he would roll out of the warm bed very much tired and sore for another day of schooling. His father would be on the couch, snoring away in his narcotic stare with heavy growth lining his rutty face. Claus expected this, because he knew his mother locked the door to the bed chambers on those nights. So Claus would have to walk in his bare feet, on tiptoe, until he left for the long walk to school. Relief came when he gently pulled the heavy wooden door closed, the white painted knob turned so as not to wake his father, who was sprawled a few feet away from the hallway.

"Claus, could you make a couple of drinks for Ma and Dad?" Gloria asked after a short, small-boned, soft-knuckled knock. "When you've finished, dear."

"Dear? Where the fuck she get that from?," he said in a loud whisper. And the word "from" echoed around the room for a moment. He sat for a while longer, this time with the tap running in the sink until Karen came pounding up to the door with her black, shiny shoes and banged wildly.

"Daddy? Daa-dee. Grandpa wants to know if you fell in?"

"Tell him to go to hell," Claus thought, but said, "All right, all right." And he closed the tap and flushed the toilet once more and retreated again, this time to the kitchen.

He didn't have to ask what they wanted to drink. They were easy to please. All they ever drank was bourbon and a bottle was always on hand just for them, Gloria made sure of that. Claus retrieved a couple of glasses up high over his head. Jimmy came stomping into the room and went straight for the fridge.

"Jimmy, go ask your mother what she wants to drink," Claus said firmly. He clomped out of the room and down the hall. Relief from the thunder came when he reached the rug in the living room. "Bourbon on the rocks, what a sick ass drink," he said to himself as he poured the rich brown liquid.

"Nothin', Dad!" Jimmy shouted from the living room.

With a napkin and drink in each hand Claus turned toward the livingroom. Just prior to reaching his destination, the voices of the in-laws coming straight into his ears, he stopped and counted to ten, took a deep breath and promised himself to be a good boy and smile a lot.

"The chairs are real comfortable, Claus," mother said.

"Yeah..." father started in but Claus cut him off.

"It was a toss up between these tweed things or all leather but I don't like sitting on cold leather. In the summer it's too hot."

Claus sat down in one of the new chairs. He felt the comfort, the softness, and the smell of new fabric filled his nose. But that physical comfort was dulled by the presence of the visitors. Father settled down with the Sunday paper, the kids were playing a board game on the floor, and Gloria was all ears—sitting on the sofa with her mother, the two generations intent with idle chatter.

It started slowly, that feeling in the eyes where the light looks kind of funny. Claus rubbed his eyes, feeling the tenseness in his forehead. The room took on a strange presence. The jabber of the kids and Gloria increased in volume then faded, up and down, in and out, louder and softer. The sounds gathered in his head as if brought to his ear by a horn of plenty—the noises revolving and swirling—slower at first and then whirling very fast. The crinkling of the newspaper was a rhythm, a percussive cadence, that melted and flowed in the same whirl of sounds. Claus sat as if waiting for something to happen, back in the chair, bolt upright, arms extended on the new fabric armrests, just looking around.

That little white dot appeared before his eyes. It followed his vision wherever he looked, like a flashbulb went off in his face. He looked at Gloria—the dot glowed; the kids—still there; at father. It was everywhere, on the white of the pre-fabricated ceiling, the rust colored rug, the cocoa paint of the walls, the heavy gold drapes. He blinked trying to clear his vision, as if he had gotten smoke into his eyes and they were smarting. But it would not leave. Then he looked at his hands. Then he knew. The dot appeared there but he did not notice it. What he saw was someone else's hands, rubberlike, mechanical, acting out commands from an alien source. Their presence was overwhelming—nothing else was in the room except these artificial hands. He could see each individual pore, a blondish hair jutting from each. As he inspected them he noticed them turn in his lap as though he were not turning them. His heart beat faster as the hands moved. His breath quickened and the swirling sounds crept back into his ears, into his brain. A queasiness melted his stomach as he looked up—saw the white dot bright, radiant, glowing on Gloria's face. But Gloria had only half a face, the glow covered the right side of her face. He blinked hard. The dot grew to encompass half his vision. His thoughts turned electric, bouncing off his brain and skull, mixing with the sounds, rising and falling, and the dot, the yellowish glow taking his sight, half of whatever he looked at. He was warm, sweat beading on his forehead. He tried to get a sense of the people in the room but the frantic pace of everything kept him at a distance, as if someone or something were holding him by the back of the shirt at the collar and pulling him up and away slowly, dreadfully slowly. He closed his eyes and the dot persisted. A breeze brushed at his face and he felt it on the skin like billowing smoke, clean smoke or maybe steam. He sat like this for a moment, eyes closed, mist caressing his face. It was his own place away from the franticness of sight, half sight and the mechanical hands and the sounds…He felt his right hand go numb, then the arm. He tried to make a fist but couldn't. He looked at the hand. Staring at the fingers canceled out the palm; looking at the palm he could only see the glow where the fingers should be. Then, as he looked at half a hand, the glowing spot came alive and burst into a sizzling light, intense, frantic. The patterns of bright white light flickered like a crazed neon sign, darting this way and that, crisscrossing, bouncing,

He looked up into the room, the people sitting around. It was on fire. The lights burned hot, forcing him to close his eyes tight to avoid the onslaught. The sounds were razor sharp cutting into his head, becoming a separate pain—the pressure in his head. Forehead pounded, the eyes controlled all. Half his body was numb and the eyes raced on with the sizzling light, and the half sight.

"Gloria," he heard a voice say from someone outside himself. Again the soft voice pleading, "Gloria." Someone came up to him, the voice piercing into his pain, his pressure. "What is it, Claus?" A strange expression, numb, cold, distant, was mounted on his face. "It's a migraine," the voice said again from the outside in a soft dreamy tone. "Could everyone be quiet?"

It was the same process every time. The pressure went to the head, the eyes. That spot—as if someone were dangling a flashlight in front of your eyes, opened wide—would follow your vision wherever you looked. If you could catch it soon enough, talk yourself out of the pressure before it consumed your being, before the white spot began to sizzle, come alive, you might have a chance to reverse the process and avoid the onslaught.

Claus had been sitting in math class, Mr. Sihocki's math class, seventh grade, when the spot first appeared. A test had been scheduled and Mr. Sihocki was reviewing at the green slate board drawing equations. It was a fast review. Something to kill time so there was less time for the actual test, Claus thought. He wasn't prepared anyway. Instead of studying the night before, he shot baskets down the block with the older boys. He could not have bowed out on a game in progress—they were winning. And going home to study was not a good excuse. Mr. Sihocki had the reputation of being a tough guy. He raised his voice a lot, shouting students into some form of motivation or cooperation, but he never, not in Claus's class at least, physically restrained a student. Though it was a fact that he broke a student's nose in the afternoon class. Violent yelling and loud crashing noises filled the hallways every afternoon with that class. Sometimes the principal would stand at the door of the class at recess to count heads and make sure all the students that went into the class came out and were still alive and walking.

Claus was nervous sitting in this madman's class. Sihocki was constantly licking his ample lips with a moist tongue. He had ample flesh from throat to Adam's apple, though it was firm. And these grey piercing eyes, intense. Claus was intimidated.

"All right! Now I want you all to do a good job on the test. I know you will not let me down," Sihocki said in a loud and thunderous voice as his piercing eyes darted around the room while he distributed the tests personally, never trusting the unsafe method of giving them to the head of the row and having the students pass them back. "All right, begin! You have 30 minutes!"

Claus hunched over the test, a mimeographed sheet still wet and smelling of chemicals, filling in the answers he knew. That took about five minutes. The rest of the time was spent drawing stick men on the Formica desk with a pencil, not daring to look about for fear of being killed. At the end of the class the pressure mounted to his head and eyes. And as he looked at the smeared white chalk lines on the green board, he noticed the spot, a soft white glow, and figured it to be a reflection of the sun off a car bumper he gazed at a little too long on the street below. But it did not go away.

CLAUS 2:

"One thing you could say about Claus was that he was good with cars and he was very loyal. But he pulled some shit I just couldn't believe." Jim stopped talking for a minute and sipped his beer while watching the wide screen TV suspended from the ceiling above the bar. A white foam mustache bubbled on his lip and he whisked it away with his tongue like a cat.

"There was this one time when a bunch of us guys were at Alice's Bar, that place over on Archer Avenue. Well, it was until Alice got shot one night by a black dude. Anyway, we was sippin' down a few brews when all at once somebody started giving Bobby Burns a hard time. You know Bobby, he's one solid mass of muscle, all shoulders. Well, this tall skinny guy with a walrus mustache started yellin' at Bobby and before you know it they was shovin' each other. The broads ran to safety behind the bar and the place just got more heated and more heated. The juke box even shut up for some reason and all you could hear was Bobby and the skinny stork havin' this argument. Me and Ralph and Toby quickly came to his defense and paired off with the guys stork was with. Alice was yellin' to get the fuck out of there and the broads were shakin' and sayin' 'Stop it! Stop it!'

"So we finally got the two out the front door and they started beatin' on each other right there on Archer Avenue. Cars were stoppin' and honkin'. One punk even threw a beer bottle. Smashed it all over the sidewalk. I got the brainy idea to tell Bobby to tell the stork we would meet him in the park at 3 o'clock. I figured it was better than fightin' on the street. So Bobby was standin' there in his dago-tee pointin' his finger at this skinny guy saying 'OK fucker, meet you and anyone you can get at Kennedy at 3 o'clock. Be there, sissy, 'cause I'm gonna whip your ass!' And his bicep was bulgin' like you never seen and his glazed eyes were mad, ready to kill. I thought things would end there, but oh no. Bobby wouldn't forget what this guy said about this girl he knew.

Jim raised his mug to his mouth again and looked around the bar and then up to the TV screen. The band was still marching around the field so he knew he had time to finish his story. He spoke up because the crowded bar was getting rowdy with talk, clinking glasses, smacking pool balls, and pinball dings and dongs.

"So we piled into a car, a station wagon. Me, Ralph, Toby, Steve, Rocko, Larry and Bobby. We drove pretty fast down Archer Avenue—blew a couple of lights as a matter of fact when all at once Bobby said, "Pull over into that gas station." 'It's closed, Bobby,' I said. I was drivin for some reason, probably cause I was the only one who could half see straight. 'Just pull over. Gimme all your dimes,' he says while fishin' through his own baggy greys. Satisfied with a handful he strides hisself over to the phone booth and slams all these dimes down hard on the little grey shelf in there." Jim slams his fist onto the table sending beer jumping out the glasses." Some of 'em went scatterin' and rollin' onto the floor. We was all pretty drunk and Bobby was pissed on top of that."

Jim had control of the guys at the table. All ears were on him. They took sips of their beer when he did.

"At that time Bobby's older brother, Mike, was the head of the Jungle, the baddest gang on the Southwest side. I mean you never wanted to mess with those guys or their girl friends because they'd rearrange your face pronto! The gang's pretty well broken up now. Most of the older guys are cops now. Man, they had sweaters and meetings and some wild initiations. There were the Jungle Bunnies, the toughest broads I ever seen and the Junior Jungle, mostly younger brothers of the big guys. So anyway, here's Bobby at 2:30 in the morning making all these phone calls—quick ones. He just said, "This is Bobby. Be at Kennedy at 3 o'clock. Get as many guys as you can—and bring the chains.' That's all he said. The last dime he saved to call Mike, his brother. That was one phone call he could count on to get some action.

Jim laughed, "I betja the operators thought the Russians were landin' or somethin' 'cause those switch boards musta lit up like a Christmas tree."

"So we was sittin' there killin' time and a few warm beers we found under the seat when Claus pulls up in his white '57 Chevy with this broad Gloria."

One of the guys tosses in that he married that Gloria girl.

"Yeah, from what I heard he had to. They had a small wedding down in Missouri," Jim volunteers. "Didn't even give him a chance to finish high school. Had to find a job to support the kid and his wife. Well, anyway he pulls up in this sparkling white Chevy, the exhaust rumblin' real low and mellow. We told him the scoop. I remember he turned to his girl and talked to her a minute and then said he'd help after he took her home. Came back squealin' his tires. He goes over to the phone and gets about a dozen guys just like that. I mean he didn't have to do it. He didn't even hang with us but...So we went in Claus's trunk. He had chains and bats with nails stuck out the sides and brass knuckles, all kinds of shit."

"So, how many guys did you have all together?" someone asks.

"Just hang on, hang on," Jim said, then continued:

"We pulls up to the park, see, and it looked like Sox Park on bat day. There was cars racin' all over the street burnin' rubber, doors slammin' and shit. And man, Bobby got an army. Musta been at least sixty guys, each and every one of them carryin' some type of weapon. Chains, boards, bats, pipes. Couple of 'em had guns tucked in their baggy greys, T-shirts pulled over to hide them. I saw the bulge. And across the way it looked as if the stork rounded up just as many guys. They were leanin' on their cars and passin' a couple a bottles around. You could hear a radio comin' from over there but other than that it was pretty quiet.

"The park was dark except for one light, you know one of them tower lights above the baseball diamonds. So that was kinda creepy, well, I mean the way it lit up the ground fog. No shit, it was like a movie—maybe like *On The Water Front*. Eerie as shit I tell ya.

"So Bobby talked to his brother for a while. Mike was very serious, listening to Bobby and watchin' him replay the bar scene. I must say Bobby exaggerated a little bit but, you know. We all got together in the dark, the fog kinda just hangin' there, and then it smelled like a bar. The guys that hadn't been out drinkin' were rubbin' their eyes cause they were sleepin' when they got the call. Mike spoke as if from experience. 'All right, the guys with the bats up front. We want to show them we mean business before we get on top of them. Wait for the word before you charge. Then pick out one dude and let him have it. That's the way we'll do it—one on one until it's over.' The whole time he was talkin' he just glared across the football field checkin' out the enemy.

" 'Let's go!' Mike yelled. He wore thin black leather gloves and carried a rusted tire iron. His face was serious. The gang moved silently, no one talked but the rattling of chains and the shuffling of feet took its place. Clouds of dust puffed up—we moved like a herd of cattle. I was in the middle of the gang, had a length of pipe in one hand and brass knuckles wrapped around the other. All the muscle was up front so all I saw as we hoofed towards the enemy was silhouettes of thick necks and tiny heads sittin' atop broad shoulders.

"Stork guys were still sprawled against their cars across the way under the lights of Narragansett Avenue. Then I guess somebody gave the word 'cause they started towards us, disappeared into the fog and darkness. As we approached I saw they didn't have any weapons. It was going to be a massacre, I remember thinkin' to myself. Most of their guys were walkin' with their hands in their pockets or passin' around the last of quart bottles of beer. So this is the enemy.

"Mike raised his hand when we was about 20 yards from them. The chains stopped rattlin'. 'Who's the fucker messin' with my little brother? Come on step out here so's we can all have a good look at ya,' Mike yelled. 'Hey, Mike, take it easy. No need to get upset.' The stork appeared. Mike didn't know who this guy was but Mike hisself was pretty much of a legend around these parts. The stork was tipsy on his feet and he slurred his words. 'It's between Bobby and me. Just send him out here and we can have it out.' Mike laughed knowing Bobby would reduce this guy to a pile of rubble. He then glanced at Bobby and motioned his forward. With a Louisville Slugger on his shoulder and smirk on his face Bobby ventured into the buffer zone. 'No weapons, Mr. Bicep,' the stork stammered. Bobby flung the length of wood aside. It hit the turf with a melodic thud.

"Bobby strode up like he was in the ring, ya know like that time he was in the Golden Gloves—his arms away from his sides, head tucked into this massive shoulder. 'I still say she gives good head,' the stork slurred. Bobby charged yelling but the stork struck first with a lightning fast karate chop to his neck. Bobby bit the dust. All of a sudden the stork was poised, alert, ready with his hands out in front of him. That drunken talk was all a front, ya know? Mike shifted his weight and mumbled somethin' to Vince Beimonte, in fact we all got kinda restless. Bobby got up and lunged at the stork and received a kick to the face. Just then somethin' hit Vito who was standin' right next to me and he fell to the ground. Claus yelled, 'Hey, they're throwin' shit, Mike let's go!' Mike looked back and then raised his hand. We broke yellin' like madmen raisin' our weapons above our heads. I ran up to where Bobby was sprawled but he was up runnin' after the stork sayin', 'Fucker! Come 'ere fucker!'"

"The park is surrounded on all sides by apartments and houses. I guess some old lady called the cops or maybe they was just passin' by but all of a sudden this blue and white comes chargin' up out of nowhere raisin' dust and flickerin' its spot light back and forth. We had the enemy on the run, chasin' them towards their cars. Then another squad came like out of nowhere. Most of our guys stopped and tried to hide their weapons behind their legs or simply drop them on the ground and walk away. The cops that came to check us out seemed to jump from their car before it even stopped rollin'. The driver was pretty tall and had his hat on which made him taller yet and his partner, a kinda short chubby guy, was bareheaded. So this short cop comes up yellin' 'What's going on here?' He was talkin to Vince Beimont. Vince said his friend was having a disagreement with this dude from across the way and he came along to watch. He said it in this innocent voice as if he were telling about watching some kids play basketball on the cement courts over behind the field house. 'Who's the leader here? If Burns is involved with this...is this his gang?' Everyone within earshot was quiet. The only sounds were that of a dusty voice coming over the squad's two-way and the guys being chased down Narragansett Avenue. Ball bats, and boards, and chains dotted the football field. 'You know the park closes at 11:00, fellas,' the tall cop said. Now this is the part I don't understand at all but anyway, Claus never dropped the bat he was carrying. It was a night he got from a pawn shop over on State Street. The one small cop was really a wise-ass, I mean he really had an attitude. He goes up to Claus and says, "What's that you got in your hand, sir?' As if he didn't know. What an asshole! Claus didn't say nothin'. Why don't you just give that club to me, OK?' the cop said as if Claus had a gun and was cornered in a dark alley. So Claus gave it to him—right over the head! I mean there was this CLUNK! and the thing broke in two. He still had the handle in his hand. The cop hit the ground like a wounded buffalo and the tall one was so shocked he just stood there for a moment. Claus started runnin'. Then everyone standin' there broke for the playground—that was one place you could go where a car couldn't follow. I just stood there because I didn't do nothin' and cause I was in shock. Claus just rapped that guy over the head like he was poundin' nails or somethin'. I was glad to see it, that cop bein' an asshole and all but...

"So the other cop races over to his squad. Didn't even check on his partner. The other car was over checkin' on the stork and his guys. '10-1, 10-1,' the cop called out on his radio. '10-1 at Wentworth Park, 57th and Narragansett.' Then he raced back over to his buddy who was out cold. I thought Claus killed him or somethin'. It was scary. The other squad came racin' over and after getting the low down the car went rippin' off throwin' dirt every which way.

"Then blue and whites, and paddies, and unmarked guys started comin' from all over. The sirens were blarin' and blue lights flickern' and I mean they weren't holdin' back on the speed either. One unmarked jumped right over a curb doin' about 65. BOOM! Smashed his axle and all but ya know how the cops get all freaked out when one of their guys gets hit.

"An ambulance came from the fire house at the opposite corner of the park. The cop was still unconscious. They grabbed me and threw me in a paddy like I was some sort of criminal. I didn't mind though 'cause I was tired and needed a rest. Plus I was close to the action."

"So what finally happened," someone asked from the group. "Did he get away?"

"Who do you mean?"

"Did Claus get the rap?"

"Well, to make a long story short, and Jesus, just in time, the second half is startin'. They caught Claus in the morning. They went to his mother's house at 9 o'clock. He was sleepin' like nothin' had happened. I heard his mother kept sayin', 'It must be some sort of mistake!' But the cops just looked at her. They took him down to 63rd and St. Louis and really messed him up."

"And the cop?"

"Oh, that asshole. He finally came around. Had a concussion or somethin' like that. Maybe if he wasn't such a jerk Claus wouldn't of hit him. I don't know. But you know the funny thing about it is that Claus didn't remember a goddamned thing about it. He knew somethin' happened when he woke up in bed with half a night stick strapped around his wrist and the cops there and all. But other than that...Crazy fucker, no shit. But man he knew his cars. This one time he..."

"Aw, come on Jim. Game's gonna start."

"Hey, listen, tell me you didn't enjoy it," Jim said. He waved his hand at the bar and raised an empty pitcher. Then he looked down at the table and said, "You know, it musta been a good story. I didn't even smoke a cigarette the whole time."

GLORIA: 3

"Maybe I'll drop the kids off at my mother's," Gloria said into the phone over the heavy-metal rock and roll.

"What?" Steve said on the other end.

"I said turn down the stereo and maybe you can hear me."

"Hang on!" the voice said and the phone boomed and banged as if Steve had just dropped it and left it swinging on the short cord to thud up against the wall like a wrecking ball. Gloria yanked the receiver away from her ear and held it out at arm's length and looked up at the ceiling shaking her head...

"Gloria! Gloria!" she heard the voice say as if there were a little man inside the plastic receiver.

"Yeah?"

"Well, wh-de-a donna do? Where should I pick you up at?"

Gloria thought for a moment. She pictured driving for fifteen minutes to her mother's—seven lights, three stop signs and lots of potholes to avoid—she had done it plenty of times before. At night her vision was very poor. "I'm legally blind after the sun goes down," she had told an old girlfriend on the phone, then laughed. Just the least bit of fog or road dust on the windshield and she would curb the car and jump out with a roll of paper toweling that was her ever-present passenger on the seat next to her. The sodium lights dotting the sky over head didn't help matters. Their orange tinge left everything in a surreal hue; so much that she couldn't see another drivers' headlights at the side road intersections. And then telling her mother she was going out shopping or to a movie or over to a girlfriend's house who simply hated kids. They would have to wait in the car. Grandma wouldn't stand for it and quickly takes the kids to the kitchen—the Holy Kitchen of Snackdom—where she puts together the sweetest concoctions imaginable and pours them into whining mouths to rot their teeth and keep them hopping until the next morning. On the drive home Gloria would have to watch her kids bounce around the car like wild monkeys.

"Well?" Gloria just hated being rushed.

Or she could call the babysitter who lived next door. Then Steve would pull in front of the house—honk once and pull around the corner and wait. But she didn't really care for the babysitter. When she would return, the kids would complain how they were mistreated. "Cindy wouldn't let me build anything with my erector set," Jimmy would shout. "Yeah, and she wouldn't let us eat nothin' either," Karen would add in a frantic tone. Gloria had been through so many babysitters it was as if the kids were to blame. The fact of the matter was her kids were spoiled brats. But Gloria would never admit to that.

"Listen Steve, could you pick me up here?"

"Hey, fine. Fine! See you in a bit," and he hung up the phone with a ker-chunk.

Gloria stood facing the wall, the phone still lodged in her ear. She heard the kids romping around upstairs—their socked feet pounding away on the bare floor. A few dishes rattled in the cupboard above the sink. Normally she would yell up the stairs to calm them down but now she just listened. There were muffled screams and shouts of joy bleeding through the closed wooden door of the stair well—kid sounds, natural sounds, children at play, she thought. Then a terrible sadness overcame her, hit her like a wave of some invisible toxic chemical. With every breath the drug pulled her under, touched every pore, smothered her into a fit of depression. God, she wanted the kids to know—about Steve, about Arizona, about all the nights of babysitting. No, she wasn't going to play bingo—that was for old ladies—or running to the store. She was seeing this very nice man who had a bright smiley face and talked to her softly and wanted to take her away from all of this—and bring them too.

The kids never play when Claus is about. Always tells them to shut up and settle down. Slaps 'em down if they don't listen. Jimmy, he's so afraid of his father. They never talk—he needs a real father, someone to look up to, not fear. Oh, Steve would be so good, so good.

The dial tone tumbled into her ear with a series of clicks. At the same time the colorful wallpaper went blurry and a tear from each eye rolled down her cheeks. Gloria hung up the phone slowly with both hands as if the tiny, hollow, plastic receiver was the weight of a bowling ball.

"Kids?" Jimmy and Karen race over to Gloria with expectant looks covering their faces. "Sit down here, I want to have a little talk with you two." They eagerly plop down on the sofa and wait her next command. Gloria stands, figuring it's the best position for the person in authority.

"How many times would you say your parents have fucked in the past month?" she asks casting her gaze between both. The kids look at each other. Karen shrugs. Jimmy looks back and says, "Oh, about seven."

"Why would you say that?" Gloria asks. Jimmy giggles.

"Well, I heard the bed squeaking a couple of nights," he says with a big ain't-I-a-sneaky-devil grin. Then "And I'd throw in a few more 'cause I fell asleep early a couple of times."

"Karen, what would you say?" Gloria asks. Karen crinkles up her face then slaps both hands onto her forehead and pretends she's hiding. She peeks through her fingers at Jimmy then lowers her camouflage and says, "Whatever he says," and shakes her head laughing.

"What would you say if I told you we only fucked once last month?"

"I would say," and Jimmy looks up at the ceiling as if searching for words, "that you and Daddy don't love each other."

"And..."

"And that's why Daddy has all those Hustler books in his bottom drawer in the bedroom."

"Remember that guy that was here? I told you he was from work? A couple of weeks ago?"

"That guy Pete?" Jimmy asks.

"Steve."

"Oh yeah, Steve. Yeah, he's real cool," Jimmy says.

"Yeah! Neat-o, Ma!" Karen yells and shakes her legs and her feet fly up and down bouncing on the cushion.

"Well, I fucked him...oh I would say I fucked him about twenty times in the last two months," Gloria says.

"Do you love him, Ma?" Jimmy asks.

"He gave me that real neat key chain, Ma," Karen almost shouts. Gloria sits down on the coffee table facing them.

"I don't know for sure but he treats me nice, ya know? I feel like somebody when I'm with him. He doesn't yell at me when I say something stupid." Gloria's face beams, "And he's so cute when he smiles." She looks off for a moment in somewhat of a trance then snaps back. "And he's gentle with me. Oh, I just don't mean when we're fucking, but when we're alone sitting at the lake in his car. His touch is warm and..."

"Ma! I got a quarter from school...from Tony Beacon for the key chain! Can you get sa-more?"

"Ma? Does he love you, Ma?"

Gloria looks down and toys with the shag rug, her toe revolving in tiny circular patterns. "That I'm not sure of either," she says quietly. And then her voice inflecting upward, "But he wants us all to go out West with him and buy a house and live there!"

"Aw, great, Ma! Let's go!" Jimmy says continuing on the upward note.

"I want to...but..." and her voice trails off.

"But what, Ma?"

"Your father. I don't know if I can leave your father."

Steam rose from the hot running water; some of it collecting on Gloria's face and the rest on the window facing her. She pulled the last frying pan from the brown, greasy water. She wished the scene that had just played in her head could be that simple. She laughed. The language she used in the day dream. Such a mouth. She stepped back from the sink, wiping her hands in a soggy dish towel. Yes, it looked good—dishes stacked in the drainer, counter clear of clutter. Claus wouldn't even notice, but then, that's the way he wanted it.

With her face painted and with her arms jutting out from her sides to relieve the sting of the deodorant on her freshly shaven pits, Gloria marched to the bedroom to pick through her so-called wardrobe. She heard the kids pounding feet above her head and the woosh and tick of the hangers sliding along the black metal pipe of the closet in front of her. It wasn't that she was indecisive, her hand parting the limp clothing was more or less an idle review of her rags. Claus never bought her anything and allotted her a scant allowance that usually went for the kids' needs. Cotton summer tops of pastel colors, a few wore-torn dresses for weddings and funerals, a collection of the same style—different color of polyester slacks and an array of sweaters to keep her body warm year-round.

"Claus, I don't have anything to wear."

"Wha-de-a mean. You can't even close the closet door now."

"You never take me any place."

"In that case you don't need anything to wear."

Gloria heaved a hanger-full of slacks out of the closet with both hands. Under the layers of colorful polyester were the jeans she wore when she went out with Steve; tight-fitting straight legs with two star bursts of colorful embroidery stitched to the ass where the pockets should be. Her black pumps were tucked away in a shoe box labeled 'KIDS PICTURES' on the closet shelf. And tonight she decided on her black cotton top with the interesting plunge and a distracting outline of a cat in silver sequins on the front. She held her breath until she zipped the jeans, fought her way into the top and slipped the pumps onto her naked, stark-white feet. She ran her hands down her sides as she inspected herself in the mirror above the bureau, ruffled her hair and waggled out of the room, her pumps scuffing the bare wood floor. Steve was so easy to please.

"Cindy? This is Gloria. Do you think you could watch the kids for a couple of hours tonight?" The voice at the other end was raspy. "I didn't wake you, did I? Good. Uh, I'm going to a dis...to aah, to a dish meeting. Yeah, you know like a tupperware thing. Right. OK. What. Oh sure, bring your homework. The kids have been quiet all night. Within the half-hour? OK, bye."

Gloria managed to make it over to the couch after flipping on the television. She thought of unzipping the jeans to breathe but figured she would have to get used to it anyway, so she eased her legs up onto the couch, cuddled her head to the rock hard pillow and watched the tail-end of "Baretta".

She awoke to sound that curdled her stomach—the low rumble of tail pipes running up the side drive. Claus was home. What time was it? Where are the kids? She jumped off the couch and dashed to the bathroom. The television set was flipping in slow revolutions, the late night announcer was signing off. She peeled off the jeans, ripped the top over her head and grabbed for the yellow quilted robe on the back of the door. The back door clicked open them slammed shut. Footsteps came up to the closed door.

"Gloria? You in there?"

"Yeah. Be out in a sec."

"Hurry up, I gotta take a wiz."

She folded the jeans into a towel and stuffed the top into her pocket and reached for the door. As the lock of the door clicked open she remembered the make-up. Shit! She quickly locked the door again and dove into a double handful of water. It was cold on her face.

"Hey, come on," Claus pleaded. "You wanna mop up the floor at this hour?"

"All right," Gloria said and gazed into the mirror. Good, she looked like hell—bags under blood shot eyes, hair standing on end—Claus wouldn't even look at her.

"How was your day at work?" she said as she rushed past him.

"Now now, Gloria," Claus said and rushed past her and closed the door. Gloria threw the clothes into the closet and dashed to the couch to retrieve her heels. Claus appeared in the doorway just as she stuffed them into her pockets.

"What are you doin' up so late?"

"I fell asleep on the couch again," she said with a guilty look on her face.

"Well, since you're up, why don't you make me some eggs?"

"OK. How do you want them?"

"You know this guy had a heart attack at work tonight," Claus said as she brushed by him.

"Oh, yeah?"

"They had an ambulance there and the whole shot. We stood around for a couple of hours just shootin' the shit. He didn't die or nothin' but it was somethin'. He was carryin' a case of bleach when all of a sudden he fell down forward and curled up around the box. I saw the whole thing. It was scary, let me tell ya." Claus pulled a chair from the table and fell into the chair. Gloria stood at the stove, her back to him, flashing a pan of butter over a full blue flame. The pumps bulged in her pockets. She was sure he would see them.

"Listen, I'm really tired. Do you mind if I just crack the eggs and you watch them?"

"Sure, yeah. It's late, I know. Naw, I don't mind." Gloria sighed a breath of relief. In her haste she broke one of the yolks. I'll hear about it tomorrow, she thought to herself. She stuffed her hands into her pockets and retreated to the bedroom not knowing what happened to the evening. "Goodnight," she said in a small voice. Claus didn't hear but it didn't matter. She didn't repeat it.

PEEPIN' THROUGH THE WINDOW
James O. Elder

Max was busy devouring his chef's salad—wilted lettuce, a wedge of
tomato, and a heavy-handed concoction of vinegar and oil that was simply
festering with garlic—and periodically glancing up at Freddie flipping
burgers, while J.B. was trying to make eye contact with the cute-pretty girl
when her father wasn't looking. So Max didn't notice the man sitting at the
straight part of the counter in the back of Nick's who was nodding over a
plate of bacon, eggs, and grits. And neither did J.B. The four people standing along the wall waiting for a seat at the counter noticed him. So did the
two truckers sitting on either side of him. And although he's watching him
out of the corner of his eye as he rings up another order, "LET'S SEE,
THAT'LL BE $3.96 OUT OF $5.00," Sgt. Marty O'Koren notices him, too.

He's hunched over the counter with his right elbow anchored beside his
plate, his right hand held high in the air, and his fingers weakly holding that
fork like he wouldn't care if it slipped, crashed, and bounced across the
counter like a fish out of water, making that funny sounding noise that only
a single piece of silverware can make when falling (hard—soft, hard-soft,
hardsoft, brrrinnggg!) and startling everybody in the restaurant to stop
eating and working long enough to look at him, knowing that he was the
culprit responsible for breaking their rhythm. If you look close, you can see
his eyelids fighting, struggling, refusing to shade his eyes. Yet slowly,
weakly they succumb to the nod. His right hand dangles toward the counter
from his wrist, the fork hovering, about to fall, teetering between weakly
clasped fingers. His head is bobbing slowly, dipping forward slowly, and
bending at the neck ever so slightly, and ever so slowly. He appears to be
swooning. To a fleeting eye, he is motionless. To a probing eye he is nodding, slowly and jerkily, his will to resist the nod fighting back at intermittent intervals, trying to keep his head erect and his eyes open, like a trucker
who's been pushing 70 for the last 400 miles and is now just 30 minutes
away from Little Rock—and SANCTUARY—but the long haul, the night,
and a renegade band of white lines have conspired to dash salt in his eyes;
and even though he knows that he's slowly falling asleep, he lies to himself
that he's not. And that's how the "nodder" nodded, slowly and reluctantly.
But with each passing second his feeble resistance diminishes more and
more, and as it does, his face droops closer and closer to his plate.

Everybody doesn't notice him all at once.

The tall man in the gray felt hat standing at the front of the line along the
wall turns and offers the lady standing behind him the newly vacated seat,
even though he came in first. She politely refuses by tilting her head to one
side and flashing this toothy, cover-girl smile, or better yet, that ridiculously benign smile worn by the little girl on the Morton salt box. Yes,
that's it, that's how she was smiling, smiling like she didn't mind going to
the store in the rain to get a box of salt; after all, she did have mommy's
umbrella, didn't she? And so what if she wastes most of the salt skipping
home in the rain; why mommy only told her to go get it—not how to carry
it. The tall man strategically places his new hat on the coat rack in the back

of the restaurant so that he can keep a sharp eye on it while eating. As he stiffly walks back past the "Morton salt lady," she turns up the volume on her smile. He grunts and squats down on the short mushroom stool with a curt smile of indifference, never realizing that she simply prefers to sit next to her man: that guy standing next to her with his fists jammed down deep into his pockets, but real cool, mind you, like he was just trying to keep 'em warm, not like he was trying to bust the bottoms out. He hasn't smiled or said a word since he came through the door; he might not have smiled in two years. But he was the first person in Nick's to know why the man in the back was nodding; he wasn't the first to notice him nodding, just the first to know why.

Nick noticed the "nodder" first, but then she always noticed things first; noticing had been the key to her survival in an all-Black neighborhood where the only Whites that exist are those that migrate to the community to work, collect rent, and make arrests. When she was a little girl, her mother told her that it wasn't good for a young lady to be so nosy. "Men are afraid of NOSY WOMEN," she said, "afraid that they're going to find out something that they don't want them to know...besides, it's just not good for a marriage to be so nosy," she continued, as if she had unmasked one too many skeletons of her own. Fortunately for Nick, she never took her mother's advice. She turned "nosy" into "know-how" and, as a result, her father saw fit to bypass two sons and a son-in-law to give her full control over all his business enterprises, which consist of three restaurants, two liquor stores, and a string of apartment buildings and real estate that only she and he know about. So it was no surprise that Nick noticed the "nodder" first; she couldn't have not noticed him even if she'd wanted to. But as long as he only nods in his plate and doesn't affect the customers, the service, or the cash crawling in the register, she won't say anything to him. Until then she'll just keep glancing over at him with those blue-blue eyes of hers, which are so seductively blue that if you didn't pay any attention to her double chin or the gray streaks in her hair and didn't concern your gaze with the wrinkled bags beneath her eyes and concentrated on the eyes alone and the blueness of them, you could very easily be sucked down a euphoric tunnel of erotic fantasy. Just so blue and deep are her blue eyes.

J.B. nudges Max with his elbow, leisurely takes another sip of coffee, then points his thumb over his right shoulder and says, "Ain't that your boy, Gus?"

Max spins half-way around on his stool and screams to himself in a whisper, "GUS!" No, that can't be Gus, he assures himself. Yet his dark, ebony face lights up with recognition as a white powdery glaze flashes across his sunken cheeks and tiny sweat pimples quickly percolate on his nose. Why he looks like a diseased animal with matted tufts of hair sticking up on his head, his shoes scuffed and worn lopsided, and that filthy orange sweater he's wearing is so putrid-looking that the sight of it makes you smell it. No, that can't be Gus. Gus would never let himself go like that. He wouldn't let the game dehumanize him; he was too quick for that, too fast, too clever...naw, that ain't non'a Gus! Max refuses to look beyond the squalid clothing for fear he'd recognize the man in them. If he did look beyond the clothing, he would see the bloated face that is not unlike that of the drowning victim who's found floating downstream a week after his disappearance; he'd see the puffed hands, swollen as large as boxing gloves with dimples where knuckles used to be; he'd see the dark, scaly splotches tattooing the skin; and he'd see the gray, ashy skin itself that's been sucked dry of all its natural juices by the heroin, the mix, or both, blanketing the bloated face and puffed hands like a piece of parched leather that was once soft and supple, but someone had left it to dry in front of a blazing fireplace too close for too long, and it had scorched and begun to smolder.

Max slowly whirls back around to his fast cooling hamburger, trying desperately to purge the sight of that filthy orange sweater from his mind. His imagination grabs it and slings it down a laundry chute to the basement of his subconscience. He shrugs his shoulders and beams a twisted, embarrassed grin at J.B., avoiding J.B.'s hazel eyes, and lifting half of the greasy, sliced burger to his mouth, only the orange sweater pops back into his mind like the clown in the jack-in-the-box that he once owned as a kid. The latch that held the top down on the box was broken, so the clown was subject to pop up at any given moment, regardless of how long or short he'd been cranking out "The Three Blind Mice" with the handle on the side, and no matter how many times he forced the clown back down into the box, it would never stay; it just popped back up whenever it felt the mood. And just like that clown in the jack-in-the-box, the orange sweater refused to stay down. He had seen the sweater and he had smelled it, and although he didn't know this at the time, he would remember that foul odor for the rest of his life. In fact, it would eventually become the standard by which he gauged all foul odors, not that this was the foulest odor he had ever smelled, nor because it was the least foul, but simply because it was somewhere in the middle, and that's where all things begin. And just as he could not forget the sight and smell of that sweater, he could not ignore the fact that the "nodder" was his friend Gus, his childhood running buddy and teenage hustling idol, the man who had taught him everything he knew about "boostin," but more importantly, had taught him about life and surviving his environment, something that his own parents had left up to God and the Baptist church. Yet he felt embarrassed that J.B. knew the "nodder" was his friend Gus and that everybody else in the restaurant suspected it, although they really didn't, and then he began to feel ashamed of himself for feeling embarrassed about knowing, knowing a man he'd once loved more than any woman, but was unable to reach down in his guts and pull out enough courage to share his humiliation with him by simply walking over there and saying, "What's been happenin', Gus?"

So Max sits there eating, but not eating, his head swirling wildly, frantically, and violently like a merry-go-round gone berserk. Finally, in a desperate attempt to cling to at least a fragment of reality, he nails his eyes down to the river of scratches criss-crossing the plastic plate holding the other half of his hamburger. Perhaps he'll discover some discerning art pattern that'll free his mind from the "Star Wars" scenario playing inside his head over whether or not he should get up from his stool and walk the scant eight feet down the counter to where Gus is nodding and say something to him; it doesn't matter what...or does it...what would you say...how would you say it...everybody will be looking at you...J.B. is laughing at you...what if Gus goes off...after all, it's been three years...you mustn't forget you've got that cocaine in your pocket and that cop is already looking at you funny....

Meanwhile Gus is nodding...and nodding...and nodding, closer and closer to his plate, a part of him having already surrendered, and the other part—the much larger part—still fighting, daring the spectators to notice that he's nodding even though they're looking right at him, his head protruding from his chest like a mounted moose; while that smaller part of him is whispering, "Gus, my man, you're noddin' your ass off! Don't it feel good? So what if they watchin' you; you don't giv'a shit about them or this little shitty restaurant. FUCK'EM! And your boy Maxwell sittin' over there with that punk Jesse-Boy like he don't know who in the fuck you is—and you was the one that put that game under his belt that got 'im them fine clothes and that diamond on his pinky; yeah, fuck'em. Fuck all them motherfuckers...just go 'head and nod, you don't giv'a shit." As he listens to the faint voice in the back of his mind or the pit of his stomach or the coffee cup in front of him, that heavy stainless steel fork slips from his swollen hand, slaps the counter like a gong, and skids to a rest against the yellow sugar bowl behind his plate. He slowly opens his eyes and straightens his posture with such a calm casualness that if you hadn't been staring right at him, you would've sworn he wasn't nodding at all; but then you were staring right at him and you know that he was. Yet he doesn't pick the fork up right away, and he doesn't look bewildered with that self-indicting countenance of the married man caught with the "other" woman; he employs the same misdirection technique he'd use if he were boosting a gold watch or a diamond ring from a jewelry case at Peacock's. While everybody's eyes are riveted to the fork, he nonchalantly picks up his coffee cup and downs a big slug of the cold mud like that's what he'd planned to do all along; only he hadn't, and everybody knew it except Freddie. That larger part of Gus had convinced him that he'd faked them all out—faked them right out of their shoes, he thought. Even as he sat the coffee cup down, picked the fork up, and started nodding again he told himself, yah, faked them right out of their shoes.

Everybody in the restaurant was watching the "nodder" now except Max and Freddie—Freddie was watching the grill—but they weren't all just gawking at him like mannequins in a State Street window who had no choice but to stare wide-eyed, even though they too had long since lost their choice of options. They glanced, gazed, and stared at him in varying styles on multiple levels of intensity, but nevertheless watching him, watching him like his humiliation and self-degradation were the key to their very salvation. Even those of them who desperately tried latching their eyes to some fixed object in the room like the steam wafting up from the coffee pot or the fly-strip dangling from the ceiling or the plastic crucifix hanging on the wall behind Nick's head, they too had no choice but to watch—just as Lot's wife had no choice but to stop fleeing, turn around, and watch Sodom and Gomorrah being destroyed, even though she had been warned that a glance would cost her her life—SHE HAD NO CHOICE. And as that smaller part of Gus seduced him more and more into the nod, so were the onlookers seduced more and more into watching him, until now his face hovers just six inches above his plate.

Max feels the ditch between him and Gus swell by leaps and bounds, and that scant eight feet that once separated them has sprouted into a mile-wide gorge so that his legs refuse to carry him and his mind refuses to demand that they do it.

A tall, gangly woman in three-inch heels, gray skirt, pink blouse, and straw hat with a pink ribbon around it inches her way into the restaurant and stands in front of the register waiting for Nick to finish bagging the corned beef sandwiches she ordered by phone. She notices the cop's eyes keep darting to the back of the restaurant, so she follows their rapt and knowing gaze until she spots the "nodder." Is he searching for something in his plate...why, I hope not...maybe he's smelling the food to see if the eggs are rotten or the bacon's rancid...hopefully not, she thinks as the bells chiming in the register snatch her attention. She looks into Marty's serious blue eyes for an answer but all she sees is the reflection of her own thick, wide-framed glasses. Walking out of the restaurant past the big plate glass window with "Nick's" scrawled across it, the sharp clacking of her high-heels pounding against the concrete, merging into the avalanche of groaning engines. blasting horns, and the barking of the paper-man in front of his newstand on Madison, she glances back just one last time, thinking, MAYBE HE'S SICK!

Angrily, Max looks at Gus again—not knowing that it would be the last time—and he sees the withered shell of a body that he once knew and loved and that once housed an enviable athlete but now, at best, houses a part-time spectator who watches games on TV between nods...between hustling...between copping...between taking off...and between nodding again; and even though he can't see Gus's eyes, he knows that the heroin has zapped them of all their whiteness and contaminated them with a ghastly, jaundice yellow that is as close to being brown as it is to being white. And as Gus's bloated face swings just inches above his plate, a thick stream of saliva froths from his mouth into his grits like a rope of spider silk, and everybody is watching, waiting—hoping—that his face crashes into his plate. A sharp, jagged-edge pain slithers inside Max's chest that he knows can't be dislodged by water or coffee, so he reaches into his pocket, ups with a ten-spot and flings it on the counter, and only J.B., Nick, and Marty notice him leave out the door, spit in the street from the side of his mouth, and light a cigarette as he walks past the big plate glass window without even peepin'.

THE GALLERY
James O. Elder

It's a small dark room with a red naked light bulb snoozing silently in the ceiling while casting two shadowy figures on the wall—a feature that any bona fide "shooting gallery" must have. The blonde wood furniture in the gallery, a dresser and a set of matching twin beds, was originally designed to be used by children, and it was Sarah Stewart who brought it home from Ember Furniture Store after making a ten dollar down payment on it thirteen years ago. But a lot of things can change in thirteen years, and usually do. Maxwell is sitting on one of the beds snorting dope off a small white plate bordered by pink roses with short green stems, while Gus is sitting on the other bed near the one narrow window in the room that has been painted black—nobody knows when or why—with a syringe of heroin stuck in his left forearm. The initials G.S.&C.S. are carved in the thick tar-like paint covering the window, and they are the only way you can tell whether it's day or night outside. It's night now, but it if were a bright and sunny day outside, those initials would stand out like a neon sign in the dark alley. The G.S. stands for Garibaldi Stewart, which is Gus's real name, but don't ever let him hear you call him Garibaldi unless you know him real well or else you're close kin to him, because Gus has busted a lot of heads about that name. A word to the wise should be sufficient; Willis Parks found out the hard way. The C.S. stands for Constantinople Stewart, Gus's twin brother who got shipped off to Nam and never came back. Their mother, Sarah, received a letter from the Army saying that he was "MISSING IN ACTION," but that's been about five years ago now and all of the American troops have since pulled out, so nobody's expecting Connie to come home except Sarah, who, when she has had one pint too many (which used to be just on weekends but lately happens with more and more frequency during the week), will tell Mrs. Woolridge on the second floor, "Connie's coming home this weekend, so I'm gone have to clean up them boys' room real good. I seen a sign and signs don't lie. Last night I dreamed I saw a flock of white geese flying north, and that can mean only one thing: Connie's coming home."

Gus is sitting on his bed with his parted feet pointing in opposite directions at a 45 degree angle, his six-foot frame leaning forward, shoulders slumped, head bowed limply at the neck, his elbows resting on his knees. He's clenching and unclenching his left hand to keep that fat vein pumped up that's shaking down his forearm like an obese earthworm while his right hand is playing with the plunger on the syringe. He pushes it in until nearly all of the murky brown juice has been forced from the clear tube, then hooks the top of his thumbnail under the rim of the plunger and pulls it back out, sucking up one part dope and three parts blood into the plastic tube. He repeats the process again, and again, and again, teasing himself and loving it.

"Ain't shootin' the shit enough?" Max cracked sarcastically "Why you gotta jack off with the fuckin' needle too?"

Gus raised his bowed head, cocked his left eye wide at Max and produced a feeble smile that only registered on one corner of his lips, and in a slow and raspy voice said, "You jack off your way, and I'll jack off my way, and I'll get to heaven before you."

"Yeah, you catch a fuckin' bubble in that syringe and you ain't gone know heaven from hell!"

"Well, as long as I go first class, non-stop, I don't give a fuck. Besides, you waste the fuckin' shit tootin' it and Lord knows I've got to have all mine, you dig."

"You fuck around and O.D. on me I'm gone drag your ass out in the alley like Chili-man did Susette and let them fuckin' alley rats eat off your nose."

"Fuck you, Max!" Gus said wearily, as he turned on the radio on top of the dresser near Maxwell and caught the first bar of Trane and the gang blowing "My Favorite Things." He shut his eyes and watched the barrage of musical notes explode into stars like fireworks at a Chinese festival. He heard each note distinctly and separately from the others, and just as clearly he saw them rocket off the launching pad in the pit of his stomach, climb a mile past his eyes, and detonate into a prismatic array of yellows, blues, reds, oranges, greens, violets, and indigos. Although he could smell the colors and taste the flavor of them on his tongue, he could not label them to save his life. Oh, he saw them as clear as you would an elephant in a sauna, but his mind's eye refused to tell him the names of the colors. Refusing to quit on the game, he lay down on his back on a red and white vinyl air mattress which was floating on a sea of black and gray mercury oil in the bottom of a goose-neck flower vase. He tried to catch the rocketing musical notes of McCoy's piano as they whizzed by him in eighth notes before they exploded overhead and showered him in sixteenth notes. He just smiled and played the game inside his head. Max and the rest of the world no longer existed, not now, not while that heroin was dog-paddling through his veins.

Maxwell says, "Fuck yourself, Brother," but Gus doesn't hear him; he doesn't even hear his mother in the kitchen washing dishes in that sagging sink that he was supposed to fix by propping a couple of two-by-fours under the front of it; he doesn't hear her singing that spiritual song, the one that he hates that Connie used to sing in church every first Sunday; and he doesn't hear her when she stops singing and washing and reaches for her beige coffee mug on the stove as white suds fall from her small thin hand like melting snow onto the floor. But what he does know is that the coffee mug doesn't have coffee in it. GORDON'S GIN AND MELTED ICE CUBES—he knows that without hearing and without seeing, and so does Max. Using his left hand as a lever Max slides back against the wall, feeling his sweaty palm press down on the gritty dirt in Connie's bed, he quickly washes the thought from his mind, knowing that's where he slept last night and more than likely that's where he'll sleep tonight. He hates to go home almost as much as he hates to see Gus shoot dope, and there's nothing that he hates more than that, not so much from fear of what Gus is doing to himself, but a fear of what it would be like for Gus to O.D. and leave him all alone. That's what he's afraid of, being alone just like he is right now, while Gus is playing hide-n-seek in a world that only has room for one. He actually envies Gus's serene solitude, but he'd never tell anybody that, not even Gus. What he would tell you is that he and Gus are running buddies, and that running buddies hustle together, get high together, and, if need be, die together. But what running buddies do most is just rap. They rap about applying for a job that they never got because some racist honky behind the front desk didn't like the way they were dressed: wide-brimmed hats, colorful clothes, and spit-shined shoes. They rap about their mops and how they quit school rather than shave them off; they rap about the first time they "bust a nut" inside a girl and how they thought they had pissed on her; they rap about boostin' gold and diamond jewelry out of Peacock's right in front of them honkies' faces; they rap about knocking some fine, sidity bitch who always turns her nose up at niggers like them and turning her out on the stroll to turn cheap tricks for a habit because she's got a hang-up about a father figure, which she don't know about, but they do, because they rap about it. They rap about niggers, they rap about honkies, they rap about old news, new news, but what they like to rap about most are players: MEN WITH LONG CARS, FINE WOMEN, AND LOTS OF CASH: MEN WHO ARE FREE ENOUGH TO DO WHATEVER THEY FEEL LIKE DOING. But what they never rap about is the pain, the pain that constantly throbs in their guts, begging for fulfillment of those abandoned childhood dreams they were bred to cherish, knowing those dreams are a million miles away and moving fast in the opposite direction. And Max knows that if Gus O.D.'s he'll be without a rappy, and heroin don't get him high enough to fill that void.

Sitting on Connie's bed, cradling the plate of dope in his lap with his back pressed against the wall, Max scoops the undated Sears bank card in the small mound of brown powder. Lifting it up to his nose, he snorts a hefty one-n-one up each nostril. Gus is sitting on his own bed, still nodding, his body limp and leaning forward, the empty blood-streaked syringe drooping from his left forearm. The needle stuck in a collapsing vein about five inches above his wrist is the only thing keeping it from just falling to the dust-and-grit-covered linoleum—the gray linoleum with the yellow rocket ships and blue astronauts which covers the old worn black and red linoleum that Max has never seen and Gus doesn't remember. Gus's right hand is hovering over the space where he once held the syringe upright—he still believes he's holding upright—and if you were to break his lethargic trance in order to caution him, he'd say, without raising his head or opening his eyes, "Don't be fuckin' with me; I'm noddin'."

Max knows better than to fuck with Gus when he's nodding, boosting, or screwing—in that particular order of importance—and that knowing when and when not to violate each other's air space is the most crucial element in their relationship; it's the thread by which running buddies hang. There are times, like now, when Max wishes there weren't any rules of the game and he could share his troubled feeling with Gus the way they used to share all of their troubles. But as it stands, Gus has his side of the room, and Max has his, and even though Max knows that a white shadow has crept into the darkened room, there is nothing he can do about it. It's like watching a three-year-old child run through the house with a butcher knife in her hand. A loud warning can be more harmful than silence. So he waits and watches, knowing that tonight will be different from all the other nights.

A laminated lithograph, *The Crying Clown*, is hanging on the wall facing Max, about nine feet from where he's sitting on the bed. His glassy brown eyes, with the dilated pupils and the sagging eyelids, watch the painting through the dusky red light as if it were the first time he'd seen it, when in fact he's seen it nearly every day for the last three years. Every time he gets really stoned and Gus has nodded out on him, he studies it with wrinkle-browed intensity. When the Gallery is jammed tight, like it was Wednesday night, and everybody is getting high and talking shit, Max doesn't even notice that there's a painting in the room. But when he's alone, he studies it with a mountain-top sense of loneliness that quivers in his stomach like an empty wagon rolling on cast-iron wheels. Sometimes he studies the red-white-and-blue-striped dunce cap which has a yellow pom-pom on the tip of it and hangs down by the clown's right ear. Sometimes he studies the white ruffled pilgrim collar which reminds him of guillotines, turkey shoots, and witch hunts. Sometimes he studies the cherry-red circles on the clown's cheeks or the white powder on his face, and sometimes it's the larger-than-life mouth with the upturned smile or the bright red ball on the tip of the clown's nose. But tonight he studies the clown's eyes, the pitiful sad blue eyes with the glossy gray tears brimming his eyelids and cascading down his cheeks, streaking his make-up into a fine thin stream of murky red, white, and blue colors slithering down a narrow path on either side of his face. Watching the painting with a pressing sense of loneliness, Max remembers when he first met Gus at the Franklin Park swimming pool, eleven years ago come summer.

THE RECTORY
James O. Elder

Connie pushed Jesse-boy to the side and said, "Fuck this!" With a violent thrust of his right leg he kicked the church door open. Both men rushed into the darkness of the sanctuary amid the muffled flickering of candlelight, their eyes cutting and darting from corner to corner and wall to wall as they waved their way through the benches, with their backs hunched low like coal miners in a fresh cut cave. Their shadows—large and ominous— flooded the walls from ceiling to floor with blackness, a blackness that slithered across the stained-glass windows and shrunk with their every step until they reached the rectory door, where the shadows were no larger than two siamese cats joined together from the neck down.

Connie slid out of his right boot the hunting knife that he'd carved from a piece of brine-soaked ebony wood, and Jesse-boy eased the .38 special from the back of his belt. They eyed each other with the firmness of a hangman asking for last words.

The nun gasped and her head flew back as the two men bolted into the room with knife and gun raised. "What's the meaning of this?" she cried as Connie rushed her, his huge black hands reaching across the mahogany desk, grabbing a fistful of her blue suit by the collar and snatching her out of her seat like a cheap rag doll. Her horn-rim glasses broke from the chain around her and shattered against the green file cabinet; her nails clawed into the flesh of his wrist as he dragged her across the desk and body-slammed her to floor. She grunted, gasping for air as the whole room whirled around her. The paperwork that had lain so neat and orderly in front of her scattered to the floor in a confused shower of swirling whiteness.

A sterile odor gushed from every part of the room, an odor so sterile that even the pungent aroma of Pine Sol couldn't hide it, mask it, or disguise it. It overpowered the aroma of every person and object in the room. They all either reeked of hospital fragrance or were smothered by it. It made Jesse-boy feel naked and uncomfortable, but Connie felt as though he'd been slapped by a northern bigot for simply being a nigger within arm's reach.

The room was a closet, compared to the mammoth sanctuary. Along with the desk and twin file cabinets in the room, there was a gray typewriter, molded by age to a metal stand of the same color, an oil portrait of the Pope, and a small ivory crucifix of Jesus on the wall, with three dried palm leaves yawning out the back of it. There was a second door in the corner of the room. Neither man knew where it led, but every once in a while Jesse-boy noticed the nun's eyes cutting toward it. Only after assuring himself that the door was not actually opening did he notice how much younger the nun looked with her glasses off. But what surprised him most was the fear that galvanized her face; it shocked him. For some strange reason that even he couldn't explain, he didn't expect to see that same tortured look of fear that he'd seen and felt so many times before—the red flushed cheeks, the glassy eyes (bugged and twitching), and that sandy pebble in the throat that swells into a dusty rock before it suddenly explodes into a boulder, lodging itself between the lungs and pressing against the heart, smothering all hope of speech beyond grunts and murmurs.

The nun was lying on the marble floor, quivering from head to toe in the grasp of Connie's clenched fist—her frail, veined, white hands still melted to his wrists as if they alone could keep her from trembling to death. Connie was kneeling over her on one knee, with the lapels of her blue jacket knotted in his left hand and the wooden knife held loose but menacing in his right. He turned to Jesse-boy, who was still standing by the door, and said, "You ever *fuck* a nun, brother?"

The words were cold and brittle, and they peeled across Jesse-boy's flesh like the squeal of old chalk on a new blackboard. Sweat streamed from his pores until his forehead glistened. The pearl handle of the .38 felt slick and slimy in his hand, the spit in his mouth thickened like paste, and the barrel of the gun became heavier and heavier as he fought to keep it pointing level. And yes, he too felt that sandy pebble swelling in his throat.

"Let's get the money and get the fuck out'a here!" he said as he sensed Connie slipping away again.

Connie laughed, revealing that twisted grin of even white teeth. And then, abruptly, he stopped. This frightened Jesse-boy even more. Like a kid mesmerized by a new toy, Connie turned from looking over his right shoulder at Jesse-boy, glanced down at the nun briefly as she closed her eyes, and then looked over his left shoulder and said in a childlike voice, "Say, Gus, do you think she's a virgin?...I don't either. What about you, Jesse-boy?"

Gus had been dead for nearly a year now and Jesse-boy knew it. He wanted to turn and run but he was afraid of what Connie might do to him if he did. So he stood there with the Pope's blue eyes pressing down on him, frozen like a hollow rock.

Connie laughed and turned back to the nun. "Yeah, I wonder if this bitch is really a virgin," he said, eyeing her with those glazed, muddy-brown eyes that didn't need words. When he placed the point of the wooden knife to her throat, she flinched and began praying through silent lips. The mahogany door in the corner of the room suddenly swung open and a priest entered. He didn't notice Jesse-boy standing by the other door as he quickly lunged for Connie. Jesse-boy struck him hard against the back of his head with the barrel of the .38 and staggered him. Connie grinned and stuck the point of the knife deep enough into the nun's throat to draw blood. "I want all the money you got in this motherfuckah, or this bitch is dead."

"OK, OK, just don't hurt her," the priest said as he frantically gathered his composure as best he could. "I'll have to get it from the other room."

"Well, DO IT!" Connie barked as he gestured with his head for Jesse-boy to go with him.

When they returned to the room, both of the priest's hands were filled with bills—mostly fives and tens. Connie stood and jerked the nun up in the air so that only her toes touched the marble floor, and with one crisp yank of his left hand he snatched her petite body toward him and plunged the blade of the wooden knife into her stomach. She could only manage to snatch a mouthful of air as the loud hiss of escaping gas flooded the room. Her eyes rolled back in her head as two of her fingernails broke off in Connie's skin, the blood trickling down the back of his wrists. Then he tugged her body even closer and began gutting her stomach. Blood and fecal matter splattered to the floor, and you could hear the splintering of bones as the knife struck her rib cage.

Jesse-boy felt eternal damnation seize him as he looked on helplessly. He couldn't go to sleep and he couldn't wake up, so he backed up to keep the puddle of blood from cresting against his shoes. The priest, stunned beyond all belief, dropped the money.

Connie slung the nun's body off the knife, and they all heard her skull crack against the marble floor. Then he turned and lunged at the priest. The priest tried to protect himself with his hands, but the force of the blow was too strong. The jagged edge of the knife's blade severed his left index finger at the second joint, before piercing his stomach to the spine. Connie held him up with his left hand as he yanked the knife out and stabbed him again and again until his body sagged limply to the floor.

Jesse-boy entered the blue-steel blackness of the house through the kitchen door. The acrid taste of vomit pulsating in his throat eroded his patience as he shoved the kitchen table out of his way and hurried to the washroom. Joyce, his wife, was in the front room watching TV in between glances at a James Clavell novel when she heard the table violently squeak across the floor. Jesse-boy ignored the repetitious chanting of "Jesse? Jesse? Jesse, is that *you*?" as he flicked on the bathroom light. He tossed the blood-soaked money that was wrapped in the nun's blue scarf into the tub. It landed in a limp but solid splat.

The fluorescent light above the mirror sputtered on and off like a neon sign about to burn out when Joyce suddenly appeared in the shadows outside the bathroom door and said in a weak, trembling voice, "Jesse, you all right?"

"Stay out'a here, Joyce!" he responded, as he palmed the door shut in her face. He usually called her Joy and she called him Jay, yet, neither of them dared to be so familiar. But in that brief glimpse before the door shut and the light sputtered off again, Joyce saw the blood. She didn't know where she saw it, but she saw it; and even though her stomach quivered in her desire to find out, she could not force her hand to open the door.

Jesse-boy turned the water on in the sink and stared into the mirror. Small, burgundy specks of blood freckled his face, as flashbacks of Connie stabbing the nun fell before his eyes like a broken window shade. He saw the surprised look on her face as the wooden knife gutted her stomach; he could hear the loud hiss of gas rush from her intestines as the knife ripped them open; and as that foul odor of unleashed excrement stormed his nostrils, the vomit erupted from his throat. Again, and again, and again. And each time he saw the knife plunge into the nun's stomach, he puked...and puked and puked, until there was nothing left to puke but the green and yellow bile that dribbled from his lips.

When he looked in the mirror and saw the blood on his shirt where Connie had pressed the bloody scarf against his chest, he began ripping away at his clothes. He snatched his shirt open in the front, popping all five buttons loose at once. He pulled the shirt over his head and tried ripping the sleeves from his wrist, but the buttons wouldn't give. So he dropped the shirt to the floor and stood in it with his foot and, with an angry thrust upwards of his arms, freed it from his right wrist and tore it loose at the cuff on his left. He kicked the shirt behind him, snatched the tattered cuff off, and flung it to the floor. He tried ripping the collar of his T-shirt but it wouldn't tear. The harder he pulled on it, the more it stretched. Finally, he grabbed it beneath the collar with both fists and yanked a hole in it. Sticking his fingers into the holes, he continued ripping it until there was nothing left but the warped collar around his neck. Next, he kicked off his shoes, unbuckled his belt, and took off his pants. He shoved the shoes and clothes into the corner behind him with his foot, pushing the blood out of sight and out of mind. All he had on now were his socks, a pair of white jockey shorts, and the warped collar of his T-shirt. And if not for the blue, octagon-shaped tile on the floor and the blue scarf in the tub that had turned a glazed purple from the blood soaked money, the washroom was white again.

Joyce leaned against the bathroom door, listening, trembling, wondering if he'd gotten into a fight, wondering if he'd been shot or cut, wondering if he'd shot or cut somebody, wondering if he was hurt bad—just wondering when she heard him turn the water on in the bathtub.

Jesse-boy got down on his knees and begin pulling detergent, shampoo, bubble-bath, cleanser, and bleach from beneath the sink and dashing them in the swiftly rising water. At first, the water turned pink from the bubble-bath and blood, but once the bleach started stripping the navy color from the scarf, the water turned an aqua-blue.

The small, white and blue, octagon-shaped tiles on the floor were biting into the flesh of his knees. Consciously, he didn't feel it, but, subconsciously he did, as he danced about on his knees, not keeping them in one place too long.

Once the suds became thick enough to hide the scarf, he shut the water off. He made sure to keep the money beneath the surface of the suds as he rubbed the mucous-like slime of coagulated blood from each and every bill before bringing it up and laying it on the side of the tub. But as his hands trolled the bottom of the tub, searching for more bills, he felt something solid and snatched his hands out. It felt like a dead mouse, but it was too narrow and too hard to be a mouse. He wiped the perspiration from his forehead with his left forearm and slowly stuck his right hand back in the water. He poked it with his finger but still couldn't tell what it was. So he picked it up and slowly pulled his fist up through the suds. He stared at his hand as it cautiously crept open. It was a human finger—thick and pale white, with a round, freshly manicured nail on one end and mushroomed and with ragged flesh on the other end, where it had been cut from the hand. It was the priest's finger. A white flame of burning heat shot up Jesse-boy's arm as he jumped to his feel and slung the finger with all his might against the wall. The finger ricocheted off three walls—thoomp-thoomp-thoomp—and bounded to a stop by his finger. He cursed Connie out loud, "You crazy-motherfuckah!" And that's when Joyce burst through the door. But Jesse-boy was a dead man, a dead man who just happened to have a heart that still pumped blood and lungs that still sucked air. He could not look Joyce in the face as she probed his body for scars or wounds, as he feebly bowed his head and walked out of the washroom like a zombie, the tears welling up his eyes and the irresistible urge to cry throbbing in the back of his throat. He walked lethargically toward the flickering TV light in the front room, Joyce hugging him around the waist, still searching for injuries, before she disappeared unnoticed and then reappeared in the front room with his pajamas and robe. Neither of them said a word as she helped him into the clothes she'd bought. He looked hollow and empty inside, and she was too afraid of what not to say to say anything at all. For the moment she was satisfied just to sit there on the couch and hold him close to her.

THE LAND
John F. Howe

The Viet Cong are magical. They can see in darkness. At night you can watch them moving around in the bush. They are shadowy clumps crawling across the jungle floor, coming at you, creeping hunched over, bending low and floating in the dark haze of vegetation. Sometimes you can hear them, mostly not, and when you do, they sound like owls and wind and falling rock.

If you take a grenade and pull the pin and hold the spoon tight in your palm, you can track them with your eyes and roll the grenade at them where you think they will be. But you must hold your breath and be very still, waiting with the grenade held tight against your chest. And you must throw it before your heart starts beating too loudly, because he can hear this and the throbbing of the ground around you and then he will disappear. It is always better to throw a grenade than it is to use your rifle, because when you shoot you always miss, and he knows that it was you that fired at him. He laughs and watches you for the rest of the night, and in the morning, when you are walking in column across the rice paddies, he singles you out and shoots you in the back of the head when you are dreaming of home. There will be a flash of blue light across your eyes, and your head will feel like all the times you fell and smacked it when you were young and falling from trees and learning to ride bicycles. You will feel the momentary pressure and see the flash and then your head will explode. But these things do not really matter because they are not lasting. What is lasting is that you feel foolish. It is the last thing that you will feel. I have seen the faces of guys that have fired at the shadows during the night, and in the morning, when we are humping and that firecracker pop echoes from the treeline where we spent the night before, they are lying in paddy muck where water buffalo and little yellow people have emptied their bowels and they look foolish. Face down, spreadeagled in dirty shit, shallow-water foolish. And when you roll them over their face is a mass of oozing gray and red strips of meat and they have emptied their bladder and bowels into the paddy too. It is not really a face any longer, but it's foolish looking just the same...very foolish and very much forever.

The Viet Cong are mystical. They turn to smoke and float over mountains. You kill them and they disappear. They crawl through rows of concertina and razor wire without making as much as a whisper. They can see everything and they know everything, even days before the rumors get to us. Where they know you will be going, they plant things in the ground along the trail that explode in loud orange and black CRACKS when you step on them, or things that go pop, real soft and fizzing like, when you trip on the wires that they string across the narrow foot paths. All of these things take your legs off, or your balls, or your hands, or other things that you need. The bigger ones are not so mean and degrading. They don't spare you anything, they just make you disappear.

The VC can swim for miles under water, and in the current look like floating reeds or patches of weed. They are haze in the morning, and distant rippling heat waves across a flat paddy in the afternoon. At night they are shadows that turn into bushes at first light. Sexton says that they can do these things because they are the land. It is a philosophy, he says. They and the land are one and the same, and I nod because now I have an understanding and I nod again because I don't want to know anymore.

Once, on a sultry afternoon hump across the valley, we spotted four VC crossing an open expanse of brown checkerboard paddies. They were about seven hundred meters away and nearing a treeline at the far end of the basin. We waited for the lieutenant to make contact with Battalion and Sexton passed the binoculars along the crouching column. I had never seen a VC before. I leaned across the dike, resting the glasses on top of the packed earth. The heat rises in wavering chorus lines in the distance. They are walking in column, rifles slung casually across the sweat-stained backs of their tan khaki uniforms, and moving crisply. The one at the rear of the column turns, looking back across the flat, and I lower my eyes from the glasses, thinking he can see me.

IMPALED MAN
John F. Howe

We come down from the mountain, single-file, ten yards apart, under a triple canopy of thick rain forest that blocked out the light of the sun. Underfoot the soft earth is damp and covered with moss. You have to keep one arm free to push away the giant hanging cobwebs and hordes of insects sent into frantic swarms by the swinging machete of the point man cutting away at the tangle of vines looping down from the tiers of vegetation above. There is no breeze. Everything hangs limply and smells like an old basement foot locker.

We trudge along and birds take up screeching in panicked flight, their calls echoing hollowly in the listless half-black emptiness. Rock monkeys chatter and roll small boulders down on our procession from the dark elevations of the ridgeline to our left. The air is heavy. You suck in at the vacuum around you through clenched teeth to keep the clouds of insects from being pulled into your mouth.

Sexton holds the platoon up and checks his compass. He motions to the point man at the head of the column to swing off to the right. We move away from the incline of the ridge and soon lose the rock monkeys, who follow cackling behind us for a while but gradually lose interest and return to their caves.

Ahead, the canopy of vegetation begins to thin out, and streams of dusty sunbeams angle through the black overhead. A few hundred meters later we come out of dense bush and there is a horse-shoe clearing facing a steep granite ledge that falls away into a large open sea of swaying elephant grass. Across the valley of grass there is another range of looming purple mountains, and thin wisps of clouds drift across the valley. The clouds are almost level with my gaze, and where the sunlight strikes the sides of the dark mountains, I can see the shadows of the clouds passing against them. A rush of cool air comes down the valley, chilling my sweat-soaked shirt, and I shiver.

From the ledge the valley below looked deserted. Two wisps of blue smoke ribbon up from the center of the hootches. On the side of the ville facing us there is a semi-circle of dark objects stuck in the ground. It is difficult to make out just what the forms are, but gazing down from the ledge, they appear to be something of religious significance. There is no movement in the ville. No livestock. No people. Nothing…It is deathly quiet and, except for the wind coming down the valley rustling the jungle on the sides of the mountains, all that is heard are the deep cries of the buzzards circling over the village.

At the base of the ledge we come into the valley of chest-high elephant grass. You cannot see to either side of you once inside of it, just straight ahead, following the man in front of you through the path cut by the point man's machete. Every once in a while Sexton raises his arm for us to halt and climbs up on the point man's shoulders to get a correct heading to the village. We change directions several times but I feel relatively safe from the ambush, because in the high grass you cannot see a man walking three or four feet next to you and the 'gooks' can never tell our position.

I plough ahead, swinging the butt of my '16 against the stomach of the grass, and suddenly I am in the clearing that faces the village that we had seen from the ledge. I crouch and look across the one hundred or so meters of open space to the brown, dried-grass hootches. There is a thin breeze now, and I can smell wet burning wood. A dog barks but I cannot see him. Sexton calls the radio man over and clicks the handset three times. After a few minutes I see the tops of the grass waver on the right side of the clearing and then the rest of the platoon emerges silently from the tall swaying grass. The radio crackles and Sexton whispers into the mouthpiece. He waves and we move out across the open space of the clearing toward a graveyard just at the edge of the ville. There is a faded pink pagoda centered in the middle of the cemetery. The rest of the markers are lopsided slate slabs sunk in the wet earth at unnatural angles.

I move off to the right of the pagoda and Sexton waves for us to stop. We lay chilly and take up positions behind the grave markers. I check again to make sure that the safety is off my M-16, and chamber another round to clean the action of the bolt. I push my helmet back and stare at the gravestone. It is faded and weather-beaten. The etching reads:

THAM NGUYEN LINH
PARTISAN
3/6 R.I.C.
MORT POUR LA FRANCE
20-6-50

When I look down the line of headstones Sexton is peering intently at a spot to the left of the ville where the half-circle of religious forms had been seen earlier from the mountain ledge. I peek around the stone and past the edge of the foreground hootch, squinting into the sunlight at the forms visible now in the clearing.

In the open clearing an old man hangs, naked and impaled, on an implanted mahogany stake. The pointed end of the stake is thrust up his arms and protrudes from a bluish gash at his breastbone. His head hangs stiffly forward, open eyes staring blankly downward at the last thing he ever saw. The body is turning black and bloating, oozing fluid from the sun-baked cracks across his stretched stomach wall, at which clouds of flies swarm. The barking dog that I had heard earlier is snapping at the old man's legs hanging down bent and just touching the earth at the base of the stake. When the dog snaps he pulls strings of purple tendons from the calf of the leg along with hunks of raw dark meat. The old man's white beard sticks straight out like it is starched, and each time the dog leaps, tearing away his flesh, the beard jerks. His testicles stand shriveled and black, and the flies setting on them scatter at each of the dog's thrusts. The cur continues to tear away at the old man, viciously shaking his head, possessed with each new hunk of flesh, and tossing the decaying meat to the side. When the dog lunges for the old man's testicles, Sexton leans his rifle across the nose of a gargoyle on the roof of the pagoda and fires one quick shot, shattering the stillness. The dog jerks mid-air in his final lunge and lands convulsing on the ground at the man's feet. After a while he becomes silent and is engulfed by a dark cloud of flies.

The radio set clicks and Sexton explains the shot that was fired. The lieutenant orders our squad to sweep through the ville from the east toward the rest of the platoon that will act as a blocking force for any VC flushed out from the ville. We walk through the hootches, kicking at scattered pieces of wicker and pottery. Marbley urinates on one of the two fires, and when we come out on the other side we are just to the right of the old man and in the middle of the circle of mahogany stakes. Next to the old man are four more pointed poles and on each of them a body impaled and hanging forward. Beside the man is a woman still wearing her conical hat. She is about the same age as the man, but fully clothed, and her arms are untied and hanging stiff along her sides. Her betel-stained teeth hang open in a slack grin as much as to say, "Fuck it." The woman next to her is younger but not very much less wrinkled. The pointed stake has been thrust up her vagina and exits through her back just below the next where the pole tears away at the rotting flesh from the weight of the straining body. The two other bodies are children and they have been decapitated. The frail forms hang from the poles, bloated out of proportion, the thin blue hands bound behind them with wetted strands of Manilla rope. The blackened heads of the children are stuck on the pole of the younger woman just below her crotch. Rolled up in the mouth of one of the heads is a Xerox photo of a smiling John and Robert Kennedy. Below this photo is scrawled: 'SUCH IS THE DESTINY OF ALL IMPERIALIST FAMILIES.'

We set up in a perimeter around the village and dig in for the night. The lieutenant passes word for no fires. Marbley huddles in our hole and shovels down a can of greasy ham and lima beans. I can't eat, and give him my beans and franks but save the can of peaches for myself. The stench of the rotting bodies on the poles in front of the lines hangs heavy like a wet blanket over us, and I have to choke back the vomit that threatens to erupt several times during the night. The sweet-sick smell is everywhere, and it takes me half of Marbley's watch to fall asleep. When I finally managed to doze, all I could see was the face of the old man and the bulging eyes of the decapitated heads, and I awoke well before my watch. I crouched in the hole, blinking at the unusual brightness of the three-quarter moon. Marbley is leaning forward against the edge of the hole. His rifle lies on the fresh turned earth in front of him next to the five grenades he has positioned, pins bent and pulled half out of the retaining holes. I rustle under the dew-moist poncho, and he turns back toward me holding the opened, half-eaten can of beans and franks, snickering and motioning me forward with a flick of his grease-glistening plastic C-ration spoon. I throw the poncho off and peer over the edge of the hole. There in the moonlight stands Sexton next to one of the impaled forms, tugging away with his needle-nose pliers at the old man's gold teeth. We watch him in the eerie half glow, Marbley spooning off the remainder of the beans and tossing the can behind us. Sexton pulls and wrestles with the old man's mouth, cursing silently in the quiet of the twin shadows. After each extraction he holds the tooth up to the moon glow for inspection, and either discards it with a flick of the pliers or places it gingerly into the first aid pouch hanging at the rear of his cartridge belt. When he is satisfied that all the wealth has been taken from the old man's mouth, he crouches and runs back to our lines. When he passes our hole he sees that we have been watching him and sneers, "Mind yer own fuckin' bizness." I couldn't sleep for the rest of the night, so I took both our watches and Marbley was more than happy to agree. Toward morning I nodded out a few times, and just after first light we pulled the stakes down and buried the bodies. We burned the village and went back up into the mountains. I was real tired all that day.

QUEEN OF EUROPE
Brendan Martin

I have been offered the position of Queen of Europe. They want to bathe me and worship me and wrap me in fine linens and it won't cost me a thing. I'll live in rich splendor amidst large dogs and sputtering flamingoes, and eat mangoes all day long. My name will be Vashya, and I will be kind. I'll rule with diffidence, and wear flowers woven throughout my hair. No one shall wear shoes, and the new form of greeting will be to touch lightly the other person's face. My ministers will all be painted, a different hue for a different cabinet. They will sing and laugh and tell jokes, and when we are all exhausted from play we will lie down in a coconut grove and nap like children.

I'll be eating dinner someday, the long table stretching before me, empty save for one plate at the far end opposite me. I'll look deeply into a candle's flame and wish for my prince, who rides a tall white stallion with a proud neck, prancing nimbly with a kind of sidestep down the road to my castle and, when my guards ask who is there, my prince replies, "It is I, and I have come for the Queen. Let down the doors to your battlements, that I may come up, and bid me entrance. Make warm my horse, and let the Queen know of my presence that she may prepare my meal with her hands, and anoint her skin with perfumes to spark the fire of my ardor." And they will do so.

And my chambers will be lit by a thousand candles, and the floors will be covered thickly with rugs, and scents from all the world shall be summoned to make us dreamy with passion, and we will make love until the candles die, and I'll lie in his arms with my head on his chest and sleep like a fat bear.

We will be awakened in the morning by the singing of the birds, and he'll kiss me lightly on the forehead and softly say my name, but I'll pretend to be asleep because I like the feeling of the moment. He will get up and walk naked to the window, and while he stands shrouded in the sunlight, with the mist of Spanish moors to soften his contours, I'll put on a false beard and hide beneath the covers. He does not know that I have cut holes in his pants, and put oil in his shoes, and when he runs to ask me what has happened, I'll spring from beneath the covers and yell, "Surprise!"

My subjects will be very loyal, and we will paint each house a different color, and no doors will be locked. They will hasten to the sowing in the spring, and work hard throughout the summer, so that we may have good crops for the year. I will hire traveling musicians and jugglers and mimes and acrobats and circuses and theatrical companies, and they will criss-cross the land with the best of entertainment. The children will learn to laugh in school, and how to be kind, and if they want kittens they will have them. When they are very, very young they will be shown the wonders of the world, so that they may think about them while they grow up. They will teach the adults to be children, and the adults will teach them the values needed to stay that way.

If someone will come to my country's door, and bang and shout and stamp and fume, and say that he wants to make war, we will ignore him, and turn our head to water the flowers. If they might be so bold as to throw something at us, we will step aside, and then scold them irritably. "We have no need for your implements of war," I shall tell them; "be on your way, for we have no desire for you to visit if you cannot behave yourselves." They might pout and whine, but it will be of no use, and my guards will stoutly refuse them entrance.

After a while they will see the error that they have made, and decide that it might be best to be friends. I shall have them send me their highest ministers and engage them in a contest against mine. They will play hopscotch and checkers and mumblety-peg, and have pie-eating contests and mudfights, and stay up all night to watch movies. They will be awarded points on a fair basis, and the ones with the most points at the end of a week are the winners. I have no need to fear that my ministers will lose because I know that they are the best in all of these things. And after we win, we shall invite them in for a celebration, and there will be music and puppetry and jousting, with prizes for everyone.

I shall have lots of wild bears in my forests, and tigers and chipmunks and snakes. They might wear coats and ties if they feel like it, or sing if their fancy strikes them so. They will get cold in the winter, and their teeth will chatter, and they'll have no place to go. Then I shall send out my men and have them brought forth to my castle, and there will be warm beds for all of them, and hot tea and delicate biscuits, with plenty of freshly whipped butter. I will sit up at night and tell the bears stories, and tuck them in after they have fallen asleep, and blow out the candles. I will bring in the snakes one by one, and whisper that they be quiet. I shall suspend them from the curtain rods and tops of doors, and tuck them under the bed, and in the sheets, and all around the bears. The bears will snooze soundly and be unaware that all this is happening. Lastly, I will place a pot and spoons in the room, and ask that the snakes bang loudly on the pot in the morning, for everyone knows that bears are so lazy. I should like to be there in the morning to see it, but I shall be throwing water on the tigers.

A proclamation will be sent out to all the land that visitors from outer space are very welcome at the dinner table of the castle. We have a very liberal space program. When they come to dine, I will ask them what of the planets, and how are things these days? I shall get them roaring drunk, and lead them around in the snow. We shall give them firecrackers to smoke and exploding matches to light them with, and put itching powder down their backs. If they have a back. If they don't we shall just get them drunk. At any rate, I hope they bring their own interpreters.

After they've sobered up the next day, we shall talk of difficult things, and knit our eyebrows in perplexity and confusion. We will speak of science over cereal, and mathematics over tea. They will show us the wonders of their worlds, and we will show them our toys. We'll take long walks through the woods and stop for a drink by a stream, where we'll take off all our clothes and play in the water. We'll put our clothes on while we're still wet, and run back through the fields in the sunshine, laughing and tugging at flowers. After a nap in the haystacks, we'll saunter casually through the markets, and collect things for dinner that night. If they like beets, they shall have beets. And if they don't, we'll get drunk.

The next day, I shall send the snakes in to wake them up, and have sandwiches packed for their flight back through the stars. They shall have plenty of beer to take along in a cooler, and hot peppers and salami. When they make ready to leave, we will all cry and laugh, and smile at each other in fond reminiscence of the things that we'd done for their stay. I will kiss each one on the cheek, and give them each presents to take back. As they wave goodbye from the door of their ships, we'll wave back, and wonder if they'll like the tequila.

NICKEY
John MacPhail

My father was a house painter and an alcoholic. The summer that I turned eleven years old, he decided that I should start coming to work with him. There were many small jobs that a boy my age could do, he told my mother; it was time that I started finding out about the real world.

So I helped my father carry ladders, mix spackling paste, and shake out drop cloths. But my most important job was pouring him the morning eye-opener as we bumped along the highway in the old Dodge van with the ladders creaking and shifting on the roof. Each day my father carefully placed a tall rusty thermos just behind the driver's seat, and when we were safely away from the house, he would reach behind the seat—with the absurd cunning of an alcoholic, his eyes never left the road—and hand me the thermos and say in a hushed conspiratorial voice, "Here, splash me a little in the cup, will ya?"

The liquid that I sloshed into the red thermos cup seared the air with a nose-wrinkling, stomach-churning bite, and I always held my breath as I poured. He called it "iced tea."

Many mornings, as we rode along in the van with the wind howling through the broken side window, and the leaky exhaust giving me a small headache behind my eyes, I would think about other boys who might be going to work with their fathers. In my imagination the contrast was extreme. These other boys rode in sleek new trucks, with all sorts of knobs and buttons to fiddle with, and the equipment in back was sorted and organized, everything in its place, and these boys had fathers who smiled and joked in the morning, who required no smoking brown liquid from a thermos, who didn't toss his smouldering cigarette among the paint cans, who might stop at a doughnut shop or a restaurant and get a big breakfast and tousle his son's hair and say to anyone who would listen, "Hey, this here's my kid." A section of rough road or some railroad tracks would jolt me out of this daydream and I would look over at my father, at the filthy painter's cap riding high on his head, the grimy overalls, the tiny flecks of yesterday's white paint on his nose and eyelashes, and if that wasn't hopeless enough, just about this time he'd hand over the red cup, cough a few times and say, "Hit me again there, buddy boy."

We were working in a new housing project near Wauconda, Illinois. These were ranch homes that were identical right down to the brass door knockers on the front door and the single wind-whipped silver maple on the parkway. Just down the highway was a tavern. It was a small building of flaking green paint and missing roof shingles. Though it was right on the highway, and you could see it from at least two miles in either direction, and though there wasn't a single bush, tree, billboard, or any other landmark to conceal it, the tavern was called Rudy's Hideaway. That's where my father and I would wind up at the end of each working day.

As the summer wore on, I grew to hate everything about the place. I hated the sound of the gravel under the tires as we pulled into the parking lot. I hated the iridescent blue grackles that were forever searching the ground around the dumpster. I hated the way the screen door banged behind us, as if pronouncing yet another doom, and I hated the beer smell, and the body smell, and the stacks of clammy cardboard coasters, and the sound of someone sliding a plastic ashtray along the bar. Most of all, I hated the bartender's bald head and his insincere sport shirt, and the way he would talk about his children with one man and pussy with another, and I hated him for coming over to my father and saying, "Hey Jack, what'll it be?"

That was the pattern for the summer. If I whined and pleaded with my father to get him to leave, he'd become irate and drink even more frantically. But I couldn't leave him alone either. If he got too drunk to drive the van, then I'd have to call my mother at work. ("Hello, could I speak to Vicky please, extension 217? Thanks. Hello, Mom, it's me.")

Some men came into the bar, had one drink and left. Again contrasts. To go home and eat dinner at the table with no shouting, no breaking dishes, a mother who didn't serve the meal with a body trembling in subdued fury, who had time in the evening to go to the carnival at the shopping center or to the Dairy Queen, whose hands weren't covered with dozens of cuts and scratches from working with the machines on second shift at Solo Cup.

I'd drink two or three root beers and play drums on the bar with a couple of drink stirrers and I'd wander around. There were always several men playing pool. Muscular men with dirty T-shirts and Marine Corps tattoos who said "fuck" a lot. Fuckin' house, fuckin' lawnmower, fuckin' old lady. Once a fat man who had two inches of hairy belly hanging below his undershirt said, "Hey man, fuck if I'm gonna fuck around with that fuckin' fuckup." I'd check the bathroom to see if anyone had cleaned off that question mark of shit that someone had smeared on the wall by the toilet. And I'd gaze up at the midnight blue eyes of the moosehead on the wall and wonder about something so big and majestic and dead. The time dragged on.

One afternoon, sitting next to my father, I began to squirm. I squirmed as though I were on fire. I banged my empty glass on the bar. I coughed. I coughed some more, I pretended I was choking. Nothing worked. My father was hunched over his seven-seven, not talking with anyone, a scowl on his face, lost in some unknowable anguish, a couple of wet dollar bills on the bar in front of him. I looked down the bar to an empty stool far across the room, and then I closed my eyes and imagined myself sitting on that stool watching us. I saw both myself and my father very clearly. I could see the smallest things. The blue paint chips in my hair, the fine dust on my arms. I could see my father's chest rising and falling beneath his overalls. And then I could see right through them, past the shirt and undershirt, and I could see that small mole that sat among the chest hairs directly over his heart. Then, as I sat with my eyes closed, watching from that empty stool across the room, I saw an older boy come up out of the hazy late afternoon bar light and sit down next to me. Quickly I opened my eyes. There was no one beside me. My father sat as before. Suddenly, I grinned and closed my eyes. He was there again, getting himself comfortable on the stool. He looked a lot like me. Sandy hair and green eyes, a T-shirt that said University of Wisconsin. If I'd had an older brother, that's what he would have looked like. As I watched from across the room, I could see myself talking with him. He said his name was Nickey. I said mine was Michael. He said he already knew my name. I saw myself laugh. We talked for quite a while, about baseball and fishing. My dad had always promised to take me fishing in Canada, and Nickey said he'd been there, and he told me about the northern pike and the big pine trees and how when you were thirsty you could lean over the side of the boat and drink right from the lake. I saw myself raising a hand to the bartender and buying Nickey a root beer with some of my father's change. Nickey used a straw. I drank straight from the glass. Then Nickey asked me what was wrong with my father.

"Nothing's wrong," I said.

"Whatta you mean, nothing's wrong? He's drunk, look at him."

"He's not drunk, he's just tired. He works real hard. Sometimes he goes to sleep when he has a drink."

"Come on, you're fooling yourself, he's not sleeping, he's had four drinks. Don't tell me you haven't been counting. You're going to have to call your mother. He won't be able to drive. Why are you so afraid to do anything?"

"I'm not afraid. Why don't you shut up."

"Oh sure, tell me to shut up. What does that solve? You're afraid of him. Admit it. It would be so easy to do something but you're afraid. Chicken, chicken, chicken."

I opened my eyes and slid off the stool. The cash register clanged. Someone laughed in a deep voice. Outside on the highway a semi truck boomed as it went over a chuck hole. My father was trying to light a cigarette and grunting. I watched his useless hands fumble with the matches. I heard Nickey yelling "Chicken, chicken," and then I lunged and threw myself on my father's back. I wanted to dig my fingers into his skin and hurt him. I pounded at the back of his head, and then I locked my hands around his neck and pulled back trying to choke him. He was trying to speak and stand at the same time, and then finally he stood upright and pried my hands loose. I could smell the sweat and the paint on his overalls. He twisted his body from side to side and slid me off his back as if he were removing a shirt. When I touched the floor I was too weak to stand, and I sprawled to my knees and started to cry. I had wanted to shout at him, but I had no voice.

I saw the paint-spattered tips of his shoes before me and next to them, a single bright dime. When I looked up, my father was looking down at me with red-rimmed eyes. His feet were wide apart as if to brace himself against a strong wind, and his cap had spun sideways on his head.

"Now you get up goddamn it and go outside," he said. When I stood up, sniffling and brushing the dust from my hands, I felt the bartender and some of the other men staring at me, and I held my tears and kept my eyes on the dirty floor tiles until just before I reached the door when I heard someone laugh, and then I broke into a run, pushed through the screen door and ran sobbing out into the parking lot. I leaned against the back of the van and beat my fist against the metal, and then I grabbed a rock and threw it at the tavern, but it sailed way over the roof. My father lurched from the building and came tilting across the lot like a leaning stop sign. I moved away from the van and picked up another rock. "Get in the truck," he said. I didn't move. I thought he would come after me, but he went straight to the van. He tried three times to open the door and then he climbed in. He started the engine and raced it unmercifully. I put my hands over my ears. Nickey was right. I was afraid of my father, of the tavern, the van, the thermos, everything. He backed up in a spray of loose gravel, then slammed on the brakes and stuck his inflamed face out the window.

"Get in here, goddamn it. Right now." I dropped the rock to the ground. I could hear Nickey saying, "Chicken, chicken." When I climbed into my seat, my father was pouring a drink from the thermos. His hands were shaking. He finished in two swallows and put the thermos behind the seat. "So you want to go home?" he roared. I turned my head to the window in an effort to duck his hot stare. "Where's your mother?" he yelled.

"I don't know."

"You know where she is, goddamn it. Where is she?"

"I don't know. She's at work."

"You're goddamned right she's at work. What do you think is gonna happen when you get home? She ain't gonna be there, is she? She's working at that fuckin' factory, isn't she?" I could feel his sour breath against the back of my neck. He seemed to be screaming right into my ear.

"You want to eat dinner? Huh? Who's gonna fix it? Tell me that." I had started to cry again.

"Please can't we just go home," I said.

"Sure we can go home. You wanna go home? Fine, let's go home." He floored the accelerator and we spun out of the parking lot and squealed onto the highway. I kept my face against the window, smearing the tears away with the heel of my hand. Halfway home my father pulled out the thermos and handed it to me without a word. As I poured, I thought of Nickey in his University of Wisconsin T-shirt, telling me about the pine trees and the clean water.

"Second shift," my father said. "She's workin' second shift," and then he began to laugh and pound the steering wheel, and when I tried to hand him the cup he waved his hand and gasped, "Hold it, hold it, wait 'til I stop laughing." So I sat looking straight ahead with the cup and the thermos in my lap while the white line on the road weaved before us as my father struggled to steer. I could see Nickey clearly in my mind and could see, as well, the houses and factories and fields beyond the highway, and could see our own house, and even my room, with my favorite yellow blanket on the bed and the friendly rotund shape of the dresser. At night when I lay with my eyes open, though I could see all these things clearly still, sitting there in the van beside my father I had the strongest sensation that I was at least partially blind.

THE DREAM STEALER
Jake Aronov

The Dream Stealer is a huge man, built like a bear, but totally invisible. He is ancient, as ancient as the hills from which he comes; he has been stealing the dreams of little children since time eternal, for he hates children. He walks very slowly and quietly, especially when he is out on a caper. His effects on people are subtle, almost unnoticeable: Every night at midnight, he leaves his cave in an old hillside, and goes down to the town in the valley. It is a fairly small town, but borders on a larger city. He goes to the first house he comes to in the town, and walks through the walls to enter. Nobody ever hears him coming. He searches the house for the children's rooms, then enters, very quietly, on tiptoe. He puts his hand over their forehead, then over their eyes, in order to feel for rapid-eye movements, and thus, determine whether or not they are dreaming. If they are, he unzips their heads, reaches his hand in, and pulls out their dreams.

His first victim is a little girl named Debbie, who is five years old. She is living a life of great luxury in a huge mansion with well-manicured gardens, two Cadillacs, and a swimming pool in her backyard. Her father is an airline executive, so she gets to travel quite frequently. One midnight, Dream Stealer enters her house, and looks up and down the second floor for an unsuspecting victim. When he sees Debbie sleeping, he enters her room on tiptoe, and feeling that she is having a dream, unzips her head, reaches in, and pulls out the dream. He holds it in his hands, and it flashes on his palms and fingers like a movie on a screen.

Debbie is dreaming about going to her uncle's farm in the country. The land is beautiful, and very serene, with rolling hills and nearby forests. Debbie's uncle helps her up on her pony, and she rides off towards the hills, and listens to the birds singing in the tress, and sees the green leaves blooming and loves it.

And the Dream Stealer sees the dream, and he likes it, too, for it reminds him of the quietness of the night which he loves so much. So he folds up the dream like a road-map and puts it in the pouch which he carries over his right shoulder. And the next morning, Debbie wakes up and feels that she is missing something, but cannot remember what. She no longer has any desire to go out to the country.

Next, the dream Stealer goes to the house of a famous military man. It is a large, elegant house, with a large, well-kept lawn, several trees, a flower garden with a fountain around the back; the owner has a full-time gardener to keep up the grounds. The Dream Stealer enters the house, and looks through all of the bedrooms on the second floor, until he comes to the room of a little boy, Johnny.

He puts his hand over Johnny's forehead, then over his eyes, and finds that Johnny is in the middle of a dream. So he unzips Johnny's head, reaches in, and pulls out the dream. Johnny is dreaming about becoming an astronaut and flying to the moon. He goes into his dressing room and puts on his space suit, helmet, oxygen tank, and other gear. Feeling like he is carrying a ton of bricks on his back, he walks out of his dressing room and goes to meet his fellow astronauts (there are a total of four astronauts on this flight). Johnny is a big man now, big in many ways: He is tall and handsome, and is greatly admired for his athletic abilities and prowess. A crowd of people gather around the four astronauts as they prepare to enter the space ship.

The countdown begins: "Ten!...Nine!...Eight!...Seven!...Six!...Five!...Four!...Three!...Two!...One!...Zero!...Lift-off!" And the rocket's engines roar as the huge spaceship lifts off the ground and heads for the clouds. Johnny waves good-bye as he looks out the window and sees thousands of people clapping and cheering as they wave their colorful flags. And just a few dream-moments later, the spaceship lands on the moon with a big "Thud!" The four astronauts toss coins to decide who will have the honor to be the first man to walk on the moon. Johnny wins. He puts his helmet back on his head, making sure that his oxygen tank fits securely; then he thrusts open the compression chamber and climbs out of the spaceship. The surface of the moon is just as he expected it to be: dark, rocky, hilly, and full of craters. He moves around slowly, looking for good rock samples to take back to Earth with him. After a while, he begins to feel hungry; he looks around for green cheese, but can't find any.

The Dream Stealer sees all this, and he likes it very much, for he loves men who do heroic deeds to honor their country. So he folds up the dream like a road map and puts it in his pouch with the other dreams. And the next morning, Johnny feels as if he is missing something, but doesn't know what, and he no longer has any desire to become an astronaut and go to the moon.

Next, the Dream Stealer goes to the house of a part-owner and executive of the electric utility monopoly. The house is enormous: it contains twenty-five rooms, and is decorated elegantly with crystal chandeliers and marble bathtubs. The Dream Stealer enters the house, and looks through all the bedrooms until he comes to the room of the little boy of the family, whose name is Jeff. (Jeff is so sound asleep that an air raid wouldn't wake him up.)

The Dream Stealer enters the room very slowly and quietly. He feels his eyes and forehead, and then unzips his head, and reaches in to take out the dream. Jeff is dreaming about becoming an executive of his father's company. He is sitting in back of his huge walnut desk, and is going over the company's latest financial statements with two other executives. A large graph hangs on the wall in back of the desk, showing that the company's profits have been soaring for the last two years. Suddenly, the room is flooded with gallons of green water, and the young executives find themselves swimming in a sea of money.

The Dream Stealer looks at this dream, and smiles; he loves it, for he loves money. So he folds up the dream and puts it in the pouch with the other dreams. The next morning, Jeff wakes up knowing that something is missing, but does not know what. He no longer has any desire to work for his father's company.

After visiting Jeff's house, the Dream Stealer is finished with his nightly caper. He walks back towards the cave, slowly, for his pouch is now heavy with dreams. He walks out of the town, down an old country road, through the old prairie, through an ancient forest with bayobab trees, and finally comes to the hill country. The air is still and quiet this night, and the moon is pale. Presently, the eerie cry of a coyote momentarily breaks the silence. The Dream Stealer approaches his hill and enters his cave. He takes his big pouch off of his shoulder, and empties it of its contents. Then he takes the dreams and locks them up in his vault for safe-keeping, so that the children won't ever be able to come and take their dreams back.

GANGBANGERS
Rod McKinney

"John, you ain't shit!!"

Now they stand nose to nose, toe to toe, their fists tight at their sides as they glare into each other's eyes.

"Well, hit me then.....come on, hit me."

A fat black girl in the crowd turns to her tall girl friend: "Girl, I ain't got all day. If they ain't gone fight, let's go. I want some french fries. John scared to fight Sonny anyway."

One of the boys turns toward her and screams, "I ain't scared!"

While the other shoves his bare shoulder into his chest and says, "Well, here I am.......come on, hit me then...sucker!!"

Someone in the crowd shoves the boys and the battle is on. They run into each other from the momentum of the push, instantly backing away to swing on each other. Neither connects, but the style is classic. Holding their fists close to their faces, they jab at each other as they circle, both intent on showing off their boxing styles. But the crowd will not have it.

"Hit that motherfucker, Sonny!" one boy yells.

"Go on and deal on that stud, John, he ain't shit!" screams another, who in his anger takes a mock swing at one of the fighters. Now they roll in the grass, neither doing any real damage, while you scan the nearby sidewalks.

Across the wide median and on the other side of the boulevard, shadowy figures loom in the dark doorways and against the red brick walls of three story apartment buildings. In packs of three to eight. You can tell that they have already carved out their own patches of cement real estate. As you look, it seems they have lined every route leading away from the school. Some wear immaculate white hats, complemented by small red feathers stuck in wide black bands. The hat bands also serve to hold toothpicks, small razors, joints, and anything else that can be concealed by the thick expanse of cloth. All of them wear their hats tilted to the side in one way or another, to the left or to the right, usually to the left for some reason. Some tilt the hat forward but never back. Adorning conked scalps, underneath the hats are red and black scarves knotted in the front. Usually they are black, for black is the base color for gangbangers. Many wear long black leather coats with a matching black leather sash at the waist. Others wear short waist level black leathers with buttons, never zippers. Zippers are for honkies, no gangbanger in his right mind would be caught dead in a zippered leather. Dark creased trousers are part of the uniform also, never corduroys and seldom jeans, except for very young and upcoming members. Here and there black khakis can be seen rolled up to reveal heavy combat boots called "Brogans." All wear black nylon socks; to wear anything else, especially white socks, is to beg for intense verbal abuse. Most keep their hands in their coat pockets, unless they're smoking, at which time the cigarette is cupped to the inside of the palm to keep the wind from fanning the coals. Only Kools and Pall Malls, nothing else will do. Camel and Lucky Strikes are considered "white" cigarettes. Standing around corners, some hold long sticks in their hands as some members of groups pass around small brown paper bags filled with pint sized bottles of wine. They take short quick gulps as the crumpled bags pass quickly from hand to hand.

Now they are streaming out of the dark gangways that separate the apartment buildings. Others approach from alleys that let out onto Douglas Park boulevard near the school. Still others can be seen cruising slowly down side streets with their dogs: large, mangy, black, and dirty grey German Shepherds, and sleek brown Doberman Pinschers. They strut slowly alongside their masters, ears perked, but never straining at the leash, for they are as cool, calm, and observant as their masters. Sitting on command, they join the rest of the predators in a quiet inspection of their next victims.

And you know this is just the beginning. As the weather warms up there will be more and more. So many, in fact, that some will get into heated battles over the corners they will control. But for now they didn't have their scenes tight yet for no one group took up in the middle of the median strip. As you begin to walk quickly toward Kedzie, more than five blocks away, you know that it won't be this easy much longer. Soon they will take to sitting on the park benches that line the asphalt walkways that crisscross the median at least once in every block. You know they will bring their dogs and sit calmly on the backs of the benches while their dogs growl and inspect everyone that goes by. They will pick their victim, and shake him down for anything and everything he has. You have seen them take coats, gloves, hats, even shoes, and of course every penny you have. Unless they want you for something else, like running away the last time they called you to stop, they usually won't beat you up. But in the spring and early summer there was always a fresh crop of young gangbangers trying to make the grade and they were liable to jump on you for anything and usually for nothing to impress the older hoodlums.

You are almost to Kedzie, having half walked, half run the entire five blocks. As you look back and breathe a sigh of relief, you know you have made it this time, but the question is, will you the next time, and the next, and the next?

MOTHER MARY AGNES
Zoe Keithley

The day dawned grey. The light crawled over the window sills and dissipated down the wall. It almost didn't reach the alcove curtains.

Helene turned in her bed. She knew it was morning by the peculiar quiet, like a held breath, that prevails just before the world gathers itself up for the business of the day. Mother Mary Agnes's beads bounced against the leg of her chair, and the whispering sound of her curtain opening stirred the air.

Helene turned again, thrusting her back to the world, and buried the side of her head in the pillow. Her heart felt like a stone. In her mind she saw the little yellow duck shivering in the rain, fluffing its feathers and trembling. Oh God, why couldn't they find it? How *could* they find it? Her feet under the blanket felt like ice. They were still frozen from last night. She thought to reach for her socks but stopped as she remembered them dropped on the floor at the foot of her bed, soaked from the rain that had seeped through her mud-caked shoes.

It was the squishing sound the shoes made against the wood of the dormitory floor that had alerted Mother Mary Agnes and sent her popping through her alcove curtain, head done up in a white nightcap.

The nun's eyes had searched her—wet hair plastered to her head, red-rimmed eyes, soaked raincoat, legs streaked with mud, white socks brown and stained, oxfords dyed black by the wet night.

To Helene's surprise, the nun didn't get mad. She just raised her eyebrows and asked in a hoarse whisper, "Any luck?" Helene had fought the tears welling up in her throat. She shook her head. "Get into something dry and get into bed as fast as you can," Mother Mary Agnes had directed her, gently but firmly closing her fingers over the knob of the girl's elbow and pointing her toward her alcove curtain at the end of the row.

Helene had pulled her elbow away. "I want to go back out and look some more. I just came in for a flashlight I have in my dresser." She had felt horrible irritation at being stopped by this religious traffic cop in a white night cap. Now the tears puckering the back of her eyeballs were tears of frustration. She started toward her cubicle, but the nun had grabbed her elbow a second time. This time her hand had been like a big hook.

"No." The white nightcap had shaken back and forth. "I can't let you go back out there. It's dark, it's late, it's cold, it's wet. It's not safe. You might get sick. You may get sick anyway, as wet as you are. You—"

"And what about that little duck!" Helene had flared back. "Aren't we responsible for her? It's dark out there for *her*...and *wet*.... She had felt the draft, restlessly pacing the dormitory floor, grip her wet ankles with icy fingers as it passed. "Even if she *is* a duck, she's not used to being soaked...and *cold*. She's from a *pet* store, she's not some Canadian goose!" Helene had felt her voice rising.

"Sh!" Mother Mary Agnes frowned and laid her finger to her lips. "We'll wake the others. Go to bed now. The duck will be fine. The duck will stay wherever it is until tomorrow."

Helene had hesitated. Then she had shaken her bronze curls. "I'm going back out. I'm responsible for that duck. *My* grandmother sent it to me. I'm supposed to take care of it. It might be in trouble. It might have been eaten.

I'm getting my flashlight." She had turned her back on the nun and headed firmly off to her alcove.

"Helene!" Mother Mary Agnes's voice had hissed out like a long lasso, like a long bullwhip. There was a terrible urgency in it, a crying, cutting edge, like an ambulance siren parting the thick, black night. Helene had spun around, surprised. Mother Mary Agnes's face had become suddenly even paler under the white nightcap. Dark shadows cupped her eyes, pulled her mouth dangerously downward. The nun was trembling all over, and when she had opened her mouth to speak again, the whisper had been a tremble too.

"Helene, you absolutely cannot go out there. It's not safe." Her white fingers reached for each other and held on together in a clasp over the front of her bathrobe.

Helene had taken it all in. The nun was afraid, like always. You tapped her with your toe, and she went to pieces. Like always. That wasn't going to stop Helene from finding her duck. "I'm going anyway," Helene told her, turning again, but watching for the nun's reaction out of the corner of her eye. She had seen Mother Mary Agnes draw a huge breath into her lungs and then drop her hands to her sides like a soldier.

"Then I'm going to wake Reverend Mother," Mother Mary Agnes had said, and her slipper had made a squeaking sound like a finger run up a violin string as she turned sharply toward the door. It had been like a bale of hay suddenly thrown in Helene's path. She had turned once again as Mother Mary Agnes headed out the door.

"Alright," Helene had said. "Alright! But if that duck dies..."

Reverend Mother slowly chewed a long thread of meat off the small drumstick that waited on the china saucer next to her. Her *gouter* was fried chicken. The nuns and girls had had graham crackers.

"My doctor. I have to eat more protein. Diabetes," she directed to Mother Mary Agnes around the bite of chicken.

Mother Mary Agnes suddenly wanted to leap up, grab the chicken leg from Reverend Mother's pudgy fingers and throw it in the wastebasket next to her desk. Small juicy noises escaped Reverend Mother's lips, and Mother Mary Agnes could feel little bumps rise spontaneously all along her arms and the back of her neck. At the same time the back of her eyeballs heated up.

"Who is this woman?" she asked herself. Was this the spiritual leader of the community, the visible culmination and flowering of thirty-five years of tending, nurturing, pruning, the representation of the ideals for which she gave up the world of dance, for which she gave up children of her own, for which she gave up a human lover?

The door to the study trembled under a gentle little rap. Reverend Mother looked up over the drumstick. "Come in," she directed to the door. The dark sheet of walnut exhaled a long breath from the hall—a faint odor of old, wet clay—as it swung inward, and a white veil and black sleeve of a habit, ending in a small silver tray and cut-crystal goblet filled halfway with trembling, golden brandy, glided in from the dim corridor. Sister Josephine, eyes humbly riveted on her shoe tops, found her way across the ruby circle of carpet and through the several delicate chairs and tables, all standing now in frozen pirouettes of some one hundred and fifty years duration, to the walnut, oak, and brass desk used by Reverend Mother alternately as a shield, confessional screen, and teller's cage.

Reverend Mother accepted the brandy in a hand she extended to the side without ever taking her eyes off the drumstick or acknowledging Sister Josephine.

Mother Mary Agnes observed the serene, carmel oval under the white veil with its dark brows of glistening Portuguese hair and a beautiful mole the color of chocolate just to the right of the sculptured upper lip. Sister Josephine's downcast eyes were fringed with deep lashes the color of her brows. Mother Mary Agnes longed for her to lift them for just a moment. She needed the company of a friendly look in the overwhelming loneliness of the sudden foreign country she found in Reverend Mother. Outside the window the November rain beat down, bringing the last of the leaves, large and dirty brown, to the sodden earth in wet, unceremonious slaps. A person might be ripping wallpaper off a room soaked by firemen. A person might be ripping wallpaper off a life. Sister Josephine glided past her and out the door without ever lifting her head or seemingly using her eyes. Something rankled Mother Mary Agnes in that Reverend Mother never thanked the Sister for the brandy. A little mouse of discontent was nudged from sleep by that and by Sister Josephine's downcast eyes and unwillingness to presume to disturb even the dust. Suddenly awake and aware of a desire to dig and to overturn, it began rooting around the foundation stones of a chapel she had built to house Reverend Mother, the earthly appearance to Mother Mary Agnes of this religious community of Jesus, the Son of God. An unwelcome thought crossed Mother Mary Agnes's mind that she had heard of Jesus being impatient with moral torpor and angry with dishonesty, but never dense to an act of love, never arrogant to the small, the poor, the humble.

The papers in a student folder rippled the wake of silence that trailed Sister Josephine's skirt and step. They jostled the little skiff of Mother Mary Agnes's thought gently and she realized she had been lost in a triangular patch of nap left like a little wound in the ruby carpet by Sister's black shoe.

A thin, wet hissing, slender as a thread, momentarily danced on the air. Reverend Mother was dislodging a piece of chicken. The papers rippled again.

"How long has the Rhenehan girl been with us now?" she asked Mother Mary Agnes without looking up. Two of her fat, perfectly groomed fingers held the end of the drumstick aloft, halfway to her mouth, as if it were a rare butterfly. Her other hand, wrist on the edge of the desk, lovingly encircled the belly of the brandy goblet, which spilled its aura along the dark, beveled walnut like a river of gold.

"Six weeks, Reverend Mother," the junior nun replied. She felt her heart jump at the question, like a rabbit startled by the sudden nose of the dog and flung by its fear over the fields.

Reverend Mother continued reading the file on Helene. Mother Mary Agnes waited. The room waited—the letter opener on the desk; the little silver bell; the sprawling, yellow telephone directory; the little porcelain Jesus with his sad, liquid eyes, delicate beard, and red pepper heart; the fan of sheet music ready for the organ; the votive candle in its deep blue, hobnail holder—all waited for Reverend Mother. Except the turning of the earth..., Mother Mary Agnes thought, hearing the womanly rain again, laundering the leaves, slapping them against the ground. Everything keeps moving, keeps turning. The earth continues, God's good servant, to do its work. No power and no pain is forever.

Suddenly bold, Mother Mary Agnes looked at Reverend Mother. She saw a squat, soft woman—porky. The head forced the honeycomb edge of the coif almost to a rectangle. The face made her think of a businessman—a longtime antique dealer, pawnbroker, or corporate head of a circus. She had seen one once with a loose, greedy mouth and pudgy, nervous fingers. He was interviewed on TV. His eyes had seemed dead, but kept shifting, as if herding hundreds and hundreds of ants.

"And the girl's father is—"

"In Europe, Reverend Mother. In Switzerland until December—Lucerne. Then he will be in Nice until April."

"H-m-m-m. Well the child is lonely, I suppose. No mother."

"Her mother died a number of years ago. An automobile accident."

"Yes?" Reverend Mother gave the mass of her head a wag and raised the brandy to her mouth. "God's ways are unfathomable," she mumbled over the lip of the goblet, and drank. Then she reamed the drumstick, set the gleaming bone hung with pink threads back on the saucer, and delicately wiped her fingertips on a linen square. She turned a few pages in the folder. Mother Mary Agnes, cut adrift again into silence, waited. Her heart was going like a trip-hammer behind her silver cross—anticipating the dog.

Finally, with a loud sigh, Reverend Mother closed the folder and pushed it away. She looked up at the slender, veiled figure stiffly upright in the chair on the other side of the desk. Why did the woman lean forward that way, so intently, as if listening for a key in a lock? And why did she work her fingers in and out of each other continually as if she were weaving and undoing some mistake? Why couldn't she keep the girl happy—quiet and happy? This was a good boarder. Long term. This kind of travelling for a parent usually meant that the boundaries of life were moving rapidly outward like an inflating balloon, and there was no going back until the thing popped. Eventually it would pop. Most likely he would have the girl at the Convent through high school *and* college. If they didn't muff it.

"Well, Mother, is there something of a serious nature? You wouldn't have asked to see me otherwise, I think."

"Yes, Reverend Mother." The young nun bent over her mumbling fingers. She seemed to shrink away, taking her voice with her down a rabbit hole. Reverend Mother felt little tucks of annoyance. She wished the woman would speak up. This was going to take all day. The bunion at the joint of her great toe began to boom. The clock in the corridor beyond the walnut door gonged four times with a resonating, metallic voice. Reverend Mother searched around under the desk with her shoe for the brick, covered with black leather, she used as a footrest to relieve pressure in her left foot. Eyes still bent on the pale, heart-shaped face, she thought Mother Mary Agnes looked like a valentine, sweet in a fluted wrapper. "Well, Mother?"

"It's been a series of incidents, Reverend Mother. I would not have bothered you with just one."

Would she ever get to it? "Constipated" was all Reverend Mother could think of as she set her foot on the brick and felt with relief her foot cool as the gorged blood flowed into the leg. "And these incidents were...?" she urged her on.

Mother Mary Agnes felt her heart pumping the words out, wobbling and graceless as ducklings. She struggled for composure. She felt a deluge of tears pressing simultaneously behind her eyes and voice box. She shored her wall. Reverend Mother's mouth, set in a hard, straight line, made her feel she did not have time for crying religious.

Mother Mary Agnes recited the two rosary incidents, the raising of the nightgown up the flagpole and delivery of the giant pizza. At that, Reverend Mother broke in. "Well. Trying to make an impression on the other girls, no doubt. It can't go on, of course—but not so unusual. What else?"

Her words stuck like burrs in Mother Mary Agnes's throat. Outside, the November sky wept unremittingly. Her fingers wrung themselves. "It's...it's her attitude, Reverend Mother. It's the belligerence. No matter what I do, the child seems to resent it, resist it, deliberately act in the other direction."

Reverend Mother watched the woman working her hands like a washcloth. Annoyance flared up in her like a paper fire. Obviously it was just a discipline problem with this girl. This simpering shrinking violet had let things get out of hand. If you let one stitch unravel, the whole sweater goes. This was the wrong occasion for martyrdom. Here was a thread rapidly fraying in the fabric, and this misdirected marshmallow was weeping and wailing instead of picking up a needle and stitching!

The older nun suddenly slammed her hand flat on the desk. The lid on the inkwell jumped and rattled. Mother Mary Agnes jumped and gripped the arms of her chair.

"I! I! I! Mother. Me! Me! Me!" Reverend Mother bellowed, her grey eyes like stones. "That's what I'm hearing from you—I, I, I."

Mother Mary Agnes dropped her eyelids against the hot sting of tears that rushed in and bent her head over the silver Jesus on her breast. Her face burned. Her hands shook on the cool, silky wood of the chair.

"Is this about *you*, Mother?" A sneer, like congealed stomach acid, slid across Reverend Mother's desk. "I thought it was a child we were concerned with, Mother, not a nun. I thought it was the *child* we serve, not *ourselves*. Perhaps I was mistaken, Mother. I didn't know that we were here for *our* comfort, that this was some kind of spiritual country club. I thought it was growth through service, through *sacrifice* we were interested in. Was I wrong, Mother? Have I made a mistake—a forty year mistake?"

Reverend Mother's voice stopped, and there was silence in the room. Beyond the windows the sky wept; beneath the silver cross, behind her tightly closed lids, the young nun wept.

When she spoke again, Reverend Mother's voice was low and hard like a rod. "Your work, Mother, is with Helene. Your own feelings DO NOT (she hissed this through her teeth), I repeat, DO NOT! enter in. Is that clear?" Then the woman heaved her bulk to her feet in a gesture of dismissal. "A firm hand, Mother. A firm hand is all that is needed. I'm sure we haven't been wrong about where we have placed you. I hope I will hear no more of this. You may go now."

"Yes, Reverend Mother." Mother Mary Agnes leapt from her chair and fled the room like an animal sprung from a trap.

Big John's shovel sliced into the wedge-shaped mass of leaves blown against the wall of the grotto and opened a grave through that strata of cast-off seasons. A cold mist, not quite ready to break into flakes, prickled the eyelids of the girls watching. It made the edges of the shovel flash against the dark loam and beaded the navy wool cap the handyman had pulled over his red ears with encrustations of tiny, unpolished pearls. The black veil and shawl of Mother Mary Agnes and Sister Josephine glowed with a chill, ghostly halo, and blooms of breath unfurled in miniature winding sheets that hung in the air. The icy dew was fast gathering on the coffin Helene cradled stiffly at her chest on a bier of her arms and secured by clamps of her freckled hands, fingernails bitten to the quick.

It was the requiem for Helene's pet duck, Billie Jean. The Virgin of Fatima peered out from the dark cave of her sanctuary with a sad, dirt-streaked face at the ragged crescent of girls, hunched and shifting from foot to foot in the raw air. The coffin was a large, square biscuit tin. It had been carefully covered with heavy, white art paper and ribboned with the names of the friends of the duck in colored pencil. These were now dissolving into a rainbow wash in the wet atmosphere. The coffin was finished with a wreath around the outside, braided of anklets—principally brown, navy, pink, apple green, and white. Each girl in the middle school had donated socks to make the wreath. When there weren't enough, Madeline and Jennifer cajoled the high schoolers and bullied the Minims for more. A gorgeous pair of purple hightops materialized at the last minute to crown everything with a brilliant bow.

Big John's shovel rang harsh on the air as it struck the large foundation stones of the grotto. He stepped into the rectangular hole to square a corner, his haunches splitting from the awkward distribution of one leg bent at ground level and the other, to the knee, in a hole. "Almost done now," he offered in his thick Irish voice, and, turning heavily with three or four loud grunts, he raised the shovel high and sliced even slabs all around the weedy, tangled earth to finish the grave.

On Helene's right, Madeline kept watch with a long-stemmed, magenta bloom that was a gift of the Minim's. It had been a labor of love—one whole afternoon of scraping every scarlet crayon that could be found, then painfully tracing the many large petals required on waxed paper, and then cutting them out in duplicate so Mother Carmel could press the shavings into a glowing mass between the wax membranes. Next the petals had to be arranged, beginning with the smallest at the center, and fastened with green tape to the unbent coat hanger, also covered with green tape, which served as a stem. Others had worked on the inscription and carefully transferred it to the white card, hung by a little gold cord from the stem, which fluttered up against Madeline's solemn face. "Billie Jean King," it read, "the Minims say Goodbye. Rest in peace. And rise with Christ." The little girls had not been allowed to attend the funeral rite.

The flower healed the raw atmosphere like oil on a wound. Against the somber tones of the sleeping earth and numbed hues of uniforms and habits, it pulsed. The petals stood out dazzling and daring, intensified by the dark, unrelenting rock of the grotto, sullen webs of bushes, and lowering, pewter-colored sky.

From her window, Reverend Mother did not like the look of the whole thing. Whatever *is* that nun doing! she tapped out on the window sill with trimmed fingernails, puffy mouth stitched with annoyance. Out at the grotto at ten in the morning, when they should be in class. And on a chill day like this! Why, they could all catch their death and end up in the too-small infirmary. That would mean the doctor, and calling parents, and the general mess of medicines and special meals and extra linens. Sickness was a great deal more trouble than it was worth. And it *always* ended up costing money.

Her grey eyebrows buckled sharply together, and she reached across her desk for the coffee—made extra strong, to her taste. Two books lay open on her desk top. One was face down on a pad of yellow foolscap. Its blue oxhide cover read: *The IRS and Private Institutions: Aligning Power and Potential Through Creative Management.* The other lay face up, open at midpoint, a dark, wine and gold bookmark given her by Cardinal Mundelein in its long center crease. Some remorseless part of her had calmly disentangled the rest from the power struggle between young, obscure Monsignor Spellman and the money-hungry land-grabbers of Upper New York State, and piped all faculties alert and to service at the window.

Behind her, the room waited hushed and thick. Only the clock broke in with its short, choked little strokes, commenting on the progressive turning of the earth and unreeling of life. A dust in that room, heavy as silt, permeated the air Reverend Mother breathed. It persisted even after Sister had cleaned. It was the dust of generations of Mother Superiors, worrying over the same books, calculating the same calculations, choreographing the complex social dances among the hierarchy: alumnae, trustees, local government, parents, nuns, and students. There was the stifling and then the relenting to the same ambitions, the pruning of spirituality one month and the letting it grow wild the next, and sometimes letting it wither in favor of bookkeeping, householding, curriculum planning. There was the noticing of grey in the eyebrows and the myriad lines, like tiny rivers, turning self-sufficient skin to a soft, surrendered crepe. Every Mother Superior knew the flag marking the final rounds was made of that crepe. Reverend Mother had seen it plainly again several days ago, her face caught by a long, afternoon slant of light and dealt back to her by a wall mirror in the visitors' parlor. If I'm going to do anything, make any difference, she had told herself, I'm going to have to do it quickly.

Now, at the window, the heat of the cup burning comfortingly into her fingers, Reverend Mother felt the presence of her predecessors pressing on her like a mantle—restless, heavy, but not altogether unpleasant. The shivering crescent of girls and nuns, splotched wreath, and brilliant trembling flower, all moving toward the grave, made Reverend Mother uneasy. A little fear, which she refused to recognize, feathered her stomach. She promptly drowned it with coffee. Had she consulted it, she would have known it was not the death and burial that made her uneasy. It was the resurrection.

Big John tossed his shovel onto the little mound of dirt he had piled up. "Done now, ladies," he offered, but so softly only the girls in front heard. He climbed out of the hole and stood to one side, his big Irish hands in a knot and his head bowed. Helene turned and nodded to Jennifer on her left.

"OK. Now."

Jennifer dug under her winter jacket and produced a black missal, marked at the readings for the Mass for the Dead. She cleared her throat and began in a thin voice, wobbling with tears.

"The Lord is my shepherd. I shall not want..."

"Nobody can hear you," Madeline hissed from the other side of Helene, cocking her head over the coffin.

Jennifer began again. "THE LORD IS MY SHEPHERD. I SHALL NOT WANT..."

Her voice trailed upward over the waiting vault, over the cluster of bowed heads, over the glistening mound of rock and the Virgin of Fatima in its womb, and joined the sad twittering of the plain brown wrens hunting seeds and tree mites in the sycamores and oaks, and ruffling themselves for warmth under the pitiless hand of the chill, wet day.

When she was done, Jennifer passed the book to Mother Mary Agnes, who had come up from the back. The nun read the gospel. "His friends came at dawn to see where they had laid him and lo! the rock was rolled back and the grave was empty..." When she finished, she fished her pitch pipe out and sounded a C as the signal for the hymn. "To Jesus' heart all burning with fervent love for men...," the girls sang, their voices sweet as mountain flowers. Only Helene stood with her lips shut in a hard, tight line. She was very pale under the carrot curls, and her red-rimmed eyes brimmed and spilled, brimmed and spilled.

The hymn was done and no one moved. Helene pressed the box tight against her chest. She felt Billie Jean inside, still a warm presence. There was no way she could give her up. Behind Helene, the girls shifted from one cold foot to the next, hands dug into their pockets, watching her expectantly.

"Come on." Jennifer nudged her towards the grave with an elbow. "It's time."

Still she couldn't move, cast in cement.

Finally, Mother Mary Agnes leaned around Jennifer and touched Helene gently on the arm. "It's time, Helene." The nun motioned to Big John. "Let John take Billie Jean now."

Still the girl did not, could not move. Her fingers gripped the box harder, and she heard the paper pop. Made anxious by the hesitation, but also concerned, the nun stepped around Jennifer and put her hands on the little coffin.

"We must finish now, Helene," she said a little sternly, and tried to draw the box gently from the girl's hands. The little movement opened a floodgate. Something tore away inside Helene. She let the nun take the box, but her face was wild.

"I don't believe in all this," she raved, gesturing to include the group, the grotto and the grave. "I just did it because everyone wanted to." Her voice became loud and harsh, laying the words down like hammer strokes. "I don't believe in God. I don't believe in any God who would do this." She pointed to the little grave. "And I don't believe in any Sacred Heart," she sneered, tears running down her face, "all burning with love. It's a lot of shit, that's all it is. And I hate it. I hate it. I hate it." Her voice rose, rapidly climbing steps, until at the end it cracked and broke. She whirled on her heel and escaped toward the grey fortress of the school. Every head followed, stunned, disbelieving. The collective pain stretched the fabric of the mourners almost to the limit.

Mother Mary Agnes passed the coffin to Big John who carried it as carefully as crystal. He knelt on the wet earth and then lowered it into the shadowed, rectangular yawn he had dug. Loud sobbing burst from many points in the circle of onlookers. Madeline hesitated, then tiptoed forward, and squatting, lay the scarlet bloom on top of the still sock-encircled box. By now, the names were only blurs of color, and the white paper had a doughy look.

"Goodbye, Billie Jean, from the Minims," she said in a loud, firm voice, executing her duty. "And from all of us," she added more softly as a tear slid down her cheek and into her mouth.

Reverend Mother observed the goings-on over her coffee cup. When one girl—the red haired one—ran off, flailing her arms, obviously hysterical, she reached across her desk to the house phone. After a pause for listening, she said, "Please send word to Mother Mary Agnes I wish to see her at noon. Thank you." Replacing her receiver, she felt nettled by the thought of another session with that pale, tense cut-out of a woman.

POET PARTY
Ann Hemenway

The poets descended on Glasscott College. Throughout the week, poets had
begun reading, pontificating in classes, but the only students who knew
about it were those who belonged to the "artsy crowd," the writing
students, the drama majors, and the strange clay-smocked creatures who sat
at potters' wheels in the large glassed-in art studio. The rest of the students,
the majority, knew nothing, but trotted blithely from class to class, from
bar to bar, beer and band to fraternity cocktail party, never realizing that
wit, culture and desperation blew around them like snow.

Elaine suspected something the week before when Anton Bradley, her
poetry teacher, seemed less disheveled and hungover in class. It seemed as
though he were saving up for something.

Elaine took poetry on the insistence of Sheila, "I know you could be a
poet, Elaine, I know you could. Take Poetry Workshop I, and you'll have
Anton. He's wonderful," she glowed, "wonderful. He's such a poet."

Anton was indeed a poet, although his actual poetry itself, the words on
the page, were incomprehensible to Elaine. Elaine realized two things after
the first class: that she was not a poet and that Anton Bradley was
undoubtedly a poet, because, above and beyond anything that was
published in *Poetry Magazine*, he looked like a poet.

His large blue eyes gazed grief-stricken beneath thick waves of
prematurely greying hair. His face, too, was prematurely grey, grey with
too many nights of wandering unconsoled through unlit streets, grey with
too much Scotch early in the morning as he wrote the violent metaphors
that littered his poetry, metaphors that Elaine didn't understand, and, she
suspected, neither did Anton.

Anton would sit in class on the floor next to the coffee table in the lounge
where all the writing classes were held for informality, and pull Lucky
Strike after Lucky Strike out of the pack beside him. He smoked with his
whole body. The cigarette would be lit immediately, and he would inhale
with relief, with hunger. His entire body seemed to curl around the cigarette
and slide into his lungs with the smoke, and when he talked, the words and
smoke mingled and swirled around the students and would rise to the
ceiling and hang there.

Usually, he had a stubble on his chin, but the week before Poet's Week,
as it came to be called, he was shaved and vaguely alert. He asked if they
were going to the readings next week, "You, ah, might go to, ah, possibly
one or two," he said, the smoke billowing around his face.

Elaine decided halfway through Poet's Week that she would go to the
reading that was taking place that night. The poet, Mitch Maddox, had sat
in on her class that day, and the class had discussed the things that made
them sad.

"Old T.V. shows," Elaine mumbled to the floor, not to anyone, certainly
not to the class, who had discussed old photographs, bag ladies, and
shuffling old men.

Mitch Maddox, who had been sitting on the couch next to her, turned to
her sharply and said, "My God, my God, me, too, and I never knew it." He

looked at her, bearded and solemn.

She looked back at him. He was about her height and she could look him right in the eye. "Father Knows Best," she said.

He nodded, frowning, "Mr. Peepers."

"Timmy and Lassie," she nodded with him.

He stopped nodding, put a hand to his mouth and said through his fingers, "My Friend Flicka."

"You know what really gets me—not the shows so much," Elaine said, "it's the theme songs. The theme songs really depress the hell out of me."

Mitch took a matchbook out of his inside jacket pocket and pen from his outside jacket pocket and scribbled on the matchbook.

Elaine didn't try to see what he was writing. Poetic privacy, she thought, it would be rude. She decided then that she would go to his reading, although she'd never heard of him before. It was the least she could do.

She went by herself. Louisa wasn't interested in contemporary poetry. "If John Donne was readin', or even Alexandah Pope, ah'd go, but who the hell has heard of Miyutch Maddox?" she said, brushing her hair, "Go and cayutch a fallin' star, Get with chahld a mandrake root...' I put that in mah high school yeahbook."

Sheila, of course, would be there, but would sit with the staff of *Blue Ravine*, and Elaine didn't want to sit with them, so she sat by herself, wondering what you're supposed to do at a poetry reading—laugh, cry, snap your fingers like they did at chapel? Before the reading began, she looked around at the people. There were forty or so, but they were hard to count because the room was large and shaped like a movie theatre and the walls were carpeted so that it wouldn't echo. The red carpeting sloped down from the large glass doorways in tiers, like an inverted wedding cake, and the listeners sprawled on the tiers. A podium was pushed up against the far wall in the center, and in its place stood a table with a plastic pitcher and glass on it. Elaine looked around at the audience, bored, and counted the bluejeans. Thirty pair of bluejeans, two denim skirts, and about seven pairs of corduroys.

Mitch Maddox strode to the center of the room, holding the tallest glass of whiskey and water Elaine had ever seen. He was small—very small—in a flannel shirt and blue jeans and heavy boots. He looked like a miniature lumberjack. The audience quieted down and he began to read, except he didn't read; he strode, stomped and swaggered in front of the table, clenching his fist at the audience and booming poems in a thunderous voice—poems about his father, about his dog, about a rock, which Elaine assumed symbolized something, but she wasn't sure what. She stared at him intently. Was that what she was supposed to do? Was she to titter at a funny part, hang her head at a sad part, smile wanly at a poignant part? She glanced around her. To her left and down one tier, Sheila had her arms wrapped around her legs and her head rested on her knees as she stared unblinkingly at the poet, who had sauntered in front of her. The boy next to Sheila sat Indian style, looking into the space between his legs, shaking his head. Elaine looked back at the poet, who had moved again, in front of *her* as she looked down on him. Did she imagine that he looked straight at her as he gulped his whiskey between poems? She looked to her right. Next to the aisle, where the tiers multiplied into steps, she saw a boy lying on his back with his eyes closed. That looked like a good idea. She stretched her legs out in front of her, leaned back against the step above her, and closed her eyes. Mitch Maddox's words, images, and sonorous tones rolled like pebbles up her toes, legs, chest, and forehead. She didn't have to listen at all; she just had to pretend she was listening, and if a particular sentence happened to roll in her ear, she would smile or wince or something.

"I'd like to dedicate this next poem to my friend Anton Bradley," the poet said in between swallows of whiskey.

Elaine popped open her eyelids and slid her eyes over to Anton. He sat on the other side of the aisle on the end of the row, chin in hand. Since class that day, his face had sagged and his eyes had retreated into their sockets. He looked as if he had finished the bottle that Mitch Maddox had started. As Mitch recited his poem about snow, or midgets, or gargoyles or whatever, Anton's face didn't move. It was as though he could feel the eyes on him, the eyes (two of which were Elaine's) that glanced from him to Mitch and back again.

The dedication to Anton ended the reading and the listeners got up, stretched, and a few of them wandered down the large steps to the table to talk to the poet, who stood leaning against the table, holding a fresh drink and looking relieved. Elaine hesitated for a moment, thinking perhaps she should go down and talk to him, but she didn't know what to say to him. Nice job? Good show? I liked the part about the dog? She decided against it and began leaping up the tiers to the doorway when Sheila grabbed her in mid-leap, "Aren't you going to the party?" she asked.

"Whose party?"

"John Malcolm is having a party for all the visiting poets. Come on. Jimmy'll give us a ride. It'll be fun. Good conversation."

"No, I've got an eight o'clock tomorrow. I can't go out and party. No, I'd like to, but I can't," Elaine said, pulling away from Sheila.

Sheila grabbed her arm again, "It's only nine o'clock. Come on, Elaine. You'll probably never have another chance to talk to these people again. Come on," she coaxed.

Elaine relented, insisting that they'd have to leave early, and she wasn't going to drink anything.

They pulled in front of John Malcolm's house in Jimmy's Skylark convertible. It was snowing and the winding road down the hill was slippery. The car had skidded a few times, bumping its left back wheel into the curb, while snow filtered into the car from the crack above the top of the windshield where the convertible top latched onto it. John Malcolm lived in the bottom floor of an old stone house that sat halfway down the hill into town. When they got inside, Elaine saw poets and students standing in clusters—a group of five around the record player waving cigarettes and drinks, another group semi-circled around the window at the far end of the living room, a woman dressed like a student in a sweatshirt, but who had a lined poet's face, pointed, drink in hand, index finger extended, as though she was shooting the snowflakes and using alchohol for ammunition. One small group stood stranded in the middle of the oriental rug. Beneath their voices the record player plunked out a folk song. It was the first party at college that Elaine had been to in which the music didn't swoop around your words and snatch them from your lips, causing you to scream "What?" at the person next to you.

Elaine, Jimmy, and Sheila stood in the small dark hallway peering into the living room. A man in a Prince Valiant haircut and unbuttoned shirt appeared and then disappeared out of the hallway with Elaine's coat.

"My cigarettes," she said.

"What about your cigarettes?" said Sheila.

"My cigarettes are in the pocket of that coat and he just walked off with it."

"You shouldn't smoke anyway," said the man in the Prince Valiant haircut, reappearing at her elbow.

Who is this man? Elaine thought. Why hasn't Sheila introduced me, or doesn't she know either? She wanted to sidle in, clinging to Sheila, hiding her face against Sheila's arm, and slide against the walls until she was miraculously in some kind of brilliant conversation. But Sheila didn't move or speak, and neither did Jimmy, whom Elaine didn't know anyway, and who had remained silent during the ride down here, occasionally stroking his goatee.

"We all have our vices, John," said Sheila, kneading her hands together.

He's the host, thought Elaine, the heavenly host, and she leaped on him with relief. It occurred to her that without her cigarettes she would be forced to bum other people's, which as anyone who had ever smoked and been in a strange place without cigarettes knew, it forced you to talk to somebody. If you saw a handsome man smoking, you could unobtrusively approach him and ask for a cigarette and then wrack your brains out trying to cook up something else to say. Elaine wondered if Mitch Maddox smoked. She hadn't seen him smoke in class, but it seemed that at parties even non-smokers smoked.

"I'm John Malcolm," said Prince Valiant, smiling down at her and taking her elbow.

"This is your party," said Elaine, wanting to crawl somewhere between Sheila and Jimmy.

"I know Sheila and Jimmy, but I don't know you," he said, his grin getting wider.

He's licking his chops, she thought. "I'm Elaine Le Maire," she said.

"Why don't all of you come in the kitchen and I'll get you something to drink," he said to Elaine.

He guided her into the kitchen, past the group in the middle of the living room. She saw Mitch Maddox hanging his head like a bad dog in the center of the group, listening. Jimmy and Sheila tagged behind Elaine and Prince Valiant, talking to each other.

In the kitchen, there were more people. Anton Bradley leaned against the counter next to the sink, folded around his tall, dripping drink. A woman with long dark hair, a poetry teacher whom Elaine didn't know, stood with her foot on a chair. Two men with beards leaned against the counter; a woman, her back to the room, mixed a drink. Words were tossed about, tail-ends of conversations.

The woman with the long dark hair said, looking at Prince Valiant, "Do you think that you can write out of anger, or do you think that the anger must pass before you write? Roger thinks you must wait, but I think that you can get a great deal of power from anger. What do you think?" Her eyes scanned all of them.

"I write a lot from anger," said Jimmy, stroking his straggly goatee.

Prince Valiant went to the counter, "What do you want to drink? Sheila?

Jimmy?" He paused. Elaine?" he said gently, turning from the counter to look at her.

"Wine, if you have it," said Sheila.

"I'll have some, too," said Jimmy.

Prince Valiant got out two glasses from the cupboard, "Elaine, Sheila, Jimmy—this is Mark, Tia, Anton (you know both of them), Roger and Craig."

Elaine looked at the people. Fred? Richard? Thelma? The names floated around the room without attaching themselves to faces. The faces smiled, nameless.

Prince Valiant poured two glasses of wine. One of the men with a beard, who wore thick black glasses, shifted his body toward Elaine. "Do you think you should write out of anger, Elaine?" he said.

She looked around briefly. Sheila and Jimmy had retreated into the living room with their wine and she was still without a drink. Alone, no arm to cling to. No familiar face, except Anton's, and his was turned towards a woman who was sitting on the counter.

"I think maybe afterwards," she hazarded.

"After the spell is over?" he nodded, his eyes drooping beneath his glasses, "Yes, that makes sense. Then you can get the kind of objectivity you need to get a clear hold on the complete emotion. Yes. Yes." His eyelids drooped lower and he smiled complacently, as if to say, "You'll do. Yes, indeed, you'll do."

Prince Valiant stood closely beside her, "And what will you have, Elaine?" he murmured.

"Just orange juice or water," she said, not looking at him.

"Oh no," he said.

"No, Elaine," said the man with black glasses, leaning towards her.

"This is a party, Elaine," said Prince Valiant.

"Yes. You can't drink orange juice at a party," said Black Glasses.

"I have a class tomorrow early."

"Doesn't matter." "No, it doesn't matter," said the men, encircling her, bandying her between them like a tennis ball, like witty conversation.

"You have to have a drink," said Prince Valiant, handing her a tumbler, and holding a bottle of Scotch. "Say when."

"When," she said at two fingers full.

"When," she said again, as the Scotch crept past the halfway mark.

"When," she kept saying as the glass was filled to one centimeter below the rim with straight Scotch.

She stared into the glass. Prince Valiant and Black Glasses didn't speak, but stood bent over her as if they, too, were looking into her drink. I'm Cathy Co-Ed, she thought as the Scotch glittered in the glass. Cathy Co-Ed goes to a poet party. Cathy Co-Ed, daughter of "Gidget goes Hawaiian." If Gidget went to a poet party, what would she do? If Gidget went to a poet party, a poet wouldn't fill her glass to the rim with Scotch. No, the poet, who would be a dark handsome man in a sportscoat and thin tie, would fall in love with Gidget and recite Tennyson to her as they sat in the arbor outside Gidget's sorority house. All those years of watching the 3:30 Movie after school hadn't prepared her for a poet party at college. Cathy Co-Ed couldn't race back to Moon Doggie after the poet had proposed by quoting Shakespeare; Prince Valiant and Black Glasses had proposed something else entirely.

Elaine looked up suddenly and both Prince Valiant and Black Glasses stepped back like two sides of a bridge parting for a boat.

"What do you write, Elaine?" said Black Glasses, raising his wineglass to his lips.

In the living room, Chuck Berry cried out from the stereo and a series of murmurs exploded into laughter.

"Not much of anything," Elaine said. She held her glass in both hands as if it was a chalice that would carry her magically from room to room as she bowed gracefully to each group, bestowing largesse on each and all. But if she drank the magic potion contained within the glass, if she even touched it to her lips, she would turn into a toad. A very drunk toad, she thought.

"You don't write," said Prince Valiant.

"Not really. I'm not a poet. In fact, my poetry stinks."

Prince Valiant leaned back even further and his eyes dropped fleetingly to her toes and then slowly dragged themselves up her body, "I can't believe that."

Black Glasses shrugged, "We don't know for certain; she could be telling the truth."

"John," someone called from the living room, "John, come here a minute."

"Excuse me a moment," said Prince Valiant, touching Elaine's shoulder.

Elaine stepped back and leaned against the table and put her drink down permanently.

"What do you do?" said Elaine to Black Glasses, wishing she had a cigarette. There was Anton, over in the corner, smoking happily. She envied him.

Black Glasses said something about management for International Harvester and how he played football in college on a scholarship and seemed very proud of the fact, which she thought was strange for a poet, but she didn't really listen to him. She knew something else and she knew that she didn't want to look back at him or a pact would be made, an agreement reached.

A man came into the kitchen and asked Black Glasses a question, and as he turned to answer him, Elaine began to slide towards the doorway that led to the living room, when Black Glasses called, "Elaine, don't leave, I'm in love with you."

She hesitated for a moment, leaning against the side of the doorway, but he was not a dark, handsome poet in a sportcoat, and she wasn't Gidget, and there was no Moon Doggie, but only Sheila, standing in the next room like a lifeboat, so Elaine smiled and slipped into the living room.

Before she reached Sheila, Mitch Maddox lurched in front of her. "I was very glad to see you at my reading," he slurred, "I hoped you would be there."

"I enjoyed it," she said, thinking that it seemed he had killed at least a bottle of Scotch singlehandedly. "You were very good. I liked your poem to Anton."

He swayed towards the overstuffed chair at his right and grabbed the arm before he fell over. "Thank you. I wanted to tell you," he motioned with his drink for her to come closer, "I wanted to tell you," he said in a loud wet whisper, "I wanted to tell you how moved I was by what you said in class. I was very moved. Very moved. You know what?"

Elaine waited for him to finish, but he just stood there, rocking unsteadily back and forth, and smiling proudly.

"What?" she asked finally.

"I started a poem about it." He swung towards her.

Elaine wondered if he was lying. "You did. Really?"

He bobbed his head up and down. "Yes. I was very moved. Very moved. Theme songs to old T.V. shows. You must write. You can't not write."

"No, I don't. I can't." She wondered if he really cared if she could write or not, but what the hell difference did it make anyway? "Now, my friend Sheila, she thinks like a poet, she even talks like a poet (whatever that means, Elaine thought), but I don't. I just take a class."

Around them, Chuck Berry shouted, but not too loudly. A bright brittle murmur played around the room. Someone whooshed, someone knocked against someone, arms clutched, apologies, a fervent discussion with head shakes, and matches flaring to light cigarettes; and past the beige curtains out the window, snow fell light and clean.

Prince Valiant brushed past them, paused, then knowing that he could not join them, moved on.

Mitch was nodding. He leaned forward closer to her and attempted to focus his eyes. "You are very beautiful. Would you like to hear the first draft of the poem?"

Elaine's thighs began to tingle. Cathy Coed, daughter of Gidget, thought to herself what the hell and said yes.

He turned, motioning her to follow, and stumbled to a small hallway, which was not more than two doorways set three feet apart, and opened the large door at the end of the hall. She followed him in. A large four-poster bed filled up most of the room. At the end of the bed, on the table in front of the window, sat a suitcase, and on top of that, a briefcase, which Mitch seized and, reeling backwards, he sat heavily on the bed.

"Are you staying here?" Elaine asked him from the doorway as she closed the door behind her.

"Yes," he said, not looking up, but ruffling through the briefcase.

"Where does John sleep?" she asked, not moving from the door. She looked into the dark bathroom at the other side of the room.

"He finds places, I guess," said Mitch, still not looking up. He patted the bed beside him and she walked over and sat down next to him, not close, but aware of the distance between their thighs.

"I can't seem to find it," he muttered as the paper jumped and shuffled in front of him. He picked one up and looked at it hard, as if his stare would command the lines of type to stop dividing, to stop dripping off the page. He blinked his eyes. "No, can't find it. Can't find it," he slurred, " hafta recite it from memory. But first," he looked up brightly, "but first a drink. What are you drinking? We forgot to bring drinks. Can't have a party without drinks. Can't read a poem without drinks. Whadyou want?" He stood up, staggered forward two steps, turned with a wobble and stared at her.

She stood up, "I'll get them."

"No, no, no, no, no. You stay here. You don't move that glorious form of yours anywhere. You stay here. I'll get the drinks. Whadyou want?"

She didn't fight him. They could battle this one out all night. "Wine, I'll have wine," she said, "and could you get a cigarette for me?"

"Wine and a cigarette. And Scotch for me. You stay right there. Right there. Don't move. I'll be back in two stitches of a cat's tail." He staggered towards the door, fumbled at the doorknob and lurched out, closing the door behind him.

Elaine sat back down on the bed. She felt stupid. She felt like Rapunzel when the witch went out to look for herbs and eye of newt. What if he didn't come back? What if, in a drunken stupor, he forgot about her and she stayed in that room, the talk and laughter and Bob Dylan bouncing against the door, while inside the room was thick, waiting silence. She stood up and went to the table and leaned over the suitcase to look out the window. Snow lay thick on the bushes beneath. Outside the door, she heard a door open and the sound of wire hangers scraping against metal. The closet was right outside the bedroom door. If he doesn't come back she thought, I'll sneak my coat out of the closet and climb out the window. But the bedroom windows were layered with storm windows. She went to the small dark bathroom. The window there was heavy and glazed and looked as though chips had been chiseled out of it; she couldn't see through it. She pulled on the latch at the top and it scraped around, then she yanked at the window. It didn't budge. She braced her heel against the base of the toilet and, gritting her teeth, yanked again; the window ripped open suddenly and she stuck her head out. No storm window, no bushes, just a pile of soft snow for Cathy Co-ed's dainty feet. She pulled her head back in, pulled the window closed, went back to the bed and sat down on it as if she'd never moved.

When Mitch kicked open the door and catapulted himself in, spilling Scotch and wine on the braided rug, she was still sitting there, smiling stiffly. She could feel her neck muscles tightening, and her hands were clasped between her knees.

"Here you are," he said, thrusting the glass of wine at her. The wine shot to the rim of the glass and dripped over. "Here's your cigarette. Took me a while to get it. Sorry I took so long." He sat down next to her. He nearly sat down on her lap. She clenched her elbows to her sides, but didn't slide over. She felt like moving over, but she didn't, she hunched her shoulders and sipped her drink and looked out the window at the snow, at the streetlight, because if she turned and looked at him she'd be too close and she'd be breathing on him. He was going to recite his poem, and she wasn't going to listen, because all she was aware of was a thigh next to her thigh. He put his glass between his knees and got a matchbook from his front pocket and lit a match and bent close to her, and now she had to look at him, and he unsteadily held the match to her cigarette, and she smelled sulphur and whiskey and aftershave and his smell beneath that smell and cigarette smoke, and she thought she couldn't stand it anymore.

He lifted his drink and tipped it to hers and said, "Here's to lovely young ladies who inspire poems." And she sipped and said, "Here's to poets." And he said, "Do you wanna hear it, such as it is?" She nodded. He began to say something about Bud and Princess and Kitten and My Friend Flicka flickering across the screen in black and blue, but he was kissing her neck and her ear and lifting her hair and kissing the back of her neck and reciting phrases and images as she came up for air or for a swallow of whiskey, and she held her glass out stiffly like an anchor, like the one last connection to shore, to land. He worked his way up her chin to her mouth and kissed her hard, open mouthed, and she held out that wineglass and that cigarette like a beacon, like a flare. He pulled back and looked at her, or tried to anyway, and said, "Ah, Elaine, you're beautiful," and she thought, "All three of me." And he took her wineglass from her hand and put it on the floor and took a swallow from his glass and put it on the floor empty and took her cigarette and dropped it in the dregs of his Scotch, and they fell back on the bed and Elaine sank, thinking vaguely of Gidget, and his hand slid under her shirt and up her breast, and as her hands slid down his thigh she wondered about Cathy Co-Ed. Yes, she was Cathy Co-Ed, and he's breathing whiskey on me and I'm feeling his hard-on and he's unbuttoning my shirt, sort of, but he can't, so she helped him. And the zippers came undone with a lift of the pelvis and hands were on back and breast and thigh and between legs and Elaine thought of Sheila as her hand slid onto Mitch's cock, what would Sheila think, and Mitch rose over her like a roof and looked at her, surprised and she saw his face turning green, but she held onto his cock, like the wineglass. Would he puke, she thought. Oh no, Cathy Co-Ed, oh no. Gidget. No, he didn't puke, but she felt something die in her hand, felt it go soft as a baby bird, and Mitch closed his eyes and pitched forward heavily and landed with his chest on her face and passed out, and she was smothering. Her nose crushed and damp hairy skin pressed her cheeks, and she struggled like a beetle on its back, trying to heave him off of her, but he was beyond moving—he was dead, he was out, his cock had shrivelled like a dead balloon and he was smashing her. She struggled longer, arching her back and lifting her knees, then lay still, her eyes wide and staring into his chest; she was blinded by his flesh; she could hear her own labored breathing in counterpoint to his snores; she was going to die. She panicked. Her stomach clenched, her shoulders clutched her neck. She kicked her legs and wriggled her hips and shoulders, not caring if she battered him. Finally, with a fishlike sideways motion of her body, though she was sure her nose and breasts would rip off, she pulled the lower half of her body out from under him and pushed at his unyielding flesh and slowly, painfully, with sweating cheeks and forehead and throbbing nose, pulled her head away and lay there on the bed, her shirt flattened and wrinkled beneath her, her bluejeans halfway down her hips, her underwear damp and sticky. She looked at him while she caught her breath. He should have flies buzzing around him, she thought.

She got up, listening at the door while she zipped her pants. She couldn't plaster a smile on her red and burning face and act as if she didn't smell of sex and Mitch Maddox. Sheila would be out there, sitting on the couch, her fingers dancing as she spoke. If Elaine came into the room, Sheila would look up and for one moment, one unconscious moment, and she would look at Elaine, Smelling, Judging, Accusing, one hard pinprick of knowing before she smiled and called to her. Because of that one short look, barely noticed, barely signaled, Elaine would not go into the living room; Elaine would not see that glance.

She cracked open the door and peered into the living room. No one was in eyeshot, so slowly she opened the door wider and felt for the closet doorknob. Her coat was on a hanger on the far side of the closet. She grabbed the arm and gently pulled it off the hanger. The hanger gave a short rasp and swung drunkenly on the rod. She flicked at the closet door and stepped back into the bedroom and shut that door, crossed the room, jamming her hands into her coat, went to the bathroom, pushed open the window, glanced over her shoulder at Mitch to make sure he was still asleep (he'll sleep forever, she thought), put one leg on the windowsill, then the other, and slid out, feet first, shooting out into the cold. She landed lightly on the snow feet first. Her tracks would be covered by the next morning, and she didn't care anyway. She leaped through the snow, past an elm tree, past the streetlight, and crossed the street. John Malcolm's front door was opening, and for no particular reason, except perhaps that she had carried deception this far, so why not carry it farther still, she crashed through a wall of bushes bordering a yard and crouched behind them. Snow flew as the branches snapped back into place and she sat back in the snow, watching through the branches as two forms stepped from John Malcolm's house.

DKE HOUSE
Ann Hemenway

Elaine and George stood outside DKE house—the rattletrap, falling-apart, plaster-cracked (where the members had punched the walls in anger or ecstasy), alcohol-sodden, hockey-playing fraternity where Chuck was a member. George had a standing invitation to all DKE functions, though he was not a member of that or any other fraternity. "Why do I have to join and pay money and live and eat with a bunch of sweaty guys when I can go to their parties and drink free booze, which is the only reason for joining anyway?" he had said and laughed. "I can't see calling anybody bro, anyway." But he called all fraternity members bros, exaggerating it, drawing out the syllable and deepening his voice, booming "BRO." Because George lived with Chuck—one of the broiest bros of them all, Elaine thought—he could go to DKE parties without getting kicked out, as the brothers kicked out most non-fraternity members who attempted to walk through the thick and battered door that screeched open into DKE House.

Elaine was female—she could get in anywhere. "And all the better if I spread my legs," she said.

They did not normally go to cocktail parties—especially fraternity cocktail parties and most particularly not DKE cocktail parties, where everyone got drunk within the first hour, and then the women took off their shoes and the men took off their jackets ("Just like Mommy and Daddy," said George, who never wore a suit or jacket to any party) and spread their tail feathers and did a mating dance.

By the time Elaine and George had walked down to the house (which sat collapsing on the edge of campus) and hauled open the door and walked across the warped floor past the rickety bannister, the strutting and preening had already begun to the thump and grind of Bruce Springsteen. Ties were unloosed and stockinged toes gripped the moldy, blue carpet. As she and George stood in the wide doorway that led to the party rooms, Elaine saw that, yes, they were dressed like Mommy and Daddy, but with a difference: If a young man was wearing a three-piece suit, he also wore a pair of scroungy tennis shoes. An olive-skinned young man with a bump on his nose wore a tie with a flannel shirt. They were in transition.

Across the room through another doorway behind two long tables that served as a bar, Chuck beckoned them, raising a bottle of vodka or gin. They weaved their way through the knots of people, George receiving punches on the arm from various directions as they worked towards Chuck. When they got to the bar, Chuck grinned at George while he poured Scotch into a glass for one of the people who lined the bar.

His smile faded as he looked at Elaine. "Elaine," he said, disgusted.

Elaine laughed. That afternoon at the library, Chuck had complained to her about how she never wore a skirt.

"Why don't you ever look like a girl, for Chrissake?" he said, his florid face turning even redder. "You never wear anything but those fucked-up T-shirts and those army pants. Can't you at least wear a blouse or something?"

Elaine didn't think that was any of his business and told him so.

Chuck closed the book he had been studying with a slap. "You're not a bad-looking chick. You could be really good-looking if you wanted to be."

Elaine had leaned forward and narrowed her eyes. "I wore a fucking uniform for almost twelve years. A jacket, a little Peter Pan blouse, and a goddamn pleated skirt for twelve years. Winter and summer. The same skirt for practically twelve years. If I don't feel like wearing one, that's my business."

Chuck leaned back and lowered his eyelids, frowning; his fleshy cheeks sagged. "Okay, okay, but if you and George come down to the house tonight, why don't you wear a skirt."

Elaine had laughed and said she didn't have one. She laughed now as Chuck looked at her Spiderman T-shirt and bluejeans and shook his head, then looking at George, asked them what they wanted to drink.

"Scotch and water," said George.

"Vodka and tonic," said Elaine and, leaning forward over the bar whispered, "I wore mascara just for you, Chuck."

Chuck pulled two plastic glasses from the stack and expertly poured Scotch and vodka into two glasses at the same time. "Thanks," he said, sarcastically, as two and a half jiggers worth of liquor splashed onto the ice in the cups.

Chuck was too busy to talk to them; young grown-ups were appearing and reappearing by the table rapidly tapping their cups, calling out, "Screwdriver!" "Two Bloody Marys!" "How 'bout a beer, Chuck?" And Elaine and George walked into the main room carrying their drinks. In this room the music was loud and clusters of skirts and pants waved arms and drinks and cigarettes and chattered wildly above the noise.

"Oh God," said Elaine after glancing around, "no food."

"Shit," said George, straining to look around the groups of strutters and preeners, "they must have spent all their bread on booze—wait a minute—there's a bowl of potato chips over there." He hoisted his glass toward the far corner of the room. "Quick, let's get them before they disappear."

They quickly edged towards the bowl and stood with their backs to it, surreptitiously reaching behind their backs and gathering up handfuls of chips.

A stocky, young man, with kinky blond hair and a red vest across the room eyed Elaine's chest. She felt, suddenly, as if they were a pair of headlights or brights, and she wished she could turn them off with a push of her toe on the floor. She slid her eyes up to George, but if he noticed, he gave no indication but looked straight ahead, his jaw jumping as he chewed. Then she noticed a thin guy with a high forehead and thick black hair flick his eyes up and down her body as he walked past. I'm being watched, she thought, as she stepped closer to George; I'm being undressed. And she felt the same way she'd felt when she was four years old and naked, and her brother had grabbed her and held her in front of the window while all the kids from the neighborhood looked on from the sidewalk.

"These potato chips are stale," muttered George as loudly as he could from the side of his mouth. The stereo had been turned up and people had begun to shriek.

"Yeah, I know," said Elaine through the side of her mouth and her third handful of potato chips. "Isn't it strange how potato chips get chewy when they get stale? Most things dry out."

George rested his arm on her shoulder; his dangling hand was greasy and dusted with flakes of salt. He stared at the wall across from them and scrawled on it in black magic marker was "CHARLIE MANSON IS MY HERO."

"George, ol' buddy!" a voice bellowed, and they saw a young man with deep-set eyes and sun-blond hair swaggering drunkenly towards them. "George, ol' buddy, how ya doin'?" And he stuck out a meaty hand as he barreled forward. He wore a tweed jacket and blue jeans. Elaine thought she saw a pimple on his square chin.

"Pretty much of a blow-out, isn't it?" he roared as George shook his hand and mumbled pleasantries that he didn't listen to. "We are going to get wasted tonight! It is going to be one brutal party night here!" He focused his glassy eyes on Elaine. "Who's the little lady?"

George let go of the young man's hand and looked at him hard, his face deadpan, then started. "Oh, Elaine, this is Chip Waller. Chip, this is Elaine LeMaire."

A tall, storky guy in a big-shouldered madras jacket came up and loomed next to Chip, just as Elaine held out her hand to Chip. He wrapped his paw around her hand, and she felt her hand shrink and grow soft and feeble until it began to disappear beneath his beefy grasp.

Chip turned back to George, still holding Elaine's hand. "Are you an art major now?" he asked.

Elaine tried to tug her hand gently from him, but he gripped slightly. She looked at George with alarm. George's jaw tightened, and there was a glitter in his eyes as he answered Chip. "Yeah, I changed sophomore year."

She pulled a little harder this time while staring at what definitely was a pimple on Chip's chin. The storky guy looked down and smirked. Elaine began to feel as though her hand were an object separate from her; an object that her wrist and Chip's huge, enveloping hand were fighting over. She tugged again and felt the hands grow sweaty; she began twisting her wrist when George said, "Chip, you want to let go of her hand?" in a deadly tone.

Chip grinned down at her. "You want your hand back?"

"Yes," said Elaine, stiff and sullen, looking him straight in his deep-set eyes, ready to spit.

He loosened his grip slightly and she began pulling her hand from his grasp, but he loosened only enough to let her pull her hand away slowly; and as she pulled, his fingertips slid slowly up the back of her hand until he caught the tips of her fingers and lingered for a moment, a disdainful smile dancing on his lips.

Elaine snapped her hand back and held it behind her back and tried to wipe it off on her jeans; her palm was still wet. As she stood there, tense, rigid, thighs clasped tightly together, the music from the stereo roaring in her ears, George swallowed the last of his Scotch, took the cup from his lips, and gripped Elaine's arm, saying through the teeth "See ya later, Chip," and led Elaine away to the bar. They marched blindly through the crowd; Elaine didn't care who she smashed into, who spilled his drink—they deserved it, she thought. They jostled through the four-deep crowd at the bar. Chuck was just getting off duty, rolling down his sleeves as they came up. A wiry boy with a mustache slid past him and began pouring. Chuck looked up from his cuff button to George's tense face. "Hold on and I'll mix you a strong one."

"No," he said, turning to a girl with barrettes and an urgent, shaking glass. "I'm off. Ask the guy with the stache."

Chuck quickly poured two strong drinks over ice and handed the cups as he slid out from between the two tables. Elaine took hers, gulped, and nearly gagged.

Chuck looked surprised; his invisible eyebrows rose and he wrinkled his forehead. "Too much for you, Elaine? I figured you guys wanted strong ones. You want me to water it down?"

"No," Elaine gasped, "it's fine."

Chuck leaned over the bar. "Bowdy. Hey, Bowdy! Hand me my coat." The bartender bent down and handed Chuck his tweed jacket, which was big enough to be a tablecloth.

"Let's get away from the bar," said George, and holding his drink high in the air, he backed through the crowd. A girl's sweatered arm knocked Elaine's elbow, and her drink sprayed onto her T-shirt and the floor.

"Fuck," said Elaine, pulling away. The girl glanced over, but didn't speak, didn't apologize. "Aren't you going to apologize?" Elaine asked, and the girl tossed her cascade of brown hair and twitched the mole above her thin lips as her eyes darted towards Elaine and back again.

"Fuck you, too," Elaine muttered and squeezed away through shoulders and arms, and she saw George and Chuck standing in a clear space against a battered wall between two walls. Chuck stood with his foot on a metal folding chair as he listened to George, who was chopping the air with his drinkless hand. As she walked up, Chuck put his arm on Elaine's shoulder. "So Waller gave you a hard time." He turned back to George. "That guy's been looking for a fight for a long time." He looked back at Elaine. "You're cold," and he looked pointedly at her chest.

Elaine pulled her chin down and looked at her chest. "Shit," she said. A blotch of wet had spread on her right breast, and her nipples pointed right through her shirt. "Shit," she said again.

"What happened?" George asked.

Chuck put down his drink and pulled at the lapels of his jacket. "You want my coat?"

"Fuck," said Elaine, watching her nipples harden even more. "No, I'd just look even more ridiculous. That thing would be huge on me. That bitch, that goddamn bitch. She didn't even apologize. She knocked me right in the arm and didn't even say a word. I'll just keep my back turned." And she faced the wall.

Chuck tried to keep his eyes plastered to her face, "So I can watch?"

Elaine shrugged and crossed her arms over her chest. What choice did she have, she thought. Chuck knew her and would at least attempt not to rip off her clothes with his eyes. George reached over and touched her face with his fingertips. "This has been a pretty bad night for you." Elaine grimaced and said nothing. She wondered why she couldn't take this in stride, why she had to cross her arms tightly over her chest and feel the wet fabric stick to her skin while George and Chuck talked about Chip Waller, while Elaine interjected snide comments miserably. "He's an asshole," she said at one point. "He's a fuck-ass," she said at another as they discussed what should be done to him (or rather Chuck did), and that was strange because she was the victim, she was the one with the grudge, with the feeling of violation, and yet all she wanted to do was avoid him as much as possible, while Chuck considered the various ways his face could be rearranged.

Chuck had begun working himself up into a fighting mood—with the help of four beers gulped in quick succession—when Louisa flew up, clutching a huge glass of something. "Whah, Ellie," she sang, "Ah didn't expect you all to be heah!"

Elaine noticed for the fiftieth time that Louisa's accent got stronger when she drank. She also noted that lately Louisa's accent had been thick as sludge for days on end.

"Ah'm Louisa Kennicot," she crowed to Chuck, "and yew ahr?"

"Chuck Watson. Nice to meet you," Chuck said, jerking his head in an uncomfortable bow. He was angry because Louisa had barged in just as his fighting mood had risen to a punching pitch. Elaine was relieved; this meant she wouldn't have to talk Chuck out of doing damage to an asshole.

Louisa, oblivious, chirped and twittered and bounced her curls and went into some wild story about how she'd ended up on the roof of "Sigma Phah with Chahlie and Timmy" and how they'd "trahd to throw beahcans into the birdbayuth from fowah stories up and those are hagh stories, too, and oh, Ellie, Ah was so scahed, but Chahlie and Timmy jest kept sayin' they'd cayutch me and pretty soon Ah fohgot all about how hah we wereah and jest kept throwin' those beahcans into the birdbayuth. Of cohse, we were so pah-faced thyat we couldn't see wheyah the dayum birdbayuth was—" and she swooped and clutched her throat and clutched at arms and tossed her head, and Elaine saw that Louisa had exorcised the fighting spirit from Chuck and he was gazing at Louisa in fascination. She nudged George and jerked her head toward Chuck, and George smiled with his eyes.

Slowly Elaine and George retreated, standing side by side, nodding, watching, a united front of observance, as Louisa spun around Chuck and engulfed him, and he began to laugh and lean forward and smile, showing his perfect, white teeth. And Louisa's glass was empty, and Chuck went up to the bar to fill it and didn't ask Elaine or George if they wanted a refill, too. They waited, preparing to leave, already outside the door in their minds, already walking through campus, already imagining how they could find something to eat because the cafeteria was closed, while Louisa chattered and they nodded and Elaine asked her where she was going for Thanksgiving and she said Coral Reef Club in Florida. Chuck came back and George said it was time for them to go—though they had nowhere to go—and Chuck said, "You just got here." But the music had been turned up and it hurled against the walls and vibrated in the cracks and the talk roared above them and Elaine knew no one there and George, she knew, didn't care to know anyone there anymore and they dug up their coats from the pile in the corner and said goodbye to Chuck and Louisa, who were laughing uproariously, and they walked through a dark hallway so they wouldn't have to pass through the crowd and they opened the door and the cold New York November seeped into their jackets, up their sleeves, as they stood outside DKE house on the hard gravel driveway.

"I'm hungry," said George, pulling an orange knit cap from his pocket.

"Me, too," said Elaine into the cold, but she was not just hungry for food. She thought of the young women inside at that party, dressed up, made up, sophisticated, as they crossed their legs and lit their cigarettes, and the young men with their jackets draped over their arms or pushed behind their wrists when they shoved their hands in their pockets. And the snatches of conversations she heard, drips and drops of talk that was forgotten as soon as it was spoken: "That history quiz was a bitch." "Did you *see* that chick? She had gold spangles on her eyes." "Why, Tommy, you look like you're ready to be Chairman of the Board of IBM." "What perfume are you wearing?" Drip, drop, drip, thought Elaine.

"I'd forgotten how bad those parties were," said George, pulling his cap firmly over his ears. "It makes me think I would have had a better time studying."

"We can still make the movie," said Elaine. "It's probably about nine-thirty."

George pulled back his cuff and looked at his watch. "Hah. Guess what time it is. Just guess."

"I said nine-thirty."

"Nope," George laughed and held his wrist out for her to look. "It's eight o'five. We were only there for an hour." He stood in front of her, crinkling up his face.

"We missed dinner for that. I'm starved," Elaine stamped her foot.

"I'm hungry and starving and I don't have any money!" George cried, taking her shoulders and shaking her.

"Neither do I," said Elaine, bouncing like a ragdoll in his hands. "And the coffeehouse is closed."

George let go of her and stared at her miserably. "I have five dollars to last me through the week. Fortunately, except for decent food and alcohol, there's no temptation to spend money in this wasteland. Elaine, what are we going to do about food? I need food!" His breath came out in snorts, puffing into the air, filling up the sky.

Elaine kicked the hard ground with her toe and it hurt, but she was only vaguely aware of it because she was loaded—vodka and tonic loaded—draped over George's arm loaded; the fresh air had hit every cell and expanded the alcohol in them.

"With five dollars we could get macaroni and cheese," she said.

George rested his arm on her shoulder and spoke out into the clear and starry sky.

"I don't want macaroni and cheese. I want steak. Steak with mushrooms and a baked potato. Steak cooked medium rare. I want real food."

Elaine let her gaze flit past George and beyond DKE house where the cemetery stretched out, its old graying tombstones jutting crookedly from the cold earth. Tombstones from old Glasscotters whose bones were rotting near the old buildings where they spent the best years of their lives.

"I want salad, too," said Elaine to the ghosts of the alumni, "with real Thousand Island dressing, not mayonnaise and ketchup and sweet relish mixed together. I want whole slices of cucumber and bits of cheese. What are we going to do, George?"

George thought for a moment, wiping his nose with his sleeve and sniffing. "Have you got a good-sized purse? Like something a little smaller than a suitcase?"

Elaine tried to concentrate, but her thoughts were not collecting; they sat like pieces of patchwork waiting to be sewn together. Her hands were going numb and, wiggling her toes, she found that they were cold, too. Time to stop wearing tennis shoes, she thought. She saw her toes through her shoes and socks, white and crammed together like dead worms. She started mentally looking around her room, under the bed with papers and old notebooks, maybe a sock coiled and ready to spring, in the closet on the top shelf. No—there it was, on the floor behind her oversized hiking boots, a brand new blue canvas book bag with snaps on the top that her mother had given her for school, and she hadn't used once; in fact, she knew the minute her mother presented it to her that she'd never use it.

"Yes. Yes, I do," she said.

"Good. Let's go get it," said George, taking her arm and marching her up the short, steep slope that led to the cemetery and beyond.

"Okay," she said, ready to be led anywhere. "What for?" she asked a minute or two later as they weaved their way through the gravestones.

George didn't hesitate a step. "Did you ever hear of stealing?"

Elaine stopped in her tracks and squatted in front of an old, crooked gravestone with scrollwork on the sides. She watched as the dim markings on the pock-marked corroded stone formed into letters and dates: Archibald Fennel, 1859-1919.

"Archibald Fennel sucks cock," she said.

George stepped behind her and looked at the stone, shaking his hands from the cold. Their breath blew steamy, like ghosts or haunts around the graveyard.

"Archibald Fennel stopped sucking cock a long time ago—long before you and I were born," he said.

Elaine's feet were turning solid, but still she squatted in front of that gravestone. "Archibald Fennel sucks bone, then—pelvis bone, or he sucks cock in heaven—that's what he does; he sucks cock in heaven."

George put his hands on her shoulders and said in resonant tones, "And all the angels and archangels and all the company of heaven came down upon him saying, 'Glory to cock in the highest. Glory to thee, Archibald Fennel, for thou hast found favor with God for thy cock sucking expertise.'"

Elaine stood up and stamped her feet on the hard, crunchy grass. "The nuns never told me that," she said, "You know, if Archibald Fennel was born in 1859, he graduated from here in 1881. My grandmother wasn't even born then. That was when this was an all-men's college. Hah, I bet he did suck cock on those cold and snowy days."

George put his arm around her and began walking up the small slope of the cemetery to the iron gate where two iron angels stood on each gatepost watching over the dead. The gate with its iron rods twisting like licorice sticks and ending in spikes, hung half-opened and was stuck with a steel peg in the earth. "Years ago," George said as they passed through the gate, unlocking arms for a moment while Elaine passed through first. When they reconnoitered, Elaine with her arm around George's waist, George with his arm around her shoulder, George began again, "Years ago, they used to plan activities so the boys wouldn't go crazy."

Elaine watched their feet—hers in boys' tennis shoes, George more practical in heavy leather hiking boots; she bent her neck and watched those two pairs of feet stomp, stomp, stomp, machine-like on the ground. "How do you know?" she asked.

"Because in October, during alumni weekend, an old alumni told me. He was a really old alumni—an ancient alumni, like class of 1911." George sniffed again, "Chuck and I were sitting in the room; I was working on a model or something and Chuck, I think, was standing in the bathroom cutting his toenails over the toilet and we heard this knock—not a hard knock, not like a pounding, but a feeble knock, an old knock, like the person on the other end was shaking. And Chuck says, 'Who the hell could that be?' So I went and opened the door, and there was this old guy standing there. He was leaning on two canes. He wasn't just old—he was *old*. Ancient." George bent over, his arm still around Elaine, and grasped an imaginary cane.

They had reached the outside of the quad in back of Baker Dorm; in a moment they would be inside the quad where students hurried like frantic shadows, dashing into lit buildings.

"Did you let him in?" Elaine asked.

"Sure," said George, "Sure, I did. He looked a little embarrassed, a little shy. He was great. He had on a tweed jacket and a bow tie," George laughed, "a real snappy bow tie and a white shirt. His clothes hung on him, he was that old. He looked at me kind of shy and said, 'This used to be my room many years ago when I was a student here. I thought I'd take a look at it.' He had a raspy, trembling voice, and I started thinking that maybe he had cancer or emphysema because he was wheezing like hell."

Suddenly Elaine wanted George to stop talking; she didn't want to hear anymore about the old alumni with cancer or emphysema; no, not with Archibald Fennel's white bones turning to dust in the graveyard, not with Archibald Fennel's school ring rattling loose around the dry knuckle bone of his right hand. Not when it was eight o'clock at night in November and earth was frozen and the leaves had fallen and the quad, even with people scurrying about, was desolate, except for the thin light shining from the windows; not when Elaine was nineteen years old in her sophomore year and the thought of an old man returning to the room of his youth, the only thing still standing from his youth, the old man in a bow tie leaning on two canes outside the door, afraid to return, afraid to bother the life that lived there now—Chuck cutting his toenails, George building, building, always building—standing outside the door and asking, but not asking, if he could come into a place that was his and not his any longer. And it struck Elaine—Elaine nineteen years old in her sophomore year—it struck her as the vodka wore off like a stone in her stomach, a stone bitter and sad, and she was sad for the pride of old men standing in doorways where they used to live. But she didn't tell George, and George, being slightly drunk and having a chuckle in his voice, grinning into the cold air, clasping her around the shoulder in such a way that she knew he wanted to tell her that he didn't want to stop, kept shaking his head as if he had water in his ear.

"So I invited him in, and Chuck came out of the bathroom and we all shook hands. His name was James Harcourt, I think, and he looked around the room, not saying anything for awhile. His eyes were blue with that film over them that old people have and finally he said, 'Hasn't changed much. Hasn't changed much at all. New paint job, maybe.' I asked him to sit down and if he'd like a drink or something, so he sat down and had a drink and started to tell us all about the old days."

They began walking on the sidewalk, heading for Elaine's dorm, which was across the street on the other end of campus, past the Commons and the Union and the classroom buildings. George called to two guys in down vests and they waved. George waved back, but Elaine only glanced up at them and then looked back down at the sidewalk, wanting the old man to rise from his chair spryly, with new juices flowing in old marrow, and throw away his cane saying, "Well, I'm off to play tennis."

George continued, "Anyway, Chuck and I are sitting there listening to old James tell us about the old days. He says, 'You know, back then there were no girls at the college, and we boys had a lot of extra energy and the administration had trouble keeping us in line. Boyish pranks, you know, just boyish pranks, like putting a cow in the belfry of the chapel.' He'd call everybody boys or fellows. He kept saying 'you boys' or 'you fellows' and pointing at us with his bent up old finger." George imitated the old man's raspy wheeze. "'So every year in late October, before it got cold, they'd give each class cans of paint, each in a different color; freshmen had yellow, seniors had blue, sophomores had red; I don't recall what juniors had, maybe green, and we'd meet out in front of the chapel at seven o'clock with our paint cans and brushes. The dean, Dean Walbridge, bless his soul (here Elaine darted a glance at George and he said, "I swear to God, he said that.") Dean Walbridge would blow a whistle, and we'd all run for the chapel and start painting.' Chuck and I couldn't believe it. Christ, the administration letting you paint all over the chapel? Chuck was really blown away, he started saying how nowadays that'd be considered vandalism. And the old guy just drank his drink and said, 'No, it was just boyish enthusiasm.'"

As she watched George shaking his head, Elaine said, "Boyish enthusiasm? Shit. Chuck's right. You try that now and you'd be a delinquent."

George tightened his grip around her and shivered, "Jesus, it's cold. Anyway, the old guy started telling us about the paint fights they'd have. Not only did they paint the chapel, they painted each other, too, whacking each other across the face, the ass. See, whatever color covered the greatest part of the chapel, that's what class won. If the chapel had more yellow than any other color, the freshman won. Except the freshman never won, they always got creamed."

Elaine stopped and unwrapped her arm. "Wait a minute. The chapel was painted all these colors? You mean in those days the chapel was yellow and blue and green and red? You're full of shit, George."

"That's what we said—only not quite that way," said George, "and old James said they painted it every year anyway, so it didn't make any difference. Then you know what he said?" George laughed. They had crossed the street and were walking toward the Union, which was two buildings connected by an overpass. Someone inside the building would rarely notice it was an overpass; they'd just think of it as a wide hallway with large windows on the sides. They stepped up onto the brick courtyard in between the two buildings.

"What did he say?" asked Elaine, sullen, cold, and hungry.

"He said," said George, drawing out the "said" and squeezing her, knowing she was crabby, "Well, he started looking over his shoulder and getting this mischievous look in his eye. 'Got to make sure my wife isn't around to listen,' he said, and he started whispering, 'Don't let my wife hear this, but I think coeducation is a good thing. I don't like boys living in the same dorms as girls, but I think that it was a great day when they brought girls on campus.' And then he started looking around even more, as if the dean had the placed bugged or his wife was listening in at the keyhole, and he hunched down in his chair and whispered (here George pulled his shoulders together and glanced around, pursing his lips), 'We boys used to go crazy up here in the wintertime when the snow would be four-foot high and the hill being as secluded as it is. We used to think terrible things would happen to us if we didn't see a girl pretty quick. We used to think it would fall off, or we'd go insane—or blind—or even worse. Some fellows used to visit town girls, but most of us fellows wouldn't stoop so low. Oh, yes, it was terrible. There were rumors of fellows whooping it up together—with each other. Now, that's probably true, but still there were rumors. Yes, don't let my wife hear you, but I think coeducation is a good thing.' Chuck and I were trying not to laugh."

"I'm glad he had a wife," said Elaine, feeling the stone lift from her stomach. They were outside her dorm. She got out her detex card and inserted it in the slot on the door. The door buzzed and she opened it.

"Ah, warm air," said George, following her inside. "Yeah, I'm glad he had a wife, too. He left shortly after that—not until he asked me what my sculptures were, though." His voice echoed in the empty lobby, bounced against all the glass, wall upon wall of glass.

"What did he say?" Elaine asked. This ought to be a good one, she thought, as she opened the door to her hall and they paraded down to her room. They stopped in front of her door.

"He asked if they were modern art," said George, rubbing his red, raw hands together as he slouched against the wall. "I told him I didn't know; I just had a good time building them and I don't worry about it. He took a long look at the one on the mantle and said, 'Stick to your books, son. Study hard.' I told him my father said the same thing. Then he situated himself on his canes and hobbled out the door. He was a cool old guy. I hope I have that many marbles left when I'm that old. But you know what was really strange?" George stopped and stared at the wall while Elaine inserted the key in the doorknob. George cocked his head and then looked sharply at Elaine. "Chuck," he said.

"Oh, Chuck," said Elaine, annoyed, as she unlocked her door. "I'm wondering what Chuck is going to pull on Louisa."

"Chuck couldn't pull anything on Louisa that Louisa didn't instigate herself," said George.

"What does that mean?" she asked, standing with the door open. They stood, George, preoccupied, sad, his forehead crinkled as he leaned against the wall.

"You know Louisa, Elaine. If anything she'll pull something on Chuck, like dragging him up to the top of DKE to throw gin bottles off the roof."

"He can handle it," said Elaine.

"I don't know. No, this was really strange," said George, looking confused again, putting his fingers to his lips and staring at the wall. "After the old guy left, Chuck just sat there on the arm of the chair, watching the door with this funny expression on his face. He was kind of smiling, but his eyes were sad. Bleak, you know?" George turned to make sure she was listening, to make sure she understood. She stood with her hand on the doorknob, her head resting against the door.

"Then he started shaking his head saying, 'Boy,' and then he shook his head again. 'Boy,' and he went into the bedroom and shut the door. It was strange." George looked beyond her head, beyond the door at the end of the hallway, across campus, staring into his own room as Chuck had closed the door behind him.

"And what did you do?" Elaine asked, putting her hand on George's arm, opening the door.

George shrugged. "I just sat there, too. I just sat there."

Still holding his arm, she led him in the door. "Come on in," she said.

HOME FREE
Polly Mills

When Bardy got to the park, he crammed himself—six-one—into a baby swing and hung there, feeling his balls turn blue. This was living. A profoundly skinny black asshole went by behind the fence, balancing a blaster on his shoulder like a side of beef, making Bardy feel vulnerable. How fast could he scramble out of the rubber seat? Not fast at all. He could be dead, if the situation turned into anything. He had a rep in this hood; it was crazy for him to make himself so vulnerable. The rush of it made him giddy. He almost cried in public. He saw Melissa Jensen, always beautiful, with all kinds of hair in her eyes, crossing at the corner, and he hoisted himself out of the seat to balance on his ass and heels on top of it.

"Hey, Melissa!" he bellowed, swaying by accident on the swing, throwing the words (but loud) away, to let her hear how much he didn't care. She was sixteen now and had big tits and a waist that gave him a sinking feeling, as the sharp sun silhouetted her (she was dressed in black) against the tarpapered houses on Ashland Avenue. There was something mature now about her hair—she was curling it or something.

She saw him waving, smiling, sitting like a chimpanzee on top of the baby swings in the park, and she remembered all about him. Once in ninth grade, on his roof with a bunch of kids, she let him kiss her, not too much, but she liked it. Bardy Tenngren was a natural enigma. He held her hand, squeezing it without letup all that night. And while Ivan and those guys were talking shit, talking reefer and boosting, Bard was rapping like the rest of them, but he kept leaning into her and whispering, "Look at the moon, Lissa, you can see the man," and "He's going, 'I see you, Lissa, hanging out with bad boys,' and 'Lissa, Lissa, Lissa, is a pretty girl.'" He even said, in secret, "Look at those morons, they can't tell what I'm saying. They think I'm talking dirty in your ear. You should probably smile now and act like I've swayed you with words."

"Hi, Bard," she said now, leaning her tits into the chain-link fence. She was nine feet away. He could see her fingers poking through the links, curly, like an eagle's.

"Whachou been doin'?" he asked her.

"Nothing. School."

"But there's school today," said Bard.

"I didn't have the heart for it. How about you, Bard?"

"I finished school at Charley Town. Got a G.E.D."

"Really?"

"Yeah."

"You were in Charley Town? I heard you were at Menard, with the psychopaths."

"I'm a minor."

"Oh, yeah." Melissa was god-damned examining him, looking at his pointy knees, then his arms, then his shoulders. "You got new glasses," she said.

"They gave them to me in jail. Gorgeous, right?"

"You look like a stockbroker."

"I feel like one," Bard said grinning; he knew he could be witty as hell. He scratched his shoulder so she would look at it again and notice that he had been working out.

"I bet," said Melissa, looking sideways at him. She had black raccoon lines around her eyes to make her look tough, but Bard thought they made her look vulnerable.

"I been working out," he said, but suddenly he felt like an asshole for saying it.

"Yeah?"

"While I was incarcerated."

"I bet it was pretty boring."

He wondered what she said that for. It was hard looking at her, with the noon sun making everything too sharp, with the long cars going by behind her, with the smell of gasoline from the station across the corner. He got this funny feeling of wanting to be someplace dark and still and warm with her, talking his head off. He thought of his crib with his big sister Allison crashed in broad daylight; forget that. The smokehouse behind Pierce School, but Melissa would never go there. "Want to go to Tastee Freez?" he asked, "get some fries?"

"I guess."

At Tastee Freez, first they smelled the fries sizzling. Coming in from the cold made the smell somehow good. They felt it in their mouths and stomachs, although in their heads it reminded them of poached eggs and fishsticks. Bard went up to the counter and told the Cuban guy there, "Two orders of fries and . . . ?"

"A Tab," said Melissa.

"And a large orange."

"For here or to go?" the Cuban guy asked. He was a shrimp, so Bard didn't freak too much about the accent, although he could hardly understand the mutherfucker.

"Here."

Bard paid and then they took their food to the table in the corner, with a sweeping view of Clark Street at Hollywood through one window and of Terry's Jip Joint through the other. Terry sold cigarettes to minors, along with candy and fireworks, and was a staple in the neighborhood. If Bard sat there long enough, he would see someone he knew coming out of Terry's.

At the table, Melissa took the plastic catsup bottle and carefully sprinkled dabs of catsup all over her fries. When she was done, Bard expelled a big glob in a corner that he had cleared of fries in his basket. He hated slimy stuff, and liked the idea of having some control. It wasn't dark at all in Tastee Freeze, with the sun cutting through the corner windows, but on the other hand, there was no one there except the Cuban, who wouldn't be listening to white people's personal shit.

"What are you going to do now, Bard?" Melissa asked, poking at her fries.

"Eat," he said, avoiding all shit.

"No. I mean now that you're out."

"Nothing. I'm not breaking the law, that's for sure. I'm getting a job. I'm getting my own crib. I'm going to college. I think Blackburne downstate. They have an excellent liberal arts program. You can design your own curriculum."

Melissa wasn't sure what liberal arts were. She thought of hippies, though, and figured that Bard was fooling himself if he counted on fitting in. "What are you going to do there?"

"Prepare for graduate school."

"Ha!" But Melissa hadn't meant to laugh. She pictured Bardy smoking a pipe, with reefer in it, and toting a load of books under his arm. It was all wrong.

"Really?" she said, sipping her Tab.

"People don't realize my potential. I have a genius I.Q."

"Right. Smart guys are always going to jail."

"You don't know me very well."

"I know you enough."

"What if I said I knew all about you, Liss?" Bard said, changing the tone of the conversation to something more gentle. "What if I said you were just a punk, smoking cigarettes before your time — and easy?"

"Fuck you," she said, gently.

"I wouldn't say that."

"You just did."

"It was hypothetical, Lissa. I was making a point. Because I know there's more to you, because I took the time to think about it. Because I know you're vulnerable, just like all the other assholes. And I know girls just smoke cigarettes, e.g., because they don't want people to know how scared they really are of getting tits and having babies and getting married and settling down in the suburbs."

Melissa laughed at him. "You're nuts," she said, grinning over her straw. "Do you really have a genius I.Q.?" she asked.

"One forty-nine."

"Is that good?"

"It'll do. It's just enough to make me feel like a fucking moron all the time."

"What do you mean?"

"I mean my head is going crazy all the time. Like maybe normal people walk down the street, thinking, 'duh, dee, duh, duh, maybe I'll feed the dog,' but I'm thinking about life and death all the time. All the time, the ideas are racking around in me. Like how we are polluting the environment. Like Agent Orange. Like Terry's is corrupting youth. Like this fucking acne will leave lifetime scars. Like motherhood is subrogated. Like . . ."

"What's that?"

"What?"

"Subrogated."

"It's fucked over."

"I don't know what you're talking about."

"You will, as soon as you settle down in the suburbs."

"You're an enigma, Bard."

He laughed; he liked that. He wanted to kiss her, right now. The Cuban guy wasn't looking; Bard saw that he had his ass to the customers and was leaning on the inside counter, grooving to his a-ooo-ga music. Bard knew enough Spanish to know the guy was believing some song about love and a sad corazon.

He stood up and leaned over the French fries. He spilled his orange into his lap, but he didn't give a fuck. He kissed her and she let him. As soon as he felt her tongue, little, wet, in his mouth, he got hard; he'd been away a long time. He heard Who music in his mind.

"I love you," he whispered, meaning every word of it, and, she couldn't help it, she laughed.

They sat there a couple of hours; Bard said his lap had to dry, but that wasn't really it. Melissa smoked a half pack of Marlboros, and Bard swiped the smoke away, just happy to be sitting close to a girl. He couldn't get his hard-on down though; even thinking of jail again didn't work. Nothing worked until he saw his best friend, Ivan, wearing the lucky plaid hunting jacket he'd lent him, going into

Terry's with some short, fucking, new guy.

Back on the street, squeezing Lissa's hand hard, his balls sticking to his Fruit of the Looms as he walked, with Lucian up ahead and the new guy, Thomas, pimp-walking to make up for his height, Bard felt better. He was back with the people.

*   *   *

When Bard got home, reeling, smiling his cocaine smile, he caught a broad, funny view of Allison schlumped on the sofa, waving *Siddhartha* at him, the book rolled up like a taco. She'd been reading it until "Jeopardy" came on.

"Aw, man, Bard," she slung the words over his shoulder, toward the front door behind him. He got no respect. "You're home one fucking day, and you're high," said Allison, with pure sisterly regret. She waited for him to answer her. He didn't. He turned the corner from the apartment's small entrance way and veered into the kitchen. Allison jumped up from the couch, leaving "Jeopardy" to fend for itself, and came into the kitchen just in time to see Bard pull a T-bone steak in a plastic wrapper out from under his shirt. "Man, Bard," she said.

"I've gotta eat, don't I?" Bard answered.

"You don't have to steal the shit."

"Where else am I going to get it? Are you gonna buy some meat for me with your paycheck?"

"Shut up."

"Get a job, Allison."

Allison, leaning against the empty refrigerator, wanted some steak, but wouldn't ask him for any, on principle. She had had it with rice and Jello, but, when she considered what was worse, Jello and a life of reclusion or meat and a life among society's assholes, her choice was a simple one. "I can't get a job; you know that," she said.

"Bullshit, Al. Go to therapy, like I told you. You can't stay here all your life."

"No. Maybe I'll go out and knock over some drugstores. Then I can get out into the world like you did, see the pleasant vistas of Audie Home and St. Charles."

"You'd never get arrested," he assured her.

Bard pulled a bottle of Worcestershire sauce out of his left-hand army jacket pocket, unscrewed the lid, and set the bottle down on the table. It spilled. He wiped it up with a dishtowel, then saved the dishtowel to wipe over his meat when it was cooked. He stooped, swaying, to light the broiler in the oven, then he slid his steak in on top of the unprotected broiler plate.

"I'm not cleaning up your shit, Bard," his sister told him. She was waiting for him to sway a little harder, then do some sort of little spin, then melt, knees first, into a puddle beside the stove, sort of à la Stan Laurel, which wouldn't be the first time he passed out in mid-sentence.

"Sure, you'll clean it up," Bard said. "You've got nothing better to do. Did you even read today?"

"I read *Rosshalde* yesterday and today I'm reading *Magister Ludi*," she said, putting a hand on her hip, jerking her bangs from her eyes.

"Well, that's good anyway. However, that book is shit."

"Which one?

"*Magister Ludi*." Bard slammed the broiler door closed, then began shuffling through Melmac plates in the dish rack to find his favorite one, the mismatched plate featuring a big-eyed puppy. "Where's Phido?" he said. "Did you use it?"

"I don't eat off of mass-media, art-for-arts-sake garbage."

"No, you don't eat off of it. You just eat it. 'And she shook when she laughed like a bowl full of Jello.'" Bard cracked up.

"It's not Jello, in the poem; it's jelly. They didn't have Jello in those days. Besides, what else can you eat for ten cents? Like, that steak must have cost two dollars," she said.

"You're fading out, Al," Bard said.

"Oh yeah. So you got your steak for free, but think about what you're costing society."

"Hey," he told her, "Steal This Book." He was bending over again, this time poking his butt in her face.

"Get out of here," she told Bard.

"Get out of here," he repeated, mimicking her in a high-pitched whine.

"Drop dead, Bard."

"Maybe I will."

"Shut up."

"Get therapy, Allison."

"Get a social conscience, Bard."

"Get a job, bitch."

"Get a G.E.D., moron."

"Hey!" he shouted. He physically wiped a smirk off his face by swiping his hand over his mouth. "I'm getting my G.E.D. I took the test at Charley Town last week before I got paroled and now I'm just waiting for the test scores. It's a mere formality, Allison. I passed that shit. Then I'm going to pre-med. I'd go to law school, but you can't get in with a record. Try doing shit with a record, Al."

"Try not breaking the law."

"I am. I am trying."

"O.K."

Bard gingerly pulled the broiler drawer open. The smell of his browning T-bone filled the room. He flipped it with a fork, then slid the drawer closed.

"Is Dad sleeping?" he asked.

"He left."

"Is he tending bar?"

"So they say. I think Cheryl just lets him work there to pay off his tab. Meanwhile, he's still drinking more than he's selling."

"Dad's got to go to A.A.," said Bard.

"Too bad they don't have A.A. for cokeheads, Bardy."

"Too bad they don't have A.A. for fat asses, Allison."

Bard pulled the broiler drawer open, crouched down in front of the open, blue flames, pulled his switch blade out from his right-hand jacket pocket and, with the fork, gingerly cut into the center of the steak. It bled. "Bloody good," he said, in a cockney accent.

"Gross," said Allison. "You can't carry that knife anymore, Bard. You're tempting fate. You're asking to get arrested. You can't carry anything anymore, Bard; you're on parole."

"Yeah."

"Plus you're high. You're high, you're stealing, and you're carrying that item."

"Have I committed any felonies in the past week, Allison?"

"No."

"Have I hurt anyone?"

"No."

"Have I smashed anyone's face in, including your own?"

"No."

"Did I get a job at Jupiter Department Store, starting tomorrow, paying eighty dollars every Friday?"

"Yes."

"Am I going to pull myself and maybe even this whole fucked-up family out of the shithole?"

"I don't know."

"You don't know shit, Al, because you won't go outside."

"I can't go outside."

"Nothing will happen if you go outside, Allie."

"Yes it will. Everything will happen. I'm too afraid, Bard."

"You're too fucked up, is all."

"You should talk."

"I am talking. But you're not listening to me simply because I am under the influence of a mind-altering drug." He laughed again.

Bard lifted his steak out from the broiler and carried it, dripping, balancing, from the tip of his knife, across the room to the dish rack, where he selected a blue and white abstract-patterned Melmac plate from the family's matched set. He threw his meat onto the plate, then wiped some Worcestershire sauce off of the dish towel onto the meat, then carried his plate high over his head into the living room, where he sat down in front of "Jeopardy." "What is the tympanic membrane!" he roared, after a moment, in the direction of the lady contestant wearing a red dress on TV.

Allison watched him scarf his steak and win twelve hundred imaginary dollars on TV. He felt big. He was a brilliant fucker.

General Essay

BLITE & WACK
Edye Deloch

There are whites who try to be black, but they don't turn out blite simply because they try too hard. They're called tryblites. Blites can't help the way they are. They are whites who mainly grew up in the black community; therefore, they naturally adopted black habits, black culture, black ways of acting. Whites who try to act black usually come from segregated neighborhoods that sheltered them from any kind of black life. When unleashed to discover the world, they discover black culture and are taken by its liveliness and earthiness, which was always missing in their white lives. They want to be a part of and identify with this new found love, but in the process, they seem fakish, because they still have that twang and those bright and fluttery eyes. And they seem to be put-on instead of real. Black folks then begin suspecting these people because they seem to want to be in their ass a lot. And you've gotta watch out for people who want to be a part of your shit so badly.

There are tryblites who don't want to be blites at all. They just talk that "Hey brotha, right-on" shit to your face, and then call you a nigger to their white friends when you ain't around. And yes, they still have that twang.

Sometimes tryblites try so hard to be black physically that they are and do it. Like for instance:

1. Wearing a severe perm in their head and calling it a gerri curl.
2. Wearing too tight polyester shirts, double platforms and too big wide-brimmed hats rakishly cocked to the side.
3. Pimping down the street with the shoulder dipping on the upbeat alongside the brothers whose shoulders dip on the *down*beat.
4. Trying to dance like the folks on Soul Train and falling down because their foot trips on their bell bottoms while doing a turn.
5. Having a conversation with a black student about how "tough" the Supremes are when you know darned well they haven't done poot in almost 10 years.
6. Doing every step of the soul brother handshake with intense feeling.
7. Trying to rap to a white girl the way the brothers rap to the sisters. (Tryblites wouldn't dare rap to a sister).
8. Trying rap #13. The "What's your phone number before what's your name" routine. (Some brothas still do that one.)

WAYS TO DISTRACT TRYBLITES

Tryblite - Say, what it is, blood!
Blood - How do you do, fellow.
Tryblite - Say did you see James Brown on TV last night?
Blood - I beg your pardon?
Tryblite - James Brown—you know (Grabs invisible microphone and sings with feeling) Please, please, please, please!
Blood - What is your problem?
Tryblite - Say man, that's an old cut from James Brown. Man, I know you heard of him. All the brothas heard of him.

Blood - (seriously) Actually, I like Cat Stevens.
Tryblite - Wha—?
Blood - Yes, he has such a laid back siren-like quality don't you think?
Tryblite - You fo real?
Blood - Why shouldn't I be?
Tryblite - I dunno. To tell you the truth I like Cat Stevens too.
Blood - Oh yes?
Tryblite - (with his real White dialect) Oh hecky yeah, forget James Brown, he's weird. Sweats too much if ya ask me. My mom bought Cat's greatest hits for me the other day.
Blood - Oh yes!
Tryblite - Yes! Gosh, I really love Moon Shadow (singing) Moon shadow, moon shadow. Say you're the only person I can talk to around here. You're swell.
Blood - (Suspiciously) Dat so?
Tryblite - Huh?
Blood - Tis so! my fellow, tis so!

I came across this female Blite many times while still at C.C. I had always noticed her in the lunchroom. Always in the lunchroom. Nowhere else. It seemed she lived between the plastic seats, printed posters, and vending machines that littered the floor and walls. She was always surrounded by blacks, the fun-loving, rowdy blacks—mostly males, who treated the lunchroom as their own paneled basement. A huge portable tape player sat on top of the table blurting out BMX. Coats were scattered over the seats, shoes were kicked off, and a deck of cards tossed its way to awaiting hands.

There she'd be, skimmed milk among chocolate faces, sitting there with her glasses on the tip of her nose, dealing the cards out, chewing on a piece of gum. Her hair, a long drab blond, was pulled back. I heard her tell somebody to shut their ass up in the most genuine black dialect. The guy shut up and made a smirky expression in mock disgust. The others laughed.

She was accepted there.

I looked at her inconspicuously while sticking 40 cents into the pop machine. I pressed root beer and then bent over to grab the clunking can. As I did that, I kicked up my feet nonchalantly and turned my head around again, as if that's part of the process of nabbing a fallen pop can. And when I turned, I saw her again studying her hand of cards, and she said cooly, "Six no." Everyone cleared his throat, and I suddenly knew two things. No. 1: They're playing Bid Whist and No. 2: She definitely knew how to play. "Six no" is a difficult bid to make. Only the most skilled Bid Whist player could pull that off.

Bid Whist is a game mostly black folks play. White folks got bridge; black folks got Bid. It's a game that's challenging and fun. It uses your strategic skills as opposed to Old Maid and Tunk, which are based mainly on luck.

Bid Whist is a game that is deeply imbedded in the culture of black people. Therefore, many whites are unfamiliar with Bid. When you find a white that knows Bid, you also know that they sho'nuff like to hang aroun' black folks. There are blacks who don't know how to play, believe it or not. They know OF it. And many gather around the table and watch from the sides. But they don't know how to play. So you know a white Bid player is a phenomenon to behold.

I beheld this phenomenon raking up all the books. Her partner giggled gleefully, as one of her fat light-skinned male opponents yelped, "She's kickin' our ass, man!"

I looked at them play as I sipped my root beer. Victory gleamed through her glasses while a soberness settled into her opponents' brows. She grunted out an "umph!" and an "ow!" for each card she flickingly slapped upon the table. I knew she had a Boston (total victory). And I smiled as a white person would smile at me flawlessly reciting Shakespeare's "To Be or Not To Be." She looked up and saw my smile. She gave me back a half snicker, the kind I'd give that smiling white person. I bit my lip and walked over to the other side of the lunch room, the section where the white folks dwell. A couple of guys with black-rimmed glasses and torn jeans talked about far-out monster flicks, while a girl studied and three others chatted away about how sickening the vending machine food tasted, as they piled chunks of vending machine tuna sandwiches and donuts in their mouths. And all the while I sat there sipping away at my vending machine pop, wondering what went on in her mind.

I saw her again, the Blite. She was in the lunchroom as usual, but alone this time, sitting where the white folks usually sit. But there were no whites around, or blacks for that matter. Only the janitor who picked up the abandoned cellophane and empty milk cartons that lay sprinkled about. Her only dinner, I thought. She was busy reading *Native Son*. Every now and then she'd push up her glasses that sometimes slipped down her nose, giving a sniffle with each punch. She sat by the window. It was dark outside, so she stood out like a picture on a mat board. The lunchroom radio was playing a Fleetwood Mac song:

> Thunder only happens when it's raining
> Players only love you when they're playing

Right then she looked how I would've imagined her at her home, had I not known her true condition—sitting at her kitchen table of her lower middle-class home, the room smelling of the Caucasian delicacy, polish sausage and sauerkraut; the TV barely audible from the living room, bearing giggling gifts to her mother and father and baby brother, courtesy of Suzanne Sommers; the radio in the kitchen battles the laughs with its mellow weapon, Fleetwood. Her book bears the title, *The Golden Notebook*, by Doris Lessing. She pushes up her glasses and sniffs simultaneously. Eyes grow bored and weak; a slice of stringy hair jolts out of place and into her eyes. A poot is heard, a slow murmuring kind that sounds like a weasel. She chuckles silently and winces at the smell. She lays the book face down on the table and stretches her legs and arms in a sacrificial pose—a victim of fatigue. She wears a cream T-shirt that has the washed up Eric Estrada on the front.

No.

It said in sparkling letters "Earth, Wind & Fire" on a black T-shirt, not cream. She yawned a deep unashamed yawn and picked up her book again, *Native Son*. The janitor edged towards her area and swept up the soup can. He threw it into the trash bag. The smell of microwave polish sausage was very prevalent. Smelled kind of good. The buzzer sounded and I grabbed my polish, which was steaming inside the oven and eager to be ravished. I tore the mustard pack open and squeezed the yellow goo onto my unbunned pole of red meat.

I threw away the pack, placed the bun back in its place, debating whether I should sit by her or not. Curiosity killed the cat, but I knew maybe I'd make a friend even if she was a bit different. Blitey. I took a deep breath, flexed my nose, and turned my body to her direction. She was gone.

DEFINITIONS

Wak: A person of Negro stock who has been raised as a Caucasian by his parents and/or environment.
Trywak: A person of Negro stock who has been raised as such, tries adopting Caucasian characteristics and customs but fails to do so effectively.

SONG: "THE LOOK OF WAK" (song to the tune of "The Look of Love")

1st VERSE	2nd VERSE
the look	the look
of wak	of blite
is in	is on
his eyes	her face
a look	the look
his 'fro	her freckles
can't disguise	can't erase
the look	she slurs
of WA-AK	her words
is saying so much more than	and combs her frizzy hair
black could ever say	with a plastic afro pick
it says he's white inside	and boogies down the street
and he's thrown the black away	oh my God, this makes me sick
I can't hardly wait to kick him	I can hardly wait to bash her
kick him in his aa-ass	scratch her in the eyes
he makes me so sick, oh	too long I have waited
speaking as a black girl…	speaking as a black girl…
speaking as a proud girl…	speaking as a proud girl…
I'm going to puke…	but she might kick my ass…

As I stated earlier, Blites do seem to come fair and blond. But there are some who are brunette and red-haired too. I had a chance to meet a red-haired Blite during my travels to the "Show Me" state of Missouri. I believe I was traveling to St. Louis from Chicago in a Greyhound, and I happened to meet this fellow on the bus. As a matter of fact, he sat next to me, which I didn't think very strange, because he seemed a chap who liked riding in the front of the bus, and I was occupying the very first row across from the driver. He was a very freckled chap, very Ivy League with crisp carrot hair cascading over his brow and tufts of carrot bristles shading his eyes. He seemed a bit tall, about six feet, and he was rather thin, but not exceedingly so. He wore a cream pullover and double-knit slacks. I could see his shirt collar peeking through his V-neck. The texture of his shirt was polyester and the pattern was NIK NIK, a shirt brand very popular among blacks in the early 70s. Perhaps that should have given me the clue that he was a Blite, but I reasoned that some whites do find NIK NIK shirts very attractive. I looked down at his shoes, expecting Hush Puppies, but they were a soft-shined leather—very slick, yet conservative. They looked new. Perhaps this should have given me another clue, but I reasoned that he probably had good taste in shoes, a gift, I find, many white men do not possess. He carried with him a small, plastic leather duffle bag—"pleather" is what the material's called. It had lots of zippers and pockets covering it. Thrown over the bag was a brown leather jacket. One can really tell what is leather and what is "pleather" when they're right next to each other. The jacket did not look at all cheap. It seemed tapered and cut short. It also matched his shoes. I remember being very impressed.

Streams of people were still boarding the bus. Two older white nuns sat opposite us. Two middle-aged black women and their two daughters and THEIR two daughters walked towards the back. A host of other whites looking lower class and tired passed us. Two college looking black girls sat behind us, and on and on and on until the bus was full. At that point I realized that there were more front seats available, but he chose to sit by me—another clue of his being a Blite perhaps, but I reasoned that I probably took his favorite seat and he had to settle for second best with the seat beside me.

After a short wait, the driver started the engines and we were off. For a considerably long time, we didn't acknowledge each other's presence. I simply read my book, and he simply sat there. All the while, however, I wondered whether or not he would say anything to me. Or should I say anything to him—What school did he go to, or what kind of work did he do? Did he think I was cute? I had on my glasses, and my hair was fixed for once. Did he think I was intelligent because I was reading a thick hardcover book? Or did he think I was dumb and ignorant, anyway, like a lot of whites think of blacks? Did he want to go to bed with me because I was a black woman? Some white guys think we're prostitutes no matter how intelligent or innocent we may look or act. Is that why he sat next to me? My mind jumped with freaked-out curiosity, even though I seemed to be so absorbed in my book. A steady wave of conversation, peppered with laughter, swarmed inside the bus. Even the bus driver was having a conversation with one of the nuns. They talked of how majestic the Pope looked when he visited Chicago.

I carefully turned my eyes away from the book to see what he was doing. I had noticed his lap; the crease was still prominent in the middle of his slacks. Whoever ironed his clothes did not, by any means, play around. As I looked at his lap, he bent down, moved his coat further to the side, unzipped his duffle bag, and proceeded to search inside for something. I looked inside, too, and saw a few magazines: *People, Sports Illustrated, G.Q., JET!* Jesus, I thought. *Jet* magazine! Two *Jet* magazines! One with O.J. on the front and the other with the Spinners. Dig that! That should have given me a clue, but I reasoned—ah reason hell! This was ground evidence that my red-headed, freckled friend here was a Blite. A Blite! So I asked casually, without thinking it was a nosy thing to do, "Can I see one of your *Jets*?"

And he said, "Sure, here's both of 'em."

Hummm, I thought, as he handed me the *Jets*. His voice hasn't the twang of a white. It was sorta low keyed and subdued. But I still couldn't tell. He looked at me and asked with a smile, "What's your name?"

I said my name shyly, like a little girl. Why did I do that? I wanted him to know that I was a strong black woman, not a babe! He said, "I'm Cliff," in a real cool, mellow tone. He sounded sexy this time. But as I gazed upon his face, I didn't see any sexiness. All I saw were freckles. But you know, his eyes did have a laid back quality to them—unlike whites whose eyes are constantly bright and fluttery. His were more fixed on my face. When meeting Blites, that is a telltale sign. It seems that this is the only nonverbal way they can let you know that they are non-white because nothing else will give it away. When I see that, I study their faces more to see whether they've got some kind of black in them. For him, I did not study long, for he was undeniably white.

He asked, "What school you go to?" I hesitated, because the dialect was finally coming in. But it wasn't plantation dialect. It wasn't ghetto dialect. It was merely nice, middle-class, college black dialect—the kind I talk. I said, "Tuxen College. You probably never heard of it."

"Noooo, nooo, noo, Can't say I have. Where is it?"

"In Chicago."

"Well, I'm from Springfield anyway, so I don't know nothing about Chicago except for Dingbats. Na I can tell you where Dingbats is." By this time his face became a little more animated, but his eyes stared fixed on my face.

"Yeah, I can tell you, too!" I replied. We both chuckled. He had a soft "heh-heh!" sort of laugh that mixed in with my frantic "hee-hee!"

We talked some more, about where he worked: At Burger King as a full-time manager. About what he likes to do: Party, as he puts it. "Hey, I like to party, you heard me? I loves to party, party, party, par-tee! You get high?"

"No," I said.

"Hey, ain't nothin' wrong with that. Nothin' wrong with that at all. Me, I'll indulge in some herb every once in a while, you know, on a sociable basis. But I don't do it everyday, now. Hey, some of my partners do it EVERYDAY. I don't."

"Well, that's cool," I said, "I don't care. To each his own."

"Yeah, to each his own. I agree with that!"

There was a mild silence. And then he said, "You think I'm strange, don't you?"

"What do you mean?" I asked knowing exactly what he meant.

"Come on. You know me! The way I've been bringing myself to you."

"Yeah, it's strange, but it's okay."

He smiled.

Then we talked about homosexuality: "Hey, I don't have anything against them muthafuckas—excuse the French—but I swear, they betta not touch me. I may not look it, but I *can* kick ass."

We talked about politics: "President Carter ain't doin' shit! I'm sorry to talk about your man, but hey, it's real. But—I don't think no president can do shit. That's what being president is all about. Not doin' shit."

We talked of women's rights: "Hey, my lady can work where she wanna work, get equal pay an' everything so long as I make more money than she do."

Racial discrimination: "Hey, of course, we're still discriminated against. I mean—ya'll are still discriminated against. WELL, EX-CUUSSSE MEE!"

About white people: "Some of my best friends are white."

About black women: "I love black women. Does that offend you? Then can I have your phone number?"

We were in Springfield by that time, nearing the terminal. So I figured he was a nice enough person, and I did like him for a friend. But I had a thing about giving out my phone number to the opposite sex—black or white. Okay, okay, maybe his skin did play a teeny-weeny part in my hesitancy. So to be fair, I asked him for his. And he willingly gave it to me, along with his address and work number. He told me to call collect if I wanted. His mamma wouldn't mind; he paid the phone bills.

Many months have passed and I still haven't called. Perhaps I will get the courage to do it someday. Blites aren't my idea of potential boyfriends. But who said he would be my boyfriend? Oh heck, after I type this sentence I'll call him up... maybe.

EUTHANASIA
Marilyn Mannisto

Advances that have been made in the practice of medicine now make it possible to save lives and to sustain bodily functions in cases where previously death was inevitable. Improved diagnostic tools, more effective drugs, and life support equipment such as respirators and dialysis machines have saved thousands of lives. However, these same advances have raised serious questions as to whether, in certain cases, it is ethical either to remove or decline to extend extraordinary measures to prolong life. In other words, does euthanasia have a place in today's system of health care?

When I was a respiratory therapy student at the University of Virginia Hospital and serving my first rotation in the intensive care unit, a 12-year-old boy was admitted in a comatose state.

Because his mother was an invalid, the family had installed a dumbwaiter so that meals and other supplies could be easily transported to her room. A few hours earlier, John had been cleaning out the shaft of the dumbwaiter in the basement, stretching up and forward on his toes to reach the farthest greasy corners, when someone unwittingly sent it back down to the basement. John was unable to completely back out of the shaft to safety before the dumbwaiter struck him on the head and neck. He was pinned beneath it, and his trachea was forced against the edge of the shaft entrance, completely obstructing his ability to breathe.

He was deprived of oxygen for at least 20 minutes from the time of the accident until paramedics successfully revived his heart.

Now we watched as an anesthesiologist connected him to a respirator. When he finished, we stood silently by his side. The tranquility and sense of repose that comatose persons emit is of such a supernatural quality that it can have a hypnotic effect. The surrounding activity of the medical staff, conversations, glaring lights, dropped equipment—none of it seems to penetrate the dim recesses of this subterranean level of sleep.

John's father would come to the hospital each day and sit silently by his bedside, waiting for a miracle—waiting for his son to open his eyes, to speak his name, to grasp his hand. Each evening John's father would leave the hospital without having had any of these hopes fulfilled. As the months passed, the strain of waiting for his son to either recover or die began to show. He became shrunken in stature, lines of worry etched his face, and mounting hospital bills contributed to the premature graying of his hair. Soon his son's body also began to degenerate: his hair thinned, ulcerous bed sores began to burrow into his flaccid flesh, and his limbs began to draw up into a fetal position as his muscles atrophied and his ligaments shortened.

For two and a half years John's heart beat, his lungs expanded, and his blood flowed, but he never awoke. He even reached the point where he could be weaned from the respirator and exist with only supplemental oxygen, but his brain was dead. Finally, pneumonia extinguished his life.

Because the paramedics had revived John's heart, the hospital did not feel justified in withholding life-support systems even though he had no discernible brain activity. The accepted medical definition of death is the complete cessation of function of vital organs—that is, no heart beat, no pulse, no respiration. The fear of legal prosecution prompted the hospital staff to use extraordinary means to prolong John's life, even though they were sure that he would never recover from his coma.

In the highly publicized case of Karen Ann Quinlan, her parents wanted Karen's respirator withdrawn after she had been in a comatose state for several months, because they had given up hope for her recovery. When the hospital refused to comply, they appealed their decision in court. In 1976 the Supreme Court of New Jersey decided that the guardian, family, and physicians of Karen could disconnect her respirator and let her die if there was "no reasonable possibility" of her ever returning to a "cognitive, sapient state." This decision was based on her right to privacy from bodily invasion.

The rights of incompetent patients such as John and Karen, who cannot express their wishes as to whether or not they want their life to be prolonged under such circumstances, need to be protected. However, medical technologies and treatments need to be used in a meaningful way and not simply for the useless prolongation of life. In 1977 the Massachusetts Supreme Court reached a decision in the case of Saikewicz that, if it were comprehensively implemented, would ensure that both of these goals are achieved.

Saikewicz was a mentally retarded ward of the state who was suffering from an incurable form of leukemia. Because he only had the mentality of a 3-year-old, his physician felt that chemotherapy in his case would cause unjustifiable suffering because of Saikewicz's inability to understand the treatment. Therefore, the hospital brought the case to court to receive permission to abstain from traditional modes of treatment. The court's decision was based on the concept of substituted judgment—that is, the court and a guardian that they appointed for Saikewicz tried to determine his wants and needs and to act on his behalf. The court decided that, based on his age (67) and the opinion of physicians that, although chemotherapy would prolong his life, his total life expectancy still was not expected to exceed that of one to two years, treatment could be withheld. Within a year, Saikewicz died from complications of his leukemia.

The use of substituted judgment can resolve the conflict that arises between the need to protect the right of the patient and the need to permit physicians to exercise their sound medical judgment. In addition, such a practice would share the burden of responsibility among the family, guardians, and physicians so that fear of legal prosecution would not override the need to act in the patient's best interests.

A few years ago in a Chicago hospital, an adult accident victim was admitted to the neurology ward. Ed had suffered severe head and neck injuries and he was paralyzed from the neck down. He was placed on a respirator, and soon afterward electroencephalograms showed that he had no brain activity.

When I came on duty a few hours later and checked the settings of his respirator, I found that the volume had been turned down to zero. Standing by Ed, you could hear him faintly gasping for breath above the sounds of the machine. I quickly readjusted the setting and reported what I had found to the resident on duty. He informed me that when they found out that Ed had no brain activity and apparently no family to consult, they had decided to "speed up" the inevitable—namely, his death.

As he told me this, he kept his eyes averted as he read a medical chart and kept his back half turned to me. "I will need written orders to that effect," I said as he began to walk away. Hesitantly, I followed him until he paused by another patient's bed. "Listen," I said, "I'm responsible for making sure that all of the respirators on this floor are functioning properly. You will have to write orders to have the volume decreased or else to completely remove the respirator." I have to admit that my legal responsibility was the reason why I had the audacity to force the issue. The class distinctions in a hospital are as clearly defined as the caste system in India. For a lowly therapist to question the actions of a resident was equivalent to a pariah speaking disrespectfully to an Indian Brahman priest. However, my boldness was surprising enough to capture his attention and force him to acknowledge me. "OK, OK," he muttered, and rapidly strode down the hall.

An hour later when I came back to the ward, Ed was gasping for breath, the respirator was making all the correct noises but not delivering any air, and orders had not been written in the chart. This time the resident said, "I'm just following the head neurologist's orders; this guy's brain is dead and we need the bed for patients that we can help." We stood glaring at each other at a complete stand-off; he had brutally but effectively disclaimed responsibility for his actions.

I called in my supervisor, explained the situation, and he set off to find the head neurologist. Finally, he was located and persuaded to authorize the removal of the respirator, but only after the resident and I had spent four hours playing tug-of-war over the respirator controls.

The next day a new patient was in Ed's bed, his file was marked "deceased," and nothing was noted in Ed's chart except for his cause of death—"respiratory arrest."

There was no "reasonable hope" for Ed's recovery, but there also was no one who cared if Ed died with dignity or not. Because of their fear of legal prosecution, the physicians charged with his care decided to act in their own interests rather than those of their patient. They tried to commit a covert act of euthanasia, and they succeeded because Ed's chart never documented the hours that he lay gasping for breath because his respirator was tampered with, or the fact that the cause of his death was a direct result of the removal of his respirator. To the uninformed, it would appear as though Ed died despite the use of extraordinary means to try and sustain his life. If brain death were an accepted substitute for the current definition of death, this entire situation could have been averted, and Ed's suffering would not have been exacerbated and prolonged.

The cases of euthanasia that have been discussed so far have all involved incompetent patients who could not voice their own wishes, but what of the patients who can voice their wishes and do not desire further medical treatment but prefer to die a natural death? To date, courts have found that "the state's interest in preserving life weakens, and the individual's right to privacy grows, as the degree of bodily invasion increases and the prognosis dims." However, if the patient's prognosis improves or if they do not have a life-threatening disease, their right to refuse treatment can be overruled by the hospital and the state legislature.

A 73-year-old terminally ill man in Florida repeatedly tried to disconnect himself from his respirator, but his attempts were thwarted by the hospital staff. He was forced to petition the court to grant his wish to refuse extraordinary means of medical treatment. Based on his right to privacy and his terminally ill condition, his wish was granted, the respirator was removed, and he died a short time later.

Obviously our courts are too overburdened to handle all of the cases in which patients want to exert their right to refuse treatment. This fact makes it that much more important that patients do know what their rights are and that these rights are clearly defined and publicized.

I became aware of the consequences of not knowing your rights to refuse medical treatment when I became acquainted with the case of a woman who had incurable breast cancer. Edith was in her late 60s, and her cancer had spread until both her liver and her spine were riddled with tumors. Her doctors decided to treat her with chemotherapy after both surgery and radiation treatments had failed to halt the progression of her disease. The devastating side effects of the drugs that she received included the loss of most of her hair, the development of painful ulcerations in her mouth and throat, and the impeded ability of her bone marrow to produce red blood cells. As a result, she began to wear a wig, eating became a painful experience, and she frequently had to receive blood transfusions. She would come to the hospital each week to receive the drugs intravenously, and the nausea and vomiting that they provoked would last for days afterward.

Her husband of 25 years had to care for her as if she were his child: rocking her in his arms when the morphine failed to ease the pain, helping her to bathe, supplying her with clean bed pans, and coaxing her to eat when the sight of food made her nauseated. Within a year, she had dropped from 150 to 80 pounds, as the cancer ravaged her body and her appetite abated. She could no longer cook, clean, shop, visit friends, take trips, or even exist without her husband's continual presence and support.

After six months of chemotherapy treatments, Edith did not want to continue receiving the drugs. She accepted the fact that they would only prolong her life and not cure her disease. Her physician persuaded her to continue the treatments, telling her that he had a legal responsibility to see that everything humanly possible was done to curb her cancer. Reluctantly, she agreed and received the drugs for an additional six months without substantial or lasting benefits. Her physician finally gave up hope and further treatments were suspended. Edith received only morphine for relief of her pain.

As higher and higher doses of morphine were required to be effective, she began to live a drugged existence that was pierced only by the pain that wracked her body between injections.

One day her clouded mind temporarily cleared, and she begged her husband to end her suffering and to give her an overdose of morphine. She wrote a brief declaration of suicide that was meant to protect him from legal prosecution, and he prepared the overdose and helped her to administer it. Her husband was charged with voluntary manslaughter, but he received a suspended sentence.

Essentially, this was a case of "active" euthanasia, which is illegal and considered to be equivalent to murder because an action was taken with the express purpose of ending life. However, it is not unreasonable to assume that if Edith had known that she had the right to refuse further treatment and pressed her case in court, her suffering would not have been as severe or as prolonged, and perhaps she would not have felt desperate enough to ask her husband to help her end her life.

The findings of the courts that have examined the issue of euthanasia need to be uniformly applied on both a federal and state level. The application of the concept of "substituted judgment" used in the Saikewicz case could successfully protect the rights of incompetent patients such as John and Ed, as well as prevent the shady manuevers that Ed was subjected to. The equal sharing of responsibility among a coalition of decision makers that includes physicians, family members, and court-appointed guardians would not only serve the best interests of the patient, but remove the fear of litigation that frequently prevents the exercise of sound medical judgment. Furthermore, the substitution of brain death for the current common law definition of death would prevent the useless extension of life-support measures and allow persons who are in a vegetative state to die a natural death. Finally, the right of terminally ill persons to choose whether they want to continue to receive medical treatment or not needs to be considered as a basic constitutional right.

Even with the implementation of the above measures, however, euthanasia will continue to be a hard issue to confront. The full burden for such decision making cannot be delegated entirely either to physicians or the courts. We must all share the responsibility of seeing that today's medical technologies and medical treatments are properly applied. To this end, we all have an obligation to support legislation that both establishes euthanasia as an acceptable practice and that clearly defines the ethical limitations of its practice. If we do not, cases like those of John, Ed, and Edith will continue to exist, and one day we may experience firsthand the same humiliation and suffering that they did or anguish and despair that their loved ones did.

EINSTEIN & FRANKENSTEIN
Michael Finger

For a period of two years, I observed the habits and lifestyles of the African clawed frog *(Xenopus Laevis)*. I owned two of the species, and they inhabited a ten-gallon aquarium. The frogs were given names that seemed to match their personalities. One frog who was perpetually busy, and quite aggressive, was named Frankenstein. The other frog was passive by comparison, and quite a brooder. I called him Einstein.

A little should be mentioned about the general habits of the species of frog. Unlike all other frogs, the clawed frog has no tongue. In order to obtain food, this frog must skim the bottom of his habitat with mouth open wide, pushing and stuffing any loose matter into the opening. The frog will eat almost anything, living or dead; the good is quickly swallowed and the bad is spit back out. This species of frog lives entirely under water, coming up only for air which it must breathe through its lungs. The frog can grow up to five inches in length, but most are only three inches or less. Frankenstein was the larger of the two and was approximately three inches long. Einstein was about half an inch shorter. Because they live underwater, frogs are extremely good swimmers and can outmaneuver most fish, a staple in their diet.

I acquired the frogs through a pet shop, and they were somewhat domesticated. They had been born and raised in an aquarium and were accustomed to being fed regularly. The only food known to them appeared daily in the form of frozen brine shrimp. At first I maintained this diet. Then after a period of three months, I introduced them to live food.

Brine shrimp comes in flat, frozen, rectangular packages. The frozen shrimp is cut into quarter-inch squares, and these squares are dropped into the aquarium. They float for about thirty seconds; then they begin to break apart and settle to the bottom of the tank. It only takes the frogs about ten seconds to know it's feeding time. They smell the shrimp and immediately begin fanning water into their mouths. Their short arms work furiously, trying to find the food to pump into their mouths. The frogs' eyes are situated on top of their heads, which are wide and elongated. Therefore, they can only see what is above and around them, not what lies under them or their mouths. Often the frogs will pass over a lump of shrimp lying directly under their bodies because they cannot see it. Frankenstein was quick to learn feeding times and often waited for me to appear with the shrimp. Floating on the water's surface with only his eyes and nose in the air, he would watch the shrimp hit the water and immediately attack it, stuffing large quantities into his mouth. Frogs have no manners or dining etiquette, the only rule being to get as much as one can eat before any other frog comes along.

After a few months of steady feeding, Frankenstein would take the shrimp out of my fingers, leaping out of the water to snap it with his toothless jaws. If I kept my finger in the tank long enough, he would try to swallow that as well, his forelimbs and mouth gently tugging until I removed the finger. I was surprised that the coldness of the shrimp never seemed to bother the frogs. If they waited at least a minute, the shrimp would completely dissolve and rise to the temperature of the water. But they just couldn't wait to eat. Whereas Frankenstein would come to the surface of the aquarium to greet me, Einstein would quickly dive to the bottom left corner of the tank every time I appeared. He never seemed to get used to my presence, even with a regularly scheduled feeding time. He would wait until the shrimp settled upon the gravel and then would move out of his corner and scavenge the bottom. Although Einstein never ate as much as Frankenstein, I don't think this had anything to do with his smaller size. Einstein didn't move that much about in the tank. He preferred to remain motionless in his corner, resting upon one of the plastic plants anchored in the aquarium floor or sitting patiently in the hole bored in the middle of a thick branch. Frankenstein never sat still and was always playing or digging in the gravel. He had the habit of racing around the tank's bottom when a light was suddenly turned on, pushing anything and everything, including Einstein, out of his way. He moved three times faster than a cockroach when you're trying to step on it. When I first got the aquarium, I stocked it with real plants and anchored them securely under the gravel. Little did I know how much the clawed frog likes to dig. It didn't take more than three days for them to uproot all the plants, and I came home to find them floating atop the water and Frankenstein underneath them, a smug look upon his little face. After that it was strictly plastic plants for them, and Frankenstein tried his best to dig these up as well.

I noticed after awhile that the frogs, Frankenstein in particular, were getting overly plump on their diet of brine shrimp. I concluded that they were in need of exercise. But how does one exercise a frog? You cannot take him for a walk, for if he were removed from water for only a short period of time his skin would dry up, and he would die. A hamster is fortunate to have a wheel to run around in and spin with glee, but no such device exists for a frog. You can dangle yarn before a kitten, but try that in an aquarium and the yarn starts to unravel and the bored frog turns red from the running dye. A parakeet even owns plastic dumbbells to lift, but what has a frog? There is nothing man has manufactured to bring exercise to his friend the frog, so I had to devise a method of trimming the bellies of my bulging pets. The only way was to logically utilize the natural instincts of the animal and its characteristic nature as an aggressive predator. If I put small fish in with the frogs, they would chase the fish to eat them; the chase would be exciting, with a number of attempts before success, and the frog, by means of the chase, would get exercise. It seemed like it would work, but I had to verify my hypothesis. I contacted the expert who sold me the frogs, and he agreed it would be a good idea. It seems that the small fish known as the guppy (*Lebistes Reticulatus*) is frequently served to domesticated frogs. I smiled and purchased a half dozen.

But would my frogs actually go after and swallow the fish? After all, they had never seen other animals, and the only food they were familiar with came dead and frozen. Would their primordial instinct to kill be suddenly recalled from the dark and untested regions of their little brains? There was only one way to find out, and that was to put the guppies into the aquarium.

I brought the guppies home in a plastic bag and set them on the kitchen table while I removed my jacket. I got my aquarium net and took the bag of fish over to the kitchen sink. I undid the knot in the bag and slowly poured the water out of the bag and into the net. This is done because it is unhealthy to mix the waters of different aquariums. The guppies were now in my net, six jumping and squirming little fish. They were very thin, almost transparent, and their mouths opened and closed rapidly as they wondered where their air had gone and what the hell was happening to them. I walked with them over to the aquarium and opened the lid. Einstein dove to his corner and Frankenstein was resting on the gravel. Neither had been fed that day, and it was four hours past their accustomed feeding time. I slowly lowered the bag of the net into the water, but kept the rim of the net above the surface so they could not escape. This was it; the hour of instinct had arrived. I looked at Frankenstein and he looked up at me, and in my best Jack Nicholson voice cooed, as I released the guppies, "Medication time."

The guppies, happy again to be in water but puzzled at their experiences, remained grouped together for fifteen seconds, and then began to explore, in clusters of two and three, their new aquatic home. Their instincts were to go to the darker areas of the tank, the log and the plants. They hovered around the air stone and the fizzing bubbles it released. Frankenstein was the first to move. He cautiously eyed the visitors and swam slowly, moving only a few inches. When he moved, the fish watched him carefully, but without apparent alarm. They kind of hovered in the water, wiggling their little bodies back and forth like exotic dancers. Frankenstein surfaced for air and floated for about thirty seconds; then he quickly dove to the bottom of the tank. For awhile nothing happened. I was getting impatient. I wanted to see a frog swallow a fish, and that's all there was to it. I was seriously considering changing Frankenstein's name to something less harsh, when he made his move. It was quick. A smaller guppy, dying of curiosity, swam right up to Frankenstein's nose and opened his O-shaped mouth repeatedly, as if greeting the frog with his own silent language. Frankenstein's reply was brief. It consisted of a lightning swift lunge forward, an even quicker opening and closing of his mouth, and a single swallow. The fish was gone. The magical frog had made the simple guppy disappear. For the first time in his life, Frankenstein felt the strange movement of live food in his stomach. It must have struggled to escape for awhile, but I didn't observe any outward disturbances on Frankenstein's underside. He didn't seem to have any bad reactions to his quick meal. He moved to the bottom of the tank and sat watching the remaining five guppies. Einstein, on the other end of the tank, did nothing and didn't seem to notice anything different in his tank-mate's behavior. But there was. The taste of food, new food with a different taste, must have been a welcome relief to Frankenstein. In twenty seconds he was up for air and ready to capture yet another guppy. Three of the fish seemed to know what was going on right away, and whenever Frankenstein moved, they swam, or tried to swim, out of his way. The other two guppies were either stupid or suicidal, because they also swam right up to Frankenstein's nose, offering themselves to sacrifice. Never one to refuse an offer, Frankenstein greedily accepted one of the guppies as swiftly as the first one. In a flash it was gone.

Now two guppies are really quite a meal for one frog, especially when that frog is no more than three inches in length and the guppies are about one and a half inches long. After his two dinners Frankenstein settled on the bottom of the tank and began the task of digesting his feast. The remaining four fish, cursing me I'm sure, learned their lesson and tried to avoid either frog. Einstein did not eat that day. He watched the fish with wonder, not hunger, and contented himself with scavenging the bottom of the tank for leftover shrimp. It was about a week later when I saw him finally lunge at a guppy. He wasn't as swift as Frankenstein and he missed. He tried once more but failed again. In all my observations of live feeding, I never saw Einstein swallow any guppies. He was happy enough to swim alongside them and share their food when it was sprinkled atop the surface of the tank. It was Frankenstein alone who tried his best to keep the rapidly breeding guppy population to a minimum.

GAY PARADE
Mary Brophy

Marge Brown and I are walking in the ragtag dyke contingent of the Gay Pride parade, heading south on Clark Street and walled in on both sides by people lining the curbs in front of shops. Far up in front of us is the head of the parade, where a uniformed marching band leads the way. A bunch of floats follow the band, lots of them decked out with big-titted drag queens with platinum hair and boobs that shake just like real tits do, because they're stuffed with birdseed.

Marge is wearing a super-wide-brimmed sombrero to keep the heat off her face, and I can feel my forehead slowly burning pink in the intensity of the sunshine. All along the curb people of Lincoln Park are lined up watching us: men who wear three-piece suits on weekdays, peck their wives on the cheek in the morning and say, "So long, hon, goin' to LaSalle Street, do some lawyering," while their wives are busy boning up for their night school classes in Oriental paper folding and French cooking at Francis Parker School. Today the men are well heeled in their barely worn fifty-dollar Adidases. They wear white Levis with sharp creases running down their legs and boldly striped rugby shirts from Land's End—no matter that they don't know what a scrum is. Their pretty wives with long tresses and summer frocks stand next to them, hands loosely gripped on baby carriages, all turned out to see the annual fag parade.

Marching along with Marge and me are about forty other dykes. We walk with our arms slung about one another's shoulders, about ten abreast on the street. We're wearing sweat-stained T-shirts, shorts from Army surplus stores, blue jeans—nothing out of the ordinary from what we'd wear on any other day. And the one characteristic that most of us have in common is our short hair.

Behind us is a float for one of the men's bars: somebody's station wagon completely covered over with white confetti and a platform on top with red drapes festooning it and a velvet couch in its center. Five guys in dick-tight bikini briefs and bare chests strut and preen and generally show off to the crowd, lounging around on the platform like beefcake homecoming queens. The float has a couple of loudspeakers that play disco music, instrumentals mostly, with the bass turned up real high so that every drum beat gives an opportunity for the beefcake queens to swagger their asses and gyrate their hips. They've all got hard-ons the size of Pepsi bottles and Margie and me keep wondering when one of them will jump off the platform and run to some alley to whack off.

The fag float keeps churning out the disco beat, while we dykes shout slogans, chanting along with a bunch of marchers in front of us. The people in front of us are about a hundred strong, and are led by a line of men holding a huge banner that stretches all across Clark Street and reads "Chicago Socialist Brigade." There are men holding hands as they walk along in this group, but there are also a couple of men and women holding hands, so you can be sure everybody in the Brigade isn't gay. There are a lot of left-wing political groups that support gay rights, and this is one of them. Off to the side of their ranks, about midway through, is a tall, sturdy, solid-looking guy with a foghorn to his lips. He has a strong, masculine voice and calls out chants that the socialists pick up and that we dykes either pick up or echo. The Brigade shouts, "COME OUT, COME OUT," their 100-strong voices in unison, and the guy with the foghorn and we dykes answer, "WHEREVER YOU ARE."

A lanky black guy from the Red Brigade sashays back to us dykes with a bottle of Mateus and says, "Wine, ladies?" to Margie and me, and passes us the bottle. I'm thinking that its coolness will be just what I want in this heat, but as soon as my fingers grasp the smooth glass neck, I can feel how hot the bottle's got from being out in the sun. But I take a swig anyway, the wine red and sweet. Around us the chant goes on: "COME OUT, COME OUT, WHEREVER YOU ARE!"

Margie and I had had some wine before we left the house, and I can feel this last hit beginning to loosen me up. She and I are in the front row of our group, about in the center of the line. As we walk with our arms all draped over one another's shoulders, I start shaking from side to side to the disco beat pounding out behind us. Margie picks up on my moves and the woman on my other side does too, so that as the Reds shout, "COME OUT, COME OUT," and we answer, "WHEREVER YOU ARE," we're getting into the rhythm and the spirit of what the parade is all about. Margie swings her hips to one side so that they bump seductively against mine, and in the midst of the marching and the noise and the crowds watching us from the curbs, I look over at her pretty freckled face and her sleek black hair, and our eyes lock for maybe a full five seconds, the longest five seconds and the shortest five seconds of the whole parade, and my voice inside my head says, "I'm in love, I'm in love," while my speaking voice rips out hoarse and loose and crazy, "WHEREVER YOU ARE, YOU ARE, WHEREVER THE FUCK YOU ARE!"

We pass by McDonald's, and a bunch of the help is out on the curb in their white paper hats and uniforms. Who would want to buy hamburgers now and miss seeing the parade go by? The curbs are lined four and five deep, with shoulder-to-shoulder crowds, the full bodies of the front lines visible, but after that a maze of heads and necks and shoulders, the layers of bodies backing one another up like successive flaky leaves of strudel, or like row upon row of fans sitting in a stadium at a football game. Sometimes people from the curb shout things at us, either friendly or taunting, but mostly they just stare and point and smile. Somebody tossed an exploding cap amid the Red Brigade back near Clark and Diversey, but it seemed harmless, just made a loud pop like a cap gun.

The Red Brigade takes a rest, but we women are feeling in the rhythm of things, so we start singing: "OH, WHEN THE DYKES, OH, WHEN THE DYKES, OH, WHEN THE DYKES COME MARCHING IN, I WANT TO BE AMONG THAT NUMBER, WHEN THE DYKES COME MARCHING IN."

It keeps us going for a while, but we're really a lot stronger with the Red Brigade and their foghorn, so after about three rounds of it, and an approving "Go to it, girlies," from a soused-out, fat old whiskered dude leaning on a lamp post on the curb, we quiet down and catch our breath.

The black dude from the Brigade passes his Mateus back to us again, and we wipe the brim with palms, swig up, and pass the bottle on, the wiping the brim a holdover from kid days of passing pop bottles. Margie takes off her sombrero and swathes the whole inside of her elbow against her forehead, which is glistening with sweat. The sun blazes down on my jeans all along the fronts of my thighs, and I wish I'd worn shorts instead. Then the Red Brigade's leader, off to the right of us and in front, takes hold of a whistle that's on a chain around his neck, and sticks it in his mouth, blurting out two small ZEET-ZEET sounds and then an enormous ZEEEEEEEEET! ZEET. Whistles, for some reason, are very camp in the gay community as of late, and the bikini-clad dudes behind us respond with ZEET-ZEET-ZEET-ZEET, staccato and quick, like somebody stomping their boots to attention and giving a stiff and sharp salute, index finger to forehead, fingers straight and pressed together.

The foghorn dude starts shouting, "OUT OF THE CLOSETS AND INTO THE STREETS," and everybody around us—*everybody*—takes up the cry: the beefcake queens behind us, we lezzies and the pinko commie fags in front of us, a contingent of parents of gays in front of them, and a bunch of dudes decked out in leather vests and chaps and motorcycle chains behind the beefcake queens. There must be five hundred of us in this one section of the parade, all of us shouting in unison, "OUT OF THE CLOSETS AND INTO THE STREETS!" I feel myself swelling and surging and swimming in the emotion of it all, and I hear my own voice shouting as one with the voices of Marge and the woman on my other side, smaller parts melding into the one big mob voice, the Goliath voice, the voice of five hundred gay people all at once calling upon all of the faggots and dykes in the whole wide world. Margie and I are holding hands now, and I can feel my pulse and hers socking against one another's in our palms.

We're on Clark almost to Fullerton, where we'll turn left and head east toward Lincoln Park, where there'll be a rally by the south end of the lagoon. The walk east on Fullerton, I know from past parades, is always the quietest stretch of the route. You walk in a cool shady canyon of high-rises, not many spectators greet you, and those few who do look like bank presidents and club wives, blue-haired women and stogie-smoking guys, who all have names like R.T. and D.L. and J.P. and wear yellow pants and have guts overhanging their belts and all own yachts.

But we haven't yet turned the corner to head east on Fullerton. On our right is this 28-story high-rise, all white and sparkling in the late June sun. On its second floor above the street level is a rooftop where cars are parked and where there's a patio with outdoor metal furniture. A bunch of people are sitting on the patio, women mostly, wearing false eyelashes and prissy dresses from Bonwit's, sipping grapefruit daiquiris. We see them and they see us, they staring cooly at us dykes, who can stir up more antipathy in their breasts than might any thousand fags. We know they'd see a lot of gay men as their playthings, whereas we incite their fear and loathing. And we hate them too, because they represent everything we're not: women whose first concerns in life are their hairdos, their nails, keeping their armpits shaved, and snagging not just one man but men enough to make up for all the emptiness they feel inside of themselves. We take one look at them and some dyke starts shouting, "OFF OF THE ROOFTOPS AND INTO THE STREETS!" The guy with the foghorn picks it up, so that pretty soon the whole bunch of us—beefcake queens, dykes, commies, parents of gays and all—are shouting out the same thing. The women on the rooftop shout back,

Mary Brophy/475

"NO! NO!" in reply, and three of them standing against a black, cast iron railing on the patio's edge seem to be shouting the most. One of them shoves her hand out straight-armed in front of her, ramrodding it toward us as she shouts, "NO! NO!" and leans over the railing, so that she's nearly falling over the side of the building, and all the while we keep marching past her and shouting all the louder and wilder, "OFF OF THE ROOFTOPS AND INTO THE STREETS!" whereas silently I'm taking in the sight of her rejection and tucking it away inside my mind, sizing it up against a hundred other times that I've been told no, that being gay is fucked-up, sick, perverted. I look at this woman's stiff-armed no and size it up against censure by parents, religious and political leaders; against electroshock treatments, beatings, imprisonments, and executions—all part of gay people's heritage. I see this woman's rejection of us and know that I must keep shouting and keep marching, because it's one sad and fucked-up world indeed that makes love a crime, and I'm sure in my whole being that loving another woman is pure and godlike and beautiful and how I was intended to be, if there is any ultimate rhyme or reason to things.

COCA-COLA
Vincent Verdooren

When it comes to Americana, Coca-Cola ranks right up alongside baseball, hot dogs, apple pie, and Chevrolet. The epic tale surrounding this sensational soda pop has been detailed by scores of scribes over the past ten decades; but because a whole lot of the beverage's history is based on anecdotes and folklore, no two accounts read exactly alike. In fact, a number of the works even contradict each other. Therefore, any spoken or written Coca-Cola chronicle ought to be taken with a grain of salt—or a grain of sugar, in the case of Coke. And the following five paragraphs are certainly no exception.

In 1886, John Styth Pemberton, an Atlanta druggist, allegedly invented the first batch of a drink that his bookkeeper, Frank Robinson, later dubbed Coca-Cola. Pemberton was a regular Mister Wizard when it came to creating medicines. His personal line of homemade pharmaceuticals included items like Globe of Flower Cough Syrup, Indian Queen Hair Dye, and Triplex Liver Pills. And the good doctor considered Coke, which was actually a revised version of a previous Pemberton concoction called French Wine Coca, to be a cure-all capable of relieving headaches, sluggishness, and indigestion. Unfortunately, the miracle drink couldn't remedy the illness that struck Pemberton in 1887. During that year the ailing pharmacist sold two-thirds of his wares for $1,200, releasing the final one-third for $550 while on his deathbed in 1888. The new owners got rid of the Pemberton business quickly, selling the entire shebang for $2,000 in 1891 to another pharmacist named Asa Griggs Candler.

Asa Griggs Candler wasn't too thrilled about acquiring the Indian Queen Hair Dye and other assorted goodies; but he did hold a great deal of affection for Coca-Cola, mainly because he often guzzled the drink to combat the painful headaches and stomach troubles that plagued him. Candler originally attempted to market Coke as a cure-all. However, a combination of bad sales and good thinking eventually convinced him to switch his strategy. Figuring that the product might generate more profits as a soda fountain drink, Candler presented kegs of Coke syrup to druggists accross the nation. He instructed them to mix measured portions of the sticky, brown juice with soda water and ice cubes and sell it for five cents per glass. Supplementing his distribution efforts with a massive dose of advertising, Candler adorned the country with Coca-Cola cups, trays, posters, and lamps. Needless to say, the soft drink soared to success. For although Pemberton had only sold a measly 25 gallons of Coke in 1886, Candler enjoyed nationwide sales of 48,427 gallons in 1893. And by 1898 Coca-Cola was jumping the border into Canada, Mexico, and Hawaii. The wildly increasing demands necessitated the construction of extra syrup manufacturing plants in Los Angeles, Dallas, and Chicago. Yet despite all the big bucks that poured into Candler's wallet, he was not without problems. An infinite mob of Coke copiers invaded the scene, sporting names like KoKola, King Cola, Gay Ola, and Kaw-Kola Dope. Candler tried to squelch the competitive crooks by registering the Coca-Cola trademark with the U.S. Patent Office in 1893. In addition, he enlisted the aid of the courts, filing countless lawsuits against the frauds.

As the product continued to reap grand rewards, entrepreneurs began to gather on Candler's doorstep to propose bottling deals for Coke. Candler at first remained cool to the idea, feeling quite satisfied with the soda fountain sales. However, in 1899 a couple of Chatanooga lawyers persuaded Candler to sign a contract permitting them to bottle Coke nearly anywhere in America. The contract, incidentally, obligated the lawyers to pay Candler a whopping sum of one dollar. Complying with the conditions of the agreement, the duo initially bought syrup from the Coca-Cola Company and then resold it to local bottlers throughout the nation. This early setup built the foundation for the mode of operation that exists in the Coke business today.

The years of reigning as supreme overlord of the Coca-Cola Company transformed Asa Griggs Candler into perhaps the most respected and best-liked citizen in Georgia. So in 1916 he quit his president job to serve as mayor of Atlanta. And in a generous gesture that turned out to be a colossal blunder, Candler gave the majority of his Coca-Cola stock to family members. In 1919, the greedy family members showed their gratitude by selling the company to a group of businessmen for the astronomical price of $25 million. The sale is still listed in the record books as the biggest transaction that the South has ever seen.

The purchasing group was led by financial genius Ernest Woodruff, who eventually handed over the corporate reins to his son, Robert Winship Woodruff. In 1923, the son surveyed the Coca-Cola Company and found it lacking any definite direction. And worse yet, the place and product were in dire need of some peppy spirit. Hence, the young Woodruff performed a facelift on the company, using soft-sell advertising to reposition Coke in the consumers' minds as a friendly, all-American drink. During World War II Woodruff proclaimed that no soldier would do without Coca-Cola; and he backed up his words by getting bottling plants erected next to all the battle fronts. He also improved employee morale, convincing the workers that quality merchandise for the consumer should be their top priority. In truth, Robert Winship Woodruff deserves almost full credit for kicking the company into the prestigious spot that it currently holds in the modern marketplace.

Now that the legends and anecdotes relating to the super soda pop have been briefly discussed, the verifiable facts may be investigated. Besides having won the respect of the American public, Coca-Cola boasts the biggest share in the soft drink category. In 1982, Coke held 26.6% of the market, while arch-rival Pepsi sat in second place with 19.5%. The headquarters, still located in Atlanta, Georgia, employs about 41,000 people. Many of these workers are involved in product research. In 1983, the Coca-Cola Company reeled in $5.89 billion from sales. But they didn't sell a single drop of the beverage to consumers. Actually, the company makes money by mixing up the secret syrup and dealing it to the 1,450 franchised bottlers. Also, the Coca-Cola Company is responsible for advertising their carbonated brainchild.

As mentioned earlier, advertising has played an integral role in pouring Coke down the parched throats of civilization. Back in 1886, John Styth Pemberton advertised the soft drink with the simple slogan "Drink Coca-Cola." Obviously, the good doctor was no Leo Burnett. Asa Griggs

Candler, on the other hand, understood the power of advertising. His earliest campaigns, circa 1880s and 1890s, were comprised of posters featuring fine lithographs of elegant people in elegant settings. Candler sought to give Coca-Cola a classy character, and he was extremely fussy about how each ad should look. However, Candler was not alone in his marketing efforts. Numerous bottlers handled their own local advertising; and Chicago was rather notorious for producing racy layouts that usually sent the mild-mannered Candler into raving fits. Nonetheless, the strategy of displaying elegant scenes continued when Candler hired the Massengale agency to produce print ads during the 1900s. The slogan in 1905 claimed that "Coca-Cola revives and sustains." And in 1906 Massengale got axed and replaced by the D'Arcy agency. The new creative force repeated the elegant concepts until Robert Winship Woodruff entered the scene during the 1920s and 1930s. Rather than concentrate on classy sights, both rural and city scenes were rendered in the hopes of relating the soda pop to the nation. However, one element in the advertising remained constant: Coca-Cola consistently showed the most cheerful side of life, disregarding any nasty reality that might spoil the festivities. The basic idea was to make people feel terrific about simply being alive. So while America's fighting boys bled and battled in World Wars, the soft drink ads pictured gorgeous girls and jovial Santas sipping Coke. In 1922, the slogan stating that "Thirst knows no season" convinced people to consume the beverage in winter as well as summer. And when the country crashed into the Great Depression, Coca-Cola unveiled its most famous slogan: "The pause that refreshes." As time went on, and Coke sales went up, a parade of slogans branded happiness and good will into the minds of all citizens. Some lines shouted at consumers and some lines sang. In the 1970s Coke reissued an old 1942 ad verse that read: "It's the real thing." After Vietnam and Watergate, the nation was serenaded with "Look up, America." Strangely enough, the recent "Have a Coke and a smile" campaign was cut because the company decided that the words didn't reflect the mood of the day. The apparently inappropriate phrase was substituted with the present slogan "Coke is it!" According to Coca-Cola advertisers, this wonderful new jingle gives unabashed product presence. If anything, it makes for a jazzy and upbeat television commercial.

The advertising slogan proudly declares that "Coke is it!" Yet what "it!" really is remains a highly guarded secret to this day. Although people have determined that Coca-Cola is 99.8% sugar and water, few know what specific elements constitute the other .2%. In fact, less than a dozen mortal men have been entrusted with the sacred recipe. Countless curiosity seekers have conducted chemical analyses of the beverage to identify the mystery ingredients. Unfortunately, no one can agree upon the results of such tests. While caffeine and caramel coloring are obviously present, other speculations include extracts from the coca leaf (sans cocaine) and kola nut, cinnamon, nutmeg, lime juice, vanilla, citrus oils, and glycerin. Since the soft drink derives its name from the coca leaf and kola nut, it might seem logical to assume that these things are part of the physical composition. However, in 1906 the company was on the losing end of a suit entitled *The United States vs. Forty Barrels and Twenty Kegs of Coca-Cola*. At that time, it became known that the drink did not feature anything "coca" or "cola" at all; and the government complained that the name Coca-Cola was therefore misleading. Following their defeat, the company apparently started putting minute traces of the two substances into their product.

The Coca-Cola Company, as stated earlier, produces the syrup to be sent to bottlers. The syrup is primarily made from the mystery ingredients and sugar. Lots and lots of sugar. Unbelievable as it may sound, the company purchases 10% of all the sugar sold in the United States. A typical finished syrup formulation for soft drinks contains about 176 gallons of liquid sugar for every 89 gallons of water. Also, about 2 gallons of additives and preservatives must be mixed into such a batch. Syrup manufacturing is based on blending, which is a cold process—as opposed to beer brewing, which is a hot process. The completed syrup is usually shipped in metal barrels. Overall, the syrup-making business relies on cleanliness and efficiency; the mechanical equipment is often sterilized daily to prevent the possible multiplication of bacteria and mold.

The soft drink bottling plants are profitable institutions unto themselves. For example, the Coca-Cola Bottling Company of Chicago recorded sales of $50 to $60 million in 1983. Operating with a pre-syrup system, Coke bottlers first pump the syrup from the barrels through filters that lead the liquid to syrupers or feed tanks. Then rows of bottles parade beneath the feed tanks and receive measured portions of syrup. Next, the bottles pass below a filler, where carbonated water is poured in. (Incidentally, carbonated water is produced by two ingredients: water (H_2O) and carbon dioxide (CO_2). The soft drink industry is the biggest user of CO_2. CO_2 dissolves in H_2O to form H_2CO_3, also known as carbonic acid. This acid is obviously non-toxic. And the process of dissolving carbon dioxide in water is called carbonation.) The full bottles remain under pressure until the cap is sealed in place. Finally, the bottles are twirled to establish proper mixing. The entire operation only takes a few seconds, since modern technical innovations now make it possible to fill over 1,400 bottles per minute.

Once bottled, Coca-Cola is delivered to distributors and stores, where eager human beings quickly snatch up a case or two. To say that Americans enjoy Coke would be the understatement of the millenium. The average citizen consumes about 40 gallons of soft drinks every year. And all over the planet Coke is served 180,000 times per minute. Considering that the company dished out $34 billion to present the country with the "Coke is it!" slogan, the least that Americans can do is buy and drink the damned soda pop.

Considine, Douglas M., and Considine, Glenn D. *Food and Foods Production Encyclopedia.* New York City: Van Nostrand Rheinhold, 1982.

Dietz, Lawrence. *Soda Pop: The History, Art, and Memorabilia of Soft Drinks in America.* New York: Simon and Shuster, 1973.

Ginsberg, Ben. *Let's Talk Soft Drink.* Springfield, MO: Mycroft Press, 1960.

Harris, Ron, and Suid, Murray. *Made In America: Eight Great All American Creations*, Massachusetts: 1978.

Kahn, E.J. *The Big Drink: The Story of Coca-Cola.* New York: Random House, 1950.

Katz, Micheal, Levering, Robert, and Moskowitz, Milton. *Everybody's Business: The Irreverent Guide to Corporate America.* San Francisco: Harper & Row, 1980.

Watters, Pat. *Coca-Cola: An Illustrated History.* New York: Doubleday, 1978.

"1882-1982: 100 Year History/Future Probe." *Beverage World.* New York: Keller Publishing Corporation, 1982.

THE HAWAIIANS AND CAPTAIN COOK
Mary Hanley

While glancing through an old grammar school history textbook, I stumbled upon this explanation of the demise of Captain Cook:

> . . . After leaving Kealakekua Bay, Cook realized he would have to return to Hawaii to repair the sprung topmast. On February 14, 1779, he was killed in an unhappy scuffle with the natives ashore.

How ironic that one of the most traumatic events in Hawaiian history, an incident that not only resulted in turning the island's culture inside out but also brought an abrupt end to the brilliant career of one of the greatest explorers ever known, should today, two hundred years later, be summed up simply as "an unhappy scuffle with the natives." Of course, since most grammar school history textbooks attempt to cover everything from the Big Bang to Watergate in 350 pages, usually nothing less than world conquests or major-scale wars weigh in at more than a paragraph. And where's the logic behind that? Wouldn't it be more enriching for young students to delve outright into only a few complex historical events, investigating each occurrence as fully as possible, rather than just turning the poor whelps into Trivial Pursuit junkies with volume after volume of sterile names and dates?

Therefore, I feel it's my duty, my sacred responsibility even, to sprinkle some breezy verbs into the vacuum of nouns and numerals that make up the bulk of grade-school history. And what better place to start than with the unfortunate account of Captain Cook's fatal run-in with the fickle Hawaiian natives?

Although the story behind Cook's final voyage contains enough plot twists, eerie coincidences and local color to flesh out an above average B-grade adventure movie, there's more to this tale than a boatload of Englishmen traipsing around the tropics. To really understand the Captain's grisly fate, we must first familiarize ourselves with his adversaries, the Hawaiians.

The Hawaiian Islands form the northwest point of the vast western Pacific triangle containing the scattered islands that make up Polynesia, with New Zealand and Easter Island constituting the southwest and southeast points, respectively. Because all the Polynesian Islands relied exclusively on the oral tradition to chronicle their histories, oftentimes myth and fact became so intertwined as to appear indistinguishable. Correspondingly, the Polynesians' distorted view of the passage of time defied most Western attempts to slap precise dates on important pre-discovery events. To most of the Islanders, who based their religions heavily on ancestor worship, the past served as more than just a timeline for easy reference; for them the past was a living presence that was completely unavoidable in day-to-day life. Tagging numbers onto the backs of their ancestors would probably seem ludicrous, if not utterly incomprehensible to them, but that isn't to say they didn't have some sort of chronology. Hawaii, in particular, provided fodder for the storyteller/poets where "current history" was concerned.

Because of its plentiful vegetation, agreeable terrain, and large size, Hawaii soon became the island of choice for many of Polynesia's highest ranking chiefs and priests. Who'd want to be high chief of a swampy little volcanic zit like Mangareva when you could have half of Diamond Head and all the coconuts you could ever want right at your feet? After a period of time, the influx of Polynesia's elite caused a rift between the upper and lower classes, which eventually resulted in a feudal system much like medieval Europe's. But, though it's safe to assume that the Hawaiian peasants enjoyed a somewhat higher standard of living, not to mention better weather, than their European counterparts, they weren't so fortunate where the political climate was concerned.

During the last few centuries before the island was discovered by Cook, the nobility and priesthood surrendered themselves almost completely to the unscrupulous pursuit of power. The laws, which included the intricate and oppressive religious taboos, bore heavily upon the common people, and their administration became more or less a matter of favoritism and arbitrariness. Not surprisingly, the Hawaiian people reacted with outbursts of rebellion which the priests and chiefs, in turn, attempted to choke by strengthening the already constrictive taboos and by increasing the number of human sacrifices in an effort to intimidate the people into submission. These extreme measures resulted in a vicious circle of unrest among the people, and more importantly, close to total isolation of Hawaii from the rest of Polynesia.

In short, Hawaii, during the last few centuries before its discovery by Captain Cook, played host to an oppressively feudal society where the priesthood and nobility managed to avoid large-scale revolution only by imposing strict taboos on the peasants and by manipulating the religious mores of the common people. These measures resulted in a fairly delicate balance between blind religious faith and political upheaval in the lower classes, a balance that could easily be upset by interference from outside sources. Wonderful, so now we can get on with the meat of this story.

When Captain Cook's ship, the *Resolution,* and his consort ship, the *Discovery,* set sail on July 12, 1776, the object of this, his third major voyage, was to examine at close quarters the northern Pacific coast of America for a possible Northwest Passage. On his two earlier voyages, Cook discovered many northern Pacific islands and successfully managed to win the trust of the natives, while collecting all sorts of geological and navigational information about the Northern Hemisphere, and his excursions into Antarctic waters provided proof that a continental land mass did exist beyond the pack ice that had stopped so many other explorers before him. Although he'd started life as the son of a middle-class laborer, Cook's successes soon made him the toast of English royal society.

The expedition began with the two ships passing through the Cape of Good Hope, then sailing toward New Zealand and the Society Islands. On January 18, 1778, Cook and his crew stumbled upon the Hawaiian Islands, where they stayed briefly before sailing north along the American coastline and then later past the Bering Strait. By that time winter had begun to set in, and Cook decided that the *Resolution* and the *Discovery* should spend the cold months in Hawaii.

The ships retreated from the icy northern waters and managed to reappear in the midst of the Hawaiian Islands in December of 1779, almost a year to the day since they'd first discovered them. Unfortunately, the hostile weather conditions forced Cook and his entourage to circle the islands for the next six weeks, until the storms finally let up and a safe anchorage became possible. But during the weeks spent afloat, Cook's crew, many of whom had sailed loyally with the Captain on previous voyages, had become restless and anxious from the lack of pork rations aboard and a somewhat high incidence of venereal diseases among the men. Cook himself tarnished his sterling reputation as a devoted and fair shipmaster more than once during his third expedition. Once, when the crew refused to drink a sugar cane beer, concocted by Cook and several of his officers, for fear the stuff may have been injurious to their health, the Captain promptly outlawed all grog on board and stomped around for days afterward convinced that he had a full-fledged mutiny on his hands. Most of these disturbances were petty and blew over quickly, but it became clear to all on board that it would be in the best interest of their own frayed nerves to land the ships as soon as possible.

That chance finally came on January 16, 1779. Cook, after sighting what appeared to be a secluded bay off the coast of the main island, took advantage of the agreeable shift in weather conditions to send one of his officers, Capt. William Bligh (yes, the same Mr. Bligh destined to get booted off the *Bounty,* but that's another story), to scout around the area to see if it would make for a safe anchorage. Always the brown-nose, Bligh piped up enthusiastically that the natives had seemed exceptionally friendly on their last sail through Hawaii, to which Cook harshly retorted, "Whatever the nature of the Indians, if it is a safe anchorage, I shall resolve to anchor in it." Coming from the man who had, over the last twenty-five years, gained the trust and respect of islanders all over the Pacific with his "beads and bangle" diplomacy, a statement of this severity must have seemed somewhat out of character.

As Bligh led his small fleet of scout ships toward the bay, he and his men were treated to an unusual welcome. The calm waters were suddenly besieged with a roaring throng of native crafts, sailing toward Bligh's ships from points all along the shore. Within moments, the Englishmen found themselves surrounded by a bustling armada of canoes, each bearing about six Hawaiians. Bligh's men started loading their muskets in alarm but were ordered by Bligh to stop; instead of wielding spears and clubs, the natives were waving feather streamers and white banners, and the roar pounding in the Englishmen's ears wasn't a war cry but rather the Hawaiians' ecstatic religious chants and welcome songs. Stunned, the British sailors gaped as the animated brown natives cruised by the scout boats, swinging their paddles in the air like batons and bowing their heads reverently toward the baffled oarsmen as they passed. Even Bligh found himself at a loss to explain the behavior of the Hawaiians; they seemed to be celebrating a festival, but with a fervor that even an old seadog like the captain wasn't familiar with. Then again, the British had come to expect big welcomes of this sort from the Polynesians, so Bligh eventually dismissed the spectacle as just an elaborate greeting.

Bligh's boats managed to maneuver their way out of the fog of canoes long enough to inspect the bay, which was dominated by a black cliff some four-hundred feet tall made of volcanic rock. A monolithic slab that almost looked like polished ebony, the cliff appeared to plummet straight into the sea but actually had a narrow beach of black rocks and pebbles at its base. Later, they learned that the bay's name, Kealakekua, meant "path of the gods," referring to the great slide from the cliff to the water.

Meanwhile, Cook and his men on the *Resolution* were astounded by the scene unfolding in the water below them; at least 3,000 canoes, by Cook's estimate, had crowded into the tiny bay and thousands of swimmers darted between the drifting crafts. Since the outbreak of venereal disease among his crew, Cook had outlawed native women on board either the *Resolution* or the *Discovery* for fear the illness would spread throughout the islands, but despite his chivalry, Hawaiian women, some with small children clinging to their backs, were diving from their canoes, paddling to the *Resolution* and crawling nimbly up the side of the ship. Before long, the deck was swarming with natives. The women showered the happily bewildered crew with leis and flowers and promptly helped themselves to the eating utensils and loose nails (iron being a precious commodity among the islanders). Many of them stayed on board the entire duration of the *Resolution*'s Hawaiian stop, a situation Cook eventually resigned himself to.

On his return from scouting the bay, Bligh informed Cook that he had "found a bay in which was a good anchorage, and fresh water, in a situation tolerably easy to be come at." As the *Resolution* sailed in closer to the shore, Cook was astonished at the island's beauty. Kealakekua Bay, a small crescent-shaped inlet stretching about a mile and a half from point to point, began as a white beach, continued further back from the tide as a lush, fragrant tropical forest, and ended in a massive black wall of jagged cliffs striped with waterfalls. Further beyond the barrier of pocked volcanic rock stood distant snowcapped mountains where sparkling blue rivers snaked from deep valleys and crevices along the hills of hardened lava. But what immediately caught the Captain's attention were the strange movements of the natives ashore. Observing the scene through a telescope, Cook saw thousands of Hawaiians amassed on the clifftops, staring out at the ships and waving white banners. The beach was carpeted with brown bodies dancing frantically or bowing toward the water; the trees were alive with natives flying feathered streamers, and the waters of the bay continued to fill up with swimmers and canoes of all sizes. Cook and his crew were used to Polynesian excitement, but the Hawaiians gave the impression of being on the brink of mass hysteria.

As soon as the *Resolution* was moored, Cook wasted no time in having himself rowed ashore to meet with the Hawaiian chiefs. Accompanied by only two of his officers, Cook found himself met on the beach by two solemn-looking priests, clad in long robes and brightly feathered headdresses and gently waving tall white poles. The priests, repeating the words "Lono, Lono" and gesturing with the poles, cleared a path for Cook and his men through the milling throng of bodies, all of whom covered their faces and prostrated themselves at the sight of the Englishmen. A narrow avenue through the crush allowed Cook to stride easily past his supine admirers, but he realized that as soon as he'd passed, the natives struggled back to their feet, staring wild-eyed and shouting "Lono!" All he had to do to see the entire crowd go down in unison was turn his head back at them, as though there was magic in his glance. He kept himself amused for the length of his walk by looking behind him every few moments until the entire throng, close to ten thousand natives, were forced to crawl after him, groveling on all fours. Hundreds were trampled.

They ended up at the center of a huge open temple, or heiau, decorated with human skulls and giant grotesque wooden idols that grimaced down at them from atop long wooden poles. Once they'd finished with a long, tedious ceremony and a massive feast, Cook and his two officers passed through the village on their way back to the ship and were baffled and fascinated by the sight of men, women, and children with their heads pressed to the ground, chanting "Lono, Lono. . . ."

What Cook didn't know at the time and never lived to find out was that the Hawaiians believed him to be the incarnation of their God-king, Lono, and his arrival was being celebrated as the greatest event in Hawaii's history. According to legend, Lono would someday return from his mystical travels during the season of abundance and relaxation. His giant canoe would sail clockwise around the island, and his arrival would be greeted with white banners and elaborate ceremonies. Cook had arrived at the appointed time, and because he'd decided to sail slowly off-shore for better trading, the *Resolution* had traveled clockwise around the island. The standard white flag that flew from the mast was taken by the natives on shore to be an acknowl- edgement of their white banners, and to top it off Cook had anchored his ship at Kealakekua, "The Path of the Gods," just as tradition had Lono parking his own miracle ship in the legendary bay.

According to Hawaiian historians, the first islanders to spot Cook's ship were a couple of elderly fishermen: "What is that great thing with branches?" asked one. The other replied, "It is a forest that has slid down into the sea." The god Lono's canoe would be like an island for one man, the poets felt, and the "gods" they saw on the distant ships were every bit as fantastic as the prophesies foretold: "The men are white; their skin is loose and folding; fire and smoke issue forth from their mouths; they have openings in the sides of their bodies into which they thrust their hands and draw out iron, beads and nails. . . ." The sheltered Hawaiians were more than ready to believe Lono had come for them at last, and Cook's timing couldn't have been better. Over the next two weeks, the Captain's actions, amazingly, conformed perfectly with the legend of Lono, and Cook's own happy acceptance of his deification by the natives only strengthened the Hawaiians' belief. With all this in mind, it's no wonder that the reception of the *Resolution* traumatized the Hawaiians into near mass hysteria. Although the natives performed their rituals and ceremonies constantly and followed the taboos as the priests commanded, no one was ready for the arrival of an actual god, particularly not the priests or chiefs.

A few days later, Cook learned that the King of Hawaii had arrived at Kealakekua Bay and wished to visit him. Cook graciously welcomed the monarch, and soon afterwards the canoes containing the high priests and important chiefs began pulling up to the side of the *Resolution*. The important islanders all wore headdresses made of feathers and elaborate cloaks, and as their canoes approached the gangway, they stood up solemnly and began chanting.

The King himself remained seated as his canoe came alongside the gangway. He was an old, bent man, almost too weak to stand by himself, and covered with festering sores as a result of a life of unrestrained kava consumption. (Kava is a drug made from a local root, widely used in the King's time among royalty, the priesthood, and trendy Hawaiians with clams to blow.) He was cloaked in a long cape of bright feathers, and he wore an extremely elaborate feather cap. The King was hoisted aboard the ship, as were his sons, his nephew, Chief Kamehameha (an intimidating character with long hair pasted down all over his face and back), some priests, and several other important chiefs.

Cook waited patiently, but wearily, for the ceremonies to begin. After a few short chants the King, shaking badly, and without any assistance from his sons, tore the cloak from his shoulders and placed it gently on Cook, then placed the feathered cap on Cook's head. The tiny man, several heads shorter than the Captain, even with Cook's pronounced middle-aged stoop, still cut a dignified figure as he looked up into the Englishman's face through red, watering eyes and grinned. He was clearly very happy.

By the end of the two-and-a-half week stay on the island, Cook decided it was time for the *Resolution* to be moving on. As things stood, the Hawaiians had burned out themselves and all of their natural resources, including their livestock and the supply of fresh fruit. It was a busy, emotional two and a half weeks for them, and though the event had given them a great amount of satisfaction, they paid a huge price for it. Some of the natives signed their situation to the crew by rubbing the Englishmen's stomachs and pointing back to the ship harbored in the bay: "You've had your fill; it's time to go." The crew had thoroughly enjoyed their stay, and many didn't feel ready to leave, especially since Cook had completely lifted his ban on native women the week before. Some Hawaiians began to grumble that their taxes were going to feed gods with men's appetites, referring to the sailors' lust for mortal women. The death and burial of one elderly British seadog added to the suspicions building up among some of the islanders, but when some of Cook's men raided the heiau for firewood and walked off with several wooden idols, the Hawaiians were openly irked. Fortunately, the *Resolution* and her crew were gone by the next morning.

After leaving the island, the *Resolution* continued north until February 8, when high winds caused the ship's foremast to split. They couldn't go on in that condition, and Cook decided that the only safe anchorage in the vicinity was Kaelakekua. Realizing that the Hawaiians may have been cleaned out during their last visit, Cook waited a whopping two weeks before returning to the bay for repairs.

Everyone on board the *Resolution* was aware of a profound change in the bay's atmosphere; no canoes bobbed on the open water, and the cliffs were altogether abandoned of watchful natives. Some time passed before a few priests came out to meet them in canoes, and then little by little the bustle returned to the bay. Only now, there seemed to be a tide of hostility brewing just beneath the water's surface, and many of Cook's men became uneasy. When the King was informed of Lono's return, he became "greatly dissatisfied."

The next morning a cutter was found missing from the ship, and Cook decided to take aggressive action against the thief or thieves. Knowing of the Hawaiians' lust for iron, and what he felt to be a natural tendency among the Polynesians to be light-fingered, Cook had an islander found in the vicinity of the crime executed to set an example. When the cutter still didn't show up, Cook decided to take the matter straight to the King. Accompanied by ten of his officers, Cook stomped ashore and promptly inquired of the high priest whether he might be granted an audience with the King. His wishes were granted, and he was led to a small grass hut on the outskirts of town. Inside were the King, his sons and Kamehameha, all of whom seemed amiable by Cook's account, and very sorry about the stolen cutter. The King (sly devil) suggested they call a meeting of the townspeople on the beach in an effort to retrieve the stolen item. Cook (the dope) agreed.

The tiny monarch, supported by a son on either side cradling his elbows, cried out to his people in Hawaiian as tears rolled down his blistered face. He and Cook had decided that the King would stay aboard the *Resolution,* kind of like collateral, until the cutter was found. By this time, a crowd of some three-thousand natives had amassed on the beach, and a hostile murmur began to fill the air. The same natives who had two weeks before prostrated themselves in Cook's presence now angrily waved clubs and spears in his face, and some of the others held swords that they'd stolen from the ship. "He has killed a chief!" came shouts as word of the executed "thief," who was actually an innocent and real popular guy, spread among the seething throng. "This is war, this is war!"

Considering the situation, you might think Cook would drop the whole cutter business and get back to the *Resolution* as quickly and discreetly as possible. Instead, for reasons forever lost to the mists of time, Cook decided to go ahead with the original plan and taking the King's arm from a shocked son, began leading the old man toward his rowboat. The suspicious murmur of the crowd suddenly exploded into a deafening roar. The Hawaiians closest to Cook, taking his actions as a threat to their King, began to advance on the Englishman. The first blow was delivered by a native standing timidly in back of the Captain. A single whack to the back of his head from the native's club left Cook dazed and on his knees. "Look," some of the Hawaiians shouted, "a god doesn't bleed." Although Cook managed to drag himself up and stagger a few yards, he was no match for the furious mob. After they'd slammed his head against a jagged rock at the water's edge, the Hawaiians hauled Cook's lifeless body up on the rocks and took turns beating it with clubs and stabbing it with daggers, all in plain view of the British sailors who watched horrified from the deck of the *Resolution.*

After a week of patient negotiations, Cook's officers on the *Resolution* were finally able to recover their beloved captain's body for a proper English burial. Well, sort of, anyway. Cook's remains arrived wrapped in plantain leaves and smelling of salt, which the priests had used in an attempt to preserve the following: Cook's hands, a thighbone, his skull—minus the lower jar—and assorted vertebrae, and odds 'n' ends. The chiefs and priests had divided up Lono's remains among themselves for the power they thought lived on in the dead flesh, so the English only got the leftovers. Kamehameha himself proudly ate Cook's heart, hoping to assimilate his god's power and courage. Shortly after, Kamehameha became King of Hawaii.

That, in condensed form, is the story of Captain Cook's final voyage and his ill-fated exchange with the Hawaiian natives. Neato, huh kids? The only problem is, why would the people of Hawaii mercilessly slaughter their most revered, beloved god? Wouldn't the natives, being as religious as they were, be terrified that Lono would seek revenge on them for their terrible crime? It's questions like these that turn this episode from a quaint fable about tact into something a bit more complex and political. The Hawaiian lower classes, as you may remember from paragraph six or so, were in a constant state of revolution, held in check only by the religious taboos imposed on them by the priests. The peasants saw Lono as their one great hope, a military-type leader who would once and for all free them from oppression. The chiefs and priests didn't even bother arguing with this, since the taboos and traditions built around the Lono legend were so complex and intertwined that the chances of someone actually fulfilling the prophesies were slim indeed. Of course, no one expected Cook to show up that winter, either. When Lono/Cook appeared in their midst, the Hawaiians were split between the peasants hailing their liberator and the upper classes gasping at the imminent collapse of their entire social and economic system. The tension of Lono/Cook's first days in the bay was to traumatize even the most hardened of the island's cynics, but it couldn't compare with the betrayal of having their own messiah—after cleaning out all the island's natural resources, every female in the bay, and the taxpayers' entire well of funds—just sail off into the night, leaving his faithful throngs even more oppressed, more hopelessly in debt to the priests and chiefs than they'd been in recent history.

When Lono/Cook returned two weeks later, he sailed right into a trap that he'd unknowingly set for himself. Considering the betrayed rage most of the peasants probably felt at the time, Kamehameha's political shrewdness couldn't have been timed better; the people were under the kind of emotional strain that could've ended in revolt had they been better organized. When Kamehameha ate Cook's heart, he in effect became the New Lono and was able to tell the people what they wanted to hear in their time of need, thus assuming ultimate power for himself and his class. It's no coincidence that King Kam is remembered fondly today as Hawaii's greatest king, the man who introduced free enterprise and Western trade to the "backward" Polynesians, and thus the person ultimately responsible for Hawaii's vast contributions to modern society—most notably those wonderful "Go Hawaiian" commercials featuring Donny and Marie—and a booming tourist trade that I'm sure we've all felt the brunt of at one time or another.

So there you have it, the history of Hawaii in a nutshell. If just one small child reads this and learns something, I'll know my destiny has been fulfilled.

BIBLIOGRAPHY

Cameron, Roderick. *The Golden Haze with Captain Cook in the South Pacific.* Cleveland: World Publishing Co., 1964.
Hiroa, Te Rangi (Peter S. Buck). *Arts and Crafts of Hawaii.* Honolulu: Bishop Museum Press, 1957.
Lee, W. Storrs. *The Islands.* New York: Holt, Rinehart & Winston, 1966.

Tabrah, Ruth. *Hawaii.* New York: W. W. Norton & Co., Inc., 1980.

Thompson, Hunter S. *The Curse of Lono.* New York: Bantam Books, 1983.

The Voyages of Captain James Cook Round the World. Ed. Christopher Lloyd. London: Latimer Trend & Co., 1949.

All quotes taken from entries in *The Voyages of Captain James Cook Round the World.*

BEYOND STEREOTYPES
Mary Moritz

They can be found sleeping in doorways, on park benches or in train stations. Their outstretched hands beg for change as America's citizens make their way to work and back home again. These are the nation's homeless. Their actual numbers are disputed: recent Housing and Urban Development estimates put the figure at between 250,000 and 300,000 but the most commonly accepted figure, endorsed by the National Institute of Mental Health, is between two and three million (Holden, 569). However, no matter how common a part of American scenery they have become, the nation as a whole appears to be ignorant and uncaring in regard to this class of people, largely unconcerned with their plight and the circumstances that force them to live on the streets.

A rheumy-eyed, scraggly-bearded wino slumping against a doorway. A dirt-caked mental patient, muttering to himself as he searches for a warm space to spend the cold winter night. These are the most commonly accepted stereotypes of the homeless. But the faces of the homeless are changing, becoming younger and more feminine. The average age of the homeless has sharply decreased to the mid-30s and the fastest growing segment is families, usually young women with two or three children (Holden, 569). Furthermore, these new destitute often confute the stereotype: they don't sleep on park benches with shopping bags bulging with their worldly possessions. In fact they often appear no different than anyone else on the street, looking as if they are on their way to work or home. The new homeless are economically dispossessed: families who are not making ends meet, young men and women who have fallen on hard times, and single mothers who have been forced to choose between paying the rent and buying food for their children.

Kerry Alston looks like any other student as he makes his way to computer class. But when Alston leaves the classroom he returns to New York City's Fort Washington Armory where he shares a gymnasium-sized room with nine hundred other men. After losing his job as a security guard a year ago, and being forced out of his apartment by his roommate, Alston found himself with no other alternative than the shelter. Says Alston, "When I first got to the shelter, I wondered what I had gotten into. I had never been in anything like this—the odor, the dirt, people all over the floor. Then I realized I had no choice" (*Time*, 27).

Rachel Hanson, 43, was a housewife in Anaheim, California, when her 19-year marriage ended in divorce a year ago. Her four-bedroom house was foreclosed upon, and with no skills and minimal savings she was forced into living in a car in a campground with her three children. The family had been living there for eight months when shelter workers discovered them. "My life simply fell apart," Hanson says. "I had everything. Why I even had a microwave oven" (Stengel, 27).

These are just two of the many case histories of America's homeless population. What is especially significant about them is that they depict the side of homelessness that many of us are unfamiliar with, whether by simple ignorance or by consciously looking the other way. Homeless people seem to be easier to deal with when they are thought of as derelicts and winos, as opposed to "regular folk," like the kid across the street or the family next door. Even President Ronald Reagan claims to believe that "the homeless are homeless, you might say, by choice" (Bassuk, 45). Actually, Mr. Reagan is being too modest; his administration has had quite a bit to do with the situation.

It simply cannot be ignored that national economic conditions are responsible for forcing people like Kerry Alston and Rachel Hanson onto the streets, and that they keep the number of homeless growing by 25 percent annually. One obvious factor is unemployment, which reached a peak of 10.7 percent in November 1982, its highest level since the 1930s. Further intensifying this is the lack of low income housing available. A recent analysis of the federal government's Annual Housing Survey by the Low Income Housing Information Service indicates that, while the number of renter households with incomes below $3,000 a year dropped by about 46 percent between 1970 and 1980, the number of rental units available to these people at 30 percent of their income also fell by an estimated 70 percent. Meanwhile, the median rent paid by those households in the lowest income bracket rose from $72 a month in 1970 to $179 a month in 1980. According to these figures, 72 percent of an annual $3,000 income is needed to cover housing expenses, leaving $71 a month to cover all other living expenses (Bassuk, 41). In New York City, for instance, the number of single-room dwellings dropped from 170,000 to 14,000 in 1971 due to the tax abatements enacted for condo conversion. Between 1978 and 1984, New York units renting for $300 or less were reduced by 715,000 units (Holden, 569). Finally, federal funds have been slashed by 78 percent since 1980, indicating that HUD has virtually abandoned the situation.

The case of Christine McDuffie, 37, bears witness to the lack of low income housing. Forced onto disability after a 1985 illness, she moved from New Jersey to New York with her 17-year-old son Paul, hoping to find public housing, as had been promised to her. Unfortunately, the promised housing never came through and mother and son were forced into a city shelter, while she tried to find a job and a landlord who would accept a welfare tenant (*Time*, 27).

Further explaining the increase in homeless families are the cuts in Aid to Families with Dependent Children. In Massachusetts the primary income for up to 90 percent of homeless families is from AFDC, but while low income housing declines, so do the AFDC payments. The average rent for a one bedroom apartment in Los Angeles is $491 a month, yet the average AFDC payment to a mother of one is only $448 (Stengel, 28). This leaves a shortage of $43 a month in rent alone, not to mention buying food and other necessities. A mother often has no other choice but to move her family onto the streets where she can at least afford to feed them.

Finally, recent cuts in government benefits may also be responsible for some people living on the streets, but a lack of data makes it impossible to draw definite conclusions. The Social Security Disability Insurance program awards payment to workers who are physically or mentally unable to perform any kind of "substantial or gainful work" for which they are qualified, whether or not such work is available where they live. However, in 1981 the Reagan

Administration launched a "crackdown on ineligibility" after a report by the General Accounting Office stated that possibly 20 percent of those people receiving benefits were ineligible. By the time the administration finally halted its review in 1984, due to charges that truly disabled people were losing their benefits, between 150,000 and 200,000 people had already been wiped off of the rolls (Bassuk, 41).

However, the newly homeless are still greatly outnumbered by the mentally ill homeless, who comprise an estimated 25-50 percent of the nation's street population; some studies indicate the figure may even be as high as 85 percent. Of these people, 35 percent are schizophrenic and 10 percent suffer from clinical depression. An additional 25-50 percent suffer from drug and alcohol abuse problems (*Time*, 103). These figures indicate that many of the people living on the streets, possibly even a majority of them, are in a psychotic or drugged-out stupor. Yet they roam the country, unprotected and unsupervised, often posing a serious threat to both themselves and society.

The roots of the mentally ill homeless problem reach back into the 1950s, when the new wave of psychoactive drugs made the possible rehabilitation and reintroduction of the psychotic into society seem especially hopeful. By the civil rights movement of the 1960s, deinstitutionalization was a hot social issue. It was an admirable idea, closing the mental hospitals, many in terrible condition, and welcoming the patients back into society where they would have more humane living conditions and greater respect for their civil rights. Also, rehabilitating patients in a community setting promised to prove cheaper than operating large state hospitals. In 1963 President John F. Kennedy signed the Community Mental Health Centers act, and what had before been therapy, getting patients out of the hospital and into the community, became policy (*Time*, 103).

Deinstitutionalization was a well-intentioned idea, but it fell through before it was even close to culmination. The first step was accomplished: the patient population at state and county hospitals is now less than one-fourth of its peak level of 559,000 in 1955. However, the intended housing, job training and transitional care were never provided, and the existing centers are primarily capable of treating patients with phobias or minor emotional disorders, rather than those with serious mental illnesses (Maloney, 55-57).

Further complicating matters are the legal reforms of the 1970s which severely limited involuntary civil commitment. Right to counsel, right to treatment, and limited duration of stays were installed in the courts, while the vast majority of states dropped their standards for involuntary commitment, focusing on the person's danger to himself or others instead of his need for treatment (Holden, 1253). These reforms were enacted to defend people against unnecessary institutionalization, and were also well-intentioned; however, they have resulted in a mentally ill class that is unable to function independently in society, is unwilling or unable to seek help, and has taken to living on the streets. There they remain, in inhuman conditions and with no counsel. Unfortunately, it is often only when a mentally ill person becomes violent against society that society takes notice. For instance, a 19-year-old New York girl who pushed a woman in front of a subway train had been recently released from psychiatric treatment, against doctor's recommendations, by a court order (Holden, 1253).

The "out of sight, out of mind" philosophy can be applied to the homeless population as a whole. The nation appears generally unconcerned with the circumstances that turn a person onto the streets, and the conditions that they live in while on them. The most immediate concern of the general population appears to be "how to keep the homeless out of my neighborhood." And every major city has its own horror stories: in New York's Greenwich Village, residents have placed barbed wire over the hot air grates in the winter to drive the homeless from the neighborhood; in Fort Lauderdale, the city commissioner has suggested thinning the street population by sprinkling rat poison on the garbage; in San Diego, a shelter has been destroyed by arson (*Time*, 103). No one incident is worse than the others, for all reflect the widespread opinion that the homeless are not actual people, just nuisances and eyesores who deserve what they get.

The city of Santa Barbara vividly illustrates this line of thinking. This prosperous oceanside resort city of 75,000 is located twenty-nine miles from the ranch of Ronald Reagan, and its citizens obviously share their neighboring president's opinion about the homeless. The people of Santa Barbara have taken aggressive measures against the city's approximately 2,000 homeless people, whom they refer to as tree people, after Fig Tree Park where many of them live. In 1979 a ban on sleeping outdoors after dark was passed, followed by a 1983 ban on drinking in public. Grocers sprinkle bleach on garbage to deter hungry vagrants, and county election officials even went so far as to deny voting rights to anyone without an address (a state appeals court struck this down) (*Time*, 29).

What makes Santa Barbara especially exemplary of the nation's view towards the homeless is the wealth its inhabitants live in. It must be a striking sight to see a scruffy man or woman begging in the city's fashionable shopping district, or sleeping on its neatly manicured lawns. The city mainly harasses the homeless, rather than using some of its abundance to help them. The mayor of the city, Sheila Lodge, has refused to fund more shelters, saying, "the general public has its rights too," and, "we don't want to become something we aren't."

This thinking has taken on an especially violent tone with the murder of Michael Stephenson, an unemployed house painter and the second homeless person to be murdered in the city in nine months. Stephenson was stabbed seventeen times and his throat was slashed; charged with the murder are two 18-year-old cadets from Santa Barbara's Northwestern Preparatory School. One of the students has admitted to the killing, but defends himself with the explanation that he was looking for some gang members who had harassed fellow students (*Time*, 29).

The homeless of America are, for the majority, not homeless by choice. They are victims of society: people who have fallen on hard times, or are suffering from mental illness, or physical disability. As a supposedly civilized society, the United States should be focusing on how to lessen the number of its citizens sleeping on the streets, not simply on how to push them into another area.

Lawsuits offer the only real hope for the homeless. "As a group that is insulated from full participation in the political process," says Doug Lasdon, founder and director of New York's Legal Action Center for the Homeless, "they don't get a fair portion of government distributed resources. Most of the resources available to the homeless today are the result of legal actions" (*Time*, 27-28).

Politically, the homeless are a non-issue, for they are mainly a non-voting population. Politicians claim that the diversity of the group and their complexity of problems make it impossible to suggest anything but patchwork remedies, such as food stamps and temporary shelters. But what is actually needed are programs that will introduce them back into society, on a productive level, through job training and job placement, as well as financial assistance that offers eventual security, rather than short-term relief.

As for the mentally ill homeless, broader commitment criteria appear to be a solution for part of the population, but this issue is being debated heatedly. Those against broader commitment claim that hospitals will be swamped, patients' civil rights will be impinged upon, and abuses will be rampant. Another remedy is the development of less costly, community-based treatment centers on a wider scale. Such centers would allow the mentally ill to function more independently in society through job training and available supervision. The patients would not be forced helplessly onto the streets with no counsel.

There are no immediate solutions to the problems of the homeless, but what is certain is that society as a whole must rethink its sentiments. The homeless must be thought of as human beings, not nuisances, who need their fellow citizens' respect and concern, not their blame and hate. The nation must accept some responsibility for the situation its homeless have been forced into, and act as the civilized society it claims to be.

BIBLIOGRAPHY

Bassuk, Ellen L., "The Homelessness Problem." *Scientific American*, July 1984.

"A Hobo Jungle with Class." *Time*, 11 March 1986.

Holden, Constance, "Broader Commitment Laws Sought." *Science*, Dec. 1985.

⸻, "Homelessness Experts Differ on Root Causes." *Science*, May 1986.

Maloney, Lawrence D., "Take Mental Patients Off Streets, Back to Hospitals?" *U.S. News & World Report*, 7 July 1985.

Stengel, Richard, "Down and Out and Dispossessed." *Time*, 24 Nov. 1986.

"When Liberty Really Means Neglect." *Time*, 2 Dec. 1985.

SMELLS: AN ESSAY
Sandra Goplin

In fifth grade, we spent a week studying the five senses. Afterwards, Mrs. Greenlee gave us a creative writing assignment. "Imagine," she instructed us, "that you woke up one day without the use of one of your senses. Write a composition about what it would be like to go for one whole day without seeing, or whatever." It occurred to me that it would be nice to go for a whole day without seeing Mrs. Greenlee, with her blue hair and cat-eye glasses, standing behind that desk like a prison warden. She rapped loudly on her desk with her pointer to get our attention and added, "And do NOT write about losing your sense of smell. Stick to one of the REAL senses, one that would make a real difference in your day." It crossed my mind that it would be nice to go a whole day without smelling Mrs. Greenlee, too, because she had the worst breath of anyone I knew, and she wore so much old-lady perfume that you could hardly breathe when you stood next to her. Maybe she was afraid we would put that in our compositions if we wrote about the sense of smell.

Until fairly recently, Mrs. Greenlee's opinion—that the sense of smell isn't worth much consideration—was shared by the science world. Yet man has used his sense of smell and been affected by the smells around him as long as he has existed, like the rest of the animal world. Some historians even believe that man is still around today because of his smell—that "protoman" smelled so bad that no prehistoric beasts were interested in eating him.[1] Smell plays a perhaps less dramatic role in our lives today, but does that mean it's any less important to us? Americans spend over three billion dollars a year on perfume alone, and virtually every product we buy is scented, from cosmetics to furniture to automobiles.[2] Researchers now know that smells affect everything from our buying habits to our sex lives to our moods and how well we do our jobs.

Perhaps the effect of smell we are most familiar with is the power it has to stir our memories. "Nothing awakens a reminiscence like an odour," Victor Hugo wrote, and it's a fact nearly anyone can attest to. You need only to catch a whiff of burning leaves, or fresh lilacs, or the cologne of your first love to know that smell and memory are closely linked. When I smell cloves, I am magically carried back to the Christmases of my childhood, when my sister and I made spicy pomanders to give to our relatives. We poked whole cloves into the skins of firm, ripe oranges until they were completely covered, then attached satin ribbons so the things could be hung in the recipients' closets to make their clothes smell nice. Our relatives thanked us profusely for the lovely gifts, but most never used the pomanders. We knew, too, because anyone who kept a clove pomander in their closet smelled like a walking spiceball. Those who told us they used their pomander, but didn't, smelled like liars, because they didn't smell like cloves. The smell of cloves also transports my mother back to her childhood, making her shudder as she recalls the days before Novocain, when a trip to the dentist meant gripping the arms of the chair and chewing cloves to ease the pain. When my grandmother smells cloves, she remembers the pharmacy where her father worked, where as a child she would perch herself on a salt barrel and watch him work while she sucked on penny candy.

Zoologist Arthur Hasler was haunted by the way salmon always returned to their birthplaces to spawn. When he returned to his childhood home in Utah after the Second World War, a rush of fragrant mountain air not only whisked him back twenty-five years, but also gave him the idea he needed to solve the salmon mystery. The smell of the air, he said,

> suddenly evoked a flood of memories of boyhood chums and deeds long since vanished from conscious memory. The association was so strong that I immediately applied it to the problem of salmon homing. The connection caused me to formulate the hypothesis that each stream contains a particular bouquet of fragrances to which salmon become imprinted before immigrating to the ocean, and which they subsequently use as a cue for identifying their natal tributary on their return from the sea.[3]

Salmon smell their way home.

When air crosses our olfactory surfaces (two mucus-covered, dime-sized areas in our upper noses), its scent is picked up by the five million cells of each surface and shot directly to the brain's limbic area, the part associated with emotion. The olfactory nerves lead right into this "feeling brain," bypassing the "thinking brain" in a way that sight and sound nerves don't. This accounts for the immediacy of odor-related memories; the brain reacts emotionally without involving regular thought processes.[4] Mountain air zapped Hasler right back to his childhood. Opening a jar of pickles once zapped me back to mine. It was like I was in high school again, the year my brother worked at the Gedney factory. He would smell so much like pickles that we could always tell when he came in from work, even if he arrived while we were asleep on the second floor. If you put your nose into a jar of Gedney dills, cover the rest of the opening with your hands, and breath in for a while, you'll know what our house smelled like that year, just from Kevin's clothes. Opening that jar brought back that whole year. Listening to Elton John records in Kev's room. Being jealous that he had a real job and got to drive the car. Laughing at our mom because she thought his pickle-saturated clothes smelled like marijuana and worried that he was "involved with drugs."

Animals also associate their experiences with scents. Norwegian rat pups respond chemically to the presence of their mothers, and can tell their own mothers from other female rats by smell alone. A study using rat pups who were taken away from their mothers at birth showed that the same responses could be duplicated by training the rats to associate certain smells with mother-like activities. The scientists pumped peppermint-scented air into the cages whenever the rat pups were being fed or brushed. Eventually the rats associated peppermint with mothering activities, and would respond to the peppermint-scented air the same way that the control rats responded to the presence of their mothers. The control-group rats had no reaction to the smell of peppermint.[5]

Like the rats who could identify their own mothers by smell (even if their mothers seemed to be made of peppermint), humans also associate people with their characteristic scents. An infant only a few days old can recognize the smell of his own mother's breast and will turn his face toward clothing his mother has worn, but away from clothing another woman has worn.[6] Scientists say that each person has his own scent, as individual and distinct as his fingerprints.[7] This natural smell—combined with what we eat, drink, smoke, and wear—registers (usually unconsciously) in the perceptions of those around us, and "even though others repress awareness of them, they are probably registering attraction or repulsion at some subconscious level."[8] Janet Hopson, a science writer who has studied how scent affects our sex lives, believes that a sense of "odor homogamy" is an important part of sexual attraction. "A would-be partner's gestalt—the sum of skin, hair, glandular scents, perfume, tobacco, foods, and home and workplace smells—must seem familiar and comfortable."[9]

Animals use smell not only to avoid mating with relatives, but also to choose the best, strongest partners. A pregnant mouse who smells a strange male mouse's urine within a few days of becoming pregnant will abort, because the smell of a new male implies a new leader in her territory. If she gives birth to the deposed male's offspring, the new leader will kill the pups. She aborts to cut her losses—to avoid a wasted pregnancy.

Female brown lemmings can smell the difference between males who have recently won a battle and those who have recently lost. The males fight for access to the females, and seem to smell different when they win. When given the choice between a winner and a loser (assuming both males are still capable of mating), the female will use her nose to pick the winner—the more aggressive male. Because lemmings suffer from crowding and overpopulation, aggressiveness is a trait needed for survival.[10] This ability to smell success may once have been a key factor in human mate selection as well. Women have a slightly better sense of smell than men have, and some researchers believe it is a trait left over from the days when survival of the species depended on the female's selecting a healthy mate. A man's smell was an indicator of his health.[11]

Perhaps it is because we don't need to sniff out healthy mates anymore, because we are *not* using our noses for day-to-day survival, that our sense of smell is so involved with our emotions. Our noses are free to work without our conscious thought, storing up memories without analyzing the smells for survival.

Compared to most animals, human smelling capabilities are weak. Sheep and deer can smell humans a mile away, and law officers have used American snapping turtles to sniff out the corpses of murder victims which were dumped into deep lakes.[12]

The actual area of most animals' olfactory regions is huge compared to those of humans. The two smelling surfaces located in the upper noses of humans are each about the size of a dime. The same surfaces in the nose of a fair-sized dog are the size of a large, unfolded handkerchief and cover most of the inside of the nose area.[13]

Even though our sense of smell can't compete with that of most animals, the human nose is surprisingly sensitive. A single receptor cell in the nose can be stimulated by as few as eight odorous molecules, and we can consciously smell something with as few as forty molecules crossing the olfactory surfaces. In studies, humans are usually able to smell the scent of an ordinary, clean footprint on blotting paper.[14] Good cooks can tell by smelling whether a dish is properly seasoned, or whether meat and produce are fresh. A woodworker I know can distinguish between different kinds of wood by their smells. A friend who works in a beer-testing facility can tell more about different beers by smelling them than he can by tasting them.

Perfumers, the scientists who develop perfumes and fragrances for other cosmetics, have noses that are trained to distinguish between various perfume-like fragrances, but most cannot tell the difference between other smells any more than any average person can. It is like a birdwatcher who can identify features of birds that an ordinary person can't even see; he doesn't have better eyesight than a non-birdwatcher, but is simply more aware of birds' characteristics. With practice and training, a perfumer can distinguish up to ten thousand separate odors. He will use over two thousand ingredients regularly, and can identify about half of these by smell alone.[15]

Most humans are not very aware of smells. We seem more interested in getting rid of our natural smells than in using them. We don't take pride in the smells that once saved us from predators, and most of us consider the term "body odor" something negative, even repulsive, rather than the attractant it is for the rest of the animal world (and for early man). Obviously, human attitudes about our smells changed at some point, probably with the beginning of civilization and the development of cities. Until about ten thousand years ago, humans traveled in bands of five or six families, small groups in which everyone knew everyone. When some of these bands settled to form the first permanent villages, people had to deal with a new phenomenon: strangers. In these larger groups, with all these strangers in close contact, something had to prevent "unwanted sexual activity," sex with the wrong strangers. In the small groups, the elders had controlled sexual access. Now social codes, rituals, and laws served this purpose. Clothing became more modest and concealing, women learned to sit with their legs together, and people started to de-scent their bodies, to rid them of sexually stimulating natural odors.[16] Regular bathing came from the need to be *less* sexually appealing, not more. We moved a step away from our animal origins.

As ancient cities and cultures grew, class distinction made different people smell different. The wealthy and powerful didn't do hard labor. They had the time to bathe all day, and the money for ointments and perfumes. Smelling clean and fragrant became a mark of aristocracy. Smelling natural was the mark of laborers and slaves.[17] Later, Napoleon would epitomize the fastidiousness of the new bourgeoisie, carrying kilos of eau de cologne on all his campaigns. In fact, fragrance was so important to him and others that its trade was responsible for the creation of the Silk Route to China and many overland and sea routes to the East.[18]

Though man had been concerned with smell for a long time, it was nearly the turn of the century before scientists began to study it, and then it began almost by accident. The French naturalist Jean Henri Fabre found the cocoon of a Great Peacock or Emperor moth, one of the largest and most beautiful European moths, and took it home. The first night after the female moth emerged, Fabre heard a fluttering of wings, and forty male Emperor moths flew in through his window to circle the female's cage. For eight nights in a row the males fluttered in, 150 of them in all.

Fabre was determined to find out how the males tracked down his single female, and he began what would become years of experiments with moths. He cut off males' antennae to see if that stopped them from finding the females. He moved the females' cages around, hid them in cupboards, and surrounded them with saucers of petroleum, lavender, and other fragrances to mask the females' smells. Still the males always found the females. One day, Fabre put a female moth inside a bell jar but inadvertently left her tray of sand and sticks out in the room. When the males flew in, they went straight for the tray and ignored the lady flying around in the jar. Fabre figured out that everything the female touched with her distended abdomen retained some mysterious love juice. "This was her lure; her love philtre!" Whatever she touched attracted the male.[19]

In 1934, in the woods of Czechoslovakia, a researcher put eighty-five female moths into sixty-nine matchboxes, tied the boxes to trees, and surrounded the boxes with flypaper. In just over two weeks, almost ten thousand male Nun moths were stuck to the flypaper. Other sex traps followed, baited with both live females and mashed female abdomens. Male moths, marked and released more than two miles away from the captive females, followed odor trails to find the females.[20]

Mammals use their natural odors as sexual signals. Male dogs go nuts over the smell of a female dog in heat. Billy goats get their "goaty odor," a smell that conveys sexual readiness, by urinating and even ejaculating into their goatees. White-tailed deer bucks ejaculate on the ground and wallow in it to absorb the smell. Porcupines urinate on their paws and present them to females in courtship. Some male camels, deer, and horses sniff and even drink the urine of females to assess the females' reproductive condition. "They swill it in their mouths and draw back their lips and nostrils in a characteristic grimace, a posture thought to increase sensitivity in the same way wine tasters swill wine about in their mouths to increase the reading of its flavor."[21]

Sows must smell androstenone, the boar steroid, before they will assume the arched-back posture necessary for mating. Farmers who want to inseminate their sows without a real live boar can buy Boar-Mate, androstenone in an aerosol can. The farmers go down a row of sows, spraying Boar-Mate in each sow's nose until she arches her back in mating stance. Then he artificially inseminates her.[22]

In 1959, German researchers coined the term *pheromone* (pronounced fear-a-mone) to describe the sex attractants that moths and other insects secrete into the environment. The word comes from the Greek and literally means "to transfer excitement." In its strictest definition, the term pheromone applies only to insects. Smell and sex are closely linked in the world of higher animals as well, though, and the word is sometimes used loosely in this context. Animal behaviorist Chuck Wysocki said, "If you take most any developing animal and expose it to odors from the opposite sex, you can advance the onset of puberty. Female animals living together in a cage menstruate together—the effect of odors. If you expose female rats to the odor of males, you shorten and regulate their cycles. And in male rats exposed to female odor, testosterone will surge."[23]

It was only a matter of time before scientists moved from studying animals to studying the effects of smell on humans. In 1971, psychologist Martha

McClintock reported that women living in a group situation, such as a dormitory, would begin to menstruate together. Two other scientists, George Preti and Winnifred Cutler, found that the one thing which interfered with this menstrual synchrony was the introduction of men. Cutler, a biologist specializing in the menstrual cycle, had already found that women who regularly had intimate heterosexual contact were more likely to have regular cycles, menstruating about once every 29.5 days. Women who had sporadic or no sex were irregular.

To test their theory that smell was responsible for this menstrual synchrony, Cutler and Preti collected daily underarm secretions from a group of women who had regular menstrual cycles. Every day, they rubbed the extract under the noses of women in a separate group. Within three and a half months, the two groups had achieved menstrual synchrony—their cycles matched. In another experiment, they rubbed underarm secretions from male donors under the noses of females with irregular menstrual cycles; in just a few months, the women had an average cycle length of 28.3 days, close to the cycle length of sexually active women. It was some smell in the underarm region, Preti believed, that "regulated hormones to enhance fertility," the way pheromones do in other animals.[24]

Several years later, a California researcher came up with what he called "Essence of Genevieve" to explain *why* menstrual synchrony occurs. A colleague of his (named Genevieve) had noticed several times that her roommates' cycles would change to match hers, never the other way around. Tests which applied Genevieve's underarm secretions (the "Essence of Genevieve") under the noses of volunteers showed that, sure enough, her cycle would dominate and alter the cycles of other women.[25] Genevieve's case is an example of what scientists call "olfactory coercion, the strong bending the will of the weak through the sense of smell,"[26] the same principle by which the smell of the stronger male rat's urine will abort the offspring of the weaker rat.

Just as women respond to the smells of men, men respond physically to the smells of women. A British scientist living alone on an island collected and weighed the beard hairs from his electric shaver every day and discovered that his beard grew "much faster" each time he returned to shore and encountered women.[27] Other scientists had similar findings and traced the cause to smell, using tests much like the underarm-secretion tests used to study menstrual synchrony.

As the research on insects was used by the pesticide industry, the research on humans and smell was quickly snatched up by the perfume industry. This research, along with the loosening of sexual restrictions in the 1960s and the "new" idea of natural scents being sexy, led to the popularity of "blatantly erotic perfumes" such as musk.[28]

It was in 1970 that I went to Connie Schulte's slumber party. Among my friends, fruit-scented perfumes and a singing group called the Monkees were all the rage. My best friend, Tina, had the whole set of Wild Tropic kissing gels, and I had a set of Monkee cards (like baseball cards but with pictures of the Monkees). Tina's favorites were Tangy Tangerine and Michael Nesmith; I preferred Positively Pineapple and Davey Jones. Connie's older sister (who was in the ninth grade and rumored to be fast) was the hit of the party with something she called musk. It was more expensive than our fruit perfumes, she said, because it was rare. It was made from the testicles of boy antelopes, so it was dirty—you know, sexy. We looked at each other knowingly, each of us pretending to know what testicles were. She told us that musk was the coolest, and that the smell of fruit was going to be splitsville real soon. We believed her, because it was she who had first told us that boys stick their tongues in your mouth when they kiss and that all our parents "did it." Then she told us the Monkees were for babies and that Neil Diamond was a real man. We all promptly adored Neil Diamond and switched to musk.

In 1983, a cosmetics company called Jovan introduced a cologne formulated on the pheromone principle, to "drive humans into frenzies of lust over members of the opposite sex."[29] Just three years earlier, a team of British scientists at the University of Warwick discovered what they thought was the long-hoped-for human pheromone, alpha androstenol. Jovan incorporated this substance into its new fragrance, named it Andron, and spent ten million dollars to promote it. In a testimonial for the fragrance, a woman reported, after smelling it on a man, "The scent went through my body . . . I wanted to let my animal instincts run free . . . My eyes were lighted with lust . . . My mouth started to fill with saliva. . . ."[30] Apparently, this woman's reaction to Andron was the exception rather than the rule; after only a mild initial success, Andron lost its popularity and fizzled out.

It isn't likely that a universally appealing scent will be discovered or formulated, because humans (unlike lower animals) respond to scents in society-influenced ways—our responses are learned, not instinctive.[31] Dabbing perfume from a twenty-dollar bottle won't make you smell any better than if you dabbed it from a jelly jar. You may think that you do, though, and that's what sells perfume.

My sister and I used to gaze adoringly at a bottle of Evening in Paris perfume that our mom kept on her dresser. It was cheap perfume, but the bottle itself was graceful and elegant. Dark, dark blue glass, curved at the top to form a long, slender neck, with a silver, teardrop-shaped cap that our mom would slowly, slowly twist open. With the touch of her perfume-moistened finger to our earlobes we were off, twirling in Paris in the arms of our true loves, gliding across the floor in crisp gowns, spun around by adoring, handsome young men. French men. Men as elegant and graceful as the letters that spelled out Evening in Paris on the silver label. Not printing, but beautiful, round, fancy writing, the letters gliding across the bottle with scrolls, flourishes, and curlicues, as we floated across the floor like princesses. We twirled, we danced, we held our heads high and let the headiness of the attic, the mothballs, the perfume, and the breathlessness of our imaginations make us swoon.

We may not be ready quite yet to pipe the smell of that romantic passion into our homes, but we have certainly come far enough to take the sense of smell more seriously than did Mrs. Greenlee. As fifth graders, we didn't argue with her when she told us smell wasn't a "real" sense, but she was wrong nonetheless. Sure, we could lose the sense and survive, but not without missing a big, important part of our world. Smells are responsible for a whole range of memories, physiological reactions, and emotional stimulation. You can't get much more real than that.

FOOTNOTES

1. Janet L. Hopson, *Scent Signals: The Silent Language of Sex* (New York: Morrow, 1979), 41.
2. Marlys Harris, "The Success of Sweet Smells," *Money,* Oct. 1985: 32.
3. Adrian Forsyth, "Good Scents and Bad," *Natural History,* Nov. 1985: 32.
4. Edwin T. Morris, *Fragrance: The Story of Fragrance from Cleopatra to Chanel* (New York: Scribner's, 1984), 37.
5. Robert Coopersmith and Michael Leon, "Enhanced Neural Response to Familiar Olfactory Cues," *Science,* 24 Aug. 1984: 849-51.
6. Hopson, 152.
7. Pamela Weintraub, "Scentimental Journeys," *Omni,* Apr. 1986: 114.
8. Hopson, 139.
9. Hopson, 140.
10. Forsyth, 31.
11. Morris, 41.
12. Ruth Winter, *Scent Talk Among Animals* (Philadelphia: Lippincott, 1977), 44.
13. Robert Burton, *The Language of Smell* (London: Routledge, 1976), 3.
14. Burton, 108.
15. Burton, 108-09.
16. Hopson, 42-43.
17. Hopson, 44-45.
18. Morris, xv.
19. Hopson, 59-60.
20. Hopson, 61-63.
21. Forsyth, 26-28.
22. Weintraub, 114.
23. Weintraub, 114.
24. Weintraub, 116.
25. Hopson, 148-49.
26. Forsyth, 30.
27. Hopson, 27.
28. Hopson, 51-52.
29. Richard Fay, "Bottled Passion," *Chicago Tribune Magazine,* 9 March 1986: 12.
30. Fay, 13-14.
31. Morris, 41.

BIBLIOGRAPHY

"Breast Cancer and Sense of Smell." *Science News,* 7 Sept. 1985.

Burton, Robert. *The Language of Smell.* London: Routledge, 1976.

Coopersmith, Robert, and Michael Leon. "Enhanced Neural Response to Familiar Olfactory Cues." *Science,* 24 Aug. 1984.

Fay, Richard. "Bottled Passion." *Chicago Tribune Magazine,* 9 March 1986.

Forsyth, Adrian. "Good Scents and Bad." *Natural History,* Nov. 1985.

Harris, Marlys. "The Success of Sweet Smells." *Money,* Oct. 1985.

Hopson, Janet L. *Scent Signals: The Silent Language of Sex.* New York: Morrow, 1979.

"International Flavors: Funding Far-Out Ideas for Future Growth." *Business Week,* 12 Nov. 1984.

Morris, Edwin T. *Fragrance: The Story of Perfume from Cleopatra to Chanel.* New York: Scribner's, 1984.

Ogle, Jane. "Exploring Scent Therapy." *New York Times Magazine,* 17 Nov. 1985.

"Sexy Paco Rabanne Turns Sober in Its New Ads." *Business Week,* 17 Sept. 1984.

"We Turned Up Our Nose at This Sensory Experience." *Consumer Reports.*

Weintraub, Pamela. "Scentimental Journeys." *Omni,* Apr. 1986.

"What Lies Behind the Sweet Smell of Success." *Business Week,* 27 Feb. 1984.

Winter, Ruth. *Scent Talk Among Animals.* Philadelphia: Lippincott, 1976.

Young, Gayle. "Lost sense of smell can be symptom." *Chicago Tribune,* 23 March 1986.

DEAH SUZY
Ada Williams

Deah Suzy,

Talkin' 'bout dreams puts me in mind me of de dream I usteh have when ah was a kid. Ah uster alla time dream 'bout goin' t'heben. Dere'd be dis long line of people stretchin' as far as ah could see—people in front of me and people behin'. We be walkin' through clouds like the meringue on top of one of yo' lemon pies 'fo' you stick it in de oven. Mist be creepin' all 'round us and evahthang looked hazy and shimmery like heat waves. Way ahead in the distance was a mountain and dat's where all de folks was headed. See, dat was the entrance to heben and de folks was waitin' day turn to get in. The word came down that we all had to stand in front of de judgment seat face to face with de Lawd to give 'count of ahselves, an' evahbody had to do it. Evahbody. What'n gon' be no sneakin' inta heben.

Now ah couldn't 'ave been no moh den six or seben, an' ah can remember havin' dem dreams right afta ah stahted goin' t'chu'ch wif Sister Belinda. Dat min'ster uster stan' up dere on his platfo'm an' rang down thunder and lightnin' on dose folks. He be jumpin' and shoutin' and his black round face be shinin' like a beacon. In one hand he be wavin' this big white handkerchief he used for moppin' his brow. A stream of water be running down the sides of his face, drippin' onto his white gown from the waterfall at the point of his chin. When he throw his head back with both hands raised to the rafters, his long, drooping sleeves would fly out like wings an' den slide down his arms an' bunch at de armpits, exposing the worn cuffs an' elbows of his Sunday best. When he really hit his stride, he'd come stompin' off the platfo'm and jump up on the pews in the front row. You shoulda seen the folks scurr'in' to get out of his way. He was sho nuf preacha. He could preach dat one 'bout "dry bones," till you mos' could see dem rise yo'se'f.

Ah done got plum carried away wif dat preacha, but he was de reason ah stahted havin' dose nightma'es. He sca'ed the livin' daylights outta me. Where was ah now. Oh, yeah. When I found out I had to look de Lawd in de face an' ansah for mah life, Lawd, but ah was scairt. Ah commenced to runnin' 'cause I knowed de Lawd didn't want no pa't of me. Ah was 'bout as spotless as a littah of delmation pups.

Ah was running mah heart out but ah what'n gettin' nowheah. The clouds had changed from white and fluffy t'wheah dey was like thick, sticky ma'shmallah, clinging to mah feet and legs. Ah looked like a fly tryin' t'scape from flypaper.

When ah'd wake up, mah heart'd be beating so ha'd an ah'd feel almos' like ah was gon' suffocate fo' ah got mah breaf.

Dear Susan,

Talking about dreams reminds me of one recurring dream I had as a child. I dreamed about going to heaven. There was a long line of people stretching as far as the eye could see—people in front of me and people behind me. We were walking through clouds that looked like the meringue on top of one of your lemon pies before you put it in the oven. Mist was creeping around us and everything looked hazy and shimmered like heat waves. Far in the distance was a mountain where the people were headed. That was the entrance to heaven and the people were waiting their turn to enter. The word came that everyone had to see the Lord face to face at the Judgement Seat. Everyone without exception had to give an account of himself. There would be no sneaking into heaven.

At the time, I was only about six or seven, and I can remember having those dreams after going to church with Sister Belinda. The minister would stand on the platform before the congregation and preach fire and damnation. When he was really wound up, he would stand on the front row pews the better to see everyone. The people shied away from the front row because they knew his habits. He was a very good preacher and could preach a stirring "dry bones" sermon—so much so you could almost see the bones coming to life.

I was utterly afraid. I began to run as soon as I heard the news, because I knew the good Lord did not want me. He couldn't want me. I was as spotless as a litter of dalmation pups. The clouds changed to marshmallow, clinging to my feet and legs, hindering my movement.

When I woke up, my heart was beating so hard I felt I would suffocate before I got my breath.

THE MISSING STORIES
Elise G. LeGrand

On a hot summer day in 1945 I was lying on my stomach on the living-room couch in front of the open terrace doors. The sheer curtains moved in the breeze from the garden. I was nine years old that summer after the war ended. Life was just beginning to settle down into a new routine in Zeist, the village where I was born in Holland.

Leaning on a doubled-up pillow I held a magazine I wasn't supposed to read. When my mother came through the kitchen door I quickly stuffed it under the pillow. I read in horrified fascination how the Jews were "exterminated" in the Nazi concentration camps. I knew that my mother's family had disappeared during the war. I did not know why or how.

Unbelieving, I read how Jews were packed into cattle cars on long trains and taken to camps where they were told to undress and take a shower. Each was given a small piece of soap. Then they were herded into showers that held no water and had no drains. The doors were closed and poisonous gas seeped in and killed them.

I read it over and over again; I finally convinced myself that this had happened to my mother's family. But I knew that I couldn't ask any questions about what I had read. I remembered how we used to visit the Red Cross office to get news of her family in the first few months after the war, and I pictured the closed look on my mother's face after these visits. I had overheard parts of whispered conversations that filled me with fear. I had a lot of questions, but my fears were greater than my desire to know the whole story. It has taken me another forty years to face the rest of the story and reconstruct what happened to Oma—my grandmother—and her family.

Like anyone else who lived through the war, I learned the story of the Holocaust. I discovered that my mother survived because of her marriage to my father who was not Jewish. I also noticed that my mother's graphic descriptions of the war always excluded her family. The only thing she would say was: "I've always hated most that my mother was not with my sister after she had spent her whole life taking care of her." I learned much later that she knew this from a letter her mother wrote her from a transit camp in Holland, Westerbork, where all the Dutch Jews were assembled before their final train journey to the extermination camps in Eastern Europe.

But I did not know the end of that story; sooner or later I would have to complete it. I would have to enter that train and travel with Oma to that cold place where she was separated from her retarded, helpless child and died, naked, desperate and alone.

Over time, I became aware of a little girl that lived inside me somewhere. I knew her perfectly well, of course. I could see her, four years old, in the bomb shelter of a friend's back yard, evacuated from her house during the German invasion of Holland in May of 1940. And four years later, standing in line at the baker's in the dark of that last winter of the war, waiting for a loaf of clammy dark bread with chaff sticking through the crust. And that same winter, standing frozen in terror at the edge of a dark hole in a hallway, listening to the sobs of a desperate woman hiding in that hole. That little girl knew far too many secrets that had to do with the yellow star on my mother's coat and the whispers in the next room.

That same little girl learned to fear many things. She was afraid of the dark, of sirens, of low-flying airplanes, of pounding on the door in the middle of the night, and of harsh German voices shouting orders.

I gave shape to the little girl by calling her Sarah and letting her write her own stories. From the moment I started this, I felt more at ease. I could finally allow the woman I am now to talk to the frightened child I used to be. Through this dialogue I gained some perspective. Keeping in touch with the frightened child enabled me to search for the facts that lay beneath the memories.

*　　*　　*

Raids, or "razzias," were part of our lives like sirens, curfews, and lack of food. Even today, the civil defense siren that goes off across the street on the first Tuesday of each month never fails to make me jump. A low-flying airplane on a dark evening makes me restless enough to question what it is doing over our house.

This is the little girl in me, remembering the sirens and the bombs one fearful stormy spring night early in the war when we sat for hours in the flimsy safety of our hallway. My parents huddled over us, and I screamed for them to get us out of there. Every few minutes a plane roared toward the nearby airfield of Soesterberg and grew silent just before dropping its bombs. Our little house shook with the explosions while the storm lashed the trees in the back yard and took the top out of the lovely birch, my father's pride and joy.

The birch tree was not the only victim of that night. I have always remembered it as the beginning of the darkness that covered my childhood and deepened when my mother went away. Early in 1943, my grandmother, her daughters Leni and Jet, who was married and had a little boy, along with all the aunts, uncles, and cousins were taken from their homes to Camp Westerbork. I don't know how long they stayed there, but I learned recently that my aunt Jet, her husband Abraham Levij van Dam, and their little son Rene Simon died in Auschwitz on February 19, 1943. Grandmother Lewine de Jonge (my "Oma") and her retarded daughter Leni died in Sobibor on March 20 of that year.

Once her family had been deported, my mother feared that she too would be taken away, even though she had a non-Jewish husband and the Germans generally made exceptions for such mixed marriages. On January 1, 1943, she disappeared from our house. My father told my brother and me that she was ill and had gone to recover in a nursing home. Actually, she lived only a few blocks away with my father's unmarried sister Anna where she kept out of sight in the house. When we would visit her on Sundays we were always told that she had just arrived there from the nursing home. After six months she could stand this arrangement no longer and came home, wearing the Star of David for the remainder of the war. Meanwhile, her family had been deported from Camp Westerbork.

Last summer on a visit to Holland, my brother and I went to the site of Camp Westerbork to search for the missing parts of our family's history. For more than forty years we had respected our mother's silence about what happened to her family after they arrived in this camp. It was a way station, a place of waiting and uncertainty. But those who left here never returned.

The low gray building was not what I expected. It is in the northern province of Drenthe, a lovely area of rich farmland interrupted by patches of forest and fields of heather. Canals slice arrow-straight through the peat-harvested land, now pasture. The sun glitters on the water in the warm, perfect summer afternoon.

It is vacation time. The parking lot is full, and many bicycles are parked in a separate area. We walk slowly, reluctantly around the building. I search the faces of the people exiting. Why are they here? Are these just casual visitors, tourists, with time on their hands on a beautiful day? Do they have a personal stake in this visit?

I'm nervous as we enter the low room filled with displays. I am not sure that I can stand to look at what we have come to see. It is a busy place. Families with small children, older couples, and groups of people shuffle along. We have to wait to get close enough to see the photographs and read the explanations. But who can explain?

A short poem on a black wall opens the exhibit:

> Come tell me tales of no more war,
> of no more people being slain,
> tell me a thousand times or more
> and every time I will weep again.

Paintings, photographs, and text tell of the long tradition of religious freedom won by Holland during the eighty-year war with Spain in the sixteenth and seventeenth centuries. This tradition of tolerance and hospitality allowed many Jews to settle in Holland after oppression and persecution elsewhere in Europe. They formed a large and vital presence in the history of Holland. The exhibit shows how the depression of the 1930s spawned the Dutch National Socialist movement that would later cooperate with the Nazi invaders. In May of 1940, Hitler opened the war in Western Europe. Shortly after the May invasion of Holland, the harassment of Jews began. Photographs of Hitler's troops rounding up Jews in Amsterdam begin a sequence leading to images of these Jews as they lived in this camp.

I stare at the faces of the Jews in the photographs that illustrate this part of the exhibit. Is that my grandmother's face? Is this my aunt, her little son? I move quickly past the videotapes of camp survivors telling their stories. These are too painful to watch. But I return several times, unbelieving, to a display of statistics that covers a six-foot-tall panel on the wall. White letters on black sum up the totals: of more than 100,000 Dutch Jews, only a few thousand returned. The names of the camps where they went on their final train journey are too familiar: Auschwitz, Buchenwald, Bergen-Belsen, Theresienstadt, Sobibor. From this last camp, only nineteen people survived of the 34,313 who entered (Westerbork 37).

In a sunny, triangular room with pleasant, modern furniture, we sit around a table while a volunteer named Ben Prinsen, a gentle young man with brown eyes, patiently unfolds more of the story of Camp Westerbork. Built in 1939 to house refugees from Eastern European nations already overrun by Hitler's forces, it contained 750 Jewish refugees when Germany invaded Holland on May 10, 1940. In 1942, expansion of the camp began as part of Hitler's plans to exterminate the entire Jewish population of occupied Europe. The camp became a transit camp. Beginning on July 15, 1942, and every Monday night until September 13, 1944, trains transported a total of more than 100,000 Jews to the "Final Solution," the ovens of extermination camps in Eastern Europe (Westerbork 36-37).

Ben Prinsen is a good listener. He tells us only what we want to know. After a while he shows us the books that cover a long shelf near the door. Forty-six maroon-covered volumes where, on cream-colored pages, rest the names of those who left this place on their last journey. And there he shows us the names of our grandmother, her children, and her sister. I have to touch the books, feel the pages. I cannot speak. Silence fills the room.

Ben offers us copies of the pages of the books. He talks about the site of the original camp, several miles away. The camp was destroyed after the war, and this commemorative center was built later. He tells us that some people return here time and again to search for their lost relatives. Their need to know has finally overcome their reluctance. It is the same way with us.

In the late afternoon we sit on the grass outside the museum. My brother and his wife and I talk of mundane matters: the busy traffic, the weather, the crowd of visitors. We do not talk much about what drove us to this low gray building.

*   *   *   *   *

Camp Westerbork was a stop on the road to the carefully designed giant killing mechanisms of the extermination camps, the brainchild of Heinrich Himmler. Titled "Reichsfuehrer" of the SS [Schutzstaffel], he controlled this fanatical, racist group of Nazis that originally served as Hitler's bodyguards. The SS based their ideology in the concepts of an old Aryan culture and neo-Darwinism, believing that survival of the fittest was the "law of nature." They aimed to raise a nation inhabited by "pedigreed humans," a race of "supermen," and believed German youth would achieve that dream. To that end, they promoted fresh air, exercise and good food. They also set about eliminating those considered culturally and racially inferior or otherwise undesirable.

Himmler's photographs show him as a slim, handsome man, a cocky smile beneath his rakishly tilted uniform cap. In reality he was a bizarre mixture of mysticism and single-minded determination, seeing himself as one of the "sons of light" in struggle with the powers of darkness for the nation and Europe ("Genocide," *World*).

In 1935, the Nuremberg laws were passed that forbade sex and marriage between racially "impure" Jews and "Aryans," white non-Jews, in Hitler's definition. These acts protected German blood and honor, and began the reign of terror that culminated in Himmler's "Final Solution." He designed this final solution after mass executions of Jews in Poland and other Eastern European countries failed to kill the eight million Jews there fast enough.

Himmler, who had never seen dead people before, visited a model camp near Minsk in 1941 to witness a mass shooting. Prisoners had to jump into a pit and were shot there. He got right up to the edge of the pit that held the bodies of those already shot, and was splashed on the face and coat by brain tissue as a new group of Jews tumbled into the pit. Himmler heaved and swayed. After this visit he concluded that shooting was "messy, distressing and inefficient." In January of 1942 he called a conference to find better arrangements. Formal minutes were kept, and detailed lists of Jews in all European countries were drawn up. The lists showed a total of more than eleven million Jews.

At this time, Himmler appointed Adolf Eichmann permanent administrator for the "Final Solution" because he had experience in transportation. He was in charge when the decision was made to replace mass execution and starvation with gassing. Dachau had been the model concentration camp. All European countries occupied by the Nazis had concentration camps based on this model. In the early months of 1942, more camps were built and re-designed to use by-products of the mass killings and dispose of the waste ("Genocide").

Valuables and jewelry (often disappearing in the pockets of the SS officers who ran the camps), shoes, artificial limbs, empty suitcases, prayerbooks and shawls, clothing, glasses and gold teeth, all were collected and sorted (Presser 487). Far more gruesome, however, was the diabolical scheme to use human hair in the fabrication of cloth, pillows, dolls and wigs. Most hideous of all, human skin was made into lamp shades, briefcases and book covers. One of my friends saw these grisly objects at a museum in Berlin in 1974. One object she described to me was a footstool made of human skin and woven hair that was supposed to symbolize how the Nazi foot was now on the backs of the Jews.

Piles of personal objects remain on display at concentration camp sites in Europe. Visitors to these camps often mention that seeing the mountains of shoes, clothing, and other personal effects made the horrors of the camps more real than seeing the empty gas chambers and ovens. The millions that arrived on the trains shed their identity with their clothes and disappeared forever.

Eichmann chartered railroad stock from the state railways to carry out the plans he had made for the "Final Solution." The trains would bring the Jews and remove the waste products. The railways charged full fare for an adult and half fare for each child transported. The trains were run by railway employees, not military personnel. Surely these people had to know the extent of the Nazis' plans for the people crammed into the railroad cars. Incredible though it may seem, enough citizens participated willingly to keep the trains running on schedule and Himmler's plans working.

Himmler visited Auschwitz in the summer of 1942. He saw and much approved of plans for the gas chambers and crematoria with their carefully designed chimneys and specially patented furnaces. Slave labor built the camp on a tight schedule. The instrument of death was a gas named "Zyklon B," fabricated by the "highly respectable IG-Farben Industrie, among the largest of German corporations" (Presser 490). Zyklon B was contained in pellets that would disperse cyanide in the air of the closed "shower" rooms where Jews were to be gathered. Meanwhile, the roundup of Jews began in the occupied territories ("Genocide").

*   *   *   *   *

The diaries of Etty Hillesum helped me fill in some missing parts of my family's story. Etty was a young Jewish woman who spent more than a year in Westerbork before she and her family went east on one of the trains. The camp was filled with desperate people, torn from their environments, thrown into filthy barracks where their previous lives did not matter. Crowded, vermin-infested cabins were their shelter. Here they could only mill aimlessly about, half-starved, dreading the next train that would take away another thousand Jews each Monday night.

The Jewish prisoners were given to understand that they were going to be resettled in a labor camp in Eastern Europe. Families were kept together and put on trains together. There were no bellowing SS guards. The camp was governed by a council of Jews, all of whom were also destined to die (Hillesum 187-196).

The camp operated on a system of false hope. Confinement in the camp was not intended to be too unpleasant. Entertainment in the form of stage and music productions was a regular part of camp life. Another anomaly was the camp hospital. By the end of 1943 it had 1,800 beds, 120 physicians and a staff of more than 1,000, all Jews. The hospital was well supplied with medications; specialists of every sort staffed the outpatient clinic, pharmacy, and quarantine stations twenty-four hours per day. "No doubt the existence of this fine hospital served to allay Jewish apprehension concerning their future in the East. Why, after all, should the Nazis take such good care of them if they intended to kill them further down the road?" The point is well taken by author Jacob Boas, who was born in Westerbork and wrote a book about the camp (Boas 50).

I wonder if Etty Hillesum and my grandmother's family ever met in the camp. They were there at the same time. Etty had a job in the Jewish council; this accounted for her long stay there. But in the end she traveled east in a cattle car to Auschwitz and died there several months later, on November 30, 1943.

According to the letter my mother received from my grandmother, she was separated from her daughter in Westerbork. But they died in Sobibor, Poland, on the same day, according to the camp's records. While I can't explain this seeming discrepancy, I think now, after reading about the workings of Camp Westerbork, that Aunt Leni was placed in the hospital there and reunited with her mother on the trip to Sobibor in keeping with the system used by the Nazis. There is no way left to ascertain what really happened.

In densely packed freight and cattle cars, men, women and children arrived at the extermination camps. A survivor of one of these camps described the arrival: "There were flames to the sky and a strange smell, as of burned chicken." Those still alive at the end of the trip were told to undress as they would be de-loused before starting work. After their showers they would rejoin their families.

They wait for hours, naked. By now some have begun to suspect the worst. Mothers hide infants underneath piles of clothes in a pathetic effort to save them. They are shut in the showers, in groups. In one camp two or three thousand were put in at once. The guards search through the clothing and throw the hidden children in on top of the mass of bodies. The door is bolted. A guard climbs on a ladder to drop the Zyklon pellets through a grate in the roof. A fearful screaming starts that lasts about ten minutes. Then it slowly gets quiet. The prison squad opens the door. A blue haze comes out. The people are always piled on top of each other, in a pointed heap. There are claw marks on the wall and the bodies are scratched and gouged. Many women miscarry during the poisoning ("Genocide").

The prison squad of fellow Jewish prisoners tug and pull hard to tear the heap of dead bodies apart. Corpses are taken by lifts to the ovens where a man removes false and gold teeth. He checks for hidden valuables in body cavities. Another man shaves women's long hair. The mangled corpses are pushed one by one into the ovens. It takes fifteen minutes to burn a corpse. Only a few ashes are left.

This was the description of the camps I had read at age nine. Seeing it more than forty years later on a TV program called "Genocide" was like an echo of a bad dream that brings back the terror of the night. This was the hidden story, my mother's silence. I cried for her and for the millions that shared our family's fate.

In July of 1944, Lublin in East Poland is liberated by the Russian troops. But 170 miles away, the ovens of Auschwitz are busier than ever. The German army is retreating on all fronts, and tries to destroy the evidence of the camps by tearing up the railroad tracks. Still Himmler urges on the destruction. Six million Jews have already been killed. Two million by shooting, four million in the more efficient camps. This is still too few for Himmler, who says to Adolf Eichmann: "There must be more than that!" and sets up his own statistics unit to check the numbers.

In January of 1945, the Russians reach Auschwitz. Later that spring, the Nazi government collapses. Eventually all the camps will be liberated. Many local Germans had known of the camps; others preferred not to know. Now they are forced to visit the camps and see. In one town, the mayor and his wife go home and hang themselves after their visit to the camp.

Some Jews survive to bear witness. A Hungarian Jew said: "I bless every day that I continue to live, because every day is pure profit." He weighed forty-two kilos (about ninety pounds) at liberation. He went about the camp with a belt, a plate, and a spoon. He counts his age from the time he was liberated. "The years before the camp don't count. I was dead in the camp," he says ("Genocide"). But he was reborn. My grandmother's life ended when the train stopped.

*   *   *   *   *

The train comes to a slow stop with hissing and grinding brakes. Oma grips Leni's hand even tighter than she has held it for the last three days. The stench in the cattle car is a mixture of mouldy straw, human excrement, and the foulness of densely packed human bodies. It no longer revolts her; it is a fixed presence, like the freezing cold, the leaking roof, and the moans of those no longer able to sit or stand. Oma opens her swollen eyelids when the door is unbolted from the outside. Harsh voices shout beyond the sudden glare of light that hurts her eyes. A gust of icy wind blows in.

Leni makes a hoarse, dry noise, no longer even a cough. Her dwarfish, misshapen little body is wedged between her mother and the wall. Filth is encrusted on her scaly yellowish face, the opaque eyes no longer seeing, her lips dry and cracked over sticky gums. Oma tightens her grip on Leni's small, cold hand.

A soldier in a green uniform has entered the car. He begins to push those nearest the door outside. People tumble and stumble through the doorway onto a cement platform. The soldier pries Oma loose from her seat. Her arthritic joints are frozen from sitting unmoving for three days on a bale of straw. She screams as the soldier pushes her roughly to the door. She screams in pain but also because she no longer holds her daughter's hand.

"Leni, Leni! my daughter, she can't walk!" She crouches on the cement platform, not comprehending anything, knowing only that she has to protect her forty-three-year-old child.

In the doorway to the train car the soldier appears, hoisting Leni under her arms. Oma screams again: "Leni, Leni!" The soldier lowers Leni to the platform where she collapses among the other half-dead bodies. Oma shuffles toward her child, her arms outstretched, as fast as the screaming pain in her joints lets her go. Two soldiers shout orders at the bewildered people on the platform. Those still able to walk are assigned by the soldiers to stand five abreast in one of two rows.

Before Oma gets to Leni, the soldiers push her into a ragged row of women and children. She pleads again: "My daughter, she can't help herself!" No one listens. Except Leni. She has heard Mother's voice. She turns her little wrinkled face toward Oma and feebly raises her left arm in a wrenching gesture. It is the last sight

Oma has of the child that has been the center of her entire existence.

The soldiers start pushing the people to walk toward a low, gray building. Frightened children cry as they are separated from their fathers and older brothers. Women scream and look around wildly, unable to take in what is happening. The wind blows cold and strong over the bare ground between the gray buildings. Slowly and painfully, Oma stumbles away from life and the train of horror that has brought her seven hundred miles from her home. It is the twentieth of March, 1943, in Sobibor, Poland.

Works Cited

Boas, Jacob. *Boulevard des Miseres, The Story of Transit Camp Westerbork.* Hamden: Archon, 1985.

Commemoration Centre Camp Westerbork. Amsterdam: Rijksinstituut voor Oorlogsdocumentatie, 1984.

Hillesum, Etty. *Het Vestoorde Leven* [An Interrupted Life]. Amsterdam: Balans, 1989.

Maass, Walter B. *The Netherlands at War: 1940-45.* New York: Abelard-Schuman, 1970.

Nieuwsbode, 7 May, 1985.

Presser, Jacob. *The Destruction of the Dutch Jews.* New York: Dutton, 1969.

Background Information

"The Allies Close In." *The World at War.* Produced and directed by Michael Darlon. PBS. WFMT, Chicago, 25 May, 1989.

"Genocide." *The World at War.* 3 June, 1989.

"Holland, 1940-1945." *The World at War.* 20 May, 1989.